CIRIE

Other books by Mildred Savage

Parrish
In Vivo
A Great Fall

CIRIE

Mildred Savage

Writers Club Press
New York   Lincoln   Shanghai

Cirie

Writers Club Press
an imprint of iUniverse, Inc.

For information address:
iUniverse
2021 Pine Lake Road, Suite 100
Lincoln, NE 68512
www.iuniverse.com

This book is a work of fiction. All events, locations, institutions, themes, persons, characters and plot are completely fictional. Any resemblances to place or persons, living or deceased, are of the invention of the author and are unintended and purely coincidental.

ISBN: 0-595-21894-6

Printed in the United States of America

To Nicholas Savage,
my dearest "Nico",
so that his name
will live on in a way
he was not able to do for himself
because there was no time.

And to Mariana Savage
and Eric Simpson

Contents

Characters

At Whitewater

The Family:

Countess Eugenie Vodovsky ("Madame")—a widow
Vassily—her eldest son
Serge—her second son
Georgii—her youngest son
Vara (Countess Laszinska)—her daughter
Stepa—Madame's brother-in-law
Elissa—Stepa's wife
Tanya—Stepa's daughter
Kyra—Madame's sister
Otto—Kyra's husband
Theo—Kyra's son
Lydia—Kyra's daughter

Guests:

Constantine Paklov—a political writer
Ilya Laranov—an agricultural expert
Prince and Princess Tchernefsky
Irene Scherevsky—their niece
General Alexander "Sacha" Borassin
Kurasin—a musician and music critic

Employees:

Gerzy—manager of the horses and country coachman
Mischa—his son
Arkady—Tanya's tutor

In Novotnii

Dr. Ivan Strengov—a country doctor
Marya—his wife
Anna—his eldest daughter
Cirie—his second daughter
Lily—his youngest daughter
Anya Dubrovna—his mother-in-law
Ulla—his cousin from Moscow
Koner—the innkeeper
Popov—a moujik (peasant)
Tessa—Popov's wife
Dr. Federin—another country doctor

In Kostyka

Dr. Legare
Petya Rossatin—a fur dealer
Oscar—Ulla's husband
General Petrov
General Renkovsky
Commander Gorshenko—Renkovsky's aide
Darius Kyrigen ("Dari")—a pharmacist
Agniya—a landlady
Alexis—Cirie's son
Christina—Irene's daughter
Marushka—a woman outlaw
Gart—Assistant Commissar of Agriculture

In Moscow

Peter Nemerov—a Soviet official
Comrade Melnikov—official at Soviet Foreign Office
Charles Wellman—official at the American Relief Office

In New York

J.K. Cannon—a real estate and construction tycoon
Norman—a lawyer

PROLOGUE

They waited on the frozen snow in the forest where the sun did not reach. The bearded man was getting impatient. "Do you hear the horses?"

The leader, a short man with a black mustache, ran his hand over his rifle. "Not yet."

Popov stood rigidly still. What if something went wrong? What if someone had seen him with these men? Tomorrow they would be gone, he would still be here. He took out a bottle of vodka.

"Put that away," the leader ordered.

Popov slid the bottle back into the pocket of his tattered coat. They could show respect, even if he wasn't from Moscow. They had asked him to take them here—to this kind of deserted spot on the road of the estate—and he did it, didn't he?

He pictured the Countess in his mind. If she were alone and if he were alone, he'd have her right here on the snow.

He spat steaming spittle. "What have you done before this?"

"I was with Koba in the South. Our bank raids paid for plenty of guns and grenades."

"He never heard of Koba," the bearded one said.

Popov's hatred came quickly. "How could I hear of him, from far across Russia?"

"Koba is the best," the leader said. "He blows up what has to be blown up. He kills whoever should not be left alive. He enjoys it. He hungers for it. Koba is the best."

All right, Popov thought. Take me to this Koba. Then the horses' hoofs clattered on the wooden bridge. The three men pulled the rags up over their faces and stepped out to the narrow road.

It was easy. Only the Countess and her maid and her son Georgii—a little boy. And a driver who did his best to fight them off, but his best was not good enough. The other two were experts. The maid screamed first. When they had taken the money and the jewels, Popov struck the first blow to the carriage with his axe, smashing the side and knocking out the door. Then the three of them pushed it over on its side. Screams, shouts, bodies flung around.

Popov could see that the Countess had fainted or been knocked senseless. She was lying across the carriage. The boy had been thrown on top of her. If Popov had been alone he would be the one on top of her. Even though she was an old woman now. Fifty at least—maybe more. For years he had watched her. Beautiful. Fancy clothes. Rich. Even now, if they would let him, he'd have her down on the snow and push into her. Slam into her.

He smashed a foot into the ruined carriage. Fuck it, he thought. One less carriage to wreck when the Revolution comes.

BOOK ONE

THE WORLD THAT WAS LOST

1914–1916

"We are the ghosts—We are the seeds."
—D. H. Lawrence

1

✿

For several miles they had traveled in silence, past fields stretching away to dark forests, past spring streams spilling over their banks, through little villages with huts and slanting sheds where thin cows and nags gnawed on brush and the bark of trees, and hungry-looking children stood beside the road and watched the sleek, well-fed Vodovsky team go by. The driver, Gerzy, a gray-bearded man bundled up in a heavy coat, as stolid and immobile as a Buddha, did not encourage conversation.

"Does the boy walk at all?" Cirie said.

Gerzy puffed on a strong-smelling Russian cigarette held between his thumb and forefinger. "How can he walk?"

"And Countess Vodovsky?"

The man studied his horses' rumps. "Some."

Cirie watched the beautiful black horses move effortlessly up the hill. She was a slender girl of sixteen with flaxen hair and startling thick black eyelashes framing cobalt eyes. And deceptively delicate features. She glanced over at Gerzy. They would be riding together for a while yet and sooner or later, before they got to Vodovsky, he would have something to say. No—Cirie corrected herself—not Vodovsky. *Whitewater*. Only her father, Ivan Strengov, one of the two doctors in the district, refused to call the Vodovsky estate by its romantic name, Whitewater. He called the vast accumulation of wealth by the name of the family that owned the vast accumulation—Vodovsky.

A little hamlet came along, a dozen crude huts huddled together with only the woodpile in between.

"The old nurse," Cirie tried again. "Is she still there?"

"There were three. All three are gone."

Cirie was not going to ask why all three were gone or anything else about life out there. She would find out soon enough. And if the Vodovskys turned out to be as bad as Strengov had said, there was nothing the coachman could do about it. And whatever they were like, she intended to get along with them. She had waited too long for this chance.

She thought of Strengov's warnings. "The sons!" he had said. "Vassily is a dull self-important man. A cold fish. He thinks too much and never laughs. And the second son laughs too much and never thinks. The line is deteriorating. The sons were dealt a poor hand all around."

He really has no use for them, Cirie thought. But how could he not be curious? What must it be like to have three magnificent estates—here and in Kostyka and one near Kazan? For many years the family had summered at Whitewater and there had been stories of picnics and dinners and balls and important guests from Moscow and Petersburg. Then the Count died and the parties ended.

The beautiful black horses moved effortlessly up the hill. Cirie watched Gerzy flick carefully at a bee buzzing over them. "These are fine horses," she said.

A light came to Gerzy's eyes. "You noticed them?"

"Many times—in town. And the troika horses, too. They're so spirited. And so beautifully trained."

Gerzy smiled like a father who has been told what he already knows—that his children are extraordinary. "It's a little different here now," he said. "With Vara in charge."

"Vara?"

"Countess Laszinska. Madame's daughter. Countess Vodovsky is addressed as Madame. But Vara, Countess Laszinska, is always called Countess."

Most of Cirie's information about the Vodovskys had come from Koner, the innkeeper, Strengov's closest friend, who talked often about the sons, but had never mentioned Vara.

"When Vassily is here, he's the boss," Gerzy said. "But Vassily is all business and is usually in Kostyka. Since the accident, Vara is in charge."

They passed a wooden church with a blue onion-shaped dome and Gerzy said that now they were on the Vodovsky estate. The road wound through the famous forests. "With Vara—" Gerzy paused. "Madame likes things to be correct but you can get along with her. When she speaks you should listen, for she doesn't waste words. With Vara, once she gets started, you have to let her run down. Always a little sore, that's Vara."

"Is she married? With children?"

"She married an old man—a Polish count—as old as her father. When he died, she came home."

"And Vassily?"

"Vassily will never marry. He wouldn't take time from his estates." The horses turned into a wide, poplar-lined drive. "And Serge is in Paris," Gerzy said. "And Georgii is only nine. I have been here thirty-five years. I watched them all grow up."

The drive wound past birches and orchards and fir trees. In the distance Cirie could see a quiet lake with a small white playhouse beside it, nestled among birches that leaned to the water. Another turn and she caught a glimpse of the river. Then the drive ended at a stately white house with wings on either side set at an angle like arms stretched wide, not to welcome the guests approaching from the road but to embrace the river beyond.

"How was this arranged—that you would come here for Georgii?" Gerzy seemed puzzled. "You didn't talk to Vara?"

"No."

"Vassily?"

"Dr. Federin came to the office and asked my father. Last Monday. Three days ago."

"With Vara—" Gerzy offered a final piece of advice. "Don't cross her for she has a long memory. And yet you can't let her push you because she'll never let up."

2

❁

"How magnificent!" Cirie whispered. "How beautiful it is."

Alone in Countess Vodovsky's study, she looked around like a child trying to see everything at once—the deep-hued Persian rugs, the little French chairs, the portraits on the walls. Some of the portraits had an old look about them of people long dead—ancestors probably, who lived in these rooms long ago. But some, she thought, are the present family.

On a long table in the center of the room was a beautiful Oriental chest and she wandered over to it. It must be teak, inlaid with mother-of-pearl and deep green—that must be jade. Before she left here, she would know all about these things. She started to touch it and checked herself—she was sure it was the most beautiful thing in this room.

She moved to the door and looked down the center hall along which the butler had led her past two drawing rooms, past several closed doors, past a dark-paneled dining room with enough chairs to seat all the guests this huge house could accommodate. She wished someone would come to speak to her. The butler had said that Countess Laszinska would see her soon, but the hall was empty.

Back in the study, she stopped before a pair of portraits—a beautiful fair-haired young woman in a low white gown and a stern-looking gentleman. Nearby was a portrait of the same serene woman, a little older, the blue eyes a little more subdued, with a dark-haired sober-looking boy standing beside her chair. Over the fireplace hung a larger portrait—the woman again, a little older still and wearing a high white gown, grouped with three children—the same frowning boy, about fifteen in this portrait, a big-boned girl a little younger, with a joyless expression on features that otherwise resembled her mother's, and a boy of about five with blond curls and merry eyes. Except for Georgii, this is the present family, Cirie thought. Countess Eugenie Vodovsky through the years, first with Vassily, and then with Vassily and Vara—the present Countess Laszinska—and Serge.

"Well, who are you?" a voice boomed and Cirie whirled around to see a giant of a man, broad-shouldered, black-haired, wearing a Russian tunic. "The new nurse!" he cried when Cirie identified herself. "For Georgii? Oh, ho!" Laughing, he strode to the door and shouted, "Tanya—Tanya, come and bring Georgii." He introduced himself. "I'm Count Vodovsky. Uncle Stepa. But you're just a child—

not much older than my own little one. Tanya—" A black-haired dimpled girl of about fifteen appeared, pushing a pale unhappy-looking boy in a wheelchair.

"Georgii, here's your new nurse—" Stepa shouted. Georgii closed his eyes tight. "The most beautiful nurse in Russia for Georgii Vodovsky!" The eyes opened and slowly lit up just as a tall, self-important woman hurried into the room. Cirie knew this was Countess Laszinska.

"I was told the new nurse was here." She was a large-bosomed, tightly-corseted woman and she stood leaning forward as though establishing a certain equilibrium. "Who is this person? Where is the nurse?"

"Right here, Vara," Stepa shouted.

"You are the nurse!" Vara's protruding eyes widened. "No, no, you won't do!" With long fingers she turned her face away, as though having just discovered a remarkable object on a nearby chair. "No—impossible. We'll have to find someone else."

Cirie stared at her. How can she say that? She doesn't know yet whether I will do.

"Why not?" Georgii demanded. "Why won't she do, Vara?"

"Leave this to me, Georgii. Go back where you came from. How did you get here?"

"Why won't she do?" Georgii's voice rose.

"Georgii, *how* did you get here?"

"For God's sake, Vara," Stepa said. "Tanya wheeled him in."

"Then Tanya can wheel him out. *Now,* Tanya."

"No!" Georgii grasped the wheel of his chair. "I want her. She's staying."

"She's not a real nurse. She couldn't handle you."

"Yes, I can!" Cirie said, firmly.

"Your opinion has not been requested."

A rustle in the doorway and the woman of the portraits, older but with the same serene face, came in leaning on a cane. Stepa hastened to help her into a chair. "Here's the new nurse, Eugenie."

"I want her to stay," Georgii broke in.

Madame's smile changed to surprise. "But Vara, she's so young. Dr. Federin said an experienced nurse."

"Yes. His exact words were, 'The strongest young woman I have ever known.'"

"That old fox!" Stepa said. "That posturing jackass may be smarter than I thought."

"Georgii is impossible," Vara complained to her mother.

"He's restless, Vara. Wait till he's on his feet."

"He could be on his feet now if he wanted to." Vara tugged on a gold bell cord and snapped at Cirie, "It's too late to send you home today. Go put on a uniform—"

"No uniforms," Georgii shouted. "That old stick wore uniforms and her hands were like dead fish. She made me sick—sick—sick!"

"We'll do without a uniform tonight," Madame said, quietly.

"Go along," Vara ordered Cirie when a footman appeared. "And be sure your appearance tonight is correct. Plain and neat and clean."

Don't answer, Cirie told herself. Smile and say nothing. She'll forget it—like a patient when the pain is over. How many times had she whispered to a patient, "It'll be over soon—only another minute."

As she left the room she heard Vara say, "We'll send her back in the morning."

"Oh, come on, Vara," Stepa said. "Why not give her a try?"

"I have too many other problems. Kyra is here already—"

"Kyra is your aunt! She grew up here."

"And Constantine will arrive any minute—"

"Constantine! Constantine is my oldest friend. He doesn't want special attention. Only good conversation which he gets from me."

Fighting tears, Cirie followed the footman down the hall. What did I say? What did I do? Then she thought defiantly, *Nothing.* They're just very unfair. Hello—you won't do—goodbye. Well, she couldn't say she wasn't warned. "A cold family, the line is deteriorating," Strengov had said. And he had not even seen Vara!

In the dining room the servants were setting the table. Silver gleamed. Crystal sparkled. The tears were back. There are going to be guests again, she thought. There's going to be life here again and I'll never see it. She won the battle against tears. "You're staying overnight. That's a start." Her mind began to clear. "They need a nurse—they've tried three others. Why send you away before they have someone else? The thing to do is give them a way to keep you a few days without appearing to back down. Make it easy for them," she told herself. "You have nothing to lose."

Leaving the startled footman, she returned to the study. "Countess—" She let a quick smile brush over her allies, Stepa and Georgii, and addressed Madame. "Dr. Federin will be calling in a few days," she said. "Perhaps it would be convenient for you to discuss it with him then."

"There you are!" Stepa boomed. "See what Federin has to say."

"Perhaps we should," Madame agreed.

"Vassily will not agree," Vara said.

Cirie told herself she should have expected trouble. For three days Strengov had been warning her. "They're miserable people. They will do damage I will never be able to repair."

Ever since last Monday.

3

❁

Last Monday. Three days ago.

Strengov had stood at his office window looking out at the snow that was vanishing into oozing patches of mud. Suddenly the air was sweet with the smells of warming earth and rising sap and nearby, at the edge of the woods, he could see his youngest daughter, Lily—who, he thought with a flash of irrational gratitude, was only nine and gave him only small problems—nuzzling her white kitten in a burst of love. In the distance there was a sound like a pistol shot—the river cracking, pitching ragged-edged blocks of ice askew, like wolves' teeth against the sky. "Spring," he said to Koner. "The season of madness."

"Listen, Strengov," Koner said in a voice like a wheel rumbling on cobblestones. "Maybe it will work out, eh?"

Strengov hunched his shoulders and felt an unfamiliar tension. Work out? For which one? Anna, seventeen, his eldest, who was going to America to marry Vogel, a man he detested? Cirie—a year younger, a lifetime older? Neither folly was going to work out.

Koner, a barrel-shaped man, a head shorter than Strengov, was sitting in his usual place on the worn leather sofa, his ruddy face sober to show he respected Strengov's problem. The innkeeper and president of the district council, Koner always said that he had seen a lot of people and knew a lot about life—although, he would admit, not so much as Strengov. Who could see more than a doctor? Especially a doctor like Strengov who always seemed to be standing to one side, observing men's deeds and passions like a critic who has seen the show many times and still reflects on what is lurking beneath the surface. "Anna is like Marya," he said. "Agreeable. Contented."

"Until now." If it were Cirie wanting to go to America, Strengov would not be so surprised. Nothing about Cirie would surprise him. And yet today he was not thinking about Anna. His mind was on Cirie.

He reached across his desk for a Turkish cigarette that his mother-in-law bought for him from traders who worked on the network of Russia's rivers. Her trading post on the river was their first stop after they left the northern Dnieper where it curved east toward Moscow.

"Bring me Turkish cigarettes," she would tell them. "For my son-in-law, Strengov, a doctor, God help us. At least if you should be taken ill here—something picked up farther south, in Odessa, perhaps—you'll have a doctor who will be kindly disposed toward you." Illiterate but the shrewdest woman he had ever known, Anya Dubrovna knew that in the dark part of every Russian soul there was a wide streak of superstition. Maybe this was a warning from God on this woman's lips, the trader would think. What if he should cheat her—as though he could—and then it should happen?

Another of Anya Dubrovna's well-worn phrases was shorter. Comparing Strengov to Marya's first husband of brief duration, she would say, "With this one you went from the ashes into the flame."

It was not Strengov's professional skill that she questioned. but the other non-sense about politics and the Tsar and God only knew what else, that went on in his head. Of the two doctors in Novotnii, Strengov was the better physician and Federin was the more prosperous. In a district where science ran a poor third to God and the local sorcerer, a doctor who did not rely on an outside mystical influ-ence—one or the other—was viewed with suspicion. And Strengov, willing enough to admit a Divine Order, could not visualize that Order as a bearded old man with priests as corrupt as the St. Petersburg bureaucrats. "I leave the chants and candles to those who need them," he would say. "Meanwhile I take care of His children who are suffering—some of them too much, I think, for God to be watching carefully." His opinions endeared him to no one, least of all Anya Dubrovna.

Strengov, for his part, would ask himself how that sharp, shrewd old woman had produced a butterfly like Marya—a gentle, pretty woman with deep blue eyes and flaxen hair, who loved pretty things—embroidered linens, a small piece of silver, her flower garden. He would look at his three blue-eyed, flaxen-haired daughters—Anna, Cirie and Lily—who all looked like their mother and were so different from each other, and he would marvel at the mysteries of heredity. Speaking of genes, not of cards, he would say, "How do you figure it, Koner, when they shuffle the deck?" It was his favorite comment on life.

Leaving the window, Strengov rummaged in his desk drawer for his gold watch that lay on top of a French weekly with a picture of Woodrow Wilson, the American president, who talked about the needs and the will of the people. The office, a small outbuilding attached to his house by a corridor, was quiet now. Cirie had gone to the pharmacy to replenish the supply of bandages and morphine used up in the accident this morning. And Greta, the handyman's daughter who cleaned the office, had not shown up today.

Strengov looked at the picture of the American president. Last week he had had nothing more on his mind than to reflect that such an event in Russia would be strange indeed—a scholar instead of a bureaucrat as Council President. And one who spoke of the needs and the will of the people would be stranger still.

Last week everything had been fine. Then Anna—Anna, his dove—had come to the breakfast table, her blue eyes shining, her long flaxen braids tied with blue ribbons—as though the bastard were right there to see her, Strengov thought now—and announced that she was going to America to marry Vogel. Vogel, whom Strengov had thought he was well rid of. "There was a letter from Karl," she said. "We're going to be married at last." And with those words Anna, usually so gentle, had turned to steel and would not be moved.

His thoughts on Anna now, he said, "How can you let a seventeen year old girl, who never in her life crossed you, travel half-way across the world to marry a man you didn't want even when he was here?"

"It's hard—I know," Koner said soberly.

"You remember him," Strengov said. "The assistant forester at Vodovsky. German. Tall, blond. When he left for America he promised to send her the passage. I thought he was just talking. Now he's sent it, God help us!"

"You calling on God?"

Strengov had no time today to worry about God. "With that one, discontent is a chronic disease. I wouldn't want him if he were right out there on the road." Strengov broke off, reminded again of the accident this morning in front of his office. "Bad news always has a mate—more bad news," he said. "Today I was worrying about Cirie."

"Cirie! What's wrong with Cirie?"

What's wrong with Cirie? Nothing. And everything.

Abruptly Strengov moved back to the window. A caravan of moujiks on sledges came into sight. All winter they were shut up in their small, overcrowded huts until one day the frozen river cracked and they said, "Old Vodianoy is waking up," and they headed for town with their winter's handiwork—kitchen utensils, furniture, dolls, all carved from the wood of these dark forests. The Vodianoy, the spirit of water, was one of the spirits the moujiks held responsible for their luck—good or bad. All winter he slept and then when the frozen river began to fire shots, they said, "Old Vodianoy is waking up," and they came into town to buy or barter for what they needed, including vodka, often drinking it down at once, washing the winter rot from their bones and ending up in trouble. Like the young man this morning, seriously injured just outside the office.

Today the road was a ribbon of mud, in another week it would be impassable. In a month it would be dust, with ruts that would shake a man's insides out and wear out his carriage and his horse. How many nights had he fallen into bed, muttering,

"If the Tsar, our little father, would like to do something for me, let him build roads!"

"Strengov, what bad news about Cirie?" Koner said.

Strengov looked around. "You saw the trouble out there this morning?"

"The blood is still on the snow. A moujik swimming in vodka, I suppose?"

"A brawl, a knife. Insanity one minute, remorse the next. The poor fellow might lose an arm. A young man—even with two arms just a step away from starvation. Fortunately Cirie saw it happen. Federin was here."

"Ah—Federin," Koner said solemnly. "Something important?"

"Very important. He wants Cirie to go to Vodovsky to take care of the youngest son who was injured last month when Revolutionaries attacked the carriage."

"Cirie to Vodovsky!" In this district the name Vodovsky was second only to that of the Tsar and Koner was its most reverent admirer. "My God, what an opportunity for Cirie!"

"An opportunity for disaster. I declined this great opportunity."

Federin, who looked like a penguin, had explained that the boy, Georgii, only nine, was not recovering properly from his injuries. "I wonder—could Cirie go out there to Countess Vodovsky as a nurse and get the boy to walk?"

Strengov and Cirie had replied in the same instant.

"Yes!" Cirie had cried.

"No!" Strengov had said. "Impossible!"

Then they heard the shouts from the street and saw the bleeding man on the snow and Strengov and Cirie rushed outside. Hoping he would not be needed, Federin lingered behind and murmured that he would be back later for an answer.

"He doesn't have to come back," Strengov said when they had cleaned up and were back in the office. "The answer is no."

"I want to go," Cirie said. "I want to see it."

"See what? They're a cold family. You'll be miserable. Mamma will need you—Anna is leaving—only Lily will be left. I can't let you go. They'll ruin your life."

She touched his arm and looked up at him with those eyes that always seemed to see everything. "What are you afraid of?"

Strengov looked into the remarkable blue eyes. "I'm afraid of the same things that you are hoping for."

"Strengov—Strengov—" Koner said. "What possible harm? A summer with Countess Vodovsky and a nine-year old boy. You declined?"

What harm indeed? Strengov turned away. Then, in the caravan of plodding horses, he saw a familiar sledge moving along at a faster clip. "Here she comes.

This old woman has been here every day, she's so excited about another one going to America."

Koner looked out the window. "Anya Dubrovna."

"To her America is El Dorado." If there was ever a chance of changing Anna's mind, the old tyrant was destroying it with her excitement. "She'll go herself one day."

"Never. Leave her store? She never leaves it now for even a day."

For the first time in three days Strengov laughed. "She's afraid the old man will give something away! Any beggar, any wandering holy man can move him to wild generosity." At the store on the river Anya Dubrovna was the business woman. Karil, her husband, was a mild open-handed man who read to her what had to be read and wrote what had to be written and, Strengov suspected, kept her honest. Left alone, Anya Dubrovna would not be above sharp practices. Otherwise, Karil yielded to her willingly, as Marya did. "The old man is a saint and the old woman is a witch."

She was a witch twenty years ago when Strengov first came here, a young man in love with the beautiful blue-eyed, flaxen-haired Marya, recently finished with a first marriage because her husband had expected an efficient helpmate. With her infant son, Anton, Marya had returned to her mother who took charge of the baby and the divorce.

Twenty years. Images rushed at Strengov out of the storehouse of the past. "I can remember the day Anna was born," he said. "I looked at the delicate features and the blue eyes and I said, 'Another Marya.'"

"And more like her every day," Koner agreed.

"A year later when Cirie was born, I said the same thing. Then the blue eyes looked back at me, already showing that uncanny confidence and self-possession, and I felt a little shock."

"Strengov, you imagine it."

"Cirie makes me believe in reincarnation. She was born knowing." Strengov laughed at himself. But he could remember vividly that instant when the blue eyes, unusually dark for a new baby, looked back and a little shock skittered through him and he said, "This one is different."

Today Cirie's eyes were darker still—a deep cobalt blue, a color one sees perhaps twice a winter in a rare, perfectly cloudless sky. And whereas Marya and Anna and Lily all had fair eyelashes, Cirie's were black—thick black brushes framing the remarkable deep blue eyes. And while the others were quiet, Cirie as a child had climbed trees with Boris, Koner's son, and raced across the fields on Koner's horses. Today her exuberance, damned up, seemed even stronger. With Cirie it was as though, in a garden of exquisite pale roses, suddenly a mutation appeared—a single bud, the same size and shape as the others but of such a vivid hue that you entertained the wildest speculation. The vivid rose was not more beautiful—it was a matter of taste, a man might easily prefer the pale and fragile—but you couldn't deny the difference, and as the color deepened and the form became more perfect, you wondered what it would be like when it opened to full flower. How would it be then among the others? How the same? How different? What recessant genes had slipped quietly through the generations and suddenly, mysteriously, combined to produce just that deep shade of blue and the thick black lashes—and the fire and the glow? How did they shuffle the deck?

"She's here." Koner nodded toward the road.

Anna Dubrovna, ramrod-straight, walked toward the house. "This is where this foolishness with Anna and America started—with this old woman," Strengov said. "It goes back nearly ten years to when the Tsar, our little father, sent an archaic fleet halfway around the world to fight the Japanese. They carried untrained crews but plenty of religious icons, which should have done the trick. Well, you know what happened. In a single day his admirals lost almost the entire fleet."

"Strengov, be careful how you talk!"

"I'm talking to you! People were already starving and when their sons and husbands were killed in this miracle of insanity, you recall, there were strikes, riots, a few things smashed—besides heads, that is."

Koner nodded soberly. "We thought the Revolution had begun."

"In Petersburg they marched to the Winter Palace to plead for bread and they were shot down. Which took care of things in Petersburg. In Moscow the trouble lasted longer. They had guns and barricades. And it was my luck that this old woman chose that moment to be in Moscow."

To this day Strengov wondered how much she saw and how much she only heard about, but she returned with a mission, convinced that in Russia her three sons would end up as soldiers or as revolutionaries. One by one she sent them to America, Lawrence, then Oscar, then Charles—each as soon as he was fifteen. And then Anton, Marya's son. "Go to your uncles in a place called Connecticut," she instructed Anton. "Families must stay together. Without family you have no one." All her life Anna had heard about her uncles who went to America. It did not seem so far. Going there did not seem so unusual. "Stay to lunch, Koner," Strengov said. "Protect me from the old witch. Come on—we'll walk around outside and enjoy the sun."

As soon as they came off the steps he saw the blood again—a ragged red blotch fading to pink in the melting snow. "You saw the accident, Koner. Did you see Cirie?"

"Cirie was marvelous!"

"Exactly." Strengov sighed. For a year now, since his old nurse, Katya, became blind, Cirie had helped him in the office. Wrapped in heavy robes, she had gone with him in emergencies to the villages, she had been at his side during deliveries and in surgery, she was a good nurse—but she didn't like it.

"Exactly what?"

"A man nearly loses an arm. Bleeds like a stuck pig. Does Cirie get sick? Does she faint? No! She holds it in place! She holds the severed arm in place so I can work on him."

"Strengov, Cirie was white. Beads of perspiration stood on her forehead."

"Afterwards I sent her to the house to lie down. She merely washed her face and changed her smock which was quite bloody. She brushed her hair—stood on her head or whatever she does. She exercises—like a ballet dancer."

"Cirie wants to be a ballet dancer?"

"No! Cirie doesn't want to be anything!"

That was the problem. All that energy, all that determination, all that remarkable, deceptively delicate beauty. And no focus. Strengov, an unreligious man, completely devoid of superstition, considered the episode, if not an omen, if not a Heaven-directed warning, at least an eye-opener. Anna was going away to get married. And Cirie would be getting married next. And to whom?

"Strengov, let her go to Vodovsky," Koner said. "She will see new things and it will be different."

"No! It will ruin her life. It will cause trouble I can never repair." What am I shouting about? If I can't stop Anna from going to America, how will I stop Cirie from going to Vodovsky?

"Strengov, Anna is going to a different world. She doesn't speak the language, she doesn't know the customs. Probably—forgive me—she won't be able to come home again. And you're just as upset about Cirie who is only going to Countess Vodovsky."

Strengov looked down the muddy road to the sleepy little town. A church, a school, a small hospital, a square with ten stores and Koner's inn, a police station, a bare little post office. And that was all. Unchanging, a little microcosm of the past, where old men passed on stories heard from their grandfathers about how Napoleon's army marched through here on the way to Moscow, Novotnii had been Cirie's whole world, and Anna's. "Think about it, Koner." He found himself wiping his eyes. "Isn't it the same thing?"

When Strengov came into the house, Anya Duvrovna, aware of how he felt about Vodovskys, lost no time in challenging him. "So—a serious accident at Vodovsky and it turns out to be Cirie's good fortune."

Strengov moved past her into the room.

"The attack is a sign of the times," Koner said, always eager to discuss Vodovsky. "And nobody has caught them."

"How could anyone catch them? They vanish in the forests. Nobody knows anything." Anya Dubrovna shot a look out the back window as though expecting to find the anarchists in the chicken yard and saw only Hector, the stubby bearded moujik who did the chores and long ago had delivered the fate of his family into Strengov's hands. His oldest daughter, Hulda, a deaf-mute, was a big girl who worked like a man beside her father in the fields. Another daughter, Gerda, cleaned the house and the youngest was Greta, prettier than the other two, who had not shown up today at the office. "Where was his other one today that she didn't come to work?" Dubrovna said.

"Greta?" Strengov shrugged. "Every year spring comes and the dog disappears for a few days and Greta disappears, too."

"Ivan, not in front of the girls!" Marya said.

With a small, uncomprehending smile Strengov regarded his wife whom he had loved passionately for twenty years. Was there ever a mother so concerned about her daughters' virtue? Which one was she protecting today from mere sexual innuendo? Anna, who was leaving her wing forever? Cirie, who probably had never paid much attention?

"What if someone comes to you from Vodovsky or another estate?" Dubrovna said. "And the girl hasn't cleaned?"

"Don't worry about it. They don't bruise their bones coming to the doctor's office. They send for him. Let him bruise his bones."

Dubrovna's eyes went to the window again. "You've got quite a collection here. The nurse is old and blind. Hulda is deaf and dumb. Greta has a different problem."

"Only in the spring," Strengov said.

"Ivan!"

Now her grandmother was pulling out pictures of her American sons, arranging them like a display of precious gems. Poor Anna should agree to whatever she said and then do as she pleased but Anna couldn't do that. "Ah, Anna," Dubrovna said, "how wonderful it will be for you!" and Anna blushed because to her the only wonderful promise of America was Vogel.

For two years she's been dreaming about going to him, Cirie thought. What could she be thinking! Vogel was handsome—one must give him that—but that was the beginning and end of it. How could Anna choose such a fate, one dull day after another with Vogel? For the rest of her life?

Cirie flung open a window. How could you choose anything for the rest of your life until you'd seen the other possibilities? How could I choose America when I've never seen Petersburg or Moscow or—surely the most exciting place in the world—Paris? And yet she knew she didn't want to see all those wonderful places in order to make a choice. There were so many things to see and do—just thinking about them made her blood race. For now she'd be happy just to go to Kostyka again to visit her father's cousin, Ulla, but Strengov considered Ulla a remarkably silly woman. And now—now—if she could make them think at Vodovsky that they couldn't do without her, there might be another way.

Outside the sun was pulling copper out of new buds and a pigeon waddled around a puddle. There was a time, Cirie remembered, when she loved it right here—the snow, the silence, the clear cold winters, the rush of spring, the white summer nights, heavy with the scent of roses and clover and hay. Wrapped in a kind of magic she would think how wonderful it was to be alive and to be right here. And she loved it still. But right here was no longer enough. Once, long ago, she would sit in the oak tree with Boris—before Boris became a radical and a fanatic—and watch the carts coming into town and sometimes a wonderful Vodovsky troika—and she would imagine that someday all of life would come down that road in a carriage drawn by three black horses. Now she knew nothing was going to come down that road.

"Tell, me, Koner," Dubrovna said with a look at Strengov, "if Vodovsky comes to the office, how does it look if the girl hasn't scrubbed?"

"Madam, Vodovsky doesn't come to me," Strengov said.

"And why is that? They pay Federin plenty."

"Federin woos them," Strengov shouted. "He poses, he paces, he strokes his chin like a man with the wisdom of Solomon."

"So he sweetens the bill a little."

"Strengov has been to Vodovsky," Koner said. "You were there when Federin was away. The oldest son was sick—Vassily."

"A dull, self-important man," Strengov said. "A cold fish. And the second son—"

"Serge—" Koner supplied the name. "Handsome. The picture of the Countess." Strengov looked at Cirie. "If he's there, you won't go even for overnight."

"He was home when you were there?" Koner said.

"No. I met him—" Strengov stopped. "Another time."

"Remember, Anna," the old woman said. "You won't see too much of Vogel until after you're married."

"Don't worry," Strengov said. "Marya warns Anna every hour not to even look at Vogel's bed until they're safely married. For my part, I'd prefer she take a good look at the bed she's going to lie in and then not marry him."

"Ivan, please!" Marya gasped.

Anna's eyes filled with tears and suddenly everyone was comforting her. But nobody was asking what would become of poor Anna who never in this world or the next would be able to take care of herself if she woke up one day and saw Vogel for what he was—handsome and nothing else.

"Anna," Cirie burst out. "When you get there, take time to look him over again. You might not like him anymore."

Anna blushed. "Why wouldn't I like him?"

"How terrible to be tied to someone the rest of your life because you made a mistake when you were too young to know better. Like a sentence to Siberia. It's so unfair."

"Cirie, most girls are married by seventeen."

"Because the world pushes them. Then when a girl sees her mistake, the world says, 'Oh, no, it was your mistake. Now you pay for it.' Not me. I won't get married for a long time."

"Cirie!" Marya said.

"They tell you marriage is a holy institution, but the rewards and suffering are very much of this world and no other."

"Cirie, you have a sharp tongue," Anya Dubrovna said in her own sharp tongue.

"Only honest," Strengov murmured.

"You don't know what his life is like over there," Cirie insisted. "You should want something more than a husband who drags himself home at night too tired to even talk and you say, 'I'm thankful to have him.'"

"Maybe you are thankful," Anna murmured.

"Over there one has everything," the old woman said.

"But everything is here!" Cirie said. "The beautiful estates and exciting people and traveling to Petersburg or Moscow. Or even Kostyka. Oh, how I'd love just to go to Kostyka again."

Anna stared at her. "Cirie, you can't have those things. They're for people with money. With titles."

"I'm sure there are ways."

Marya gasped. "Cirie, you worry me when you talk this way."

"Do you think you'll find all that in Kostyka?" Anna said.

"When I've seen what's in Kostyka, I'll go to Moscow."

"How? How will you go to Moscow?"

"How do I know?" Cirie laughed. "I'm still trying to get to Kostyka."

Walking back to the office, Strengov thought that he always reassured Marya that Cirie was well indoctrinated. But he wondered. It was hard to imagine Cirie accepting anything on blind faith, not even her mother's dire warnings on which she had been raised. If Cirie didn't see the logic in an idea, she simply left it alone on the counter of rejected merchandise. Like a seed falling on hard ground, it failed to take root and blew off on the next wind. More than once Strengov had wondered about the process by which she reached her conclusions. She seemed to perform lightning calculations intuitively, appraising the pros and cons, the odds and the risks, and to reach instant decisions others might arrive at only after days of deliberation.

"Poor Marya," he said to Koner. "Cirie is too much for her. Anna accepts life and Lily accepts instruction. That she can understand."

"And Cirie?" Koner said.

"Cirie accepts nothing."

Another pistol sound came from the river and Strengov sighed. Anna going to America. Cirie going to Vodovsky. In the maple tree a starling screeched its maniacal cry. Strengov smiled a smile, not of life beginning, but of things ending.

4

It was dinner time when Vassily locked his office door and walked to the drawing room, ready to decide whether the nurse had to be dismissed at once or could remain until he returned from Kostyka.

Vara had lost no time interrupting him to tell him the woman would not do. A systematic meticulous man—dark hair, mustache and beard all clipped to precisely the same half-inch length—he had just finished a meeting with Antychek, his manager, and was enjoying a cigar, while he reflected that soon the river would be alive again with ships that would carry his grain to Moscow and Petersburg and his lumber to ports as far away as the tip of Africa. Then Vara burst in, keys jangling at her waist, complaining before she had the door closed. "The nurse is here and I'm furious."

"Already?" How many times had he asked her not to interrupt him in his office? At every minor crisis she was in here. "That must be something of a record."

"You'll have to find someone in Kostyka. This person is out of the question."

Vassily clamped his teeth. He'd had enough of this war between Georgii and the nurses. Since their father's death he had accepted responsibility for the boy, and for Serge, too, expecting in return only respect and obedience. He had shaped Georgii's life, guided him, molded him into what a Vodovsky ought to be. Then a few thugs stepped out of a forest and now Vassily hardly recognized him. How could a boy change so much? One day quiet and cooperative, the next day a devil. "What's wrong with this one?"

"Everything! She's too young. She's too—inviting."

"Inviting!"

"Not pretty. There's something strange—the hair is very light and the eyelashes are black. But pretty enough to be unacceptable. It would be dangerous to have her in the house." Vara's tone suggested there were other considerations which Vassily must surely understand. "Stepa shouldn't have let Georgii see her before I had approved. Now there's no reasoning with him."

Vassily's cigar stopped short of his mouth. "Georgii wants her?"

"What's important is that we can't have her in the house," Vara said, pointedly. "Remember, Vassily—Serge will be home."

"When? Do you know when? I ordered him home weeks ago."

"It would be asking for trouble. I've told her she's to leave in the morning."

"And will you have a replacement in the morning?"

"No! And the burden will fall on me. No governess—no tutors—Georgii's driven everyone away. You'll be in Kostyka. And I have enough to do. The servants are so careless—the house is full of guests."

The house was not full of guests. Stepa and Elissa were in their cottage with Tanya. And Kyra, his mother's younger sister, was here. Even though Vassily had little patience with Kyra's endless chattering, he had urged her to come because he wanted company for his mother while he was in Kostyka and now she was here, only a day late which for Kyra was very good. And Stepa's oldest friend, Constantine Paklov, the most respected political writer in Russia, was expected today. Six extra people. To Vara everything was difficult.

"Maman feels we should give her a try because her father has called here," Vara said. "Naturally I couldn't discuss with Maman how rash that would be, although perhaps I should."

"Don't be ridiculous!" Discuss it with Maman! Maman, who was certain her children would never do anything improper. They might have their little ways, Maman would say, but they could be depended on to do the correct thing.

"Maman says we should consider her feelings and—"

"Her feelings, if she has any—" Vassily cleared his throat which became constricted when he was angry, "—are not my concern. Georgii probably wants her because you're against her. A few days and she'll leave like the others—eagerly."

"Not if Serge comes home."

"Vara, let me explain this to you. A young horse has to be broken. You pull him up ten, twenty, a hundred times, and then he understands. Georgii has to understand that he'll have a nurse until he walks. Meanwhile, there will be more victims. Let this woman be one of them. Victim number four."

"Are you saying she's to stay!"

"I'll decide that when I'm ready. My time is important, not hers."

"And Serge?"

"Serge won't become involved with some moujik woman in his own home. He has more taste. And he knows I wouldn't stand for it."

Vara changed her tactics. "If Stepa hadn't interfered, this wouldn't have happened. When you have a problem with her, you can thank Stepa."

This thrust found its mark. Vassily did not like Stepa interfering in his decisions about his brothers—Stepa, who had spent his whole life doing exactly as he pleased, supporting artists and musicians, playing his violin, writing an endless book about the Russian people. "Saints, Sinners and Survivors," he called it. Stepa had not even managed to marry without a scandal! He had become openly involved with Elissa, the tall, striking Countess Rette, while she was still married and after she became pregnant they retired to Whitewater until Count Rette died, when the relationship and the child were legitimized. To this day Vassily would ask himself what compulsion had driven them to flaunt their illicit relationship. They could have had a private discreet affair—if their great passion was so irresistible. Personally, few women had interested Vassily even moderately and he certainly had never experienced an all-consuming passion that could have driven him to compromise his standards. He was sure he never would.

As he approached the drawing room Vassily heard Kyra's high-pitched voice above the rest. Kyra was one of those sweet, birdlike, relentlessly boring women who imagine that every shred of gossip is endlessly fascinating to one and all—busy or idle, dull or quick-witted. "They're in the morning room," Madame said in response to Vassily's inquiry about the nurse. "I gave them permission to finish a game of checkers."

Behind him Vara gushed, "Now, Constantine, tell us the news from Petersburg." With Constantine here, she was very lively tonight, splendidly turned out in a red dinner dress and jewels. No jangling keys. Rather different from a few hours ago.

Constantine Paklov, Stepa's old friend, was a tall spare man with white hair and young bright blue eyes, as slender and reedy as Stepa was husky and broad, as soft-spoken as Stepa was boisterous. Smiling patiently he bent over to listen to Vara. Just as though he were interested in what she had to say, Vassily thought. Socially, Constantine was mild-mannered and charming but in his political opinions, eagerly anticipated and widely read, he was sharp and uncompromising. Quite courageous, really, Vassily admitted. Too liberal, but he was always supremely well-informed.

"I only know political news," Constantine said. "You know the Tsar appointed a new President of the Council. Kokovtsev was the best man we had but the Tsar told him he needed someone fresh and replaced him with Goremykin."

"Goremykin!" Stepa scoffed. "Seventy-five years old. Lies around all day reading French novels. In these serious times. I suppose we have the Empress to thank."

"She's so suspicious of anyone intelligent the Emperor is left surrounded by flatterers and inferior minds."

Vassily turned to his mother. "Is this the nurse's idea of what's expected of her? A game of checkers?"

"Vassi—" His mother touched his arm. "Georgii is smitten with her."

Vassily nodded, agreeing to consider the woman, which he was prepared to do if they ever happened to complete the checkers.

Now Constantine was talking about the former Council President, Stolypin, assassinated in Kiev, in the opera house before the eyes of the Tsar. Constantine who had been Stolypin's friend, was so obsessed with the murder he was writing a book about it, which Vassily thought was carrying things rather far.

Vassily was annoyed that this nurse presumed to keep him waiting. "We'll send for Georgii," he said to his mother.

"Here they are now, dear."

For a minute Vassily stood absolutely still. His throat constricted. Federin had sent a child! A girl so young she could hardly be considered responsible for herself! He lit a cigar and stood before her. "Did Federin interview you before he sent you here?"

She raised her eyes which Vassily saw were quite startling. The fact was not relevant. "Dr. Federin has known me all my life."

Vassily put a veil of smoke between himself and the eyes. Perhaps the fact *was* relevant. Those eyes probably explained a lot. With Georgii and with Federin, too, the old fool. "I may interview you later," he said. "But I don't think you'll do."

"You won't do—you won't do," Cirie said to herself at dinner. "Is that all they can say?" Well, if they didn't want her, she didn't want them.

But even now Madame's sister, Kyra, a little birdlike woman with a gossipy voice, was describing a banquet the Emperor gave for some foreign dignitaries. "Prince Bolkanin said the room was a shower of jewels. Only the Westerners were drab."

"Nothing can equal the splendor of the Russian court," Vara said. She moved her long fingers, jingling her own jeweled bracelets. "And the Empress?"

"Prince Bolkanin doesn't repeat gossip about the Empress." Then, lest anyone be unaware of the gossip, "Her reclusiveness, her German background—"

"Her staretz—Rasputin," Stepa put in.

"The Empress wore a diamond tiara and her throat was a mass of pearls, with diamonds and rubies." Kyra's high-pitched voice dropped. "Of course, she finds these functions difficult. By the end of the evening she was quite pale. Her breathing was heavy."

"Probably bordering on hysteria," Stepa said.

"The Emperor—" Kyra's voice picked up again, "was magnificent."

"The Emperor is always magnificent," Vara said.

"The best thing this magnificent Emperor could do is become deaf to his wife, eh, Constantine?" Stepa said.

Everyone seemed to pay a lot of attention to this mild-mannered new arrival, Constantine Paklov, with bright young eyes and a warm smile, asking him questions when they already knew the answers just to have their opinions confirmed.

Constantine shrugged. "The Tsar is a mild man. She's ten times more intense." The Emperor, the Empress, jewels, banquets, diamond tiaras, Cirie thought. Yesterday the Tsar was only a photograph on the wall of the post office. Now she was sitting with people who knew him, who spoke of him intimately. Only Tanya's tutor, Arkady, seated opposite her, seemed bored and hostile. A thin, loose-jointed young man, Arkady had an elfin quality about him—a quizzical smile and a bubbly manner—that seemed at odds with his more serious side. Tanya had told Cirie he was a revolutionary. At dinner he kept his eyes on his plate, only looking up when something particularly outrageous was said.

"What about *him*—Rasputin?" Stepa said. "Is he still riding high?"

"Why do you think Kokovtsev was dismissed? He dared to tell the Emperor that Rasputin is a lecher and a drunkard who is involving the royal family in a serious scandal. He showed him police reports—Rasputin drunk in public restaurants, Rasputin receiving actresses, seamstresses, one society woman after another in his rooms."

"This drunken lecher welcomes any woman who can climb the stairs," Stepa said. "His appetites are legendary."

"What goes to the Emperor goes to the Empress," Constantine said and smiled. "Predictably, she responded to the reports by getting rid of the reporter. To her, Rasputin is a saint, persecuted as Christ was persecuted. Meanwhile the rumors go on." Madame's eyes were fixed on the crystal goblet she was fingering. The suggestion that the Tsar, selected by God and guardian of the Church, was controlled by the fanatical ideas of an unstable wife, who in turn was controlled by an immoral uneducated peasant, obviously upset her.

"Rumors about his adventures with society women? Or his adventures with the Empress?"

"Stepa," Vassily warned and Stepa, unoffended, changed the subject.

"You don't understand." Kyra shook her head vigorously. "The Empress believes Rasputin is sent by God to save her son. And after Spala, how do you know he's not?"

Startled, Cirie looked at Kyra. Everyone had heard about the incident at the royal hunting lodge at Spala, where the Tsarevitch injured his leg in a minor fall and, because of his affliction, lay close to death. Soon it was being said that he was saved through the intercession of Rasputin, but Cirie had thought that only the moujiks believed that, turning it into one of those miracles they loved. But apparently the Empress believed it, too. And Kyra, too!

"All hope was gone," Kyra said. "The last sacrament had been given. Then the Empress sent a telegram to Rasputin in his village in Siberia, begging for his prayers for the boy's life."

"Kyra, everyone knows this fable," Stepa said.

"Yes, well, people say he hypnotizes her, but he can't hypnotize her from Siberia. He telegraphed, 'God has heard your prayers. The little one will not die.'" A hush came into Kyra's voice. "At once the Empress became totally serene. And the next day the boy began to recover. So how do you know he's not a man of God? What happened, happened."

"He's a cool gambler," Stepa muttered. "He bet his whole stake on one card. But the problem was there long before Spala. They were always a susceptible pair."

Vassily was not listening to this nonsense. He was asking himself whether they could make do with this so-called "suitable woman," who was not suitable and was not a woman, just until he returned from Kostyka. He ran his finger back and forth compulsively, tracing the scrolls on the carved arm of the chair. Probably Federin wanted to do this girl a service. These local bourgeoisie were all alike. They were flattered at your patronage, but they considered it almost an obligation to put something over on you. He would deal with Federin later, but that didn't solve anything now.

"There were others before Rasputin," Stepa said. "They always had someone."

"Remember that Frenchman," Elissa said. Stepa's dark-haired elegant wife was as irreverent as he was. "Philippe, the Magician. From Lyons. He held seances for them."

"A graduate of a butcher shop that produced pork and chickens for the citizens of Lyons. And a magician for the Tsar of Russia." While the white-gloved footmen moved silently around him, Vassily let his eyes travel down the table. They were all here and there was no one to find a new nurse. Maman was not well enough and Vara would not be satisfied with the best of them. And Maman's aged aunt, Aunt Vayana, who had lived with her for years, was senile and a bit daft. Certainly not Stepa. And not Elissa, with that air that assured you she would do as she pleased and didn't care what you thought. Or restless birdlike Kyra. They were all here, busy with each other, and no one would have time for Georgii. At least when this girl spoke to him, he answered her, he wasn't fighting her. Vassily watched her smile at him and Georgii actually smiled back. Maybe, Vassily thought, just until he returned—

"Philippe the butcher held a seance for the Tsar every week," Stepa said. "The Tsar believed he was in touch with his father's ghost who was communicating important decisions to him."

"Ruling Russia with some important raps," Elissa said.

The girl was talking to Georgii, smiling at him again, waiting while his face lit up in response. Why, she's wooing him! Vassily thought. Even though she's been told to leave, she intends to stay! He had better dismiss her at once.

"So you see, Kyra, the seed was already there," Stepa said. "At Spala it germinated and put out a poisoned plant. But this neurotic woman was already devoted to Rasputin, already writing him adoring letters and getting rid of ministers who spoke against him."

"Stepa, Stepa," Kyra protested in her insistent nasal voice. "You don't understand. The Empress believes the Tsarevitch's life is in Rasputin's hands. He holds out that promise and he makes good on it."

"It's like a Greek tragedy," Stepa said, sadly. "A disastrous combination of character and circumstances. A strong Tsar could resist a neurotic Tsarina and her medieval mysticism. A sound-minded Empress could compensate for a weak Emperor. Look at Catherine the Great. The Emperor was mad—she had him killed. A healthy son and there would be no Achilles heel through which this pathetic couple can be frightened and dominated. Russia might have a chance."

Russia might have a chance! Cirie thought. A chance for what?

"Russia is a ship on stormy seas and the captain doesn't know how to handle her," Stepa said. "The Tsarevitch's health is a dagger in her heart. He's a pleasant little boy—he doesn't mean to be the messenger of death to Russia. But he is."

A silence fell over the table and a few of them exchanged glances, more embarrassed by Stepa's abandon, Cirie thought, than worried about what he said. She felt Georgii tugging at her sleeve. "Do you believe that story?" he whispered. "That he saved the Tsarevitch when he hurt his leg?"

"Oh, Georgii—probably you should ask your mother about that."

His eyes accused her of betrayal. "You're just like the others. You won't talk to me—only tell me what to do."

Cirie glanced around the table. They believe that story here and if I show a lack of faith, they'll send me packing. But if I'm to get him to walk, I can't have him waiting for a Rasputin and a miracle of his own.

But already they were talking about more expected guests. Vara was chatting about some prince and princess and their niece, Irene, who, Vara was sure, had been the most beautiful young woman at the balls this winter. And Vassily was expecting a government man—an agricultural expert—in June. "A fellow named Laranov," Vassily said.

Constantine looked up with that warm smile. "I know Laranov. An interesting fellow. Very dynamic personality."

Vassily shrugged. "A dynamic personality is a hollow coin. I'll wait to see if he knows anything."

Why, they can't send me away with all these guests, Cirie thought. They can't find another nurse in Novotnii and it'll take at least a week to get someone from Kostyka. And they're all too busy for Georgii—during this entire dinner nobody has said a word to him. Oh, in a week I'll think of something!

She turned back to Georgii. "I believe the Tsarevitch was very ill," she said. "But do I believe that Rasputin interceded with God to save his life? No, I do not. I don't believe God requires an intermediary. I believe He expects us to help ourselves. I think that's the only way it works."

The hostility left Georgii's eyes and he was an agreeable nine-year old again. "I don't believe it, either."

"Well?" Vara demanded after dinner.

"Well, what?" Vassily said.

Vara nodded toward Cirie across the room.

"Vara, don't worry, she won't last long," Vassily said. "After she's gone, I may have Federin send out a few more. Why bring them from Kostyka just to send them back?"

Amused at Vara's shocked expression, Vassily said, "I never intended her to stay. She's only a number."

5

From the top of this little hill, fields stretched before you to the distant brown block of forests and, if you looked back the way you had come, you saw the mansion and the service buildings, far in the other direction.

In the white light of sunrise Cirie sat quietly on Pegasus, the horse Gerzy had selected for her after Madame gave her permission to ride two mornings a week provided she returned by seven o'clock. In the east the pale light wrapped itself around slender birches and the lake was an opaque mirror beside the children's playhouse—the first thing she had noticed that day three weeks ago, riding in from the district road.

Three weeks. How different it was from what she had expected—the estate so much more, the people less. She could not have imagined the splendor. Enough buildings to make a town—four guest cottages, two kitchens, one for the family's food, a second for the servants' food—laundry and sewing and dairy cottages, stables and the carriage-house and all the farm buildings. In the orchards the apple trees were beginning to flower, the peach blossoms were ready to open, the late summer pears were still only a promise. And in the mansion, sparkling chandeliers, the Oriental chest—moved yesterday to the center hall—a thousand pieces of table silver and English china, the zakuski table in the dining room where the family gathered before dinner to enjoy hors d'oeuvres of fresh caviar, smoked sturgeon, salmon, meat and fish pates, sometimes a suckling pig. She had expected it to be beautiful and it was. And she had expected the people to match. And they did not.

Cirie stroked the horse's neck, feeling his warmth against her leg. They didn't like her here, especially Vara who directed a never-ending barrage of criticism at her. "I suppose, Cirie, you're doing your best?" Vara would say. "Well, when Vassily brings a more qualified nurse…" And, "Cirie, you must be more careful of your appearance. I don't know how you can be so careless. And so bold." And, "What are you smiling at?…Try to be more discreet…Your laughter is too boisterous…You speak too loud…You speak too softly…Do not speak at the table unless you're spoken to…What are you smiling at now?"

To Vara, Cirie realized, her smile was a sore irritation, although not the worst. That came when Constantine spoke to her, as he did last evening before dinner. Even though Cirie replied as briefly as possible, without even a hint of a smile, a terrible confrontation with Vara followed.

"If you ever again carry on such a disgusting flirtation, you will be out of this house within the hour." A deep flush gave a coarse look to Vara's face. "Night or day. Is that clear?"

Dumbfounded, Cirie stared at her. The trick is not to listen, she told herself. The trick is just to say, Yes, Countess, and not hear anything she says. Easier said than done.

"We really can't continue to have you at the table. We'll have to make other arrangements."

"But, Countess, he spoke to me!"

"Only out of charity! Answer and turn away. You can't say anything that could possibly interest him."

After Georgii was asleep Cirie flung herself down on her bed. This was not working out—any of it. She had hoped that by the end of the summer they would feel they couldn't do without her and they would take her to Kostyka. And none of it was working out. Tears gave way to anger and she poured out her indignation in a letter to Ulla.

"They are cold, unkind people," she wrote. "And next month when I go home to say goodbye to Anna, I will stay there. *I will not return!*" She read the letter and tore it up. She would not admit defeat even to herself. Instead she went down the hall to the upstairs sitting room where evenings Arkady, Tanya's tutor, was teaching her to play cards.

Arkady flipped a deck of cards as she entered the room. Serious and sober all day, Arkady came alive at cards. "Tonight I'm going to teach you vingt-et-un."

"Arkady, tell me about Constantine Paklov," Cirie said.

"Now you're catching on."

"To what?"

"Paklov is a famous political writer. A man of reason." Smiling his pixie smile Arkady looked up from the cards. "To me he's the enemy because if the Tsar would listen to him, things might improve and we wouldn't get a revolution. But the Countess—our irresistible Vara—has her hard eye locked on him, so you'd better not even look at him."

Arkady shuffled the cards expertly.

"Where did you learn so much about cards, Arkady?"

"Revolution is my life's work. I'm very serious about it. But cards! My father was a gambler. I could play cards before I could read. I may teach you how to cheat."

"Why would I want to cheat?"

"Any skill is worth having, dearie. You never know when you'll use it. Besides, if someone is cheating you how else will you know? In vingt-et-un you have to learn to count the cards. You have to remember what's been played."

This morning, sitting on Pegasus, watching the sun push up over the forest, Cirie thought about how different these joyless people were from what she had expected. Vara, who kept everything locked because she was certain all servants were thieves. And Madame, always beautiful and serene but insisting in a quiet voice that everything be correct. Why must every little thing be exactly as someone decreed a hundred years ago? And restless feather-brained Kyra, always fretting about where to travel next. And Kyra's pompous self-satisfied husband had arrived, Otto, who had the face of a scheming cherub and seemed to accidentally brush against Cirie so often she was careful to step out of his way. And poor Georgii, who was fighting back with the only weapon he had. He refused to walk.

"You want to try?" she had asked him yesterday over checkers. He only shrugged. "We could practice in your room. Just you and me. Our secret." He had shown a flash of interest but it was too soon. He didn't trust her enough yet.

Now the sun was showing the top of its head and the lake was still and birches gleamed and the world was bathed in the damp promise of a new day. And suddenly the manor house with its fussy, eternally talking occupants seemed far away and unreal, like puppets she had seen as a child, carried about by a family of wandering actors. The curtains would part and the puppets would pop up on the stage and jump and hop around and say silly things in high squeaky voices or in deep, threatening voices. They would laugh at bad jokes or weep with shallow emotions and then their allotted time on stage would be over and the curtain would close. She ought to be starting back.

From a bluff overlooking the river she watched a steamer move downstream that later would go past her father's house and an oppressed feeling swept over her. She longed to go home and put these cold unloving people behind her. She did not delude herself that they liked her. She did not delude herself that she cared.

But she wanted to go to Kostyka with them so she had better find a way to get along, even with Vara. And stay away from Constantine, much as she would like to talk to him. He was so pleasant and soft-spoken and his bright blue eyes twinkled when he spoke to her. The trick is to feel nothing, she told herself. The trick is to be immune. They can't hurt you if you won't let them.

A sing-song phrase that Lily used to chant came to mind. "Draw a magic circle and in it—" She didn't remember the rest. That's what you have to do, she told herself. Draw a circle around yourself—and that is the defense line that no one gets through. And inside that line, I am in command—the ruler, the autocrat, the Tsar. And as long as that is mine, I can survive. No one can make you cry if you refuse the tears. No one can humiliate you if you refuse to be humiliated. *No one can touch you if you won't let them.*

On the river the upstream steamer came into sight and turned toward the Vodovsky dock, revealing luggage on the side of the deck to be put ashore. Probably some new guests arriving that she would be told not to speak to. She moved the reins and Pegasus headed for the stables.

*   *   *

On the porch of the guest cottage that he occupied at Whitewater Constantine sipped his coffee and read the manuscript that he worked on only intermittently now because he knew he would not publish it for a long time, if ever.

He had started to write a short book about his friend, the former President of the Council, Stolypin—his accomplishments and his assassination—calling it "The Two-thousand Days."

He wanted to explore the unanswered questions: Why had Stolypin had so little protection that day in Kiev while the security around the Tsar was massive? And how had the assassin, an extremist named Bogrov, managed to walk unchallenged down the aisle of the crowded opera house and stand in front of him and fire the gun? And why was Bogrov executed so quickly, before anyone could get the whole story? He had been a double agent, a radical extremist who also worked for the police—not uncommon in Russia. But for which of his two masters was he working that day, the left or the right? Was the assassination, as officially stated, a revolutionary plot or, as Constantine suspected, a reactionary police plot?

Then the book began to change. Sometimes an event occurs in which all the cross currents of an age seem suddenly to coalesce so that the event has a sickening sense of inevitability and becomes a symbol of its time. Stolypin was killed because, wrestling with the sins of a century, he was a threat equally to the extreme right—the police, reactionary nobles, anti-Semites, the Black Hundred—and to the extreme left—the hot-eyed terrorists willing to blow up the whole house for the sake of their own power. Constantine found he was writing a study of the political winds that had blown in Russia from the time of Alexander II, the "Tsar Liberator," who freed the serfs in 1861 and gave them land but not enough to sustain themselves, so that nobody was satisfied—neither the estate owners who lost their serfs and a third of their land, nor the moujiks who gained the land and with it a burden of taxation that imposed a different kind of slavery.

Over the next twenty years there were seven attempts on the Tsar Liberator's life. In 1881, when Constantine was fifteen, the seventh attempt succeeded. He remembered the day vividly. A terrorist bomb was thrown under the Tsar's carriage, wounding the horses and a bystander, but leaving the Tsar unharmed.

Alexander II should have hurried away. Instead he walked back to inquire about the wounded and another radical rushed up and threw a second bomb directly at his feet. His body was ripped open, one leg blown away, his face torn. The Tsar Liberator whispered that he should be carried to the palace to die. His son stood in the bedroom and watched his father's death and became Alexander III.

The assassination was a turning point. The father had been the most liberal of the Tsars and he had died at the hands of the radicals. The son slammed down the lid. A giant of a man, six feet four inches tall, with great physical strength and an overpowering personality, for thirteen years Alexander III ruled with an iron hand and preserved the absolute power of the Tsar. He expected to reign a long time. He died at forty-nine.

When Constantine reached the reign of his son, Nicholas II, the present Tsar, he knew he was writing a Gotterdammerung—the twilight of Romanov Russia.

Standing at the railing that early morning, Constantine looked over at the rose garden. At daybreak he had seen Cirie going to the stables and he was watching for her to come back. At first he had not noticed her, although now he wondered at his own temporary blindness. It was not until Vara began harassing her that he looked to see what Vara found so upsetting and saw that she was a rare beauty.

A minute later Stepa came striding along the path, returning from his morning walk with Lupa, the wolfhound, and Talley, the yellow mongrel, bounding along behind him. "What a morning!" Stepa called. "You're not writing this morning?"

"I've arrived at the present reign. It's an old story—a strong father, a weak son."

Stepa sat down on the porch, ready for a good talk. "Even physically the contrast is unfortunate. Alexander was a giant, a dynamic personality. Nicholas is small and shy."

"Many small men make you forget their size. Look at Napoleon. This Tsar is a weakling. He can't make a decision and stick to it."

Stepa shrugged. "He believes God selected him and God will run things. A true mystic. And there's his superstitious reverence for the memory of his father. Everything must be done exactly as his father did it."

"Russia—behind in everything, screaming for change—ruled by a man who can look in only two directions—backward to his father and upward to God."

"With a mediocre mind and no taste for the job."

A movement at the rose garden caught Constantine's eye and he smiled. "Here is something more pleasant to consider."

Stepa looked around. "Cirie?"

"She goes to the stables at daybreak."

"Eugenie allows her to ride twice a week as long as she's back before Georgii gets up."

"Does anyone count?"

"As you and I are the only ones up, who's to count?"

Constantine watched her as she came along the walk. Whenever he spoke to her she all but melted into the walls, letting just a hint of a smile break through. But the eyes—the eyes alone would carry her far if she had even a grain of sense. He was almost afraid to talk to her and find she was a simpleton. "She may be just a little girl from the district town, but she walks like a countess."

"She looks like a countess."

"Does Vara know she rides?"

"Ah, so you've noticed, too, how fond Vara has become of her."

"What does she have against her?"

"I suppose if Vara had a third of Cirie's beauty she'd be easier to please about a lot of things."

Stepa stood up to go back to his cottage and Constantine went down to wait for Cirie and then was puzzled that she seemed startled and eager to escape. "Do I frighten you?"

"Oh, no, monsieur. I'd like to be able to talk to you."

"Then why do you edge away?"

She lowered those incredible black lashes. "You're an early riser, monsieur." She glanced at the house. "I see your light." With all the art of a duchess she had avoided his question.

"I rise early to write."

Again a delay and then the marvelous smile. It always happened the same way. You had all her attention, but she held back that smile for just a beat, like a musical theme in which a pause gathers your attention, heightens your anticipation, before something wonderful happens. She glanced at the house again, deciding whether to escape or to stay.

"When I was about your age," he said, "I was walking only two blocks away when Alexander II was assassinated. I ran the two blocks and I saw the demolished carriage and the wounded horses and, from a distance, the dying Tsar."

"You saw it!"

"That day I saw the extreme hate on both sides and the tragedy it had produced and my passion for the study of politics was born."

Many times he had voiced far more fascinating thoughts that had not been half so warmly received. It was always like this. The eyes warmed and widened with appreciation of *you*. And you found yourself reading in them how clever, how charming, how thoroughly excellent you were. "And you, Cirie—what are you after so early in the day?"

"Only a horse."

He hardly heard. He was waiting for the reward—the delayed smile—and now it came. "Do you realize how charming that is?"

She was genuinely puzzled. So it wasn't a trick she had learned.

"Your smile. The way you hold back for just an instant and then make it seem like a reward."

She burst out laughing. "I'm not *supposed* to smile. Countess Laszinska doesn't like it."

Oh, she was quick! She saw at once the humor in it—that Vara had unwittingly contributed to something others found charming.

"And I'm not supposed to talk to the guests. That's why I was edging away."

Constantine felt that he was not really talking to a child. "Does that bother you? The way the Countess is always—making suggestions?"

"No," she said. "It's just her way."

He did not believe it but he gave her credit for a nice pride and a stiff spine. She saw Vara exactly as she was—a nagging stupid woman. It was Vara's way. With more to do or less to do, that would still be Vara's way.

"The steamer's here," she said.

The boat was at the dock and two young men stood on the deck ready to jump off. Stepa came hurrying back. "Ho!" he shouted.

"Ho!" came the reply.

"More guests, apparently," Constantine said as Stepa hurried past.

"Guests!" Stepa said. "It's Serge! Serge and Theo are home."

They came along the broad tree-lined path, Stepa walking between the two slender, fashionable young men, all three talking and laughing. Serge was blond and as tall as Stepa, Theo, Kyra's son, a little shorter and sensitive-looking with dark hair and eyes. Just as in the portraits, Serge was the image of Madame from his blond hair and blue eyes to the classic beauty of his face.

They greeted Constantine and Serge turned to Cirie and smiled. "So it's you!" he said. "I've seen you before."

Cirie met his eyes and a startling unfamiliar sensation shot through her.

Lupa and Talley raced up to him and he reached down to them while his eyes lingered on Cirie. "Haven't we, Theo?" he said. "We've seen her in town."

"Yes," Theo said. "Many times."

"The doctor's middle daughter," Serge said. His eyes held hers, as though there were just the two of them.

"Well, come along to the house," Stepa said. "Everybody's been waiting for you. Some people are put out that you're late."

A minute later Cirie raced down the wide center hall, impulsively running her hand over the Oriental chest as she passed it, and ran up the stairs to her room. Things could change in a second. Only a few minutes ago Whitewater had seemed so dull and hopeless. Now everything was different. Now her blood raced. And suddenly Whitewater was magically, unbelievably beautiful.

6

Clutching Vassily's letter, Vara hurried down the center hall, head thrust forward as though to butt aside anything in her path. He would return in about a week, Vassily wrote, and Prince and Princess Tchernefsky and their niece, Irene, would visit in July. Less welcome was the news that he had seen General Borassin who, on learning of Maman's accident, had said he would arrange at once to visit her. No surprise there, Vara thought. And even though Sacha Borassin's own estate was only a few hours away, Vassily had invited him to stay at Whitewater. And that government grain expert, Laranov, would be here in July. Vara could only pray that he would not turn up at the same time as the Prince. But what troubled Vara most was what the letter did not say. Not a word about a new nurse.

Vara decided she would have to discuss the problem with her mother, who didn't seem to notice the way the girl forgot who she was and with her eyes persuaded everyone else to forget it, too. Or the way Serge never took his eyes off her and spent hours with Georgii just to be near her. The way they all looked at her—Serge—Theo—Constantine!

Approaching the study Vara arranged a smile on her face and then, finding the room empty, abandoned it. She searched quickly through her mother's desk and continued on down the hall. Even if informed about Serge, Maman probably would not believe it. To Maman, in Serge a fault did not exist. And now she liked this girl. Whenever Vara raised the question of dismissing her, her mother put off discussing it. Her mother did not always make that much sense—she only *sounded* as though she did. She only managed with a soft voice and a well-chosen gesture to *appear* to be right. To Vara this was an exhilarating discovery.

She turned into the sun-drenched morning room and blinked. To her this room, filled with flowers and plants, was always too bright with its white wicker furniture and cushions of lilacs and green leaves on a white background. Kyra was here alone, working on a piece of French petit-point.

"Vassily is inviting too many people," Vara complained. "Sacha Borassin. And that government person, Laranov. I wish he'd tell them both to stay home."

Kyra put down her needlework. "Oh, Vara, Vassi couldn't do that. The Borassins are a very old family."

"And that agricultural person will be coarse and rough-spoken. I can see him now. He's sure to be a peasant. And Sacha Borassin might as well be, the way he roars and shouts and insults people. I don't know how Maman can put up with him."

"Eugenie won't be pleased if you make Sacha feel unwelcome, Vara," Kyra said. "He's a dear friend."

Vara looked at Kyra sharply. This wasn't the first time she had spoken this way about General Borassin. "What do you mean?"

"We knew him as children. Sacha was devoted to Eugenie, even then."

"He's at least five years younger!"

"Yes, but Eugenie was so beautiful—and Sacha always had a weakness for beauty. He still does."

Well, he just might be disappointed this time. All her life Vara had suffered in the shadow of her mother's beauty and charm. At twenty-four she had escaped by becoming the third wife of a man as old as her father and for six years she had supervised his health and his home, which was all an elderly man could expect, and after his death she had returned home. Now since the accident her mother had aged, pain had traced lines in her face, her beauty was fading. And she herself, Vara thought, was in her prime—and not at all an unattractive woman.

All at once Vara saw Constantine on the terrace with Serge and Theo, all with their heads turned, looking at something. With a smile Vara prepared to join them. Then the smile died. The something they were looking at was Cirie, reading to Georgii and Tanya and, of all people, ancient white-haired Aunt Vayana. And they were all watching her—Serge, looking like a lovesick goat, and Theo, just as enchanted. And Constantine! "I detest that girl!" Vara burst out.

"Heavens, Vara, who?"

"But as long as Georgii is happy, Maman doesn't care what I want. It's always Georgii. And Serge. And Vassily, of course."

"Vara, what's happened? Why are you so upset?"

"If I want to get rid of her, that should be enough!" Vara started to leave and came back. "Kyra, have you considered that Serge and Theo have just come from Paris where girls were available on all sides. A certain type to be sure—but Paris is a very emancipated city."

"Oh, Vara, I wouldn't worry. It's good for young men to have their fling."

You could absolutely depend on Kyra to miss the point. "I'm not talking about what they did in Paris! Kyra, Theo is your son. Do you see any young women here?"

"Well—no-o."

For a long moment Vara stared at Cirie whose hair in the sunlight was the color of flax. "There is one," she said, sharply. "Attractive and unsuitable."

Kyra followed her eyes. "Oh!"

"You hear all the society gossip, Kyra. How many stories do you hear about affairs with nurses?"

"Well it's true one hears—but she's so young."

"The countryside is sprinkled with the illegitimate offspring of these affairs. We have to think of the girl, too. She shouldn't be placed in the way of temptation." If there was one thing Vara knew it was that in the flush of an easy affair with a beautiful young girl, a young man—or an old man—could be blinded to a woman of more suitable qualities.

"Oh, Vara, what should we do?" Kyra said.

"What we should do is get her out of here." Vara leaned closer. "Talk to Maman, Kyra. Get rid of her before she spells trouble for either one of them—Theo or Serge." She was happy to see that Kyra looked worried.

Meanwhile she intended to know where that girl was every minute, watch her from the minute she and Georgii came down in the morning until they retired at night. And, she thought suddenly—after that, too. It was Serge and Theo—and more.

Cirie felt Serge's eyes on her across the dinner table. When you can't talk with words, you talk with your eyes. You ask questions with your eyes, you make promises. Serge could never speak to her because Vara was always there, a hand away, policing, but whenever Cirie looked at him, she would find his eyes waiting for hers.

Vara was talking about the expected visit of Prince Tchernefsky. "I know you'll be delighted, Constantine. I suspect you've become just a tiny bit bored with us." She paused to await his protest. "The Prince will liven things up for you."

She smiled aggressively. Was there ever a woman who could work herself up with such intensity, Cirie thought. Give her a target, whether it was Constantine or Georgii's life or Serge's eyes, and she focused on it with maniacal determination. Even when she was quiet, you felt that her mind was whirling. Some plot was hatching, some scheme was brewing. Even sitting idly on the terrace, she would snatch up her little black poodle, "Petite," and hold it on her lap, clutching her like a vise, and presently the two faces, Vara's and the dog's, would take on similar expressions of resentment.

Serge's eyes were talking to her over his wine glass. Don't look at him, Cirie told herself. This is dangerous.

"And the Princess, too," Vara said.

"Imagine—the Princess!" Kyra said. "And she never leaves Petersburg except for her annual trip to Biarritz!" Vara lifted her chin, savoring this social triumph.

Leaning past Cirie, Georgii whispered to Tanya. "Someone else is coming, too. Lydia." He flopped his head back and stared at the ceiling and he and Tanya broke into smothered giggles.

"Sit up, Georgii! You're getting worse every day." Vara threw Cirie an accusing look and said to the others, "Vassily will bring back a nurse who'll get Georgii under control."

Serge's eyes snapped over to Vara. Unconcerned, Georgii resumed his story. "Lydia pretends not to hear you. Then later she says,'Oh, I wasn't here. I left the room.'"

"She means she was in a trance," Tanya whispered. "She's Theo's sister. And Kurasin's love. He's coming, too."

"*And*," Georgii said, "she loves Rasputin." More laughter.

"Georgii, behave or I'll be blamed," Cirie whispered.

He stopped laughing. "They can't send you away. I won't have anyone else."

"What ever happened to Prince Tchernefsky's son?" Stepa said. "The one they call the black sheep."

"Maxim," Theo said. "He's in Paris, living with a delightful French woman."

"Not the sort, I suppose, one would marry," Vara said. "At least he remembers who he is."

Serge's eyes went briefly to Vara. "She's absolutely charming. She left her husband, a wealthy industrialist, and took a studio on the left bank to paint. You could always see her in the cafés with the painters and writers. Then she met Maxim and they fell in love—instantly. It can happen," he said, softly. "It can happen."

Cirie locked her eyes on her plate.

"What a lovely scandal!" Kyra turned to her husband. "Otto, I will definitely go to Paris this year for an extended stay."

"Kyra, my dear," Otto said. "You couldn't endure an extended stay anywhere. You can only enjoy a visit while you dream about the next place and all it promises to be and never is."

"I can't tolerate being bored," Kyra said. When I'm bored, I go where there is something interesting. Well, why not?"

"Russians are wanderers, Otto," Stepa said. "The upper classes go to Paris, London, the Riviera. The lower classes simply wander about Russia, traveling hundreds of miles, begging as they go. What for? Who knows? They couldn't tell you themselves."

Vara changed the subject. "Did you hear that Serge sent back a motor car? A Benz."

Suddenly everyone was asking questions about the car. It was always like this. From the moment of his return Serge had become the center of life here, the chord to which the others vibrated. He would play tennis with Theo and everyone would go to watch. He would sit with Georgii and call him "the old man" and suddenly the others found time for Georgii, too. At dinner, dressed in immaculate white French suits, he and Theo would tell stories about Paris and everyone would be a little possessive as though claiming a piece of the rich experience for their own. Theo read a great deal and thought seriously about life. Serge, unworried and unquestioning, lived it.

"Russia can never have a motor car industry until we have more paved roads," Otto said. "That's the problem. Paved roads."

Stepa was more interested in his own subject. "Sometimes I think it's the great distances. Something beckons them across that endless space. They'll tell you it's God's will. To a Russian everything is God's will. Or fate. We go to the West and we pick up some tendency toward rational thinking. We return to Russia and we revert. What do you say, Serge? Don't you find it so?"

"I'm happy either place." Serge's eyes moved slowly to Stepa and came back to Cirie. Making promises. Playing games. Cirie felt Vara's eyes fastened on her like the vise in which she clutched poor Petite. Dangerous games, she warned herself. Don't look at him. Don't encourage this flirtation—the price will be too high. For him there's no risk. For you, it will cost you everything.

After dinner Serge sat far across the drawing room, smoking. Now the game was over. Now he ignored her.

"To a Russian logic is a foreign language he never heard," Stepa said.

"We're as God intended us, Stepa," Kyra said.

"There you are. It's God's fault. Or the Devil's."

Without even a glance toward her, Serge moved farther away to sit with his mother. Aunt Vayana took a seat beside Cirie and nodded toward a portrait of Madame's father. "He was my brother," she said. "He felt a great responsibility to the poor. When he died he was deeply in debt."

"A Russian doesn't think about how he could help himself," Stepa said. "If things don't work out, he says, 'Nitchevo—it wasn't important. It doesn't matter.' His favorite expression. 'Nitchevo.'"

"Vassily made this estate profitable," Aunt Vayana said. "He's not so open-handed although he knows his responsibility."

Cirie wondered why Aunt Vayana was running on like this. Across the room Madame's face lit up when Serge spoke to her.

"Vassily gives his brothers everything," Aunt Vayana tucked in a strand of her white hair. "Except the right to decide anything for themselves."

Slowly Cirie turned to look at her.

"Russians have no sense of cause and effect," Stepa said. "That an action has consequences and that he could act to prevent them, this doesn't occur to him. It's always Fate."

Cirie stared at Stepa. *Listen*, she ordered herself. *Listen and think*. He's *warning* you. If you encourage this flirtation, and get yourself sent home, will you say that it was Fate? It will not be Fate. It will be *you*. *Fate* is that the scales are out of balance. *Fate* is that you came fifteen miles up a muddy road and he stepped off a boat from Paris. *Fact* is that to him this game is amusing. To you it will be expensive.

"A Russian will pray all day for God's personal intervention," Stepa said. "But does he spend even an hour figuring out what he can do about his own fate? Never!"

And will you pretend you didn't know these looks and smiles would give Vara the ammunition she wants? And when she fires you, will you say, "It doesn't matter, it wasn't important? Nitchevo?" Don't play this game. Don't smile when he smiles or even let him see that you are holding back the smile that is all too clearly there. Don't pray for God's intervention. God will not help you and this game, even if only when he chooses to play it, is a game you can't win.

She watched the clock until it was Georgii's bedtime and then, grateful to escape, she pushed the wheelchair to the door. In the soft light, the doorknob gleamed against the dark wood. As she turned it, a hand covered hers. "Let me help you," he said.

She froze under his touch. Then, firmly, she withdrew her hand.

"Come on, Serge," Georgii said. "Open the door."

In the hall, Serge whispered, "Cirie, meet me later at the river."

"No!" She rang for a footman to carry Georgii upstairs before Vara followed Serge as she surely would.

"In an hour."

"No!"

The door flew open. "Serge, go back inside," Vara ordered. "How do you think this looks?"

"I'll be right there, as soon as I say goodnight to the old man," Serge said.

Hardly hearing, Vara lashed out at Cirie. "What are you up to now?"

"We're waiting for a footman to carry Georgii, Countess."

"Don't play the innocent with me! I've had enough of your devious ways. Remember you'll be leaving soon." When Cirie didn't reply, she said, "Would you prefer to leave at once?"

"Vassi will be back next week, Vara," Serge said, half-reasoning, half warning, and led her back to the drawing room and closed the door behind her. He hurried back to Cirie. "At the river."

"No!" *You can't win—you can't win*. Suddenly she didn't believe it. But rushing to him tonight was not the way.

"In an hour," he said. "I'll wait for you."

"No. Don't wait, Serge."

She was at the stairs when the door flew open again. When she looked around, Serge had followed Vara into the drawing-room.

7

On a moonless night in June a band of men—some said they were radicals, others that they were just hoodlums—burned a barn on the estate of an old Prince who had squandered his fortune and lived today as a recluse, forgetful of more than his traditional duty to his moujiks who hated him. On the night of the fire, the orange sky could be seen for miles.

At daybreak Strengov was summoned by the Prince's only remaining servant, who told him that as the flames painted the sky, the old Prince had collapsed because of his bad heart, which turned out to be an accurate diagnosis. As Strengov rode out along the river he could see clouds of gray smoke billowing up into the white sky. Ordinarily such heavy smoke would mean that an entire village was burning. The moujiks built their huts so close together that a fire in one meant a fire in all. After an inspection the police would issue letters confirming the loss and granting official permission to beg for the means to rebuild. So much for the government's idea of compassion. Some begging trips covered a thousand miles.

"Revolutionaries," the Prince choked out when he saw Strengov. "It's starting again. In the Japanese War we had radicals behind every tree. Now again!"

"Nonsense," Strengov said. "We don't have radicals behind every tree. You shouldn't get excited."

"Why should the moujiks deliberately burn my barn?" the Prince mourned. "I have so little left."

Why should they deliberately burn anything? Strengov knew there was no simple answer. After twenty years of treating battered wives and patching up wounds inflicted in a senseless rage or a drunken brawl, he knew them and he knew there was no understanding them. The moujik was an uncontrolled mass of contradictions. In a transformation as quick as a magician's hand, he would leap from one extreme to the other—from gentleness to brutality, from resignation to rebellion, from saintliness to lust. In a fit of fury he would burn down an entire village, then beat his breast with remorse and set out on a pilgrimage, begging his way to the Holy Land. He loved his children and forced himself on his daughter-in-law.

When he left the Prince, Strengov continued along the dusty road. On these long trips, alone on these narrow dirt roads where nothing changed from one village to the next or from one year to the next, he would talk out loud to himself, commenting on life, asking himself questions that had no answers. "Where will the long fingers of this fire reach?" he said to himself. "Who else will suffer?" He crossed a bridge where the river ran between high banks. "Just as radicals attacked the Vodovsky carriage and I, who never did them harm, am presented with a fear that never leaves me." Cirie, his prize, had been out there for six weeks. What was happening to her?

Her letters, delivered when Gerzy came to town, told him too much and too little. He had sensed happily at first that she was disappointed in the place. Then something changed. Strengov suspected the worst. A picture flashed across his mind of Serge Vodovsky, a year ago, when he came to the office with his cousin. "Frivolous dandies," he said aloud. "Elegant, graceful—*joking*."

He came off the bridge. If he turned north, he could be at Vodovsky by noon and see for himself what was going on. "And if he's there, then what?"

"If he's there, she comes home today," he answered himself.

"And how will you manage that? By pleading? By coaxing? Or will you tell her what you know? And will you tell her all of it? Or a little more than all? Or a little less?" And how would he do it and what would it accomplish?

Strengov turned his horse south and headed home.

The sun was higher now and he tilted his hat over his face. When he traveled these roads in the mesmerizing heat, he would lapse into the illusion that he was standing still and the familiar scenes were moving past him like a string of photographs—the dilapidated huts with crooked sheds attached, stinking with animal smells, teeming with flies. Inside, a single small room where the moujiks slept on the floor or on benches, covered with parasite-infested rags. They ate, everyone from the same pot, using big wooden spoons. Everywhere it was the same. Poverty. Dirt. Ignorance.

A peasants' field came along, divided into long narrow "strips," each strip worked by a different family. The land was owned in common by the village—the "mir"—and redistributed every twenty years based on the number of men and boys in a family. A moujik with only daughters fared badly. Altogether a family would receive three or four strips, each in a different field, several miles apart. In the summer they left home at daybreak and walked for miles to their strips, some wearing "lapti," shoes woven of tree bark, most of them barefoot. It was dark when they walked home again.

Then in winter they were shut up in the crowded little huts. A result of the close quarters and the long nights was incest. The father-in-law's rights with his daughter-in-law, especially if the husband was away working or in the army, was a Russian scandal, common enough to have a name—snokhatch estro—and the boy a man called his son might very well be his brother. Syphilis produced deformed and imbecilic babies. (And does not recognize class distinctions, Strengov thought.) Drunkenness was epidemic. Vodka was nectar and nourishment. Strengov could read the story of their lives in their bodies—coarse, thick, heavy-muscled. "Life is habit," he said as his horse lurched across a dry gully. "But when the habit is ignorance and drudgery, hunger and cold, drunkenness and disease, what then? The Prince's fire? The attack on the Vodovsky carriage?"

Coming up to Popov's ramshackle hut, Strengov saw Tessa, Popov's wife—barefoot, pregnant again, throwing slop to a pig. Last winter he and Cirie had brought Tessa's last child into the world in a difficult delivery. Strengov remembered Cirie's face that night. She had known Tessa as a child—a pretty little girl who came irregularly to school when the roads were passable. Then she married this lazy conniving Popov and already she looked worn out. Strengov knew what Cirie was thinking that night. Whenever she saw one of these poor women, overworked, abused, a child at her legs, a child in her arms and another on the way, everything about her would say, "No thanks—not for me—" and dream of a life as different from this one as she could imagine.

Popov's yard was filthy, the pig was pushing at the hut, the whimpering baby in a basket was dirty and had a bad rash. Strengov reached into his bag for his sulphur ointment. "Tessa," he called. "Will Popov come in for lunch? I want to talk to him."

Tessa regarded him with suspicion. "Popov was late today. He won't be in." Then Popov strode out of the hut and greeted him with a booming voice and a broad smile.

"Popov, build a shed for the animals a little way from the house," Strengov said. "Your children will be healthier. And you, too."

"Eh!" Popov said in a loud voice. "And who will give me even rotten boards?"

"Write to the landlord and ask if you can cut some trees. I'll help you with the letter."

"Eh! And who will do my farming while I'm doing all this work?"

Strengov continued on his way. Suddenly the memory of Serge Vodovsky was back—the handsome smiling face, the graceful lounging body. The story of his life was in his body, too. On that day last year he came with his cousin—the two of them joking but nervous, passing the ball back and forth about which one was sick. Strengov thought of Cirie's face that had said, No, thanks! Not for me—I have better dreams.

"And after Serge Vodovsky finishes with her, what will be left?" Strengov mourned out loud. "What kind of life? What kind of dreams?" Overhead crows cried and grasshoppers hummed in the long grass. "If he gets her pregnant? Or worse?"

At the Inn, people were talking about the Prince's fire. "There'll be investigators from Petersburg," Koner said anxiously.

"Don't worry," Strengov said. "Even if Boris should come home tomorrow, he wasn't here last night."

"I don't know if the Okhrana is that reasonable," Koner whispered. Then he said, "I had another letter from Laranov. He'll be here in a few weeks." After a minute Strengov remembered—a bureaucrat from Petersburg who had written to Koner as head of the local council. "Also Gerzy left a letter from Cirie."

The letter was full of trivia—more guests expected, a highly prized mare about to foal. But nothing about the one thing he wanted to know. If she would write that Serge was expected later he would feel he had a reprieve. There's no reprieve, he said to himself. He's there.

"Do you think, Strengov, that Laranov could come to dinner while he's here?" Koner said. "I feel he should talk to you."

Isn't it enough that I'm losing one of my daughters forever and the other one is walking into serious trouble or already in it? Do I have to put up with this bureaucrat, too? "The house is in a turmoil with Anna leaving soon. My cousin Ulla will be here. But if he can stand it, he's welcome."

"Ulla is not without a certain charm."

"Ulla is as silly and as busy as ever. Talking—fussing—she misses her telephone as though it were a pet dog." In the hotel dining room the plump pink-cheeked waitress rushed in from the kitchen carrying fresh-baked black bread and piroshki and borsht. Strengov nodded toward the driver of the post carriage. "Did he bring anyone today for Vodovsky?"

"A man and a young woman. No, not Serge. An older man—fashionable. Gerzy called him M. Kurasin. The young woman was very thin and limp. Her name was Lydia."

"Are you sure Serge hasn't come home, Koner?"

"I haven't seen him. If it's so important I'll ask Gerzy next time he's here."

"Do that," Strengov said.

"You were at the fire?" Anya Dubrovna said when Strengov came into the house with Koner. "Be careful. They'll be around to question you."

"I was summoned to a patient. I don't refuse to go because some drunken vandals start a fire."

"Drunken vandals! Anarchists! These radicals tell the peasants they need a revolution. When they get their revolution, they won't know what to do with it." She shot a look at Strengov waiting for an argument. "Suppose I gave them my store?" She argued, anyway. "And I said, Divide it fairly. Do you think they would? Never!"

"If you gave them your store," Strengov said, "the man in charge of dividing would take the largest share for himself, his assistant would come next, his family would get a few favors, and you'd have a new bureaucracy. It would be a small share for some."

"For once you're right." She looked up as Lily came in, carrying her white kitten. "Where were you all this time?" Lily buried her face in Strengov's shoulder and he stroked her hair. Shy little Lily, eager to please, always a little overwhelmed.

"Where do you go?" Anya Dubrovna demanded.

"This little mouse plays with her kitten," Marya said. "Or she goes to the square and talks to the moujiks whom she adores. Or she sits at the edge of the woods and dreams."

"A dreamer. Very Russian, but it doesn't pay."

"Marya, Koner's expecting a bureaucrat from Petersburg. He'd like to bring him to dinner."

"He's probably the Okhrana coming to investigate," the old woman warned.

"Laranov is traveling around talking to the moujiks, on the theory that if you want a good harvest you should talk to the people who grow the grain," Koner said.

"A remarkable theory for a bureaucrat," Strengov said. "Are you sure he's from Petersburg?"

"Give them a little power—" The old woman was still arguing. "And it will be like vodka."

Strengov had stopped listening. All day he had been flirting with the memory and now that scene a year ago came rushing back.

"We've just returned from Paris," Vodovsky had said and smiled at his cousin as though it were a game. Strengov waited. If they were ill enough to travel seven miles to a doctor, it was no game.

"And we haven't been feeling too well," the cousin said.

"The long trip doesn't always agree with you, does it, Theo?"

"And Paris doesn't always agree with you."

It's serious—they're very nervous.

"We've heard we can trust you," Serge said. "Dr. Federin talks a lot. Especially to my mother and my brother."

"Who is sick and what is the problem?"

They exchanged glances. Maybe both, Strengov thought. But Vodovsky is more worried than the cousin. Why did this young fellow bother him so? Strengov had a pretty good idea what the problem was going to turn out to be. He looked at the tall graceful body, the Paris clothes, the polished boots. He's human, like everyone else, he thought. He'll grow old, like everyone else. And he's utterly useless. And he never thought this could happen to him. In the end there was only one patient. Vodovsky.

And now he's been in Paris for another year, raising hell. And he's out there. And he's found Cirie.

*   *   *

Cut trees! Build a shed! Popov had better things to do! Today he felt a sense of elation he had known only once before in his life—three months ago. Then they had waited on the frozen snow and he had been nervous. But as the carriage overturned, he had felt the rush of hate and the thrill and in that instant he had seen his future.

Last night was hot and Popov was the leader. Last night they didn't pay for any guns or bombs but he watched the flames and felt the hate and tasted the thrill. That was the same.

8

❀

A week later the police came to Whitewater—the district chief and a special officer from Moscow who suspected a link between the Prince's fire and the attack on
the Vodovsky carriage by terrorist revolutionaries. No more pretense about
drunken hoodlums.

When Constantine came onto the terrace at noon they had just left and the
family was discussing their visit. In the music room Kurasin was playing Chopin.
Across the terrace Serge lounged on a chaise, devouring Cirie with his eyes while
Vara, on guard duty, sat closeby. Cirie, Constantine was happy to see, was ignoring
both.

"The special officer is the Okhrana," Stepa said.

"He didn't say so," Otto said.

"He wouldn't say so! Secrecy is their lifeblood!"

Officially, the Okhrana went back two centuries to Peter the Great but its
methods were inherited from Tatar chiefs who ruled Russia long ago with their
Tatar specialties—spies, torture, secret accusations, secret trials, secret executions.

"Peter the Great added some German efficiency, but the Okhrana is still
shrouded in secrecy," Stepa said.

"In Petersburg I used to pass their headquarters—that yellow building with
barred windows," Theo said. "And I'd always think, what evil have you been up to
today? Who have you spied on? Who have you violated?"

"But Theo, they're not evil," Madame said. "They're necessary. They arrest people who want to kill the Tsar and overthrow the government."

Constantine smiled. The statement was accurate and it was an over-simplifica-
tion. The Okhrana's zeal in protecting the throne was legendary. During the 1906
uprisings, they were everywhere, arranging assassinations, whipping up pogroms,
fanning the fires of fanaticism, reminding the moujiks that the Tsar was a reincarnation of Christ. All to divert hatred away from the Tsar and into other channels.

"The Okhrana is a centipede with a hundred long arms," Stepa said. "It's everywhere. Even abroad! If there's a conspiracy against the Tsar in Paris, the Okhrana
is there. London? It's there. Geneva or Zurich? The Okhrana is listening."

Kurasin was playing Tchaikovsky now and Serge stirred a little, giving himself
up to the romantic mood, caressing Cirie with his eyes. This was something you
could feel—the magnet between these two—and Constantine wondered how far

it had gone. He's so much more experienced, he'll destroy her. But she—he reassured himself—she is smarter.

"A hundred long arms and a head of its own," Stepa said. "The Okhrana answers to no one. It's outside the courts. It manipulates the Tsar. Only a strong ruler could curb its power. Not this one."

Theo shrugged. "Without it he couldn't survive."

Vassily, who had returned yesterday, had come outside and was becoming annoyed. "Are you criticizing that?" he demanded. "With Revolutionaries thick as flies! What right do they have to attack our carriage? Look at Maman. Look at Georgii." He cleared his throat. "That scum should go to Siberia for life! Not just five years. Life!"

Vassily was irritable today. Probably this automaton of efficiency had discovered some error committed in his absence. Constantine studied him—the high peaked forehead, the cold eyes, the carefully clipped beard, the start of a stomach bulge due more to poor posture than to corpulence. He was a strange man—still young but old in spirit, a man who worked tirelessly, not out of necessity but out of sheer passionate love for the process.

Vassily's anger escalated. "These anarchists have one goal. To murder the Tsar and plunge Russia into chaos. They're well-organized and supported by international revolutionaries. Well, thank God the Okhrana is organized, too."

"Organized!" Stepa said. "They're everywhere. In a hundred disguises. They're on the street selling newspapers and watching, driving public coaches and watching."

"I rejoice in it!" Vassily said.

"They're working in restaurants and theaters and on railroads. They're in homes as domestic help. You may have some here. Always watching."

And keeping lists, Constantine thought. And opening mail. And observing who goes where, who meets whom, who changes his address too often. Keeping track of every revolutionary leader in Europe. One professional against another.

"With the rabble, the end justifies the means," Vassily said.

"That's their philosophy!" Stepa said.

"With these people it's necessary. Don't forget. *The person of the Tsar is what holds Russia together.* Without a Tsar it would fall apart into a hundred pieces. You'd have anarchy. The Russian people can't govern themselves."

"Well, they've never had the chance," Theo said.

Vassily glared at Theo and turned suddenly on Serge, who had not said a word. "You're not going back to Paris. You get too many liberal ideas there."

Startled, Serge pulled his eyes away from Cirie. "I don't get involved in them!"

"You can study law in Petersburg. Get up there and register. I'm going to London in August and I want the matter settled."

"All right, Vassi. Any special time you'd like me to go?"

"I'll tell you when you'll go. I'm going myself, soon. We can go together."

This had been an argument in which everyone was right, Constantine thought. It was true that the secret police were the protectors of the Tsar's power and were necessary to thwart the plots against him. And it was true that Russians probably could not govern themselves and it was also true that they had never had a chance to learn. And it was true that the person of the Tsar held the Empire together. And that, he thought, is the most serious problem of all.

He glanced back at Cirie. With that cool self-possession, (How had it happened, without training, in a little district town given to emotion?) she appeared to be totally oblivious of Serge. But he was looking at her and plotting his moves. And clever as she was, with so little experience would she be able to recognize them for what they were?

After lunch Serge lay on the grass, his head against the chestnut tree, and let his half-closed eyes go where they always went these days—to the object of all his fantasies. He spent all his idle hours—and most of his hours were idle—in a turmoil, watching her. He had waited in vain at the river that night, with a new moon rising and the smell of honeysuckle and the sound of the water lapping the shore. He had escaped the drawing room and he had waited under the shower of a million stars while the water whispered and crickets called and she didn't come. Serge had told himself that it was because dear old Vara had posted herself on police duty—she would come to him the next night or the one after that. He waited. She did not come.

Through the trees the sun cast a mottled light onto the terrace. Serge watched while his love bent over to speak to Georgii. The sun danced on her pale hair. She sat erect again, like a ballerina, and looked up to reveal the cobalt pools of eyes. Serge stirred. It was agony to be near her and not be able to move nearer still. He could not believe that since he spoke to her she had not come to him.

Ordinarily Serge was not curious about other people's reasons for doing as they did. He was more absorbed in his own feelings. He loved to be in love. He loved the game, the pursuit, the conquest. Lying here now, with the heavy oleaceous scent of the warm lazy June day stirring his senses, his thoughts drifted back to Paris and other love affairs in which obstacles had only whetted his appetite. When a suspicious husband or a jealous lover—his or hers—had introduced the excitement of intrigue, it had added spice to the game. He would pour all his energy into outwitting the enemy. This time the obstacles were too frustrating. He was never alone with her, never able to touch her or to feel her hand in his.

Snatches of the conversation on the terrace reached him. "Don't forget the affair with the ballerina—Kchessinka. He built her a magnificent palace."

"After he became Tsar, Kchessinka became the mistress of his cousin, the Grand Duke Sergei."

Cirie spoke to Georgii, gave him a dazzling smile, touched his hand. In an agony of jealousy, Serge closed his eyes. Oh, God! Just to be alone with her, to touch her hair, her lips, her arms where the fine white down showed in the sunlight.

The rush of desire engulfed him. He felt it lift him from the realm of ordinary sensations and he slipped into the fantasy that had become so familiar. In his seething mind he was on the soft-scented grass beside the river under the guarded glow of a thousand stars. He touched her hair where it sprang from her temples, he untied the ribbon and spread the heavy hair on the soft grass beneath her and twined his fingers through it. He could never make love to a woman whose hair was tied or pinned. Light fingers explored the delicate planes of the face that had bewitched and enslaved him until the willing lips opened and yielded to him. Firm hands moved quickly to the warmer softer smoother rises and hollows that waking or sleeping he had dreamed about and he knew them at last. In his reverie the little white blouse and the full skirt fell away effortlessly. She was quickly and smoothly brought naked, the down above her wrist transformed to the down first known on this voyage of discovery when her legs parted to his insistent hand as her lips parted to his lips.

A fire drove his fantasy forward. Magically unclothed beside her, he guided her hand, shy only at first and then braver, stronger…And then the joyful yielding, while he moved in total oblivion of night and stars and the scent of grass and the river, to have at last what he had burned to possess every hour since he first saw her and now—now—

"Serge—" Theo said from a million miles away.

He couldn't answer. He flung himself over and felt the hard ground beneath him. Oh, God! He buried his contorted face in the hollow of his arm. He suffered. He burned.

Theo sat against the tree. "Serge, are you still dreaming of Jeanne?"

"Jeanne?" His tone was light. His voice was hoarse. "I don't remember what she looks like."

She was standing now—about to take Georgii somewhere. Where was she going? Inside—out of his world from which all color drained when she left it. The sun touched her hair where it sprang free of the ribbon. She bent over to pick up Georgii's book that had slipped to the ground and the young breasts moved against the thin cotton blouse. Too soon she straightened up. She spoke to Georgii who was always only a hand away, who touched her freely, who accepted her caress with such a careless evaluation of the treasure bestowed on him.

"Then *who*?" Theo said.

Serge stood up. "What shall it be, Theo, tennis or croquet?"

"Serge, I *know* you."

"I'm dreaming of a vision—so beautiful she can't be real." He had to have a moment alone—if he couldn't be with her, touch her, hold her, he would be with no one.

"Serge—!

"Let's make it tennis in half an hour."

"Serge! She's not fair game! She's had no experience!"

Serge turned to stare. "You're in love with her yourself!"

"Everyone is in love with her. You—me—Constantine. She comes into the room and soon everyone is glancing at her. You can feel it. She lowers those fabulous eyes and everyone is waiting for the vision when she raises them. But nobody is touching her. Nobody is leading her on."

"Get Stepa and Constantine and make it doubles."

"Serge," Theo said sharply. "*Have you*—?"

"When? How? I'm never alone with her."

But he would find a way, he would have her. "I'm in love, Theo," he said, as though that explained everything. And besides, without her, what would he do all summer?

9

❀

"Cirie—" he called in a low voice.

He was here. She had known that one morning he would be here at daybreak when the world was still wet and a chunk of a waning moon showed low in the sky—here on this little hill where she came each time she rode and looked down on fields where nothing moved and the only sound was the bright talk of birds that was different at daybreak.

"Cirie—" he called in a hushed voice, as though they were not far from other ears.

She had known that one day he would be here ever since the afternoon that Georgii insisted that Serge take him to see the horses and Vara hastened to say they would all go along. "You haven't seen the horses this year, Constantine."

At the stables Mischa, Gerzy's son, came over to lift Georgii onto a docile horse. In the next stall Pegasus, aware of Cirie's presence, neighed and pawed at the straw and Cirie scratched his ear and murmured, "How are you, my love?" Beside her Serge whispered, "I've waited for you every night at the river." As Cirie turned, Constantine's alert blue eyes telegraphed a warning. Too late.

"How do you know Pegasus?" Vara demanded.

Theo stepped up beside the horse. "Everyone knows Pegasus. He's such a beauty."

"But how do *you* know him?" Vara persisted.

Cirie would have lied gladly if she had thought it would work. "Madame gave me permission to ride him, Countess."

"When do you have time to ride?"

"Before anyone is awake, Countess."

Serge turned away to conceal his triumphant expression.

"So now you're keeping secrets. We'll see about this," Vara said.

"What secrets?" Stepa said. "We early risers see each other."

"Am I to rise at daybreak, then, to know what's going on in my own home?"

"I think, Vara," Constantine said smoothly, falling in beside her, "that a horse's morning exercise is hardly a reason to rise early when one is absolutely disinclined to do so."

"Well, if you put it that way, Constantine." Vara laughed and turned to him. "I detest sneaky servants. I don't know why Georgii is so taken with that girl."

"Just ignore it," Theo murmured, still at Cirie's side.

Outside the stable, the entire party moved to the top of a small hill and looked down at the handsome cattle, grazing in the pasture. Then they all marched back to the terrace to resume their talking.

Now, in the first white light of day, he was here.

Prince Igor bounded up the hill and without a word Serge took her in his arms and there was no question but that they had been waiting too long for this moment. "Where were you?" he murmured. "Where were you?"

She looked at him, puzzled.

"Where were you yesterday—the day before? I've been here every morning since that day at the stables." His lips found her face and her hair and moved to her lips. "Why didn't you tell me?"

She couldn't answer. Unfamiliar feelings, wilder than she had known or even suspected, surged through her.

"Cirie, darling, you're driving me mad. I can't get through the days for wanting to touch you, to hold you—" He untied her hair ribbon and ran his hands through her loose hair and held a thick tress against his face.

How could she keep her head when it was already lost?

"Darling, can't you see how I'm suffering? I'm half out of my mind with wanting you."

Some deep-seated instinct told Cirie that he was moving too fast, that she couldn't move at his pace, that she needed time to catch up. Run away, an inner voice whispered. Leave while you still can.

"Cirie, I want you so!"

She forced herself to move out of his arms. "I have to go in, Serge."

"Don't move."

"I have to. I'm late." Dull as a thud.

"No!" He reached for her again. "I've waited so long."

If she didn't leave now, she would be lost. Safely on Pegasus she reached down to touch his bewildered face. He seized the bridle. "Serge, let go."

"Cirie, *why*?"

"Let go, Serge."

"Tell me why."

She started down the hill without looking back.

"Cirie," he called after her. "When will you ride again?"

She didn't answer. He would find out at the stables.

In her room Cirie closed the door and leaned against it. "I can't believe how I feel," she said, softly. She looked in the mirror. She was a different person. Since she looked in this mirror two hours ago she was transformed. All he said was,

"Darling, you're driving me mad…Can't you see how I'm suffering…I'm out of my mind wanting you." And she was in love. And she would never be the same again.

She lay back across the bed. "I can't believe how I feel!"

10

❀

She lived for the mornings. All of life was those mornings when she would lead
Pegasus out of the stable, snorting and tossing his head in the sweet smell of the
start of the day, and ride to the hill overlooking the lake to meet Serge. All day she
would remember how he had looked in his white linen shirt and fawn-colored
riding trousers, and the way his eyes would light up when he saw her and the way
he protested that for no one else in the world would he get up at such an hour.
Evenings, while she played cards with Arkady, she would remember the touch of
his hands and his lips. She would lie in bed and remember how it felt to be closed
in his arms.

At Whitewater life had become everything she had imagined it could be.
Writers and musicians came to visit Stepa and an artist arrived to paint a new portrait of Elissa before she left for Paris. Lydia, Kyra's dark-haired languid daughter,
separated from her husband, was having a "romantic adventure" with the slender
white-haired music critic, Kurasin, who had a look of pursuing the fountain of
youth with total dedication and addressed everyone of his own class as, "My dear."
General Borassin, a Count who was a famous military man, was expected any day,
and Prince and Princess Tchernefsky with their niece, the Countess—Irene. And
the government grain expert, Laranov, whose visit Vara dreaded.

At dinner the men talked about the rumblings of aggression in Europe. "The
Kaiser is blustering and belligerent, but in Vienna Franz Josef is old. Eighty-five."

"He began his reign when Alexander II was on the throne in Petersburg and
Queen Victoria in England."

"Now Victoria is gone and her son, Edward VII, is gone. And Alexander II and
Alexander III are gone and still Franz Josef goes on." Surviving his wife, surviving
his son. The heir to the Austrian throne was his nephew, a stocky man with a walrus mustache married to a commoner, the Archduke Franz Ferdinand. The men
spoke of strategic meetings—English ships visited Russia, the French president
was coming to call on the Tsar in July.

Lydia and Kurasin talked about the glorious social season of the past year—a
year filled with ceremony and pageantry to celebrate the three-hundredth
anniversary of the crowning of the first Romanov Tsar, Michael, in 1613. Michael
Romanov's grandson was the legendary Peter the Great and Peter's grandson was
Peter III, succeeded by his Empress, the German-born Catherine the Great.

58

Because of Catherine's chilly relationship with her husband and her long series of lovers, it was possible that the Romanov bloodline ended with Peter III. Catherine's grandson was Alexander I who fought Napoleon, and Alexander's great nephew was Nicholas II who celebrated the three-hundredth anniversary.

"The Tsar was greeted everywhere by wildly cheering subjects," Kurasin said. "On his pilgrimage to Michael's birthplace, the moujiks fell to their knees to kiss his shadow. To them he's a reincarnation of Christ."

Constantine looked at Stepa. "The aura of well-being lingers on. Now the upper classes have gone abroad or to their country estates. The Grand Dukes and Duchesses are playing in Paris or Biarritz—with the feeling that all's right with the world."

"Marvelous," Stepa said.

"And a million and a half workers are out on strike."

"The Emperor was quite overcome by this great show of love," Kurasin said. "I heard it myself from one of the Grand Duchesses."

It was all more than Cirie, only a short time ago, had dreamed possible. Now this bright sophisticated world seemed a shadow world and the only reality was Serge.

On a morning in late June, she waited for him on the hill. In the damp woods the air was redolent with the smell of ripening vegetation that was different from the fresh smells of spring, and a warm breeze warned that the July heat was moving in. She listened for Serge's horse but except for the talk of birds and the drone of insects the woods were perfectly quiet. Nearby a cluster of gnats hovered over a bush.

In the distance the road was a narrow line following the river to Novotnii where Anna was packing. Tomorrow Cirie was going home to say goodbye and then Anna would be gone forever. A feeling of loss swept over her. Two months ago she had not understood at all the passion for Vogel that drove Anna to give up everything she loved and travel across the world to him. Now she understood. But this was different. Serge wasn't a dull clod like Vogel. If Serge were to go out of her life, she thought suddenly, there would be no life left.

She dropped the reins over a limb a little distance from the gnats. Down below, the white light gave a ghostly character to the swirling mist. Her thoughts drifted back to the bizarre conversation in the drawing room the night before. In hushed voices, Lydia and Kurasin, who were part of the Rasputin set, had been telling stories of the occult—of sorcery and communication with the dead and transmigration of souls and dead nurses roaming corridors during thunderstorms.

Half-reclining on a sofa, Lydia took on a dreamy faraway look. The conversation shifted to Rasputin and his power over people and his affairs with society women.

"His incredible pale blue eyes see right through you," Lydia said in a hushed voice. "If you don't look away you are hypnotized."

"It was the Montenegrin Grand Duchesses who presented him to the Tsar and the Tsarina," Kyra said in a nasal gossipy tone that contrasted with Lydia's hushed whisper.

"Those two ladies are always seeking new sensations," Stepa said.

"Oriental magic is all the rage now," Kurasin said.

Constantine laughed. "Petersburg is full of silly restless women running from a clairvoyant to a seance, from church to a sorcerer. An hourly worship of a different oracle."

Lydia gazed at a candle on the table.

"The most beautiful women submit to him eagerly," Kyra said. "They consider it an honor to be chosen."

Cirie snapped out of her reverie about Serge. Had Kyra actually said what she thought she did?

"Father Gregory preaches that repentance is the road to salvation," Kurasin said. "So when God places temptation in your way, it's your duty to yield. You must sin in order to repent."

"And he elects himself the temptation!" Stepa laughed. "The itch is there. He makes it a religious experience to scratch."

A religious experience! Cirie would love to hear what Mamma would say to that.

Kyra began to talk about a Countess Sophie somebody-or-other, very fragile and beautiful, (and simple-minded, Cirie decided as the story unfolded) who had caught Rasputin's eye. "Every day people wait for hours outside his door seeking favors. Sophie called on him with some friends. She looked particularly beautiful that day with her fabulous red hair swept high. He selected her at once for a private session."

"Kyra, do you think you should talk about this?" Madame said.

"She talks about it herself, Eugenie! When his attention continued, a friend asked if she intended to favor him if she were invited to do so." Kyra lowered her eyes briefly to underscore the nature of the invitation.

Cirie saw Serge watching her, amused, and she looked away.

"And Sophie smiled radiantly and said that the honor had already been bestowed on her! She had already accepted! They're overjoyed. And their husbands, too! It's considered an honor to both if the wife is selected."

Suddenly, in the incredulous silence, Georgii let out a whoop and pointed to Lydia who was lying motionless in a corner of the sofa, in a trance. How long the trance lasted Cirie did not know because Georgii was shouting so gleefully she had to wheel him out of the room.

Later in her room Cirie considered the conversation. Ever since her arrival here, she had heard that the rules of society were rigid, that a young man could ruin his future by marrying beneath himself. "And yet," she said to herself, "there's Rasputin—an unkempt moujik with disgusting table manners if what they say is true—accepted by the best society, with the silly ladies of Petersburg calling it an honor to sleep with him. And Lydia is having an affair with Kurasin and nobody is upset about that. And Kurasin says society ladies entertain their lovers in their boudoirs with gypsy music playing in the next room. Obviously," she told herself, "if you're a lady and can afford a boudoir and gypsy music, that makes a difference." She thought of Lydia and told herself, "The rules are different for the rich and the poor." She thought of Rasputin and told herself, "The rules are what you make them."

Now the sun had moved above the trees and the mist had lifted off the lake and still Serge had not arrived. Cirie stepped onto a low stump where old roots traveled above the ground and tried to see across the silent woods. Uneasily she wondered if something had gone wrong. Had someone found out about them? Lately the fear had haunted her. We can't go on like this without being caught. Sooner or later it will happen.

A gull dropped to the lake and rose again. We leave at different times, by different paths and we tell ourselves we're safe, but one day we're going to be caught. And then? Will Serge stand up to his family—to Vassily and Vara—and tell them he loves me?

She told herself to stop worrying. "There are so many people here, everyone is too busy to notice. And if that Prince ever gets here, nobody will notice anything but him. And they all stay up so late that nobody gets up early." In a game of chance, Arkady had said, when they spin the wheel, your number doesn't come up very often. Serge was here.

"What a night!" He closed her in his arms. "I thought I'd never get away."

"Where were you?"

"In the summer house. They stayed up to see the sunrise. They're all still there."

A stab of alarm. "Did they see where you went?"

"How do I know?"

"Serge, be careful!" Her eyes swept the path in the distance, near the house.

"I'm careful!" He ran his hand roughly over her hair and her face and she suspected that he had been drinking vodka all night. "While they all talked, I spent the night thinking about you. I imagined how you looked at each moment, asleep with your hair spread out on the pillow—" He broke off. "My God! All day I'm careful. Nobody knows a thing."

"The stable workers know."

He threw back his head and laughed. "Cirie, darling. With stable workers, a few rubles and they haven't seen a thing."

She knew the moujiks better than he did. A few more rubles from someone else would open their eyes fast enough. Below, the gull dove to the lake and rose up with a fish in its mouth—a fish that had lain on the bottom, thinking itself well-hidden. Cirie stared at the fish that flapped desperately in the gull's mouth. Soon it would be gone—as though it had never been. "Serge, we're going to get caught."

"If you spend your whole life worrying about getting caught, you'll never do anything." He laughed but his mouth was set in a tight line.

"Would you stand up to them?"

"Of course." He spread his jacket on the ground and drew her down. He began to loosen her hair. "Last night I thought about your hair until I could feel it against my face—" He buried his face in her loosened hair. "Then I thought about your eyes and when I could see the color of your eyes, I thought about your lips and when I could feel your lips—"

He was restless and rough today. He pulled a thick strand of her hair, possessively, until it hurt and talked about his hunger for her and Cirie sensed that he was demanding what he had not demanded before. Other mornings he had coaxed, pleaded, argued that they were in love. Today he intended to have his way. Uneasily she realized that he had been working himself up to this all night. His mouth bit into hers and traveled to her throat and she eased out of his arms.

"Don't pull away from me!"

"Darling—"

"You want me as much as I want you. I can feel how you move in my arms."

"Darling—" She touched his lips that showed no trace of a smile. "Stop now."

"Stop!"

She stood up and he leaped to his feet and walked around without speaking. The warm breeze that smelled of the end of spring came out of the woods. A fear swept over her that she was losing him.

Then he was smiling again. "Cirie," he murmured, taking her in his arms. "I love you. See how easily I say it. Usually I talk all around it. In Paris girls would say, Do you love me, Serge? and I would say, How could anyone not love you? Or they would say, Tell me that you love me, Serge, and I would say, 'I am so dazzled by your beauty, I can't speak.'

"Serge," she whispered. "You're too experienced for me."

"In Paris I said many things but never, I love you. To you I say it easily. I love you."

He drew her down again and buried his lips in her hair. "Cirie, I'm in love. Wildly, hopelessly in love. All day I look at you and I want you." The black mood settled over him again. "I'm coming to your room tonight."

"No."

"Darling, it's only natural. We're so much in love. Oh, God, Cirie, don't leave me like this. Let me have that to live through the day."

"Serge, you can't—"

"I'll be there at midnight."

"Wonderful, darling," she teased. "It'll be a busy place because Vara will be right behind you and Vassily and Heaven knows who else." She saw at once that it was a mistake. His anger flared and he forced her back, pressing against her, unbuttoning her shirt with suddenly clumsy fingers. She pushed him away. He ripped it open and his hand closed over her breast.

"Is that all this means to you?" she cried. "To come to my room! Don't meet me anymore—"

His mouth bit into hers.

Fires flared and she thought, Why not? We're in love! It's natural. Deep inside, a cold hard voice warned her. She argued against it. Why not? Why not? The cold hard voice won. It was not her mother's preaching—that bell that had tolled warnings over the years—that spoke to her. It was her own hard certainty that his victory would be her defeat. She tugged at his hands. He pinned her wrists to the ground. His lips found her breast. Struggling against her feelings Cirie wrenched free and pushed him away and ran to her horse. Furious, Serge lunged after her and stumbled and took a crooked step sideways and caught his heel on the bared root and pitched into a growth of brush.

His howl shattered the silence. A cloud of gnats rose out of the brush and covered him and swarmed over to the horses. Cirie tightened her grip on Pegasus and seized Prince Igor who had reared at the onslaught. A gnat stung her wrist. "Serge! Quick."

Slapping, flaying his arms, Serge leaped onto the horse. Cirie beat the gnats away from her face. "Move, Serge. Quick!" She slapped at gnats that had settled on Pegasus. At last Serge found his wits and the horses raced for the stable.

The instant the house came into view in the distance, Cirie saw the problem. "Serge! There's someone outside!"

"What!" Small welts peppered his face. She could see that he was in agony.

"On the terrace. It must be Vara looking for us."

Disoriented, he stared at the house. Then he said, dully, "She can't be. She just went to bed."

"You go first." Cirie's arm and hand stung, but he was in agony. "Use some cold water. I'll try to get you some ointment."

"You have to go first," he said.

"You can't wait."

"I have to wait. She doesn't know I'm out. She'll only wait for you."

As Cirie hurried along the path, she thought that this was probably the first time in his life Serge had suffered and endured the suffering to let someone else go first. She scanned the terrace anxiously. Unbelievable luck! It was empty.

She was almost at the door when a voice startled her. "Good morning!"

She whirled around. A tall man with dark hair and a dark mustache came onto the terrace. "Good morning," she said. Who is he? What is he doing here at this hour?

He came toward her, black hair, heavy black mustache, eyes black as a pirate's, looking her over, openly pleased at what he saw. "I didn't think anyone around here got up so early."

He couldn't be one of Vassily's friends—this man and Vassily would have nothing in common. He was as relaxed and amused as Vassily was stiff and humorless—and he looked as immoral and reckless as a buccaneer and Vassily was so proper. And even in his well-cut suit, his body had the look of a man who had done physical work and probably would not hesitate to do it again. Whoever he is, she thought, I've got to get him out of here. "Have you just arrived?" she said. "Come inside. I'll find someone to help you."

He smiled, as though he knew her plight. Somewhere in the distance a moujik was singing a love song. The voice came rich and faint across the fields. Serge came rushing around the corner of the rose garden and stopped short when he saw her still outside. Horrified, she looked back at the stranger who was saying that yes, he had just arrived. "On the steamer. My name is Laranov."

"Oh!" she said. "They're expecting you." At the rose garden, Serge jerked and shuddered and paced frantically back and forth. "Perhaps Vassily is up."

"I doubt that. I'll just enjoy the famous beauty of Whitewater for a while," Laranov said.

"Then walk to the river. It's even more beautiful there."

"I arrived on the steamer," he reminded her. His smile said he had caught on that something was afoot.

She remembered that Constantine knew him. "M. Paklov is always awake by now. He's in the first cottage over there."

"Constantine is here?" he said, pleased. "But I wouldn't disturb my old friend so early. I know his work habits."

Then it was too late. Face flushed and swollen, Serge rushed across the terrace and disappeared into the house.

"That's Vassily's brother," she said. "He must have been riding."

Laranov's bold eyes traveled down over her own riding outfit and he laughed at her icy stare. The moujik was singing again, a little closer now, about a better life to come.

11

❀

On this warm sunny afternoon Madame sat with a view of the Italian garden where workers were trimming the trees, and reminisced with her sister. "I can remember when father designed our sculptured garden," she said. "It was 1870, the year of the uprisings in Europe. Father thought they would spread to Russia."

"Well, thank God they didn't," Kyra said.

"It might have been better if they had." For Madame this was a disturbing thought. She believed the old ways were best—they had worked for generations. And yet the attack on her carriage and the Prince's fire had combined to make her wonder. And Constantine talked about strikes in the cities and riots in which the moujiks had stolen all the grain. "Back then the problems might have been easier to solve."

"Eugenie, don't be ridiculous! You get these ideas because you're alone too much. You should come abroad with me this year."

Madame's eyes settled on Georgii who looked healthy again—brown, bright-eyed, not so terribly thin anymore—and she wondered whether there was anything to Vara's accusation that he was secretly walking. "They're scheming together," Vara had insisted. "They go off in a hay cart with only Tanya along. Tanya wouldn't tell us. One day they came back with baskets of wild flowers. Who do you think picked them? One day they went fishing. He can walk. He only pretends he can't."

"Oh, Vara, why would he do that?"

"Because of that girl. He doesn't want her to go home. And she doesn't want to go and leave—" Vara checked herself. "All this."

Madame, who didn't like to believe such deception, hoped it was true. "I promised Georgii we could stay here into the fall," she told Kyra.

"Here!" Kyra glanced at Vara. "You know he only wants to stay because of Cirie."

"I'm becoming fond of her myself. I'm thinking of taking her back to Kostyka."

"Eugenie, Vara will be furious!"

Madame sighed and looked past Vara to the chaise on which Serge was lying. Poor Serge. What an unfortunate accident—to have his horse upset a nest of gnats. All day, wearing a scarf and a long-sleeved shirt to cover his welts, he had suffered his discomfort without complaint. She saw that Vara was scowling, first at

Cirie's reading group under the tree and then at the servants who were bringing out the tea service and had rattled a few dishes. "Poor Vara," she said. "She likes everything to be just so. If only she had Serge's disposition, I'd worry less about her. But I'm afraid she holds a grudge. She always did."

On this warm fragrant June day Vassily had planned his trip to England and conferred with Laranov about a new American thresher.

"Vassi, I want Eugenie to come to Paris with me this fall," Kyra said when he came out for tea. "You can buy some new gowns, Eugenie, and perhaps a piece of jewelry. I must buy Otto a new diamond stickpin. Evenings we'll go to the ballet or the opera. Vassi, do leave for London soon so you can get back."

"I can't leave while the Prince is here," Vassily said, curtly. "Then I'll need a week in Kostyka. I'll go in August."

"Oh, Vassi, can't you skip Kostyka?"

"I cannot. It's my policy, after an absence, to go over every detail. If I neglect one man's work, that man will think I trust him and he'll grow careless or dishonest or both. When I check his work again, I can guarantee there will be errors."

"Don't hurry away, Vassi," Madame said. "These are the best days of the year."

"I can't agree," Vara said. "I have too many problems."

On this sunny June day Vara, complaining because Laranov had turned up at this particular time, just when he said he would, was surprised to learn that Lydia and Kurasin knew him.

"Everyone knows him—or did!" Lydia said. "He was a great favorite. So brilliant and—irreverent."

"What do you mean irreverent?"

"Don't misunderstand me, his conduct was above reproach—but I suspected his thoughts were outrageous." Lydia indulged in a rare smile. "He's a master at being charming without letting you know what he's really thinking."

"I haven't seen him yet. He was off with Antychek before I awoke." Vara's tone sought to establish Laranov's position as inferior before he reappeared to defend it. "He's an agricultural advisor now, working in the provinces."

"If he was off to such a good start, why's he out in the hinterland?" Otto tilted the long cigar in his mouth. "If he's out with the crops, he was pushed out."

"That's hard to believe." Lydia arranged herself on a chaise. "Here's Constantine. What's Ilya Laranov been doing, Constantine?"

"Traveling, I believe."

"I remember him quite well, my dear," Kurasin said. "Society ladies were mad about him. He was considered a great catch. Everyone said he would marry money."

"But I thought he was a moujik!" Vara was uneasy when people's labels came loose.

"His father was a moujik who made good," Constantine said. "His mother was the rebellious daughter of an impoverished country nobleman. Laranov is quite a fellow."

"When they shoot up like that, they can't stay there. A fast climb and a fast slide," Otto said.

"He was so irresistible—so clever—maybe he chose to do this," Lydia said.

"Nonsense. An ambitious young man doesn't leave the seat of power willingly. He did something serious."

"Somehow I doubt that," Constantine said. "The last I heard, he'd gone to Siberia."

"By choice or otherwise?" Otto roared with laughter.

Vara glanced at the group under the chestnut tree. Today they were reading a book about the American West that Aunt Vayana's grandson had sent from England. Vara decided that she would choose the next book herself and enlist Constantine's help.

She turned to Vassily. "Where is your agricultural person? I haven't seen him yet."

"Laranov," Vassily said. "His name is Laranov. He's talking to Antychek."

"I hope he won't stay long."

"He's leaving tomorrow evening on the steamer and—"

"Thank Heavens for that!"

"And he's coming back. I'm satisfied that Laranov is very knowledgeable. I want him here at least a week."

"Then he'll be here when the Prince and Princess are here!" Vara protested. "Just the wrong time."

"Not for me," Vassily said.

On this hot oppressive June day, Serge lay on the chaise and studied two exposed welts on his wrist as a barometer of his condition. He saw that they had swelled in the last half-hour. Miserably he stared at Cirie. Only when he saw her long sleeves and bandaged hand had he realized that she, too, had been stung. Now, watching her reading to her little group on the lawn, he marveled at her. Not once this whole day had she scratched or even touched her bandaged hand. Serge was in awe of so much control. And all day she had ignored him! And she knew he was suffering!

Serge was not proud of that wrestling match this morning. But he'd been up all night and had consumed a fair amount of vodka. And besides, what did you expect of a man? Until today he'd been practically a saint. This affair wasn't going at all the way he had intended. He had done everything right, he was experienced enough to know that. Usually he succeeded too well. Women he had intended only as a passing diversion were always falling in love with him, making it necessary to disentangle himself. Not that he wanted to hurt them, but once you were bored it was kinder to break off. With Cirie, at first he had enjoyed the game—outwitting Vara, leaving by different paths, bribing the stable help. At first when she didn't succumb, it had added zest to the chase. Now it had gone too far. *She* was the obstacle—more than Vara. Anxiously, he wondered whether she was right that people suspected them. She would forgive him, but if other people knew about them, her days here were numbered.

Kurasin was speaking to him. "So you're going to study in Petersburg. What's wrong with Paris?"

"Paris is full of liberals," Vassily said.

"Liberals!" Kurasin said. "In Petersburg he'll find radicals. In Paris, students are in the full bloom of youth. In Petersburg they're wretched. They look starved, stooped. They're dressed in rags. They have a feverish look in their eyes."

"What do you expect?" Stepa said. "They look starved because they're starving. In winter they freeze. Their minds are feverish—they hallucinate. Dostoevski knew what he was talking about."

"I suspect that in Paris Serge was more interested in the ladies than in the liberals," Vara said, all charm.

"In Russia, some of the best radicals are women!" Kurasin said. "Some of them quite handsome. Watch out."

Serge laughed dutifully and turned away. Presently Theo sat beside him. "What really happened?"

Serge wished he could talk about it. In Paris he used to report every detail of an evening's adventures to Theo. It had been like living it twice. Even this past year while Theo had begun to grow more serious about the world, he would listen and laugh with him. But Serge had no desire to talk about this. "I told you—Prince Igor upset a nest of gnats," he said.

"And Cirie's hand?"

"Russian women make passionate Revolutionaries," Stepa said. "Why I can't explain. But it's true."

Kurasin smiled. "Russian women live by their emotions. They thirst for excitement. They're easily bored. They adore heroes and bravery and their hearts break for the unfortunate. So—the revolutionary movement satisfies all these emotions, does it not?"

"Be fair, Serge," Theo said. "Stop now. You'll only hurt her."

"I can't stop!"

"It's a game neither of you can win."

He knew that but he could not bear to think of losing. "It's gone past that."

"How far?" Theo flushed with anger. "How far past that?"

Serge tried to make light of it. "Then she would quickly become a bore, wouldn't she?" The words had a false ring. "She won't let me! She laughs at me. She's driving me crazy. I'm in love with her."

"You always think it's love."

"At first it was a game. For the summer. Now—" Serge raised troubled eyes to Theo. "Now she has a power over me."

On this hideous interminable day, Cirie closed the book about the American West, ending the reading period. She could hardly believe it was only tea time. In her room this morning, she had applied Strengov's yellow ointment and loosely bandaged the tell-tale welts and put on a long-sleeved blouse. She knew these gnat bites. They were small at first but now they were beginning to swell. By evening they would subside. She forced herself not to even touch her hand lest Vara detect the itch and deduce the rest.

"The American West is like Russia—vast spaces, people close to the land," Aunt Vayana said. "Primitive, hard-drinking."

Vassily had come onto the terrace and Cirie wondered what had become of Laranov. She could still see his knowing look and smile this morning when Serge hurried past. She hoped he had left.

"I love Russia," Aunt Vayana said. "I wonder how anyone can leave it. Tanya, wheel Georgii over for tea."

Serge was lying on a chaise, obviously miserable, and Cirie's heart went out to him as she remembered that he had tried to let her go in first.

"But my daughter went to England," Aunt Vayana said. "She resented the way her father was treated. My husband was a minister of Justice. He made speeches about the need for a more democratic government. Tanya, wheel Georgii to the terrace," she said again and Tanya turned the chair around. "He went to jail once. In Russia it's safer to write articles than to make speeches because the moujiks can't read."

Cirie flexed her fingers, feeling the skin taut over the swollen bites. Serge was moving about uncomfortably, rubbing his arm, a desperate look in his eyes. He scratched his hand and Cirie resisted the urge to scratch, too. Laranov came onto the terrace.

"Cirie, be careful of Serge," Aunt Vayana said suddenly. "He'll break your heart. He's done it to others—an English governess—a French music teacher."

She knows! Cirie struggled to hide her alarm. All day, with a relentless exercise of will, she had concealed her discomfort. Even when Serge tore at his arm and she itched unmercifully, knowing how he felt, she had sat perfectly still with her hands in her lap. Now it took a greater exercise of will not to show panic. On the terrace Serge's hand was at his neck. His face was flushed.

Aunt Vayana answered the unuttered question. "I'm a poor sleeper. And an early riser."

She knows! And Laranov knows! And Constantine has surely seen us and if he knows, Stepa knows. And Theo. Panic clutched at her throat. I'm done for—I'm finished. She looked at Serge with a silent cry for help. His face was puffed, one eye nearly closed. He rolled up his sleeve and tore at his neck. Cirie flew to the terrace.

"Madame—Serge is in pain," she whispered.

Madame gasped. "We must send for the doctor."

"I have an ointment," Cirie whispered. "And a pill for the pain. The doctor will give him these same medicines." Serge tore off his scarf and rushed across the terrace to the house. "Shall I try them?"

"Yes, yes—take them to him."

Cirie hesitated. "To his rooms?"

"Yes. Oh! No!" Madame stopped. "Yes. Just don't let Vara see you. Hurry."

Cirie hurried past Laranov but as she ran up the stairs, the image of his knowing laughing eyes went with her.

Serge was thrashing about in his sitting room when she came in, his face and hands red and swollen. "Oh, Serge—" she rushed to him. "I'm so sorry."

"Cirie, forgive me!" he murmured through swollen lips and held her close. "Cirie, I love you so! Just tell me you still love me and I'll suffer anything."

"Serge, Aunt Vayana knows about us. And Laranov knows. What shall we do?" He continued to kiss her as though he hadn't heard. "Serge, I can't stay here. I only brought the medicines."

"Cirie, I have to talk to you. Ride tomorrow—"

"I'm going home tomorrow!"

"Going home! What happened?"

"Anna's leaving next week—I'm going to say goodbye. I told you—"

"My God, how you frightened me! I thought I was losing you. Cirie, I love you so. I want to spend the rest of my life with you. Before I found you my life was nothing—just a colorless prelude—" He broke off. "Aunt Vayana knows?"

"And Laranov, too. Be prepared if anything is said."

He drew her close again. "Swear that you'll come back. Swear that you'll never leave me again."

She drew back to look at him. "Serge, are you willing to do the same?"

"Yes!"

"Swear that you'll never leave me?"

"I swear it. Cirie, swear that you'll spend the rest of your life with me. Every day. Forever. Swear it." To her astonishment, Serge's eyes filled with tears. "From this day forward your life is mine. Swear it."

"I swear it, Serge."

"When you said you were going home the thought of losing you actually made me ill. Can you imagine! How my friends in Paris would laugh! Serge Vodovsky!"

"Serge, I have to leave. I can't be found here."

"You're right." He kissed her and released her. "From now on we belong to each other. Nothing can ever change that."

Just before dinner, while the others were at the zakuski table, Madame drew her aside. A flash of alarm subsided when Cirie realized that Madame would not discuss anything unpleasant in the dining room. "I want to speak to you before you go home, Cirie, so you can discuss this with your father. Georgii has become so fond of you. We all have. Would you like to come back with us to Kostyka? If your father will permit it."

Cirie felt only a passing twinge when she assured Madame, while Laranov watched with mocking eyes, that Strengov would have no objection.

A thousand miles away that long summer day, the Archduke Franz Ferdinand, the stocky man with the walrus mustache, heir to the Austro-Hungarian throne, and his morganatic wife, Sophie, rode in an open car in a parade in Serajevo, the capitol of Bosnia, and were shot to death by a Serbian patriot.

12

At first when you traveled across Russia you were struck by the differences. You saw the Empire as a hodge-podge of unrelated nationalities and tribes and religions, incongruously bound together by an incomprehensible fate. What did the Baltic peoples with their German blood have in common with the descendants of the Tatars who swept across Russia five centuries ago? Or the Poles with the descendants of the armies of Tamerlane? Muscovite, German, Lithuanian, Latvian, Estonian, Finn, Pole, Ukrainian, Georgian, Armenian, Tatar. Orthodox, Catholic, Jewish, Lutheran, Moslem. Changing, always changing as you traveled east.

To Russians in Petersburg, Russia was European, but when you crossed into Asia, three-quarters of Russia still lay before you. Mingrelian, Uzbek, Kirghis, Azerbaidzhan, Malmuk, Mongol, Chinese, Korean. Dozens of semi-Nomadic tribes. Ilya Laranov spoke five languages—Russian, French, Polish, German, and English. In most of Russia he needed an interpreter. The Russian Empire—more than a hundred and fifty nationalities, two hundred languages and dialects—one-sixth of the earth's surface.

Laranov sat on his horse and watched the scene below where barefoot women and children were loading logs onto a barge. Out on the river men and women fished, kneeling in dugout canoes, and gangs of men and boys poled rafts of logs downstream. All over Russia it was the same. They came to the river with their logs, they came to the river to work like animals for an extra ruble, they came to the river for food.

And clusters of huts huddled together on dirt roads, that too was the same—isolated from the world, isolated from ideas. In Petersburg men took comfort in this isolation. With communication so difficult, they said, with few paved roads, with railroads going mostly east and west—north and south the rivers were the railroads, frozen half the year—with telephones only in the major cities, there could never be a revolution all across Russia.

The moujiks here were the same as all the others—suspicious, superstitious, stubborn. Among the upper classes it was fashionable to say they were mystical and philosophical, dreamy and very deep. Laranov had seen too much to be sentimental. They were poor, abused, hungry and drunk. They farmed with methods so primitive that the yield had not improved in three-hundred years. When Laranov talked to them about better ways to farm, they regarded him with suspicion because he was from the government.

They lived marginal lives, making slaves of their wives, needing sons for land. Because daughters did not merit land, many parents delivered them while they were still children to brothels in the cities—Moscow, Petersburg, Kiev, Odessa. Prostitutes at thirteen, in ten years they were old and finished, ravaged by alcohol, syphilis or tuberculosis. Some returned to their villages and married and bore diseased or imbecilic children. When the moujik traded this hard life for factory work in the city he only sank into deeper degradation.

For several years Laranov had kept a diary and over time he had found that on some desolate steppe or frozen wasteland a vivid memory would surface, evoked by this place but not of it, and combine with other memories and, the umbilical cord tied always to Russia, a deeper insight would be born.

Here beside the river, Laranov thought of the living quarters he had visited in St. Petersburg factories. In his diary he had written: "Thirty people—husbands, wives and unmarried men—living together in one large room—not a shred of privacy. Beds piled to the ceiling—three feet by six feet of living space alloted to each human being, and even that not exclusively his but assigned to a worker on each shift, occupied nights by one worker and days by another. The stink is overwhelming, the noise unrelenting. Women bear their children right there, their only privacy improvised with cardboard and rags. Even more pathetic are those who have no separate quarters at all but live and sleep on the factory floor.

"And into these filthy holes the Bolshevik organizers come to tell the workers that the factory owner is rich and that a larger share of what their labor produces should be theirs."

No revolution?

Today Laranov had talked to a moujik who owned a little patch of fourteen acres, a wooden plow and an old horse and complained that he paid too many taxes. "My grandfather got this land in 1861 and we have paid for it again and again in taxes. It's too small—we can't live off it. It's time we had more." Even if they didn't own their land, it was time. "We've slaved for years. We should have more. It's time."

And into these rural pockets of hunger and hopelessness the Social Revolutionary organizers came and told them there were great estates in Russia and the poor had the right to take the excess land of the rich.

No Revolution?

Laranov looked down at the river bank. A heavy woman glanced up at him and he saw that she was quite young. Here in the country he didn't look to see whether they were young or old or pretty because, whatever they were now, in a few years their bodies would be thick and their faces coarse and they would be old. He took up the reins. Koner had said they were going to the doctor's house for dinner. What was he going to ask the doctor? If his patients were sick, hungry, drunk, diseased? He knew the answers. He had seen them all over Russia.

He moved on. In a few days he would finish here and return to Vodovsky and then he would go home to Petersburg where the women created illusions with silk and lace and French perfume, where their bodies were soft and supple, where they were beautiful and bored and thirsted for excitement and wanted him. Petersburg, where the wine was smooth and the vodka was strong and the women had the power to excite him if only for a little while. It had bored him once and it would bore him again. But for now—God, he would be glad to be back.

*   *   *

"So how was it out there for Cirie?" Koner said.

"She said fine. It sounded more like wonderful."

"This bothers you?"

Strengov sighed. Every morning he counted one day less until Anna would be lost forever. And now Cirie had come home with dreamy eyes and a private smile and the kind of glow that says in another part of the forest fires are raging.

"I thought when Cirie came home the house would be lively again. Oh, it's busy, with Anna packing. Ulla is here—talking too much as usual. But Cirie—" He broke off. Why am I still reviewing the symptoms? The diagnosis is clear.

"So she's smitten with them. She'll get over it."

"And Marya's mother. For weeks she turned up every day, like a rash you couldn't get rid of. Now, suddenly she's missed three days. Marya is frantic. Tomorrow I'll have to drive her out there to see what's wrong."

"Is it still all right to bring Laranov tonight?"

"Why not?"

"Listen, Strengov, soon they'll go back to Kostyka and Cirie will be safely home and you'll see it was a fine experience."

She would not be home because they had asked her to go to Kostyka and she would not be safe because the damage was already done. Strengov thought of the two dandies, lounging in their fine clothes on these old leather chairs. *We've just returned from Paris…Do we have your word that you won't tell my mother?*

You don't even know he's out there, he argued with himself. It was no good. He's there—and she's suffering from the deadliest of diseases—infatuation—and you have only a few days to cure her or she goes back to certain disaster. He made up his mind. He would talk to her tonight after Koner and his bureaucrat left. And what are you going to say—what magic words to change the heart of a young girl with a severe case of first love? What truths? What lies?

"Koner," he said. "If Boris came home from Zurich, you'd try to talk some sense into him, wouldn't you?"

"I'd try. I don't think it would work."

"And if you had to tell a few lies—" The thought bothered him. He had never lied to Cirie. "Half-lies—a story not quite as it happened but not entirely false—?"

"To save him! How can there be a question? I'd do it!"

For once Koner was right. How could there be any question? Whatever it took, those dreamy eyes had to be opened before it was too late.

Any hope that he was mistaken about Cirie vanished at dinner. Here was this Laranov, a very attractive fellow—with his reckless air and a sense he communicated in the fluid motion of his powerful body of energy spilling over, energy to burn—a man who had traveled all over Europe and all over Russia, more remarkable because it was more primitive, and Cirie had hardly looked at him. Cirie who had spent her life dreaming of far away places. When Laranov arrived she had been startled to see him and Laranov, equally surprised, had bowed and said, "Why, it's the pretty nurse who rides so early in the day!" Now, although Marya had carefully placed him next to her, Laranov could have been dining in the barn for all Cirie cared.

But Ulla was thrilled with him. Strengov marveled at the energy she was pouring into this flirtation. "Ilya, you say you're traveling over all of Russia. But why?" A vivacious smile. "Why are you doing this?"

"Because in Petersburg people have no idea what all of Russia means. To them it's only a map." Laranov's black eyes feasted on Ulla's red hair and green eyes. Ulla had always been attractive, just as she had been silly and over-busy. She had married well—her husband was a lawyer in Kostyka who loved to indulge her—and now at thirty she was as gay and frivolous as ever. "So I decided to go and see all of Russia for myself."

Not for the first time Laranov's eyes drifted over to Cirie, who had discovered an object of total fascination just north of her plate.

"But surely you don't mean all," Ulla protested. "That would take a lifetime." A puff on her cigarette. "Where have you traveled?"

Strengov looked at Marya who was worrying about her mother. He was a little concerned himself. Tomorrow, if he found the old woman well and healthy, he would speak seriously to her.

"From the Arctic Circle to the Black Sea," Laranov told Ulla. "And from Germany to the Pacific Ocean."

"But your friends must never see you—how unfair! How did you go? What routes did you follow?"

Laranov settled back in his chair. He had the shoulders of a bull and the grace of a courtier. "I sailed the Black Sea and I traveled the borders of Turkey and Afghanistan and the deserts of Persia and still there was Russia—" His voice spoke of unimagined mysteries. "And I traveled across Siberia to Vladivostak and down to the tip of China and still it was Russia." Granted he looked like a cousin to Lucifer but he had them spellbound. Everyone except Cirie.

"All this wandering about!" Marya said. "Your wife doesn't object? Your children—" Shades of the old woman. Neither shyness nor a natural reticence will deter a woman with an unwed daughter over sixteen.

"I'm not married, Madame. Nor do I wish to be while I'm still traveling."

At last Cirie gave up the contemplation of her plate. "How far is that? To the tip of China?"

"After you've put the Urals behind you, it's four-thousand miles across Siberia. In Vladivostak the day is seven hours older than in Moscow. In winter, when the sun comes up over the Kremlin, the day is over at the other end of Russia."

Strengov looked at Laranov with curiosity. Traveling by boat and train and horseback and probably on foot, too, over some of the worst roads one could imagine—what did he have in mind? He wasn't a bureaucrat—Koner was right about that. With a bureaucrat there was always that stifling sense of a man careful not to break any eggs. This Laranov would break eggs and never look to see where they splattered. What was he doing in the government?

"What's it like in Siberia?" Cirie was succumbing at last.

"You mean the part they talk about at Whitewater—where the Tsar sends his political prisoners?"

"Across four thousand miles there must be more than a railroad and some prisoners," Cirie said. Her low voice made Ulla's seem high-pitched and shrill. Strengov wondered why he had never noticed how seductive it could be. Or was this, too, something she had learned at Vodovsky? She had changed so much he wasn't sure anymore how to talk to her. Now when it's important, he thought, I don't know her.

"In the south there's a rich black belt where people farm," Laranov said. "And north of that, enormous forests where trappers catch animals for furs—wolf, fox, lynx, mink and magnificent sables." Laranov's eyes shone as though he could see it now. "And far north of that is tundra, permanently frozen, where the only life is polar bears, wolves and ermine for an Empress."

"Oh, I hear about those Siberian furs from a dear friend," Ulla said with a shake of her fluffy red hair. "Petya Rossatin—a fur merchant who travels there. Cirie, when you come to Kostyka, I'm going to introduce you to Petya. He's so handsome, everyone adores him. Of course, you already know the handsomest man in Kostyka, and I understand in Petersburg, too. They say every girl dreams about Serge Vodovsky."

"He's there, then," Strengov said.

"He's been home for weeks!" Ulla said.

Cirie was staring at Ulla and Laranov, amused, was looking at Cirie.

"And he's gorgeous." Suddenly Ulla realized that she had talked too much. "Cirie, tell me about Whitewater. What do they do all day?"

Cirie recovered and said hastily, "They talk. About their friends and society. After the Prince's fire they talked about the radicals."

"Radicals! Have they had problems this summer?"

"Only with gnats, I believe," Laranov said, soberly.

"Only the day you arrived," Cirie countered sweetly, and their eyes met.

What's going on out there? Strengov thought. That little exchange was not about gnats.

As soon as she could escape, Cirie rushed outside. Ulla! She should have known better than to write one word to Ulla. Anyone who talked so much had to come out with the wrong thing. And Laranov! Smirking as though he knew everything. She hated him—he was so smug. And tomorrow he was going to ride out in the country with them as far as Red Emilianov's and then come to Anya Dubrovna's for dinner and a ride home. All that time with Strengov—he could say anything! With alarm, she wondered if he had said anything to Vassily after she left.

Under the oak tree she stopped, her blood pounding, and looked at the reflected glow of the sunset over the house that after Whitewater seemed smaller. Then she saw Anna coming toward her. Poor Anna. She would be among strangers and she would have only Vogel.

"Anna, be careful!" she cried when Anna reached her. "Vogel might have changed—you might have changed. Don't marry him just because you're lonely."

"Cirie, I'm going there to marry him."

"Anna, start to learn English the minute you land. You can get a job."

"Karl has a job. And when he knows English better, he'll get a better job."

Two years—he should know it by now! "If you hear about a job that you can do, tell them you did it here. You draw and paint so nicely—say you taught here."

"But I've only taught Lily."

"Tell them anyway. How can they check?"

"You could do that, Cirie—I couldn't."

"Try it. It'll work."

"Cirie, I know you'll marry someone important and have more than I will. But I've never wanted a lot. And you've always meant to have everything."

Voices on the porch told them Koner and Laranov were leaving.

"We should say goodnight," Anna said.

Cirie shrugged. "We'll see him tomorrow."

"Why don't you like him?"

"My God, did it show?" That was a mistake—that was just plain foolish—he was going back to Whitewater. As she watched Anna walk back to the house she told herself that tomorrow she would have to be more agreeable.

As soon as Koner and Laranov left, Strengov headed for the back yard to find Cirie.

"Poor Anna," she said as he came up to her. "Someday she'll stop seeing Vogel's good looks and see only the sullen man behind them and she'll have no one."

"Cirie, what's going on between you and Serge Vodovsky?"

"Nothing! Nothing's going on."

"Don't evade with me. Have you done anything foolish?"

"No!"

"Cirie, Serge Vodovsky will never marry you."

How could she protest without giving herself away?

"You weren't born a princess or a countess or a millionaire's daughter. I'm a poor rural doctor." Wearily he sat on the weathered bench. "Even if Serge wanted to marry you the other one, Vassily, wouldn't let him. He's only playing with you for the summer."

"He's not! He loves me."

"Maybe. But he won't marry you."

"He will!"

Anguished, Strengov hunched forward on the bench. "My prize is his plaything," he mourned. "To use and break and throw away."

"Don't say that!"

"He knows he can't marry you. And if you become pregnant, in your eyes the baby would be a Vodovsky—not in theirs. He still couldn't marry you."

"What baby? What are you talking about?" She tried to humor him. "If you keep saying these things Mamma will hear you. Then we will have a problem."

Strengov lit a Turkish cigarette. "Cirie, he'll never ask to marry you."

"He has!"

"To marry you?"

"Yes."

"Then he's worse than I thought. His words mean nothing. He's a weakling." He stood up and paced in front of the oak tree. "You're too ambitious, Cirie. For a girl it's dangerous. Men take advantage of her." The aroma from his cigarette filled the night air. "Who is going to hold Vodovsky accountable for what he says to you?"

"He will!"

"When his family objects, his promises will go up in smoke. And they're not the only ones who would object. I, too, would be against it."

"You!"

"When he lets you down, you'll be hurt but you'll recover. If he were to actually marry you, he would hurt you more."

"You don't know him. You've always disliked them."

Strengov stared at the dark woods. "I know him."

"How? How do you know him?"

"He came to me once with his cousin." If the story were the whole truth, however unpleasant, he could tell her. But a lie? "Cirie, you never miss a thing—sometimes you see too much. Now, when it's important, you're blind." Against the last purple band of the sunset they faced each other, the one all anguish, the other all defiance and passion. "Give him up. He'll ruin your life!"

"I love him!"

"Cirie, I ask you not to go back."

"I would go back to him," she said, "if I had to walk."

Strengov was almost at the door when she stopped him. "Papa—what did he come to you for? Was he sick? Was he hurt? What was wrong?"

She's *asking* you. There won't be a better chance. He stood a minute, shoulders hunched. *Only a half-lie. Tell her.* Then the shoulders sagged. "I don't remember—" he said. He went into the house.

For a long time, with the first stars coming out and the frogs starting up, Cirie stayed outside. Her father didn't know how it was between Serge and her. He had always said people should stay with their own kind and maybe he believed that. And maybe they believed that at Whitewater. But for Serge and her, their only world was their world together, beyond all those unimportant people. How many times had Serge said that without her his life would be nothing? Of course he would marry her.

Upstairs Ulla was waiting for her. "Isn't that Ilya Laranov gorgeous?" she said when Cirie came into the room.

"He looks like a pirate."

"That's what's so gorgeous! And I'm sure he has the heart of a pirate. I could be wild about him!"

"To me he only seems arrogant."

Ulla became serious. "Cirie, you must forget about Serge. He'll never marry you. That's expecting too much."

"Ulla, did my father tell you to say that?"

"No! Cirie, at best you would be his mistress. And being a mistress before you are married isn't a good idea. Afterwards, an affair is another matter." Ulla sat beside her on the bed. "Cirie, my love, I'm driving a knife into your heart—I know it—but Serge is going to marry a countess."

"You sound like my father. He's not going to marry any countess."

"Not any countess. One particular countess—Irene Scherevsky."

Cirie caught her breath. Irene! The countess Vara talked about so pointedly. "That can't be true!"

"It's been understood for a year now."

"He doesn't love her!"

"But he's going to marry her. The Scherevskys are an old important family and their fortune is diminishing. It's a good match on both sides. For Vassily this means a connection to one of the oldest and most respected titles in Russia."

It can't be true! "Ulla, have you seen her?"

"Oh, my sweet Cirie, she's very beautiful. I saw her once with the other countess—Vara. She's quite extraordinary. Tall, graceful, blonde hair that she wears in the French style, drawn back with a few strands of curls. When she stands it's almost as though she were leaning backwards. She's positively regal."

In a panic Cirie rushed down the stairs. No! It can't be true. Outside again, under a shower of stars, she brought her panic under control. Serge loved her. She was sure of it. Ulla was just repeating gossip. Didn't he say that before her everything was meaningless and that without her his life would be meaningless again? And how frightened he was when he thought he was losing her. Then her mind cleared and she understood. Those arrangements were made a year ago! Now things had changed. "From now on we belong to each other," he had said. "Nothing can ever change that."

If I'd come home a few days earlier, I might be alarmed, she told herself. When I get back I'll ask him and he'll laugh at this.

          *   *   *

Vara hurried into her mother's sitting room. "About that girl," she said. "Now that she's gone, she shouldn't come back."

"But I want her back," Madame said. "The Tchernefskys and Irene are coming. And Sacha Borassin."

Of course! Vara thought spitefully. Time for Sacha Borassin is more important than my feelings. "This girl upsets me! She's common. You know these peasants—pretty at sixteen and at twenty they're fat and coarse, that girlish laugh becomes a cackle—" Vara let her eyes sweep over her mother's desk. "I'm sure some of the other maids were once prettier than she is."

"Vara, I must tell you—" Madame said, troubled. "I've asked Cirie to come to Kostyka with us."

Vara grasped the desk. "I can't believe this!"

"My dear, I wish you could be more generous about Cirie. You've allowed yourself to become vindictive."

"I won't have her in Kostyka!"

"I know you're unhappy. I know what it is to be a widow. And you're so young. But I must be honest—"

"Honest! Well, I can be honest, too! I didn't want to upset you but she shouldn't even come back here because there's something's going on between Serge and her." Good—it's out. Vara saw that she had found her mark.

"Vara, do you know that? Or do you only suspect?"

"I know Serge."

Madame's composure returned. "I know Serge, too. He's so gracious, even to a servant. But he knows better than to lead Cirie on."

"Then you admit she's a servant. Maybe if we treated her like one, Serge would see a distinction."

"I think Serge knows the difference."

"Maman, Irene is coming. What wonderful gossip for Petersburg! Countess Scherevsky sharing her fiance with a servant. They were on the verge of announcing the betrothal but the young man showed a preference for a servant. Serge Vodorvsky—rich, handsome, but apparently rather common."

Furious, her disorderly mind in a turmoil, Vara stormed out of the room. Her mother didn't begin to know how it felt to be a widow. Eugenie Vodovsky! Married, single, widowed, all her life men had fawned and fussed over her. And now the girl had to stay because Sacha Borassin came ahead of everyone else. Well, Vara had her suspicions about that. She had tried to get the truth from Kyra but Kyra always played dumb. Naturally! Kyra probably had a few skeletons in her own closet that Maman could rattle if she talked too much. Someday Vara would confront Kyra. "You might as well have told me," she would say. "You see, I know that Sacha Borassin was Maman's lover."

Vara shuddered. It was easier to think the words than to cope with the image— her mother lying in her cool dark boudoir with Sacha Borassin—submitting to him—permitting him—! No, probably not in her boudoir, she was always so discreet. Then where? Borassin, heavy-boned, bull-like, passionate, *male*—the image came into sharp focus—her mother and Borassin coupling—like animals—like! Vara's heart pounded. Even animal breeding upset her. And her mother! *How could she?*

Downstairs Vara darted into her mother's study and rifled through this desk. All she needed was some proof. Then things would be different. Then it would be Vara's wishes that would be heeded, not those of a silly old woman who wove spells with a smile and a soft voice. And that loathsome, blue-eyed tart would be gone and they would all—Serge, Georgii, Constantine—*all* have to get along without her. If not for her, Constantine would have spoken by now. Vara was sure of it.

"Serge "

Madame had debated with herself whether she ought to speak to Serge. Vara's accusation could be based on nothing more than jealousy, but it was too serious to be ignored, especially as the Tchernefskys and Irene would be here any day. Not that the Prince was a particularly amiable man. Completely self-absorbed, he expected others to adjust to his schedule. But Madame had never chosen her friends out of affection. She accepted them as part of her social circle, like a tree in her Italian garden, standing in its proper place, conforming to the pattern. She would have to confront Serge. Better she than Vassily. Better now than when it was too late. A little before dinner she called him to her study.

"Serge, what are your feelings toward Irene? You do care for her?"

"Why do you ask, Maman?" Serge smiled disarmingly and crossed his legs. "Isn't she the most beautiful woman in Petersburg?"

Madame asked herself if that was a satisfactory answer. Irene, with her lineage and her cool beauty, was the most eligible young woman in Russia. If there was even the most innocent flirtation between Serge and Cirie, she would have to send word to Cirie not to return.

"Serge, I don't know how to say this tactfully—Serge, have you been—indiscreet—with Cirie?"

"Cirie!"

"Vara feels there is—something of an attraction—between you."

Serge's laugh did not entirely dispel her fears. "Is that how Vara put it? Something of an attraction?"

"I believe Vara said, 'Something is going on.'"

"I'm sorry, Maman." Serge stopped laughing. "Vara's imagination is working too hard again. Cirie is always with Georgii or you. She's pleasant. I'm pleasant."

Did she detect a hint of alarm? "She's a very pretty girl."

"Yes, I suppose she is. But not like Irene. Well, why go into it? Irene was educated in Paris—her grandmother attended the Empress. I imagine Cirie has never been out of Novotnii and her grandmother trades with sailors on the waterfront. So what are we talking about?"

Is he protesting too much? Cirie is more than just a pretty girl and she doesn't appear to be that old woman's granddaughter. "Serge, you know how much Vassi wants this marriage between you and Irene."

Serge shrugged impatiently. "Maybe Vassi should marry her."

Momentarily distracted, Madame said, "I've often wondered what kind of woman would attract Vassi. Well-connected, of course. And not frivolous."

"It wouldn't matter whether she was beautiful—he'd never notice."

Madame's thoughts came back to her immediate worry. "Serge, can you assure me there's no problem?"

"Maman, do you really think I'd become involved with a servant?"

No—and yet. In age, you might remember the foolish things you did long ago, but not the passions that drove you to them. "While Irene is here, you must not so much as glance at Cirie. No looks, no smiles. Do you promise?"

"Certainly I promise, Maman. It's no problem.

13

Laranov and Strengov walked into the field where "Red" Emilianov was working. Named for his red hair and beard, Emilianov was that rare moujik who had struggled out of absolute poverty. His house on the river had four rooms and a rug and flower boxes at the window and he had a dory with iron sheathing to protect it against the spring ice. In his yard fishing nets were spread to dry. His thriving fields were separated by a pole fence from Popov's shabby little place, both farms worked on shares for an absentee landlord. Popov saw them and suspended work in favor of conversation. "Not good," he said when Strengov asked about his crop.

Laranov squinted at his scrawny field of rye. "Get better seed next year at the cooperative."

"I was using this seed before you were born." Popov roared with laughter but his eyes were narrow. Always that reluctance to try something new.

"And plant deeper."

"Eh? And who will give me a new plow?" Hate sat in Popov's eyes as he surveyed his filthy barnyard where his pregnant wife was tossing garbage to a pig. "Also my horse is very old. One horse is not enough. A team is better." Then the eyes changed as they settled on Cirie, fresh and cool-looking in a flowered dress and a straw hat and Laranov frowned at what he read in them.

Popov became aware of Laranov's hard look and turned to Strengov. "The baby has a bad rash," he said and Strengov went to his wagon for some yellow ointment.

"The baby is no cleaner than the rest of the place," Emilianov said as they moved away from the pole fence.

"His place looks worse for being next to yours," Cirie said.

Emilianov cheered up. "I'll have boots for you before winter, Cirie. The most beautiful boots I can make."

She rewarded him with a smile. "Then they'll be the most beautiful boots in Russia."

One more knight who would die for her. Laranov had watched them at Whitewater. She collects them with that smile and those eyes of which dreams are born and an instinct for finding just the right words to make a man feel like a king. Every man except Ilya Laranov, who had the bad luck to stumble onto her secret and could betray her to Vassily or her father. And maybe he should—it would be a service to her. But not to himself.

Walking with her to the wagon, Laranov said, "You're looking at your future."

"You mean Emilianov?"

"I mean Popov."

"But it's Emilianov who works so hard."

"Emilianov produces miracles. Popov will hear promises that if the landowners are removed he'll have more land and a better plow and another horse, too. And his barnyard would still be filthy."

After the wagon pulled off, Laranov and Emilianov walked across the field.

"I have slaved to improve this land next to his," Emilianov said. "Winters I raised logs through the ice. I worked nights as a watchman on the river. I made fine boots. And I saved enough to buy a good plow." He picked up a clod of earth. "I removed stumps. I rotated crops. Now my wheat is as high as Vodovsky's. But the landlord could sell my land and I would be out. And others, even this lazy Popov, could shout loud enough to the mir to get my land and the good of my work."

I must own my own land.

"The mir would give me only a few poor strips because I have only daughters. A daughter is a mouth to feed, too. A daughter is a child to love. My land should be mine—for me to gather the fruits of my hard work and to give to my daughters." His fist tightened around the clod of earth. "*I must own my own land.*"

As Strengov came around Anya Dubrovna's store—a log hut with three additions—he was startled to see the old man, Karil, a little distance away, staring at the river with such an attitude of grieving in the sag of his body that he thought Anya Dubrovna must have died. A moment later the old woman came out the door, fairly bursting with health and an air of high excitement. This shrewd old witch has made another good deal, Strengov thought, relieved and then resentful at the anxiety she had caused. Already she was pulling out her latest batch of photographs from America. "Lavrentii has a business," she said. "He's a merchant, selling coal. Not a peddler. A merchant."

"An apple that dropped close to the tree," Strengov muttered and Cirie smothered a laugh. She had not said a word about their disagreement last night. Even with Laranov she had been more agreeable today. She couldn't stay mad—she was in love.

"And a new picture of Anton," Dubrovna said, retrieving a picture of Marya's son from the pile.

Out of relief at finding her mother alive and well, Marya burst into tears. "Oh, Mamma, so many have gone. What will I do without Anna?"

"They're better off," the old tyrant insisted. "Strengov should go, too. You hear, Strengov?"

This was a new suggestion. What scheme was she hatching now? Anya Dubrovna darted into the store and returned with a small unwrapped brown box. "Here, Marya, a gift for you." Opening the box she displayed six little silver spoons, each adorned with the figure of a cellist with his bow across his instrument—a gift probably acquired long ago and saved against just such an unhappy day. Marya's most prized possession was the fine lace tablecloth her mother gave her when Anton left. "Very heavy. Very fine pieces."

Marya gazed at the spoons and Strengov knew that in her mind she saw herself in an elegant setting, serving tea to a guest, placing a little silver cellist across the saucer.

Dubrovna's eyes settled on Lily and impulsively she stroked the little girl's long fair hair. "Cirie, you must always look out for this little one," she said. "She's like Marya—a dreamer, a kitten. When I'm not here, remember that."

"Mamma, don't talk like that!"

Embarrassed by her moment of weakness, the old woman began to straighten some boxes of cabbages and potatoes. "A captain from Constantinople says there's unrest in Europe. An Austrian Archduke was shot. Somewhere in the Balkans. And there are strikes all over Russia. There's going to be trouble. You hear, Strengov?"

"There's always unrest somewhere, Mamma."

"Nobody worries about it, but they should," the old woman grumbled. "I'm glad I won't see it."

Strengov looked up quickly. This old woman didn't repeat herself without a purpose. "Why won't you see it?"

Anya Dubrovna, who ordinarily could not be persuaded to stop talking, suddenly was speechless.

"Where will you be? What's the matter with Karil?"

She was like a courier who has ridden for days with his message and now cannot find the voice to speak.

"Mamma, what's wrong?" Marya said.

The voice was found. "I'm going!"

"Going where?"

"I'm going!"

Strengov understood at once.

"I'll see my sons!" A fanatical glint sat in the old woman's eyes. "I'll see America before I die!"

"Mamma!"

"Don't cry, Marya. It won't be right away. I only sold the store yesterday."

She meant it! By God, she meant it. That was what she'd been doing these past three days—selling her store! How many times had he said she would go? How many years had he hoped for it?

"There's a lot to do," Dubrovna said. "Your father has to get used to the idea."

Strengov turned to look at Karil mourning beside the river. An old man, over seventy, he had lived his whole life in this house—and now this ageless, fearless harpy would uproot him and drag him to a place he wouldn't understand, that wouldn't understand him. Strengov started over to him and Cirie fell in beside him. "For years I hoped she would go," he said. "Did I really believe it would happen?"

"Probably not."

"Cirie, Mamma will be miserable, losing Anna and her mother at the same time."

"I've thought of that." She met his look, already refusing.

Marya can take a silver spoon, Strengov thought, and for a little while she lives in a dream but she knows it's a dream. But Cirie—even without the spoon, Cirie imagines herself with the whole silver service and the world it belongs in and once she has dreamed it, it becomes real, it becomes possible, it's waiting for her to claim it—she has only to find the way. "Cirie, only Lily will be left."

She looked at him, troubled. "I can't give it up!"

Give up what? The world isn't there for her to claim! The spoon that shines for her is tarnished! "Cirie, the world is full of handsome young aristocrats who amuse themselves with pretty nurses until they become bored—and then marry a woman of their own class."

Her chin came up, defiantly. "It's not like that."

Strengov stopped walking. If he was going to say it, this was the time. "Cirie, I told you he came to me once—he was sick—"

"You said you didn't remember whether he was sick or hurt—"

A rough-looking sailor on a boat feasted watery eyes on Cirie. Strengov moved between her and the look of lust. "I remember."

"What was it?"

He searched for the right words.

"What was wrong with him?"

There were no right words. "He thought he had syphilis."

Was it love or fear that drained the color from her face? Had she already exposed herself?

"Did he—" Her voice gathered strength. "Does he have it?"

Strengov hunched his shoulders.

"Does he have it?"

The bulbous-nosed sailor moved and Strengov moved again.

"Papa!"

His shoulders sagged. He couldn't go through with it. He couldn't lie to her. He had thought he could do it and he believed that he should and he could not. "The microscope showed a simpler type of rash. But he was very worried. He was certain he had it."

"But he didn't!" Her voice leaped with relief.

"Cirie, he *believed* that he had it. Think what this tells you about him—his habits—his morals—"

But she was only thinking that he had intended to deceive her. "That wasn't fair!"

"—His character. You're going to be hurt, Cirie. It's a cold family. They don't care what happens to you."

"He didn't have it!"

"Cirie, have you considered how much this will cost you? In unhappiness and worse if you're reckless?" But he knew that in her lightning calculations, she had. She had considered the cost if she failed and the prize if she won. And she had considered the loss if she didn't try. She wanted the man and she wanted his world and she had always wanted it and it was not in her nature to turn away. "Cirie, don't give in to him. I tell you this not as your father, but as a man."

She laughed. "I know that. Don't you think I know that?"

He felt that he had betrayed her by not lying—just a small lie, a half-lie. "Send for me when you need me," he said. "I won't say I told you so."

She smiled and touched his arm. "Neither will I."

The sunset tinted the sky as Laranov walked with Cirie along the waterfront. All through dinner he had endured the tears of the family crisis he had stumbled into, knowing well enough the reason he had allowed it to happen. And she was only a child—an inexperienced lovesick child.

From the river bank came the call of the watchman guarding the logs. "All's well." The cry was picked up by another guard down the river on the opposite shore and then by another, farther away. For centuries, all over Russia, the watchmen on the rivers had called to each other all through the night. "What about you, Cirie?" he said. "Are you going to America, too, someday?"

"Never!"

She said that now because everything she wanted was here. But what about later when everything she wanted no longer wanted her? His thoughts moved briefly to the old woman. Usually those who went to America had little to leave behind—a hovel for a home that was easy to turn your back on, possessions so meagre they could carry them in a sack. "Your grandmother is an exception. Usually people go to America because they're poor or persecuted or without hope. A trade of the past for the future can't turn out to be a bad deal."

"She thinks America is Paradise."

"Their welcoming monument is a Statue of Liberty. Can you imagine a monument to liberty in Russia—with the words, 'Give me your tired, your poor, your huddled masses'"

"You'd give them most of Russia."

Laranov smiled, surprised. He had not suspected she might be political. "Does she know anything about it?"

"I think it's mostly imagined."

Every paradise is only imagined.

"All's well," the watchman called.

As dusk deepened they moved along the dock, past narrow ships riding the quiet water.

"Whenever I'm here on the river," she said, "I imagine that these ships have seen the whole world—India, China, Africa, America—and now they'll sail to the wonderful places in Russia."

She was Marco Polo bound to this poor district and longing to see the world. Laranov realized how little he knew her.

"Have you ever seen any of those wonderful places, Cirie?"

"I've never been anywhere! Once I visited Ulla in Kostyka."

At the end of the dock, where the water lapped the posts, they stopped and he stood close to her.

"There's a fair at Novgorod, where ships do come from everywhere—sailing ships, steamers, barges, Chinese junks—a city of ships, anchored so close together that you can cross the river by jumping from one to another."

"You can walk across the river on the ships?"

Laranov nodded without speaking. He wanted to hold this girl, feel her body close to his, her lips under his lips. Go home, Ilya, you've been away too long.

"What do they bring to the fair?"

"Furs from Siberia, tea from India, silk from China, cashmere from Persia—" His words wove a magic spell and she listened, mesmerized, forgetting that she resented him. "And the riverfront is even more crowded, with shops and stalls and all kinds of merchants—Turks with fezzes, Arabs, Indians, Persians, Chinese. There's a whole market for tea and one for intoxicating luxury furs—lynx, mink, ermine, sable. Persian rugs and Arabian horses. Markets for every trade. And bells—all kinds of bells. People take turns ringing them. You can go from market to market and never see it all."

She hung on his words, not at war with him now and not thinking about Serge Vodovsky. "Have you seen it, Laranov?"

"Yes, I've seen it." The moon had pushed up out of the water and masts and ropes of ships were silhouetted against the sky. "Someday," he said, softly, "if we are all the same as now, I'll take you there to see it."

We won't any of us be the same, he thought. And nothing will be the same for us. "All's well."

Later, in his room at Koner's Inn, Laranov poured a glass of vodka and drank it and thought about her. After a while he opened his diary and re-read his last entry, written at Whitewater after talking most of the night with Constantine. "Constantine knows the Tsar's days as absolute ruler are numbered and he hopes the changes will be peaceful. I see the faces of Russia—worn, hungry, drunk, diseased—and I ask, How can the changes still be peaceful?

"The question is not, who loves the Tsar enough to give him time? The question is, who hates him enough to fight and die to be rid of him? And who will seize that hatred and use it for his own ambitions?

"These will be the shock troops—damned now and doomed later. But a man will hear that he has the right to breath, demand, seize control—and his blood will race. He will die, but he will have had something more than rotting in a factory, starving in a hole, the slow deadly march to nothing. For one moment he will feel glory and for that, willingly, eagerly, he will let himself be used. For that, he will welcome death."

Laranov gave a humorless chuckle. What is death to a Russian? Death is an old friend. Now—later—it's all the same.

Now he wrote: "Like death the hatred is there—an old friend. Now he hates his exploiters and takes it out on his neighbor in a drunken brawl. But offer him the privilege of hating in a cause and you give him back his wasted life. For one glorious moment before he is disillusioned—before he learns that the magicians in this world are ambitious—he will know what it feels like to be a man."

Cirie pushed back into his thoughts. "Have you seen all those ships, all those places?" she had said. In the darkening day, beside the tall ships, her delicate features had had a carved cameo look. Every paradise is only imagined.

He resumed his writing. "All over Russia there are people who believe that what has been will always be because it's God's will. And all over Russia other people are laying plans to see that what has always been will be changed."

The watchman's cry sounded. "All's well."

Laranov raised his glass in the direction of the river. "A matter of opinion, my friend."

"All's well."

14

Prince Tchernefsky, frail-looking, pink-cheeked, jowls like an old rooster's sagging over a stiff collar, would hold court each evening with the attitude of a man who recognized his obligation to instruct the less meticulously informed. Entering the drawing room before dinner, the Princess' jeweled old hand clutching his arm, he would bow to the ladies and kiss their hands and then, taking up a position in the center of the room, he would deliver a monologue, pausing only to correct anyone who disagreed with him. If conversation actually developed and took a bad turn, he would say, "Ordinarily I would not select this matter for discussion but since you raise it, I realize my thoughts would not be unwelcome," and he would begin another monologue. Seventy-two years old, the Prince parroted the ultra-conservative doctrine—the absolute authority of the Tsar and the Orthodox Church, inextricably bound together, neither open to question or change.

The effect of the Prince's presence was a general dispersion. Stepa and Constantine retreated to their cottages and wrote their books. Kurasin and Lydia left for the Crimea. Constantine did not listen to the Prince because he considered him an idiot, but Stepa was like a man who couldn't keep his hand away from the flame. He could listen to the nonsense only so long before erupting.

Only Vassily was more in evidence, forsaking his office to spend many hours with his guests, determined that nothing would upset his plan to marry Serge to Irene and link the Vodovsky name to this venerable family.

In the drawing room before dinner Vara and Kyra were fawning over the Princess, all dry and powdered and jeweled, who accepted their ministrations as nothing more than her due, and the Prince after adjusting his pince-nez, was droning on about God's special love for Russia.

Cirie glanced at the door. Since her return a few hours ago, she had looked everywhere for Serge, hoping to question him quickly and be quickly reassured, but he was nowhere about. Nor was Irene—although Gerzy's son Mischa had said she was here. Mischa had made the trip into Novotnii because Gerzy refused to leave the mare, Penelope, even though she was not due for another three weeks. "He's even starting to sleep in the stable," Mischa grumbled. "A lot of fuss over a horse."

"This foal is supposed to be very special," Cirie said. "You know how Madame feels about it."

"I have no feeling for horses." Mischa scowled. "This Penelope is pampered like a princess. Or this Countess we have now."

Cirie's stomach tightened. "They're here, then?"

"The Countess and the mare are of equal importance. Which is saying something for the Countess."

Now, in the drawing room before dinner, Cirie still had not seen Serge, but Vara was watching her, eyes bulging with anticipation.

"Russia has to change," Stepa shouted at the Prince. "The West is alive with new ideas—scientific discoveries, economic progress—"

"Don't talk to me about the ungodly West!" In the Prince's cheeks, two irregular pink spots dribbled down like spilled ink. "Talk to me about pious Russia, bound to the unchanging rituals of the Church."

The door opened and Constantine and Theo came in and the Prince nodded as though conceding their right to be in his presence provided they did not attempt to be equal. Everyone was here except Serge and Irene, and it didn't take a clairvoyant to know they were together.

"Of course you don't mean political changes," the Prince said.

"Political changes and other changes," Stepa said. "We're old, we're obsolete, we're a century behind the West."

Vara's eyes were riveted on the window that was just a white square of sky from where Cirie sat.

"Political changes are out of the question!" the Prince cried. "The Tsar received his authority from God in the sacrament of the Coronation. To challenge it is heresy." His pale eyes swept the room, daring all heretics to make themselves known.

"This is reassuring to hear," Madame murmured.

"Oh, yes," Kyra said and the Princess' parchment face cracked into a smile.

Cirie saw that Vara was watching her like a vulture ready to swoop down and bloody its prey. And Constantine was watching. And Stepa had stopped arguing and fastened his eyes on her. My God, what a spectacle!

Then Serge was here, standing in the doorway, and on his arm Irene, cool and beautiful, blonde hair drawn back just as Ulla had described her, her head so high that she did indeed seem to be leaning back. She paused, collecting attention, with a smile that didn't quite reach her eyes, and took a chair and Serge stood behind her. Cirie stared at Irene's elegant beige dress trimmed with matching lace and at the gleaming pearls at her throat and her eyes dropped to her own homemade cotton blouse.

"I purchased it in Paris," Irene said, in reply to Kyra's admiring inquiry. "I feel quite a different person in it."

Cirie stared across the room at nothing. Once Serge met her eyes for an instant and looked carefully away. He remained standing behind Irene's chair. If his attention strayed even briefly, Irene summoned it and it returned.

"The social events of the past year were a delight," Irene said at dinner. Names flowed from her lips—Tchaikovsky, Chekhov, the Little Theatre, the opera, the ballet. "And there was the scandal about Nijinsky," she said to Serge. "I'm sure you heard about that."

Serge sipped his wine and nodded.

"In the eyes of God, Russia is unique," the Prince said. "Everything that happens in Russia is God's plan."

"In honor of the Tercentenary," Irene said, "the Emperor and the Empress appeared in robes of the early tsars and tsarinas, covered with gold and jewels."

"The Empress' robe weighed seventy pounds," the Princess said, as though confiding a state secret. "She was quite fatigued."

"I've never seen such gowns…Faberge was extremely busy…I'm torn between M. Faberge and my jeweler in Paris…I can't describe my feelings…"

"Tell me, Irene dear," Vara said. "Did you enjoy Whitewater by moonlight? You and Serge took a very long walk last night."

"My feelings are quite indescribable," Irene said. "I told Serge a sky showered with stars is all I require to be totally content. I simply feel everything around me."

As they left the dining room after an interminable dinner, Arkady fell in beside her. "Cards?" he said.

"Not tonight, Arkady."

"They're cretins," Arkady muttered. "You haven't been here all week. Come on down and play cards."

She had to do something. "All right—in an hour."

After Georgii was in bed Cirie flung herself down on her bed, fighting tears. The smell of the summer night came through the open window. Summer at its peak. Soon to pass. *Forget about Serge…He's going to marry a countess—it's all arranged…He's amusing himself with you for the summer*—Forget about Serge and all that the summer was and all its promises. A picture of Irene danced before her eyes—the elegant coiffeur, the angle of the chin. *She's very beautiful—positively regal…He's only playing with you for the summer.* "I won't cry," Cirie said to herself. "I refuse."

Half an hour later she entered the card room, her neck arched in an imitation of Irene.

"That's a nice angle to the chin, dearie," Arkady said with his pixie-grin. "I like that."

"It's no great trick," Cirie said. "You don't have to study in Paris to do it."

"Tonight I'll teach you more about how to cheat." Arkady flipped the deck of cards. "All of life is cheating, you know. Play it straight and you'll get nowhere."

He's going to marry a countess. Who wears pearls and Paris dresses.

"I don't think I can teach you how to fix cards," Arkady said. "I learned that from a magician and it takes years of practice, but cheating is a matter of natural-looking signals. Pay attention and I'm sure you'll learn very quickly."

"Oh, I'll learn," Cirie said. "I simply feel everything around me."

But later in her room, without warning, the tears were back. *"A promise from Serge Vodovsky means nothing. Who is going to hold him accountable? The world is full of handsome young aristocrats who play games with pretty nurses until they become bored. Then they marry a woman of their own class."* She looked at her three white cotton blouses and slammed the drawer shut. *"A promise from Serge Vodovsky means nothing...He's going to marry a Countess."* How could he have loved her all summer, loved her only a week ago—she couldn't be wrong—and marry Irene, elegant as she was, and a countess?

At daybreak, she told herself that she would not ride today. She would not wait on the hill while he didn't come. She flung her cotton shirt back into the drawer. Then she took it out again. It's important to ride today—now—as though Serge had never come home, she told herself. Ask Gerzy about Penelope and ride along the river and come back. Penelope, named for that woman who waited all those years for Ulysses to come home. Paklov had told her the story. Silly woman—she probably had a hundred rivals along the way if he took all that time getting home. The tears were starting again. This is too much, she thought.

At the stable Gerzy said, "She's due in about three weeks but I'm sleeping here."

Cirie stroked the big dark mare. "For three weeks?"

"Prince Igor was General Borassin's best stallion and he gave him to Madame to mate with Penelope who is our best." Gerzy indicated a cot in a corner. "I'll take no chances."

"You're right, of course."

Later, probably, Serge would ride with Irene—in a Paris habit, no doubt. And they'll go to our hill and Irene will tell him that she feels—feels—feels everything just standing there, looking down at our lake. Cirie flicked her crop at a broken branch. Maybe there'll be gnats again. That'll be quite a different feeling, too.

Harvesting had begun and the moujiks had left home at five o'clock and were already working. At midday they would rest for two hours in ditches beside the fields and then work until dark. Arkady and Boris are right, Cirie thought. Why should these poor people work from dark to dark while that pompous prince drones on and Irene examines her silly feelings? And when she is with Serge on our hill, will he hold her as he used to hold me? At the river, Cirie stared at the morning steamer. It would have been better if they had sent her home that first day and she had never seen Serge. Now, for the rest of her life, what was she to do?

The sun was up and she started back. I did what I said I would do, she thought. I didn't go near the hill. The stable came into sight. Keep going, she ordered herself. But what if he's there? He's not there, she told herself. And isn't it better to think that maybe he came than to know he did not? No. All day I'll wonder. All day I'll be looking for a sign that he was there. She stopped. All right, then—go and look and he won't be there and you won't have to look for signs or anything else. Pegasus climbed the hill.

"*Where have you been?*"

"Oh, Serge!"

"I've been here an hour. I knew Pegasus was out." He kissed her lips and her hair. "Darling, I've missed you so. I've ached for you." Serge looked hastily toward the stables. "Darling, we can't meet here, anymore. The Prince rides early. If he sees me I'll be stuck with him every day. Go to the playhouse tomorrow—the other side—where we can't be seen."

The tears that had waited all night finally had their time.

"Darling, what's wrong? You're always so controlled."

"Serge, you're going to marry her!"

Bewilderment and hurt chased across Serge's face. "Is that why you didn't come this morning?"

"Everyone says it's all settled."

"Marry her! When I'm so much in love with you? How could I?" He kissed her as though making up for every lost moment. "Darling, we have to be careful. Vara is suspicious. My mother is asking questions."

"Serge, it *looks* as though you're going marry her. You act as though you're going to marry her."

He laughed and kissed her worried face. "I can see you have no idea how I feel." He looked deep into her eyes and told her he loved her. And she believed him.

Vassily's mind was jumping from one grievance to another tonight. He was tired of Prince Vladimir's endless lectures. Why didn't Serge talk to him once in a while? Only what could Serge possibly say? He didn't know anything. But what did the Prince know? Vassily knew this mood. It was as though someone were scraping his nerves with an emery. When it gripped him, nothing helped.

In the drawing room Serge was with Theo and Vassily signaled him to move over to Irene.

"Don't talk to me about a constitutional monarchy," the Prince said, flicking his hand as though waving away something offensive. "With the Tsar only a figurehead and the Duma in charge."

By dinner Vassily's nerves were raw.

"The social season this winter was breathtaking," Irene said. "A steady stream of parties."

Vassily clamped his teeth. Next it would be her jeweler in Paris. Who was she fooling? The Scherevskys had long since squandered the kind of fortune it took to buy jewels. Why did she irritate him so? Vassily had no desire to marry—he had a satisfactory arrangement with a widow in Kostyka—but he usually found a beautiful woman agreeable for a while. Irene only upset him.

"Really, I wish you'd been there," Irene complained to Serge.

"Well, I was in Paris," Serge said, without taking his eyes off his wine.

"Don't talk to me about concessions," the Prince grumbled. "In 1861 my father lost a third of his land. He never recovered from this bitter blow."

"All the same, you should have been there," Irene said, sending a signal to her uncle.

"I assume Serge will be in Petersburg this winter," the Prince said to Vassily.

"I'm sure Serge will love it," Vara put in.

She always has to have her say, Vassily thought. You can't shut her up. "I'll think about it," he said. Then he caught a glimpse of Cirie's face and frowned. What was that reaction about?

"Perhaps by next winter Serge's proper place will be in Petersburg," Vara said, pointedly.

Serge should have just kept quiet, which was the thing he did best. Instead he selected this moment to speak up. "Theo and I will be back in Paris."

And Vassily, tired of the Prince and irritated by Irene and Vara, turned on Serge. "I told you I would make that decision."

"Yes. But then you didn't so we assumed—"

"Am I on some kind of schedule then? Am I to obtain your permission to attend to my affairs? Tell me," Vassily's voice rose. "Is that the way you see it?"

Serge reached for his wine. Vassily got hold of himself. "I'll decide when I'm ready to decide. And I'll let you know my decision."

Serge only smiled. "All right, Vassi."

Vassily looked back at Cirie. She was chatting with Georgii, looking perfectly composed. Maybe he had only imagined that quickly checked reaction.

In the morning, beside the playhouse, Serge denied everything. "The Prince talks—Vara talks. What right do they have to decide I should marry her?"

"And Vassily? Does he have the right?"

"To tell me who to *marry*! Why should he?"

"Is that a question, Serge, or a cry of protest?"

"Neither," he said angrily. "I don't want to talk about it."

Cirie stood with her back to him and stared at the reflection of the playhouse in the lake. "Do you know what it looks like, Serge? A business transaction. The Prince strutting about, instructing everybody. Irene posing all day long in her Paris gowns. Vassily giving up his office to spend hours with them. Both families displaying their wares."

"Cirie, cut it out!"

"And you're the property being negotiated for."

"Yes, well this property is not for sale.!"

In the quiet water a mirror image of the playhouse was beginning to catch the sun. Serge came up beside her but still she held back. "Look at the reflection in the water, Serge. Here it's an ordinary playhouse—but the reflection gives it a kind of majesty—as though it were the center of the world—and the sun is rising on its day."

"Oh, Cirie, you're my whole world—" He buried his face in her hair. "Without you the sun would never rise again for me."

When she looked again the sun was higher and the water had grown busy and the perfect image was blurred. "In a different light, everything changes."

"Cirie, don't you believe that I love you?"

"Yes, I believe it."

"Then how can you think I would marry Irene? You don't know me very well."

I know you, Serge—I know you. And I know you don't know what to do.

"The week you were away was like a year. I love you and I'll never give you up," he said.

And she believed him because she wanted to.

"Stepa, what's going to happen to Cirie?" Constantine said as they took their evening stroll along the river front.

Stepa frowned. He, too, had seen Cirie's face when they were talking about Serge belonging in Petersburg. "There are women in this world, Constantine, who are magnets to men, like honey to the bee. From the time they are little girls men fall in love with them—they don't even have to do very much—and when they are fifty, men are still falling in love with them. To a man it's like seven notes on the scale and she is the eighth note. The missing piece to the puzzle—with her the picture is complete."

"Are you saying that Serge might find the courage?"

"Who knows? The question of the femme fatale is one I've thought about—the famous irresistible women of history. It's more than beauty. Irene is beautiful—is any man in love with her?"

"Certainly not Serge."

On the river a boat passed, the voices clear in the quiet night. "Eugenie in her day was adored, but not the way I'm talking about. Look at what's happened this summer with Cirie. Serge, Theo—Laranov noticed her—"

Constantine smiled. "You and I have not been immune."

"I think even Vassily has not been completely blind," Stepa said. "Why else is she still here? She was supposed to go home the next day. With Cirie you're tempted to say it's the eyes."

"It's more than the eyes."

"Yes. It's that indefinable, magical—*something*. A siren song. And she's still very young. She doesn't know her own power yet."

"What about Serge? Can he find the courage?"

"Who can say? He's had affairs with other nurses and governesses. This time he would like to, I think. But Cirie will be all right. When she turns around, she'll find someone else who's in love with her."

Constantine frowned, The problem is who will be there when she turns around. In this little district who is there for Cirie?"

"There'll be someone—and someone else after that—and then still someone else," Stepa said. "Because, unless I'm totally misreading, Cirie is one of those women."

15

❀

The day had dawned hot without a trace of a cooling breeze and by ten o'clock the sun blazed in a cloudless sky. Vara, worried that the Tchernefskys were becoming bored, had planned a picnic for today. She had thought Constantine would welcome the opportunity to converse long hours with the Prince, but Constantine was preoccupied with his book. And Stepa only argued. And Sacha Borassin, when he arrived, would be worse. Vassily had agreed readily to the picnic. It was time to show the Prince the vast estate with its magnificent forests. At the northern edge of the estate a glade was kept groomed for such outings.

Two open carriages stood near the terrace. The servants had loaded a haycart with meats and smoked fish and pates and cakes and fruit. "Where is everyone?" Vara said. "It's almost time."

Earlier Irene had seemed depressed—thanks to Serge, probably—and if she begged off, the Prince and Princess would stay home, too, and the picnic would be canceled. Vara had warned Irene that Cirie should be sent home. "Serge is devoted to you—anyone can see that," she had said. "It's just better to be rid of that type." A word from the Prince to Vassily would do it.

Holding straw hats for the trip, Cirie sat in the mounting heat with Georgii. Vassily was already here and Madame and Kyra with their white parasols. Vara touched her handkerchief to her forehead. "It'll be cooler when we get started," she said. Cirie doubted it.

A moment later Irene, in a cool white dress, stood poised like a bird in the doorway. Long neck arched, the bird moved out onto the terrace and constant companion moved automatically to her side.

"We'll need more than two carriages," Vara said.

"Theo and I are riding horses," Serge said.

"Cirie and Tanya and I are going in the haycart," Georgii said.

"The lunch and the servants are in the haycarts," Vara said.

"I always ride in the haycart."

"Send for another haycart, dear," Madame said to Serge.

Suddenly Irene noticed the parasols. "Why I've forgotten my parasol," she said. "Perhaps Cirie could run up and get it."

Cirie sat perfectly still, waiting for Serge to speak up, but Serge only wandered off a few steps. Instead it was Georgii who protested. "She can't. She's my nurse. Send Tika."

"I'm sure you can do without a nurse," Irene said, coolly. "And I'm sure you can walk. Vara says you can."

"Vara doesn't know anything."

Irene smiled at Serge. "Is Cirie going for my parasol?"

"I believe Tika's getting it," Serge said.

Cirie turned away. Serge should have spoken. He should have resented the demeaning remark—as I resent it when Vassily embarrasses him. She smiled at Georgii. "You're my hero—my knight in shining armor."

Georgii grinned and looked narrowly at Irene. "I hate her. I hope they won't visit us much after Serge marries her."

Calm, Cirie told herself. Calm. She didn't trust herself to speak and she couldn't remain silent. "Serge is going to marry her?"

"Everyone knows that—" Georgii said, puzzled. "He has to! Vassi says so. She's ugly. Don't you think she's ugly?"

"No" Cirie groped for the rail and went down the steps. "She's not ugly at all."

Only this morning, only three hours ago, Serge had denied it again. "Talk!" he had said. "How can they decide what I will do? Why should they?"

Cirie had felt a stab of fear. Was he edging closer to admitting that they were planning his marriage and that he couldn't fight them all? If they love him, how can they want such a life for him, she had thought—just for an old family? Every family is old! In Novotnii elderly moujiks boast that their great grandfathers watched Napoleon march through here.

"Cirie," he had said. "I can never part from you again. Whatever anyone says, I'll never let you go."

Only three hours ago.

She walked blindly toward the chestnut tree. The heat was oppressive. Bugs flitted. The thought of this picnic was stifling. I don't want to have to look at them all day—any of them. I never want to see them again. I want to go home. Tanya's cat rubbed against her leg and settled down to watch a bird on a low branch. This cat spent hours in this spot, on motionless alert, ready to pounce, but the right moment never came.

Constantine came up beside her. "Do you think that cat ever catches a bird?"

"No. He just dreams." Everyone was moving to the carriages. "They're getting ready to leave."

"Cirie, are you all right?"

What can I say? That I've been toyed with—lied to—betrayed? She forced a smile. "I'm fine." Somehow I must get through this hot bumpy ride. Somehow I must live through this awful day.

"Good," Constantine said, taking her arm even though Vara was staring at them. "It's going to be a hot day."

Scowling, Serge walked with Theo to the horses. He was beginning to feel like a high-wire artist in a circus, as though his life were a balancing act, while he tried to keep everyone happy—Irene, Vassily, Maman—Cirie.

"Don't hang back too far," Vassily called.

"Don't worry, General," Serge muttered. "Your trained dog is performing. Your monkey is jumping on a string."

"You're cheerful today," Theo said.

"Oh, hell."

The carriages moved down the poplar-lined drive, the ladies in their white dresses, parasols opened against the hot sun, the gentlemen in white suits and straw hats. Serge saw Irene look back. "The Octopus is searching for her prey," he muttered. "Those busy little tentacles are always ready to snatch, lest I get away for five minutes." He wished he could eliminate her from his sight forever. He couldn't wait for her to go home.

When the procession turned onto the district road, Irene looked around again and Vassily signaled to him. "Messages from headquarters," Serge muttered to Theo. When he passed the haycart Cirie ignored him. Serge dropped back to Theo again. The road entered a thick forest and the ladies closed their parasols in unison. "Does Cirie seem upset to you?"

"Serge, when you started this you knew that in the end Cirie was going to be upset."

No, he had not known that. Serge was not accustomed to thinking ahead. He expected difficult questions to resolve themselves without him. Meanwhile he told people what they wanted to hear. When he lied to Cirie about Irene he thought it was all right because <u>he</u> was doing it. Out of love.

They came out of the forest and the ladies opened their parasols. Serge rode on in silence. Here was a trio of giggling moujik girls going down to swim naked in the river. He glanced at them but they didn't interest him. The taste of life had gone flat.

Here a caravan of gypsies had stopped to trade. On a tree stump a gypsy woman sat beside a display of wooden dolls. A gypsy with a cigarette hanging on his lip played a violin, and a young woman with snarled hair banged a tambourine. Other gypsies came to the roadside to beg. Irene called to Serge to buy some dolls and he tossed the woman a few rubles and scooped up her entire display. He gave four to Irene and brought the other three to the haycart. His smile died when Cirie handed her doll to Tanya.

At the picnic glade the slow movement from the carriages to the chairs had a dreamlike quality and, once seated under the trees, everyone seemed stiff and motionless, like a group frozen in time in a photograph. Birds were still. Not a leaf stirred. In the whole landscape of river and forest, nothing moved.

Cirie had disappeared over a grassy knoll with Georgii and Tanya and as soon as he dared Serge followed and found them picking daisies, Georgii and Tanya on their hands and knees, Cirie following with a basket. "What's wrong?" he whispered.

"Not here, Serge."

Ignoring him she started away and he seized her arm and quickly let go as Georgii looked around. "Cirie, I'd have straightened it out in another minute."

"No, I don't think so."

"If I'd spoken up at once, they'd have known there was something between us."

"Serge, she knows now. Why do you think she did it?"

Alarm shot through him—he hadn't thought of that. Georgii and Tanya were watching. "Darling, I have to talk to you."

"Serge, Georgii told me! After all you've said, you're going to marry her because Vassily says you have to."

"Cirie, it's just a charade! For our families." He forced a laugh. "I'll have to tell Vassi to let up on Georgii. If he thinks that if Vassi wants it, it has to be—that's going too far."

"And don't you feel the same way?"

Serge wiped his face with his handkerchief. He hated this heat. "Cirie, Vassi has a very quick temper. If you don't argue with him, he gets over it."

"And when he tells you to marry Irene, do you argue about that?"

"About marrying her? I'll certainly argue about that."

"And will you know how, Serge, when you've never done it?"

Serge wiped his face again. "God, it's hot. Cirie, it was true once. You know that. Everyone wanted this match, and I tried. But I can't go through with it." He had to get back. And Georgii and Tanya were watching, fascinated, damn them! "Darling we'll talk about it tomorrow. Come out early."

"No."

"Why?"

"Serge, at first you said you loved me and I believed you—"

"But I do."

"Then you told me again, and I let myself believe you because I wanted to."

"Darling, I do love you."

"Now I don't believe you."

What could he say? "Cirie, I'm going to tell her."

Georgii's voice came across the field. "Why are you bothering her, Serge?"

"I'll tell her it's all off. She must know, when I love you so much."

"Serge, when you said we'd always be together, what did you mean? Together married or together as—"

"Lovers?" He gave a short laugh. "I know better. You've made that painfully clear." She looked at him coldly, in a way he had never seen before. Damn her control! If he didn't know better, he'd think she was ice. Serge had a feeling that she knew so much more than he did. "When will you ride again?"

"After you tell her, Serge."

"It's all right, then. I'll do it first chance I get—as soon as the time is right."

Back at the glade, Serge sat at the edge of the hot motionless little group. Once he looked around and saw Irene sitting erect, on display, between his mother and Vara. He stared at her as a victim stares at the weapon he knows will destroy him. Someday, somehow, in the distant future, he would be married to Irene. When he thought about it, which he did not do often, he imagined her exactly as she was this summer—sitting on display in a drawing room, talking about the same things as now—a new dress, a piece of jewelry, the latest gossip. He never imagined Irene in the morning. He never imagined her undressed as, to his distress, he did Cirie. He never imagined himself in her bed.

Desperate, he motioned to Theo to walk with him. "Are you leaving again?" Vassily called.

"Just for a minute." Serge turned to Theo. "What am I going to do?"

"This time I can't help you."

Serge sat on a fallen tree and put his head in his hands. "At first it was fun. Now I'm lost."

"For you, every time is different from all the others." Theo sat on the tree trunk and fiddled in the dirt with a stick.

"In my life I've never felt like this. With Cirie there's an explosion."

Theo's head snapped up. "That, too? You're cruel, Serge."

At first Serge didn't understand the accusation. Then he grew defensive. "You never asked me that in Paris."

Disgusted, Theo threw down the stick. "When there were no complaints, I knew you'd succeeded."

"And now you hope I haven't?" Serge said, lightly.

Theo's dark eyes blazed in his tanned sensitive face. "I hope you haven't and I hope you won't."

Suddenly Serge could pretend no longer. When he thought of marrying Cirie, he knew it was impossible. When he thought of giving her up, he knew he could not. "If I could never have another thing I would want her. To have Cirie the rest of my life I would give up everything."

"Don't say that lightly, Serge," Theo said. "Because that's exactly what it would mean."

As they were finishing lunch the first lick of wind danced across the table, lifting a corner of the tablecloth and flipping it back onto the Princess' plate. A waiter hastened to set it right. During the trip home the wind blew steadily, a hot horizontal wind, raising swirls of dust off the dirt road.

At home two footmen hurried out to carry Georgii and the wheelchair and Cirie crossed the terrace and found that Laranov was back.

16

✿

By evening the wind hissed past the window as though rushing with dark messages to a distant destination. In the drawing room Cirie told herself she had only to get through dinner and she could escape to her room, steaming hot, not a breath of air, but still a refuge, and give herself up to the wounds that all day she had kept anaesthetized—the sting of betrayal, the bruises of the rude awakening. After today she could not stay here. She would have to go home.

The Prince's eternal drone had begun. "Don't talk to me about changing the life of the moujik," he said with that small flick of his hands, waving off the disagreeable idea. Nobody had tried to talk about the moujiks. The Prince always retired to his rooms to rest before dinner and Cirie had decided that he spent that time planning his evening monologue.

She glanced at Laranov, as elegantly dressed tonight as Vassily or the Prince and perfectly at ease in their world. In dinner clothes his powerful body suggested the reined-in energy of a prize stallion, controlled, ready to run. He's always in control, she thought. He listens more than he talks and he misses nothing. Even now he looked at her and then at Serge, amused. As though he knew everything that had happened, she thought—as though he knew ahead of time that it was going to happen. What did I do to deserve him?

At dinner she found that Vara—an effort, no doubt, to clearly mark class distinctions—had placed Laranov beside her.

"The moujik is as God intended him," the Prince continued at dinner. He used the term as a label—more than a hundred and fifty million human beings—all the same.

Cirie turned to Laranov with a bright smile. Serge would see no signs of a broken heart from her. "He saw them harvesting today," she said. "It's his subject for the evening."

"There's a new doctor in Petersburg who's all the rage," Irene said. She had changed into a sheer white dress and her blonde hair, softened by the heat, framed the classic beauty of her face. "Badmaiev. He's not an ordinary physician. People speak of him as a magician."

The candles flickered and the voices blended into a steady hum, talking about people she didn't know, talking about people she did know as though they were identical ants. I'm a stranger here, she thought—alone in a world of strangers who have closed a door that can never be opened. To them she was forever outside their world.

And to Serge, too. And so he could play with her, lie to her, amuse himself as he would never do with Irene. That's the meaning of the classes, she told herself. People in another class aren't valued the same and need not be treated the same. They're less human. There's a lesson there—remember it, she told herself. Only Laranov was as alone here as she was—and Laranov, she sensed, needed no one. Outside the wind hissed and a shutter banged—a hollow sound from another world.

"Badmeiev works wonders with rare herbs and magic potions from the East," Irene said. "One of his potions, Elixir de Thibet, is a miracle in cases of depression. They say the relief is immediate."

Magic potions? And yet everyone seemed to consider this so-called doctor very important. Laranov was listening with a mocking smile.

"Did you see this magic potion in the East?" Cirie said. Every time she spoke to Laranov Serge, his face flushed from the heat and too much wine, glared at her.

"Not this one," Laranov said.

"Elixir de Thibet isn't an ordinary medicine," Irene said rather sharply to Serge, as though he had failed to grasp its importance. "They say a sense of relief fairly rushes on one."

Serge, flushed and resentful, drained his wine glass before he answered her. "What is it?"

"Dr. Badmeiev brings it back from Tibet."

"But if it's not a medicine what is it?" Serge insisted.

"Nobody knows what it *is*. It's a magic potion," Irene said.

"Elixir de Thibet," Laranov said, "is cocaine."

A silence fell over the table and everyone stared at Laranov who had said, after all, that some of their most respected friends were engaged in an unacceptable practice. The Prince dismissed the outrageous suggestion. "Your remark is in poor taste."

"Why on earth would you say such a thing?" Irene demanded.

"Badmeiev's rare Eastern medicines are morphine and cocaine," Laranov said. "And sedatives and anesthetics. He's carrying on a thriving narcotics business—very popular in a society that is always looking for a magic solution, whether from a clairvoyant or a soothsayer or Oriental potions."

"Are you aware that Dr. Badmeiev has treated the Tsarevitch?" Irene said, icily. "So clearly you are mistaken."

Laranov smiled. "These days it seems that every charlatan in Russia can find the key to the palace."

"I hope you don't mean Father Gregory!" the Princess warned.

"Oh, Rasputin makes the other charlatans look like amateurs."

"A man of God!" the old lady gasped. "And you speak of him this way! You have no chance of salvation."

"Probably not," Laranov agreed. "As for Rasputin, I don't worry about his conventional excesses of drunkenness and lechery. I worry about his power."

The Princess and Irene exchanged offended glances.

"If he were just another mystic I'd say let those who wish find comfort in him," Laranov said. "But this cunning debauched staretz is the *Tsarina's* mystic. He is autocrat over the Tsarina's mind. And she is autocrat over the Tsar's mind. This holy fraud—"

"Holy fraud!" the Princess gasped and her husband cautioned her not to upset herself.

"This holy fraud," Laranov repeated, "has power over the police. He controls the department of justice. He can make or break a government minister. And nobody defies him because they've seen what happens to people who do. That's not the role of a man of God. That's power."

"And the incident at Spala? Was that a fraud? For a week, until the Empress wired Father Gregory, all of Russia prayed for the Tsarevitch's life. I myself went twice daily to our Lady of Kazan."

"Twice daily?"

"Yes!"

"Perhaps then, Princess," Laranov said, "it was not Rasputin's prayers that were answered, but yours."

Cirie suppressed a giggle and the Princess looked startled.

The Prince returned to his subject for the evening. "You, sir—you know the moujik," he challenged Laranov. "Now he accepts the Tsar's authority. He calls him little father. But if he's given a little power over his own affairs he will erupt. If there were trouble he would join in."

The Prince grew agitated. Laranov remained calm. They can't touch him, Cirie thought. He doesn't need them. Whatever he is or whatever he wants, they are not a part of it. She wondered whether anyone was a part of it.

"Join what?" Laranov said.

"The trouble," the Prince said, impatiently. "I remember 1905. Can you say as much?"

"I remember 1905."

"In Petersburg there was chaos. Food disappeared. Electricity was cut off. Crowds marched, waving red flags. Barricades blocked the streets."

Arkady looked up. This interested him more than God's will.

"In the country the moujik raided estates, burned, killed. And if trouble comes again, he will do exactly the same. Burn, kill, destroy."

"Give them something to protect and you'll have less to fear from them," Laranov said. "Give them land."

Vassily looked up sharply.

"The lesson of 1905 was not to yield an inch," the Prince cried. The pink spots in his cheeks deepened. "They have land in the mir. The mir has worked for generations."

"Has it? When a man feels the land is his today and someone else's tomorrow, he doesn't break his back to improve it. He doesn't buy equipment. He doesn't use new methods. The mir is against every law of agriculture."

"They don't know what to do with the land they have," Vassily snapped. "You've said yourself you can't teach them anything."

"They don't trust me."

"And why not?" the Prince said.

"Because I'm from the government. They think my advice is a trick to make them lose their land. Just as in an epidemic they don't trust the doctor. They think he's spreading the disease to kill them so the large landowners can get back their land. The same with the census taker. They think it's a plot to increase their taxes or send them into the army—so the landowners can get their land."

"Nonsense," the Prince said.

Laranov regarded the old fool with curiosity. "Doesn't that say something to you—that ninety percent of the Russian people don't trust their government?"

"The mir is a bulwark against revolution," the Prince said. "It keeps the moujik in his place."

"The mir is no bulwark! It's a gate! Mir land belongs to no one and to everyone. And that, sir, is the basis of communism! And if the land problem isn't solved, the gate will burst open."

This was the statement of a fear too awful to articulate and for several minutes the diners were stunned into silence. Then they began to talk quietly among themselves.

"What's the good of giving more land to someone like Popov?" Cirie said to Laranov. "He doesn't do anything with what he has now."

"I just wanted to shake up this pious fool," Laranov said. "If we give it to them now, we'll manufacture a famine. They have no equipment, their methods are three-hundred years old. They can't handle more land."

The Princess began to talk about an elderly countess who had held a seance for the Tsar.

"Besides," Laranov said, "there are twenty-five million families in European Russia alone. To divide up the land would take fifteen years and by then you'd have another five million families and you'd have to start all over."

Her room was an oven and on the north terrace below it, the vines made an eerie sound in the hot wind. Cirie went outside and walked to the river and came back to the sun dial where the six paths fanned out to the different parts of the estate. All day she had told herself she would leave here. Now she thought, No! She would not run away. She would stay and she would ignore Serge. No more questions—no more accusations. And she would go to Kostyka.

A moment later Laranov came along the walk, still looking trim in spite of the heat. "Are you waiting for your lost Adonis?"

"I'm not waiting for anyone." In the house someone was playing the piano—a listless performance. "Adonis?"

"In Greek mythology Adonis was a beautiful young man. He didn't do much but he was very beautiful. He was devoured by a boar."

Let him talk. "I'm here because my room is hot."

"It's hot everywhere. It'll end in a storm. On second thought, I don't think the Countess can be likened to a boar." His pirate eyes laughed. "More a snake. Head arched. Cold-blooded. Coiled to strike."

"I admire the angle of her chin," Cirie said. "I think in a crisis it could work wonders—almost as much as Elixir de Thibet."

Laranov laughed out loud. "Cirie, haven't you gotten tired of listening to that stale trash—what they bought in Petersburg or Paris, what happened in the latest seance? You're too smart for that." He looked at her, not unkindly. "Your poor Serge has a problem he can't solve, you know."

The listless music had started again. "Was that true about Dr. Badmeiev?" she said.

"Why do you doubt it? He's in the narcotics business with a Petersburg druggist. And he gets away with it because he's a friend of Rasputin."

Laranov always made her realize there was a whole world of corruption and intrigue she knew nothing about. "How do you know these things?"

He laughed. "There's always an underground of information, Cirie. Not all my friends are so respectable."

She suspected that he was not always so respectable himself. "Have you ever seen Rasputin?"

"Many times."

"They always talk about his women and his drinking. But what gives him that power over people?"

"Rasputin is disgusting," Laranov said, after a minute. "When I first saw him seven years ago, he was filthy. Long greasy hair. You could have picked an assortment of food and dirt out of his beard. His nails were black. People said he slept in his clothes and never changed or washed—and I believed it because he smelled like a pig sty. He ate with his hands and had a foul mouth. And yet, even then, he was accepted in the best homes."

"But why? And how can these ladies bear to touch him?"

"I see you've heard the interesting gossip. He's cleaned himself up now. The Empress makes him silk tunics and he wears fine boots and a magnificent gold cross, also from the Empress."

"But what gives him that hold on people?"

"Everyone says the same thing—that it's his eyes. When his eyes pierce into you, you fall under his spell."

"They must want to fall under his spell. I think Irene and Lydia love it. It's a thrill."

"I have a friend, Count Sergei Scherevsky, Irene's cousin, although he's been disowned because of his radical views. Sergei loathes him. And yet he says that when his eyes met Rasputin's, it was like being sucked into a whirlpool. He had to struggle against being hypnotized."

"But the Tsar should know better."

Laranov laughed. "Cirie, the Tsar is a good husband and father, the least essential qualities for a strong ruler, but he has no idea what should be done. He accepts all misfortunes as God's will and that reinforces his inclination to do nothing. Are you sure you're not waiting for someone?"

"I'm not waiting for anyone."

"I thought I saw someone on the path."

"Probably Arkady. He goes to the stables to talk to Gerzy and get the Prince out of his system."

Bugs floated on the heavy air and crickets called. "It's that story about Spala," Cirie said. "They believe it—that Rasputin cured the Tsarevitch. I wonder what really happened."

"Maybe he cured the mother."

Cirie stared at Laranov. That could be it! The Empress was hysterical, so the boy was probably like a clenched fist from head to foot. Then Rasputin's message arrived and the mother became serene. And the fist unclenched. It struck Cirie that Laranov always knew what to expect. "You should give them your interpretation when the story comes up again."

"To them it's gossip. They don't know it's history."

Laranov closed the space between them and for a fleeting moment Cirie thought he was going to take her in his arms. She never knew what Laranov was thinking. Serge she understood—but Laranov was an enigma.

"Cirie, you don't know it," he said, "but you can be reached."

She looked at him, puzzled.

"You are less consumed by Serge than you think." He stood over her, close to her. "You could be just as dazzled by another man."

"I am not dazzled by anyone," she said coolly.

Then a figure came toward them and this time Cirie saw him, too. "Well, it was a short wait," Laranov said. "Here's your Adonis."

"I wasn't waiting!"

"Then it's a happy surprise."

Laranov walked away in the direction of Constantine's cottage.

Serge hurried up to her. "I can't stay. I'll be missed"

"Then go!" Cirie burst out angrily. "Why are you here, anyway?"

Taken aback, Serge stared at her. He had expected to be welcomed. "Who were you with? Is that Laranov?"

"Yes, it's Laranov. Why not?" She felt a tug of disappointment that Laranov had not even looked back.

"Cirie, do you think I meant to hurt you?"

"You can't hurt me anymore, Serge. Nobody can touch you if you won't let them, do you know that?" She started away. If she stayed, she would say things she would regret. "Stay with your class, Serge."

"Cirie, wait!"

To her own surprise she cried, "There won't always be this difference between us!"

"Wait." He caught her arm. "I've brought you a gift."

She shook off his hand. "Give it to your fiancee, Serge."

"Cirie, I've never seen you like this." He looked resentfully after Laranov as though it were all his fault. "After dinner I went to my room—it took me a long time to choose just the right gift. Come, let me show it to you." He led her toward the shadows of the river front. In the bright moonlight he held out a small blue velvet box.

Cirie kept her hands at her side.

"Take it."

"No!"

"Cirie, open it. It's yours."

"No!"

Serge opened the box and held it out to her and Cirie stared at the most beautiful ring she had ever seen—a large diamond encircled by six sapphires. "It's for you."

The water whispered on the shore. Frogs croaked.

"Darling, this was my grandfather's first gift to my grandmother."

"Serge, this isn't fair!"

"It's my promise." He slipped the ring on her finger and struck a match and in its flame the clear white diamond glowed, the sapphires found hidden depths of color. "After my grandmother died, my grandfather gave it to me. I give it to you because I love you more than anything in the world." The water whispered on the bank and was quiet and whispered again. "Cirie, now" he insisted. "I love you so. Why should we wait?"

She looked at him with eyes that held no protest. Yes, why?

"Cirie, it's all right." At her small gesture of hesitation, he whispered. "Why should we deny ourselves when we're so much in love? We should have everything."

She turned away, struggling to regain the control he had almost dispelled.

"Oh, God, Cirie!"

She held out the ring. "If I'm found with it, someone will say I stole it."

"Who will find you with it? You don't have to wear it."

"Give it to me when I can, Serge." She struggled against desire and love. "That's the difference between Irene and me."

"That's not the difference between Irene and you," he said with a bitter laugh.

"If you gave it to Irene, she could show it to everyone to admire because it's so beautiful. But I would have to hide it. It would be a secret—and a danger."

"It's not like that."

"It's like that, Serge."

"Cirie, I told her! I told Irene I can't go through with it. She wasn't upset. She knows it's not working. Why are you looking at me like that? Don't you believe me?"

No, she didn't believe him.

"We agreed to continue the charade while she's here," Serge plunged on. "When she gets home she'll write me and break it off. I think she has someone else."

"When?" She felt he was working out the story even as he told it. "When did you tell her?"

"Tonight. Just now. After she leaves, I'll tell my mother."

She held out the ring again.

"I don't want it back! This is my promise to you."

But what could he promise? "Serge, what if you tell them—"

"I will!"

"And your mother won't hear of it—and Vassily forbids it?"

"My mother! She loves you!"

"Will you give me up?"

"Never!"

"Then what? Will we go away together?"

"Go away!"

She understood his alarm. He had never been without everything that money—and Vassily—could buy.

"Go away!" Serge backed away from the idea. "Where could we go? What would we do?"

"We'll find a way. If we have each other we can do it."

"In Russia! Without money—without connections!" Then he recovered. "It won't come to that. Just let me give them a little time. But if we have to go away, we'll do it."

She put the ring in his hand and closed his fingers around it.

"Cirie, soon it will be different," he promised. "We'll be married before the year is out. And you'll live here—not just as a nurse—and in Kostyka, too." He held her close. "Someday this will all be yours."

"So you, too, have succumbed to arguing with our idiot Prince," Constantine said as Laranov came up to the cottage.

"Once in a while you have to say something or they'll think you're plotting against them. Just keep it simple. Don't confuse them. That's my advice for weathering the storm."

"You're cautious."

More cautious than he would admit. "There's a new climate, Constantine." Laranov sat in the other rocking chair. "A new breed of organizers. Men who came up from the factory floor. They're building an army in the factories—the foot soldiers of the Revolution. They're a rough crew but they offer hope—and the thrill of shaking a clenched fist." Through restless trees Laranov could see the hard bright moon without a cloud drifting over it. The heat would go on a while before there was rain. "After all, what does the government offer them? Not hope, certainly. I suspect the Tsar has little hope, himself."

"Not much." Constantine's chair squeaked as it rocked. "Stolypin told me a pathetic little story. The Tsar complained one day that nothing he did seemed to succeed. He reminded Stolypin that his birthday—the sixth of May—is the Saint's Day of the Prophet Job and said that he had a premonition. He applied Job's words to himself and said 'Hardly have I entertained a fear than it comes to pass and all the evils I foresee descend upon my head.'"

"Premonitions—seances with old Countesses. Three incongruous superstitious people—the two of them and Rasputin—holding a sixth of the world in their hands. And not a realist in the pack. But in Zurich a realist is waiting—Lenin."

The hot wind sliced across the porch and Laranov longed to go to the river for a swim. Youthful memories drifted back of hot days and nights when he would head for the river as soon as he had finished studying—the classics with his impulsive, Petersburg-educated mother, and scientific farming with his dynamic, self-educated father. An incongruous match that had worked.

Then Stepa and Arkady came onto the porch. "Arkady has been telling me his general plans," Stepa said, mildly. "The moujiks are to rise up and destroy everything. Then a new regime will establish absolute equality by means of force and terrorism."

"Is it the Prince or is the idea in the air?" Laranov said.

"Everyone will be equal," Arkady cried. "The moujiks will have all the political rights that Prince Tchernefsky has—or Vassily. Why not?"

"Sit down, Arkady," Stepa said.

Another idealist thrilled with his own ideas, Laranov thought. "They want land, Arkady," he said. "And lower taxes. They want to educate their children. They're not interested in politics the way you're interested."

"They don't know what's good for them!" Arkady cried. "They're ignorant. We have to educate them. First we'll seize power by any means—violence, terrorism. Then we'll explain that it was best for them."

"Arkady, listen to yourself!" Laranov had heard all this before. "You're talking about an elite corps with power—who will kill all their enemies and make great changes. And on some future golden day things will be better."

"With no aristocrats and capitalists, the people will live in justice and harmony!"

Laranov put his hands behind his head and leaned back in his chair. "This ignorant moujik, who doesn't even know what's good for him, for the first time on earth is going to establish justice and harmony?"

"Correct."

"Have you looked at this moujik? He drinks until he falls down, he steals, he fights, he burns, he rapes."

"Because he's oppressed."

"You're not going to get justice and harmony. You're going to change the hand that holds the whip."

Arkady's mouth set in a defiant line.

"Your new elite corps will give the moujik what they think is good for him. How is this different from Prince Tchernefsky who thinks poverty is good for him—it's part of God's plan?"

"You can say that!" Arkady leaped to his feet.

"Easy, Arkady, we're only talking," Stepa said.

"That's the oldest hoax in the world, Arkady," Constantine said, patiently. "Give up liberty today and get it back tomorrow—more glorious, more perfect. But if you kill off all those enemies without justice, with each stroke you build a new tyranny. And with tyranny, the other side of the coin is slavery."

"Without force and terrorism, you'll never have a revolution!"

"Would that be so bad?" Stepa said. "If we could get steady improvements, educate the people—"

"Then they won't rise up!" Arkady cried. "So many people will be better off, the Revolution will never take place!" Furious, Arkady took the stairs two at a time and hurried away.

"I envy Arkady his passion but his reign of terror shocks me." Stepa gave a rueful laugh. "I seek reforms I don't know how to bring about. I oppose a revolution I don't know how to stop. I would side with the persecuted before the persecutors, but I can't join them. The eternal Hamlet—questions without answers. Arkady terrifies me with what he proposes."

"Then why do you keep him to teach Tanya?" Laranov said.

"How can I turn on a man who is fighting for the poor and mistreated?"

"For the sake of his revolution, Arkady will forget them quicker than you will,"

"It's more than that," Stepa admitted. "My little one is my life. If trouble comes, understanding it will be the best weapon I can give her."

"Why not send her to Paris for a few years?"

"I don't want to make her an exile from Russia for fear of something that might not happen."

It will happen, Laranov thought. It's ready—waiting. It will come when the match touches the tinderbox, when the explosion blows off the lid. The only question is what form it will take.

A gust of wind rattled a window behind them. Constantine's rocking chair squeaked faster. "What about you, Ilya? You've removed yourself from the seat of power. You know that out of sight is out of mind."

Know it? He was counting on it.

"Where do you stand? What are you for?"

"Me?" The hot wind beat the trees. "First," Laranov said softly, "and in the end, I am for Russia."

Walking back to the house, Laranov thought about Arkady. In the name of liberty, Arkady would destroy anyone who disagreed with his prescription for liberty. In the name of equality, Arkady would put everyone equally into chains. In the name of love for his fellow man, Arkady would kill all his fellow men who objected to his fanatical means of showing his love. Arkady will not create Utopia—only victims. But Arkady is not an original thinker—he is somebody's disciple—so when Arkady speaks, we should listen.

From his window, Laranov looked out at the sundial. Where did that spineless bastard, Serge, find the courage to duck out tonight and come looking for her?

Constantine's question came to mind—*What are you for?*—and at his table, he wrote: "First and in the end, I am for Russia—a creature of beauty, vitality and infinite variety. I am caught by her challenge—I am tantalized by her possibilities—I love the promise of how magnificent she could become."

He smiled at his folly, knowing he was writing only partly about Russia, and he went to the river.

The next day the heat climbed and the wind carried dust. Old horses moved listlessly across the fields, dragging water barrels to the workers. Vara's poodle lay in the shade against the house and Lupa and Talley heaved themselves from one place to another, seeking a cool spot. At midday the workers needed an extra hour of relief and lay for three hours under trees or in deep ditches between the fields—any place where there was a patch of shade.

All day and all night the hot wind continued.

On the third day of the stifling heat, General Alexander Borassin arrived with the news that Rasputin had been stabbed.

17

❀

An erect deep-chested man with great vitality and a roar of a voice, Borassin strode into the morning room where the curtains were drawn against the hot sun. "Tell me what I can do for you, Eugenie." When he spoke to Madame, his voice was soft as a summer breeze. "I'd have been here sooner but there are problems. The Austrian assassination—"

Vara looked on as though something contaminated had blown in on the hot wind.

"Ah, Eugenie, you're more beautiful than ever! Don't you agree, Vara?" He acknowledged the others, Vassily and the Tchernefskys formally, Serge with an affectionate clap on the back. "So—" he said to Georgii, "life is good to you these days."

"Why do you say that?" Vara objected. "He's a cripple!"

"You've got yourself a beautiful nurse! You're a clever fox. What's her name? What's the matter, you won't tell Uncle Sacha the name of your beautiful nurse?" Georgii shouted with glee. Irene snapped a fan rapidly before her arched neck. Borassin nodded to Cirie. "A pleasure, mademoiselle."

"What's the news in Petersburg, Sacha?" Kyra said.

"The news is that Rasputin was stabbed!"

Irene's fan stopped. "We were talking about him only last night!" she gasped. "It's an omen."

"Why?" Serge said, so irritably that Borassin looked around to see what was wrong.

Princess Tchernefsky grasped Borassin's arm. "Tell me he's alive!"

"He's alive," Borassin obliged her. "For several days it was in doubt, but it seems, unfortunately, that he'll recover."

"When did it happen?"

"The day the Austrian Archduke was shot—or the day before. He was in his native village in Siberia. A Petersburg prostitute stabbed him in the stomach and cried, 'I've killed the Antichrist!' She knew him. He'd been her lover. A typical Russian prostitute—Gusseva—a drunkard, religious. Afterwards she tried to kill herself. They led her off to a madhouse."

"I should think so," Vara said.

"You think she was so crazy, Vara?"

"Certainly."

The Princess' yellow jeweled hand still clutched Borassin's arm. "And you're sure he will live?"

"I have not moved mountains to be sure! They say he'll live. The Tsarina is in constant touch by telegraph so that should do it. Meantime Gusseva, who should be considered a patriot, was carted off to a lunatic asylum—with Vara's full approval."

The Prince gave his head a testy little shake. "And you want to give these people more rights."

"More rights than what?" Borassin demanded. "This was one more girl from an impoverished district. There isn't a civilized country where women are worse off than in rural Russia. When they go to the city streets, they figure it has to be better than the life at home."

"Nonsense. At home they could live simple, hard-working lives as God intended," the Prince said.

"Prince Vladimir!" Borassin said, heatedly. "These women are slaves in their own homes. They do the heaviest work. They're worn out, they're sick—they've had more than a dozen children and buried half of them. Their husbands get drunk and beat them like they whip their horses. They're victims of the husband's lust, the father-in-law's lust. You think it was God who conceived this wonderful life for them?"

"I'm sure the nurse has seen these attacks all her life," Irene said suddenly, working her fan again. "After all, these are your friends, are they not?"

"My father treats their injuries, Countess," Cirie said.

"I'm sure you've seen many." The fan moved faster. "And what do you tell your friends while he's treating them?"

"If they're in pain I tell them it will soon be over." What is she getting at?

"But these are your friends. You don't just send them on their way, however rough they may be, however low their station." Irene smiled a condescending smile. "I'm curious. What do you say?"

Cirie smiled back, a wide-eyed innocent smile. "I tell them," she said, sweetly, "to hit back."

Serge closed his eyes. Vara's hand turned her face away. Borassin roared with laughter. Serge's eyes remained closed.

Prince Tchernefsky was questioning Borassin as though the only purpose of his visit was to report to him personally. "What's the climate in Petersburg?"

"There's talk of war. The Kaiser was in Vienna. The French President is coming to Petersburg. It all smacks of examining alliances."

"There won't be a war," the Prince said, testily. "Germany won't attack Russia, France and England combined. What help is Austria? Franz Josef is old—Austria is unprepared."

"Russia is unprepared!" Borassin cried. "We have no industries. The Kaiser is pushing Austria to invade Serbia and Russia has promised to protect Serbia, which is madness."

"It's Russia's destiny to be protector of all Slavic peoples," the Prince said.

"We can't protect Serbia! We're drowning in our own problems. We'll only sacrifice our men and our future. For what? The freedom of Serbians to choose their own government? Russia is full of people who have no freedom at all—to choose their government or anything else."

"I see you're still a trouble-maker, Sacha," the Prince said, severely. "A compassionate God spared the old Count, your father, from seeing his son become a disloyal and dangerous man." His face pink from agitation and the heat, the Prince bowed to Madame. "A thousand pardons, Countess, for my blunt words to your guest, but anything less would be treason."

"Don't try to put me on the defensive, Prince Vladimir," Borassin roared. "I'm as loyal as any man." Madame touched his arm and cautioned, "Sacha—" and Borassin smiled good-naturedly and said, "That's all I have to say on the subject."

But it was not all the Prince had to say. He snatched off his pince-nez. "Loyal— but you want to lead us into democracy! With a revolutionary, we know what we're dealing with. Lenin makes it clear. Rob—destroy—kill. You liberals are more dangerous!"

"Mon Dieu, I am more dangerous than Lenin!" Borassin laughed.

"You're traitors! The Russian people need an absolute authority. That's all they know." The two blobs of spilled ink darkened in the Prince's cheeks. "The Tsar <u>cannot</u> give up his absolute authority! It comes from God. And it's to God that he's accountable. To God! He isn't free to give up his absolute power even if he wants to!"

"Prince Vladimir, this theory might have worked a few centuries ago," Borassin said. "But the clamor is becoming loud and dangerous."

"It must be dealt with!"

"How? What's your remedy? To send every man with ideas to Siberia?"

Unintentionally, Borassin had hit the nail on the head. A glint burned in the Prince's faded eyes. "I have faith," he said, "that God did not put Siberia at the gates of Russia for nothing!"

Hastily Madame murmured to Borassin that they should visit the stable and Borassin seized on the suggestion. "What a foal this will be! How many years did we plan for this, Eugenie?"

Cirie was walking back from the river with Arkady that hot evening when she caught the first whiff of smoke. A minute later, through the trees she saw the flames flare in the strong wind. "Arkady, it looks like the stables!" She grasped his arm. "They'll need help with the horses."

Arkady froze.

"Come on, Arkady."

"I can't! I can't be seen there!" Arkady rushed off toward the house.

In the stable the heat slapped Cirie's face as though an oven door had opened and she saw thick smoke massed in a far corner where Gerzy was beating a blanket against the smoldering wall. Alekei, a stable boy, was leading two nervous horses out of their stalls and Cirie rushed in to lead out two more. Back inside, she saw that the fire was almost out. Through a crack in the wall the wind fanned some embers and Gerzy smothered them with the burned blanket. Cirie seized a water bucket and doused the smoldering wood. "Shall I take them all out?" she shouted.

Tears mixed with sweat on Gerzy's blackened face as he beat at the dead fire. Cirie stared at him and gasped. His hands were raw and bleeding. She tugged at his arm. "It's out," she shouted. "It's all right. It's out."

At last Gerzy allowed her to lead him to a stool. "They didn't know I was here," he moaned, rocking with pain. "They didn't know—"

"Wait here," Cirie said. "I'm going to get some medicine for your burns." When she returned, Gerzy was still rocking on the stool and moaning over and over, "They didn't know." She applied the ointment and wrapped his hands in gauze. The acrid smell of wet burned wood filled the steaming stable. Rivers of perspiration ran down Cirie's face. "Who didn't know?"

"They didn't see me. They didn't know I was sleeping here because of—" He remembered the mare. "I have to see if she's all right." His hands were two bandaged stumps. "Take the lamp."

The beautiful Penelope tossed her head and wrenched away when Cirie tried to stroke her. Talking to soothe the horse, Gerzy looked her over and suddenly cried out, "God help us!"

"What is it?"

He raised a bandaged hand to feel the mare's flank and realized that he could not and lowered his face to her body. Sweat showed on the flank—the first sign of labor.

"Maybe it's just the excitement," Cirie said.

"Alekei," Gerzy yelled and the slow-witted boy came running into the stable. "Get Mischa."

"Where's he at?"

"Go to his hut. Tell him to come running. And Boro, too. Run." Babbling a prayer, Gerzy looked around helplessly and stumbled to the door and screamed, "Mischa!" although Alekei could not yet have reached his hut.

"Gerzy," Cirie tugged at his arm. "If Mischa doesn't get here, I'll help you. You can tell me what to do."

"Did you ever see a mare deliver?"

"I've helped with babies. If you tell me what to do we can take care of her—"

"Mischa will be here. I pray he's not too late."

The mare moved about her stall. Cirie propped the lamp securely in a corner. Suddenly the stable was quiet. The wind that had blown relentlessly for three days had stopped. Just as the mare's water broke, Mischa rushed in. Cirie's heart leaped with relief and then dropped. Mischa was drunk. The mare lay down. Glumly Mischa took up his place beside the horse he hated. Cirie started to tell him to wash his dirty hands. Then she saw there was no time. The mare was starting to deliver. A second later Mischa roared and reeled away. "It's the ass!" he shouted. "The ass is comin'."

"Get back there," Gerzy ordered. "Push it back in and turn it."

"Fuck it! I can't push it in!"

"Bastard! Push it back," Gerzy yelled. "It'll die!"

"Fuck it! It wants to get born ass first, let it!"

"It can't!" Furious, Gerzy tried to grab Mischa and winced with pain. In a rage he kicked him and Mischa reeled and went down flat and lay in the dirt without moving.

By now the breach presentation was horribly apparent. Carefully Cirie knelt between the legs of the huge mare and pushed and the foal slipped back inside. She began to turn it. "I can feel the rump and the hind legs."

"It'll never get out like that. Turn it—turn—"

The mare struggled in vain to deliver. Turn—turn—slowly—slowly—

"They'll die—both of them," Gerzy babbled. "Turn it all the way around—the head first—turn it—"

The door squeaked. Someone was coming. Maybe Boro or Alekei—anyone who could help. Cirie looked around as Serge and Theo hurried in and her heart sank. She was drenched, her blouse was sticking to her back, her hair was matted. This foal is enormous. For a minute she felt dizzy from the terrible heat. The stall swam before her eyes. She had to force herself to concentrate. Turn—turn. This foal must weigh a hundred pounds.

Serge and Theo came up to the stall and Theo said, "Can we do anything?"

Gerzy waved them back. "When she gets it in position, she may have to pull it out—a hundred pounds—maybe then—" He shot them a look, fearful lest in this crisis he had gone too far.

The head was almost around. She was exhausted. Before her eyes the lantern receded and returned. Just a little longer. Don't give up now. Turn.

Then Laranov was kneeling beside her. "Move over," he said. "I'll do the rest."

The foal was standing, feet spread, nursing, and the other horses, aware in their own mysterious way, were craning to see the new arrival. Leaning against the wall, Laranov blotted Cirie's drenched face with a handkerchief. "Tired?"

She nodded. "But isn't that a wonderful little foal—standing on her wobbly legs?"

Now that the wind had died, the stable was eerily quiet. Boro had arrived and was measuring the placenta. Laranov motioned Cirie over to a window. "We're only in the way here." He struck a match to light a cigarette as a flash of lightning stabbed the sky.

"The storm's coming," Gerzy muttered. "It'll cool things off, thank God."

A loud clap of thunder broke overhead and Cirie started and Laranov put an arm around her. The first raindrops tapped the roof. Then lightning lit up the world and thunder crashed and the sky opened up.

It had been a hard fast storm and the night air smelled wet and fresh. Too exhilarated for sleep, Cirie and Laranov walked along the river. "He couldn't have helped you, you know," Laranov said. "He had no idea what to do." Cirie realized that she had not thought of Serge all evening—not since his arrival at the stables when she thought only that he could be of no help. She didn't know when he left. She had not seen him go.

From downstream the smells of a campfire and roasting meat drifted into the night air and shouts and laughter came across the water. "It's the river men," she said, "putting up for the night at one of the clearings."

Laranov guided her around a wet low-hanging branch. "Many nights, I've sat around campfires with river men, talking and drinking while they cooked a cow they'd stolen."

"My grandmother says they drink their wages and steal their food."

"She knows them. They carry the bare essentials—bread, salt, tea—and steal the rest." Someone began to play an accordion. "At every campfire they're the same—some rough and heavy-muscled, some old and stooped from years on the river—some with heavy beards, some faces bloated from vodka. And some are just boys who in time will become like the others,"

"The river men are heroes to the boys in the villages. As soon as they smell the fires they go to the camps."

"They're enticed by the camaraderie," Laranov said. "And the stories of the river life. 'Come with us,' the men tell them, 'and you'll ride on every river in Russia. Come with us and you'll see what it means to be free.' And in the morning the boys leave with them. There are a million men living on the rivers, creating a legend about themselves. To those who have no freedom, they're free."

Laranov was different tonight—warmer, less cynical. "Cirie, you're worth ten of him," he said, suddenly.

"What could he do?" she said. "He'd never seen anything like that before."

"Had you?"

"That's different."

The red lights of a barge moved on the river. "It's easy to like him," Laranov said. "His good looks, his pleasant nature. But that's all there is. He's a symbol of his class. Charming, playing at life—emotional, unthinking, helpless. They're victims, too, because nothing they say or do can change anything. You think that you love him—and you think you want them—but neither would satisfy you for long. Cirie, you have too much fire—you could be magnificent!"

For a minute Cirie almost forgot to deny everything. Then she said, "I don't know what you're talking about."

"I'm talking about your life! Forget him! Forget them!"

"That's easy for you to say when you've seen the whole world!" she said with a low laugh. "I'm only trying to get to Kostyka."

"What's Kostyka? Cirie, I'm leaving in the morning. Come to Petersburg with Ulla and we'll ride through the snow in a sleigh behind horses with their breath freezing in the winter air and I'll show you the whole world including heaven."

He moved as though to take her in his arms, just as he had a few nights ago. He was only waiting for a sign of acquiescence that she couldn't give.

At the house the watchman let them in as the kennel workers were putting out the watchdogs for the night.

In his room Laranov's diary lay open as he had left it when he smelled the smoke.

Tonight he had written: "The Prince is right that an absolute ruler is all the Russian people know. But he adds up the figures and gets the wrong answer. The Tsar is not the only ruler who can be absolute."

A cool breeze teased his senses with smells of wet leaves and grass. She is so quick and intuitive, he thought—why can't she see he's a fool? He laughed at himself—it wasn't because she was quick and intuitive that he wanted her. And that makes two fools, he thought. Tomorrow he would leave here and in a few nights he would be out on the town in Petersburg and he would forget her. His thoughts moved to the fire and he wrote: "The Revolutionaries are reaching these moujiks just as they are reaching the factory workers in the cities. If someone can move them to rise up *together, at the same time*, Russia will see a catastrophe beyond anything we can imagine."

Vara was certain she had found the opportunity she had been looking for. The day after the fire she confronted Vassily in the study. "So—he's a radical! I suspected him from the start." The police had informed Vassily that Arkady was a radical known for his fiery speeches at the University. "We'd have realized it sooner if we hadn't had to watch *her*."

"I've been trying to remember," Vassily said. "I don't think the man ever said a word in my presence."

"Stepa brought him," Vara reminded him. "I didn't hire him. And I didn't hire *her*."

"Well, he's leaving. Although he didn't set the fire. He was with Cirie when she smelled the smoke."

"I might have known! She's so low! Delivering a foal like a common stable hand! And living in our home—dining at our table! She's not fit to be around a young boy."

"Not now, Vara," Vassily warned as Madame and Sacha Borassin entered the study followed by Serge and Theo.

But to Vara this was an opportunity not to be missed. Now she had grounds for dismissing the girl. "Do you know about it?" she confronted Serge and Theo. "Your little peasant, of whom you're both so fond, performed the disgusting task of delivering a horse!"

"We were there," Theo said. "We smelled the smoke. By the time we reached the stable the fire was out and the mare was in difficulty."

"And she was in charge of the delivery!"

"Gerzy was directing her. There was no one else until Laranov showed up."

"She looks just a little common now, doesn't she?" Vara leaned close to Serge. "A little disgusting?"

"Disgusting! Oh, no, not disgusting," Serge murmured. "She seemed so small beside the big horse, her eyes were bright, her face was wet in the lamplight."

"I thought Cirie was kind of magnificent," Theo said. "She must have been frightened. Penelope weighs at least a thousand pounds. The foal weighs as much as Cirie."

"She's not a fit companion for Georgii!"

"Vara, that's nonsense," Madame said.

"I don't see what the foal has to do with Georgii," Serge protested.

"I won't explain it because she'll be out of here today."

"No!" Madame cried. "Absolutely not!"

"What kind of madness is this?" Borassin demanded. "She's a sweet pretty little girl who helped in an emergency."

"She saved the mare and she saved the foal," Madame said, firmly. "I don't know how we can repay her."

"Can't you see how base she is!" Vara cried. She couldn't believe they were opposing her on this.

"What do you object to, Vara?" Borassin shouted. "What bothers you? That the mare was in foal? That it was her time to deliver? That she had difficulties? That Cirie kept her head and helped? What is it that has you so upset? If she had panicked or refused to get her hands dirty and the mare and the foal were dead, would you be happier? Let's have it. Where in this logical progression do we run into a problem?"

"She knew how! She must have grown up wallowing in a barnyard. I doubt I could eat at the same table with her. I don't know how any decent man could touch her!"

Borassin laughed out loud. "For that matter—" he started and then let his words hang in mid-air.

"She grew up in a medical home," Madame said, calmly. "And she chose to help with a life. To discharge her would be wrong. We're on our way to see the new foal and we'll continue."

When they were out the door, Vara leaned across the table to Vassily. "Get rid of her. Get her out of here." Vassily only started to leave the room. "Vassily, did it ever occur to you that Maman is especially doting on Serge?"

"He's been away for a year."

"No—always. I think there's a reason for this." Vara's mind was seething. "Aren't you curious about what the reason is?"

Over the summer, since the idea first occurred to her, Vara had convinced herself that she was right. Sacha Borassin had been her mother's lover. Now another idea had entered her head. She had decided that there had been a child of that liaison. Serge was not a Vodovsky! He hadn't a shred of Vodovsky aloofness or sense of superiority. Of course, you couldn't tell from looks—he was the image of Maman. It could be Georgii. No—she felt it—it was Serge. And if Vassily knew this, would he still think his mother was next to divine—always to be sheltered, her wishes always to be considered first?

"Well?" Vassily said.

Vara opened her mouth to say it: Serge is a bastard—Borassin is Serge's father. The words wouldn't come. Some vestige of sense restrained her. But her day would come. Somewhere there was proof and she would find it. And then, she promised herself—then we'll see.

"Goodbye, dearie," Arkady said when Cirie came to the river where the flag was up for the steamer.

"I'll miss you, Arkady."

"And I'll dream about you. I'll see you playing cards and beating everyone with what I taught you."

"Where will you go?"

"To Moscow. Now that I've lost my position, I'll earn my living at cards. If you're in Moscow, ask for me at one of the Casinos. Someone will know me."

"It's not fair. You didn't start the fire."

"If Russia were fair, dearie, I wouldn't be a revolutionary. Cards are more amusing, anyway, and I couldn't have stood that pompous penguin, Tchernefsky, much longer."

Arkady gave her a sheepish smile. "What good did it do to play it safe? I should have helped with the horses. Don't play it safe, dearie. It doesn't help anything." The steamer came into sight and Arkady kissed Cirie's hand. "And remember— cheat when you have to. Life is a game to be played and won."

*   *   *

A few days later, on July 25th, on a crystal clear morning, a telegram was delivered to General Borassin at breakfast. "Austria has sent Serbia an ultimatum," he said, soberly. "And has given her forty-eight hours to reply." He left the room and within an hour he and Constantine had gone.

"There will be no war," the Prince reassured everyone. "Germany is bluffing." Nevertheless, the next day the Tchernefskys and Irene left and Kyra and Otto returned to Moscow and Vassily hurried to Kostyka, hoping the crisis would pass and he would be able to leave for England.

For a week the governments worked in vain to put out the fire. On the evening of August 1st, Germany declared war on Russia.

On Sunday, August 2nd, in the huge St. George's gallery in the Winter Palace, the Tsar responded with Russia's declaration of war. Reaching back to 1812, he prayed before the icon of the Virgin of Kazan, as Kutusov had prayed before going forth to fight Napoleon. Then he took the oath taken by Alexander I in 1812—never to make peace so long as one of the enemy remained on Russian soil.

Afterwards, wearing a plain khaki uniform, the Tsar appeared on a balcony of the Palace. Below, a huge crowd packed the square, waving flags and icons and portraits of the Tsar. At the sight of him, the people fell to their knees and sang the national anthem. All politics, rancor and grievances were forgotten—everything but their worship of their Emperor, appointed by God—their undisputed leader, religious, political, and military. He was their master, their father, their Tsar.

Watching the wildly cheering crowd with Constantine, who had come out of St.George's Gallery, Laranov said, "Nine years ago they came here to their Tsar, appointed by God, to plead for bread. That time they were shot down in this same square."

18

To Serge the war offered a way out. If he went to the university in Petersburg, he was doomed. He would never escape from Irene. But Theo was going to volunteer, even though university seniors were not being called, and to Serge that seemed the answer. As an officer in the Tsar's army, he would be his own man. "I'll go with you," he said to Theo as they walked back from the nearly empty stables. "And then I'm going to marry Cirie."

Theo walked on a minute. "God knows I don't blame you for wanting to, but Vassi will never let it happen."

"I'll do it and tell him later."

"He'll be through with you for life. And if you tell him first, he'll block it the way he would defend his property."

"Damn it, I'm not his property."

"You'll have to give up everything. Even your mother won't stand by you."

"I can't give up Cirie." He had promised her. She believed him again, she trusted him. She loved him.

"What about Irene?"

The world came into focus again. "I'd be satisfied—almost—if I could keep Cirie in beautiful luxury for the rest of her life as my mistress. But Cirie won't hear of it. I'm going in to tell Maman."

"About Cirie!"

"No! About volunteering."

Serge walked across the deserted terrace. Everything at Whitewater had changed. The guests were gone, Vassi was gone, the horses were gone. At the call for men and horses Maman had ordered all the Whitewater horses rounded up and delivered with several cartloads of hay to the mustering place outside Novotnii. Serge and Theo had gone along, hoping to save at least Prince Igor and Pegasus and had returned on the steamer without them. Of all the splendid riding horses, only Penelope, the mare, remained.

Stepa kept informed about the war news. The Tsar's distant cousin, the Grand Duke Nicholas, a dynamic military man, six and a half feet tall, had been appointed Commander-in-chief. Mobilization, in spite of great confusion, was progressing better than anyone had expected. Constantine had written that the Russian people were united with a religious fervor and a total dedication to the

Tsar. They believed they were protecting Holy Russia against the German hordes, and they were confident of victory.

Stepa read the letter aloud. "'The *people* have risen to the sacrifices of war. The *Bureaucrats* are unchanged.

"'The Minister of War, General Sukhomlinov, is a sly slippery old man with a young wife. To keep his job, he flatters the Tsar and cultivates a friendship with Rasputin. Trained in the last century, he thinks wars should be fought with sabers and bayonets and feels that the German war machine with its artillery and machine guns, is not quite gentlemanly! So much for the War Department.'" Stepa looked up from the letter. "I know Sukhomlinov. His vanity and stupidity can only cause trouble."

"Sabers and bayonets!" Theo exploded. "I'll fight for Russia. I'll volunteer. But I don't want an idiot making the decisions who thinks you can fight the Germans with bayonets."

Puzzled at Theo's outburst, Serge studied him. Every day Theo was growing more sober and serious.

"He saw Laranov," Stepa continued reading Constantine's letter. "'He's a captain in the War Department, working to procure supplies. An intelligent appointment, for a change. Laranov knows all of Russia and has friends everywhere, even in Asia, to sell him supplies and tell him where he can get more. We agreed—the numbers are on our side, but Germany has the machinery and the efficiency. And we have the Bureaucracy.'"

Serge found his mother in her study and without wasting a minute, he blurted out that he was going to volunteer.

"But Serge, Vassi says it will be a short war—Germany can't fight on two fronts at once. She'll soon make peace and you'll have upset your life unnecessarily." When he didn't answer, she said, "Go to Petersburg and finish your studies. You'll be close to Irene—"

"I don't want to be close to Irene! I don't want to be anywhere near Irene!"

"Serge! Don't say that!"

"I can't stand Irene. That's why I'm joining the army. Theo is joining as a patriot—I'm joining to get away from Irene—because I'm not going to marry her."

Madame's hand went to her throat. "Serge, you can't do this to such an important family."

"Maman, how can you ask me to marry Irene? Don't you want me to be happy?"

"Serge, you didn't feel this way before. I knew you didn't love Irene but I felt that love would come later."

"Love Irene!"

Madame was silent a minute. "Serge, is there someone else?"

He had not intended to tell her now. He had intended to wait for the right moment. "I want to marry Cirie."

"Serge, that's impossible!"

"I thought you liked Cirie!"

"As a servant, yes. But as a wife for my son? That would be totally unsuitable. Vassi would never hear of it."

"Vassi—Vassi! It's my life—"

"It's impossible. Oh, Vara said this would happen. Serge, is the girl pregnant? We can make arrangements for the child—even legitimize it in time—"

"What are you talking about? There's no child!"

"Then what has prompted this insanity?"

"I love her!"

Relief flooded her face. "You're infatuated. You'll get over it!"

"Maman, don't say no until you think about it. Think about how wonderful Cirie is."

"Society will never accept her, Serge. I can't let you ruin your life. I'll explain to Cirie and we'll send her home at once."

"Explain! Explain what? Don't say a word to Cirie!" Serge stared at his mother and rushed out of the room.

*　　　　　*　　　　　*

LARANOV'S WAR DIARY

On August 9, a week after war was declared, Laranov wrote: "Germany has moved with lightning speed to try to knock France out of the war before Russia can get into it. Our mobilization is slowed by our great distances and our lack of roads and railroads. The early defeat of France would remove Germany's greatest worry—having to fight on two fronts at the same time.

"Our size is our strength and our weakness. Against Napoleon Kutusov fell farther and farther back, stretching Napoleon's lines until they could not be sustained. Going the other direction, the distance is the same. Our troops from the Urals and Siberia won't reach us for another month."

Two days later Laranov stood on a small hill west of Moscow and watched the chaos below. The railways could not carry all the troops and supplies and artillery. Laranov shaded his eyes against the rising sun. To his left trains had been shunted onto sidings to let other trains pass. Trucks and horse-drawn wagons carrying troops were bogged down in mud. Traffic on the unpaved roads was at a standstill. Trucks spilled over into fields. Germany was a fraction of Russia's size, but it had ten times the railway track.

A week later the French army was in full retreat and the German steamroller was driving toward Paris. Frantically France pleaded for a Russian offensive to divert German troops.

At the War Office in St. Petersburg a debate raged. The Tsar and the government felt Russia could not leave its ally in such grave danger. The generals at the front warned that Russia was not ready. General Samsonov, commander of five divisions, reported bluntly that a major offensive would fail.

"The generals are overruled," Laranov wrote. "To take the heat off France, the Grand Duke Nicholas will launch two offensives in East Prussia—one directed toward Berlin, the other toward Vienna.

"If France falls, Germany will throw her whole massive war machine against Russia."

In East Prussia the line stretching south was three hundred miles long. Laranov thought of the trucks and horses and wagons jamming unpaved roads that could not hold them. He hoped the Russian troops were strategically well-placed. If not, how would they be moved?

"The offensive in East Prussia will start soon—around Soldau."

*   *   *

When Cirie heard Strengov's voice in the study, her first thought was that there was trouble at home. Then she heard Vassily's voice and apprehension swept over her. Vassily had returned unexpectedly and Serge must have told them.

The voices became clearer. "I'll get right to the point, Dr. Strengov," Vassily said. He was speaking quietly—that was a good sign. "You have three daughters. You might like to be able to do something for them—"

"Did you call me all the way out here to discuss my daughters?" Indignant. He could never forget his feelings toward them. He carried them about like a flag. She'd better get in there before he said the wrong thing. Serge and I must remain calm.

"…Rather than see them rot in Novotnii—" Vassily persisted. "With no futures, really."

"My daughters' futures are my concern!"

"Not entirely!"

"Vassi—" Madame cautioned. Madame was there, too.

"*Really!*" And Vara! Where is Serge? Are they deciding our lives without him?

Vassily struggled to clear his constricted throat. "This is my concern, Dr. Strengov, because my brother has become involved with your daughter—enamored of her. This attraction is upsetting to my mother and to me. I have nothing against the girl, she's quite—"

"Cirie. Her name is Cirie."

"Cirie—" Vassily conceded. "She's pleasant enough and Georgii is fond of her."

"As is Serge, apparently."

"She has her ways!" Vara said. Pure acid.

"These things happen to young people," Madame said. "I'm sure you understand."

Serge should be there, defending us.

"What is it I'm to understand?"

"There's more to marriage than infatuation," Vassily said, sharply. "Background, social position, similar interests—"

"What are your brother's interests besides my daughter?"

Vassily ignored the question. "If someone could terminate this unfortunate infatuation, it would be a service for which I would be generously grateful."

Cirie hurried into the room. Madame ignored her. Vara threw her a look of hatred. Serge was here! Sitting huddled over, with an expression in his eyes of a wounded dog. Cirie rushed to her father and he gathered her in and looked defiance at this family who would devalue his prize.

Vassily smiled his thin smile. "I consider it an illness. I'm prepared to pay a large fee for the cure."

Strengov was tense with anger. Cirie flew over to Serge. "Serge, tell them!" Serge only looked at her with dull eyes that said he had given up. "Serge—no!"

He lowered his head again. What have they done to him? How have they threatened him? "Serge, defend yourself!"

He seemed to draw himself into a protective shield.

"If you won't stand up for yourself now, you're lost! We're both lost!"

With a crooked half-smile of resignation—not a smile, a habit—Serge avoided her eyes.

Vassily continued. "Now—your fee, Dr. Strengov—"

A terrible rage burst in Strengov. "Fee! For my daughter! I don't want this match any more than you do. It's beneath her!"

"Papa!" Cirie whirled on Strengov. Vara strode to the bell cord to have Strengov removed.

"I'll have my say!" Strengov warned her. Vara hesitated.

"Papa, be careful! We'll work things out—"

"This is no time for politics, Cirie!" Strengov turned back to Vassily. "I don't want your brother! For Cirie—for one as exceptional as Cirie—I would insist on high intelligence and sensitivity and strength of character equal to hers." Fifty years of his standards were in Strengov's face. "Your brother has none of these. He's not acceptable…"

Strangely, Vassily did not erupt. He merely regarded Strengov coldly. "My brother is young and irresponsible."

"I know your brother is irresponsible."

Serge's eyes shot up.

"What do you mean?" Vassily bristled. It was all right for him to say it but not a stranger.

Serge looked at Strengov, alarmed, and suddenly Cirie remembered the suspected disease and understood that he had not anticipated this moment when Strengov could betray him. Why can't he understand that if Vassily were sure he could control him, he wouldn't be looking for help. If he'd stand up to him now, he might win.

Strengov said only, "It's apparent to me that he's irresponsible."

"You don't know my brother, sir, I demand an apology."

"It's all right, Vassi. Don't press it." Serge spoke for the first time.

Madame smiled at her generous son but Vassily, as always when he had to rein himself in on one front, exploded on another. "You stay out of this," he ordered Serge. "You've caused enough trouble." His temper was riding out of control. "When I want you to be understanding, I'll let you know! And when I want you to amuse yourself with the servants, I'll let you know! This isn't the first time you've caused this kind of trouble but, by God, it's the last. Do you hear me? Do you understand what I'm saying?" Vassily was shouting now. "*Answer* me. Say something. I don't expect you to use your head because you don't have a head, but I expect you to use your voice even if you're a fool! *Answer me!*"

Serge flushed. Kneeling beside him, Cirie seized his arm. "Answer him back! What's the matter with you, Serge?" Panic swept over her. We're lost. It's all gone. "Tell him we're going to be married. Tell him he can't stop us!"

Vara towered over her. "Get out of this house, you whore. You're not fit to breath in these rooms!"

"Watch how you speak, Countess!" Strengov roared.

It's over. It's all gone. Why was she crying? She knew better than to cry. "Witch!" It was someone else's voice, not hers, screaming at Vara. "You're jealous of Serge—

you're jealous of me—you're even jealous of your own mother—you hate every-one that anyone loves because no one could ever love you!"

Vara's face darkened. She raised a hand and Cirie thought she was going to strike her. Instead the long fingers groped for the flushed face and turned it aside.

Rivers streamed down Cirie's face. "Serge—if you love me, tell them. We'll go away like we said we would. We'll manage. Together we can do anything."

Serge stared at her fingers digging into his arm. "I can't," he whispered. "I can't go away."

"You never meant it!" Cirie's tears turned to rage. "You were playing with me! You said you loved me—we'd be married before the year was out—you gave me a ring!"

"A ring! What ring?" Vara demanded.

"Don't worry. I gave it back."

"I demand an answer. What ring? Where is it?"

Cirie's whole world was falling apart. Vara's shrill voice was a hundred miles away. I'm probably going to die—I can't live through this. "You're weak!" she screamed at Serge. "My father was right. You have no courage. You have a beauti-ful smile and you're so charming! And so good with words—that are only lies. But you're a coward!" She released his arm. "Can't you understand that they can't get married for you? They can't love for you? You're afraid to admit that because then you'd have to fight and you don't know how. You don't even know how to begin."

Over her own shrill voice she heard Vassily. "Get to your feet, Cirie. Go pack your belongings and leave this house."

Cirie only looked at him. "Oh, you're cold! You have to rule everyone! You abuse everyone until they jump to your whip. Then you're happy! You hide behind that black beard so no one really sees you, but oh, you're cold."

"We have never witnessed such a scene in this house!" Vara cried. "I'm having this trash removed." At that moment the door opened and Tanya pushed Georgii into the room. "You're just in time to bid your nurse goodbye," Vara flung at the startled boy. "She's leaving."

Georgii looked at Cirie who was weeping convulsively in her father's arms. "Cirie!" She didn't answer. Georgii turned to his mother. "Is that true?"

Madame nodded. "I'm afraid she must."

Vara stood over him. "She never cared about you. She just used you—"

But Georgii wasn't listening. He was running across the room to Cirie.

"I told you!" Vara screamed and pointed to him. "I told you he could walk! You wouldn't listen!" Vara was flushed with triumph.

"Oh, Cirie," Madame said. "I trusted you."

Cirie resented Madame more than Vara. Vara had always hated her but Madame had pretended to be her friend. "What did you trust me to do, Madame?" she said, coldly. "Get him to walk? I did that. Why do you think he didn't want you to know? Any of you? Or did you trust me not to fall in love with your son?"

"That goes without saying. I'm sure you know that."

"Did he know it, Madame?"

Strengov urged her toward the door. "Cirie, get your things. I'll wait for you outside."

At the door she turned. They were all staring at her as though she'd sneaked into their house with the plague. All except Serge who was slumped forward again, drawn into his shield. And except Georgii who was clinging to her, crying.

Gerzy came up to Strengov's old wagon—Gerzy, who had been here thirty years and was not surprised. "It was good you were here, Cirie." He held out his hand where the burns were still bandaged. "I hope someday you'll be back."

At the drive Cirie turned. "I'll be back," she addressed the white mansion where nothing moved. "Someday I'll be back."

Past several villages Strengov remained silent. In the road the autumn rains had produced deep ruts that would freeze soon. It would be a hard winter—hard on his wagon and hard on his bones. And hard with long hours. Already they had started to bring in the wounded from the war. There had been a battle in East Prussia—at Soldau—and Russia had lost a hundred-and-twenty-thousand men. Twenty-thousand killed and wounded, the rest taken prisoner. All those men who had marched off confident of victory, dedicated to Russia and the Tsar. A hundred and twenty thousand lives—a hundred and twenty thousand souls. The mind could not absorb it. Some of the wounded were being carried all the way to Novotnii.

Cirie had stopped crying but her streaked face and red eyes gave her such a pathetic look Strengov ached for her. "Cirie, you wanted too much." His words didn't touch her. "You wanted everything—money, society, adventure. If you hadn't wanted so much you wouldn't be so crushed."

"I want him," she said, dully.

"Not only him. You wanted everything that went with him."

No answer. The wagon bumped and groaned along, a far cry from the Vodovsky carriage. A wounded officer had told Strengov that for a week after the battle at Soldau was lost, the Russian army had retreated slowly to tie down German troops intended for France. Now the Germans were approaching Paris. If Paris falls, he thought, can France be far behind? What will the world come to if the Kaiser is to rule Europe? A fresh burst of tears from Cirie. "Cirie, he's not good enough for you."

"He's good enough for the Countess."

"Is she so exceptional?"

"Not in any way. She's stupid and cold."

"Then he's good enough for her."

"They're all like that. Boring, selfish people."

"You've learned something, anyway."

"There's really nothing special about them at all."

Good. She was getting back a little spirit. "And him?"

"He's different."

How can love be so blind? "Cirie, he wouldn't fight for you."

"He was frightened."

"Were you frightened?"

"That's different."

"Why? Because you have courage and he does not?"

"He does! He'll change. He needs time."

Is it possible that she still believes in the childhood myth that the good live happily ever after?

"He loves me," she said. "He'll be back."

God forbid. Then he thought, No—he won't be back.

Until midnight the sound of racking tears came from Cirie's room. "Is it possible that all these years I've misjudged her?" Strengov said. "Is she just another ordinary girl with adolescent dreams of love?"

"I wish she were," Marya said.

Strengov raised worried eyes toward the sobs upstairs.

"She wants everything," Marya said. "And when you and I are gone, Ivan, Cirie will still want everything. And she'll always rush in first and pay later with tears. She doesn't think."

When they shuffled the deck Marya shouldn't have drawn a hand like Cirie. She would never understand her.

In the morning Cirie faced herself in the mirror. She had behaved like a fool! She had panicked. She had fumbled her only weapons—her wits and her charm. "Never again," she vowed. "I will never lose control again. Nobody cared about your tears—nobody cared about your wounds. *Nobody cared.* As long as I live—I will never panic again."

She started to dress to go to the hospital. "He'll be back. Someday, I'll see them all again. And next time it will be different. I'll have him in the end."

LARANOV'S WAR DIARY

15 September, 1914

"The battle of Soldau was lost to the German railways. Germany diverted troops already headed for France and raced them on the railways to East Prussia while we were bogged down in transportation problems and could not bring all our troops together.

"The Grand Duke Nicholas retreated slowly, all the way to the border, accepting heavy losses, to buy time for France. General Samsonov, who had warned we would lose, who moved only after repeated orders, whose army was destroyed, went into the woods and shot himself. And Paris was saved.

"Against Austria-Hungary it's a different story. Brilliant Russian victories—disorderly Austrian retreats. Austria has lost a quarter of a million men.

"St. Petersburg is now Petrograd. Petersburg was too German.

"And Rasputin is back, boasting that his remarkable recovery from his stab wounds is due to God's special consideration. He is very anti-war and predicts disasters."

1 October, 1914

"Turkey, supposedly neutral, closed the Dardanelles. For Russia a disaster. Shipping on the Black Sea is cut off and we are left with only two ports—Archangel in the north, ice-bound eight months of the year and already frozen, and Vladivostak, four-thousand miles across Siberia, on the Pacific. Our lifeline to our allies is cut."

In October the action shifted to Poland and all through the fall the battle see-sawed. The Germans retreated, launched a fierce counter-attack, were repelled again. Russian spirits were high. Laranov wrote: "I am at the front at Lodz, west of Warsaw, where a million Russians and Germans are locked in battle. The terrain is flat, the weather raw and cold. From a small rise near the river I see bodies littering the snow-covered fields. I hear the heavy fire from sunrise to dark.

"Now it is night. The quiet will last until first light when the guns will start again. Enormous quantities of ammunition are being consumed. Russian factories cannot replace it. And supplies from our allies cannot get through. Russia is isolated from the world."

On the day Laranov returned to Petrograd, the government announced a great Russian victory at Lodz. People were radiant. At a restaurant where Laranov was waiting for Constantine, a fellow diner said, exuberantly, "The war will soon be over. We'll be rid of the German menace once and for all."

When Constantine arrived he said, "Russian spirits are soaring, but at the first setback, people will plunge into despair again."

"The Germans will be back with reinforcements," Laranov said. "The cost in men and ammunition is staggering."

Constantine ordered a French wine and Laranov thought Russia should have stocked up less on French wine and more on French ammunition.

"There'll be other military problems," Constantine said. "Rasputin is agitating at the Palace against the Grand Duke Nicholas. He tells the Tsar and the Tsarina that the Grand Duke is incompetent and he warns them that he has his eye on the crown and that his popularity is growing."

An exhilarated gentleman stopped at the table. "We're on top now. We'll finish off Germany and then take care of the Turks. The Dardanelles and the Black Sea will be Russian. Lodz was a great victory."

He moved on and Laranov said, "His joy is premature."

4 December, 1914

"The battle at Lodz goes on. The Germans rushed in reinforcements and the balance has shifted again.

"On these short dark days, spirits are very low. The Russian people are saying that hundreds of thousands of Russians are dying for Poland. And the Poles are saying that their cities and farms are being decimated for Russia. Defeat sees grievances everywhere."

Four days later the Germans took Lodz.

25 December, 1914

"The Grand Duke Nicholas has halted operations. The people are despondent. Now you hear, 'Our troops have suffered too much…Long frozen marches in the snow…The wounded lying, miserable, in the bitter cold because we can't transport them.' And—after only five months—'This terrible war is too long. When will it end?…The Grand Duke Nicholas is incompetent…The Tsar is born to bad luck…The Empress is German—she is in constant touch with Germany.'

"Rasputin tells the Tsar he is spilling the blood of his people and God is abandoning him. The halt to operations cannot be blamed on God. The reason is our lack of rifles and ammunition. Sukhomlinov, the War Minister—that devious bastard—assured the government there was an abundant reserve—he was ready for anything. There is no reserve.

"We have no rifles. With nearly a million men in training stations, we have no rifles to train them. Our factories turn out 100,000 a month. We need a million for the trainees alone. We're trying to buy them abroad—a million from Japan and America—and we hope for a few hundred-thousand from France and Britain.

"The ammunition problem is even worse. Our entire supply is gone. Our factories can produce only a third of what we need. Orders placed abroad won't reach us for months and still won't fill our needs."

Laranov looked out at the street where snow was falling. "The people despondent and tired of war. The troops untrained and unarmed. Hundreds of thousands of men lost in Poland. Rasputin mixing into the war effort. More than just the year is coming to an end."

19

❊

Patients—hundreds of patients. In one day and out the next—dead. Or out a week later—an arm amputated, a leg, a hand, a foot—patched up, moved on to a hospital farther away from the battle. Get ready for the next cartload from the front. Cots had been set up in halls and storerooms and in the farmers' meeting hall next door.

There were not enough doctors. Federin put in his hours but emergency medicine with no time for pacing and conferences did not appeal to his best talents and Lubochev, a stocky young army doctor, son of a moujik, was slow and methodical. Cirie marveled at his detachment. No injury was awful enough to upset him, no line of wounded men waiting for help, relief, life even, was long enough to persuade him to hurry. Strengov saw the lines and felt the suffering and he was exhausted.

The hospital smelled of ether and disinfectant and gangrene and sixty bodies. At night Cirie would lie in bed, the smell still in her nostrils, and hear the distant mournful whistle of a train and imagine a lone trainman going about his war work in the cold night and she would think, Is he delivering more men to the front to die? Or is he hurrying back with more wounded—more bodies with legs or stomachs or faces blown apart, more shell-shocked men screaming at their private horrors? And is one of them Serge? Cut down before he can write me that he's an officer now, fighting a war, and Vassily can't run his life anymore. She would toss in bed and wonder where he was. She would search the newspapers, which arrived about once a week now, for reports on General Borassin's army and she would wonder whether Serge was still with him. She would tell herself that Serge would write to her soon with answers to all her questions.

On a map in the doctors' room, Strengov kept track of the fighting with pins and bits of colored paper. Most of his information came from wounded soldiers, who knew where they had been, and from Boris Koner who had come home to fight for Russia and got a leg full of shrapnel at Lodz. Gaunt and gangly, he would limp into the hospital to talk to Cirie or Strengov. The pins on the map moved west as far as the German section of Poland. Then the direction changed and the pins moved steadily east. Like a sluggish metronome, first left, then right as Russian troops retreated. Small retreats in January. A major retreat in February. By spring Russian troops were falling back along a three-hundred mile line, from Lithuania south to Poland.

"More reports today that the artillery is out of ammunition," Strengov said. "Also the infantry is out of rifles."

He moved to a cot to dress an arm he had been forced to amputate above the elbow. The soldier, little more than a boy, whispered, "I had a rifle." He was heavily sedated and he looked without seeing at the arm where the hand had been that had held the rifle. "Not everyone had a rifle, but I did. I'm a good shot—I don't miss. And he grabbed my rifle the second I was shot. Before I hit the ground."

"They wait like vultures," Strengov said as they walked away. "They're sent into battle without rifles and they watch for others to die or be wounded."

"I suppose it's natural," Cirie said.

"For vultures, it's natural, too. Will they start to kill their Russian brothers for their rifles? How long before vultures turn into cannibals? In Russia it's happened before."

"What kind of man sends men into battle without rifles?" Cirie looked back at the boy. Soon he would be screaming. "Who decides these things? Some pompous old fool like Prince Tchernefsky who tells them it's God's plan?"

"In Russia that's always the question," Strengov said, wearily. "Who decided? Who did something? Who failed to do something?" They headed for the doctors' room, a bit of walled-off privacy where they stored the records and locked up the medical supplies that were dwindling like the rifles and ammunition. "Who took us into war, knowing we were unprepared? And if they didn't know, why not? And what about the 'little father' who passes out the power, guided by a neurotic wife and an evil monk? Where does it end? Where does it begin?"

Cirie put on her cloak. Every day at lunch time she went to the post office looking for a letter from the Vodovsky bastard. "Do you ever think," she said, "about how much cruelty there is in the world?"

"Frequently," he said.

Alone, Strengov sank into a chair and lit a cigarette. It was snowing again, a fine snow that would continue all night. Still, when you could see out the lower windows, winter was on the way out. Presently he saw Cirie coming back, walking briskly in the snow. Drawing on his cigarette until he could feel it in every nerve in his tired body, Strengov watched her. Some people, he thought, in the melancholy of a broken heart, become too lethargic to move. And some become martyrs— brave, suffering. Cirie worked. She made the rounds, she kept the records, she assisted in surgery, murmuring words of encouragement. ("Another minute—it'll soon be over—we're almost done.") She had taught Greta to help with the nursing and showed the deaf-mute, Hulda, how to clean the ward. An inspiration. Hulda didn't hear the moans and screams. But when she spoke of all the cruelty in the world, was she thinking only of the war? Not once all winter had she mentioned the bastard.

She stopped to greet someone and Strengov recognized Gerzy. Good. Maybe she'll hear the bastard is married. A fait accompli. Probably there would be hysterics—maybe for a few days, even—and then it would be done with.

When she came in, she offered nothing and Strengov said, "Did Gerzy have any news?"

"Not really." She began to unpack the supplies that had finally arrived.

"Cirie, you have to talk about it! You can't keep it bottled up. A wound must be drained."

"There was no news! The family is in Kostyka. Georgii is at school in Petrograd. And Gerzy misses his horses."

Hardly the news Strengov was hoping for. "Did Serge get married?"

"He's not going to get married."

Strengov looked up, alarmed. "Did Gerzy tell you that?"

"We didn't talk about Serge. We talked about the horses."

"Cirie, stop living on hope. Serge won't come back to you."

"He'll be back."

What else could he say? Even Koner had not been able to come up with the information and offered only platitudes. ("Listen, Strengov, it's always darkest before the dawn.") What a gift—to be able to live by such nonsense! In some lives there are few dawns. In some times, there is little light. He looked at the map where the metronome was not starting in the other direction. Sometimes the dawn is late in coming.

A minute later Boris limped into the room—Boris, the Jeremiah, the study in moods. As a boy he had had a sunny nature but revolutionary zeal had produced a darker side and the one mood would invade the other. With Boris it was either bright sunshine or the dark side of the moon. He was Cirie's oldest friend and Strengov was delighted that he was home but he was no help with the Vodovsky problem.

"Things are stirring again in the Carpathians," Boris said, brushing off the snow. Thin and pale, with fiery eyes, he looked more as though he had been in Siberia than in Switzerland. Strengov motioned for him to change the pins if he wanted to.

"You can't move a pin on a map for a few feet! Can you imagine the cold and snow in those mountains? Russian soldiers are dying for every foot."

Cirie looked up from counting the supplies. "Not enough morphine."

"If we capture the passes, we can sweep down on Hungary. Against the Austrians we might win. With the Germans it's always retreat. Last month we lost fifty-thousand men in East Prussia."

"Boris, here we struggle to save some part of a hundred men delivered to us," Cirie said. "Don't tell us about fifty-thousand!" She opened another box of supplies. "Not enough ether."

"Whatever is there, I'm glad to have it," Strengov said.

"Not enough morphine, not enough ether!" Boris cried. "No rifles, no ammunition. Don't you think the people know what's going on?"

"If we know, they know," Strengov said.

"People hear their sons and husbands are just cannon fodder—sent to war without weapons. How do you think they feel?"

Strengov took a bottle of vodka from his desk and poured an inch into a glass and drank it. Since mobilization, vodka had been illegal—an effort to sober up Russian workers for the war effort. Koner kept him supplied and Strengov asked no questions.

"It's only a matter of time until the Germans are right out there." Boris pointed a bony finger at the window. "Walking around on the street."

"Boris, we have enough to worry about without that kind of good news," Cirie said.

"This is the route to Moscow!" Boris cried. "Napoleon came this way. Do you know where the Germans are now?" He tapped his bony finger on the map. "Right here—a hundred miles from Vilna. And after Vilna, we're next."

Cirie was watching Strengov. "Go home," she said. "Lubochev is here. A few nights' sleep and you'll feel better." Then the boy screamed and she snatched up the morphine and rushed out.

Strengov poured another half-inch into the glass. He wished she would hear that the bastard was married.

*   *   *

Lily wished people would stop calling her the little mouse. Or the little kitten. Anna was going to have a baby and that would be the baby now.

Mamma had cried at the news and Papa had said he hoped now Vogel would manage to be of some use in this world. Lily felt sorry for the baby. Probably this was how they had greeted her own expected arrival. Once she overheard Ulla say that Lily, too, had been an unwelcome baby. "Your little mistake didn't turn out too bad," Ulla said and Mamma hushed her up and told her not to talk that way about her kitten. Lily was stung with guilt to think that she had intruded on everyone and they had not even wanted her. She felt that she had to make it up to them. But if they hadn't wanted her, maybe no one would ever want her.

"Mamma, do you think if I go to the hospital they'll let me fix the trays?"

"Probably."

"I want to help Papa, he works so hard."

"Papa doesn't fix the trays."

"But I can never help as much as Cirie!" Just as she would never be as beautiful as Cirie, no matter how hard she tried. At her mirror she would practice Cirie's smile, but it was not the same. Sometimes she hated Cirie. No, she didn't! That was a sin. Especially now when Mamma said Cirie was going to have a broken heart. She didn't hate Cirie—she loved Cirie—and she would try to be more like her. Except that she wasn't remarkable at all—she was just plain Lily—shy, timid, ordinary.

"If I can't help with the trays, maybe I can write letters for the men who are wounded or don't know how to write," she said.

Passing the office, Lily saw a man standing at the window and she hurried on. Then she stopped. No wonder they called her a mouse, if she was too shy even to tell a patient that Papa was at the hospital. When she reached the door it opened and a lieutenant, his arm in a sling, stood there.

"I'm delighted to see you," he said. "I was about to leave." He was thin and his hair had grown long.

"The doctor's at the hospital," Lily said.

"Will you direct me there?"

"I'm going there now to fix trays or write letters."

"Then it will be my good fortune to have a beautiful guide."

As they walked together in the snow, the lieutenant smiled down at her. He had a fresh scar on his left cheek and dark brown eyes and Lily decided he was the most beautiful man she had ever seen. "What's your name?" he said.

"Lily——" She met his eyes—for her an unfamiliar act of courage. "My name is Lily."

"How do you do, Lily." He took her arm to guide her around a snow bank. "And my name is Petya Rossatin."

At the hospital Petya explained that he had been wounded during the latest retreat and his arm was not healing properly. "There were thousands more seriously wounded," he said. "There wasn't much time for a bullet in the arm." When his train was shunted onto a siding outside Novotnii, Petya remembered that both

Ulla and his old friend, Ephraim Pointer, had spoken of a good doctor here. Pointer was Strengov's old friend, a brush manufacturer who had left for America during the pogroms of 1906. As a boy Petya Rossatin had met him often in Siberia where Petya's father had traveled to buy furs and Pointer to buy bristles. Then Strengov remembered. This was the friend Ulla had talked about last summer.

"What a coincidence that you knew our friend, Ephraim Pointer," Marya said to Petya. Delighted to have a guest for dinner, Marya had taken out her best table-cloth and had invited Koner and Boris who were always hungry for news.

"There was a letter from him in Kostyka when I was home on leave." Petya was a soft-spoken man with a sensitive face that was pale and drawn now, making his eyes seem unusually large. "Pointer has prospered in America."

"When did you have leave?" Boris said. If it was recent he would have a million questions.

"In January. I was in Moscow when Rasputin was run over."

Cirie looked up. "Rasputin was run over!"

"In Petrograd. By a troika going full speed. Anyone else would have been killed. For this bull it meant only a slight head wound. You can't kill him."

"Are people in Moscow fed up yet?" Boris demanded.

"There's a different mood. When war was declared there was a thrill in the air. The people forgot their grievances—the only enemy was the Germans. Now they're depressed about the endless retreats. They blame the Emperor, the Empress, Rasputin. They call the Empress 'Nienka'—"

"The German woman," Boris said with contempt.

Petya nodded. "They say Rasputin is in German pay, which is not likely since he can get anything he wants from the Empress."

"Have they had enough yet?" Boris said impatiently.

"They're tired of war, but still they say we shouldn't make a dishonorable peace. We must go on to the end."

Strengov wondered who had such lofty principles. Not the soldiers he talked to, who had lost arms, legs, sight, faces—for Russia.

"You're in Moscow so much," Marya said. "Is your wife in Moscow or Kostyka?" Cirie's eyes flew up. Not again!

"My entire family is my father and a sister in Kostyka."

Cirie hastened to change the subject and asked about Pointer's son, Danny. "Boris and Danny and I were good friends."

"He's studying law," Petya said. "I'm glad Pointer's not still here. These retreats are making things very rough for the Jews. When the battle draws close, the Cossacks say the Jews will cooperate with the Germans—even though there are a quarter-million Jews in the Russian armies, fighting as bravely as any other Russians. The Cossacks drive them out of their homes and force them onto trains to be taken away. While their pious Orthodox neighbors stand around waiting to loot their houses."

Strengov liked this man—solid, rational, still young. He wished Cirie seemed a little more interested. The problem was she was still waiting for the other bastard to find a little courage.

"But where do they go, these poor souls?" Marya said.

"They're pushed off at some railway station," Boris cried. "Forced to live out-doors until they die of hunger and cold."

Accustomed to Boris's exaggerations, Marya turned to Petya.

"It's true," Petya said. "Russians are susceptible to hysteria. When there are reverses, the people look for a scapegoat. And the Jews are elected."

And that sums up the news, Strengov thought. The people are tired of retreats (as who is not?) and they blame the government (as who does not?) and take it out on the Jews—the historic scapegoat. And neither a prostitute with a knife nor three galloping horses can kill Rasputin.

All evening he had been on the verge of asking the question. Now he said, "In Kostyka did you hear anything about the Vodovskys? Cirie worked at their estate here last summer."

Cirie looked at him, horrified.

"In Kostyka everyone knows about the Vodovskys," Petya said. "Ulla says, with a peculiar relish, that it's a lonely house these days. Only Countess Vodovsky and Vassily are there."

"Where's the little boy—Georgii?" Strengov prodded.

"In school in Petrograd."

"And Serge?"

"In Galicia, I believe, with General Borassin. And Vara is with relatives in Moscow. My news is two months old," he apologized. "No—wait—there was something else. Serge was wounded—nothing serious. And that's all."

Wounded! Cirie paled. "Is he all right?"

"He was supposed to get married," Strengov persisted. "Did he get married?"

"I didn't hear that."

Damn the bastard. Wounded. Now Cirie would spend her days and nights wor-rying about him, everything forgiven.

In the morning Strengov removed a fragment of shrapnel from Petya's arm. "Just another minute," Cirie murmured while he worked. Petya was wet with pain.

Ether and chloroform were saved for only the most serious surgery. "We're almost through."

Strengov finished and then he saw the way Petya was looking at Cirie. Ah, he thought, can it be that Koner, the old fool, is on to something? That when it's darkest, there will soon be a dawn? "If you pass this way again let me check your arm," he said.

Maybe by then she'll hear that the bastard is married.

20

Yellow threads of willow trees gleamed in the sunlight and snowflowers pushed up through the snow and the Russian retreats continued.

Laranov questioned wounded soldiers. "We retreat and turn and fight," the soldiers said. "And then we retreat again." Laranov asked about artillery and rifles. The soldiers said, "No artillery. No rifles. Bayonets." Reports of an alarming German buildup in Galicia warned of a spring offensive. Laranov went to Galicia to see for himself the shortage of Russian arms.

On the first of May the Germans fired fifteen-hundred guns against a single portion of the Russian line and the expected offensive began. Russian troops had nothing to fight back with. From the hill where he watched, Laranov could see enemy fire for miles. Russian trenches were completely blown up and every man in them was blown apart.

Reinforcements were rushed in. And wiped out. In the Russian trenches nothing moved. The Russians lost forty thousand men and retreated.

The Germans followed with an offensive in the north. In a period of ten days Russia lost a hundred and forty thousand men.

"Enough!"

"Enough retreats!"

"Enough of the Tsar."

On his way back to Petrograd Laranov stopped in Moscow and found himself in the midst of a riot. Red Square was packed and men and women pushed and shoved each other—men missing a hand, an arm, a leg.

"Enough! The Tsar can't run the war."

"The Tsar can't run the government."

"Throw him out. Abdication!"

"Abdication! Abdication!"

Men leaped onto boxes and were knocked off. Men and women were knocked to the ground and lay in the square bleeding, trampled on by rioters. Sticks and pitchforks appeared. Fires were started and stamped out. Fights began.

"The retreats are on the Tsar's head."

"The Tsarina is the cause! Nienka! German woman!"

"Rasputin is the cause. Kill him!"

"The Empress is mad. Send her to a madhouse."

"Our troops are unarmed."

"Abdication!"

"Hang Rasputin! Hang the bastard!"

"Give us the Grand Duke. The Grand Duke Nicholas!"

"Enough retreats!"

Before Laranov's eyes the bearded and flushed and muddied and bloodied faces swam together. Like the soldiers in Galicia. The soldiers without rifles in the trenches in Galicia, waiting for the Germans. And blown up. The trenches where no one moved.

"Warsaw will fall," a man shouted in his ear.

Laranov nodded and moved away.

"And Nicholas will fall," the man shouted. Laranov could not see his face. All the faces, men and women, were the same. And all the faces in the trenches were the same before they were blown apart.

At the end of May Laranov was back in Petrograd. Waiting for Constantine one evening at the St. Honore, an elegant restaurant known for a pair of chandeliers said to have belonged to Marie Antoinette, he stopped to speak to his old friend, Sergei Scherevsky and Sergei's mistress, Marina, a beautiful fiery radical. Sergei resembled his cousin Irene, but he was so restless and hot-eyed, the likeness was not readily apparent.

"Have a glass of champagne with us," Sergei said. "I heard you were in Galicia when they uncorked the offensive. Pretty bad?"

"General Belaiev said our army was drowning in its own blood, and that's how it was." Laranov recognized that something inside him had changed. He heard that his voice was hoarse and drank down a glass of champagne. "And you?"

"Poland," Sergei said. Already a little drunk, he reached for Marina's hand. "It's my first leave. We went to Moscow to test the temperature—savor the discontent. Very heartening. Then we came here. Just heard the latest story about Rasputin—the Empress' savior—the society ladies' voodoo staretz."

Laranov glanced around for Constantine. "Which one?"

"Gave a stellar performance at the Yar," Sergei said, referring to the smart Moscow restaurant. He refilled Laranov's glass. "Old Grigoire turns up at the Yar with three society ladies. Gets very drunk in a private room. Boasts about his sexual conquests in Petrograd."

"Named the women," Marina said. "Called the Empress 'the old girl,' which doesn't bother me. We call her worse than that."

"Finally Grigoire gets so drunk he proceeds to expose himself. At the Yar! Management calls the police. Police are afraid to arrest him. So Grigoire—free as a bird—all of him—staggers out into the main dining room, converting the affair into a public spectacle, talks about the Empress and says, 'I can do anything I want with the old girl.' And that's all I know. After that we came to test the climate here. Wonderful. People horribly fed up with retreats. It looks very promising. A few more disasters at the front, a little more help from Rasputin and the people will be ready to invite us in."

When he joined Constantine, Laranov heard rest the rest of the story. "The Tsar ordered an investigation and the Tsarina was told the story was true. Can you guess her reaction?"

"I've given up on that."

"With some incredible mental gymnastics, she saw it as a victory of Good over Evil for Rasputin. 'The Powers of Evil set a deadly trap for our holy friend!' she said. 'Without help from Above, he would never have gotten out of it so cheaply!'"

In spite of his somber mood, Laranov burst out laughing. "It's fantastic and ridiculous. But very serious."

"The Tsar's been forced to call the Duma, you know," Constantine said.

Laranov nodded.

"The Tsar told Rasputin to be out of the city while they're in session. And the Tsarina told him he could return as soon as they adjourned so his absence would be brief. Rasputin told her he can get along without her but she can't get along without him because—the same old card—her son will come to harm."

The orchestra began to play an old Russian song.

"He's working relentlessly against the Grand Duke," Constantine said. "He tells them the Russian armies can never succeed with the Grand Duke in command. He says, 'How could God bless the undertaking of the man who betrayed me—the man of God?'"

"His whole crowd has taken up the cry. I heard it at a reception last night."

"At Countess Nina Bragaw's?"

"Constantine, at heart you're a gossip. Yes, at Nina Bragaw's."

"It's all over town that she's taken with you. Is this a serious development?"

Laranov laughed. "Nina Bragaw, with her luxurious black hair and her dazzling black eyes, is as beautiful as Irene Scherevsky and very much like her."

"And are you smitten?"

Laranov only shrugged.

Constantine looked over at the orchestra. "The orchestras don't play much French music anymore. People feel our allies have let us down. When the Germans threatened Paris, we sacrificed ourselves for them. We moved before we were ready and suffered enormous losses. Now we need them to launch an offensive to give us that same kind of relief and they say they can't do it."

A chorus of tziganes appeared in front of the orchestra and began a gypsy song. "Ilya," Constantine said. "In your travels have you been near Novotnii? Have you heard anything about Cirie?"

Laranov's hand stopped on his glass. "I can't believe she's still there. She wanted more than anything to get out."

"I told her to write to me but she never did."

"You told Cirie to write to you?" Laranov said, curious.

Constantine's young blue eyes laughed. "She cast a spell over me, I admit it. That slow smile that was like a reward and those remarkable eyes."

Laranov was startled at the way desire announced itself at the introduction of her name and her face in his mind's eye. "I haven't been near there."

Constantine returned to the serious news. "The Empress and the bureaucracy are up in arms about the Duma. I'm not optimistic that the Duma can get the upper hand."

"I'm not optimistic about any of it. The bureaucracy is a swamp of corruption. Our troops are facing German artillery with bayonets. When they had guns Russians were brave soldiers. Now desertions are way up."

"Warsaw is lost?"

"The Germans will take it any day. And they're only thirty miles from Riga. Their western front is quiet. This hot summer of 1915 is marked to knock us out of the war. And they may succeed. It's the Duma or Revolution, Constantine."

Constantine glanced around the room and leaned closer. "Never have I heard so much talk about revolution—from people of all classes. They believe it's the only thing that will save us. They think we'll have a few months of chaos and then Russia will be healthier—reinvigorated."

"They don't know what chaos is. Things are easy to talk about—but different when you see them. Before I went to the front, I read all the reports—no guns, no shoes, the wounded left to die where they fell in front of the trenches because they couldn't be rescued." Laranov tossed down another glass of wine. "Now I've seen it. Those wounded men scream for days, crying out for God's help, not to save them but to endure the horror they know is ahead of them until they die."

Constantine listened soberly.

Laranov's hand trembled. "I thought I knew what to expect. What I saw was a hundred times worse. Revolution won't mean a few months of chaos. Revolution will mean anarchy for years. And tyranny."

Laranov stopped. He'd said enough. Then he added, "Russians never had any trouble with violence and this war is breeding killers."

The orchestra played on, unenthusiastically—a Russian folk song. "I'm leaving to visit Stepa for a few days," Constantine said. "I'll be back for the Duma."

"To Whitewater?"

"Kostyka. They didn't go to Whitewater this summer."

"At Whitewater and Novotnii they'll hear German guns before the summer is over."

In May Russia had lost 350,000 men. In June they would lose another 350,000. And July would be worse.

21

Cirie was catching a few minutes of fresh air on the hospital steps and listening to Boris who had returned last night from Moscow where he had actually seen riots. "You should have been there," he said, gleefully. "Huge mobs in Red Square!"

Cirie turned her face to the sun. This morning before dawn, six carts that had traveled all night had arrived at the hospital with sixty-seven casualties who were still alive and seventeen who had died on the bumpy trip from the front. Daylight was just sifting through the windows when they began to work. Six more men had died on the table. The hospital was full, the farmers' hall next door was full and there were some wounded officers in Koner's Inn. Now, at one o'clock, this was her first break.

"The mob wants the Tsarina locked up in a convent!"

"Boris, the Tsar isn't going to lock up his wife in a convent."

"He may not have a choice! They want to kick him out. And hang Rasputin!"

Even out here you could smell the ether. Cirie was filled these days with a hollow feeling of living with no purpose other than to patch these poor men together. She worked mechanically, numb and detached, trying to save lives and trying to save her father who looked more exhausted every day. And waiting for Serge. In her fantasies, as soon as he had leave he would come to her. He would come here and they would walk along the river and find a secluded spot and she would be in his arms again. But he did not come and there was no letter and the fantasies were fading. They did not return so often—and nothing replaced them. She was drifting. Without Serge she had no goal.

"Have you been to the post office yet?" Boris said.

"I don't go every day anymore." She stood up. "I'm going for a walk."

"I'll come with you." Boris was too excited to stand still.

At the bridge she stared at the river that was a shimmering ghost, empty and deserted. She thought of the night she had stood with Laranov beside the tall-masted ships and he had told her about Nijny-Novgorod where so many ships came together you could walk across the river on them. What had become of Laranov? And all the others—Constantine, Stepa, Theo? Serge?

"All those ships that used to pass here," she said. "Hundreds of them. Now it's empty."

"No one can get in!" Boris cried.

"A Russian steamer now and then—that's all we see," she said. This deserted river, glittering in the sunlight, only reminded her of her own isolation. No one can get in and no one can get out. Russia is cut off from the world, she thought. And so am I. Oh, Serge, where are you? Did they send you home with your wounds? Back to Vassily? It was her greatest fear.

"Cirie, it's spring," Boris said, with his old exuberance. "Let's go climb the tree and see what's coming down the road."

He was just talking. Nothing came down that road anymore.

"Who knows what wonderful things we'll see!" Then the cold hard look of the revolutionary returned. He reminded her of Arkady. What had become of Arkady? What would it have been like to fly through the streets of Petersburg in a sleigh? ("I'll show you all the world, including heaven," Laranov had said.)

"Germans, maybe. Or Russian deserters," Boris said. "Warsaw is going to fall,"

Had Serge's wounds healed? Was he back at the front? "Is General Borassin defending Warsaw?"

"Whoever is defending it, it'll fall. We'll lose all of Poland."

Cirie didn't care about Warsaw and she didn't care much about Poland. She only knew that the number of casualties rushed to the hospital was climbing because the war was coming closer. And one day, one final retreat would bring the battle too close and they would haul the wounded men past Novotnii to a hospital farther from the front and for her the retreats would be over.

"I'm going over and tell your father some more about the riots," Boris said.

"No," Cirie said quickly. "He needs this half-hour for rest, not riots. Come on, we'll go to the post office." Serge, she thought, are you even still alive?

She saw the letter at once among the other letters and newspapers.

"Darling Cirie—" Serge had written the letter in a hospital in Kiev. "How I miss you! Here I think only that I can't live without you. I love you and I'll always love you."

Cirie's hand shook. She had known Serge could not forget.

"These months without you have been hell. If you remember last summer you must believe that I have never loved anyone as I love you. I was wounded in the leg by a stray bullet while carrying a message for Sacha Borassin. It's not a bad wound and soon I'll be discharged and will limp back to Kostyka. I must see you. We must find a way. I'll try to come to you before I go back to the front. You are my life. I love you. Serge."

Cirie leaned her head back against the wall. He's coming here! I'm going to see him.

Boris was looking rapidly through the newspapers as they walked back toward the hospital. "These papers are too old," he said. "They're full of German victories on a river called the Dunajec."

"In war unknown places become important because men die there." Thank God she could be sure Serge was not there. Then she remembered there was a letter from Ulla, too.

"Dearest Cirie, I have not slept in two nights—"

Cirie smiled. Leave it to Ulla to dramatize her problems.

"But I feel you must be told. Serge married Countess Scherevsky this past week in Petrograd…"

As he read Ulla's letter, Strengov's heart pounded. The bastard—the bastard—

He dropped the letter on the desk and tried to collect himself. He took out his handkerchief. "Cirie, you would never have been happy with him." His eyes were wet. Her eyes, he saw, were dry. "You were infatuated—"

"Infatuated?" she said, coldly.

"With his good looks, his charm—" He gestured helplessly. "All that will pass. What is beautiful at twenty-one is not so beautiful even five years later. A man has to grow—and his growth is stunted." He hated the bastard so that his hands were shaking. "Cirie, there are standards!"

She looked at him indignantly. She thought he was talking about class distinctions.

"Look at what you do here—taking care of these men. You help with surgery, you dress their wounds, you find words of encouragement. You give them a little peace until they die. Who at Vodovsky would do all this? Certainly not Serge."

"I don't know what he would do. I don't care."

"I'm talking about character. What a man will do and what he will not do. Serge Vodovsky wouldn't touch these men. Cirie, in time you wouldn't be able to stand him."

"Why talk about it?"

"Because it *must* be talked about!" Strengov gestured helplessly. He picked up Ulla's letter to finish it. Ulla was inviting her to Kostyka.

"Serge is not here," Ulla wrote. "And if you should see Madame or Vassily, you can ignore them. I hope I will be there to see it." Ulla was an idiot but occasionally she had her head on straight. "In Kostyka there'll be some life for you. You'll meet people—" Strengov stopped reading. "Do you want to go?"

"Not now! Maybe when the war is over." Cirie took out a second envelop. "There was another letter today."

Strengov frowned. From Serge?

"Darling…how I miss you…I'll always love you…"

Strengov looked at the date and saw that Serge's letter was written a month ago. He looked at Ulla's letter—dated a week ago. So this great man—this tower of strength—had limped back to Kostyka and allowed himself to be whisked off to his wedding. The bastard—the bastard—

"Cirie, someone will come along who will really love you—" The letter shook in Strengov's hand. "Not like this."

"No, I won't make that mistake again."

"Love isn't a mistake. He was a bad egg. Petya has fallen for you." Petya Rossatin had been back on the pretext of having his arm checked.

"I don't want to marry Petya."

"You'd have a good life—" He broke off. Now wasn't the time to argue Petya's case. He handed back the letter. "Tear it up! Throw it out! Don't re-read it until it's stained with tears. Don't cry over it."

"I am not crying," Cirie pointed out. "I have no intention of crying."

Strengov had thought that when the news came there would be hysterics. Instead he was the one filled with tears of rage. He would talk to her about it, reasonably, when he had control of himself.

Walking home that evening Cirie was impatient when Strengov brought up Petya again. "Cirie, he would take care of you. You'd be in Kostyka. In time you'd grow to love him."

"Love?" she said, coldly. "Love is a matter of convenience. I love you if no one objects. I love you if there's something in it for me—a little fun in a boring summer, a temporary intoxication you can always sleep off."

"Cirie!"

"Love passes like the seasons. A beautiful spring. A hot summer. An autumn cooling. And a long winter." Then she saw how haggard Strengov looked. She shouldn't torment him. But the words poured out, stored up all afternoon while she worked. "All those silly people," she said, softly. "And he gave up his life to them without even a fight."

"Cirie, you're hurt." Strengov slowed his pace a little. "You're disillusioned—"

"No—" All winter she had looked at the snow stretching into the silent woods and had thought that once she had loved it and now it only depressed her. She had told herself that summer would be better. Now it was summer. The woods smelled sweet. Hector had let out the calf. And still this town was a barren trap. "Not disillusioned—" she said. "But I can play that game too. I'll love whoever will give _me_ what I want. And I won't settle for Kostyka."

"Cirie, don't think about him. Don't think about them."

"When I think about them, I think only one thing."

"What's that?"

"I think," she said, calmly, "that one day I'll even the score."

"Ah, Cirie, that's a mountain you can't climb!"

The beautiful deep eyes met his. Cold, controlled, no hint of passion. One minute she had thought of it and the next minute it was seared into her heart.

"Cirie, you won't hurt them! Only yourself!" He shuddered at the determination in the cold clear eyes. "Cirie, don't live for revenge. What do you think you can do to them?"

"Nothing now."

"Exactly."

"I can wait."

22

❀

In the General Store a moujik woman was trading for food and the proprietor, a stocky woman with frizzled yellow hair, took a small axe and chipped a chunk of sugar from a high block.

"Look at the shelves," Cirie whispered to Boris. "There's nothing here."

"What do you expect?" Boris said. "Before the war we imported everything from Germany. What do you need?"

"Needles and thread for Mamma." Marya spent her life sewing these days.

"Buy extra. Needles come from Germany."

"So the Germans will be in Vilna soon, God help us," the proprietress said.

"If it's God's will, they'll be there," the moujik said. "Maybe it will be God's will that Russians will turn them back."

"We haven't turned them back yet," Boris said. "They're almost there."

"Probably it won't happen," the peasant agreed. "But if it's God's will, he'll send a miracle."

"Can you believe that?" Boris said as they left the store. "They live their whole lives thinking someday God will spread around a few miracles. They don't understand that after Vilna, we're next."

They came out into the sunlight. In the distance, a carriage moved along the winding road coming into town—a heavy carriage, not a peasant's cart. That was unusual this summer. The war had kept most of the families away from their estates.

Across the street two men stood leaning against the Inn, smoking cigarettes. The bright hot sun gave a white glare to the dusty street. The horses drew closer now and Cirie started as she recognized the Vodovsky carriage. Someone must be at Whitewater. Gerzy would not use the troika himself.

As the carriage approached the square, it slowed down and an arrogant black-bearded face looked out at her. Vassily! Their eyes met and the carriage rolled on to the telegraph office down the street. Without realizing what she was doing, Cirie started toward it.

"Cirie, no!" Boris caught her arm. "What would you say to him?"

What indeed? Would she tell him again how much she hated him? He knew that. Even if she had not screamed it at him—oh, he would know! If a person is hated as much as I hate Vassily, she thought, he would have to feel it even across great distances.

"Cirie, I'm leaving soon," Boris said. "I'm going to Moscow."

Was Serge here, too—only a few miles away? Or was it only Vassily, making sure no one had stolen anything or cut a few trees in his precious forests? She started back to the hospital.

"Cirie, wait a minute. Do you want to come to Moscow with me"

"Boris, don't be silly."

"You were always talking about getting away from here. Where do you want to go?"

"*Anywhere.*"

"Then come on. You can't stay here and rot!"

"No, I can't stay here."

"Then what will you do?"

"*I don't know.* But have you looked at my father lately? I can't go away now."

Up the street she saw the familiar sight of stretchers arriving and she hurried on to the hospital.

Federin had given up at midnight, saying he could not go on. At a quarter to three, Lubochev turned from his last patient and vanished. Strengov sat down, too tired to walk home, and Cirie wondered whether she should fix a cot for him in the office. A few minutes passed. Then a furious pounding broke the silence. The door flew open and Popov stood on the stoop, doubled over, with Tessa supporting him.

"Help me, I'm dying!" Popov vomited on the doorstep.

"Popov, are you drunk?"

"He's sick!" Tessa screamed.

Retching and shouting obscenities, Popov let Cirie lead him to the examining room. Strengov sat still, too weary to move.

Tessa pushed him. "Aren't you going to help him?"

"Yes, I'm going—" Every bone in his body rebelled as Strengov dragged himself to the examining room and Cirie turned up the light. It took only a minute to realize that Popov was suffering from an appendicitis.

An hour later, white and sick, Strengov finished sewing him up and turned from the table and collapsed.

23

❀

LARANOV'S WAR DIARY

10 August, 1915

"In the Duma there has been a steady outcry for an end to corruption and incompetence. Even though appointments are a disgrace the blunders are not corrected because the Tsar believes that to admit a blunder would diminish his prestige. This Tsar who has done nothing but blunder believes that appearances must insist that, for him, a mistake is impossible.

"The gulf between the government and the people is widening and the Germans are approaching the Russian-Polish border.

"The Germans entered Warsaw on August 6th."

25 August, 1915

"On the Polish front the slaughter is overwhelming. Bodies of Russian soldiers are piled so high the advancing Germans have to clear them away in order to see. The dusty Polish earth is soaked with blood.

"And the refugees! Long lines of people, already suffering, moving slowly east. Carts full of children. And most of those children will soon be dead."

Laranov prided himself on his discipline but this was an image he could not erase. No way to move the refugees, no place to send them. The hungry bewildered faces of children no one could save.

"The Grand Duke, like Kutusov before Napoleon, retreats and retreats, trying to save his army. The last Russian fortress in Poland has fallen. Soon the Germans will be on Russian soil.

"And so the old Russia is slipping away."

The disasters of August continued. The Tsar decided to dismiss the Grand Duke and assume command of the armies himself. "According to my sources, the Tsar hesitated," Constantine said when he told Laranov the news. "But the Empress drummed it into him that it's God's intention that a ruler be at the head of his army when his country is in danger."

"Why?" Laranov said.

"Rasputin backed her up. Together they convinced the Tsar that all these disasters are the fault of the Grand Duke who, they say, is only interested in seizing the throne."

Laranov considered the impact of this news. "He has a genius for making the wrong decision at the worst possible time."

"Rasputin fed him a lot of mumbo-jumbo about taking on himself all the sins and suffering of his people. And the Emperor himself added an even more occult and more frightening reason because it shows such total resignation. He's going to be the scapegoat needed to save Russia."

"A scapegoat! Needed by whom?"

"By fate, apparently. He's offering to sacrifice himself. He's given up completely to the idea of predestination. God has already decided everything and he accepts it. He leaves for General Headquarters in about a week."

"There couldn't be a worse time," Laranov said. "In Poland the Germans are at the Russian border. And in the north any day now Vilna will fall. The fighting will all be on Russian soil."

Constantine nodded. "When the first Germans are on Russian soil, the Tsar will be blamed for everything. Every retreat will be a double crisis—military and political."

They fell silent while the waiter poured the wine. This was not information for other ears.

"By the way," Constantine said. "I've had word of Cirie. Her father died."

"Her father died?" Laranov put down his glass. "How did you hear that?"

"Stepa was here last week. Vassily went to Whitewater to salvage some papers and a few prized possessions because it's not far from Vilna. He was there when it happened."

"I met her father once," Laranov said. "He was a good man. You say Cirie is still in Novotnii?"

"She was there that day."

Laranov frowned. "There's only a rather helpless mother. And a very young sister—a little girl. And Cirie."

In his war diary Laranov wrote:

"The troops are demoralized at the dismissal of the Grand Duke for whom they felt loyalty and affection. Desertions are climbing.

"The people are furious. After only six weeks the Duma, which they regard as their voice in the Government, has been dismissed. Factories have gone out on strike. On all sides you hear, 'If they want a revolution, they'll get it.'

"In August we lost 450,000 men, bringing the total since May 1 to a million and a half.

"In a few days all of Lithuania was lost. Soon the Germans will take Vilna."

24

❁

Fear gripped the town. Rumors flew. Vilna was under siege—Vilna was ready to fall and the Germans would be here any day—Vilna had fallen, the Germans were on the way. On a gray day in September Cirie sat alone in the hospital office, working on the records. Already the first hint of winter was in the air. Soon these last patients would be moved deeper into Russia and no new wounded were being brought in. As Strengov had said, that's when we'll know there'll be trouble. Cirie thought. We're too close to the front. It isn't safe here anymore.

Her thoughts moved to her own wounds. When she lost Serge she had been able to martial a whole medley of emotions. There had been people to hate and in a strange way that had helped. Grieving for Strengov, she had no one to hate except fate. And she was left with a distraught mother who sewed compulsively all day and an eleven-year old sister who kept running away. "She runs away because you have become her father and her mother," Marya told Cirie. Cirie understood that, but who else was there to decide anything?

Greta rushed into the office and nodded toward the window. "Did you see him?"

Across the street a ragged stranger was slouched against a building, eating sunflower seeds and staring at the hospital. His uniform was so torn and filthy she could not identify it.

"Is he a German?" Greta whispered.

"Every stranger isn't a German. Greta, is Hulda here yet?" Today for the first time Hulda had not come to work.

"If Hulda was here, I wouldn't be cleaning." Greta's eyes were glued on the straggler.

The square was empty. Everyone was at the General Store or the Inn, discussing Vilna and the Germans. "Greta, what's wrong with her?"

"I don't know," Greta mumbled. Cirie realized she had spent the night with Lubochev and had not been home.

She stole another look at the straggler. She ought to warn Marya and Lily to stay inside. As soon as Lubochev finished the surgery, she would run home.

When she came out of the hospital at three o'clock the stranger was gone. But when she reached home she saw two more stragglers in rags at the edge of town. Inside Koner was with Marya who was sewing the lining of a coat and crying.

"Where's Lily?" Cirie said.

"She's just outside the kitchen door," Marya said.

"Call her inside until I get back. The town is full of strangers."

"Cirie, you can't go back!" Marya burst into fresh tears.

"What happened?" Cirie said. "Why are you crying?"

"It's the deaf-mute," Koner said.

"Hulda? What about Hulda?"

"She was raped!"

"Oh, God!"

"Last night—going home from the hospital."

"Oh, poor Hulda! Oh, God, she couldn't even cry out."

"She killed them!" Marya cried. "Two men."

"She's a strong woman," Koner said. "All her life she worked like a man. She slammed a heavy limb at their heads—first one and then the other. They're both dead."

"Oh, God!" She could picture Hulda trudging along in the dark, not hearing the men approach. She could hear the awful guttural gasps, which were all Hulda could utter. "Where is she? She's not in jail?"

"Who would arrest her? They can't talk to her. And under the circumstances—"

"What will become of us? Who will take care of us?" Marya wailed.

"I'm taking care of you, Mamma."

"Cirie, I'll come to the hospital at six o'clock to bring you home," Koner said. "Marya will be worried."

Thank God for Koner, Cirie thought as she hurried back to the hospital. She wished he would divorce his wife and marry Marya. She pushed aside a twinge of guilt. Why guilt? His wife is a complainer and a recluse who prefers her own company to all other. That's why Koner lives at the Inn while his wife and younger son live at the farm. Why feel guilty? Why worry about what other people might think? That's Serge's game. And what did it get him?

She was almost at the hospital door when the straggler in the ragged uniform appeared from nowhere.

"Can you give me something to eat, little sister?" he said. He wasn't German. He was Russian. She should have known from the sunflower seeds. His eyes bored into her. Suddenly he grabbed her wrist.

"Of course," Cirie said softly. Don't panic—keep a grip on yourself. "Go around to the kitchen. We have a hundred of your wounded brothers here. You can't get through this way."

Still the straggler held her wrist in his filthy vise. Beady eyes glittered. The square was empty. Even Koner was not across the street at the Inn. No one in this whole world sees us.

"There's a good thick soup and black bread." She hoped he was starving. "I'll get you a loaf of bread to take with you. The soup is fresh and hot. Right that way."

He wavered. She wrenched free her wrist and darted into the hospital and told an orderly to feed him at the back door. "And give him a loaf of bread."

In the office Cirie put her head in her hands. Our world is suddenly dangerous. Now we can't go out on the street alone. Her eyes fell on the map where the pins were still west of Vilna. The Germans were closer than that. You didn't need a map to know it. She took it down and put it in the pocket of her cape. She would keep it as a memento—that's all it was good for. A thud came from the ward and she went to investigate. Across the room, Hulda was huddled over a mop.

"Hulda!" Cirie hurried up to her. At her touch Hulda burst into guttural tears. Oh, this poor soul, hasn't anyone at all let her know that they feel for her? For a long time Hulda clung to her and Cirie just patted her shoulder because words were useless.

It was ten o'clock and you could cut the fear in this room. "Marya, I don't think you're safe here—you and the girls," Koner said. "Even if our army is still in Vilna, it won't hold out much longer."

Marya's needle darted in and out of a quilt.

"We must decide what you should do," Koner said.

"But what can we do!"

Do? Cirie thought. When war comes close the local population flees! Everyone has heard of the long lines of refugees, walking or riding in carts in searing heat or freezing cold, going nowhere! No, thanks. I'd rather take a chance with the Germans. But what about Marya and Lily—a helpless woman and a helpless child?

The sound of men's voices cut into the quiet night. "Oh, my God! Cirie, put out the light."

"They've seen the light, Mamma." Cirie shaded her eyes and looked outside. In the black night she saw nothing. Marya started to cry.

Voices again. To Cirie every man out there was the straggler gripping her wrist. "It's probably just some men walking into town. Don't be nervous."

"How can we not be nervous? Cirie, where are you going?"

"To Papa's office."

"You can't go outside!"

"I'm going through the corridor."

"They'll see you there. Why are you going to the office?"

"Mamma, there are medicines there." Not much. The yellow skin ointment, pills for pain and fever, quinine, bandages. "Medicines are scarce. Someone will break in and steal them." And if we have to leave and wander they will be something to barter.

Men's voices again. The sound of breaking glass. Lily chewed on her handkerchief and shook with terror. The voices grew louder. Orders. An argument. A shot. Silence. Loud knocks on the door.

"Sit still," Koner whispered. "Don't move."

The hard knocks continued. Cautiously, Cirie moved to the window beside the door.

"Cirie, don't move!" Marya gasped.

"The lamp is burning, Mamma. They know we're here."

The knocks rattled the door. "Cirie—" a familiar voice shouted. "Open up, damn it! Cirie, open up."

Cirie flung open the door and threw herself into his arms. "Laranov!"

"Cirie, you have to get out of here. *Now.*"

"Now?" Laranov was here—Laranov who was strong, Laranov who was clever, Laranov who always knew what to do. Laranov was here and everything would be all right.

"*Now.* You're not safe here. The Germans took Vilna yesterday. Russian troops are on the run. It's dangerous here for three women alone—especially you."

"Surely German soldiers won't be so barbarous!" Marya protested. Reluctance to leave had erased the memory of Hulda.

"Russians! Not Germans! Deserters move fast. Looting, killing and *raping.* Leave now."

"I don't want to lose my home," Marya wept.

"It's as good as lost now. They'll break in and take what they want. And Cirie will be raped. More than once. Koner, have you got a wagon and a good horse?"

"I had wonderful horses. They took them all. All I have left is an old nag."

"Hitch it to a cart. Drive them to the railway station tonight."

Koner closed his eyes and nodded.

"Fill the cart with hay. Hurry."

"Must we go in the dark of night?" Marya said. "Maybe tomorrow."

"By tomorrow you'll walk. The trains are coming from Vilna with the wounded and the refugees. Tomorrow you won't get on."

"All right," Marya said abruptly. "I'm ready."

"Leave your doors open. They'll only break them down. Where are you going?" He whirled on Cirie as she moved toward the corridor.

"To the office to get the medicines."

Laranov understood immediately what she was saying. "I'll go with you. Hurry. There's no time to waste."

"What are you doing here, Laranov?" Cirie whispered as they hurried along the corridor.

"The War Department needed officers to help stop the flood of desertions at Vilna. I volunteered. Why, I don't know. My job is to find supplies, not men."

While Cirie threw the medicines into a sack, Laranov stood at the window, his hand on his pistol. "Cirie, listen carefully," he said. "In the cart you ride under the hay. If Koner is stopped, don't make a sound. Don't look out to see what's happening. Koner will give them some reason for taking your mother to the train. You don't move."

"All right."

"If anyone starts to check the hay, shoot him. I brought you a pistol. Don't wait for him to find you. Don't think you can talk him out of it."

Cirie looked around at him.

"If a deserter wants a woman, talk isn't going to do any good. Shoot him."

The medicines were packed. "Laranov—thank you. But why are you doing this?"

"Why am I doing it?" Laranov crushed her against him and kissed her hungrily, as though there would never be another chance. "Because like Constantine I'm under your spell. You're worth more than a Russian deserter."

How many days—how many weeks—have we been on this train? Moving east, moving south, shunted onto sidings in the middle of nowhere. Packed in like animals with the Vilna refugees—filthy, stinking of every kind of human odor, thieves ready to steal anything. Cirie and Marya took turns staying awake to guard their possessions, less meager than Cirie had expected. All those weeks Marya had been sewing her prized possessions into quilts and the linings of clothing and packing them into a small trunk—her silver, her lace tablecloth, her linens.

Three freight cars with wooden shelves for the refugees had been attached to a train carrying wounded soldiers. The air was stale, the smell unbearable. At the crowded stations the door would be opened, letting in welcome fresh air, but Cirie was afraid to leave the car. She would never get back through the mob fighting to get on. When the train stopped outside a town, moujiks appeared with food for sale. Cirie had bought bread and cold piroshki and water. The last of the food had run out two days ago.

Lying on an upper shelf, Cirie could feel Laranov's pistol in her pocket, next to Strengov's map that she studied at station stops, trying to figure out where they were. But the names of small stations did not appear on a map of Europe. The train had picked up speed. We're in the middle of nowhere, racing across this vast space to some other nowhere, and no one in the whole world knows or cares who's in this train. A refugee has no identity—no name—not even a number.

She opened her eyes. In the dim light the faces in the car had the grotesque quality of a nightmare. Old men with swollen noses and loose mouths and runny little eyes, toothless old women in babushkas with thin lips and beady eyes and dirty clothing, screaming and whimpering babies, a vicious-looking young woman with Mongolian features who pinched her children until they screamed and watched for every opportunity to steal, a filthy old woman across the aisle on the shelf over Lily, who scratched incessantly. Lily had dozed off. Cirie leaned over to look at her mother on the shelf below her. Marya was awake, drawn into her own thoughts, staring at nothing.

Cirie moved the map into a blade of light that sliced through a crack in the wall. The crowd at the last station was not so large or so desperate. We must be in safer territory. People here are not fleeing so why should we? At the next station I'll buy food and find out how far we are from Smolensk. On the map Smolensk was the most important city between Vilna and Moscow. We'd have known if we had stopped there. Marya wanted to go to Ulla, their only remaining relative in Russia, and Kostyka was southeast of Smolensk. If Kostyka is on a railway and if Smolensk is a railway center, sooner or later there will be a way.

Suddenly Lily screamed and the worst odor Cirie had ever smelled went through the car. The old woman on the shelf above Lily had emptied her bowels and the excrement was dripping down over one of Lily's flaxen braids. Marya cried out and snatched up the screaming Lily and ripped off her sweater and searched frantically through her bag. The black-haired Mongolian-featured woman moved silently toward them to take advantage of the chaos.

"Get away!" Cirie snapped and the woman retreated. With scissors from her bag, Marya cut off Lily's braid and threw it on the floor. The black-haired woman slithered back.

"Get away!" Cirie screamed. She seized Lily's bag and reached up for her own bag and the sack of medicines and flung them down beside Marya's trunk where she could watch them. In Marya's arms Lily stared at Cirie, her eyes flooded with tears.

"We're almost in Smolensk," Cirie said. "We'll get off there." The only way to end a nightmare is to wake up.

"But we should stay with the others," Marya protested. "Someone someplace will take care of us."

"No," Cirie said. "We'll get off and we'll take care of ourselves."

Three days later they climbed out of the horrible freight car in the Smolensk station. The waiting continued. Railway schedules were ignored. Trains arrived when they arrived and left when they left. At last they boarded a train bound for Kostyka and the delays began again as they were shunted aside to let trains carrying more important cargo go past.

It was October when at last they put the trunk and the bags and the sack of medicines down on Ulla's doorstep.

25

Questions circled in Constantine's mind—questions without answers. Revolution was not the answer, although more and more it was what he heard. Abdication? He heard that, too. But abdication in favor of whom? The legal heir? And who would be regent? That was the rub. Assassination? Assassination was a synonym for Revolution.

In Constantine's mind, abdication had already taken place. Except for a few major decisions, the Tsar could not rule from Army Headquarters. The Tsarina ruled in his name and did as Rasputin directed because she believed his orders came directly from God. Constantine turned out of the March wind and entered his club where Stepa was waiting.

"I've just come from Kostyka," Stepa said cheerfully, warming his hands at the fire. "I spent a day in Moscow and now two days here with Tanya and it's back to my train."

All his life Stepa had gone from one enthusiasm to another—his violin, Elissa when the affair was new and torrid, his book about the Russian people—always longing to be totally committed to something. Then with the coming of war it happened. Equipping a Red Cross train at his own expense, Stepa supervised it on every trip that carried wounded men back from the front, and he was dedicated as never before. "My train is having an overhaul," he said. "I keep it in top condition, which is more than you can say for the government railway wagons."

"Or anything else." They moved to the dining room. "How are they in Kostyka?"

"The house is like a tomb. Eugenie is ill and stays in her apartment. Only Vassily is there. Serge is back with Borassin. Serge has changed—he doesn't care about anything. How long he'll endure this marriage I don't know. He wanted a divorce the next day. And dear Vara hasn't found the road home from Moscow to her ailing mother. Of course, if you were there she would fly to her side."

"Is she visiting Kyra?"

"Why?" Stepa laughed. "You want to call on her? What about you, Constantine?"

Constantine leaned forward with a wry half-smile. "I've had a new experience. I can't get published anymore. Three papers have turned down my latest piece."

"What! What do you say in it?"

"That the Tsar's exit from Petrograd to take over the army is the beginning of the final act."

"It's probably true!" Stepa glanced around the dining room. "On the train we don't see the papers regularly or talk to anyone who knows much. But the stories we hear!"

"Rasputin is giving the orders. The new Council President, Sturmer, is his tool and fool. Conniving and totally dishonest. Sturmer is not an administrator, he's not a statesman. He's nothing. And his assistant, Manuilov, is a former convict and a former Okhrana agent—a former thief, spy and swindler. He's known as the policeman-convict. But in his shady career he's performed many services for Rasputin."

"The Tsar knows this?" Stepa said.

"The Tsar has all but abdicated." Constantine lowered his voice. "He's just given up. Even in his most gullible moments how can he believe that Rasputin is a man of God? He knows all about his disgusting private life. And yet for peace with his wife he's turned the country over to him."

"He accepts the easy way."

"The Tsarevitch's latest attack didn't help." While on tour with the Tsar, the boy had suffered his worse hemorrhage since Spala at the very moment Rasputin was angling for more power. "Twice he was given up for lost. Rasputin prayed and told the Empress, 'Praise be to God. He has given me your son's life once more.' The next morning, as the train neared home, the boy began to improve and by evening the bleeding had stopped. How do you fight that? In some general way he seems able to predict—"

"What did he have to lose? If the boy recovers, he claims the credit. If the poor little fellow dies, he's finished, anyway—he loses the key to the deranged mind of the mother." Stepa looked sober. "In three days I've been in three cities and I can tell you, Constantine, people are very depressed. The retreats, the terrible losses in life. Prices so high they can't get by." He paused. "Fears of typhus and famine—like Serbia."

"We went to war to save Serbia. Now we can't even save ourselves," Constantine said.

"The poor Serbians. Their retreat on foot across the ice-covered Alps is the worst story I ever heard. Blinding snowstorms, no food, no shelter, so many dying on the way. And the few who struggled home found their country starving in the grip of a terrible famine and their people dying of typhus. People are frightened that this is a warning of what will happen in Russia. 'The rich will be all right', they say, 'but what about us?'"

"If it comes to that, the rich will be worse off than anyone else," Constantine said. "It will trigger revolution."

"And Rasputin rules Russia," Stepa said. "It's too much to bear."

"The papers will print none of this," Constantine said. "Not a word against the government. They're afraid of Rasputin. Sturmer is his man. The Director of the Police is his man. He controls the Church. When he wants a minister dismissed, he tells the Empress, 'This man is a liberal, friendly to Revolutionists.' The man is out and Rasputin's man is in. It's like watching a scene in a madhouse. An inmate who thinks he's Napoleon, lining up the idiots and giving them their orders. The only encouraging news is that he's predicting his own approaching death."

Stepa looked up hopefully. "He's ill?"

"He predicts that he'll be murdered—that soon now he'll die a terrible death."

"Let us pray the prediction is right on the mark," Stepa said.

"He's also had a vision of piles of corpses—Grand Dukes, Counts, Princes. He predicts the Neva will be red with blood."

"I'm afraid that one, too, may come to pass."

Constantine feared it, too. "Russia is racing to disaster like a runaway horse without a driver."

26

Ulla had always said that Kostyka, a city of thirty-thousand inhabitants, was like a small Moscow. A large park with flowers and fountains and a bandstand adorned Elizabeth Street, the broad main street lined with fashionable shops, tearooms, churches and yellow brick public buildings. Turn off Elizabeth Street opposite the park onto Gleb Street and you came upon smaller stores offering whatever merchandise they could get—clothing, housewares, woodenware, foodstuffs, tobacco—and merchants hawking their wares and people bartering on the streets. Around another corner, on Vanya Street, the open-air food stalls. Retrace your steps and bear right at the top of Elizabeth onto St.Stephens Street and you came to the hospital, one block away.

Kostyka was busier than Cirie remembered. A military center for the war in the south, the streets were filled with officers and soldiers. War-wounded men walked about aimlessly and the war-weary population wore expressions of just trying to live through another day. The last time she visited here she had spent hours with Ulla in the shops on Elizabeth Street. Now the shops had less to sell and she went there only at lunch time, racing down the block from the hospital to read the lists of casualties posted in shop windows, searching for the familiar names—Serge first and then, her heart pounding with relief, the others she knew from Whitewater and from home.

On a June evening Cirie stood on the hospital steps, waiting for Petya. Today she had assisted Dr. Legare, the chief surgeon, with an operation on a soldier whose face was so destroyed his own wife would not recognize him. In the corridor after the operation Dr. Legare, a small bony man with skillful hands, had drawn deeply on a cigarette and said, "They're developing facial prostheses for these poor wrecks. There's going to be an exhibition of them in Moscow." Now, hours after the surgery, when the poor wreck lay bandaged with only holes for his one remaining eye and the place his nose had been, the words still ran through her mind. "They're developing facial prostheses..." So many faces have been blown apart we're developing false faces. False legs—arms—faces! For what? *For what?*

Petya was late, probably because he was leaving tomorrow for Siberia to buy furs for his shops in Kostyka and Poltava. He would be gone a month and Ulla was having them to dinner tonight because, she had said pointedly, we'll all miss him.

And she would miss him, Cirie admitted. He was so devoted. Every evening he came to the hospital to take her home and nights when she returned to work extra hours he was there again at midnight, concerned, begging her not to work extra hours again. But with prices going up every day, it was the only way they could get by. Unless she married him.

For a week after arriving in Kostyka they had stayed with Ulla and then moved into a tiny one-room apartment on Muscovy Street, a narrow unpaved road parallel to St. Stephens, where Marya sewed for Ulla's friends while Cirie worked at the hospital to get a nursing certificate. After two months she had persuaded Dr. Legare that the training program had little to teach her except hospital regulations and Dr. Legare, desperate for good nurses, had expedited her certificate and brought her into surgery. When she began to earn more money they had moved across the hall to a two-room apartment where Marya and Lily slept in the bedroom and Cirie on a cot in the living room and where Ulla and Marya talked to her regularly about Petya. "Cirie, any girl in Kostyka would love to marry Petya," Ulla would say. "They'd jump at the chance. And he adores you." And Marya: "He's such a good man…he'll always be devoted to you…He's the best kind of husband you could find." And Ulla again: "I never saw a man so much in love. He'll give you anything. Marry him."

And why not? He was kind and attractive and his suits from Moscow were always well-tailored. And that scar on his face was actually glamorous. Why not?

Petya was here apologizing for his tardiness. In the carriage, he turned to her. "Cirie, I don't want to leave you—"

She touched his arm. "I'll be right here when you get back, Petya."

"If you would marry me you could get away from all this." Petya motioned toward the hospital. When she didn't answer, he said, "Is it because of my arm?"

"Your arm!"

"Because I still haven't regained the full use of it. Do you feel I'm a cripple?"

"Your arm!" Cirie gasped. "Petya, my God, after the horrors I've seen—" She stopped and collected herself. "Petya, it isn't you—it's me. I'm numb from all the horrible wounds and burns and death I see. Today was a bad day. I'll try to give you an answer when you get back."

At dinner, Ulla's husband Oscar, a smart lawyer with a taut pugnacious look about him, was talking to Petya about what seemed a strange decision—to send Russian troops to fight in France. Last winter the French had asked the Tsar to send them four-hundred-thousand men right away which, Oscar said, was impossible.

"The French don't understand the northern Russian winters," Petya said. "The White Sea was frozen over and the Dvina for sixty-five miles below it. The troops would have had to walk to the boats in total darkness and sub-zero weather."

"We don't have ships to transport four-hundred-thousand men," Oscar said, flatly. Then, as if issuing the order, "We'll send ten-thousand men a month and see how it works out."

"It won't work out," Petya said. "Our moujiks are fighting for Mother Russia. They won't understand that in France they're still fighting for Russia. That's beyond them."

"Oscar, dear heart," Ulla cooed. "Tell me, love, why should we send our poor Russian soldiers to fight in France?"

"The French have suffered terrible losses, darling," Oscar said.

The French have suffered terrible losses! Cirie thought. The French!

"They should worry about rising prices, not sending Russian soldiers to France," Marya said. "Today I didn't buy butter. Even soap has gone sky-high."

"France has been bled white at Verdun," Oscar said. "They've lost the flower of a whole generation."

So have we! Cirie thought. We're making prostheses for faces that have nothing left but holes. There's going to be an exhibition in Moscow. This is a bad night for you, she told herself. Tomorrow you'll feel better. Or the day after. Or as soon as there's a let-up.

Petya was looking at her as though he understood that she was suffering and wanted to help her. ("If you would marry Petya he would take care of you..." "...If you would marry me these bad days would all be behind you.") I'm going to have to do it. Why not? He loves me and he isn't worried that someone will know about it. And he'll never betray me or abandon me for someone else. Time changes things. Before the war, I wanted to see the world, but then we weren't wanting for anything, except maybe excitement. Now we're poor and if prices keep going up we'll be needy, and seeing the world doesn't seem so important. Mamma can't make enough with her sewing and Lily is only twelve. Now it seemed that just to be free from ghastly wounds and nightmarish operations and worrying would be all she would ask. ("If you marry me, you'll get away from all this.") She shook her head to dispel the seductive thought. Just hold on, she told herself. The tide will turn.

"The French think we have enormous reserves of men," Oscar said. "But our reserves are untrained."

And men are still sitting comfortably in Petrograd sending them into battle unarmed, Cirie thought. They see lists—those cruel, ambitious old men in Petrograd—but they don't see the wounded or the mutilated or the dead and they don't lose any sleep over them. A wave of nausea swept over her. She could stand the wounds, she could go on all day in surgery, no matter how horrible they were, but deliberate or thoughtless cruelty sickened her.

"In the reserve camps they just live in overcrowded, smoke-filled barracks and listen to revolutionary speeches all night," Oscar said. "We don't have trained men even to replace our own losses."

I think the wounds are worse this year, Cirie's mind ran on. No—it's me. I have to train myself not to see them.

"I'm going to have a job, Petya," Lily said. Cirie was always amazed at the way Lily's shyness melted away in front of Petya.

"What are you going to do, my little friend?" Petya said.

"I'm going to play with Ulla's friend's children on Saturdays when their nurse is off."

Marya sewing, Lily taking care of children, and with prices going up, it doesn't mean a thing. I'm going to have to marry him. There's no other way.

Later, as they rode along the riverfront in Petya's carriage, Cirie said, as she had said to Strengov, "Petya, have you ever thought about how much cruelty there is in the world?"

Petya took her hand. "Everyone sees cruelty on all sides, darling. Especially in Russia."

"Why should one human being have the right to play God with the life of another—thoughtlessly, frivolously?"

In the soft night Petya closed her in his arms. "Cirie, marry me—let me take care of you. I love you so. You'll never have to see anything cruel or ugly again. Cirie, I can't go on like this. I have to know."

Tell him. In the end you're going to do it. Instead she said, "When you get back, we'll talk about it, Petya."

"Cirie, if you would marry me, the bad days would be just bad memories."

At home Marya was waiting up for her. "Cirie, how can you pass him up? I don't understand it."

"I haven't passed him up, Mamma. I'll probably do it. I'll marry him."

"He loves you. He'll take care of you. What are you waiting for?"

Certainly not to fall in love. She'd washed her hands of that.

"He asks so little—just for you to live in his beautiful house and wear his beautiful furs and let him take care of you. Where will you find someone like Petya again?"

And have his children. And then what? Then everything will be finished. A dead end. And what do you have now?

The bearded gray unconscious patient was wheeled into the operating room and the nursing trainee lifted the sheet from the battered body and gasped and turned white. Dropping the sheet, she held onto the table and swayed and ran from the room. The poor wreck's organs—penis and scrotum were almost entirely shot away. A field doctor had inserted a little tube where his penis had been.

Dr. Legare looked at Cirie. "Will you be all right?"

"I'm all right." Train myself not to see? How do I do that? If he lives, what misery this poor soul will know for the rest of his life.

After the operation, Cirie sat on a bench in the corridor. I've stopped feeling. I'm numb. She thought about Petya and didn't feel anything. I'm thinking of marrying him and I don't feel a thing. I have to go in there for another operation and I don't feel a thing. I can't even cry. Nothing. She went back into the operating room.

The patient's assaulted flesh hung loose off his ribs. He looked as though he would die. They all look as though they will die. The last one would be better off if he did die.

A door opened and the head nurse came up beside her. "Cirie, Count Vodovsky wants to speak to you. I'll take over for you. He's waiting."

Serge! Cirie's heart leaped. Serge had come for her at last. But that couldn't be true.

"Count Vodovsky has been very good to this hospital," the nurse said. "We can't keep him waiting."

Not Serge. Vassily. "If he can't wait, ask him to come back." Dr. Legare looked over his mask with approval and she handed him a clamp. "Please tell him I'm in surgery. I'll be down when we've finished."

Vassily? How did he find me? What does he want? Can he possibly think I would do anything for him? Can he think I've forgotten? For nearly two years the thought of revenge had burned in her. For nearly two years she had told herself, someday I will even the score. My chance will come. They had felt they were too good for her. Well, they were never going to feel too good for her again. And now Vassily had come to her. Vassily wanted something. Now it would be her turn.

In the Director's office Vassily, dark hair and beard still trimmed to half an inch all around, was sitting on a hard chair, reading an old newspaper. Staring at him through the glass, feeling the surge of the old hatred, Cirie was tempted to go back upstairs and send down a message that she could not see him. Then she thought, No! I'll see him and I'll be as cold as Irene, as cold as Vassily himself. I'll show him exactly how much I hate him. She reached for the door and stopped again. *What for?* You swore you would never lose control again. Nobody cares, you said. And does he care now? Will it bother him? Less than not at all. What's to be gained by insults? She forced herself to smile and opened the door.

"Vassily," she held out her hand. "We were in the middle of operating on a poor soldier when you arrived."

Relieved at her cordial greeting, Vassily gave a little bow. "Cirie, how are you? We were sorry to hear about your father. Maman sends her sympathy. We had great respect for him."

Of course you did, Vassily.

"Isn't this very hard work for you here?"

"I don't stop to think about it. There are so many who are suffering so terribly."

"You look marvelous!" For Vassily this was an amazing performance. He was actually trying to behave like a friend. "Prettier than ever."

Cirie turned her shiny cobalt lights with their thick black lashes on him. Vassily cleared his throat. "Maman isn't well," he said. "She suffered a heart attack. We've had a terrible time getting a good nurse."

Quick images chased through Cirie's mind. Serge at daybreak, dismounting from Prince Igor...Serge lying beside her near the lake, sunlight dancing on his blond hair...Serge that last day, shrunk into his chair, unable to look at her...The man lying on the operating table with his organs blown off...Vassily telling her to get out...

"The doctor has sent several," Vassily said. "Moujiks with only a few months training. Their ways are hard on her."

...Serge holding her and swearing they would never be apart...The man with a tube where his penis had been...

"She was always so fond of you." Vassily was a devoted son. For his mother he would even swallow his pride. "Cirie, can I persuade you to come out to Rivercliff to take care of her?"

If Madame was ill Serge would come home! Fate was sending him back to her! Oh, no—nothing of the sort, she warned herself. Fate is setting a trap. She spread her hands in a gesture that said it was impossible. "There are so many wounded patients—"

Vassily nodded as though he had expected the answer, but still he persisted, speaking softly—no anger, no orders now. "Maman is bewildered at the harshness of these people. They order her about gruffly. Poor Maman is such a gentle soul—"

Except when you love her son.

"If you could help her even for a short time—I'm sure I can arrange a month off for you."

Yes, you could arrange it, Vassily. You can arrange anything.

"Cirie, I don't mean to appear to bribe you, but I'll happily double what they're paying you here."

If he'll go double, he'll go higher. Shades of Grandma! Well, what of it? "Vassily, how can I leave? I'm a surgical nurse. We have so many soldiers with awful wounds."

"I didn't realize—I didn't mean to make a paltry offer. If you're a surgical nurse, four times the amount would be fairer. A month's wages every week."

You just bribed me, Vassily, and I can't afford to think of the wounded soldiers.

"Because you'd be Maman's constant companion," Vassily hastened to gloss over the bribe.

This was a sensitivity Vassily had never revealed before. Still she shouldn't make it too easy for him. "I'd like to help Madame, but my conscience tells me I must stay here. Can you give me a few days to think about it?"

"Of course. Cirie, we'd be so grateful—Maman and I."

Cirie took out Strengov's watch. "I should get back—"

"I know you're working terribly long hours here. I've seen you several times going into the hospital and coming out. A young man accompanies you."

Petya! Now she could put off the decision about marrying Petya. How can I marry Petya when just thinking about seeing Serge makes me feel alive again?

"In time such hard work will wear you out. Come to us for just a little while. Shall I come back tomorrow for your answer?"

"That will be fine. Goodbye, Vassily. Please tell Madame of my concern for her."

Ulla was there with Marya when Cirie got home. Warm-hearted Ulla had brought Marya some butter.

"You can't!" Marya cried when Cirie told her. "You can't go back to those people!"

"Cirie, I wouldn't go back to those Vodovskys for anything," Ulla said.

"Oh, yes, you would. Vassily is going to pay me a lot of money."

Then she went into the bedroom and, to her own astonishment, burst into tears. Why am I crying? For Serge and what might have been? Or for the man with no face—or the man with no penis—or is it just relief at getting away from the hospital and the worries about rising prices—or at having a reprieve from having to decide about Petya—or is it just because I can feel something again? It's everything, she thought as fresh tears came. It's all of them.

27

❀

For sheer splendor the mansion at Rivercliff eclipsed even White-water. The high-ceilinged, marble-floored entrance hall was several times larger than the average drawing-room, larger than several moujiks' huts combined, larger than the two rooms where Cirie had left her mother and sister. Gold-framed mirrors reached to the ceiling and a wide marble staircase rose like a huge throne with wrought-iron banisters in which intricate figures of animals—lions, tigers, monkeys, panthers—played among trees. Ornate detail was everywhere—in French and Italian antique furniture, in Persian rugs and damask drapes, on doors carved in geometric figures or painted with bucolic scenes. In the library, shelves of fine leather bound books—English, French, German and Italian—and the Oriental chest of teak and jade and mother-of-pearl, removed from Whitewater before Vilna fell. On the wall, a portrait of Serge.

The house was polished and immaculate and empty. Georgii was at school for the summer, the curriculum having been accelerated, the sooner to train the young gentlemen as officers for the Tsar's army. Vara was with Kyra in Moscow and Stepa was on his Red Cross train and poor old Aunt Vayana had died and Madame remained in her apartment. Only in the stables did Cirie find a familiar face—Gerzy, who had brought his brood mares here from Whitewater and had six new foals he hoped to conceal from the army. Life at Rivercliff was like a half-recalled dream in which the principal characters had failed to appear.

For a week Cirie had dined in silence with Vassily, he at the head of the table, she far down the side. A wide diamond-paned window looked out on an Italian statue of three women pouring water from pitchers into a pool. Beyond the pool, gardens stretched almost to the river.

For just the two of them there was no zakuski hour. Tonight the white-gloved waiter served cold sturgeon with caviar at the table. Cirie looked at it and at the butter on her bread plate and the wine and caviar and thought it would be a mistake to linger here too long. All this would be too easy to get used to again.

Then one night Vassily broke the week-long silence. "My mother seems better."

"She should come downstairs," Cirie said. "Especially as there's a lift. She should go outdoors."

"Why doesn't she?"

"She takes a few more steps each day but she doesn't want to leave her apartment."

The waiter served a madrilene. Vassily said, "Is that what you did with Georgii—a few more steps each day?"

"Yes." Cirie met his eyes. She was not apologizing for anything. "I think Madame is lonely. Perhaps Kyra could visit her."

The next night Cirie's chair was closer to the head of the table. "The newspapers arrived today," Vassily said. The arrival of newspapers had become an event. "The Brussilov offensive is going well in Galicia. We took two-hundred thousand prisoners."

Outside the Italian statue caught the glow of the summer sun, still high over the gardens.

"Everything is so beautiful here," Cirie said. "Would you mind if I looked into the drawing rooms that are closed up?"

"I'll show them to you myself."

After dinner Vassily opened and closed doors to luxurious unused rooms, ending at the largest drawing room. French furniture was grouped around the room—brocade sofas, small straight chairs, fine tables. At the windows, carved vertical beams formed alcoves where small groups could gather. Chandeliers, gold sconces, magnificent old Italian paintings. On the wall a portrait of Serge holding Prince Igor. Careful to reveal nothing, Cirie turned away. "It's a beautiful room."

"Yes, it is. We haven't used it in a long time."

At dinner the next evening, Cirie's chair was at Vassily's right. "There's a shortage of help for harvesting." He began the conversation at once. "The men have all gone to war."

"In the hospital we heard the estates were being offered the use of German prisoners."

"I wouldn't trust them. Still, I suppose one man with a gun could guard a whole field."

"You speak German so fluently. You could talk to them and decide. They couldn't fool you."

A few nights later Stepa arrived and Madame came downstairs and Cirie's chair was back in the middle of the table.

After dinner the purple sunset cast a glow over the garden of rare shrubs where Madame sat with Stepa and Vassily.

"Eugenie, you should have more company," Stepa said.

"Vara and Kyra are coming, although I'm not sure when." Vara was reluctant to trade Moscow, however melancholy these days, for Kostyka and an ailing mother. And Madame was not eager to have her here. "And Irene, probably, if Serge has leave."

"I'd like to have Tanya join me here next time," Stepa said. "And Constantine, too. Although I must warn you he may be headed for trouble over some articles. The papers refuse to print them."

Vassily's cigar stopped in midair. "Constantine hasn't become a radical?"

"He's attacking some political appointments. With the Tsar at Headquarters, a sinister group has formed around the Empress. They call it her 'Camarilla.'"

"Camarilla! Who is in this camarilla?"

"Speculators with ties to German bankers and industrialists. They want a separate peace with Germany—any kind of peace—so they can get back to the business of making money."

"Traitors!" Vassily said. "And they're advising the Empress?"

"Through Rasputin. Rasputin is an uneducated moujik—he isn't capable of ruling Russia but she thinks his decisions come from God. So this Camarilla tells him what to do and he sends out orders to bankers, government ministers, even the Empress. He scrawls her a note saying, 'Get this done for me!' And she does it. Don't look for any hint of this in the papers. They won't print it. They're afraid of him. Ask Constantine about it when he's here."

Madame had a sudden thought. "If I write Vara that Constantine will be here, she'll come running. And yet if I don't write her, she'll never forgive me."

Stepa laughed. "Constantine can take care of himself. Eugenie, I was delighted to find Cirie here."

"Have you noticed how poised she's become? I wonder—were we partly responsible for it that summer when we were too busy to notice?"

"Who was too busy? Everyone noticed. When she entered a room everyone's eyes would light up."

"Did they really? What about you, Vassi? Did you notice that summer how unusual she was?"

"Not then and not now," Vassily said. Rather quickly, Madame thought.

"I'm concerned that Vara will be hard on Cirie," she said. She needed this girl whom once she had wronged. No!—we didn't wrong her. It was only proper. Yes, we did. Suddenly she felt that she had built her house on sand. "I suspect that now Cirie won't put up with it."

"She needs the money, Maman," Vassily said. "She supports her family."

"That won't hold her if Vara harasses her." If Vara came home there would be trouble. "I feel that I need her strength."

*　　　　　　*　　　　　　*

Something is wrong here! Vara studied her mother and Vassily, shocked. They were both on that girl's side. When Irene, quite properly, treated her like a servant, Vassily treated her like a guest of honor! When Vara made clear that the careless intimacy that had obviously prevailed here was at an end, Maman reinforced the intimacy. The girl had bewitched everyone. Even Vassily. When he spoke to her, he paused and waited for her smile. And Vassily smiled, too—Vassily, who never smiled at anything!

Vara ignored the strawberry ice that the waiter placed before her. If she had known the girl was here, she'd have come home sooner. Thank heavens Lydia wrote from Petrograd that Constantine was going to Rivercliff or she wouldn't be here now and who knows what the witch would have accomplished in another two months! If she had a shred of decency, with Irene here she wouldn't be at the table. Anyone could feel the tension, even with Kyra chatting away, trying to ease it.

"What a hero Sacha Borassin has become!" Kyra said. "Who would have expected it?"

"I would expect it, Kyra," Maman said, and Vara threw her a sharp look.

"His name has become a household word—along with General Brussilov's," Kyra ran on. "And have you heard about Ilya Laranov?"

Cirie looked up at that. So she was involved with him, too.

"He's regarded as a hero, too. He's working night and day to supply the troops. Traveling far and wide looking for food, boots, clothing. He'd find ammunition, too, if there were any. People say if Laranov can't find it, it doesn't exist in Russian."

"I remember Laranov," Maman said. "He was charming."

"Everyone seems to think so," Kyra said. "Lydia says he turns down hundreds of invitations when he's in town."

Vara saw an opportunity to take the girl down a peg or two. "He's been pursuing Countess Nina Bragaw, who is a great beauty. They say she's rather taken with him, for some reason—and he is simply smitten with her. More understandable, of course."

The girl betrayed no reaction. No reaction when Irene talked about Serge, no reaction to the news of Laranov and Countess Bragaw, or of Constantine. She just plays with them—and promises things with her eyes they have no business wanting. And when Constantine arrives, she'll start all over again.

"Vara, I don't want her at the table," Irene said as soon as dinner was over. "I don't want her in the house while Serge is here."

"Irene, Serge adores you."

"I won't have him tempted."

If she can't keep her husband's interest, what can I do? "Don't worry, Irene. I'll get rid of her."

In the drawing room Vara studied her mother. She's getting old, she thought. Tonight no one would think she'd been a great beauty. Well, no one lasts forever. And—Vara caressed a familiar thought—she has lots of money. A moment later Cirie came in. Time to tuck in the elderly patient for the night.

When Vassily left to go to his office, Vara followed him. "I realize the war has exacted compromises," she said with an indulgent smile. "But this is going a little far. Now that I'm here I expect her to leave. After all, she insulted me."

"She insulted all of us. And we insulted her."

"Oh, she doesn't know the difference."

Vassily took out a thin cigar. "You think she doesn't remember? She remembers every minute."

"Then why is she here?"

"We needed her enough to offer her a good salary and she needed the money. She supports her mother and her sister. Her father died. He worked himself to death taking care of Russian soldiers."

Vara sat up sharply. "You've certainly changed your tune! Remember, Vassily, I have rights in this house, too."

"Let me know, Vara, when you're ready to give Maman every minute of your time. Day and night."

"There are other nurses."

"None so totally satisfactory."

"To whom?" Vara said, pointedly.

"To Maman. And to me."

"Irene won't have her at the table. It's insulting. And you treat her like an equal!"

"Do I?" Vassily smiled. "In many ways she's superior. Don't interfere, Vara. Maman needs her."

Furious, Vara hurried out. In the hall she saw Cirie coming toward her. "What are you doing here?"

Cirie looked at her calmly. "I have never been asked to explain my presence in any part of this house, Countess."

A little chill skipped through Vara. "Don't talk back to me! Where are you going?"

The girl only smiled and lifted her chin. As though she were Irene! Vara had half a mind to go back to Moscow. But Constantine would be here any day. "Step aside and let me pass."

"Certainly, Countess."

"And remember your place when M. Paklov is here. Control your vulgar smile. I had to speak to you about that before."

Is it possible that this ridiculous woman still thinks she can intimidate me, Cirie thought as she continued on to Vassily's office. Vassily is on my side now.

When Vassily opened the door, he smiled with relief. "I thought it was Vara again. Come in. Sit down." The inner sanctum had comfortable chairs and magnificent old Italian paintings and pieces of sculpture on pedestals. Vassily circled a snifter of brandy in his hand. Here in his private domain he seemed more relaxed. "I don't like people coming in here and telling me what to do."

"I only wanted to ask you—"

"I didn't mean you. Will you have some brandy?" He poured a glass and brought it around the desk. "Now, what do you want to ask me?"

"Madame was too tired tonight. Can you remind the ladies that in her presence things should be serene?"

"I should have warned them when they arrived. I didn't think they'd start so soon." Vassily stopped circling his glass. "Don't let Vara upset you. Nobody can please Vara."

"She asks me not to smile but sometimes that can be hard."

Vassily actually laughed. "Why shouldn't you smile?"

"She finds it vulgar."

"Oh, Vara—Vara!" He finished his brandy. "I'll speak to them first thing in the morning. Vara's disposition will improve. Constantine will be here soon."

After Cirie left, Vassily poured another glass of brandy. Vulgar! She seemed more a countess than either Vara or Irene. They were so nervous while she was so serene. Their voices were nasal while hers was soft and low-pitched. What did she ever see in Serge? She's too smart for him—she has too much spirit. In six months she'd have been bored to death.

"What a delightful coincidence that you chose precisely this time to visit," Vara greeted Constantine. "Just when we've arrived to cheer up poor Maman, who has to put up with so much these days."

Now the characters were all back. Except for Georgii and except for Serge. And Serge was always present, less in the portraits than in Vara and Irene's pointed reminders.

"We've a hundred questions," Vara rushed on. "In Moscow we're not so cut off as here. Or at Whitewater, which was worse. When I think of that desolate little town! I marvel that anyone could live there."

"Have you ever seen such a performance?" Tanya whispered to Cirie. Tanya was seventeen now and looked like her mother, the tall dark beauty who had become bored with country life in Russia and had gone to France and remained there.

Vassily was discussing the war with Stepa and Constantine. "General Brussilov began brilliantly but now he's short of ammunition," Stepa said.

This is where we were two years ago, Cirie thought. Does anyone actually believe we can still win this war?

"The ammunition is actually on the wharves," Constantine said. "French ships delivered it in June, but the Railway Department is bogged down in corruption and inefficiency and claims it can't move the munitions because of a shortage of railway cars."

"Stepa," Vara said in a commanding voice. "You say you saw Serge. He's so eager to see Irene. When will he be here?"

"When he has leave, I presume."

"We're having trouble shipping logs," Vassily said. "The government should pay attention or the cities will feel it. It'll be cold soon."

"What government?" Constantine said, bitterly. "The government is the Camarilla working through Rasputin and his lackey, Sturmer. With its ties to German bankers the Camarilla wanted control of the Foreign Office. The Empress went willingly with Sturmer to Headquarters to talk the Tsar into it. She hated Sazanov because he refused to kowtow to Rasputin and had no use for Sturmer. So now Sturmer is not only Council President but Foreign Minister, too."

"The Tsar dismissed Sazanov, a man he liked and trusted," Stepa said soberly, "and gave the Foreign Office to Sturmer, a man he despises, all because he hasn't the courage to stand up to his wife."

"When it comes to handling the Empress, Sturmer knows all the tricks." Constantine spoke softly but his voice betrayed anger and sadness and disgust. "He flatters her, he tells her she alone can save Russia, he sends her letters, supposedly from her subjects, full of love and admiration. He writes them himself. And she's thrilled. So you see, Vassily, there is no government interested in shipping logs or anything else. The government is a bunch of thugs."

*   *   *

"Cirie, what's happening out there?" Ulla said when Cirie came into Marya's apartment. "I hear everyone's back."

"Everyone?" Marya said quickly.

"Not Serge, Mamma."

"Petya's waiting for your answer and you're waiting for the other one!"

"The other one is married, Mamma."

"Would that stop you, the way you plunge first and think later? You always think somehow it will work out. Things don't always work out."

Cirie turned to Lily who was becoming quite pretty. "The streets are full of deserters. Don't speak to strangers."

"I don't. But sometimes they speak to me."

"I'm sure they do. Don't answer them."

Marya held out a letter and a photograph from Anna. "Anna's expecting another baby. Maria is almost two. Grandma wants them to move in with her so she can look out for them."

Cirie took the letter. Anna wrote, "But Karl won't do that. He feels superior to Grandma and the uncles. I don't know why. Germans have become unpopular here. There's a feeling that soon America will be fighting them."

Poor Anna, who had thought she would be happy just to have her husband there, tired, at the end of the day. But Anna's husband was not tired because he didn't work very often and Cirie suspected that Anna was not so happy, anymore, to have him there. She handed back the letter. "Mamma, are you managing all right? I hear prices are going very high."

Marya groaned. "Eggs, butter, soap—everything. Now they say there will be a famine." But today Marya's mind was not on prices. "It will be different when he gets there, Cirie."

"Mamma, I'm not waiting for him. He has a wife who's waiting for him—anxiously." She opened a drawer to get some sweaters. Mornings there was already a chill in the air.

"I don't understand it. Aren't they worried having you there?"

"They might be worried about their own. Serge or Irene. Not about me. That might have bothered me once. No more."

"Cirie, you must be careful not to be too hard!"

"No, Mamma! I must be careful not to be too soft!"

When she left, a stolid woman in a babushka and ragged sheepskin coat was waiting for her on the street. It took Cirie a minute to recognize her. "Tessa! What are you doing in Kostyka?"

"Popov's brother, Evgeny, is here. He came years ago to work for Madame."

Cirie struggled with the thought that Popov had killed her father and knew it was not literally true.

"Cirie, my little girl, the one with the rash—Popov said maybe you have some ointment. She scratches and cries—"

Tessa took out a small wooden jar, caked with yellow ointment. Images rose up of containers like this one on a shelf and a young vigorous Strengov mixing the ointment on the worn counter. Cirie fought back tears. "Come inside, Tessa. I'll get you some."

Tessa shook her head. "I'll wait out here."

As she took down the sack of medicines from the closet shelf, Cirie saw Marya's mind working. "Don't barter the medicines, Mamma," she warned. "They're valuable. Medicines are scarce."

"Cirie, you should come home until he leaves."

"Mamma, I don't even know that he's coming. I don't think about him anymore."

She didn't think about him anymore. And she told herself she didn't love him anymore and some of the time she believed it.

Vara was taking advantage of Cirie's absence to speak to her mother. "It's just like Serge not to write when he's coming," she said. "Irene is quite put out."

"Irene is put out much of the time, Vara."

"She doesn't enjoy having that girl here."

Maman smiled that practiced tolerant smile. "We've enjoyed Irene's visit, but if she's unhappy she should return to Petrograd."

"And leave her husband alone with that witch! You don't think Serge takes this marriage seriously? Did you see his face at the wedding?"

A cloud crossed her mother's face, as though she regretted this brilliant marriage. She's as dotty as Aunt Vayana, Vara thought—and ripe for that girl to mesmerize! The witch shouldn't be here. Maman could adjust to someone less pleasant. "And now he's with Sacha Borassin who is hardly a good influence," Vara said. The picture of Borassin never entered Vara's mind except as a repellant image with Maman. "But you know more about that than I."

"I imagine Sacha has more important things on his mind."

She never gives herself away. Not even a flicker of alarm lest I've found her out—nothing. "Maman, you must be realistic. Serge is a thoughtless and very immoral man."

When Vara came downstairs, Irene said, "They should discharge her out of regard for my feelings."

"Irene, I told you I'd find a way."

"Every day she has more authority here. I've heard of these devious women, but I didn't expect to find this in my husband's home."

Vara bristled. Is she suggesting we're not good enough for her? You have a short memory, Irene, she muttered to herself. Who floated on air down the aisle and who had to be dragged?

"I'd go home but Serge would come here, anyway."

"Irene, something will happen soon," Vara snapped. "And if it doesn't, I'll make it happen."

*　　　　*　　　　*

By October, when Laranov returned to Petrograd, the cesspool of politics had spit up another bizarre addition to the Camarilla—Protopopov, a practitioner of the occult sciences, especially spiritualism—always a first-class ticket to the Empress. The slippery Sturmer's convict-assistant had been arrested for blackmailing a bank and Sturmer, himself, was saved only by the intercession of the Empress. Once cleared, he got rid of the Interior Minister who, as head of the police, had caused his troubles and came up with Protopopov. Rasputin assured the Empress that Protopopov was a Heaven-sent savior of Russia.

As the result of an incurable disease, Protopopov suffered nervous disorders, talked incessantly, had an unusual glitter to his eyes, and wore an outlandish uniform with high boots and a sword-belt. One more mad-man in the government, Laranov thought. His doctor was the infamous Badmaiev, the quack who dispensed narcotics as Eastern "magic potions." It was Badmaiev who introduced Protopopov to Rasputin, and the friendship between Badmaiev and Rasputin had been formed at the bedside of the Tsarevitch. Things had come full circle.

The city was crawling with rumors about power plays and assassination schemes. On his first day back Laranov heard that Sturmer was plotting the Tsar's assassination or, as an alternative, was planning to force him to abdicate in favor of his son. The Empress would be regent. They could handle her.

At the St. Honoré, the Marie Antoinette chandeliers still sparkled and the tables were full. Watching Laranov down a glass of vodka, Constantine thought that his endless moving about had taken its toll. He had lost weight and had a lean, almost grim, look about him.

"No, I'm not tired," Laranov said. "I've seen too much. The smell of death is in my nostrils. I've seen such enormous piles of bodies. I've seen men go mad from the horrors they've witnessed. I hope I never see anything like it again." Then he shook off the grim mood. "In Petrograd I'm going to love or gamble all night for a week." He drained another glass of vodka. "Petrograd is wild with rumors, Constantine."

"Mostly true."

"Sturmer and his mad ally, Protopopov, are plotting with pro-German interests?"

"That one I believe." In his pocket, Constantine's hand rested on one of his unpublished articles. "I've heard Sturmer is plotting to deliberately cause a famine—to provoke strikes and riots and make it impossible to continue the war."

Laranov looked up from his caviar. "A very dangerous game."

Constantine nodded.

"The Revolutionaries sense that their time is here," Laranov said. "They're meeting. They're planning. The peasants are talking about dividing up the estates. Soldiers are deserting to get home and get their land. This is no time for manufactured problems." Laranov turned back to his caviar. "I've a whole new appreciation of good food after some of the things I've eaten this past year." He smiled the old irreverent smile. "And a lot of days I've gone without."

"Are you saying the threat of famine is real?"

"The threat is from the government." Laranov ate his caviar with relish. "Harvests were good this year. But if the government won't straighten out the distribution mess anything can happen."

"Add it up, Ilya," Constantine said, soberly. "The Council President is a traitor. The Emperor has given up. The Empress is melancholy."

"And we're not supplying our armies or feeding our people."

"Vassily Vodovsky said there's trouble shipping logs. This winter people will be cold as well as hungry." Constantine started to take the article from his pocket and hesitated, asking himself again whether it was right to involve Laranov. "By the way, Cirie was at the Vodovsky's."

Laranov showed his surprise. "The idiot came to his senses?"

"She's there for Eugenie. And Vassily is extremely courteous to her. I must say I applaud Cirie for pulling this off."

"As you say, she casts a spell."

"If you're in the area, stop and see them."

"I would but I won't be near there. I'm looking for winter supplies for the army." The grim look returned. "In a Russian winter, an army is miserable. Men are paralyzed with cold. I've seen hands freeze to the gun barrel so that their skin comes off. The soldiers need so much that we can't give them—food, shoes, gloves—"

Constantine took out the article. "Ilya, you're always in touch with the nether world—"

"In the nether world a lot goes on."

"Do you know an underground publisher?"

"I know a hundred! The police smash their offices and they start up again somewhere else."

"Can you get this published? I hesitate to involve you—"

"Don't worry about me." Laranov scanned the article. "I can do it, but this is a futile gesture, Constantine. The problems are too enormous. There's too much momentum."

"Do you really believe there's still time to equivocate?"

Laranov slipped the papers into his pocket. "There's no time for anything. When it's published, you shouldn't be in Petrograd."

"I've promised to take a trip with Stepa on his train," Constantine said. "Let me know when to go."

A few days later Laranov watched striking workers rioting in front of a factory. Barricades had been set up, telephones poles knocked down, windows broken, and now there were brawls and fires and explosions. The police sent for help and two infantry regiments arrived. Shots sounded in the cold gray afternoon. Then Laranov saw that the infantry soldiers, called to end the riot, were actually siding with the strikers and firing on the police! At last the Cossacks arrived and drove the soldiers back to the barracks and restored order.

Laranov walked on. When it comes, he thought, this is how it will start.

28

❁

On a raw November day Vassily went to his office in town. Snow-flakes drifted out of a slate-colored sky and disappeared before they hit the ground. A government man was coming today to buy grain and Folker, his grain manager, urged him not to sell. "A shortage is developing," he said. "Grain will go sky-high."

"The government is cornering the market to create chaos and end the war," Vassily said.

"I only know a shortage is coming."

"I have no desire to profit from the misery of starving Russians and I'm not interested in selling to traitors," Vassily said.

At a little before noon an explosion racked one of the warehouses. Charred walls collapsed. Fires hissed and crackled in the cold wind. While Vassily viewed the wreckage, the snow turned to rain. The police chief told him that the explosion was probably an ill-directed protest against the grain shortage and warned him not to reenter his office until the building had been searched. Angry, drenched and cold, Vassily went home and found that Stepa and Constantine were back.

By dinner Vassily had developed a heavy cold. The hot soup had no taste. The conversation annoyed him.

"Constantine, you're probably delighted to get away," Kyra said. "It seems a lifetime since I've been abroad. I go to the Crimea and come right home. I used to say God made Russia so big to give us places to go, but it's not the same as Paris."

"I'm making a trip with Stepa on his train," Constantine said.

"Everyone is restless and unhappy, Kyra," Irene said. "Every week in Petrograd we hear about another suicide."

"Suicide is becoming an epidemic," Stepa said. "Especially among the young. College students. Children, even. Prisoners and prostitutes. It's a symptom of the hopelessness at the heart of Russia."

"And the divorce rate is climbing, too," Kyra said. "But that's not a sign of hopelessness. That's hoping for something better." At Vara's chilly stare, she protested, "Everyone is getting divorced, Vara. It's become very common."

Vassily's head throbbed and his eyes filled. He saw that Cirie was watching him. At least someone was concerned.

"The Tsar is close to a nervous breakdown," Constantine said. "He can't eat or sleep. He feels God has abandoned him."

"No longer!" Irene cried. "My aunt wrote that the Emperor saw Badmaiev and is taking Elixir de Thibet. The Empress insisted. Now he's filled with a feeling of well-being—even of optimism."

Vassily's lips were parched. Immediately after dinner Cirie was at his side. "You should go to bed. I'll bring you some medicine."

In his apartment Vassily rang for Simon, his valet, and poured a brandy. Snow was piling up on the window sill. When Cirie came in, he said, "Do you remember what Laranov said about Badmaiev's Elixir de Thibet?"

"It's cocaine."

"Three centuries of Romanov glory ending in a cloud of cocaine."

"I'm going to take your temperature," Cirie said.

As she opened her kit Vara burst into the room. Must she always enter this way? Vassily thought. He waved her away. She confronted Cirie. "What are you doing here?"

"Get out!" Vassily shouted. "I don't want you here."

"What is she doing here? I thought you were going to bed."

"Is that what you came to say? All right, you've said it." Vassily whirled about and knocked over the glass of brandy. "If you had eyes, you'd see she's brought medicines. Now get out. Go downstairs—go flirt with Constantine. Be your usual delightful self. Get some more practice. And Vara—don't carry your complaints to Maman."

Flushed and furious, Vara fled. Cirie bent down to pick up the pieces of broken crystal.

"Leave it," Vassily said. "Simon will clean it up."

"I'm afraid you'll cut yourself." She left the broken glass on a paper. "Take these pills. If you're ill during the night, send for me."

At two o'clock in the morning when Simon awakened Cirie, she found Vassily tossing in bed, drenched and burning with fever. She gave him an alcohol rub and changed the sheets and at four o'clock she sent Gerzy to the hospital for Dr. Legare.

Vara awoke at ten o'clock to learn that a doctor had been summoned. "Why wasn't I told at once?"

"At four o'clock in the morning?" Stepa said.

"Who sent for the doctor?" In Vassily's absence she was always in charge.

"Cirie was with Vassi most of the night. At four o'clock she decided a doctor should be sent for."

"*She* decided! Who is she to decide?"

"Vassi is very ill," Stepa said. "I hope the doctor will get here soon."

"Well, what's keeping him?"

"I presume he's attending to some wounded men. Meanwhile Cirie says Vassi should sleep. She wants us to stay out."

"Of course she does! I have no intention of staying out."

"Don't make trouble, Vara. Cirie says he has pneumonia."

"Another trick." At that moment Cirie appeared in the hall and Vara ordered her into the study. "What are you up to now? What are you doing up there?"

"I'm taking care of a patient, Countess," Cirie said, coldly, "who has developed pneumonia and is burning with fever."

"So—you're a doctor now!"

"Excuse me, Countess." Cirie started to leave.

"I'll excuse you when I'm ready! What are you doing to him?" Cirie continued into the hall. Vara leaped forward so aggressively that Stepa and Constantine moved to Cirie's side. "Don't touch him!" Vara cried.

Cirie turned. "Who is going to touch him if I don't?"

"Come on, Vara, we're all worried." Stepa said. "Don't take it out on Cirie. She's doing all she can."

There were things seen only when there was time to see—the way the snow looked as though it would ride the wind for miles before it touched the ground, the way branches moved like shadows across the window, the way Vassily seemed suddenly vulnerable, small in the wide bed, his black beard flecked with gray, burning with fever and struggling to breathe. Cirie drew a quilt around herself and settled into a chair to spend another night at his bedside.

Between Dr. Legare and Vara there had been an unpleasant scene. At the end of an anxious day, the bells of the sleigh sounded at last. From Dr. Legare's drawn gray look Cirie knew he was exhausted. To Vara, if she noticed, it had no meaning as she berated him for not coming sooner.

"We have dying men, Countess," he muttered and turned to Cirie. "Take me to the patient."

"We might have a dying man here," Vara flung at him.

Madame gasped and Cirie saw Irene's mouth twitch. Sitting apart, Irene affected her usual aloof manner but her mouth betrayed that she was not quite so detached. Cirie looked at Vara's bulging eyes and wide greedy mouth and back to Irene who had brought the telltale twitch under control. She took Dr. Legare upstairs where he confirmed that Vassily had pneumonia.

When he came downstairs again, Vara was waiting. "The instant you get to the hospital, arrange to send us a trained nurse."

Dr. Legare barely looked at her. "You've got a trained nurse."

"She's not really a nurse!" Vara had assumed the doctor would be on her side.

Dr. Legare was already leaving. "She's been in surgery for two years, working on every kind of wound you can imagine."

At the unseemly implication, Vara's hand turned her face away.

"And she ought to be back there," the doctor grumbled. "She's needed. Meanwhile she can give a sick man his medicine and an alcohol rub. If the weather weren't so bad I'd move him into the hospital where we have oxygen. Tonight that's out of the question."

After the doctor left Vara turned on Madame. "Did you hear what he said! She's positively indecent."

"If she were Florence Nightingale I suppose it would be all right!" Stepa shouted and even Constantine forgot his usual tact. "An interesting definition of indecency," he murmured. But Vara, her mind whirling, was too preoccupied to notice.

Now, at Vassily's bedside, Cirie could still see Irene's twitch and Vara's less quickly controlled eyes and greedy mouth. There are things seen when there is time to see and things revealed only in a crisis. They want him to die! Irene because Serge would become head of the family and she would have Vassily's fortune. And Vara because she's greedy and because she hates him. She simply cannot understand that Vassily is taking out his frustration on her. As he used to do with Serge.

And how does he treat Serge now—now that he followed orders and married Irene? Don't waste time wondering because you'll find out any day now. He's overdue. You can tell by the way everybody is getting nervous.

And when he gets here, what then? Will he look the same? Will he still be the champagne at the party? Weeks ago Cirie had decided that she would greet him like the stranger he was now. She would hold out an untrembling hand and say, "How nice to see you, Serge. I hope your wound has healed." Could she do it? Of course she could do it. She would be ice. Nobody can upset you—nobody can touch you—if you won't let them.

Hearing Vassily's labored breathing, Cirie thought about how much he had shielded her since Vara's return and that now, for a while, that protection would be gone. And in this house, except with Vassily, Vara got her way. Like the Empress, she thought, she pours so much maniacal passion into her schemes, no one can stand up to her. Her mind worked around the problem. There'll be a confrontation before the day is over, she told herself, and you'll have to find a way to hold your own. You can't give an inch. You can't woo her and you can't reason with her. Whatever she says, you'll have to face her down.

Then Vassily began to cough and she felt that he was drenched again. He was no better. While she gave him an alcohol rub she thought again about Irene's telltale twitch and Vara's bulging eyes. Out of pure greed they want him to die. Well, we'll see about that! It takes more than greed to kill a patient.

In the morning a brilliant sun glittered on white fields where the marks of a sleigh revealed that someone had either arrived or gone out early. At nine o'clock Vara opened the bedroom door and motioned Cirie into the sitting room. "I'm sending for another nurse. You'll be relieved as soon as she arrives."

"For Vassily or for Madame, Countess?"

"Madame doesn't need a nurse."

She's such a bad seed—would she deliberately send for someone incompetent? "A nurse will have to be approved by Dr. Legare."

"I'm not satisfied with Dr. Legare, either. There'll be a new doctor and a new nurse and you will leave here today. By noon."

What's the rush? Cirie thought. Her mind raced over the problem and found an answer. They've heard from Serge. "Vassily hired me, Countess, and I'll wait for Vassily to discharge me. I won't leave while he's so ill."

Face flushed, Vara leaned her large torso forward. "I want you out of here by noon!"

"I will not go!"

"You'll go!" Vara screamed. "There's no room here for your kind, even as a servant. First you took advantage of a gullible romantic young man, then a half-dotty old woman and now a dying man—"

"Please lower your voice, Countess."

"You dare to speak to me like that!" Vara gasped. "Who do you think you are? Trash! Trying to take over everything! The world is full of women like you who'll do anything to climb out of the filth they were born in. Where are you going?"

Cirie lifted her chin. "I can't be away from my patient any longer." At the bedroom door, she stopped. "Cancel your orders, Countess. Dr. Legare is the best doctor in Kostyka. If you try to replace him I'll tell Vassily the instant he recovers. And he is going to recover—you can be sure of that. He's not going to die."

Back in the bedroom, Cirie's anger erupted. Once she swore revenge and she almost forgot! Well, now she remembered! Vassily thrashed about restlessly and she seized the bottle of alcohol. Then a new thought broke through her anger. Vara was sure to carry her complaints to Madame, wake her if necessary, and before she was through there would be two patients in bed. As Cirie reached Madame's apartment she heard Vara shouting and Madame urging her to calm down.

"When she's out of my house—when I've seen her for the last time—that's when I'll calm down."

"Vara, I want you to be reasonable—"

"Reasonable! You're not reasonable, anymore. You're half-dotty—you're senile—"

"Oh, Vara!"

Cirie hurried into the room. Madame had not even summoned her maid yet. Vara had awakened her.

"Get out of here!" Vara screamed at Cirie.

"Madame shouldn't be upset, Countess," Cirie said.

"Out of this room and out of this house!"

Madame motioned to Cirie not to reply. "How is Vassily this morning, Cirie?"

"His temperature is still high but he's no worse."

"All right, you've given your report," Vara interrupted. "Get ready to leave."

"Wait in the hall, Cirie," Madame said. "We'll discuss this calmly, Vara, without saying things we'll regret."

Madame was herself again, serene and dignified. Vara was not. "I'm sending for another nurse and I want this trash out of this house. I'm not asking you, Maman. I'm telling you. I've discharged her."

"No, Vara," Madame said, firmly. "She'll stay with Vassi until he's recovered. Then she'll come back to me."

"And Serge? Is she to take care of him, too? Because he's not deliriously happy in this marriage?" Vara's voice was shrill. "It would be different if Sacha Borassin were so mad for her!"

"Vara, these veiled suggestions are unseemly."

"Don't think you fooled me all these years. I've known about you a long time—and why you always favored Serge. Sacha Borassin was your lover and Serge is his son—a bastard! And just as immoral. He's not a Vodovsky—"

"Oh, Vara!" Madame gasped.

"I've known for years!"

Cirie started toward the room. She couldn't allow this to continue.

"Vara, I've seen your mind take strange turns but never like this," Madame said, sadly. "I'm going into my bedroom. I don't want to see you again today."

Waiting in the hall, Cirie knew this wasn't the end of it. For two years Vara has been hinting at this, she thought, and she won't rest until Madame admits it or collapses. Vara can't possibly be sure. But if by some wild chance it's true, why did she decide on Serge? It could be any of them. Even Vara.

Even Vara.

Vara came out of the room. "What! Are you still here?"

Why not Vara? Cirie met her eyes. "Vara, don't you realize—"

"What? Realize what? What are you trying to say?"

"Vara, it was you!"

"It was me what? What are you talking about?"

"If there was such a child—" Cirie pinned her with her eyes. "If it's anyone—it's you!"

Vara stared. She had not quite grasped the implication. "Go downstairs and out the door. We'll deliver your possessions to you."

Still Cirie held her with her eyes. "You're the one like General Borassin—" she whispered. "Big bones—great height! The others have slender bones. You're the one—"

Suddenly Vara understood. "*You tart!*" Her color was ashen—the color of the dead. Her whole body sagged. "Whore! Filthy thoughts…Not fit to live with decent people…Trying to take over everything—" Gasping half-sentences, Vara straightened to her full height and then, as though suddenly conscious of it, she sagged again. "You're a whore! Everyone knows what you are." Babbling, she pushed past Cirie. "A common whore! Go back where you came from. You don't belong with decent people. You taint them with your presence!"

Back with Vassily, Cirie snatched up the bottle of alcohol and with a vengeance started a rub. Once she had vowed that nobody was going to talk to her that way ever again—nobody was going to claim to be too good for her or her family. Well, this time she wouldn't forget. Strengov had said that revenge was a useless emotion. "You'll destroy yourself and you won't touch them," he had said. "That's a mountain you can't climb." And she had said, "I can wait." Well, she'd show Vara who was not good enough. She had no idea what she would do but she intended to think of something.

Vassily opened his eyes and she gave him a ravishing smile. His eyes sought hers and she said, softly, "It's all right. You're going to be all right." He closed his eyes again and she continued the alcohol rub on his chest and stomach, gentler now that she knew he was conscious. Then she put down the bottle of alcohol and turned back and stifled a gasp. Under the sheet Vassily had an erection!

Hastily she drew the blanket over the sheet. His eyes were closed. His hands lay limp on the sheet. Cirie had seen this reaction in patients before and Strengov had explained that it could be personal or involuntary—sometimes the patients were not even conscious. But she had not expected it here. Not Vassily!

So he's human, after all, she thought. He's human and he's a man. She sat perfectly still on the edge of the bed. A mountain I can't climb, indeed!

A few minutes later she heard someone in the sitting room and she hurried to the door. If Vara was back, she didn't want a scene at Vassily's bedside.

And there was Serge. Serge in his uniform. Serge with his wonderful good looks, his carved features, his blond hair, his clear bright eyes. Serge unchanged—looking at her, smiling at her.

"Cirie—" he said, softly. His eyes told her that he had missed her and wanted her more than ever. "Oh, Cirie—" He moved to take her in his arms. They were alone. It seemed only natural.

Her hands went out to him. This was Serge—not a portrait on a wall, not a fading memory—this was Serge, alive, warm, smiling, exactly as she remembered him. Then her hands stopped and with a great effort she drew back.

"Darling, I just arrived and learned you were here! Nobody wrote me—I came right up—"

"Serge, you should come in and see Vassily. You can only stay a minute but he'll be happy to see you."

In the bedroom Serge stared at Vassily, shocked. Weakly, Vassily held out a hand and for a moment Serge stood paralyzed before he forced himself to touch it. Then he backed off. His eyes shifted away. It was as though he couldn't believe this was Vassily, as though his mind couldn't grasp that Vassily could be so weak and frail, that Vassily who had always managed everything was almost helpless, struggling to breathe. Then slowly a different look came over him. Shock was replaced by resentment.

"That's enough, Serge," Cirie said. "Come back tomorrow when Vassily feels better." In the sitting room she said, "You shouldn't have avoided looking at him, Serge. He noticed."

"I don't like to look at dying people."

"He's not dying. He's going to recover and be just as he was before. So when you go in again, speak to him."

He reached for her again, in the way she knew so well, and all the old feelings of loving and of belonging together surged up out of the past and she thought that if she didn't belong in Serge's arms, she didn't belong anywhere. But any minute someone would come in here. "Serge, you're married now."

"But I don't want to be married!"

"Go downstairs, Serge. You can't stay here."

"I never wanted to marry her. I was wounded. I didn't have the strength to argue. I hardly knew what was happening."

"It happened," Cirie said, flatly.

"Didn't you get my letter? I wrote you that there could never be anyone for me but you."

What did he think that could mean after he'd married someone else? And yet he looked so miserable it was all she could do not to tell him they would find a way, they would work it out.

Suddenly Serge threw an angry look at Vassily's door. "He's just like any other man!" he said with contempt. "He always had to be in control. He made himself into a God. Do you know I never saw him in his bedroom—I never saw him undressed—not once in all these years. He's just a frail little man—getting older. He's not a rock—he's not iron—he's not a Tsar—he's a man!"

"No, Serge, for you he's not like any other man because you're dependent on him."

"He took my life!"

"No, even without Vassily, you wouldn't have had the courage."

"I would! Cirie—"

Suddenly Cirie understood what she had not seen before. She had always thought that Serge felt as she did—that he must want to live life to the hilt, to be free, to have new adventures. Now she realized that he did not. He needed Vassily. To be free to live his own life was not what he wanted at all.

"Cirie, I love you so. What can I do? How can I—"

"Serge!" The door flew open and Irene burst into the room—Irene, awakened and told her husband was home and with the woman he loved. "Serge!" she screamed. Then she collected herself and moved gracefully to kiss him. With dull eyes Serge accepted the kiss and barely returned it. Cirie went into the bedroom and closed the door.

She was thankful that Vassily was asleep. For a long time she sat in the chair, overwhelmed by a sense of final loss. All those years she had let herself believe that Serge wanted to be free of Vassily. Now she saw that Vassily was his rock and his strength. Vassily had made all things possible—life, luxury, play. The only freedom Serge had wanted was to romp in green fields as long as fortress Vassily was there behind him. He had never wanted to stray any farther than he could step back. And a moment ago when he had thought that the fortress might vanish, he had been paralyzed with fright. He still loved her—but if he were to lose Vassily he would miss him more than he would ever miss her. And she would never be in his arms again.

The next day Vassily's temperature broke and Serge kissed his mother goodbye and left for Petrograd with his wife.

For a week Cirie poured all her charm, all her wit and passion and indefinable magic into captivating him until Vassily, whose life had always been so orderly, so planned and correct, was left literally helpless to determine his fate. He was like an adolescent. When she left his bedside he missed her and when she returned he felt a soaring exhilaration that was totally foreign to him. Unaccustomed to these emotions, Vassily delayed his reentry into the household while he tried to think clearly. But his efforts always ended in one overwhelming obsession—he had to have her.

He told himself that he had saved her from Serge, that she was too much for Serge, too amusing, too beautiful, too rich a prize. She was a prize for him. He couldn't imagine life without her.

At last all the flickering arguments against it died before this strange unfamiliar heat and at the end of a week, Vassily begged her to marry him.

29

Moscow. Golden city of the East. City of churches, city of commerce, city of gardens and parks. Ancient city of gilded spires and onion-shaped domes and golden crosses against a brilliant blue sky.

Gaudy city of contrasts. Broad boulevards and crooked little streets and alleys. Palaces of stone and brick and wooden houses painted every color you could imagine. Fabulous shops with fashions and perfumes and jewels. And crude markets for poultry, eggs, flowers, dogs, fish, sausages, and street vendors and peddlers. Clean shaven merchants in European dress and bearded moujiks in traditional Russian dress and all the peoples of the Empire in their native dress and coachmen who raced their horses and shouted and sang old Russian songs. And dominating the sprawling city, the ancient Kremlin, a city within a city, of palaces and churches and monasteries and cathedrals with gold and silver domes gleaming in the sunlight.

Vassily was intoxicated with her. She had stood beside him in the little church on the estate, in a magnificent wedding gown that he had ordered from Moscow and there were candles and icons and the young priest. And Madame, smiling, and Kyra and Otto and Stepa and Constantine. And Marya and Lily, awed by the splendor much as Cirie had been that first day at Whitewater. Except that Lily looked self-conscious and miserable and Marya was already worried about whether this could work, while Cirie that day had had no doubts. Vara had remained in Moscow with severe headaches and Irene in Petrograd because she was pregnant and considered herself an invalid. Serge stayed at Headquarters with General Borassin. Cirie had stood in a daze, the words running through her brain, "This is Vassily, not Serge! Not Serge—Vassily. Vassily! How did this happen? What has fate done to me? Not fate! *You.* Your fate is yourself! And Vassily—not Serge— is your husband and tonight not Serge—not Serge—but Vassily will be your lover."

On Vassily's arm, she walked through the huge mirrored marble-floored reception hall filled with flowers, and down the wide hall lighted with hundreds of candles and into the formal drawing room with crystal chandeliers and gold sconces and brocade hangings and Renaissance paintings, and flowers everywhere. Once at Whitewater Serge had said, carelessly, "Some day this will all be yours." Today Vassily extended an arm and said, "Now you are mistress here."

In Moscow Vassily bought her gowns and furs—sables and blue fox—and adorned her throat and her hair and her gowns with jewels—pearls, sapphires, a diamond and emerald brooch.

They went to the ornate Bolshoi Theatre where the people in the audience lost themselves in the magic of the ballet, their melancholy problems of war and unrest forgotten. They dined at the Yar and at the Strelna amidst tropical palms and waterfalls, and drank champagne with slivers of ice while gypsies played and snow fell outside.

Vassily took her to museums of ancient Russian and Renaissance art and Stepa came home to Moscow and escorted them to the brilliant private collections of the Moscow millionaires that included hundreds of French Impressionist paintings—Monet, Renoir, Cezanne, Degas, Matisse, Picasso—and daring works of the Russian avant garde painters—Malevich, Oarianov, Goncharova, Kandinsky, Chagall.

At dinner Stepa discussed the latest news. Sturmer was out and the new Council President, Trepov, had been double-crossed by the Tsar. "Trepov accepted on condition that Protopopov would go. But the Empress was furious about Sturmer's dismissal and insisted that she must have Protopopov. So the Tsar went back on his word. Trepov tried to resign but the Tsar said, 'You'll stay and you'll govern with the people I give you to assist you.'"

Great cries arose in the Duma demanding that the Empress should be put away as a lunatic. "Russia is being ruled by the occult!...A recommendation from Rasputin raises the lowest creatures to the highest office...Tell the Emperor this crisis cannot go on...Tell him Revolution threatens...Tell him that an obscure moujik shall govern Russia no longer."

That night at dinner Stepa said, "Every day you hear that the Tsar can no longer govern—that he should abdicate in favor of the Tsarevitch with one of the Grand Dukes as regent. Even members of the Imperial family are saying it. Also that he should remember the fate of Paul I."

"Assassination from inside the Palace!" Vassily said.

Stepa nodded soberly. "At the start of the war, all Russia rallied behind him. Then first he lost the Left, then the Center and then the extreme Right."

"And now even the members of his family?" Vassily said.

"I understand he's in terrible condition," Stepa said. "A faraway look—long silences. He's resigned himself to the disaster he knows is coming and he's ready to be the sacrificial lamb. They say he knows the dreams he had for Russia, whatever he imagines they were, can never be realized."

          *   *   *

Petrograd. St. Petersburg. Golden city of the North. City of water. Venice of the North. The Neva River, three-quarters of a mile wide, canals, lakes, the Gulf of Finland—all frozen now. City of ice with short days and heavy snows and fog. City of Government. The Winter Palace. Government buildings. Bureaucrats. Wide straight boulevards and islands and parks. Golden spires and domes and crosses.

Wrapped in a fur robe, in a sleigh behind a shouting sheepskin-wrapped driver, Cirie saw the great palaces built by former rulers—Peter the Great, Elizabeth, Catherine the Great—the Winter Palace, turquoise with white columns, more than a thousand rooms, and the Tauride Palace, given by Catherine the Great to Potemkin, once her lover and for years her closest advisor. And the palace of Kchessinka, the ballerina, the Tsar's mistress while he was still Tsarevitch and later courted by two Grand Dukes, and the Fortress of St. Peter and St. Paul, sometimes called the Romanov Bastille. Vassily bought her masses of pearls and sapphire earrings to match her eyes and rare black pearl earrings set in diamonds as a tribute to her heavy black lashes.

They dined with Constantine at the Restaurant Contant where, at a nearby table, the extravagantly chic Countess Danoy sat smoking and drinking champagne with two army captains. As she was leaving she spoke to Constantine and after she moved on he said, "Now she'll play all night—theatre, ballet, parties with gypsy music and dancing. She has divorced twice and now she plays until dawn. And yet she's warm-hearted and courageous and a great patriot." Cirie was not so much interested in her warm heart. She had watched her easy sophistication and her confident gaiety and the way her escorts were her slaves.

When they had been in Petrograd a week Serge came home just in time for a ball at the palace of Prince Evgenoff, where people seemed to forget their anxiety even more than at the ballet. Cirie wore a black velvet gown made for her in Moscow and her black pearl and diamond earrings and the blue fox wrap, and Constantine and General Borassin, home for a week, treated her like a Grand Duchess. She danced the first dance with a count and the second with Prince Evgenoff and the third with a Grand Duke while Vassily watched, torn between jealousy and pride that this beautiful creature, whom everyone found so enchanting, was his. She danced the fourth dance with Serge.

"Are you happy?" Serge scowled as he led her away from Vassily and Irene.

She had dreaded this encounter. "Yes, Serge, I'm happy."

"Cirie, how could you do it?"

"Serge, this isn't the place—"

"You don't love him! You love me!"

"Serge, people will hear you."

"Can you forget?" he demanded. "Can you forget those days we had together?"

Oh, Serge, she thought, how can I forget? The smallest crack in her control and she would be weeping in his arms. "Didn't you forget, Serge?"

"Never! Not for a minute. I think of them every day of my life. They're part of me."

And they're part of me, Cirie thought—and I intend to forget them. "Vassi is very good to me—and very loving."

"Vassi!"

"He loves me."

"Wait until he decides you're his property," Serge said, bitterly. "Wait until he starts to own your life—every minute, every move—you won't find him so loving. Have you forgotten how he can be?"

No, she had not forgotten, but she had made up her mind that he would not upset her. She would agree that he was right and do as she pleased. How could he upset her if she refused to be upset?

Serge lapsed into a sullen silence. Then, abruptly, he said, "He's watching. I can't be close to you and hold you while he's watching." As they danced back to Vassily, Serge said, "I can never come to Rivercliff again. I can't think of you in his arms. I can't think of him sharing the bed that should be mine."

"Serge, it was all a long time ago."

"You have forgotten!"

"Yes," she said. "I've forgotten."

On the way home, for all his pride, Vassily could not resist reproving her. "You should not have made yourself so available."

"But darling, these are your friends!"

"I would have expected you to decline occasionally."

"Darling, if you had told me, I would have declined as many dances as you wished!"

Vassily smiled. "Perhaps just once or twice."

Cirie leaned her head on his shoulder. "Darling, I felt that their attention was respect for you. I knew you would want me to accept it that way."

Vassily felt better.

Cirie had half expected to see Laranov at the ball and the next day at lunch with Constantine, she inquired about him.

"I've been wondering where he is, myself," Constantine said. "I haven't seen him for a while."

"He hasn't been wounded?" Cirie said. "Or taken prisoner?"

"I don't worry about Ilya," Constantine said. "He has an uncanny instinct for keeping himself in one piece—physically and politically. He has friends everywhere. He always knows what's going on." Then, seeing Vassily's annoyance, he changed the subject.

"I don't want my wife inquiring about strange men," Vassily said when they were alone.

"But darling, I only asked if he had survived. I'm sure Maman would inquire about someone who had once saved her life."

"I think you make too much of the incident." Vassily's temper flared. "Cirie, why do you argue with me? I have more experience and you have a lot to learn. When you're uncertain you should consult me."

Cirie bit back a retort. She wasn't uncertain about anything, least of all that already Vassi felt that he owned her, as he had owned Serge and Georgii and his estates and his factories, and that he was very jealous of his property.

Petrograd. Where, during the early hours of December 30th, 1916, Rasputin was murdered.

The names of the murderers were quickly known. Prince Yussupov, twenty-nine, heir to the largest fortune in Russia, married to a niece of the Tsar, slender, somewhat effeminate, frivolous—but cool enough during those early morning hours, in a cellar room of his palace, to converse calmly with Rasputin while he fed him three cream cakes and three glasses of Marsala, each one laced with enough cyanide to more than kill an average man, and then shoot him twice when the poison did not finish him off, while upstairs his accomplices played over and over an old record of Yankee Doodle; Grand Duke Dmitri, twenty-six, son of the Grand Duke Paul and grandson of Alexander II, man about town, a fervent and courageous patriot; Purishkevitch, the ultra-reactionary leader of the extreme Right, who fired the final two shots.

On the street when people heard the news, they cheered and kissed each other and went to the Cathedral of Our Lady of Kazan to light candles. They spoke of nothing but the murder. Wild rumors spread. One claimed that three society women had been present, a second that the woman present was one of the Tsar's daughters, disguised as a lieutenant, to take revenge against Rasputin for having attempted a sexual attack on her. A third rumor embellished the second—that to satisfy the Grand Duchess's desire for revenge, Rasputin was castrated before her eyes.

The body, disposed of in the river through a hole in the ice, was not found for three days and discovered then only because one of the staretz's overshoes had fallen off and remained on top of the ice.

The Empress wept and covered the corpse with icons and flowers and saved Rasputin's blood-stained white blouse as a holy relic on which, she believed, depended the future of the dynasty and of Russia. Rasputin was buried in the Imperial park at Tsarskoie Selo.

The deterioration of the government continued. In icy weather food lines grew longer and a spirit of rebellion increased. Protopopov consulted nightly with the ghost of Rasputin.

The British ambassador told the Emperor of his government's concern about German agents, especially Protopopov, in the inner circle of the Empress. The Emperor refused to listen. "I take advice from no one in choosing my ministers," he said. The British ambassador also expressed concern over the people's growing lack of confidence in the Emperor. The Emperor responded coldly, "You tell me that I must deserve the confidence of my people. Isn't it rather for my people to deserve *my* confidence?"

The members of the Imperial family sent the Emperor a joint letter, warning him that his policies were exposing Russia and the dynasty to extreme danger. He replied with apathy and indifference, saying that he allowed no one to give him advice. Infallible to the end, which was very close.

"The crisis is already here," Constantine said as Cirie and Vassily prepared to leave Petrograd. "He has known it and has been resigned to it for a long time."

"Will you try to keep us informed?" Vassily said.

"We're in for a bad time. I'll write and hope the letters will reach you," Constantine said.

By the time they left Petrograd Cirie had observed and listened and learned a great deal about the elegant women of the capital with their poise and their daring chic and their self-assured flirtations.

And by the time they left Petrograd she was pregnant.

In Kostyka, the moujiks felt differently about the murder of Rasputin. "Grishka was one of us—a moujik," they said. "At the palace he spoke for the people. The enemies of the people killed him. It's an omen." The often-repeated prophecy that Rasputin had made to the Emperor and the Empress had reached their ears. "If I die or if you turn your backs on me you will lose your son and your crown within six months." The moujiks took it seriously.

A little more than a month later, in March,1917, Cirie and Vassily turned into Elizabeth Street and beheld an amazing sight. The street was thronged with moujiks dancing, cheering, kissing each other, many of them drunk, many dressed in gaudy outlandish costumes, some cavorting in costumes for two—costumes of horses, donkeys, pigs, bears, elephants, with a man at the head and a man at the hind. At first Cirie thought the war must be over. While they stood there, a bear wrestled on the snow with an elephant and then the men scrambled to their feet and began to dance to the music of an impromptu band of horns and balalaikas. In front of the band, waving his arms and shouting for the musicians to play louder, was Popov.

A pair stuffed into a donkey costume ran past, clumsily chasing a pig. Then the fore part of the donkey recognized Vassily and the pair waddled back. When the donkey stood squarely in front of Cirie and Vassily, the fore part reared up and shouted, very close to Vassily's face, "We've gotten rid of your Nicholas! Your Nicholashka!"

The Revolution had begun.

BOOK TWO

REVOLUTION

1917–1926

"The day shall come when one prodigious ruin shall swallow all."
—Homer. The Iliad.

30

The Revolution was here and nobody was ready, not even the leaders who had worked for it and fought for it and gone to prison and to Siberia and into exile for it. Lenin was in Switzerland, still planning it. Trotsky was in Brooklyn, New York, editing a Russian newspaper. Even the liberals in the Duma were taken by surprise and then terrified at the speed and violence of the eruption.

On Thursday, March 1st, bread rationing began in Petrograd. Leaving his apartment early that morning, Constantine stopped a moment at the door to speak to Feodor, the superintendent. "A cold morning for lines," he said.

"Forty-three below," Feodor said.

On the street, Constantine passed long lines of women who had waited all through the freezing night to buy a few ounces of bread. The weather was as cold as he could remember, so cold the railway system was paralyzed. Engines froze and broke and there was a shortage of replacement parts because of strikes. Heavy snows blocked the tracks and there was a shortage of labor to clear them.

"The bread shortage is worse and there's a wood shortage," Feodor said that evening.

Shortages everywhere, shortages of everything, Constantine thought. A warning of the trouble to come.

On Thursday, March 8th, International Women's Day, a week after bread-rationing began, masses of women, joined quickly by men, poured into the streets to protest—ninety-thousand hungry citizens. They shouted, "Give us bread!" and "Down with autocracy!" They sang the Marseillaise.

The next day, Friday, the number of protesters doubled. Bakeries were looted. Workers went out in a general strike. Barricades sprang up. Cossacks arrived to restore order but their sympathies were with the protesters and they merely walked their horses through the crowd. The madman, Protopopov, conferred with the ghost of Rasputin.

On Saturday, red flags appeared, proclaiming:

"DOWN WITH THE GOVERNMENT!"
"DOWN WITH PROTOPOPOV!"
"DOWN WITH THE WAR!"

On Sunday, day four, the protests flamed into Revolution. The Government ordered the police to shoot to maintain order. Disorder escalated. The infantry was sent but the soldiers, mostly peasant and worker conscripts, held their fire. That night the Volhynian Regiment killed their officers and went over to the Revolution and drove wildly around the city, calling on other soldiers to follow.

On Monday, March 12th, the fires began. All the hated symbols of Romanov law went up in flames—the Courts, the Arsenal, Protopopov's Ministry of the Interior, the Headquarters of the Military Government and of the detested Okhrana. Police stations were wrecked and weapons seized. Prison doors were flung open and all prisoners released—Revolutionary leaders and common criminals alike. The Winter Palace was occupied.

Telegrams went out to the Emperor, warning him that Petrograd was in a state of revolution and his throne threatened. His reply: "I command you to restore order."

Drunken soldiers with machine guns raced around the city in armored cars, murdering officers and the police. The palace of Kchessinka, the ballerina, was occupied—Kchessinka, the former lover of the Tsar and still showered with Imperial favors—a symbol of Romanov power.

It had started as a spontaneous eruption. Now leaders took over, turned loose when the jails were emptied—former factory organizers and street fighters, who knew the importance of nerve centers and ordered the telegraph and railways seized.

Frantically the Duma rushed through reforms, trying to save the government. The Soviet, representing workers and soldiers—the real power, if there was one—set up headquarters at the Finland Station. The mutinous army troops seized the Fortress of SS Peter and Paul and concentrated on anarchy.

On Wednesday, March 14th, there was a test of power between the Soviet and the Duma. The Soviet won. It forced the Duma to issue Prikaz #1—an Order of the Day for the army. Each regiment was ordered to elect a Committee which would seize all armaments—arms, machine guns and armored cars—and make all military decisions. All rank was abolished and any differences of opinion between soldiers and former officers would be settled by the Committee.

In a corridor of the Tauride Palace where the Duma met, Constantine read the order, surrounded by a shouting mob. Was it possible that anyone believed this could work in the army? In the middle of a war? No officers, all military decisions made by an untrained, unschooled, uninformed committee of peasants and workers? With Prikaz #1, for Russia the war was over.

That same day, March 14th, the Tsar attempted to return to the capitol. His train was stopped by workers who had seized control of the railways. Re-routed, it was stopped again. It came to a final halt at the military headquarters at Pskov. A delegation from the Duma arrived and met with the Tsar in his railway car.

The next day, March 15th—two weeks after the start of bread rationing, one week after the protest marches began—Nicholas abdicated in favor of his brother, Grand Duke Michael, who was persuaded by a delegation from the Duma to refuse the crown. For the first time since Ivan the Terrible came to power in 1547, Russia was without a Tsar.

And without a Government.

*   *   *

The moujiks were at the gate again. Every day they gathered there like a flock of crows, going through the motions of dividing up the Vodovsky lands. They would point to a wheat field or a section of forest, laying their claims. They would discuss their selections, they would nod their heads. It was settled. They were owners. Then the next day they would go through the whole procedure again.

The daily pantomime was driving Vara crazy. When they first turned up she ordered them to leave. The crows refused to be shooed away and the next day they were back. And the next.

"We have to get rid of them!" Vara confronted Madame, speaking so sharply that Lupa, Serge's wolfhound, moved away. "Well, don't you care?"

Madame was too worried to care. Since the Revolution there had been no word from Georgii in Petrograd nor from Serge at the front. Nor from anyone else—Kyra or Stepa or Theo. "We don't even know where they are," Madame said, tearfully.

Terrifying rumors reached Kostyka of riots in Petrograd, elite schools shut down, government officials arrested, people shot on the streets. "If the school is closed, how is Georgii surviving?" Madame said. "Why hasn't he wired us?"

"Wires don't seem to be delivered, Maman," Cirie said.

"But how is he existing?"

"Georgii is resourceful, Maman."

Vara was too preoccupied with the peasants to listen.

Madame tried to push away her worst fears. "Why would anyone harm Georgii? What could he do?"

The police everywhere had been overthrown. The Provisional Government in Petersburg was only a figurehead and all power lay with the local Committees— thousands of little local authorities, "the powers on the spot," in villages, towns, and districts, each doing exactly as it pleased on its own spot.

"Is Serge still at the front?" Madame continued to agonize aloud. Rumors from the front brought horror stories about the collapse of the army and officers tortured and murdered with a drunken exuberance. Too late the Soviet had agreed that Prikaz #1 should not apply at the front. It applied—it applied. "If I heard that Serge had been tortured, it would be more than I could bear." Cirie, pregnant with Vassily's child, felt sick at the image of Serge dead, mutilated, his golden hair soaked with blood, his smile frozen forever.

No, Madame did not care about the moujiks at the gate. But to Vara they were a magnet. "I'm ordering them to leave!"

"Don't do it, Vara!" Cirie looked up quickly. "There are no police. Who will you turn to if things get out of hand?"

"They don't worry me!"

"Vara, all they ever cared about was getting their own little piece of land. Now they've been told the miracle is about to happen." In their dreams they were riding to glory.

"I'm not surprised that you understand them so well!"

"They're simple moujiks. They've been told it's theirs now—not ours."

"It was never yours!"

Cirie saw Vassily, of all the most altered, pacing in the hall. Most people, even conservatives, had greeted the Revolution almost with relief. When elderly Prince and Princess Krastov and young Count and Countess Rostovich visited from neighboring estates one weekend, Cirie had been surprised to hear that even they believed it was necessary and might work out.

"A revolution in the middle of a war will not work out," Vassily had told them. "It's like major surgery on a patient already bleeding to death. Changes require careful planning."

Vassily had always turned to business as another man might turn to cards or chess or tennis. Efficiency had been his refuge and his relaxation. Solving a problem gave him confidence in the order of things. But today Russia was reveling in chaos. Vassily's ship was set adrift. He withdrew into himself, speaking only to take out his frustration on the only available targets—Vara and Cirie. Tyranny over his family was the only power left to him. With Cirie he was domineering and suspicious. When she visited her mother, he would imagine that she had seen other men and on her return he would confront her with questions and accusations and fresh orders. He slept alone. She had hardly known him when she married him and she hardly knew him now.

"I'm about to order those vultures to leave," Vara said when Vassily came into the room. "Although they have the sympathy of your wife who, of course, understands them better than I."

"So far they're only looking and pointing," Cirie said. "We shouldn't look for trouble. Their hatred is old and deep."

"Hatred! What hatred? We were always good to them!"

How could he understand the hatred of the poor for the rich? Or imagine the things said on long winter nights in crowded huts? "They're easily aroused, Vassi. For years they've believed the land was rightfully theirs because they worked it."

"Well, I intend to straighten them out!" Vara cried.

"Stay where you are!" Vassily exploded. He cleared his throat and turned to Cirie. "Spare me your advice. You don't know as much as you think. Just because you were one of them."

"I'm trying to explain them to help you protect yourself."

"Don't explain them. They're not worth understanding. Don't help me. Just keep quiet. Don't speak unless I tell you to."

"As you wish, darling." What did it matter? She didn't care whether she spoke to him or not.

"And don't speak to those people again—ever."

"Vassi, we should try to get along."

"Do as I say. Don't go out to take care of them. Or their children. I don't want my son around a lot of children sick with God knows what disease."

Cirie shuddered. Every day Vassily issued new orders in the name of his unborn son. What if the baby was a girl?

Vassily turned on Vara again. "As for you, with these people you maintain your dignity. Now dignity may come hard to you but you are not to stoop to their level. Can you understand that?"

He looked at the moujiks who were pointing at his fields, pointing at his forests. "We'll fight for what's ours!"

"Darling, don't let them hear you say that." He didn't look ready to fight. He looked old and burdened and worried.

"This land has been ours for three hundred years!"

"I know, darling."

Suddenly Cirie saw Vara outside, striding toward the gate. She knew the exact moment she ordered them off. Vara pointed and shooed. The moujiks laughed and jeered. Someone threw a stone. Then they spat at her! Vara fled. She stumbled and fell. The moujiks hooted and applauded. How can I still feel sorry for her? Cirie thought. A moment later, hysterical, Vara flung herself into the house and collapsed. The peasants resumed their pantomime, crows at the gate, riding to glory.

*   *   *

As Stepa's Red Cross train approached a station, he could see a mob of soldiers storming the train ahead, throwing off passengers to take their places. The effect of Prikaz #1 had spread across Russia like a bloody stain.

"Deserters," Stepa said to the engineer. More than a million deserters were roaming around the country, going home or to Petrograd or Moscow to see what was happening. They commandeered trains in transit. At overcrowded stations, they threw off all the passengers and forced the station master at gunpoint to switch the train to wherever they wanted to go. Meanwhile the ousted passengers were stranded, left to wait for days, sleeping on the floor, filing up and down in roped-off lines, to get permission to buy a ticket, permission to board the next train or the one after that. Or sometime. All his life Stepa had believed in the essential goodness of people. Now he recognized that something was happening to obliterate that humanity.

Stepa's train came to a halt a hundred yards before the station and he opened the door for a better view. Watching the soldiers storming the train ahead, he decided he had better wake up Laranov who had turned up at a field hospital, bleary-eyed from lack of sleep like most officers these days, and asked for a lift as far as Stepa was going. He had been in the south and was trying to get back to Petrograd. Stepa was taking his wounded men to Moscow and then he was going to Petrograd to pick up Tanya.

Anxiously Stepa saw that twice too many soldiers were pushing into the train ahead. Soldiers appeared on the roof of a car. If the first train would roll he could race past this mob, but the other train did not move. Another wave of shouting deserters rushed around the side of the station and spotted the Red Cross train. Stepa told the engineer to get Laranov.

Minutes later, ten filthy rag-tag deserters with rifles announced themselves to Stepa as "the Committee of the soldiers who are taking over this train."

"This is a Red Cross train!" Stepa protested. What were the rest of them doing? Disturbing the patients? He thought of the nurses.

The spokesman's slicked-down black hair contrasted with the rest of his appearance. The bottom of his coat was torn away, his boots and ragged pants were muddy, his hands were dirty and had crusted blood under the fingernails. His own or somebody else's? "Show us the officers," he ordered. "We'll throw them off first."

"We have no officers."

"We'll leave them on the station floor," a thick-set man with warts on his chin said. "One less officer on a shelf will make room for four of us." He started toward the door.

"Don't touch them!" Stepa shouted. He searched the faces for an eye that showed some humanity. There was none. He could feel his gun in his pocket but they were armed, too. "These are your wounded brothers!" he said. Behind him the door opened. He was relieved to see that Laranov had brought his gun.

"No officers?" the leader sneered.

"This is an assistant."

"We'll kill the officers and throw them off."

"That way they won't suffer." The heavy man with the warts laughed. Dirty toes showed through his boots.

"The Committee will decide what to do with the officers and the train," the leader said.

"No committees here," Laranov said.

"Hand over that gun. We're taking this train."

"You are taking nothing!" Laranov raised his pistol. The man's hand inched along his rifle.

"Now why not take a ride—deliver these wounded men to a hospital first?" Laranov's voice became persuasive. "What's your hurry? You'll just get to someplace where you'll be recruited again and sent back to that miserable front."

While the man fingered a wart and thought about that, in one swift motion Laranov seized his rifle.

"Jackass! Fuckin' bastard!" The leader spat at his comrade. He jerked around to face Stepa. "In the name of the people we're taking your train. We'll tell you where you're going, Comrade Conductor."

"This train will deliver these men to Moscow." Stepa's hand closed over his gun. "Then you can arrange what you like."

Suddenly the man with the warts, smarting at the loss of his rifle, seized a comrade's gun and fired and Stepa and Laranov fired and the man jerked and crumpled at their feet.

In the next second Stepa realized that he was waiting to be shot, himself, but the men only stared at the pool of blood forming around their fallen comrade and at his toes sticking grotesquely through his boots. The train ahead lurched forward. If they were going to switch this train, the soldiers had to act now. The leader threw a quick look at the window. Laranov raised his pistol in one hand, the rifle in the other.

"Moscow is four days away," the leader sneered. "You can't hold a gun on us for four days."

"We can do it for a month," Laranov said.

The Red Cross train jerked and began to move. The leader ran a hand over his slicked-down hair. Then he looked away.

Saddened, Stepa sat in his car with Laranov. "I've known these moujiks my whole life," he said. "What has happened to them?"

"The war turned them into killers and the Revolution has removed all restraints," Laranov said.

"In that whole gang there wasn't one man who would stand up for the wounded and dying who had fought beside him."

"They march together. If one gets out of step, they'll kill him."

Stepa felt terribly depressed. "If this is what the Revolution has done, who will control them?"

"Another tyrant." Laranov took a deep drag on a cigarette. "Another tyrant will control them."

In the chapel at Tsarskoie Selo, under cover of night, a band of soldiers exhumed Rasputin's coffin and took it to a forest outside Petrograd. There they set the coffin down beside a pyre of logs and forced open the lid. Working with long sticks for fear of putrefaction, they raised the corpse onto the pyre and soaked the pyre with gasoline and set it on fire.

Constantine had learned of the plan earlier in the day. That night, concealed by trees, he looked at the faces of dozens of horrified moujiks standing beside the pyre, witnessing the sacrilegious spectacle, and then across the pyre at the wildly abandoned soldiers working themselves up to a frenzy. The old Russia facing the new across the stench of the pyre, the one superstitious, hypnotized by the flames destroying the ancient beliefs along with the body of the "Man of God," the other atheistic, exhilarated, drunk on power and anarchy. Constantine was as horrified as the mute bewildered moujiks while he watched the old ways turn to ashes along with the cremated corpse and asked himself where this new abandon would take crumbling Russia.

For six hours the pyre burned. The moujiks stood transfixed, watching the flames devour the body of the "Man of God." In the morning the soldiers buried the ashes and the moujiks went home.

After a bloody night of battle in which he had fought not only the Germans but also the Soldiers' Committee to get ammunition and reinforcements, Theo had been ordered home by his colonel, who had somehow held onto a little authority, for a rest. "Get out of here before they kill you," the colonel said. Theo ripped all decorations and signs of rank from his uniform and waited for a train that was scheduled to leave at midnight but would probably not even arrive until morning. In the station restaurant the counter was greasy and flies covered the food but

Theo had not eaten for two days. He ordered black bread and tea and carried them to a table in a corner.

A soldier with the shifty neglected look of a deserter took a seat beside him. The stink of his body and his blood-smeared uniform, with sweat stains across the chest and shoulders, assaulted Theo's nostrils. Theo nodded and reached for the black bread.

Spittle landed on his hand.

Without a word Theo wiped his hand. He knew that the stinking deserter had spotted him for an officer and wanted to provoke a fight. He continued eating. The man spat on him again.

Theo's hands were shaking, not from anger or fear but because his hands had been shaking for several months. He slipped the bread into his pocket and walked to the door leading to the station yard. He did not have to look to know the man was following him. At the door, the deserter spat on him again. Theo walked out into the dark night. Hand on his pistol, he turned. "Are we going in the same direction, Comrade?" he said. "We can travel together—"

He looked into the barrel of a pistol three inches from his face. He had understood all along that the man intended to kill him. He continued talking. "There's no argument between us, Comrade. Why not travel home together—it's a long trip—"

Still talking, in a swift motion Theo slammed his knee into the deserter's groin and seized his pistol and killed him.

In a dark corner of the station yard, he stripped off the dead man's bloody sweat-stained coat and left him there.

A month after the Revolution began, Laranov came home to a city of speeches and processions and no police and no bread. On every corner a speaker stood on a bench or a pile of snow and shouted. However long the speech, the audience listened, spellbound, and when he finished another speaker took his place and the audience listened to him, too. The people had waited centuries for free speech and they could not get enough.

On the streets Laranov saw crowds of soldiers and sailors. No officers. And no police. The only police were the "Red Guard," made up mostly of former criminals and social outcasts. In his rented room Laranov put on an ordinary workman's clothes and left his uniform in a closet and went out to the streets again.

At Constantine's apartment house the superintendent appeared to remember his tenant only vaguely. "Is M. Paklov in?" Laranov said.

"Not that I know of, sir."

"Do you know when he'll be back?"

"That is information I don't have, sir."

"Did you see him leave this morning?"

"I don't recall, sir."

Laranov sensed a need for caution. "Tell him that Ilya is in Petrograd," he said.

He walked about the city, witnessing the exploding energy of the Revolution. Every day new processions filled the streets—processions of Christian religious pilgrims, Jews, Mohammedans and Buddhists and teachers and orphans and deaf-mutes and prostitutes.

The people were drunk on freedom. On the streets carriages collided all through the day because some drivers drove on the left and others on the right and they refused to try to agree because they were free.

The food shortage had become a crisis. People had no bread. And yet the lorry drivers refused to unload wagons of flour. The Soviet published an appeal: "Comrade Lorry-drivers. Do not repeat the crimes of the old regime. Do not let your brothers die of hunger! Unload the wagons!" But the Comrade Lorry-drivers refused because they were free and they did not feel like unloading. When they finally unloaded the flour, the bakers refused to bake. Another appeal: "Comrade Bakers. Do not let your brothers die of hunger! Make bread!" But the Comrade Bakers refused because they did not feel like baking bread and they were free!

Laranov walked over to the Marie Palace, where the Provisional Government sat—the beautiful Marie Palace, gift of Nicholas I to his daughter. Filthy now, with unswept staircases covered with litter, broken windows, bullet holes in the paneled walls and unshaven soldiers lounging about, smoking, dropping ashes and cigarettes everywhere. The spectacle struck a faint chord in Laranov that he had thought was dead after three years of horror—a regret for lost beauty.

While he stood there, Kerensky came in, full of nervous energy, young, thin, pale, bristling black hair, sharp half-closed eyes that darted everywhere. Kerensky, a lawyer and the Minister of Justice, was the Soviet's man in the government and a dazzling orator.

After that Laranov attended several of Kerensky's speeches to the people. In his diary—his Revolutionary Diary—Laranov wrote, "Kerensky is a marvelous speaker—in Russia a golden key to the people because most of them can't read. When Kerensky talks to them he is their friend—comrade—teacher—ruler. He is fevered, passionate—at times almost hysterical. Reading his speeches in a newspaper is not the same. You have to see and hear him—his personality is part of the act. With his marvelous voice, his piercing eyes, his maniacal intensity, he holds them spellbound."

He thought a minute and added, "But whether there is much substance behind the histrionics is hard to say."

He went back to Constantine's apartment. "Have you seen M. Paklov?"

"I don't recall, sir."

"Did you give him my message?"

"What message is that, sir?"

Then Lenin came home.

With his entourage he arrived late at night at the Finland Station. He had traveled from Switzerland through Germany in a sealed box car, like a diseased organism. Outside the station searchlights from the Fortress of SS Peter and Paul, "the Russian Bastille," flooded the building. Workers and soldiers and sailors packed the square. Bands played the Marseillaise.

Lenin walked quickly through the Finland Station to address the welcoming crowd. "Don't believe the promises of the Provisional Government!" he shouted. "The people need peace! The Government gives you war!"

The crowd cheered.

"The people need bread! The Government gives you hunger!"

Cheers.

"The people need land! The landlords are still on the land!"

Louder cheers. Wilder cheers.

"We will fight for the complete victory of the proletariat! Long live the world Socialist Revolution!"

Later that night at Kchessinka's Palace—now Bolshevik headquarters—Lenin appeared on the balcony to address another crowd. "We don't need any bourgeois democracy!"

Cheers!

"We don't need any parliamentary Republic!"

Cheers! Cheers!

"We don't need *any government* except the Soviet of Workers and Soldiers and Peasants…!"

For two hours he delivered a violent brutal speech that Laranov recognized as nothing more than the primitive anarchy of the last century. But the crowd cheered wildly, their faces aglow, their eyes on fire. The promise of violence and anarchy was what they wanted to hear.

Because of the war, the Provisional government could not keep its promises of reforms and the people were growing impatient. They had fought a revolution and nothing had changed. Lenin called for an immediate armistice. "No reparations—no annexations—just peace."

"The exploited and oppressed masses cannot go on living in the same old way," he shouted.

Cheers.

"And the *exploiters* cannot be *allowed* to live in the same old way."

Cheers! Shouts!

"The new class must *smash* the old machinery, *crush* it, *wipe it off the face of the earth*—" Always violent, always extreme!

The Provisional Government was terrified. The Mensheviks in the Soviet worried that they would be pushed aside. The more moderate public was scared to death. But for the masses, it seemed to be exactly what they wanted.

Or was it?

Standing on a corner of the Nevsky Prospect one day, Laranov watched a different kind of procession. The war wounded—the "mutilés."

Thousands and thousands of pitiful souls poured out onto the streets, protesting the growing demand for peace at any price. Crippled men struggled along on canes and crutches. Empty sleeves were fastened into pockets. Shattered, bandage-wrapped bodies were transported on lorries. The blind were guided by Red Cross sisters. A military band played martial and patriotic music. Red banners proclaimed:

"LET NOT OUR GLORIOUS DEAD HAVE DIED IN VAIN!"
"LOOK AT OUR WOUNDS! THEY CALL FOR VICTORY!"
"THE PACIFISTS ARE DISGRACING RUSSIA! DOWN WITH LENIN!"

An awed silence greeted the "mutilés." Heads were bared. People wept. Women collapsed. Wild cheering broke out, even among Lenin's strongest supporters—the workers. And then the "mutilés" struggled on and were gone.

Two days later, on May 1st, there was another massive day-long demonstration. Workers, soldiers, moujiks, women and children marched to the square. A dozen bands played the Marseillaise. Red banners proclaimed:

"DOWN WITH WAR!"
"PEACE NOW."
"LAND, LIBERTY AND PEACE!"

And they, too, were greeted with wild cheers by the same people who had cheered the banners of the "mutilés" that had demanded no peace without victory.

From Petrograd Lenin addressed moujiks everywhere.

"For years the owners have occupied the land that is rightfully yours. Take it."

"For years they have cut trees in the forests that are not their trees but *your* trees. Take them! Seize them!"

"Don't wait for the government to find a way to give you the land. Take it! It's your right. Seize it now!"

31

❀

Elizabeth Street was suddenly deserted, shops closed, gates drawn across doors and windows. This was the way it always happened. Even before you saw the soldiers or the gangs of hoodlums or revolutionaries, you knew that somewhere in the city there was trouble.

Cirie stopped on the steps of the post office. A gang of ragged soldiers ran past, waving rifles. Shots sounded. Terrified pedestrians pressed into doorways. Another gang appeared. Cirie stepped back into the post office. Every day someone from Rivercliff came here, hoping for a letter bringing news of Georgii or Serge. Vassi had written and telegraphed to Irene and to Constantine in Petrograd and to Stepa in Moscow, although no one knew whether he was there, to ask if they had seen Georgii. There had been no replies. Had the letters and wires been lost or delivered to empty houses or had the replies gone astray? From Dr. Legare Cirie had learned that when the Red Cross train brought wounded to Kostyka, Stepa was no longer aboard. Who would have thought so many people could just disappear?

Outside the post office a bomb exploded and the street was suddenly littered with ragged bleeding men. A moujik, holding his neck, fell onto the post office steps. The looting began. Soldiers raced along the street, breaking into stores and robbing and abusing people. Is this what they fought a revolution for? Cirie thought. Is this the freedom they dreamed about all those years? Early in the war, you helped any soldier you saw. Now you were afraid of them. They were deserters or Bolsheviks or both, gangs roaming the country, looting and stealing, in tattered lice-infested uniforms.

During a lull in the fighting, men with carts appeared and wheeled the wounded off to the hospital and Cirie raced to Marya's apartment.

"Who's fighting today?" she said, darting in as the shooting began again. Every town's power-on-the-spot changed every week—new rulers, new rules and new atrocities.

"Every day it's someone else," Marya said. "Socialists, Bolsheviks. Some are just thugs. They rob everyone and move on."

"Any Monarchists?" Cirie said. If there were Monarchists, Vassily would surely get mixed up with them and bring trouble on the family. How could Vassily survive against these street fighters?

"We've had everything else. We'll get them, too." Marya was working on a wedding dress. "For the daughter of a moujik who has mastered the tricks of the black market. That's the most important lesson you can learn today, Cirie. For this I'll get chickens and eggs and a pair of boots he bought for his son who was killed at Vilna—near us." Marya sighed, remembering. "How are things out there, Cirie?"

"We're all right. The soldiers go through and steal. But the cellars are stocked. And we have wine and vodka and champagne. What do you want with a pair of men's boots, Mamma?"

"What do I want! I can feed Lily for a month with them. Guard the wine and vodka, Cirie. With vodka you can get anything."

Then Lily burst in, dismissed early from school during the lull in the fighting. "The streets are full of maniacs," she said. Lily was thirteen now and looked more like Cirie every day. "They're not really soldiers. Just bandits. Some of my friends talk to them to get cigarettes. You can get anything with cigarettes."

The Revolution has accomplished wonders, Cirie thought. Mamma has learned to drive a hard bargain. Lily knows the soldiers are bandits and that you can get anything with cigarettes. All anyone thinks about anymore is what is good coin for barter.

"How many gangs do you think there are in Russia today?" Lily said. "There's even a woman gang-leader—Marushka. Ma-roosh-ka!" She rolled the name off her tongue. "A huge woman—a giant—who looks like a man and acts like a man. But worse!"

"Lily, where do you hear these things?"

"At school. She's very famous for being so rough and cruel and dangerous. Ma-rush-ka!"

Marya sighed. "Well, maybe soon things will get better."

Cirie doubted it. With no real authority and people running wild, who was going to make things better? And how?

The next morning, at Madame's urging, Vassi and Cirie set out to check on Prince and Princess Krastov. The few members of the aristocracy who were left on their estates tried to stay in touch with each other and it was three weeks since they had heard from the Krastovs.

Even before they reached the Krastov mansion, they heard the riot and then, around a curve in the drive, they saw the mob, hundreds of moujiks and soldiers storming the house in a drunken frenzy, piling tables and chairs and sofas on the lawn, tossing China and silver into the air in wild excitement. They seized the loot indiscriminantly and piled it into their carts. They dragged chests to boats on the river. They were shouting, reeling, sweating, racing in every direction, like religious fanatics you heard about who danced and whipped each other all night in mounting hysteria until they dropped. "And only yesterday I was shocked at the gangs and the looting in town," she said.

"Swine!" Vassily spat out. "Filth!"

The baby kicked. Cirie looked at the faces contorted with hatred and greed. A moujik, howling like a wild animal, appeared at an upstairs window and flung a delicate table to the ground where it smashed into splinters. A second moujik heaved out the mate. Two men attacked a window with axes until it came loose. They ripped it out and threw it on top of the broken tables.

"They're insane," Cirie whispered. "They've gone mad." The baby kicked again.

Suddenly there were moujiks at all the windows, moujiks at the doors, moujiks crawling on the roof, like a cloud of locusts attacking the house, chopping, ripping, tugging until the beautiful mansion, emptied of furniture, stripped of windows and doors and floors and roof tiles, was a shell.

"Criminals!" Vassily cried. "They should be shot—every one of them should be shot."

Cirie saw Princess Krastov in a corner of the garden, her white hair still in place, staring in shock at the destruction of her home and beside her, the tall, white-haired Prince, his face a mixture of defiance and stoic acceptance of this insanity. As Cirie started over to them, she saw that the moujiks had made torches out of pieces of drapery and broken window sash and were converging on the house.

"Don't burn it!" she cried, rushing up to them. "You can use it for something!"

A leader waved his fiery torch and thrust his red sweating face close to hers. In the heat of the flame, the bloodshot eyes and red-veined nose swam before Cirie's eyes. "We burn it," he cried in a mad frenzy, "so they can never come back!"

Faint and dizzy, Cirie clutched momentarily at a woman standing beside her who shook her off as though she were a leper. Shocked and horrified at this display of hatred, Cirie stared at her and at the insane mob with torches. Why are we still here? she thought. We should have left long ago. Things aren't going to get better. The old days won't come back. The people have had a taste of anarchy and they love it and you can't stuff the evil genie back in the bottle. We should leave. We should go now—as soon as possible.

As they helped the Krastovs into the carriage, Cirie looked back and thought that these were not war-hardened soldiers who had been turned into killers. These were simple moujiks who had moved very fast from dreaming to acting and had come a long way from standing at the gate. And there would be no going back.

Back at Rivercliff they found that Gerzy had brought a letter from Constantine. Vassily scanned it quickly and said there was no news about Georgii or Serge, only about politics. After the Krastovs had been put to bed the family gathered in the study to hear Vassily read it.

Kerensky had come to power, Constantine wrote, but Lenin was growing stronger every day. How strong was hard to say because his organization had always been secret. But Trotsky had returned from America so he had another talented leader at his side. It's the same everywhere, Cirie thought. Every changing wind brings a change in power.

"'The Emperor is referred to as Citizen Romanov,'" Vassily read, "'and the Empress as Alexandra, the German. The family is confined at Tsarskoie Selo, almost completely alone. I'm told that the Emperor has accepted his fate stoically, is even relieved to be free of his burdens. He spends his days reading newspapers, playing with his children, doing puzzles, taking walks when permitted around the grounds. He has been seen sweeping snow and breaking ice in the garden. The Empress has retreated into religion. She believes God has sent her these trials for the sake of her eternal salvation.

"'We're seeing enormous protests against the war whipped up by Lenin. The Government, too, would like to end the war but Russia is bankrupt and the Allies bribe her with promises of loans to continue to fight. Meanwhile the Bolsheviks are growing more aggressive. The most violent are the sailors who recently held two hundred officers at Kronstadt, where they humiliated, abused and then massacred them. Against such murderous passions, how can the moderates survive? A terrifying thought but I'm afraid the extremists will win—'"

Suddenly Vassily was interrupted by a commotion at the side door and a delegation of about twenty peasants and soldiers appeared in the hall. The soldiers leaned brazenly against the tapestries, hands on the triggers of their guns. The spokesman was Evgeny, Popov's brother, a short man with a weathered face and slits of eyes. Popov stood beside him, urging him to speak.

"We have come to announce—the Soviet has declared—" Evgeny paused. Out of habit he took off his hat and then remembered that times had changed and put it on again. Vassily stared at the delegation in silence. Before, when they were inferiors and came to him with requests, he had spoken to the moujiks easily enough, but then they had come with low bows and respect. Now that they considered themselves equals, he received them with haughty silence. Vara hovered in the background, trembling with rage.

"You no longer have any rights here," Evgeny blurted out.

"You have no rights to anything," Popov sneered. "The fields—the forests—nothing. For hundreds of years you used the forests and land that were ours, not yours."

"Yours!" If the thought even crossed Vara's mind that they were in danger, she ignored it. "This estate is ours! Get out!"

Popov spun around to the soldiers. "Shoot them! Who'll stop you? Who cares for them now?" He poked the soldier beside him. "You've killed for less reason. Kill them!"

With an angry look Evgeny silenced his brother—more, Cirie thought, because Popov was trying to steal the show than because he cares whether we are killed. Evgeny continued his speech. "Everything on this estate belongs to the people."

A soldier leaning against a tapestry struck a match and held it a minute. Cirie watched, horrified. Did they catch the fever from the Krastov's moujiks? she wondered. There have been so many fires—is this how they happen? Someone challenges them and the match is struck in anger and touched to the hangings and then—The soldier dangled a cigarette on his lip and moved the match to it. "Vara," Cirie said softly. "Go to Maman. She must need you."

"Don't tell me what to do!"

"Go!" Vassily said and Vara hesitated and then strode off.

Evgeny continued. "We will not drive you off at this time, even though nothing is yours. You can remain until the government sends a paper telling us how it is to be divided among the people."

"A—ah!" Popov turned away in disgust.

"We have to take an inventory," Evgeny said. At the sight of Madame coming up to them, he removed his hat again. "This is the people's property. We have to make a record."

"Nothing here is the people's property!" Vara cried. "These are our personal possessions!"

"Personal possessions!" Popov shouted. "Did you hear what happened to your friends who also formerly had personal possessions?"

"We have to make a list," Evgeny persisted, doggedly.

Vassily stood in icy silence. Madame looked faint. Vara's hands jerked, showing she was losing control. "Evgeny," Cirie said. "Come in and tell me what you're required to do. Ipat—" she turned to a soldier with a nervous trigger finger. "Stand your gun there in the corner so you won't forget it. I'll put on the samovar and you can tell me over tea how I can help you."

Half an hour later, with those who could write carrying paper and pencils, the ragged group spread out over the house, counting, conferring, listing the contents. It was an almost impossible task, they were unfamiliar with so many objects, they could never agree on the count. In the large drawing room they were completely confused. "What kind of table is this?"

"It's a small sofa table," Cirie said. "It stands behind the sofa."

"It's not a small table," a moujik protested.

"You like it—take it," Popov put in.

"For a sofa table it's small," Cirie said, devaluing it. "Usually the table is as long as the sofa."

"And this, Madame?" A moujik pointed to a gold sconce.

"Just a wall light. There are eight of them. Otherwise these areas would be quite dark. Write down eight lights."

"Over here, Madame." A moujik pointed to the Tintoretto painting.

"To me this painting seems very gloomy," Cirie confided. "What do you think?"

"I agree. But what do I write?"

"Why, it's a picture of two old men."

Three hours later they still had not finished. The lists were almost illegible. "We can't possibly finish today," Cirie said, making herself one of them. "Perhaps we should do the rest another day."

They nodded willingly. "You can't sell anything," Evgeny warned.

"Madame has sold nothing since her husband's death. She took a solemn oath." She embellished the story. "At the very hour at which his soul went to rest with God."

It seemed a sacrilege to argue.

"Save your lists." She hoped they would not realize that the lists were meaningless unless deposited together in one place. "Ipat, how is your baby?"

"He's all right now," Ipat said.

"Don't forget your rifle," she said.

Exhausted, Cirie returned to the study. Vassily ignored her. Vara, in tears, ignored her. Cirie put her head back. "Vassi, we should leave here."

Vassily's jaw set. "I will not be driven out of my home."

"You will be driven out, Vassi."

He did not answer.

"If you insist on trying to stay, you should start to hide things." Still he refused to speak. Cirie closed her eyes, feeling the ache of fatigue all through her body.

"Do you recall my orders, Cirie?" Vassily demanded suddenly, his finger tracing the scrolls on the arm of his chair. "You were not to speak to these people. You were to maintain absolute dignity at all times."

"Darling, I thought of nothing else. I did exactly as I knew you would wish the entire time." Didn't he understand what he saw at the Krastovs?

"You treated them like guests!" Vara cried. "I have never been so disgusted."

Cirie closed her eyes again.

"Cirie! When I speak to you, I expect an answer! Do you hear me or have you gone deaf? Or after three hours in such excellent company do you no longer speak to us? Answer me!"

"I am very tired and you are going to have a stroke. What are you talking about, Vassi?"

"I'm asking," he said, with grinding calm, "how you could stoop to such a level. Since we've been married, you've required so much instruction, I've had time for nothing else. If I hadn't been so busy instructing you, we might not be in this terrible position!"

He's incoherent, Cirie thought. He's having a nervous breakdown.

"Why did you escort that filthy horde through my house?"

"Vassi, you saw one riot today. Wasn't that enough? These men had guns and matches and some of them were drunk and they were in a dangerous mood. How were you going to stop them? This way they roamed around and made a lot of lists that no one can read and they left."

Vassily stared at her and cleared his throat again. "It may come as a surprise to you, Cirie—you may have trouble believing it—but we managed very well without you for a long time." He was opening and closing his fist as though in time with a beat pounding in his brain. "Now I see such a gap between your standards and mine that I'm alarmed. If you can't learn, I'm not sure you'll make a fit mother for my son."

Cirie opened her eyes.

"My son will be raised my way. And if you continue to defy me, I will not permit you any access to him. Is that clear?"

Cirie sat up straight. Oh, yes, it was clear.

"Or do you have trouble understanding even that?"

"What is clear," she said, coldly, "is that every day there are new expectations for this baby who hasn't even been born."

"You dare to speak to me this way!"

"It's not hard!" She had seen Vassily break Serge and try to break Georgii. And one thing I am certain, she said to herself, is that he is not going to break my son, if it is a son.

"We're very late for dinner," Madame said. "We'll go in now."

In the dimly lighted dining room the drawn curtains were a momentary shield against a hostile world. The baby kicked as though to remind her and Cirie thought, What am I to do with you? How can I protect you from a father who is rapidly going mad? She looked at Vassily, brooding at the head of the table, his drawn appearance exaggerating the obsessed look he wore these days. A madman who thinks he can fight a revolution with silence. Who even after today thinks he can simply refuse to leave his house and these maniacs will let him stay. He has gold to get us all to safety. And he is furious at me for suggesting it.

Well, let him stay! I'll leave him! And I'll leave Russia!

But how can I get away? And when? And where can I go? Her mind whirled around the idea. She had toyed with it before, fleetingly, in the back of her mind. Now it had surfaced, bright and strong. If I go now he'll track me down relentlessly. For that he'll use his gold. And if he finds me, he'll bring me back until the baby is born and then take the baby and throw me out. And if I wait, he'll follow me and take the baby. To leave him I'll have to disappear. But when? Right away, she told herself. Leave before the baby is born. So that if he has a son, he'll never know.

She saw that Madame was too ill to eat. "Maman, let me take you upstairs," she said. "Have a tray in your room."

Vara threw down her fork. "Why wouldn't she be ill? You helped them count her things! It was so disgusting and offensive! I wouldn't have helped them if they shot me for refusing!"

Vara's bravado was interrupted by a loud pounding on the door. "They're back!" she screamed. "They've come to kill us!"

"Sit still!" Vassily ordered.

Not again, Cirie thought. She heard Simon cautiously crack open the door and then a thud as someone slammed it open and threw himself into the house. An unkempt bearded man in a torn soldier's coat with caked mud and blood and old perspiration stains across the chest entered the dining room.

Vara swayed and clutched the table. "Sit up!" Vassily ordered and stared at the intruder.

The man looked exhausted but he stood expectantly, waiting for someone to speak to him. His eyes devoured the food on the table. He can't hurt us much, he's half dead, Cirie thought. And starved. She stood up.

"Sit still," Vassily ordered her. "Not a word."

"Vassi—" she whispered as she passed behind his chair, "you can't fight your way through a revolution with silence. He's exhausted but he has a gun." She moved toward the stranger. "You're hungry. I'll get you something—" In the dim light, she broke off and stared. "Theo!"

Madame cried out and Vara gasped, "Theo, why are you in this condition? Where is your uniform?"

"I got this off a dead man." Theo's voice was hoarse. "It was my safe-conduct pass."

"Orders from Petrograd! In the army nobody cares about orders from Petrograd." Theo laughed, scornfully. He had washed and shaved and found his clean clothing where he had left it and now in the study, he was talking about the war. "The Soldiers' Committees are running everything!"

The once gentle Theo was a hard bitter ghost of his former self. "The front is a lunatic asylum and the inmates are criminally insane. Nobody cares about the war. They just want to go home and get their land."

At the mention of land, Vassily's head jerked.

"The army is a bunch of goons and murderers. Officers are fair game for anything—humiliation, torture, murder." Theo's dark eyes had a haunted look. He tossed down a glass of vodka and poured another. "I was in the middle of a battle—my men were being slaughtered, I needed reinforcements and ammunition. And they were available behind the lines. I called for them all night. Where were they? The Committee was having a meeting! Discussing it! For a whole night I had to economize on my fire. I watched my men die. And ammunition was just a few miles away. It turned up in the morning, after the battle was over. Then the Committee held another meeting and reprimanded me for going easy on the Germans by economizing on ammunition!"

"Theo, are you a deserter?" Vara said.

"I'm on sick leave," he said, dully. "Rank doesn't mean anything anymore but my colonel has managed to hold on and he said, 'Get out of here. There's talk of an offensive. If you try to take them into battle they'll kill you.' An offensive!" Theo laughed, wildly. "*How*? With *what*? A disintegrating army that fights by vote? No arms, no morale, no leaders."

Theo's hands shook as he reached for his glass. "An officer is in more danger from his own men than from the Germans. What the gangs of soldiers are doing to officers is one of the bloodiest chapters in all the bloody history of Russia. They murder them—shoot them in the back—torture them while they're still alive—eyes, ears, hands—I won't tell you all the obscene ways—"

The room was still, everyone thinking the same thing, Cirie knew. We're all seeing Serge in our minds, maimed—tortured—dead.

"Now I know there's something worse than war," Theo said. "An uncontrolled mob with its passions running wild. Until you've seen that, you don't know what hell is."

He reached for his drink and dropped it. The shattering glass broke the silence and at the sound, Madame fainted into her chair.

After Madame had retired, Vassily resumed reading Constantine's letter. "'The government isn't getting a grip on things and people are alarmed at the violence.

Many have gone south, those who can, hoping to leave the country that way, and others have gone to Sweden. A few say we cannot desert Russia in these desperate times but more and more my friends' homes are empty. Including Ilya Laranov's apartment, although I doubt he has left Russia—he was her most passionate lover.

"Many conservatives feel we should support Kerensky as the lesser evil, the alternative being Lenin. I think it will take a stronger man than Kerensky. The economy is paralyzed, peasants are demanding land <u>now</u>, the provinces are seceding. We're split into too many factions—Mensheviks, Bolsheviks, Anarchists, Social Revolutionaries, Tsarists, who are quiet for now but whose hopes have never died."'

Vassily looked up with an unfamiliar gleam in his eye and Cirie thought, He's getting involved in something.

"Support Kerensky, indeed!" Vara burst out.

"There are other choices," Vassily said.

"What makes sense is that people are leaving," Vara said.

"We can't leave! Maman couldn't survive the trip. And what about Georgii? Would you have him make his way home and find no one here? And we don't know anything about Serge. Besides—" the light flashed in Vassily's eyes again— "our turn will come!"

He can't understand that they had their turn and it has passed, Cirie thought. But he's right that Maman probably could not survive the trip. And that we can't abandon her. Or Georgii. And I can't abandon Mamma and Lily. For the first time she thought, When I leave I'll have to take them along.

At last, his earlier tirade apparently forgotten, Vassily indicated it was time to go to bed, suggesting that Cirie must be tired. While she was brushing her hair there was a knock on the door between their rooms. For a moment Vassily stood in the doorway, looking miserable. "These atrocities against Theo," he said, coming into the room. "Imagine—an officer sent home on artificial sick leave to escape his own men."

"It's not artificial, Vassi. Theo is close to the breaking point."

"Aren't we all?"

It would be simpler to cure Theo.

Without meeting her eyes, Vassily said, "It was bad enough when they were fighting on the streets of Kostyka. Now they've invaded our home." In his own way it was an apology, but it didn't dissolve the wall his threats had erected. Underneath the remorse was he actually thinking that she should not be allowed to raise her own child? And once the seed was planted in his mind, would it grow? She had seen him become obsessed with ideas before.

"In our own home," he said, "we're drowning in an ocean of enemies."

"Vassi, if you won't leave, at least hide your gold. They'll steal it."

"Maybe the worst is over. Maybe the government will get things under control."

"The worst isn't over."

"Theo spoke of an offensive. Maybe some good will come of that." For a moment Vassily held her. "We have to believe that."

"Vassi, the people have had a taste of running wild, seizing whatever they dare, destroying what they hate. They won't go back to the old ways."

"But why should they hate us?"

"Vassi, the only question is how much further will they go? The next time they come here will they still be peaceful? And after that?" And what is going to happen to all of us—together or apart?

The next day Cirie sewed her jewels into her mattress—she would take them out when she left—all the diamonds and pearls and sapphires and emeralds and the two black pearl earrings.

In Petrograd Lenin addressed his growing masses of followers:

"The State is an organization of force and violence—for the suppression of some class of the people!...Until now States have used this force on behalf of the *possessing classes! Now* the State should use force and violence on behalf of the *people—against* those whose rule was based on exploiting them.

32

"We have to do an inventory." Two days after completing the first inventory the moujiks were back.

"But Comrades," Cirie said. "We just finished an inventory two days ago." Protesting gently, Vassily thought, instead of letting them know firmly that once was enough.

"That inventory was for the other committee," the hoodlums said. "We fired them. They were dishonest."

"We have to do an inventory."

Every week it was the same. They went through his house, filthy swine, with their grubby stubs of pencils and scraps of paper, taking inventory. And a lot more than inventory. They pawed through dressers and closets, they accused him of stealing his own possessions when they missed an article that was in use or in the laundry. Dishonest! They were all dishonest. Stealing more every time they came, carrying off priceless Vodovsky possessions in their filthy carts and boats—chairs, tables, sofas, rugs, silver, china. The Oriental chest from Whitewater. "We'll use it for a log bin!" they said. The oversize Persian rug in the formal drawing room. "We can share it. We'll cut it up into pieces."

And always the same words. "We fired the other Committee. They were dishonest." Like parrots. Why not? They weren't interested in eloquence. They were interested in stealing.

They shifted their attention to the land. Their blade became broader and swifter and their mood uglier. Accompanied by an official, they took half of the Vodovsky hayfields and pastureland. Vassily immediately sold half his cattle and horses to an opportunistic dealer. He wouldn't be able to feed them on the land left him and he wasn't going to watch those splendid animals starve. Then the swine returned in a rage and accused him of selling the people's property!

Cirie gave them one of her honeyed speeches. "But we thought we were expected to get rid of them when there was no longer enough hay to feed them. After all who gains if an animal starves to death? You wouldn't want that."

They didn't know what they wanted. They wanted whatever they could steal.

They returned for more land. A mob of fifty hostile peasants with an official from Kostyka, descended on him at dawn and for an entire day they argued with Cirie and threatened, violent-tempered, foul-mouthed brutes, calling the Vodovskys pigs, thieves and leeches.

"For years you used the land that is ours. Now we'll take it all!"

"And your horses, too. And your barns and your house. We have let you live too long."

"Leave them nothing. Take it all. The land belongs to the people."

In the end the official figured how much hay, in his opinion, Vassily would require to feed his animals through the winter. His opinion was wrong. It was not enough.

"I'll set a price you'll be paid for the land we're taking," he said. "And we'll confiscate the money. You can't be allowed to make a profit from this."

Profit!

"And for the land you use, you must pay rent!"

This time they didn't wait for him to sell the horses. They took them at once, leaving Vassily only what he would need for plowing his few fields. Again in the official's opinion.

"Comrade, look at these fields," Cirie wheedled. "With your experience, you can see we need two more."

"Liar—liar," the moujiks screamed. "They don't need them. Don't give them to her!" And she had always gone out to take care of the monsters! Well, no more! In the end she talked the official out of two more horses. No pay for the horses. But what was the difference if they were going to confiscate the money?

On a morning in August, as Vassily made his way into the city with Cirie and Theo, the peaceful silver and gold countryside of ripening oats and rye seemed a mockery of his losing war with the moujiks in which every battle went against him. After a morose silence, he said, "I should go to Petrograd to look for Georgii and Irene. Serge's child will be born soon. But I'm afraid of what these maniacs will do while I'm away—take the little that's left and throw everyone out."

Terrible questions about his brothers haunted him. "Where is Georgii? And where is Serge? Are they starving? Are they abused? Are they even still alive? A twelve-year old boy lost in a violent lawless city? A Paris-educated young man who—let's face it—never did a thing in his life, among soldiers who are murdering their officers."

"Serge will do as well as anyone else against them." Theo defended Serge without conviction. "And Georgii is clever."

"All these years I've accepted the moujiks because I didn't think they could be any different," Vassily burst out. "Now I've seen what they can be and I despise them."

"Be careful, Vassi," Cirie warned. "We should try to get along."

"For what? Where is the justice that my land should be given to people who will ruin it? Where is the sense? I can produce so much more. They'll only starve. I've lived such a restrained responsible life. Where is the justice?"

"Who's talking about justice?" Theo said.

They were at Vassily's office. "Give me a few hours," he said. "I'm expecting some Government people to purchase paper."

"Justice!" Theo said as he and Cirie continued into town. "In Russia we've lost our chance for justice."

"It's not justice we need. It's power. But how do you get close to power when no one is strong for more than a day? He's seen those paper buyers before. Afterwards he's all keyed up."

"Monarchists?"

"I think he should be very careful. And you, too."

"I'm not mixed up in anything. All I do is walk along the river." Theo looked across the green countryside. "Shall I tell you what I've decided on my long walks? As an officer and an aristocrat, I don't know how long I'll stay alive. But I'm going to dress like a peasant and live like a peasant and I'm going to fight these madmen who have their hands on Russia's throat. And I'm going to help as many of their victims as I can. I won't fight like a gentleman but I hope I'll be smart enough to do some good. Does this shock you?"

"You don't shock me, Theo. Even that summer at Whitewater you seemed so honorable."

"My thoughts weren't so honorable." He smiled at her surprise. "We were all in love with you. I wasn't the only one. But your eyes were somewhere else."

Cirie pushed away the memory. He was just one man, she thought, who had been pampered and then tested by fire, who had suffered and come out stronger, and he had thought about this new world that had destroyed the old and had found the only place in it that could be his. "And now I think you're quite wonderful. And very brave."

For a moment he was silent with his thoughts. "I know what Vassi means," he said. "Moujiks I knew and liked have turned vicious. They hate us more now than they did when we had power."

"My father used to marvel at human nature," Cirie said. "He used to say, 'How do you figure it when they shuffle the deck?' He was talking about genes and the differences between people. Now I think that all the cards are in every deck and under the right conditions, the worst comes out in almost everyone. Greed, cruelty, revenge, hate.

When the men entered his office Vassily looked up, thinking they were the "paper buyers" and saw instead some of the workers, accompanied by three soldiers, who announced they were taking over the factories.

"You don't know how to operate these factories!" Vassily said.

"Don't tell us what we know. The people are running things now."

Vassily summoned his paper and grain managers. "Tell them how complicated it is to run these factories," he said.

"These are your managers? Bourgeois! Out!" The soldiers pushed the managers out the door.

"Stop! These managers have had years of experience,"

The spokesman leaned close to Vassily's face. "Why should we have the shitty jobs and they're managers?"

"Because they're trained. They know their jobs."

"Let them have the shitty jobs. We'll be managers!"

"You can't produce! You don't know how."

"And you are out, too." They pushed Vassily away from his desk and one of them sat in his chair and four others sat on his desk.

Vassily was walking toward the center of the city when Cirie and Theo came along.

"Now just keep quiet—" he ordered Cirie after telling her about the outrage. "They're sitting at my desk! In my office! Now don't speak. For once don't say anything." Vassily looked straight ahead. "This power on the spot is going to change."

"Be careful, Vassi," Cirie whispered automatically.

"Don't talk. Don't say a word." He glared at her. "My son will have my estates. My son will have my factories and my railway. My son will be an aristocrat—not a Comrade!"

"Vassi," Theo said before he realized this was not the time. "It might be a girl."

"I'm going to have a son!" He threw Cirie a look, warning her not to deny him this. "My son will manage the estates and the factories as efficiently as I do. I'll train him until he's the most efficient man in Russia. Don't say a word. My plans for my son are not open to discussion."

Cirie shuddered. Three more months. And then, if it is a son, will we each be plotting to take him away from the other?

When they reached home she watched Vassily disappear into the house—a man who had been stripped of his possessions and, worse, his occupation. She thought of the Tsar playing with his children, doing puzzles, relieved to be free of his burdens. Vassily's reaction was exactly the opposite. His work had been his life and his habits were shattered.

"What will happen if it's a girl?" Theo said.

"I don't know," Cirie said. "But I'm counting on it."

"Cirie, you can't live with him."

Cirie hesitated. Theo was his cousin.

"There's never been much feeling between Vassi and me," he said.

She met his eyes. "I have to leave him, Theo. But it's hard to find out anything—where I can go, how I can get there."

"Going anywhere today is dangerous and hard. And he'll follow you. He must still have gold. He'll pay someone to find you."

"I'll have to lose myself in a big city. Moscow or Petrograd. Until I can go to America."

"Moscow and Petrograd are in chaos."

"I know."

Theo hesitated for only a second. "If you want to, you can come with me and I'll try to take care of you."

For an instant, although she knew better, Cirie brightened at the thought of a solution and a possible escape. Then she said, "Theo, you're my only friend, but I can't do that to you."

"Cirie, you'll need me. You can't let him find you."

"If he finds me I'm done for. But one thing I'm certain. My son, if it is a son, is not going to have to take to a wheelchair to fight his tyranny. Or escape behind a shield of vodka."

"Or marry someone he hates. When will you leave?"

To get away now I would walk, she thought. "I can't walk a baby into a famine. And I probably wouldn't even get to the railway station before he caught up with me. We'll be three people. I can't leave my mother and sister behind. If I don't leave soon I'll have to stay until the baby is born. Then I'll think of something."

*   *   *

Then, for a brief period, Vassily became a man full of hope. From Folker, his former grain manager, he heard about a planned counter-revolution. And General

Kornilov, a war hero and the new commander-in-chief of the army, a colorful fig-ure, son of a Cossack, was going to lead it.

Vassily was flooded with optimism. He began to plan next year's planting in fields he no longer owned and the breeding of animals that had already been taken from him.

"Vassi—" Cirie tried to summon him back to reality one day at lunch. "If we don't finish harvesting we'll starve this winter."

"Kornilov is going to lead a counter-revolution," he said.

"Darling, they've ordered us to give them part of our rye. If we don't, they'll throw us out." She broke off. Three beggars appeared around the corner of the driveway.

"Kornilov will make short work of these usurpers," he said.

"Vassi, three beggars are coming."

Theo took his gun and started outside. "I'll try to head them off."

"You'll have to give them something to eat," Cirie said. "I know that hungry walk."

"Then feed them and get rid of them," Vassily said.

Cirie looked again. They were half-starved, dragging themselves up the drive, but they weren't beggars. Georgii and Stepa and Tanya had made their way home.

They were a rag-tag trio but bright-eyed and exhilarated—three comrades who had shared a dangerous adventure and lived through it—firm-looking and confi-dent, especially Georgii who had survived by dodging street battles and stealing.

"I'd go down a street," he said, while he ate the gruel and berries Cirie hastened to put out, "and suddenly there'd be a battle with machine guns and people firing from roofs. So I'd try another street and run into another battle—"

"Where were you going?" Vara interrupted.

"To Tanya's. The Revolutionaries closed our school. They thought we were armed. In my school uniform I had to be careful so I hid in the day time and moved around at night."

"How long were you on the streets?" Madame said. "What did you eat?"

"Only what I could beg or steal."

"Beg!" Vara said.

"I'm pretty good at that. Stealing, too." Georgii had a new and harder look about him.

"Why didn't you go to Irene?"

Georgii looked surprised, as though the idea had not occurred to him. "Then guess who I saw one night. Laranov. At first I didn't even know him. He looked like a factory worker, the way he was dressed. I ran after him and asked if he had anything to eat. I told him I was trying to get to Tanya's school and he said, 'You'll never make it tonight,' and he took me home with him. He said Stepa was coming to Petrograd for Tanya as soon as he finished arguing about his train."

"They took it away," Stepa said sadly. "They were afraid I would use it against the Revolution. Maybe even help officers."

Georgii grinned. "Laranov isn't afraid of anything. He took a gun and a club and went everywhere, but he wouldn't let me go with him. The next day he got me these old clothes and took me to Tanya's. Then Stepa came and we spent our time trying to get out of Petrograd."

"In Petrograd we stayed at a dirty little hotel," Tanya said. "No one would clean or even give us a light bulb."

"Everyone was out demonstrating," Georgii said.

"I tried to find Constantine but he's disappeared," Stepa said. He looked up from his gruel. "The first hot food we've had in months. Wonderful."

"Did you see Irene?" Madame said.

"When I could get through the streets I went to see her. She was still in her apartment with only her old nurse who thank God has stayed with her."

"Has she heard from Serge?"

"I'm sorry to say she has not. She cries continually. My heart goes out to her but she does so little to help herself. She refers to her unborn child as her fatherless baby or her poor orphan. I wanted her to come with us but she felt she couldn't travel. She should be thinking about getting that baby out of Petrograd, but she doesn't have the courage to move."

Cirie glanced quickly at Theo and saw that he was watching her.

"Then we started our long struggle to get on a train. We took turns waiting in lines. We knew we would probably be forced to walk part of the way"

"And you started out!" Vara said.

"We told ourselves that for years the moujiks have walked great distances across Russia and now we would find out what it was like. We went to Moscow first—a little longer, but I was afraid of running into the fighting."

"Is riding the trains any better these days?" Theo said, with a glance at Cirie.

"It's terrible. The soldiers throw everyone off."

"And they steal the lanterns and candles so the cars are all dark," Georgii said. "At every stop more soldiers pile on and it gets hot and crowded."

"And it smells awful," Tanya said. "Because they're all dirty. You can hardly breathe."

"And they scare the women." Georgii's eyes were bright. "Two ladies were in a locked compartment and the soldiers broke down the door. And if anyone has any food they take it because they're hungry."

Georgii and Tanya had never looked so animated, Cirie thought. Like Lily, they were at an age when they found the anarchy exciting.

"We were lucky," Stepa said. "We were thrown off thirty kilometers before Smolensk and again only about eighty from here. After that we walked or begged rides with moujiks. They didn't object—by now we looked like comrades."

Georgii laughed. "It's the only way you're safe."

"What's happening in the cities?" Vassily pressed Stepa.

"In the cities the people are facing starvation."

"Politically. What's happening politically?"

"Starvation is political, Vassi. In Moscow and Petrograd this winter millions will die."

So much for Moscow and Petrograd.

After lunch Stepa tried to answer Vassily's questions. The last offensive was probably the most unpopular offensive in history. A disintegrating army. Generals ignored. No supplies. Desertions were epidemic. The government bowed to Allied pressure because they wanted those loans but the offensive was a disaster.

But because of it Lenin had lost ground. On the day the Germans launched a counter-offensive, thousands of workers in Petrograd, Lenin's followers, poured into the streets to protest against the war and the Provisional Government. A serious violent protest with shooting and looting. For two days it threatened to explode into a more extreme Revolution. Then Lenin spoke to the marchers from the balcony and told them this was not yet the time. "His words urged restraint but his tone applauded them. The protest showed that Lenin and his Bolsheviks were in control of Petrograd. People understand that for the masses it's not over and they're very frightened.

"But for once the Government fought back. It published evidence—authentic or forged, who knows?—that Lenin, Trotsky and the other Bolshevik leaders had stirred up the riots on orders from the German government. Officers were sent to arrest Lenin. Too late. He had escaped to Finland. But Trotsky and other Bolshevik leaders went to prison. Their supporters, the Bolshevik factory workers and soldiers, felt they had been used in the German cause. And suddenly Bolshevik fortunes were at rock bottom."

"Then is Petrograd quieter now?" Cirie said.

"A little—for now."

"And Moscow?"

"Quieter than Petrograd," Stepa said. "But they're still both facing starvation."

"I understand," Vassily lowered his voice, "that other people are working for a different kind of change."

Stepa looked up quickly. "If you mean Tsarists, Vassi, be careful."

"Do you think the Socialists have a monopoly on change?"

"They have the numbers. And right now they have the government."

"And what has Kerensky done with it? Nothing!"

"All Kerensky does is talk. But for now the Soviet is content to stay behind the scenes. There are so many problems no one wants the power openly. Except Lenin. Kerensky rules by default."

"And General Kornilov who was to lead a counter-revolution?" Vassily said, eagerly.

"I don't know much about Kornilov. A short tough man—Oriental features." Stepa shrugged. "To some he's a hero but not to the workers and street fighters."

"He's a great military man," Vassily said, upset that Stepa's hopes for General Kornilov did not match his own. "And if Kerensky is weak and the Soviet backs away from taking power—and if Lenin is in Finland—" Vassily leaned forward over the table. "When will we find a better time?"

Suddenly Kornilov was the man of the hour and Vassily's hopes soared. Kerensky called a conference of all classes in Moscow and General Kornilov arrived like a conquering hero, carried off the train on the shoulders of red-cloaked bodyguards and greeted by cheering men and weeping women. Why?

At the Moscow conference Kerensky made two speeches so histrionic and hysterical that he left his audiences in despair and ready for a strong leader and General Kornilov captured their imaginations as just the man to save Russia! And he liked the idea. He intended to lead the counter-revolution against Petrograd and seize power.

Even Laranov was surprised at how quickly the pot boiled up. Within two weeks of the Moscow Conference, he wrote:

10 September, 1917

"Kerensky and his own appointee Commander-in-Chief, General Kornilov, are plotting against each other. Every day Kerensky makes melodramatic speeches, as though he knows the only thing he does well is talk, and all night he walks around the Winter Palace singing Grand Opera. Yesterday he ordered Kornilov to turn over his command and the General replied by ordering his men to move.

"Anyone who thinks all this nonsense will succeed should take a look at what's happening in Petrograd. The Soviet, alarmed at both Kerensky and General Kornilov, is arming the people, including the Bolsheviks, to defend the city. The Bolsheviks have come to life again and are pouring into the streets, erecting barricades and digging trenches, ready to fight to defend Petrograd against the counter-revolution."

In the end Laranov described Kornilov's effort in a paragraph. "The trade unions spread the alert and the railway workers, just as they did last spring with the Tsar, stopped Kornilov cold. They halted his trains, sent them in the wrong direction, cut him off from his troops, sent cars of supplies and artillery to the wrong stations or lost them altogether. Telegraph workers intercepted messages. The General never reached Petrograd. Today he was imprisoned in a monastery. Inside Petrograd, not a shot was fired. The attempted counter-revolution was a fiasco."

By the end of September the cauldron was boiling again. A new Revolution was in the air. Laranov heard about it everywhere. And heard, too, the arguments about whether it could succeed.

Lenin was busy again, writing letters from Finland, urging his people to prepare to seize power with arms—*now*. He sent detailed instructions—all the tried and true methods: Organize into small groups, each with a specific target during the uprising—take over the railway stations, the telephone or telegraph buildings, arrest the General Staff and the members of the Kerensky government. The time is here, he urged — the time is now.

"The peasants are the key," he warned. They are 90% of the population. Without their support a Revolution cannot succeed. And all the peasants care about is the land. They're tired of waiting for it. They're up in arms—burning and killing. And they're turning to the Bolsheviks.

"*Seize this mood*," Lenin said. "*Act now*. Because once they get their land, they'll be satisfied. They won't be revolutionaries—they'll be landowners. They won't support a more extreme revolution. And in Russia, without the peasants, no Revolution can succeed."

In his diary Laranov wrote: "The question is this: Can Lenin's proletariat—less than 1% of the population—succeed in taking over the country?

"Moderates say they cannot. But what if the rest of the country is floundering? And what if the 1% has a strong leader and that strong leader has a plan? What if the 1% are trained and organized and dedicating their lives to his Revolution? And if he has, for the moment, the allegiance of his unnatural allies who are 90% of the population—the moujiks who want their land? Lenin is still in hiding in Finland but if he acts in this brief flash of time when the moujiks are with him, then he can do it. He will take over the country."

Two weeks later Lenin came in disguise to Petrograd to argue for immediate action. "I am told a serious disagreement divided the Central Committee,"

Laranov wrote. "Trotsky supported Lenin. Kamenev opposed him. Stalin, the Georgian who used to be known as Kuba, the bank robber, and has joined the inner circle, remained on the fence until he saw how the wind was blowing. The argument went on for ten hours and Lenin won.

"Lenin returned immediately to Finland but a second armed Revolution is in the air. Everyone knows the Bolsheviks are going to move. Only the date is uncertain."

33

In Kostyka a cold wind sliced down the street and most of the shops were closed, not because a new gang was looting the town but because there was nothing to sell. Signs in windows listed the merchandise the store was out of rather than the merchandise for sale. In a dry-goods store a few blocks from Elizabeth Street, a sign read:

No Needles
No Thread
No Buttons
No Wool
No—

The bottom of the sign had been torn off, a final gesture of defeat, and today the store was closed. No one had bothered to lock the gate. There was nothing left to steal.

As Stepa guided the horse around a frozen rut, Cirie's eyes lingered on the torn sign that said so much. "No wool," she said. "But the moujiks have wool. They just won't sell it at the government prices."

"Can you blame them?" Stepa said. "Government prices for goods they need are going sky-high."

"What the sign says is that when the government fixes the prices everything disappears," Cirie said. "When government agents come around, the moujiks hide their sheep in the woods."

"They're old hands at self-preservation against the government."

The sign said the moujiks were taking care of themselves and would let everyone else starve and freeze. They were weaving their wool into cloth for their winter clothes and bartering what was left. The sign said money was useless. You could get what you needed only by barter. And to barter, you had to have something that somebody wanted, hidden away where the authorities could not lay their hands on it.

Which Cirie and Stepa were trying to do, late at night after the spies had gone to bed. All the old servants except Gerzy and the aging Simon had been expelled and a dozen lazy drunkards were in their places, not working but spying. Last summer, after the first inventory, Cirie and Gerzy had removed valuable paintings from their frames and substituted magazine pictures, and replaced gold sconces with iron brackets found in cellars and stables and Gerzy took them and the paintings, rolled in newspapers, to his hut for safekeeping.

By the time Stepa came home and became an enthusiastic fellow conspirator, everyone's interest had shifted to food. After a bad harvest, people were talking about nothing but bread. A disorganized rationing had begun. Everything was given by cards. Officially everyone was to receive five pounds of white flour a month, a pound of sugar, a little tea and a few matches. But there was no sugar and if you had rye flour you got no white flour. "We'll hide flour and cereals first," Stepa said and Cirie agreed. She had taken her own food inventory.

"We have three bushels of squash, four bushels of carrots and beets and two kegs of sauerkraut to last until the next harvest," she said.

"Georgii and I will fish through the ice," Stepa said.

"And we'll get eggs from the few chickens and a little milk from the cows." They were carefully tending three old cows, all that remained of the huge dairy herd that once had supplied half the district.

"We should hide most of our allotment," Stepa said. "Before long there will be bread riots and they'll come to take back the little grain and flour they allowed us. I've seen bread riots. People behave like mad dogs. If the Revolution can't stop hunger, what good is it?"

Finding a hiding place was the first problem. "It has to be a place that won't burn," Cirie said. "Half the countryside has been in flames."

The usual hiding places for valuables were of no use. Safes and locked rooms would be smashed open and a piece of furniture was out of the question. You never knew what desk or chest or sofa would be requisitioned for an official's office or stolen for the hut of some moujik with a little temporary power. Already the house was more than half empty. They settled on the ash dump in the cellar under the banquet kitchen, of little use in a revolution, and late at night they would mix small bags of jewels and gold coins into the flour and cereal they had smuggled past the spies during the day, and pack it all into the ash dump. On nights when they had not been able to slip flour past the spies, they worked in the wine cellars, storing the vodka and wine in old boxes on high shelves and sifting ashes over them to give the shelves a look of having been undisturbed for years. Even Vassily, dazed and depressed after the Kornilov fiasco, had reluctantly turned over some gold and jewels.

Last night their work had been interrupted by a "visit" from officials and soldiers with an order—the usual scrap of yellow paper. "The forests are no longer yours," the leader announced. "You cannot cut even a tree in the forests from which for generations you have stolen the people's trees."

One more rule to find our way around, Cirie thought. If we don't cut trees, we can't heat or cook.

"To cut a tree you have to prove you need it and get permission from the Committee." Another crumpled scrap of yellow paper. "This order says the people can go into the forests any time they want and cut trees for firewood."

Vassily sagged at this new defeat. "I'll have them marked," he said in a dull voice.

"Marked for what?"

"The trees that are ready to be cut. I'll have them marked."

"The people are free—they can cut whatever they want."

"Comrade," Cirie said. "Certain trees are cut to give others room to grow. The people's forests should be taken care of—"

"We'll decide how to take care of them. If you want to cut one of the people's trees, you can try to get permission."

"And if you freeze it's not so serious," a soldier said. "We're going to have to kill all the aristocrats and bourgeoisie, anyway, so it'll be a few less we'll have to kill."

This morning when Cirie came downstairs Vassily was already at the window, eyes riveted on the nearest section of forest, where dozens of moujiks were hacking away at trees, large and small alike. With every blow of an axe, Vassily seemed to wince. Already the edge of the forest was just a field of stumps.

"It's not a problem that they say we can't cut any trees," Stepa said as they bumped over the rough road toward Elizabeth Street. "Gerzy and I will go deep into the forest at night, where they don't go, and cut what we need for our house and his house. We can outwit the villains."

"You can't go into the forests at night. There are too many wolves."

"We'll take guns. One of us will watch for wolves while the other works. We'll take turns." Stepa had adjusted better than anyone to the revolution, Cirie thought. He played his violin, he waxed enthusiastic over any food that was edible and he took special delight in outfoxing the villains.

"For Vassi, the problem isn't that they'll take a few hundred trees," he said. "He always gave that and more with few questions. The problem is that they won't let him mark the trees. The section they attacked this morning is ruined for years."

On this raw windy day the once elegant Elizabeth Street was drab and dirty. The streets were not swept or washed anymore. Old newspapers clung to buildings. On the corner a shivering woman was trying to barter a lacy dress, a relic of her former life. The wind blew a newspaper against her leg—one more trial visited on her by the Revolution—and she stepped around it. Near her a peasant woman in a babushka was offering a few dirty lumps of sugar.

"How long since we've seen sugar?" Cirie said to Stepa as he helped her down. "If we had anything to barter would we trade for it?"

"We would not. It's filthy."

"I'll stop to see my mother and then walk over to the hospital."

"I'll come with you," Stepa said. "I don't want you walking around alone—"

He was interrupted by the sound of gunfire and people ran for cover. A huge figure on a horse rose up in front of them—the leader of the gang, wearing shabby trousers, cracked boots and a heavy belted tunic. Cirie saw Lily racing toward her. Nearby, two ragged soldiers began to abuse a victim, poking him with rifles to the cheers and laughter of a crowd.

The huge drunken leader yelled orders. "Again! Poke him again!" The horse pranced nervously. The crowd parted to avoid the jabs of the rifles and Cirie saw that the victim was a gray-bearded Orthodox Jew. With the butts of their guns the goons were shoving him back and forth, sending him reeling from one to the other. The giant on the horse shouted and cheered. The crowd yelled. The scene took on a manic quality. "Hey—hey!" the leader shouted. "Harder! Harder!" The horse reared and the leader let out a wild yell. With horror, Cirie realized suddenly that the huge figure on the horse was a woman! An Amazon with mammoth breasts spilling over the belt of her tunic.

"Marushka!" Lily gasped. "It's Marushka! The woman gang leader who looks like a man. There couldn't be two."

"Again! Again!" The leader screamed. "Push him back. Roll him around! Again! Again!" Her face was the face of madness—wild-eyed, flushed with excitement, teeth missing in her loose mouth. She snapped a whip, jerking her head each time it cracked the air.

"Hey, Marushka!" the goons screamed.

"Hey—hey—don't stop!"

"She's insane!" Cirie gasped.

"Push him again!" Marushka yelled. "Poke him. Shove him—roll him around. Faster."

The two goons pushed faster. The old man stumbled.

"Hey! Hey!" Marushka yelled. "What's this! You want to lie down? Hey, what's this? Maybe you want to lie with me!" She laughed a sex-crazed laugh. "Hey, you want to lie with Marushka tonight? I'll give you a thrill—I'll show you things."

The floundering old man looked at her, horrified.

"You want me, eh?" Marushka laughed wildly. "It's on your face. You're shaking for me!" She cracked her whip. "Let's see him shake harder."

The old man stumbled again. The butt of a gun slammed his back. Another gun hit his nose. Blood streamed down his face. Marushka's whip sliced the air. A gun slammed him again. "Stop!" Cirie cried, hardly realizing what she was doing. "You're killing him!" She started to rush toward the crowd and Stepa pulled her back.

"Cirie, no!"

The horse reared over her and Marushka's ugly mouth hissed. "Aristocrat! I'll kill you instead!" She cracked the whip and Cirie felt its sting on her ankle as Stepa pulled her back hard.

Marushka yelled and raised the whip again and Stepa stood in front of Cirie, his arms folded defiantly, his own giant frame drawn up to its fullest height, and stared at Marushka until she wheeled her horse around and rode away.

"Like in the Bible, we're being stoned," Cirie said as Stepa lifted her into the carriage to go home. He had carried her to the hospital where Dr. Legare had numbed the pain and treated the welt on her ankle and ordered her home to bed. "In the Bible when the mob turned against people they stoned them to death." She winced as she moved her ankle. "Have you ever seen so much evil in a face?"

"Not a beauty, I'll admit," Stepa said.

"We've become a jungle where only the most vicious can survive. Constantine wrote us that months ago—the extremists will win. Civilized people can't survive."

"Cirie, Marushka is a thug. A big hard-drinking gangster, more man than woman. Forget her."

But she couldn't forget her. She put her head back and the picture rose up again of the reeling bleeding old man and the goons enjoying the sport and the crowd laughing and the grotesque face of Marushka—the big, red, wild-eyed evil face of Marushka—the face of the Devil. "The thugs always win. I think that's probably a rule of life."

"Don't dwell on it, Cirie. We'll get you home and put you to bed."

"Nothing gets in their way—that's why they win!" She poured out her bitterness in jerky sentences. "They have power—and they can carry out their threats. And no one stops them. No one even stops a maniac like Marushka because she has power with her gun and her whip. Brute power in the hands of the rabble."

"There's always been a rabble, Cirie. High or low, rich or poor, people without principles are a rabble."

"The question is, how do you beat them?" Cirie said, suddenly cool, and Stepa looked at her surprised. "Or must you become like them to survive?"

The question is power, she told herself. How do you get close to power? Somewhere there's a way, she told herself. There has to be a key. Somewhere there's a key.

As Stepa guided the horse up the drive, Cirie thought that, like the city, the house looked forlorn and neglected. And only a year ago it was one of the most beautiful mansions in Russia. What gives a house that look almost of being abandoned—of life having stopped? She turned away. Maybe it's all in my head. Maybe it's this terrible day. Her ankle throbbed, her back hurt, she was exhausted and all she wanted now was to go to bed. Tomorrow I'll look and it will be beautiful again. At the door Tanya came rushing out to tell them there was a mob of women out back, taking the grain.

Near the barn the screaming threatening women were waving bags in the air and Vassily and Georgii, surrounded by soldiers, were trying to face up to them. Cirie limped over to the threatening crowd and found the official. She didn't know his name. They never lasted long enough for you to know their names. Beside him was Popov, who seemed to be everywhere lately, and at the head of the women was Tessa, his wife, her old school friend. The official explained the problem. "They heard you have extra flour. They heard you're selling it at a great profit."

"Selling it!" Cirie cried. "We haven't enough for ourselves."

"Don't lie to us!" Tessa screamed. Tessa, to whose bedside she had ridden with Strengov in the snow to deliver a baby that would have died without them.

"Liar! Liar!" The women were all yelling now. "Getting rich while we starve!"

Tessa spat on the ground. "Aristocrats!"

Marushka! Marushka's face on fifty thick bodies. Marushka's face over a sea of fists lashing bags like whips. Cirie's ankle hurt. Pain stabbed at her back. She felt ill. As she reached for Stepa's arm, she saw some strangers in the distance, walking along the river. More trouble, she thought with a numb feeling. Today strangers always spelled trouble. She hoped they would turn off to the road before they reached the barn to reinforce this ugly mob.

Tessa brought her face up close. "We're here for your grain and we'll take it all!"

"And more than your grain!" Popov said, menacingly.

"We'll leave you nothing!" A soldier moved his gun. He had a dirty patch over one eye.

"After the barns we'll start on the house." Another soldier waved a hand toward the house. The hand was missing three fingers.

"We'll teach you to cheat us!" Tessa screamed. "We'll burn you down."

"Go into the barn and weigh our grain," Cirie said to the official.

"We're doing that and we know what we'll find," Tessa said.

Cirie saw then that soldiers in the nearest barn, surrounded by a crowd of hawk-eyed women, were weighing the grain. "There was an official paper, signed and witnessed," she said firmly. They respected official papers. "It stated our official allotment. And that's all we have."

"Liar! You were seen!" Tessa screamed. Tessa, to whom she had given medicines for her children and jars of the yellow ointment for the child she had helped bring into the world.

"We were not seen because it didn't happen," Cirie said. She glanced up the river. The strangers had drawn closer and to her horror she saw that they were very young officers, tired and hungry—she knew that walk of hungry men. She looked back at the blood-thirsty soldiers and peasants, itching to loot and burn and kill. The young officers noticed the frantic scene and hesitated. Some of them wore ragged bandages or slings. "Go tell them not to stop," she whispered to Georgii. "Tell them to move on."

Too late. The soldiers had seen them. Almost casually they sauntered up to the boy-officers and brought them back at gunpoint and lined them up against the barn to wait until the matter of the grain was settled.

"They're wounded," Cirie said. "Let them go to the house so I can take care of them."

"Oh, no!"

"I always take care of the wounded in these villages." She looked hard at Tessa, whose face showed only hatred. "And the sick, too."

The soldiers who had been weighing grain emerged from the barn to report their tally. "Really, they have no extra grain," the official told the women. "They have very little."

The women waved their bags and screamed. "They're hiding it. They're liars. We'll kill them for their grain."

The official motioned Cirie to one side. "I'll have to give them something or they'll loot your house for revenge."

"But we have only the amount you allowed us."

His eyes went to the mob. "They're out of control. They expect grain." In the end he told the women that he would take forty poods of Vodovsky grain and divide it among the truly needy.

Leaning on Stepa's arm Cirie turned to go to the house and felt a blow on her shoulder.

"I'll tell you this—" Tessa screamed.

Stepa turned on her. "You would strike a woman about to have a child!"

"We'll be back!" Tessa brought her face up close. "Whenever we need grain we'll be back." Tessa, who had been so pretty, was coarse and heavy now. In Russia the past has no relation to the present.

"Let these wounded men come to the house now." Cirie made a last effort to save the young officers but she knew in advance what the answer would be.

By the time she reached the house, she knew that the day had taken its toll and she told Stepa to send Gerzy for Dr. Legare, hoping he could get away from the hospital. If not, she would have to depend on Gerzy's wife, whom she had trained as a midwife when doctors became scarce.

Walking, limping, in her bedroom at sunset, she saw the moujiks and soldiers on the cliff over the water, tormenting the young officers. Two soldiers were nailing a sign to a tree. In the fading light she stared at the crude sign until the words came into focus: ELITE DIVE PLATFORM. Shots rang out and screams died in the night air. The boys were being shot and pushed, still alive, off the cliff into the river. This sign said more than "No Wool." This sign said, "Darkness Has Fallen." Cirie turned from the window and threw up and began to weep uncontrollably. "It's too late," she sobbed. "There's no way. There's no key to find."

At eight o'clock Dr. Legare arrived and at a little past ten Vassily had his son. He named him after his father—Alexis.

On the night of November 6th, the Bolsheviks moved. Trained squads fanned out across Petrograd with the usual targets—the railways, the telephones and telegraph, the army barracks, the important government buildings. The takeover was quiet and bloodless. No barricades, no street fighting, no fires, no looting. No resistance. Kerensky escaped from Petrograd in a car with American flags flying, borrowed over the protest of the American embassy. Besieged in the Winter Palace, the officials of the Provisional Government held out for two days and then gave up and were arrested.

On November 7th Lenin returned to Petrograd. The next day he was elected head of the government. "We will now proceed to construct the Socialist Order," he said.

For centuries democracy had been the dream of the great Russian Revolutionaries. At the end of November, elections to the Assembly were held. The Bolsheviks received only thirty percent of the votes while twice that number went to the party of the moujiks—the Social Revolutionaries.

The Bolsheviks' answer to the election was to sabotage the first meeting of the elected delegates and throw them out of the hall. The pattern was set. The dream of democracy ended.

34

❀

Lenin's first step was to abolish all private ownership of land with no compensation to former owners. "It's no great change," Vassily said. "How is it different from taking it and confiscating the money they pay?"

"The difference is that the moujiks are included in the order," Stepa said. "They thought that after centuries at last they would own their own land. Now Lenin says no one will own land. They've been double-crossed."

"The moujiks!" Vara cried. Hunger and humiliation and the steady loss of possessions were taking a toll on steadier nerves than Vara's. "What about us?"

"We didn't help with the Revolution," Stepa said. "But without the moujiks it couldn't have succeeded. Lenin told them, 'It's your land—take it.' So they supported him. If the Bolsheviks try to enforce this, they'll run into serious trouble."

For weeks after the Bolshevik coup there was no news. The telegraph was not working, the mails stopped, newspapers were not published, trains did not run. Rumors flew—all of them about violence—rumors of Revolutionary fighting and personal assaults in Petrograd and Moscow, rumors of the Germans advancing deep into Russia, rumors of chilling massacres of Russian officers. And not a word from Serge, who seemed to have vanished like so many others—Kyra, Irene, Constantine.

A new delegation, Bolshevik now, arrived to enforce the new order. And heading it—leather boots, leather cap, treading heavily with his new power—was Popov.

"This estate passes into the hands of the Committee." Popov threw Vassily a look of hatred and let his eyes rest defiantly on Madame, with the look of a man challenging a woman who had been so far above him.

Popov, who could not read, produced the usual yellow paper. "This says you agree not to sell anything on the estate or kill any animals or try to take anything away." He crooked a finger on the paper in front of Vassily. "Sign it."

"You've taken enough!" Vara cried. "The little that's left is ours!"

"Nothing is yours! Cows, horses, pigs, tools—nothing is yours. Even to kill a *chicken* you must get permission! Even your clothes are not yours. We'll leave you what you're allowed and take the rest." He thumped the paper. "Sign it."

Vassily's hand froze.

"And don't try to steal the people's property. Any moujik can stop you—I can stop you—at any time and demand to know what you are carrying and you must show us. Sign."

Cirie touched Vassily's arm. "Sign it, Vassi."

"Peasant!" Vara screamed at her. "How can you be so cold? Bitch!"

"Sign it, Vassi." Sign it—what's the difference? It's all over.

Vassily scrawled an illegible line and Popov snatched up the paper. "You are allowed to live here until another paper comes. We'll take an inventory."

At the door Popov stopped and Cirie was shocked at the way he looked at Madame. "Do you hear that, Madame Countess? I am going through your house."

"If you wish," Madame said, quietly.

"And I will decide what will be yours and what will be mine. No more everything for you and nothing for me. No more."

Popov had left Vassily in shock. "Thieves! If you're robbed at gunpoint, you don't give up claim to what's been stolen. I'll get it back! And I'll pass it on to my son."

"Vassi, someone should go through the house with them."

"That's right—go through the house with them!" Vara said. "You're in league with them. They take our things and give them to you! Go earn your share!"

"Vara, in their presence I want dignity," Vassily mumbled.

"When your wife is so sweet to them, is that dignity? She's in conspiracy with them. What does she do for them to get these favors?"

"Vara," Stepa said sharply. "This is nonsense and I, for one, am sick of it."

"Then why are we still here?" Vara uttered the question they were all asking. "They keep saying, 'It isn't yours—we're taking it all away.' Then they let us stay. Why? Ask her. She gets favors from them. She's sweet to them. She always knows their names. None of our friends are left. But we are! Why? Why?"

"Vassi," Cirie said. "We may have to leave here at a moment's notice. We should plan. We should be ready."

"I will not leave my estate! I will not leave my home!" Vassily's hatred, stirred up by the Bolsheviks, focused on Cirie. "And if you're not entirely satisfied here, you can leave. I'll raise my son without you."

"Vassi, who is satisfied anywhere today?" Stepa said.

"I'll do it, anyway, as soon as he's old enough to understand my orders. Now—" Vassily struggled to clear his throat. "Do you want to stay or do you want to leave?"

Cirie heard them tramping up the marble stairs. "I am going to watch the inventory."

"As soon as he's old enough to understand!" she muttered to herself as she hurried into the hall. "We'll be long gone before that. As soon as things are a little quieter. As soon as there's a little more food." These days you couldn't just leave home and disappear into the vast convulsive countryside. People on the roads starved to death. They wandered for weeks until they dropped, unable to find a single morsel of food. "And when we leave, we'll go where you can't follow so easily." Her escape was always on her mind. "All the way to America."

But going to America was no longer so simple as when Anna went, when all you needed was passage money and someone who wanted you or would say he did. Now it was harder to leave Russia. You couldn't get an exit visa and you couldn't take along any money or jewelry to tide you over. And there had not been a letter from America since before the Revolution. And there was the problem of Marya and Lily. Uneasy about what Marya's reaction would be, Cirie had not yet spoken to her. She didn't want to give her time to think and worry about it and line up arguments against it. She wanted to wait until she could tell her when they would leave and how.

Then everything seemed to come apart. Food was nationalized and private trade was forbidden and, as though Aladdin had rubbed his lamp, everything vanished. According to Lenin's plan, everyone would receive food and clothing as payment for labor. So far the plan was all on paper. The government took the food but the second part of the plan did not follow. Rations were never on time and never enough.

The relentless effects of hunger were everywhere. People were nervous and lethargic and sick and you doled out your supply of food carefully to make it last the winter. A typical meal was sour cabbage, thickened with gruel, and tea made of dried apples or berries. Breakfast coffee was made of rye, roasted and ground.

Marya took to saying, "Tonight we eat a pillow case." Marya had been bartering Grandma's linens that she had hoarded. "Tonight we eat a pillow case," she would say. Or, "This week we eat a sheet."

There had been a poor potato crop and what they had was being eaten.

"There'll be nothing left for seed in the spring," Vassily said.

"They'll throw us out before spring," Cirie said.

The black market flourished.

As the food shortage worsened, peasant women began to go south for flour for their starving families. Women who had never seen a train pushed aboard overcrowded lice-infested cars where they sat on floors and steps and platforms and roofs. In the south, epidemics of Spanish flu and typhus raged. Along with the flour, the women brought home lice and disease. Almost every night a moujik knocked on the door and begged Cirie to come out to treat the sick. She took along an empty medicine bag. Her supply was almost gone and there were no new medicines to be had.

"If you can see the lice, it's typhus," Dr. Legare told her. "A rash, diarrhea, vomiting—all typhus. Fever, chills, aching muscles, it's probably Spanish flu." Dr. Legare was thinner and grayer. "I have no medicines for them and I don't know of any that work. We can't accept the people here. We're a Red Army Hospital now." Kostyka was becoming a military center for the Civil War in the South. The generals were here and the prisoners and the wounded were brought here. "You're as well off with home remedies. Liquids and rest. And sweat them on the stove. Cirie, you don't want to come back to work?"

"As soon as we're thrown out, I'll have to find us a place in town," Cirie said. "It'll be soon."

The women riding the trains had acquired a name—"baggers"—and soon they developed a trade. They did not just go south for flour, anymore. They got hold of flour and vegetables and salt beef that the moujiks had hidden away and smuggled them into Moscow or Petrograd where they sold them for more money than they had ever expected to see. Then they brought home city articles that the moujiks were crying for—material, needles, soap, matches—and bartered them for more food and they were off again on the lice-infested trains, back to the cities for more deals. Until, inevitably, they came down with typhus. Some of them died on the floor of some distant railway station. Others brought the lice home. And the disease.

"The baggers have killed hundreds of thousands in the epidemic they've spread," Dr. Legare said that day. "And yet they've probably saved as many lives as they've taken. They've fed the cities single-handedly. Without them, hundreds of thousands would have died of starvation. A bizarre balancing of good and evil."

He stood up to let her go. "Be careful of the lice, Cirie," he said. "Pick them off at once. It's the lice that carry typhus."

So she went with her bag and pretended to make a diagnosis and poured very hot raspberry tea into them and had them moved onto the Russian stove and told the families to give them liquids and keep them in dry clothing. They believed she was treating them and they felt better and many times, when she got to them early enough, it worked.

"I'm like Rasputin," she thought. "I'm a faith healer."

In Marya's apartment Ulla, drawn and thin, was visiting today. "Marya, I came to tell you—" she said. "We're moving to Poltava. No one knows us there. Petya went to Poltava but if he's still there, he won't give us away."

"Ulla, things are no better in Poltava."

"There we'll be like everyone else. Here we live in fear. They hate anyone who was formerly connected with the law." Ulla shook her head—an old gesture, once flirtatious, now distraught. "Here we sleep with our ears open, always listening for that awful sound next door. They never stop in front of the house where they're going to make an arrest. Always next door. Cirie, don't they come to you, too, in the middle of the night?"

"Usually about nine o'clock." Cirie looked at Marya. "Popov now. In a leather cap and boots. Suddenly powerful." The visits, called Control Visits, were searches for alcohol and counter-revolutionary literature. "Night is their favorite time to turn you out."

Ulla shuddered. "We hear awful stories. People thrown out of their homes and allowed to take only what they can carry in their hands. My God."

"Why have they left you alone?" Marya said suddenly to Cirie.

"They haven't left us alone. They just haven't evicted us."

"If everyone else has been turned out, why are you spared?"

Again the question Cirie had asked herself so many times. Surely not for love of the Vodovskys. "Mamma," she said. "Do you have an old sheet that you haven't eaten?"

Marya brought a sheet from the bedroom, where she hid her treasures. "What do you want it for?"

"Can you make me a long smock? All the way down to the floor, with a high neck and long sleeves?"

A look of horror crossed Marya's face.

Cirie nodded. "The better to see the lice."

Marya groaned. "Do you remember what Grandma used to say?" she said while she went to work on the sheet. "When it comes it will be like vodka—they'll go crazy. She was right. No food—not even a needle or soap. Not even kerosene for a light at night. Now lice." She sighed. "I wonder if they're all right. Grandma and Anna and my grandchildren I haven't even seen."

Cirie wondered if this would be a good time to talk to her. After Ulla left, she moved closer and lowered her voice. From the way Marya talked today, she might even welcome the suggestion. "Mamma, we have to go to them. To America."

"You can't go to America anymore!"

"Yes, we can!"

"You can't get a visa to leave Russia. You can't buy a ticket. You can't take money."

Not legally, Cirie thought. But there are ways. When the time came she planned to use her jewels for bribes and passage money. Selling jewels was probably dangerous and not easy but someone would want them.

"Even if a miracle happened and we got out," Marya wailed, "how would we exist—stranded in a foreign country—no money to get to the boat? We'd be beggars. We'd starve."

"People who leave manage to take a little with them."

"Smuggle!"

"Just enough to exist." She said it only to reassure Marya. She didn't intend to leave a stone behind.

"Do you know how they search at the borders!" Marya cried. "Do you know what they do if they're suspicious—the way they search—even women. Body searches! Everything!"

"There are body searches here, too." She didn't tell Marya about the hands that searched her on every control visit or the way she clamped her teeth together to keep from crying out or spitting on them.

"It's better than Siberia!" Marya said.

"We won't go to Siberia. Officials take bribes."

"Bribes!" Marya's needle flew in and out of the sheet. "Cirie, you'll kill us all. You have a helpless baby. How can you bribe and smuggle and sneak four people across the border in times like these? You always plunge first and think later. How can we live though a trip like that when all they want to do is shoot us?"

"Mamma, we can do it. We have to plan carefully."

"I won't go! I won't be shot in the back!" Marya's voice rose. "Or starved or sent to Siberia. I won't go!"

"All right, Mamma." Cirie had not expected such extreme opposition. "We'll talk about it some other time."

She wasn't planning to move four people together across the border. Moving in secrecy and bribing for four people would be hard. When she found a way, the only solution would be to send Marya and Lily first. And Marya would have to go because Cirie couldn't go off and leave her in Russia.

"Dear Anna—More than a year since we heard from you." Because of the paper famine, Cirie was writing in small script on a scrap of paper. Even public documents were written these days on scraps or on wrapping paper, and newspapers were no longer printed for private circulation but, with little news and most of it lies, were posted in town.

Outside a shot rang out. Cirie steeled herself as Tanya rushed in and burst into tears. "They've started killing the dogs."

Another shot and a horrible yelping cry. And a shot to put the animal out of its misery. Cirie steeled herself. Rather than watch the dogs starve, Stepa and Gerzy were killing them—all except Vara's little poodle, Petite, and except for Lupa,

Serge's wolfhound. The family had decided they couldn't kill his dog when they didn't know whether Serge was alive or dead—or maimed or crippled or a prisoner. And if I leave, that will be all I'll ever know, Cirie thought. And they were trying to save the mongrel, Talley, who was a marvelous watchdog and gave them their first warning of a control visit. Two shots. And one more. Tanya was shaking and weeping hysterically.

"Tanya, watching a dog starve to death—and look to us for food when there is no food—is worse."

Tanya nodded. Another shot and yelp and she began to shake again.

"When they throw us out we won't be able to take them with us. And nobody here will take care of them."

Tanya tried to stop shaking. "Did you hear that the Bolsheviks said that all former landowners who want to plow will have to go to Siberia unless the local villages vote to let them stay? We have to plow to eat."

No village here is going to vote to let us stay, Cirie thought.

Presently the shooting stopped and Cirie began to write again. "Mamma is depressed. There is little food or kerosene and evenings she sits alone in the dark. Here we burn a single lamp for dinner and one hour more and then put it out.

"Ask Uncle Lawrence to try to send for her. You wrote that his brother-in-law, Harry, in New York has political connections." (My God—to have political connections!) "Mamma can take Lily—she is a minor. If you can arrange it there—" She stopped. Mamma had to go first—there was no other way. If they could work it out there, she would find someone here to bribe for an exit visa. "I'll help somehow at this end."

Another shot. I do not intend to go to Siberia.

35

❀

When the dogs began to bark early on a summer evening, Cirie's first thought was that their turn had come. Then the barks turned to frenzied yips of delight that could mean only one person and she threw open the door to Serge. Serge, able-bodied and well. Not wounded, not disfigured, not massacred. Serge, holding his child, with Irene on one side, grim and thin as straw, and Kyra on the other, looking gray and sick.

"You're alive!" Serge kissed his mother. "All of you!"

At the sight of her sister, Kyra burst into tears and cried that Otto was dead. "He was arrested twice. He was in Lubyanka. He was sick. He was tortured. And he died there."

"Tortured!" Madame said. "Oh, Kyra, if I'd known, I'd have come to you."

Serge held Cirie close. "Are you all right?" he whispered and Cirie nodded and moved away.

"They said he was communicating with the British," Kyra said. "The first time they took him I paid an enormous bribe. Fifty-thousand rubles. Lydia and I sold my jewels." Fifty thousand rubles! Cirie thought. That would pay for passage around the world for four people and a lot of bribes besides. At least jewels were still changing hands and bribes were still possible.

"It took us days to sell the jewelry. It's not so easy."

"How could you sell it at all when nobody has anything?" Vassily said.

"Speculators! Some people still have money. They're just different people. I paid the bribe just in time. Otto was marked for death. Then a month later, they came back. They said he was telling men not to join the Red Army because the British and French were coming and—"

"Is that true?" Vara cut in. "We've heard that, but where are they?"

"You hear rumors about everything," Serge said. "But Otto wasn't keeping anyone out of the army. They're flocking to join up. In the army they eat. Have they left you any wine or vodka?"

Vassily hesitated. Stepa hesitated. Cirie remained silent. "I suppose you had a hard trip?" Stepa said.

"Oh, it was marvelous," Serge said. "We stood in lines for days first for permissions, then for tickets. We got them only because I'm a glorious Red Army soldier.

260

Then we got onto the lice-infested train. They're really running the trains for the lice, not the passengers. I hope we haven't brought you anything."

"You should check quickly—they carry typhus," Cirie said. The lice could get into anything—furniture, draperies, clothing—and you'd never get rid of them.

"The train ran out of fuel and all able-bodied men were ordered out to find wood. We tore down an old barn."

"You broke up a barn to make the train run!" Vassily said.

"If a train works, which is something of a miracle, they send it out. When it runs out of wood, the passengers get out to find more. But they do carry axes. That shows some foresight. Well, Irene, do you have of any of the little darlings crawling on you?"

What's happened to him? Cirie thought. Stepa left the room and she knew he was going to get him a drink.

"Tell us about Otto, Kyra," Madame said.

Kyra burst into tears again. "After he came out of prison the first time, he just stayed home and didn't talk to anyone but they arrested him again, anyway. And a week later, they came a third time. Lydia said, 'How can you arrest him when he's already in your prison?' They're so disorganized they don't know who they've arrested or who they've let go."

"They already had him when they came to arrest him?" Stepa said.

"Yes! One of them was our former footman. I drew him aside and said, 'Don't they know they already got him?' I gave him my gold watch and he said he'd try to find out something. At least he knew someone he could bribe. No one does anything without a bribe. He came back and told me Otto was dead."

"Does Theo know?" Stepa said.

"We don't know where Theo is." Kyra lowered her voice. "He didn't go back to the army. He said he had work to do."

Cirie remembered the day Theo had told her his plan. "I'm going to look like a moujik and live like a moujik," he had said, "and I'm going to fight these people with their hands on Russia's throat, and help as many of their victims as I can." Had he joined the Whites? Or was he working alone? And where? And how?

"Oh, Eugenie, the things I've seen!" Kyra found a fresh river of tears. "People arrested with no explanation. Bombs thrown right into our apartment house."

"In Petrograd there's no food!" Irene wailed.

"I saw a woman, a well-dressed genteel woman, forced to take off her dress on the street by a soldier who wanted to give it to his girl-friend. The poor woman was hysterical, half-undressed on the public streets. We're not people, anymore. They even call us non-people. We have no value."

Cirie remembered that Prince Tchernefsky used to say "the moujik" as though they had no individual identities, Cirie thought. Now we have no identity.

"Last winter there was no wood," Irene wailed. "There was an old man who tore down fences for fuel and I had to deal with him myself. There was no one to help me. And people are eating their dogs!"

Dry-eyed, Madame stared at Irene. Madame didn't cry anymore. She knew she could not fight these enemies but with her own disciplined pride she would not let them reduce her to tears.

"Our allies—our former friends—should help us," Irene wailed. "We can't help ourselves."

"They'll help when they can," Madame said bravely. "They won't forget that we sacrificed for them."

"Our allies can't help us!" Kyra said. "All Europe is Bolshevik—and America, too."

Cirie's heart dropped. America, too! Is that why there have been no letters?

"I don't believe that!" Stepa said.

"The papers say so!"

"It happened here!" Irene cried. "Constantine always said the Bolsheviks were only a small minority—and look at them."

"If it's true, we have nothing to hope for," Madame said.

If it's true, Cirie thought, there's nowhere to go.

At their meager dinner the next night, with Serge seated opposite her, Cirie thought that everything had changed and nothing had changed since that Whitewater summer long ago—could it be only four years?—when dinner had been six courses and Serge's eyes had come to her across his wine glass. Now wine was saved for barter and dinner was squash thickened with lentil gruel, a half-pound of bread for the entire table and raspberry tea. But Serge's eyes still stayed on her and Vara and Irene still watched.

"In Moscow, everyone is fighting," Kyra said. "Monarchists—Bolsheviks—Anarchists. Moscow has its own Civil War."

"We had nothing to eat—I thought the baby would die." Irene's cool languid manner had given way to a perpetual nervous anxiety. "We ate a little cereal and salt meat that was so old it smelled. And they turned us out, didn't they, Serge?"

His eyes went to her, grudgingly. "I presume so, Irene."

"Well, you know we weren't in our apartment!" Her hair was drawn into a careless knot, her manner distraught. "The baby is Christina," she said, as though they had never been given this information. Cirie wondered whether Serge realized his wife was on the verge of a nervous breakdown. "And Serge wasn't there," Irene rushed on. "Constantine took us in or we'd have died. But we weren't safe there, either."

"You've seen Constantine!" Stepa said. "Is he all right? I've written him a dozen times and had no answer."

"That was last year. He was under suspicion! He's considered a Monarchist because of some articles—something about a Constitutional Monarchy."

"Those articles were very liberal!" Stepa said. "Laranov got them published in an underground press."

"He was arrested but he got out. I don't know how. When someone is arrested, no one ever sees him again. But his days were numbered. I felt he was being watched. I was never at ease there."

"We should write him to come here," Cirie said.

Stepa looked around for the family's consent.

"No, don't!" Irene cried. "He's not still there. It would be dangerous. They're after him."

"Nobody's after him here," Cirie said.

"Another mouth to feed!" Vara said.

"And Serge has to stay in the army because of the Civil war." Irene gave her head a desperate shake.

"We thought maybe you'd gone over to the Whites where you belong," Vassily said.

"If you join the Whites, your family is held responsible. How would you like to hang by that kind of a thread, Vassi?"

He's tired, Cirie told herself. And four years of war would change anyone. It had changed Theo. And yet in Theo she had sensed a kind of wounded love. In Serge she sensed a veiled hate. And when he spoke to his wife, not so veiled. Seeing him again she thought, do I feel anything besides memories stirring? The truth was that her emotions were anaesthetized. Except toward her baby, Alexei, she didn't feel anything. Not hate—not love—not fear. She was numb.

As soon as dinner was over Irene, her neck arched in the old manner, pushed back her chair. "Serge, may I speak to you?"

Serge's eyes shifted but he didn't move.

"Serge—" Madame reproved him. He stood up reluctantly and joined Irene in the hall.

At first the argument was inaudible. Then Irene's voice rose. "You know I didn't want to come here. I want you to leave her alone!"

"I've hardly spoken to her!"

"You look at her all the time. You wanted her once—that doesn't show such high taste."

"Lower your voice, for God's sake. You're talking about Vassi's wife!" Serge's voice was heavy with hatred. "Irene, I'm only staying a few days and I won't be back for a year. By then you can find us a palace to live in—just the two of us—in eternal bliss. Or two tickets to Paris. Or better still—" his voice took on a hard edge—"one ticket to Paris!"

Talley's sharp alert ended the argument. The door slammed open and Popov burst in, wearing his leather cap, with a gang of soldiers and moujiks behind him. Is this the night? Cirie thought, automatically. The men were racing around, opening closets and drawers, and ripping pages out of leather-bound books to use for rolling cigarettes.

"Are we just in time for the final curtain," Serge said at her elbow.

"I don't think so. It looks like another raid to steal."

"Where's the wine?" Popov shouted.

"They searched for our wine long ago," Stepa said.

From the reception hall came the rasp of a saw. "That room is empty," Cirie said. "What are they sawing?"

The sound of breaking glass gave her the answer. "They're cutting up the high mirrors."

"Why?" Serge said.

"They're too big to fit into a moujik's hut."

"Those mirrors in a moujik's hut!"

"The Oriental chest went for a log bin."

She was deciding whether to try to save a few mirrors to barter when a new mob burst through the door, already drunk, cheering and shouting in a kind of celebration.

"What is it?" Popov shouted.

"The Tsar! The Tsar!"

The Tsar? Had the Tsar somehow returned?

"The Tsar?" Popov shouted above the noise.

"Dead! Executed! Yee—ach! And the Tsarina! And the whole family. Finished!"

"The children, too?" Madame whispered.

"All of them. In Siberia. Shot. In a cellar!" They roared with laughter. "The Tsar and the German woman. Dead in a cellar."

Kyra and Irene burst into tears and struggled upstairs to their rooms. Madame, white and trembling, sat frozen in a chair. The news triggered a new abandon in Popov's men. They rushed to the cellar where a crash and wild yells announced that they had broken in the door to one of the wine cellars. More men rushed down the stairs, knocking over other men struggling up, their arms full of bottles. Curses, fights, and the sound of breaking bottles filled the air.

Cirie saw Tanya pressed into a corner. Through the mob that kept shoving her back, she reached her and told her to hurry upstairs. Then she saw that Madame had not moved. She was still sitting dazed in the same chair, and Popov was strutting in front of her, laughing, shouting at her, making obscene gestures. Madame's glazed expressionless face revealed that she was totally unaware of him. Cirie pushed through the mob to her side. "Maman, come with me."

Shakily Madame stood up and Cirie took her arm. Popov danced around her, blocking her path.

"Did you know, Madame, that I watched you?" Popov sneered and leaned toward her. "I looked at you for years."

Staggering, he started to perform an awkward dance. "Beautiful. Your clothes! Your dresses. Your necklaces. Hats! Beautiful! You passed in your carriage. Like a goddess." He danced in a drunken circle. "A goddamned goddess. A Madonna. And I watched." He swayed toward her. "I was the animal at the side of the road. I stopped working in the dirt to look at you. An animal couldn't touch you. *Then*." He bent close to her face. "But I can touch you now."

Cirie shuddered. Madame moved to step around him. "Excuse me, Popov." Still Popov blocked her path.

Suddenly, over the shouting, sweating, reeling mob, Cirie saw a drunken soldier staggering down from the second floor carrying a pile of her clothes. With alarm she thought of Alexei asleep in her room.

She saw Ipat nearby with his gun. Ipat had lost an eye in the war and returned to gain some power among the moujiks. He never parted from his gun. Even in his hut where Cirie went to see his sickly youngest child, he carried it about. "Ipat!" she shouted.

Ipat came over to them. "Come on, Popov," he said.

"I'm busy," Popov said.

"Come on, there's wine down there."

"Later." Popov reeled close to Madame and thrust out his genitals bulging under his baggy pants. Madame, suddenly aware of him, looked horrified.

"Popov—" Ipat nodded toward Cirie. "Don't go too far."

"To hell with her."

On the stairs the grubby soldier still stood holding her clothes, watching the drunken scene below.

"The people won't like it, Popov," Ipat warned.

Popov hesitated and Ipat seized his arm. "Come on, we'll have a drink. There's wine."

With a tight grip on Madame's arm Cirie rushed her up the stairs so she could get to Alexei. The grubby soldier, legs spread apart, stood in her way. She tried to squeeze past him and he dropped the dresses and caught her. She pushed Madame ahead of her. "Don't stop. Go to your room."

Downstairs the drunken mob had broken open the doors to the large drawing room, unused since the day of her wedding, and were cavorting around like donkeys. Cirie wrenched away from the drunken soldier but he caught her in a hard grip. She screamed. In this mob no one would hear her or care. Where was Serge? Why didn't he save her? Or Stepa or Georgii, or even Vassi? No one was here. Sweating profusely in the hot night, the soldier pushed her against the wall and pressed his foul-smelling body against her and groped for her breasts. She screamed again and he silenced her with his mouth. The foul smells of his body and breath assaulted her nostrils and her stomach cramped. She choked and gasped for breath and vomited on him. Stunned the soldier backed away and Cirie broke away and ran up the stairs to her bedroom where Alexei was sleeping soundly, unharmed, oblivious of the bedlam downstairs.

A minute later, from Madame's room she heard a rough animal-like growl and she rushed across the hall. In her room, Madame was lying on the floor, immobile, senseless. And Popov was on top of her. He had ripped away her dress. Her exposed body was thin and white, her skin like paper, her arms like skeletons.

Popov's pants were down, his massive bulk half-naked.

"Popov!" Cirie screamed.

He ignored her. He was working himself up. "A goddess—a goddess—a goddess. And I watched!"

Cirie pushed and kicked him.

"A Madonna—a Madonna—"

Cirie rushed back to her room and picked up an old cracked pitcher and immediately threw it aside. It would be useless against the massive Popov. She seized her medicine bag and rifled through it. She had nothing sharp—no knife, no scalpel with which to stab him. Her hand closed over her last bottle of chloroform. It was almost empty. She had not used it for a long time. She did not know whether it was still good. She seized a piece of cotton and rushed back to Madame's room.

Madame was nearly naked. Popov was nearly naked and pumping faster.

Cirie poured the chloroform onto the cotton and rushed over to the heaving Popov and held it under his nose, praying it was strong enough to make him groggy.

With an animal growl, Popov pushed her off. She lunged around his arm and thrust the cotton under his nose again. Madame lay so still she could be dead. If she had known what was happening she had probably suffered another heart attack.

Then suddenly Popov shook his head—like a dog trying to shake off a bug. He shook it again and his pumping slowed. He sagged.

Cirie pushed at him and he rolled over on his back. She carried Madame to her bed. Popov's eyelids fluttered open and closed again. Cirie grabbed his leg. He was a dead weight—at least two-hundred and fifty pounds.

Then Tanya stood beside her. Popov's genitals were exposed and Cirie tried to cover him with his baggy pants. "What happened?"

Cirie shook her head.

"He hit her," Tanya said. "Her face is bruised."

Cirie nodded.

"Her clothes? What's that smell?"

"Chloroform."

Without another word Tanya took Popov's other leg. Vara and Kyra came in and Irene hovered just outside the doorway.

"Bathe Maman from head to foot and douche her and get her into a nightgown," Cirie ordered.

Vara looked shocked that this was expected of her. Irene drifted away. Kyra moved to Madame's side.

"Help her," Cirie snapped at Vara. She leaned close to her. "Do it!" she screamed. Vara moved to Madame's bed.

With Tanya's help, Cirie dragged Popov out of the room. In the hall they passed Irene. "Get in there and help!" Cirie ordered her. "Now!"

They dragged Popov to the stairs. "We should throw him down," Cirie said.

"He might be killed," Tanya said.

"Good."

"If anyone sees us they'll come for revenge. Even if they hate him."

Cirie dropped Popov's leg. "We'll leave him here. Go back to your room. Bolt the door and don't open it."

The same drunken soldier came out of her room again, carrying more of her clothes and her medicine kit that she had left on the bed. Cirie stepped over Popov to try to get to her room.

The soldier grabbed her. Not again! I am so sick of them. An army of degenerates with their leader naked and drunk on the floor. The soldier was so reeling drunk she should have been able to push him away but he held her fast. She screamed, even though she knew no one could hear her. Sweating rivers, the soldier backed her into the wall with his foul-smelling body over hers. She screamed again and he clamped his wet sour mouth over hers. As she kicked wildly at his shin she realized that he was fumbling with his fly. Revolted she dug her nails into his throat until he slammed her wrist against the wall. With all her strength she slammed her knee into his groin and he grunted and swung the medicine bag at her head to knock her senseless. Faces swam before her eyes. She saw drunken men watching, laughing. She saw Stepa rushing toward her and then saw him knocked to the floor.

"Get away," she screamed. The foul-smelling soldier raised the medicine bag for another blow to her head. Dizzily she made out Ipat below with his gun. "Ipat!" she screamed.

The soldier forced her up a step. She bit his hand. He swung the medicine bag. Suddenly Ipat shouted, "Not that bag!"

Ipat came up the stairs. Sweat poured down the soldier's face. "Drop it!" Ipat pointed his gun at the bag. "It's her medicine bag!"

Still gripping the bag, the soldier elbowed Ipat aside. Ipat snatched the bag. The soldier snatched it back. "What the hell!"

"These are the medicines," Ipat shouted. Gripping Cirie's wrist, the soldier swung out at him. "She needs them to take care of us!" Ipat shouted. "And our children. There's no doctor."

To Cirie's astonishment the soldier capitulated. "Oh," he said. "Oh." He put down the bag.

"Leave her alone," Ipat ordered. "Come on—come get a drink." He slapped the man's back and the soldier allowed himself to be led away.

In her room Cirie locked the door, although she knew a man could break it in, and sat on the edge of the bed, shaking. She asked herself whether she had chloroformed Popov in time. Head in her hands she tried to think through the horror. Whatever happened, Madame had been unconscious. She did not know and she should never know.

Her mind whirled. Who are they down there? Bolsheviks? Moujiks? Red Army men? Or all of them? We're helpless here—we're like ducks in a shooting gallery. Anyone can attack us—anyone can degrade us—and all we can do is stand there and let it happen. The image of Popov lying over Madame had left her in shock. Suddenly she remembered poor Hulda on that night long ago, raped by two men and unable to scream, who had seized a limb and killed them. If the chloroform had been strong enough to kill Popov she would have let it. All her life she had heard about rape in Russia, moujiks and soldiers raping girls, farm wives, their own kin. Sometimes it had seemed like a Russian epidemic. To them it doesn't mean anything. Raping me is no more serious than stealing my clothes. And the Revolution gives them the right.

She sat on the bed and shuddered. She felt a need to touch someone she cared for, to be held by someone and healed, and there was no one. She picked up the sleeping baby who nestled into her shoulder, and walked around the room with him. "I'm going to take you away," she whispered. "We're going away from here and if we die trying, it's better than living like this. We're not going to stay here, just waiting for them to kill us. What have you ever done to them?" she whispered as she circled the room. "But they'd think nothing of killing you because you're the child of an aristocrat. And we're going away from here."

There was a knock on the door and she started to shake again. Hastily she returned the baby to the crib and seized the old pitcher for a weapon.

"Cirie, are you all right?" Stepa called softly. She put down the pitcher and unlocked the door. "Are you all right, darling?" Under Stepa's eye where he had been struck, a cut was starting to swell. Without a word she stepped into his arms and stood there, shaking.

When Cirie arose at dawn the house was silent. Downstairs men lay on the floor where they had collapsed amidst bottles and spilled wine and a terrible stench. On the terrace she stepped over more men, some so still and white she didn't know whether they were alive or dead. She didn't care. She saw her medicine bag on the first step. Probably someone else had tried to steal it and Ipat had saved it again and left it where she would see it. She walked past it and kept walking.

"Now I know," she said, talking out loud to herself as Strengov used to do while he wrestled with a problem that had no solution. Not only the image of the half-naked Popov was burned into her mind. Not only the stench and flesh of the grimy sweating soldier on the stairs. Also frozen in her memory was that gesture of capitulation when he put down the medicine bag.

"Now I know why we're still here," she said. "We haven't been thrown out because they believe that I am all that stands between them and death—and their children and death—from typhus or Spanish flu. That's why they've spared us. And as soon as I leave, everyone here will die.

"They'll be thrown out to wander and beg. Or thrown into prison or sent to Siberia to die. Or be shot. Or raped. Or forced into slavery. Everyone here is hanging by the fragile thread of my medicines—my magic potions, no more scientific than Badmeiev's Elixir de Thibet—my potions which are mostly raspberry tea served up with a lot of instructions. How can I leave? She was trapped by her medicine bag.

The sweet smell of July came out of the woods. This fragrant dawn could have been daybreak in that carefree innocent summer at Whitewater with Serge lying beside her on the hill instead of upstairs, asleep beside his nervous distraught wife. She ached for someone to hold her, to love her, to heal her wounds and give her strength. She had not loved or been loved for a long time.

She started back. The morning sun slanted across the lawn and touched the Italian fountain in the pool, neglected relics of the golden days. Last night two men, too drunk to see the accumulation of rain water, had poured vodka into the pool and jumped in to drink it. Now she saw two pairs of legs sticking up over the edge. They've drowned, she thought. They're dead. She kept walking. Two more lives had come to an end. And that's the way this mob will feel. If everyone here dies, no one will care any more than I care about the men attached to those legs who died happy, drowning in vodka. It will be just a few more lives come to an end. And if I leave, it will happen.

Back at the house Stepa, his bruised eye almost closed, came out onto the terrace to report that he had checked the cellar and found the wine and the vodka untouched around the ash dump.

"Good," Cirie said dully.

"About a hundred bottles. After last night they'll think they've found it all."

"Who is they? Next time it will be a whole new mob we've never seen before."

She looked back at her medicine bag still on the terrace and burst into tears.

"Cirie, we can only try to go on." She nodded and cried harder and Stepa looked at her, puzzled. "Cirie, did Popov harm you last night?"

She got control of herself and, because someone ought to know, she told Stepa the ugly story about Popov's rape of Madame. "He struck her. She fainted. She should never know what happened."

Stepa sat on a battered sofa that reeked of wine, his head in his hands, as though he had taken all the blows the Revolution had dealt him but this one was too much. Then with a heavy sigh he said, "No, Eugenie should never know. No one should know."

"Tanya helped me drag him out."

"Tanya won't say anything."

Cirie nodded and struggled against the tears that were starting again. "We're so powerless. We can't do anything to save ourselves. We have to find someone with more power than Popov—steady permanent power." But who? And where? Finding someone with steady permanent power was like chasing moonbeams. She realized that she was not talking like someone who was leaving soon. She went out to the terrace and picked up her medicine bag. For now it was the only permanent power she knew.

*   *   *

"Cirie!" Serge called.

All week he had been trying to talk to her alone. Now, returning from a patient, Cirie found him walking among the linden trees, waiting for her. "Cirie, I have to talk to you."

Like the eyes speaking to her at dinner, like the scent of the summer night, his words were an echo of the past. "Serge, there's nothing to say."

"Cirie, I can't leave you like this." He moved to take her in his arms. "I love you. I've never loved anyone but you—"

"You've said all this before, Serge."

"Be fair! I've been to war for four years! Do you think I'm the same man?" He drew her into the dark shadows. "Darling, I should have fought for you. I can never love anyone else—"

As though he had never held her like this before, kissed her like this before, new life awoke in her. She felt whole again. Loved again.

"Darling, it's our last chance. Let me love you now."

His hands moved over her face and into her hair as they used to. "I won't be back for a year. We should have each other while we can."

Inside, upstairs was Vassily, the man she hardly knew and never thought about anymore and here in the opalescent night was Serge and she was in his arms again in the shadow of the black grove where tall trees blocked out the moon and erased the years and she thought, Why not? Why not—he was all she had ever wanted. Why not? Tomorrow we may all be dead. Why not? In all the world we have nothing else. We belong together—we've always belonged to each other and wanted only each other. "Yes," she whispered.

"Serge—" Irene's harsh voice shattered the quiet, sweet-scented night. They pulled apart to see her, indistinct in the doorway. "Serge—"

"Don't move," Serge whispered.

"Serge—" Irene's voice grew shrill.

"Go to her, Serge." Cirie's blood pounded but she was alone again.

"Will you meet me later?"

Another echo. "No."

"It's my last night! You still want me as much as I want you. I can feel it."

You could always feel it, Serge.

"Cirie, I'll be back in a year. Promise you'll wait for me."

"Wait! Wait for what?"

"Serge—" Irene came down the walk and Serge stepped out, impatiently. "What do you want, Irene?"

"What are you doing here?" Accusation spilled over in Irene's voice. Serge strode past her toward the house. "You were meeting her."

Hands in his pockets Serge walked angrily to the house and Irene hurried along behind him. "Irene, this is my home. I have walked here at night for years— *alone*—and I will walk here now—whenever I please—*alone*."

Irene began to cry.

"Am I going to have to listen to that all night, too?" Serge went inside and slammed the door. The dogs began to bark and he quieted them and, quieter himself, opened the door to Irene.

Then Serge went back to the army and his wife and daughter remained behind, a nervous mother and a baby who cried a lot, and life became an unchanging gray line again, one day like another. And the worst of it is that we hope it will stay that way, Cirie thought as winter approached, because any change can only be for the worse.

*   *   *

6 November, 1918

"Dear Anna—We do not hear from you. Famine and kerosene drought worse. Mamma is hungry and depressed by lack of light."

After Kyra's news that America was Bolshevik, Cirie had stopped writing to Anna. Now, half-heartedly, she resumed because if America was Bolshevik, there was nothing to hope for. She had to believe they were still free.

"Ask Uncle Lawrence, ask Anton—ask anyone who can help—ask Uncle Lawrence's brother-in-law, the one with political connections—"

In December new officials came, wearing black leather jackets and black leather caps and boots, carrying briefcases, and produced the usual yellow paper. In the spring the estate would become a State Soviet Farm. All land, barns, animals and agricultural machinery were included in the order and all moujiks would participate equally. Only the Vodovskys were excluded. They could work the two small fields and the patch of garden alloted to them last year, but they could not use the equipment. They would be allowed one horse and one cow but there would be no ration of feed for the animals. No mention was made of the house. With gloating looks that spoke of years of hatred and the sweet taste of new power, the officials handed Vassily the yellow paper.

Every change is for the worse, Cirie thought. You can depend on it. Not yet evicted, they settled down to the cold of another long, dark, hungry winter.

36

❁

Stepa and Georgii, covered with snow, their faces pinched with cold, came in from attending to the horse and cow. "I wouldn't send a Commissar out tonight," Stepa said. He stood at the kitchen stove and fumbled in his pocket. "Gerzy brought a letter from Serge. He opened it because it was addressed to him."

Cirie turned around. "From Serge to Gerzy?"

"Probably thought a better chance it would be delivered. Serge has been wounded."

The scrap of paper was in Serge's handwriting. "This is news of your friend, S.V. who knew you in your stable. He is in hospital—a bullet in his shoulder. Recovering from pneumonia. After surgery on shoulder, he will go home. Tell his friends."

Flooded with relief that the news was not worse, Cirie handed back the letter. "Give it to Irene."

"It makes Gerzy sick to look at the horses," Georgii said. Georgii had stretched out this year and had a look, on this winter's meager diet, of no meat on his bones. He moved his arms to warm up and the wick in the kerosene bottle flickered. They no longer used a lamp but burned kerosene in a bottle with a wick through the neck—not so steady a light—the slightest breeze or vibration extinguished it and matches were scarce—but it consumed less kerosene. "The workers took the best and now they don't take care of them."

"It's true," Stepa said. "All those splendid animals. Thin now, with bad coats. Our old horse and cow that Georgii and I care for so lovingly are in better condition."

"That will cause trouble. The workers will resent it."

"What can we do? We can't neglect our animals as they neglect theirs." When Georgii had left the kitchen, Stepa said, softly, "Cirie, I know Serge pursued you while he was here. I love Serge but he's not for you."

Cirie shrugged. "Anything between us was a long time ago."

Stepa hesitated. "Marriage is a mystery, Cirie. Elissa and I were so much in love—and now we're apart. I doubt that Eugenie loved my brother when she married him but she applied herself and it wasn't a bad marriage." And Sacha Borassin? Cirie thought. Or was that part of applying herself—marriage in one place and love in another? Why not? If there is no love in the marriage? She had heard that the Bolsheviks had made divorce easy. The only good thing they'd done.

At dinner, Irene read the letter and burst into tears. "Oh, my poor Serge!"

"He says he's better!" Stepa said. The storm rattled the windows. "Tonight we don't have to worry about a visit. Nobody would move in this blizzard."

"Thank God Serge is safe and will be home soon," Madame said.

"Yes!" Irene cried. "And I am the one who will take care of him."

At her mother's unrestrained weeping, Christina began to wail and Alexei joined in. "Silence," Vassily shouted at his son. "Conduct yourself properly." Understanding the tone if not the words, Alexei cried harder.

Then Talley began to bark and raced to throw himself at the door. The familiar apprehensive silence fell over the room. "They can't put us out on a night like this," Irene cried. "They can't—I'm not well."

The barking grew more excited. A faint thud sounded at the door. "Was that a knock?" Stepa said.

"Whoever it is can hardly move," Cirie said. With Stepa beside her, she opened the door to an old man, bent with exhaustion, covered with snow—an old man with a full snow-white beard, wearing a ragged sheepskin coat, supporting himself with both hands on a rough stick. He looked as though the next gust of wind would blow him over.

"Come in, come in!" She reached out to help him.

With an effort the old man, frozen and shaking, struggled inside and raised his head and Cirie looked into the feverish blue eyes.

"Constantine!" She threw her arms around his chattering body. "Constantine!"

A little at a time, over several days, Constantine told his story. After ten feverish days in bed, he sat wrapped in a blanket near the fireplace where a single small log burned. The entire family hovered over him except Irene and Vara, the one fearing for their safety if they sheltered him, the other keeping her distance from this once-powerful man, reduced now to a white-bearded skeleton by Bolshevik prisons and months as a fugitive.

He was in prison twice, released once in error. The second time he escaped while being marched with other prisoners through the streets to a different prison. "A violent disturbance at a busy corner gave us a chance to save ourselves. Probably staged by some unsung heroes."

Theo, Cirie thought. Was Theo one of them? Is that what he's been doing in the year since he went away?

"The underground used to be Lenin's men. Now it's a handful of brave men and women who are trying to save Lenin's victims."

"After I escaped I went into hiding and lived like a beggar," Constantine said a few days later. He was so emaciated, he looked ancient but his eyes were still young. "I looked for Laranov. He was the only one I could trust, but he had disappeared."

"Constantine, we thank God you made it safely to us," Stepa said. Cirie looked at him, curious. Madame had thanked God that Serge was safe. Is it only a Russian habit or do they still believe God is looking out for them? God is not looking out for Russia and God is not looking out for us.

"What happened to Laranov?" Georgii said. "He helped me in Petrograd."

"I never found out. His specialty was supplies. The Kerensky government welcomed him, so today he would be the enemy—marked for prison or liquidation."

Laranov in a Soviet prison! Cirie thought with a shock. Or dead. Laranov who was so dynamic, so clever. It couldn't be.

"The Bolshevik Cheka is more sinister than the Tsar's secret police," Constantine said. "A trial today is a farce. It's called a Revolutionary Tribunal. Anyone can hear a case and pass sentence, even if he can't read. The defendant never sees his lawyer—"

Laranov wouldn't wait around for that, Cirie thought. Laranov would find a way to disappear.

"Lenin's people see enemies everywhere, trust no one. And are untouched by violence. The prisons are full of tragic cases," Constantine said. "People neglected, cold, starving, eaten by lice, and finally either shot or shipped to Siberia. By the time the end comes, it's usually welcome."

"Is Lenin really so cruel, then?" Madame said.

Constantine smiled. "I forget that here you don't get the reports. Lenin is brilliant and ruthless. He's wiping out all his enemies, real or imaginary—even the Socialists who were once his friends. His pattern is to kill an enemy and blame it on another enemy and kill him, too."

Every change is for the worse, Cirie thought. Only a short time ago people were praying for a strong government to put an end to anarchy and street crime. Now there's a strong government and the government is committing worse crimes.

"We heard rumors that there was an assassination attempt against Lenin, himself," Stepa said one morning at breakfast. They ate their meals in the kitchen now where the stove gave off some heat. "By a group of Counter Revolutionaries."

"It wasn't a group. It was one lone woman who felt he had betrayed the revolution. Fanya Kaplan."

"Too bad she didn't succeed," Stepa said.

"She was almost blind or she might have. The bullet is still in him. In Lubyanka, even though Lenin knew she had acted alone, this poor woman was tortured for information she didn't have and then shot in the head. Then publicly Lenin blamed the Counter-Revolutionaries and launched a campaign of terror against them that he'd planned long before. In his mind any deception is acceptable because his goal is a better world. His way."

"There's your steady permanent power," Stepa muttered to Cirie in a low voice.

Cirie turned to look at him. "If it's the same here," she said. "If it's no longer a new mob every day, maybe someone can be reached."

"Cirie, don't even think about it!" Stepa said.

This interested her. "However dangerous they are," she said coldly, "maybe something can be done—"

A loud frantic knock on the door interrupted them...

"Cirie, thank God you're here!" Tessa said when she opened the door. Tessa! Tessa, who had threatened to take her grain and burn down her house. "Cirie, my children are sick. Popov is sick." Popov, who had performed unspeakable acts in this house! Cirie shook her head.

"You can't get a doctor."

"I know you can't get a doctor." Better men than Popov were dying.

"Cirie, he's very bad!"

Good. The image that refused to die rose up in Cirie's mind, as sharp and revolting as the night it was formed. For days she had watched for signs that Madame remembered. Apparently she did not. "Tessa, I won't go."

"Cirie, those things I said—the others expected it. I was the leader—Popov was the leader."

"Popov is still the leader. And he has led mobs of people against me. And he will again."

"He won't. Cirie, we were once good friends. My children are burning with fever."

"Tessa, I will not go out for Popov."

"Cirie!" Tessa screamed.

Then Georgii came to the door. "Cirie, please can you come in a minute? Vassi needs you."

She left Tessa and returned to the kitchen where the sober frightened faces told her they had heard the conversation. Now she supposed Vassily would order her again to have nothing to do with these people. For once she agreed. Instead he said, unhappily, "Cirie, you have to take care of him."

"Take care of Popov!"

"If you don't he might die."

"Think what he's done to us!"

Stepa and Tanya were watching her, deeply troubled.

"If he lives he'll hear that you refused," Vassily said. "He'll take revenge on all of us. And if he dies, the others will avenge him. They'll say you're elitist—you thought you were too good to touch Popov."

"I take care of them all."

"Since when are they reasonable?"

"Cirie—hurry!"

"Understand this." Cirie lowered her voice to a whisper in case Tessa was eavesdropping. "I do not want to save Popov. Popov is a degenerate. He's disgusting and obscene."

"Cirie, life and death is not your decision to make," Madame said.

"They make it theirs."

"It's God's decision."

Cirie looked at Stepa for help. He returned her look with troubled eyes and remained silent. "You, too?" she said.

"Cirie doesn't decide about life and death," Tanya spoke up. "God decides. If it's revolting to her to go, we shouldn't force her."

"And when they come to avenge themselves on all of us for her fine sensibilities?" Vara said. "What then?"

Nobody spoke.

"Do you deny that they will?" Vara looked at Stepa.

Stepa sighed. "No. Almost surely they will come, whether he dies or lives, if Cirie refuses to treat him."

In spite of her revulsion, Cirie understood what they were saying. If I don't go to treat him and if he lives, as he might, he'll come here with murder in his heart. And he'll destroy us.

"Cirie, for God's sake, hurry—" Tessa called from the other room.

And if he dies, even if they hate him the others will come to avenge him because the Leader must be respected. And because a Vodovsky cannot be allowed to decide that a man is worthless. Either way, if I don't go, we are dead. They won't even let us flee from here peacefully.

And if I do go, after what Popov did, how do I live with myself?

Then Constantine, who had remained silent, said, "Cirie, in Petrograd, after I escaped the second time—"

"Sh-h-h—" Cirie motioned toward Tessa.

"In Petrograd," Constantine whispered, "I existed with a false identity card. I had sneaked back to my apartment house early one morning to ask about messages and my building superintendent, Feodor, was shot dead before my eyes."

"Cirie—" Tessa wailed,

"The murderers fled and before anyone else arrived I took Feodor's card. I was shocked at what I had done—" Constantine paused. "But I was a wanted man and I was determined to live to tell the world what the Revolution was like. And I didn't want to go back to prison. So I took it. My name now is Feodor. This is what the Revolution has done to us—our fine scruples are compromised."

He stopped and everyone was silent, except for Tessa wailing in the hall.

"Our scruples are a luxury," Constantine went on in a low voice. "They make us feel clean in a dirty world. Sane in a world gone mad. But there are times we close our eyes to them to survive."

Seated beside Popov's cot, Cirie made her deal. "Popov, I have always taken care of you—my father always took care of you." She did not touch him. She did not touch her medicine bag. "I helped bring your children into the world. And you turned against me—"

Feverish, eyes dull, Popov waved a hand to protest.

"There are no doctors." She anchored Popov's gaze with cold hard eyes. "I won't save your life to have you turn against me again."

"Cirie, he won't!" Tessa cried.

"If I take care of you, remember this. If you ever act against me or my family I will never come again."

"Cirie, give him something."

"Not even if your children are dying. You may think with your new power you can force me. But you'll never know whether I'm treating them or taking revenge. Do you want to live with that fear?"

Hate sat in Popov's eyes.

"And if you get rid of me, you'll have no one. You have your power." Still she anchored his eyes. "And I have mine. Agreed?"

Popov begrudged her a nod. She took out her lice apron and her thermometer from the medicine bag.

Outside Popov's hut she stood in a rut in the snowy road. *This is life,* she thought. Constantine said it. We compromise to survive.

But this compromise was different. This touched something deep inside her. She tried to shake it off. Get used to it—make friends with it—it's life, she told herself. You win something, you lose something. What does it matter? But something had changed. Something was gone and she felt that she would never be the same again.

She started home, walking in the rut in the snow. "Why is it so important?" she said to herself, "What's the difference when all of life is compromise? Especially today. Especially in Russia. It's how we survive."

She looked back at Popov's shabby hut and walked on in the rut in the road. "What does it matter?" she said. "Nitchevo."

37

❀

Now that it was spring the band concerts had started in the park. At lunch time the music floated out over Elizabeth Street and people congregated around the bandstand and young men and women laughed and flirted and for an hour you would never know that anything was wrong in Russia. Whenever she could, Lily went to the park with her friends, Olga and Tina, to listen to the music and watch the people. Olga was tall and a little heavy with brownish blonde hair and Tina was dark and wiry. It was Olga who first noticed the tall, polished, extremely handsome man on the other side of the bandstand. "There he is," Olga whispered. "Isn't he gorgeous? He looks as though he comes from Paris."

"He's very mysterious looking," Tina said. "Everyone flocks around him, but he just smiles and shakes hands and turns back to the music. All the girls are after him. Including Olga."

"Really, Olga?" Lily said. Olga was sixteen, more than a year older than Lily, but the man was at least twenty-five.

"He has dreamy eyes," Olga said.

"I think he's a playboy," Tina said. "He's charming to all the girls but he's not interested in any of them."

"I know his name now," Olga said. "I followed him yesterday. He has a pharmacy on Gleb Street and the sign says, Darius Kyrigen, Pharmacist."

Lily marveled at such courage. Two pretty girls smiled up at Darius Kyrigen and Lily thought, What must it be like to be so adored, to have everyone smile at you and wait for a smile in return? The way they do with Cirie. Some people in a lifetime never saw that look given so readily to Darius Kyrigen.

"They call him the Persian God," Olga said. "He's part Persian."

Darius Kyrigen's eyes traveled across the crowd and stopped a moment on Lily and her friends and moved on.

When the concert was over Lily hurried out of the park. She still had to do the lines. This morning in the bread line, as the young man handed her a loaf of bread, he whispered, "Come back this afternoon after we're closed." Lily understood that he was saying that later he would give her another loaf. And she had heard that today there would be butter. And then in the cigarette line she would have to smoke a cigarette to prove that she smoked. If she got butter, she would trade the cigarettes for sugar and salt. If not, she would trade them for butter.

Back at the bread window, the young man handed her another loaf. "Where do you live?" he said.

Lily blushed and waved a hand. "Over there. With my mother."

"Can you get out at night?"

"I couldn't!" If only she could think of a clever reply or just give him a slow smile, like Cirie. But, no! She just blushed and the words rushed out. "My mother would be hysterical. I'm all she has. I can't leave her."

The young man smiled. "Don't be nervous. I won't hurt you."

"Do you want the loaf back?" Lily blurted out.

"No! I saved it for you because you're so pretty. I don't want you to get thin and haggard like the others."

Lily couldn't believe it! People said things like that to Cirie and did special things because she was so pretty. But she had never expected it to happen to her.

$$*\qquad\qquad *\qquad\qquad *$$

Cirie stood at the window waiting for Georgii to bring up the horse and cart. A few days ago Lily had seen Gerzy in town and sent a message that a letter had arrived from America! "But it didn't say anything important," Lily had said. Still, a letter! Vassily had promised her the horse for a few hours this morning to go to her mother's to read it.

She looked out at the mist rising in pockets over neglected fields, where the workers' horses and cows had not yet been turned out and thought that the damp shroud reflected her own mood. You could hold on a long time in the face of hunger and cold and darkness and abuse and then, suddenly, you felt you couldn't go on. Not only the animals had had a hard winter.

Vassily and Stepa came in from the field, where they had been working since daybreak, and sat down at the rough round kitchen table for breakfast. They farmed these days with the most primitive tools—the workers had taken all the modern machinery—and yet Vassily's fields were plowed and planted and the contrast to the workers' fields was all too striking.

"I talked with Boloshin," Stepa said. Over the winter the estate had become a Soviet farm and the government representative, Boloshin, had moved into the manager's cottage. "I think he must be a former land owner who managed to get on the Bolshevik team."

"He knows farming," Vassily said. "But he can't control the workers."

"Still, maybe he can save the estate from total ruin."

Vassily turned to Cirie. "How soon can you get back?"

"I'll try to hurry." She knew he was thinking about the horse. "I have to stop at Gart's. Dunka was here. He's sick again."

Vara and Irene exchanged disapproving looks. "I'm surprised at Dunka's concern for a man who is taking advantage of her daughter," Vara said. Before the Revolution Dunka had been a Vodovsky cook. "She always seemed quite moral."

Ignore her, Cirie told herself. You're depressed enough today. Still she said, "Dunka is one of the few moujiks who has never lifted a hand against us. I think she's very moral."

Dunka even left little packages of food at night, not daring to antagonize the others by bringing them in daylight. There would be a light tap and when they opened the door they would find a little milk or a fish on the doorstep. The only time Dunka had remained at the door was the night she asked Cirie to visit her daughter's lover who was ill, begging her not to tell Madame about the relationship. Roza, a plump pretty girl, was living with a man whose wife and children were back in his native district. The lover, it turned out, was the Assistant Commissar of Agriculture and he had typhus. His name was Gart.

"The girl is an unkempt slattern, living openly with a married man," Vara said.

"It never bothered you when your society friends had what they called affairs of the heart."

"You mean Roza's arrangement doesn't offend you?"

"Who does it hurt?"

"Is that your only criterion?"

"I think so, Vara," Cirie said. "To me someone who doesn't hurt anyone these days is a person with very high standards."

"Cirie, I don't know that you should go to that house so often." Vassily looked up from his rye coffee. "I can't approve of this Gart. You must be very ill at ease there."

"Gart has more power than Popov," Cirie said, pointedly.

"Oh, I'm sure Cirie is quite at home there, Vassily," Irene said.

Cirie laughed. "I wouldn't think of missing a visit to Gart. I've learned a lot from him. Gart is the most outrageous person I know—and that's the only way to be these days."

The horse picked his way through the cheerless mist, ignoring an airplane that passed overhead and disappeared into a low cloud. Why do we cling to every shred of hope? Cirie thought. Things will be better if Boloshin can make the estate work again. Things will be better when the Civil War is over, when the border wars are over, when the government can turn its attention to problems at home. How will they be better? Today things never get better. At the end of a hard winter with too little food and too much disease and now a letter, awaited like a love letter, that said nothing, she was tired and hope was at a low ebb. "I think this will be our last year here—they won't let us stay much longer," she had said yesterday to Constantine. "We could be ready to leave on a moment's notice. But where can we go?"

With just Alexei I could go alone, she thought. With just Alexei I could find a way. And I may have to do it. Leave everyone, leave Mamma and Lily and go. The airplane was back, flying very low now, and Cirie tightened the reins. But the horse didn't protest, anymore. He was getting used to it.

"Anna has given up on Vogel at last," Marya said as she handed Cirie the precious letter. "She's taken the children and gone to Grandma. And Uncle Lawrence gave Grandma a store. They don't understand why we don't write."

Our letters haven't reached them. Not one! Quickly Cirie scanned the letter. What can we do to get through to them? Once you would have found someone who knew an official. Today you didn't ask an official anything for fear of calling attention to yourself. And you certainly wouldn't say you were trying to send a letter to America.

"A very nice neighborhood store," Anna wrote. "People say Uncle Lawrence is a hard-headed businessman and not above sharp practices, but he denies his mother nothing."

Cirie looked up. "Mamma, Grandma has a store! And Uncle Lawrence supplied the money!"

"He won't regret it. If anyone can make it pay, Grandma can."

"It's a *private* store. And Uncle Lawrence has *private* money. America is still free!"

"That letter is six months old, Cirie. The papers say things have changed."

"The papers are lying! Constantine says the government spreads the rumor to destroy hope. If you can hope for outside help, you hold out. If there's no hope, your resistance crumbles."

"I don't know," Marya said doubtfully. "Your Constantine used to be in a position to learn things. Now—"

"Mamma, they're free! We can go there."

"If we can get papers, if we can get out of Russia, if we can get there with no money, if—if—" Marya had no hope of surmounting all the obstacles.

"Since America went to war the women here seem more daring," Anna wrote. "Many have cut their hair—some very short, others to the shoulders...."

While Cirie was reading the rest of the letter, Lily came in with two loaves of bread. "The man at the bread line gives her extra because she's pretty," Marya said. "It's nice that something is still normal."

"He doesn't want me to become thin and haggard." Lily was in high spirits today. "Olga is in love with a man she sees at the concerts."

"And is he in love with her?" Marya said.

"He doesn't even know her!" Lily laughed very hard. "He's very handsome. All the girls flirt with him."

How many centuries is it since I laughed like that? Cirie thought.

"Cirie, I have a present for you," Marya said. She took a tortoise shell comb and brush from her sewing basket. "You said they took yours in one of the visits." It was her own comb and brush. "A Commissar's wife gave them to me. I fixed over a dress for her."

It was probably one of my dresses, too, Cirie thought. "Do you think cutting their hair really makes American women feel more daring?"

"I think it would make them look fast," Marya said.

When she came out of Marya's apartment, clouds had moved in and the world seemed back in winter, with the trees bare and spindly and threads of willows beaten by the wind. Even the birds were still. The world is falling apart, Cirie thought, and yet schoolgirls still get crushes. And Vara and Irene reassure each other of their superior standards. And Dunka worries that Madame will know that her daughter has set up housekeeping with a married man. And what difference does any of it make? Everyone is the whole show to himself—the center of his own little universe. Even the Communists, who claim to be interested in the welfare of mankind. Especially the Communists who are supposed to be interested in the welfare of mankind.

She was at Gart's.

*   *   *

"Gart, I told you to stay indoors another two weeks," Cirie said. "Now look at you."

"Cirie, I was pining for you! I wanted you to come to see me again. Isn't that so, Roza, my beauty?" Even with a heavy cold, the boisterous exuberant Gart had not lost his spirit. He stroked his black mustache and his eyes twinkled. "The truth is, it's a beautiful spring. I wanted to check on the mating season for the sake of Russia's future."

"Gart, you're insane, you know that."

"Of course—of course! It's what saves me. Who but a madman could keep his sanity today?"

Cirie sent Roza to make some raspberry tea. Very hot. "And build up the fire. Get up on the stove, Gart, and pour hot tea into yourself or you'll get pneumonia and I won't take care of you."

Gart gave her a broad smile. "The truth is I had to sacrifice myself for the cause. Lenin and Trotsky were in despair—without me the anti-Bolsheviks would be back and we would all be slaves again when now we're so free. Isn't that so, Roza, my beauty?" he shouted.

Roza giggled. "Tell her the truth, Gart."

"The truth!" Gart doubled over with laughter. "The truth is I was arrested!"

"Don't be silly, Gart." People who got arrested disappeared and you never saw them again.

"It's true!" Gart shouted. "Someone has it in for me. You know how it is—whenever I can steal something, I steal it. Listen, that's what you do these days. If I'm ordered to close out an estate or conduct a domiciliary visit, if I didn't steal a few things, who would respect me? They'd say I wasn't fit to be a leader."

"Of course." Cirie laughed.

"And most of what I stole I kept in Dunka's hut—an unpretentious little hut—who would have any use for it? Dunka is happier with my little Roza. And somebody squealed on me." Gart leaned forward. "And that Commissar is so dishonest! While I was sick he went to my unimportant little hut and took everything. Cleaned me out! Then he sent four soldiers to arrest me. When I was led into his office, there he was—splendid in a new suit, sitting behind a splendid desk, wonderful boots, a pistol on his desk with a pearl handle, a gold letter opener, although he doesn't open his own letters because he thinks it's important that the secretary slice them open and besides he can't read. And this splendid creature, this unshaven pig, was ready to line me up against the wall—after all, the distance from an arrest to the wall is very short these days. I'm standing there thinking, what prison is going to have the pleasure of my company? We have three prisons in Kostyka now."

"Three! I hadn't heard three."

"They say each is for a different type of offense, but the fact is, the only question is where is there room, because they're all filled to overflowing. They can't ship the prisoners to Siberia fast enough. I took one look at this Commissar—this thief—and I roared with laughter. I slapped the desk, I seized his hand and congratulated him. What a capital joke! Every single splendid thing about him, everything he wore, his desk and everything on it—the silver, the gold—was something I had stolen that he had stolen from me! That's how dishonest he is! I laughed until I cried. I congratulated him. Pretty soon he started to laugh, too. He decided that he was very clever. I assured him that he was. And he told me he liked my taste in thievery and he sent me home. In the rain. So I caught a cold and, if not for you, I would come down with pneumonia. Meanwhile he cleaned me out. I have to start over."

Cirie couldn't remember when she had laughed so hard. "Gart, you're the most outrageous, unscrupulous man I've every known."

"Of course, of course!" he said. "How else do you survive?"

Roza brought the hot tea and Gart, on top of the stove, began to drink it and to sweat profusely. Dunka came in with butter cakes and strawberry jam and Cirie ate them ravenously. They were the first sweets she had tasted in months. Nobody had butter or sugar or jam except Commissars. Already she felt her spirits reviving.

"Have some chocolates," Gart said. "Someone brought them to the Commissar as a bribe. I stole a few when I was in his office."

Cirie shook her head at Gart's irrepressible bravado. Then she said, "What do you think, Gart? Will these be our last days here? Are they getting ready to throw us out?"

"I think it will be soon," Gart said, sadly.

"How can we save some things, Gart?"

"You must do it! You'll need bribes or you won't survive." Gart looked sober while he considered the problem. Then his eyes brightened. "Listen, Cirie, it's time for another inventory. The last one is useless. We're so efficient now that we must have things straight." Gart howled at his own joke. "I'll supervise it myself. It will be in pencil—who can get a pen these days? There'll be plenty for everyone. For me to steal from you. For you to steal your own things. I'll bribe some people to help you smuggle them out. The inventory will show only half of what's there. I'll fix it up myself. Our present inventory is worthless because so much has been stolen or requisitioned. We might need something and we won't know whether you have it or we've stolen it already." Gart coughed and doubled over at his plan. "Believe me, Cirie, it's a good plan."

"It's a great plan, Gart," Cirie agreed. "A plan of genius."

When she came out of Gart's house, the clouds had moved on and the sun was bright and new green showed on trees and Gart had reminded her of something she had almost forgotten. There are ways, she said to herself. Somehow, somewhere, there are ways. This is the new morality—everything comes to those who have power, everything belongs to those who steal it. And something can still be done. As long as you believe that if you take the first step there will be another step

someplace. Like Gart you might find opportunities where there are no opportunities in sight.

At home she put away the horse. A warm soft breeze blew in her face. In her
pocket she felt the comb and brush that Marya had given her. Better than a white
smock to show up the lice. Suddenly she felt almost whole again. It was Gart and
the spring and, she thought realistically, the sugar in the cakes and candy that had
restored her energy. Impulsively, she went upstairs and, in front of a small cracked
mirror, the only one she had left, she cut her hair and felt young again and daring.
Is it possible, she thought, that I've found another little well of hope?

38

Serge did not touch reality these days any more than he had to. He relived his memories and his memories were of Paris—of those carefree days when he was young and rich and loving and loved—and of his one idyllic summer with Cirie. Now, whenever he saw her the desire was the same, fresh and strong as though he had never felt it before. The dream of having her gave him his reason for living.

On a day in late July, when he had been home a week, he sat on the edge of the pool and smoked his home-made cigarette rolled in a scrap of an old book. The statue of the three nubile young women pouring water into the pool was broken—hands missing, a head gone, a nose smashed—and the dry pool was littered with debris—twigs, broken bottles, even a little manure. How did that happen so far from the fields? Serge looked around him. How did any of it happen? The estate was in ruins, the crops scrawny, the animals half-dead, the moujiks hacking down the forests, although they didn't do much other work.

The government man, Boloshin, was here to advise, not to issue orders—one of the dividends of this great new god, Equality. The workers thought Equality would take care of everything, like the spirits they believed in. They couldn't see it was a god of total destruction. Every morning the equal workers met and voted on the jobs each would do in the morning and the jobs each would do in the afternoon. The vote had to be unanimous and all the workers had to have a turn at all the jobs, in the stables, in the fields, even maintaining the machinery, whether they knew anything about it or not. They were managers. As managers they had taken the leather belt from Vassi's American threshing machine and used it to make shoes and now when the thresher was needed, they couldn't get another belt so the machine stood idle and they threshed with the most primitive of methods—with flails. It didn't upset them. They loved being managers.

Serge braced his arm on his knee to relieve his shoulder. Over in the little patch of garden he saw Vassily straighten up and work his back muscles and he thought that he ought to go over to help him—he could weed with one arm—but for now he sat and smoked and let the memories begin. It was almost August and in Paris August was still summer and shops were closed and people went away on holiday. In Russia by mid-August they began to prepare for winter. Did they still set the birches to mark the road and the river in the snow or did that practice disappear with the rest of civilization? His reveries settled on Cirie.

Every time he found her alone, she rebuffed him and denied that she still loved him. He did not believe her. She was young and passionate—who knew that better than he?—and more beautiful than ever, as though the fires of adversity had flamed the metal and polished it to a fine glow, and she was stuck out here with Vassily. A dull husband, two old men, two old women, two jealous younger women and a teen-age boy and girl. She was starving for love—he could feel it. And he loved her more than ever.

Walking toward the house, Cirie didn't notice Serge until she came up to him. Automatically, she shot a quick look at the house. "Hello, Serge."

"Cirie, wait!" he said. "Talk to me a minute."

She didn't want to be alone with him. "You ought to be helping someone, Serge. Even Irene is working today."

"I'm going over to help Vassi in the garden." With his good arm, Serge motioned to the scrawny fields. "Cirie, this place is falling apart."

She sat a little distance from him on the edge of the pool. Over in his garden she saw Vassily straighten up to survey his vegetables. "Vassi has tried to tell them what they should do but they won't listen." Vassily could no longer look at the ruin around him. He had taken all that expertise that had produced three of the most productive estates in Russia and concentrated it on his garden—a small patch in the community vegetable garden. Every day, after he had worked in the field, he turned to his garden. He fertilized, he weeded, he carried water from the river. Next to the workers' unweeded desert of stunted squash and carrots and beets, it was an oasis.

"He's in that garden every spare minute," Serge said.

"He's in love with it. It's his perfect creation."

Serge looked narrowly at Vassily. "Cirie, remember that summer we were in love? Those mornings at sunrise when the whole world was just the two of us." He touched her hand and she drew it away. "If he hadn't torn us apart, it would still be just the two of us. We'd be out of all this. We'd be in Paris."

Cirie stood up.

"Don't go!"

"Serge, can't you see how things are here?"

"I have only to look around—"

"That's not what I mean."

"The horses are the worst," Serge said, sadly. "I can't go near the stables."

"Nobody takes care of them!" she said. "If they don't get their unanimous vote on who's to do it, nobody waters or feeds them. And they work them all morning, anyway. Then at noon they just leave them and go to their own lunch. And other people work them all afternoon. Still no feed or water. It breaks your heart. They're emaciated, they've all got a horrible skin disease. Stepa and Georgii have tried to water them but the workers won't let them interfere. They left us our old horse and cow because they were the worst of the lot. Now they're the best. Just like our two little fields and the garden."

Vara came out of the house and saw them and hurried back inside.

"Just like old times." Serge grinned. "We always worried about whether Vara had seen us."

"Yes, and it will stir up trouble, the same as then."

She moved to leave and he touched her arm. "Stay a little longer. I'm going over to help Vassi in a minute." It was getting hot and Cirie took off the kerchief that she wore in the fields and shook her hair. "I like your hair," he said. "It makes me want to touch it."

"Don't."

"But don't cut it any shorter. I want to feel it across my face."

Without warning, feelings she had told herself she did not feel and could not feel and had every reason not to feel, shot through her.

"Cirie, meet me tonight. Go out to see a patient."

"No!"

"When then?"

"Serge, there can't be anything between you and me again. Don't let it get started."

"It never stopped. Cirie, I love you!"

"Serge, we're struggling just to survive here, all of us together. We have nowhere to go. If there were something between you and me, we couldn't all go on living together this way."

"Nobody has to know."

"They would know. They knew that summer—everyone knew—and they would know now."

A breeze blew her kerchief to the ground and she bent over to retrieve it and at the same moment Serge reached for it and his hands closed over hers. "Cirie, come away with me."

Cirie withdrew her hand.

"Elope with me. We'll go to Paris. We can do it. As long as we have each other, we'll find a way."

"Once I used to say that to you, Serge. But now I have Alexei."

"Vassi and Maman will take care of him."

"Leave Alexei! I'll never do that!"

"All right, we'll take him."

"It's more than Alexei, Serge. I can't abandon my mother and my sister."

"Once we're in Paris we'll send for them. An underground is working all over Russia now, smuggling people out."

"Who?" she said quickly. "Where?"

"Cirie, look at this place. Everything is gone. There's nothing left but you and me. We have a right to live. We belong to each other."

"Where is this underground, Serge?"

"We'll find them," he said. "Irene will leave me soon. She's going to her sister in the south. She feels that from there they can get out."

"She's going to leave you!"

Serge nodded.

We could make it, Cirie thought. The nightmare would be over. The nightmare of this mean life and the nightmare of a loveless marriage.

"Darling, you do love me. I can feel it."

The despair would end at last.

"Tell me you still love me."

"Of course I still love you! Of course I do!"

"Then you'll do it! You'll go with me!"

"I don't know—I have to think—" She broke off as she saw Vassily's head snap up. His attention was riveted on something across the field. "What's he looking at?"

"Cirie," Vassily shouted and started to run toward the fields.

Without knowing the problem Cirie ran too. Then she saw it. A worker was viciously whipping a horse that lay on the ground without moving. The worker shouted and cursed and the sounds of the whip cut the air. The horse lay still, eyes dull, accepting the lashes on its scaled and bleeding hide.

"Stop!" Vassily shouted.

The whip sliced the air. The horse uttered no protest. He made no effort to rise. Cirie saw that it was the stallion, Mita, once the best of the work horses, now just a helpless skeleton covered with stiff sores. The worker raised the whip again and Cirie shuddered. His look was like that look of total cruelty, the symbol of evil, that still haunted her—the face of Marushka. She seized his arm. "Gosha, if you kill him it will be your back, not his, that will do the work!"

Impelled by his own momentum, Gosha raised his arm again and then lowered it and flung away the whip. The horse lay panting, his eyes glazed.

"When was he last watered?" Cirie said. "When was he fed?"

Gosha shrugged. "That's not my job."

"Go get some water now, even if it's not your job."

"I have water," Vassily said. "I brought it for the garden."

As they bent down together to hold the bucket to Mita's mouth, they saw that he was dead.

"I'm afraid of what they'll do now," Boloshin said that evening. "Gosha will report the dead horse and lie about how it happened. The workers are already complaining that your horse and cow are better. And your rye. And, my God, your garden! The Commissar says your presence is upsetting to them. You're living too well. It's a bad example."

"A bad example!"

Vassily couldn't understand but Cirie knew what Boloshin was saying. We took the worst and made it the best and they resent it. It's the sickness of the times.

Two days later, soldiers arrived to take Vassily and Serge "for questioning." All night the family waited for their return. The next morning Dunka brought a message from Gart that they had been arrested.

Stepa broke the frightened silence that followed. "I'll go into town to see what I can find out."

"They'd probably arrest you, too," Cirie said. "I'll go." The thought of Serge in a filthy Bolshevik prison chilled her. She should have loved him while she could. Now he might be lost forever.

"Which one are you thinking about?" Irene screamed at her.

And poor Vassi—so fastidious, clinging through everything to the standards of the lost civilization—held prisoner, perhaps even tortured, by ignorant power-crazed men who had once bowed low to him. Tortured! Serge tortured!

"They don't need any excuse to arrest you," Constantine said to Stepa. "They can just decide you're an enemy."

"Then I'll go along and I won't get too close to them."

Cirie looked at Madame, erect and dry-eyed, and she reached out to touch the thin, blue-veined hand. "We'll find out what prison they're in and what must be done," she promised.

"Nothing can be done," Irene sobbed.

"Take food and clean clothing," Constantine said. "Sew a message into a seam. Other prisoners will tell them to look."

Stepa decided they should not start at the prison for political prisoners. "In case it's a political charge, if we go there first, it will appear that we know something. We'll assume they've been arrested on the false charge of killing the horse."

In Kostyka they went first to the prison for common criminals, behind the stalls of the outdoor market. At the windows dirty degenerate faces, crowded together, peered through bars. Outside, a long line of women waited with bundles.

"They're not allowed anything but food and clothing," a woman in line told her. "No books, no paper, no pencils. Not even a clock."

Serge—immaculate, fun-loving Serge—stripped of everything, wedged in among the degenerates at the window. I should have loved him! He was right—tomorrow we may all be dead. If I ever get him back, I'll meet him, I'll go to him, I'll love him. And I'll elope with him to Paris. There's so little left—of life, of everything—I won't waste it again.

"This prison is for thieves and murderers," the woman said. "My husband was a shopkeeper. They put them wherever they have room."

"Did they tell you right away that your husband was here?"

"When they've got a record, they'll tell you, but that doesn't happen right away. Yes, he's here, they'll say. No more."

Then it will be easier to do something before there's a record, Cirie thought. Time is important. It was noon before she reached the gate and was told that Vassily and Serge were not here.

She found Stepa and they hurried to the Cheka prison for political prisoners, behind Party Headquarters. Here there was an atmosphere of extreme caution, as in an occupied city. Again in the crush of faces at the barred windows she searched for Serge and Vassily. At three o'clock she reached the gate. "No, they're not here."

"I suppose Serge could have been sent to the military prison," Stepa said. "But why Vassi?"

"In the lines they say they're sent where there's space."

"The military prison is the largest," Stepa said. A sprawling depressing structure, it stood next to a mansion that housed the high command.

Coming out onto Elizabeth Street, passing the Party Headquarters, Cirie wondered aloud about going to Gart. "I suppose it could cause him a lot of trouble without doing any good."

"It could cut off a source of information we may need later."

Cirie stopped. "We need the information now. Later may be too late."

"Try the military prison—it's the last one," Stepa said. "If we don't learn anything there, we'll know they're not telling us and we'll come back to Gart."

Cirie hesitated. Even two hours could be important. Then she saw Gart coming out of Party Headquarters with some other officials. "Comrade Commissar—" She approached him cautiously.

"What! What is it?" Gart shouted nastily, looking at her as though he'd never seen her before. "Oh, it's you! Pestering me again about your cow that has been requisitioned!"

"But, Comrade, where is my poor cow?"

"Your cow is where it's needed. What do you think I did with it—sent it to the military prison?" He seized her arms and turned her around. "Now go—there's nothing I can do—don't bother me again."

"Comrade—" Cirie said, softly. In the dim light of the office, she gave the slender young man at the table a slow smile and an innocent look. The young man stood up. His uniform was neat and even his hands and fingernails were clean. Another well-bred idealist, who had turned his back on his former life in the name of the cause. "The guard was good enough to let me come in. I promised not to trouble you more than a few minutes."

"It's no trouble," the young man assured her. "I'm Comrade Tovarin, Pavel Tovarin." He pulled up a chair for her.

"I am Comrade Vodovsky and I'm inquiring about two prisoners—my husband and his brother."

"Vodovsky?" He went to a file drawer. "They're not here."

"They were brought in only last night."

"Oh, just last night. Then their names wouldn't be in the file." He picked up a list on the table. "Why do you think they're here?"

"By sheer coincidence the horse of a friend reared at a sudden noise last evening quite near here. Did you hear the disturbance?"

"I wasn't here, but a sudden noise isn't unusual these days."

"And as our friend, a moujik, was quieting his horse, he saw my husband and his brother being taken into the prison." She lowered her black eyelashes and raised them again. "We were fortunate that they were seen by our friend. We were able to reassure my husband's mother, a gentle old woman in the final years of life, that her sons were taken, even though in error, to the military prison where they would surely receive justice, rather than to a prison for criminals or enemies of the State."

Pavel Tovarin watched her, smiling. "Why do you say in error?"

"My husband is an older man who keeps to himself," Cirie confided. Pavel settled back in his chair. "The only thing he knows well is agriculture. At that he's an expert. I haven't heard the charges against him."

"That will be taken care of in the next day or two."

"What could he have done, an older man who is an expert only at agriculture? It must have been in error." She looked into his pale eyes and Pavel was transfixed. "What do you think?"

"Perhaps someone gave information against him by mistake."

"That could be it!" Cirie exclaimed. "How lucky I am to have found you! You know how it is—when everyone is working in the fields, it's so easy to confuse one person with another. And his brother is a soldier in the Red Army, only recently wounded. I'm sure you're right. It's a case of mistaken identity. I can't tell you how you've helped me."

She closed her eyes and he hurried to her side. "Are you all right?"

"Of course."

"You look weak." Pavel closed the office door. "Let me give you some brandy."

From under the papers in his bottom drawer he took out a bottle of Napoleon brandy and Cirie wondered if it had come to him as a bribe. She sipped the brandy. "Comrade Pavel—?" She let her eyes ask the question.

Pavel's smile said he was enjoying this lovely interlude and was not at all put out by the suggestion. He read the list again. "What are their names?"

"Vassily and Serge."

"Vodovsky—no, the names are not yet on the list—"

Cirie smiled and waited.

Pavel reached a decision. "I'm on duty tonight until midnight. Come back after dark. I'll come out for some fresh air at ten o'clock."

"Oh, Pavel. "She looked deep into his eyes. "Thank you."

"The records are terrible—no one will notice," he said, as though reassuring himself. "As long as they haven't been charged, I may be able to do something. There's only one problem. We have a new general next door who turns up at any hour. If he's here, I'll have to deny everything."

"Is he in charge of the prison?"

"No, he's just always looking around."

"I'm sure he won't be here, I've been so fortunate until now." She held out her hand. "Thank you, Comrade Pavel. I'll see you tonight."

"You'll have to know the password. When they stop you at the gate, they'll say, 'Red Glory.' Your response should be, 'Death to the exploiters.' He walked out with her. In an office across the hall, a stocky scowling man was hastily signing papers without looking at them.

"Is that the new general?" she whispered.

"No, he's a prison official."

"What are all those papers he signs without looking at them?"

Pavel looked over at the stack of papers. "Death warrants."

He held open the door. "Be careful tonight. After dark the streets are danger-ous. The patrols shoot without warning. Or you could be stopped and arrested without explanation. These are difficult times—there are enemies everywhere."

At a little before ten o'clock Cirie left Marya's apartment. Wrapped in a hooded black cape, she stood in the shadow of the building until she was certain the street was empty. Then, hugging the buildings she proceeded cautiously along a series of narrow alleys, stopping whenever a patrol passed on the main street. At the prison gate, she said, "Death to the exploiters."

The gate squeaked open and she slipped into the yard. At the prison door, Pavel stood erect, examining the stars. "Good evening, Comrade," Cirie whispered. Pavel did not reply. He gave no sign of recognition. He did not move a muscle. Something had gone wrong. At a side door of the mansion, she heard the click of a heavy lock. Pavel's eyes slid over to the door. Gunfire sounded in the street. The door groaned open.

"The general?" Cirie whispered.

Almost imperceptibly, Pavel nodded.

The smell of tobacco filled the cool summer night. What lies can I tell this general who has already seen me—at least has seen a figure in a black cloak? The general moved toward her. Cirie ordered herself to be calm. She arranged her face in an expression of bewildered innocence, drew a deep breath and turned—and looked up into the face of Ilya Laranov.

"Cirie, what the hell are you doing here?"

Laranov closed the door and swiftly took her in his arms as he had the last time she saw him, that night in Strengov's office while she packed the medicines. "Let me look at you. God, Cirie, how do you do it? You're more beautiful than ever!"

For a second, while Laranov kissed her, Cirie wondered whether he was responsible for Serge's arrest and put aside the suspicion. She was as bad as the Bolsheviks, seeing enemies on all sides. Then she reminded herself that you saw enemies everywhere these days because you could trust no one. "Laranov, how long have you been here?"

"Three days. How did you know I was here?"

"I didn't." Laranov was just the same—bold dark eyes, dark hair and mustache, his tall body still suggesting energy to burn. "Everyone's been wondering about you," she said and checked herself. Constantine was a fugitive and Laranov was a Bolshevik general. "Irene and Serge came from Petrograd last year and everyone asked if they'd seen you."

"That must be interesting. Your old lover in the next bedroom."

Cirie swallowed a retort. He had never liked Serge—and now he held Serge's life in his hands. At his desk, Laranov poured himself some vodka. "I'm surprised you're still at Rivercliff. Why have they left you alone?"

"We cooperate. We don't do anything to upset them."

Laranov laughed. "Well, I'll hear the reason soon enough. Do you want some vodka?"

"Laranov," she blurted out, "you've got them here."

"What do I have here?"

"Vassily and Serge."

Now Laranov understood why she was here. Standing at his desk he studied her.

"Laranov, they haven't done anything. They haven't even been accused of anything."

"They'll probably be accused of counter-revolutionary activity. Especially your husband."

"How could Vassi be involved in counter-revolutionary activity?" Cirie coaxed him. "He only knew how to control things with money. He's no threat to anyone. He hardly speaks to anyone. He hardly speaks to me."

"It sounds like a loving marriage." Laranov regarded her with curiosity." So it's your husband you want?"

"I want them both!"

"I thought so."

"They're equally innocent!"

From across the room Laranov watched her, his dark eyes enigmatic, laughing. Laughing at what? At her plight? That she had come to him to beg for Serge. Cirie shuddered to think that he had power over them. And he's not vulnerable like other men, she thought. He has no weaknesses—nobody can touch him. Across the dimly-lighted room, he said, "If I can only give you one, are you prepared to choose?"

"I can't choose one! I can't go home and tell Madame that one of her sons is lost. They're all she has left."

Laranov moved around the room and Cirie started as he passed a chest in the corner.

"What's the matter?" he said.

"That chest."

He didn't recognize it.

"It's the Oriental chest from Whitewater. I used to touch it for luck." She saw other furniture from Rivercliff—a sofa, and the desk and chair from Vassily's office. "It was one of the first things the moujiks stole. They filled it with silver and China and carried it down to a dory. They were going to use it for a log bin."

"Shall I send it back to you?"

"No, Laranov. Send back my husband and his brother."

Laranov smiled. "You always had spirit, Cirie. You can have the chest if you want it. I didn't furnish this room."

"Your desk and the sofa are ours, too. And the paintings."

"I'd give them back but someone will only take them again."

He came close to her. "Cirie, I want to love you. I've wanted to love you from the minute I saw you—when you were hurrying back from a rendezvous with another man. I envied him when he came along, even though he'd been eaten by gnats. I've thought of you every day and wondered if I'd ever see you again. I thought of you the minute I was assigned here." He touched her face. "Don't tell me it shocks you that I want to make love to you."

Shock her! From the moment she saw him, she had been counting on it. That night in Strengov's office, he had said, "I'm under your spell." She prayed the spell was intact. Still, she should appear to be shocked. "Laranov, you know I'm married."

He burst out laughing. "Don't be coy with me, Cirie. You came here tonight to talk someone into giving you your lover and your husband. What did you have in mind? That boy outside who was dying to talk to you and afraid to say a word after I came outside—how were you going to persuade him to help you?"

"Laranov, that night in Novotnii you risked your life for me. Why won't you give me two men who haven't done anything?"

"That night I didn't have time to ask for anything. Tonight I do."

"There's not even a risk. No one knows yet that they're here."

"Darling, in normal times I'd be willing to woo you, but these aren't normal times. We don't any of us know if we'll be alive tomorrow or next week and certainly not next month. I want you tonight. And if I find myself inside the prison next week instead of outside, or if I find myself in Siberia next month, it'll be my most cherished memory."

"That's all anyone says these days," Cirie cried. "Tomorrow we may be dead. Only today matters."

"Who else says that to you? Your precious Serge?"

"No!"

"Doesn't he know you're married? Poor Serge—married to the woman his brother picked for him and lusting for the wife his brother took for himself. I'm surprised to hear that he has to plead his case to become your lover again. Or is he pleading for more than that? Does he want you to run away with him to Paris? That's everyone's dream today. Cirie, he'll never go through with it. It's a rough trip. You could make it, but he couldn't. If you decide to go, leave your lover behind."

"Laranov, why do you keep saying that? He was never my lover."

"Are you serious?"

"Yes."

"Why not?"

There was no point in lying to Laranov. "Because I intended to marry him."

"And you thought once he'd had you, he might not marry you?"

"Yes."

Laranov smiled. "Cirie, has it occurred to you that you really don't think much of him?"

"He was very young then!" She checked herself. His opinion of Serge didn't matter as long as he set him free.

"Cirie—" Laranov took her in his arms again. "Come let me love you. You're alive—you're young—and you're married to an old man you can't possibly care for. And the man you think you love isn't a man at all. You don't even know what it is to be loved."

He pulled her close and crushed his mouth on hers and she thought again of that night in the office and her own fleeting fire in those few seconds when danger was all around them. She broke away. "Laranov, think! Think what you're suggesting!"

"God, I know what I'm suggesting!"

She stared at him. "You want me to buy their lives and that's the price!"

"You want me to take a chance for your precious Serge. Cirie, the worst thing that could happen would be for you to get your Serge because you'd be disappointed."

It could have been Strengov talking.

Abruptly Laranov went to his desk and tossed down a glass of vodka and poured another and took it to the window and stood looking out at the prison. "Achilles absent is Achilles still," he murmured.

"What?"

"A Roman writer wrote that two thousand years ago. Serge Vodovsky may be over there in the prison but I can't get him out of this room."

Cirie waited but Laranov remained at the window, drinking his vodka and staring at the hideous sprawling building where Serge was locked away from her. She picked up her cloak and left.

She made her way back through the alleys, more slowly than before, asking herself if there was any other way to save them. But if Gart had the power, he would already have helped her and she didn't know anyone else. Nobody knew this mob in control today. But she couldn't just let Serge and Vassi die or be sent to hard labor in Siberia or languish for years in a lice-infested prison. She had heard about these prisons—and not only from Constantine. Everyone had heard about them. Twelve men and women in a filthy stinking cage meant for two. The only facilities were two buckets—one of dirty water for drinking, the other a toilet. They slept on the floor that was crawling with lice. In the shadow of a building she stopped. "How can you do it?" she whispered to herself. "How can you abandon Serge and Vassi to that? Is your so-called virtue worth so much?" Virtue!

"It isn't even virtue you're thinking about," she confronted herself, without illusions. She had never been concerned about virtue—except as a weapon. The only man she had ever wanted and resisted was Serge and virtue had nothing to do with it.

In the narrow alley she stared at the dark houses. Does anyone know whether these houses shelter virtue or evil? Even if there are saints inside, does anyone care? And is there any greater evil than the cruelty in Russia today in the name of a supposedly virtuous cause? On Elizabeth Street shots erupted as patrols of soldiers rode around in open cars firing as they pleased, cutting down lives for no reason. Is there any conceivable virtue there? In the dark alley she waited for the shooting to stop and then she retraced her steps to the prison. Walking slowly, she asked herself whether, if Serge were not involved, if it were only Vassily in the prison, she would go back and she thought, I would go back for a stranger!

Laranov went back to the desk that was her husband's, and filled a water glass with vodka and returned to the window, staring out at the prison that held the man who had blocked his way to the only woman he had ever wanted for more than a night. The man who still stood in his way. The only woman who had ever aroused his interest as well as his passion. Radiant, desirable, elegant even in her black cloak, she was so strong, so clever, so perceptive about everything else—how could she be obsessed with that idiot, Serge? For five years!

Laranov drank down half of his drink and unlocked a drawer in the desk. In his diary, he turned to the page he had copied from an entry he had written that summer at Whitewater. Since the Revolution he had re-read it so many times it had come to define him. "...I am for Russia...She is a creature of beauty, vitality and infinite variety. I am caught by her challenge. I am tantalized by her possibilities. I love the promise of how magnificent she could become...She is in my blood." He remembered the moment when he knew that with no changes he could have written the words about Cirie.

He was staring at the prison again when he heard the light tap and she walked in. He waited for her to make one last effort at a deal other than the one he had offered. But she simply stood there, radiant, as though she were the victor. He saw that she had no intention of speaking—she had triumphed over herself—and she had come back to pay his price. Damn her!

With great tenderness, he touched her face. "Are you so reluctant?"

She only looked at him out of those incredible eyes.

"Tell me how you feel," he said, softly, his feelings naked for her to see. "I have to know."

Still she didn't speak. He grasped her wrist. "Cirie, apart from all the rules, apart from what your mother taught you, apart from the fact that I was temporarily insane and made it the price of their lives—" He stopped speaking and let the rest of the question ask itself.

"Laranov," she said, softly, "when I first came to Whitewater, they weren't nice to me and I was very unhappy. And one day, riding alone at daybreak, I told myself, There is a little part of me, deep inside, that no one can touch—the part of me that is <u>me</u>. There it is my world and I am in command. I am the ruler, the autocrat. And as long as <u>that</u> is alive, I am alive. And untouched. And free."

Astounded, Laranov stared at her. "Damn you, Cirie!"

She looked up, startled.

Suddenly he laughed. "Do you remember the night you delivered the foal? I never loved you more than that night. I thought then that no one would ever get the best of you. And neither would I!"

He released her and went back to the window that looked out on the prison, knowing he had lost. At last he turned back to her. She was calm, serene, not frightened—and not wanting him. "Take him," he said, from across the room. "I won't play his cards for him. If I let you make this enormous sacrifice for him, you'll cherish him more than before and cling to him forever." He came back and drew her close again. "Damn you, Cirie, and your hold on me."

Through the dark alleys she hurried Serge and Vassi to Marya's apartment and herded them into the bathroom to rid themselves of lice with soap and water and precious kerosene and to change into the clean clothing she had brought and now they sat in the tiny living room, waiting for the first light, to go home.

Traumatized, Vassily sat absolutely silent in a corner, erect, head high, as though convincing himself that he was still who he was and not degraded by the horrible experience. In an hour he had not spoken a word. And in an hour Serge had not stopped shuddering. He sat slumped forward, head in his hands, and every few minutes he would tremble and shudder. Once before Cirie had seen him slumped forward like that—on that awful day when Strengov came to Whitewater.

"Serge, do you need something?" she said. He needed a glass of vodka, but Marya had none. Serge shuddered again. "Serge, did they torture you—that you're shuddering like this?"

"It was all torture," Serge whispered. "Day and night we lay on that filthy crawling floor. No air and that horrible smell. We couldn't wash. And the lice! Men, women, criminals, prostitutes—all crowded into one cell—the buckets—the stink—" Serge choked with tears and began to tremble.

Horrified, Cirie looked at him—he was a broken man, as though he had been in prison for months, like Constantine, instead of a day. His blond hair was matted and disheveled, the light was gone from his eyes and the warmth from his face. He seemed older. ("Cirie, he's mortal," Strengov had said. "He'll grow old—and he has no strength. A man must grow and his growth is stunted.")

She stared at Serge. And I was going away with him! Laranov was right—he couldn't escape to Paris. He couldn't make it. And then she thought, he was just dreaming. He never intended to go any more than the last time. He doesn't take chances. He promised only in order to make love to me—the same as last time. Nothing has changed!

"I never harmed anyone in my life," Serge whimpered, looking up at her. "How could they treat me like that?"

His eyes were dull, his mouth was slack. He was only a shell, with dark circles under his eyes. Cirie looked at him and saw a man she had never seen before.

39

It was only September and already the untended lawn outside the study was a field of brown weeds, dead and gone by. "And tomorrow we'll look at it all for the last time," Madame said to Kyra. "And then we'll be gone, too."

Tonight, in a sentimental gesture, she had put out a few rye rusks and weak tea brewed from apple leaves, one last "zakuski" before they left. Vara and Irene, teary-eyed, were whispering together and in the hall Vassily was pacing for the last time. "Poor Vassi—" Madame said. "For such a long time he refused to give up and then his resolve just collapsed. When Cirie heard we were to be evicted I felt that Vassi had already accepted it. I remember when he was so fussy he accepted no compromises. Now he seems numb. He accepts everything."

"There's certainly enough intrigue around here," Vara said. "Strangers moving our things at night, deliberately taking them to the wrong place. Are they moving them or stealing them?"

"Serge doesn't know," Irene said, bitterly. "Or care. Serge doesn't care about anything."

Another complaint, Madame thought. But it was true. Since his night in the prison Serge had slipped even further away. And soon he would have to return to the army. The Civil War was still raging, and the border wars with Poland and the Baltic Provinces.

For Kyra moving had evoked the old wanderlust. "Wouldn't it be wonderful to be packing to go to Paris or Biarritz? Instead of to a few rooms in a dilapidated house in town? Even though we're lucky to have them." Then, lapsing into her greatest worry, she said, "If only I knew Theo was alive, I could accept anything."

"How did Cirie get that house, I'd like to know," Vara said.

"However she managed it, we should be grateful," Madame said. "Without it I don't know where we'd go."

"I believe she and Stepa searched until they found it," Kyra said.

"It just happened?" Vara gave a sarcastic laugh. "The same way she happened to hear that we were to be driven out—two weeks before anyone else knew? Don't be so gullible." As Vassily passed the door she called out to him, "Vassi, when your wife visits patients, are you sure they're always patients?" She turned back. "And that business about the cow. Tell me how she managed that."

Madame restrained a smile. She had only admiration for the uproarious plot to keep the cow. "If Cirie plots and schemes to hold onto our things, as far as I'm concerned, that's fine."

"She's gotten hard," Vara said. Stepa and Constantine came in and she hastened to confront them. "Tell me, Stepa. How did Cirie get that house?"

"I've no idea."

"You were with her!"

"I stayed with the pram."

"And what's got into the moujiks?" Vara persisted. "First we were murderers and bloodsuckers—now they're helping us move."

"Maybe they see that the Bolsheviks are a worse enemy than we are," Stepa said. "But they're helping us because Cirie promised to pay them each a pound of salt over the next year."

"Salt! Where is she going to get salt?"

"I suppose she has something in mind."

"I'm sure she does!"

"Do you think she's gotten hard, Eugenie?" Kyra said.

"Only very cautious. But she accomplishes miracles."

When Cirie came into the study, Vara said, "We're all so curious, Cirie. How did you hear we were to be evicted?"

"The Agriculture Commissar told me," Cirie said, innocently.

"And I suppose he helped you with the cow?" Vara said. "And that house?"

Cirie smiled. Laranov had given her both the advance warning and the tip on the rooming house and if there was one thing she had learned from all this, it was the importance of influence. He had sent word through Lily telling her to come to his quarters after dark—that it was important.

"How much time do we have?" Cirie had asked when he told her they were to be evicted.

"About a month." It was a warm September night and a light breeze rustled a branch across the window. "Do you have anywhere to go?"

"When people are evicted, they try to go where they're not known."

Laranov moved closer to her. "Are you going to stay with him?"

She didn't answer. Until she arranged to send her mother and Lily out ahead of her or decided finally to leave without them, she would not complicate things by leaving Vassi just to leave.

"Why?" Roughly Laranov drew her to him.

"I won't stay with Vassi forever."

"Leave now. This is the time. Make a clean break!"

Cirie looked into the demanding dark eyes. "I will—soon."

Abruptly Laranov moved to the open window where pale leaves dipped in the light wind. When he spoke again, his voice was impersonal. "A block past the grain mill on River Street, there's a house that belonged to my mother's cousins. They left in 1917, but their housekeeper still lives there. Agniya. She rents by the night to transients who come to buy food."

"Would she take permanent tenants?"

"You'll have to persuade her. Transients pay better. But this Agniya would sell her mother for a good bribe."

"What should I offer her?"

"Have you got half a million rubles?"

"Half a million!"

"Why are you so shocked? All those jewels I heard Vassily showered on you would bring millions in Moscow. But don't sell them for rubles. Get something of value." He laughed. "I'm only teasing you, darling. This old lush can be had for a few bottles of vodka. If you don't have any, I'll give you some."

"We have a little," Cirie admitted.

"Then I'm sure you'll persuade Agniya. Now listen carefully, Cirie. Hold onto as much as you can, even if you're crowded. You'll need it for barter and bribes. Move your woodpile to some dark concealed spot. And hide your grain. People are hungry already and this winter they're going to freeze." Laranov drew her into his arms again. "And be careful, darling, about moving the things you've hidden. You wouldn't enjoy prison and I don't want to have to think of a way to get you out."

"Why do you think we've hidden things?" Cirie said, carefully.

"Everyone has hidden things." Pulling her close, locking her against him, Laranov made no effort to conceal his passion and Cirie started as, unexpectedly, desire shot through her. Struggling to put out the fire, she told herself this could be dangerous. The half moon dipped over the treetop and the branch whispered against the window and she thought she couldn't move out of Laranov's arms if she wanted to, and she didn't want to.

Then suddenly Laranov drew away, dark eyes questioning and then astonished. He touched her face and her hair and a different smile warmed his face and he said, "Doesn't Serge live here anymore?"

She bribed Agniya with vodka, but it was her hint of influence that closed the deal. With four bottles under the mattress of a pram, she and Stepa went into town and found the large house—once rather elegant but shabby now, with boards nailed over a broken window. A look at Agniya's flushed complexion and bulbous nose and Cirie produced a bottle of vodka. "If you will rent to us," she

said, carefully, "and if you will let me measure our rooms, I will repay your kindness with a bottle of vodka."

Agniya snatched the bottle.

"And if you can find a concealed space near a window for our small woodpile
and a shelter for our cow—for that another bottle of fine vodka." They would have
to bring their small stoves to replace the larger ones—less heat, but less wood. Two
mice scurried across the room and she made a mental note to bring the cat.

"Where do you get such bribes?" No nonsense about kindness for Agniya.

"Sometimes it's wiser not to know too much," Cirie suggested. "A friend, an
important official, sent me to your house."

"He knows my house!" Agniya made the sign of the cross. "I don't want any
part of him."

"Naturally, he wouldn't want this discussed. Officials can be vengeful." Then to
insure that the old woman wouldn't take the vodka and double-cross her or steal
the possessions they would have to move early, she added, "He's waiting to hear
that it's all arranged."

The old woman made the sign of the cross again and snatched the second bottle of vodka. There was no threat like the threat of influence.

When Cirie went to Gart to ask how she could keep the cow, he reflected
soberly a minute. "Are you also trying to keep the horse?"

"We couldn't feed it, but without the cow we'll starve."

"The Commissar has been complaining about his horse which truly is not in
very good condition." Gart's eyes brightened. "Maybe we can trade your horse for
your cow which belongs to the people, of course."

"Of course." Cirie knew Gart was just beginning. "But we have to be careful.
We'd be shot if it sounded like a bribe."

"The Commissar could just take your horse, and he'll probably think of that
any minute. The last time he was out there, he noticed it. We should get your horse
out of the district and I know a moujik who will do that for a bottle of wine. Then
I'll tell the Commissar I saw a fine horse in a neighboring district that he can have
for a half-million rubles—".

"A half-million! Is everything a half-million rubles these days?"

"It's the going price for a horse or cow. He'll agree. What does he care? He'll just
accept another gift from someone. Then you'll call on him and ask permission to
keep and feed the cow which is the people's cow. You'll tell him you realize that
these arrangements will involve a great deal of paperwork for him and you'd like

to pay him for his valuable time. He'll say the paperwork will cost a half-million rubles. You'll say it's a fair price—you'll try to arrange it. He'll give me the half million rubles to buy the horse. I'll bring you the money and you'll pay him with his own half-million for the use of your own cow. So in the end you'll be trading your horse for your cow." Gart broke up with laughter. "Believe me, Cirie, it's a plan that will work."

"Gart, I don't doubt it for a minute," Cirie said. "I think they're wasting a great talent leaving you here as Assistant Commissar."

"Ah, Cirie, mine is not the only great talent being wasted. On the other hand—" He began to laugh again. "I enjoy a good deception. The more devious, the better."

Then the faithful Dunka, who never let her leave without offering her a delicacy, came in with a piece of chicken and bread and butter and a dish of salt. Salt! The Civil War had cut them off from the salt-producing districts and there was no salt. Except for some.

The moving was almost completed. Gerzy and two peasants had smuggled out furniture, kitchen utensils, curtains, clothing and other miscellaneous items, carrying them at night to a temporary storage—again on Gart's advice. "Wait for a visit before you touch them," he told her. "The authorities will check what you moved. Already they're going over our last inventory on which I made a few modest changes, and they're cursing the peasants and former commissars for stealing so much." Gart roared with laughter. "Take along a few things that they can steal—after all, a visit has to produce something. Then, gradually, we'll move the other things."

The precious vodka and wine would go tonight and Stepa and Georgii would bury them under the woodpile. Last night Cirie had taken the jewels and the gold from the ash dump and sewed them into her mattress. An unwritten Russian law forbade depriving even debtors of bed and mattress. Tomorrow Gerzy would take the beds and chairs and the watchdog, Talley, and the cat and the cow. And we'll be gone, Cirie thought. And horrible as it is, without Laranov and Gart it would have been much worse. At the thought of Laranov, a new feeling went through her as she remembered the iron lock of his arms and his hungry mouth. She was puzzled and uncertain. Were her feelings only the stirring of life where there had been only emptiness—passion awakened by his passion—or was she falling in love with Laranov?

"What are you smiling about at a time like this?" Irene snapped.

Cirie closed the door on her reverie with a stern reminder. Caring for Laranov could be dangerous. And letting him know it could be even more dangerous. If Laranov were sure of her, everything could change. And she needed him to want her passionately, hungrily, as he did now, because he was the only man she knew with real power.

She had seen what influence could do. She had seen what even the suggestion of influence could do. And she did not intend to ever be without influence again.

40

In Kostyka everything was broken down and neglected. The tram line was no longer operating. The streets and pavements were piled high with snow—it would stay there until spring, there was no one to shovel it—and the people walking in the middle of the road were in rags. Aristocrats and bourgeoisie had been forced to fill out cards listing their clothing, and most of it had been taken away. In place of boots, women wrapped strips of old curtains around their feet. Men wore suits stitched together by their wives from any material on hand—scraps of bright green or blue cloth, sewn with thread of any color—red, green, orange. Everyone's shoes had holes. At the hospital the wards were cold and the patients under-nourished. The moujiks, with no horses, no machinery and no incentive, had planted fewer acres and after a bad harvest, the specter of famine loomed.

At Agniya's, they had already suffered three "visits." ("How much did you move? What did you hide? Where is it? Stand aside—we'll find it.") Searching their persons with rough hands. Cirie cringed when their hands moved intimately over her breasts and down her body. She would grit her teeth and stand rigidly still, refusing to show any emotion other than cool hatred. They would search closets and dresser drawers, throwing articles on the floor, pulling mattresses off beds, trampling on clothing to see if anything was concealed in linings, helping themselves to what they wanted. "Where is your important official now?" Agniya said, viewing the shambles left behind by the last visit. If Cirie was going to keep the myth of influence alive, she had to find a way to stop them and she hadn't seen Laranov since they moved.

Usually during the morning break in surgery Cirie sat on a bench and smoked a cigarette, if she had one, or sipped cold ersatz tea. Today she walked past the bench and took the stairs to another corridor to the only remaining private room. For a month she'd been waiting for a general or a commissar to come into the hospital and yesterday they had operated on General Petrov, the most powerful general in the area. The general's nurse cracked open the door.

"How is General Petrov today, Risa?" Cirie whispered.

"He's had morphine. Generals get morphine. He's asleep. Can you sit with him while I have a cigarette?"

"I have fifteen minutes," Cirie said.

General Petrov reminded her of General Borassin although Borassin was tall and Petrov was short and stocky, but he had the same bull-like quality to his body and good-humored lines around his eyes.

Through the spotted window she saw that it was starting to snow and her thoughts went to the walk home tonight. Even if the trams were running, as a former aristocrat she would not be given a pass. Mornings she walked to work in the dark, passing shabby figures moving furtively to some illegal deal, the trade of some precious possession for a little bread or grain to survive another day, and evenings it was dark when she walked home. Every day she saw mindless destruction—books seized and left out in the rain, china and crystal broken as it was tossed into carts. At Agniya's, Professor Erlat, a professor from Moscow who had come in search of flour, had offered her sugar in exchange for an old plate. In the house he had once owned and now was permitted to occupy along with other workers, he and his wife were reduced to only one plate for the two of them.

But of all the senseless destruction, the most shocking was the careless neglect of food. Precious rye rotted on dirty floors of bins that no one had bothered to clean. Before the river froze, piles of requisitioned potatoes lay around on docks, soaking in the fall rains, freezing at night until, wet and already half-rotten, they were packed onto the steamer to be shipped to the cities. Each new report was devastating to the unhappy family that was always hungry even though most of them were working—Vassily at the grain mill, Stepa at the fisheries, Constantine and Georgii sweeping floors and carrying wood at the office of a Commissar, Tanya as a waitress in the restaurant at the Metropolitan Hotel, patronized by officers—a hungry bewildered family trying to form new habits.

General Petrov stirred and Cirie turned him and rearranged his pillows. For a few seconds he opened his eyes and she bent over him and smiled. The lines around his eyes deepened. Then he was asleep again.

Cirie looked out at the snow, letting her thoughts go back to the family. Vassily had become irritable and domineering again, especially toward the two babies, Alexei and Christina, whom he was trying to mold into what a gentleman and a lady had been in the glorious days that were gone. And Serge, bitter, trading his last possessions for vodka, had taken to forcing arguments with Vassily, pouring out the accumulated resentment of a lifetime. Samson's hair had been cut—it was time to even the score.

"He didn't wake up," Cirie said when Risa returned. "I'll come back later."

"What's your interest in General Petrov?"

"We check on all our patients, Risa," Cirie said, innocently. "You know that."

Back upstairs the hospital supervisor, a large woman—a party member—with red hair flying about her flat bumpy face, was inflicting more forms on Dr. Legare.

Every day they had to struggle through a flood of questionnaires—about the surgery and the shortages and their political awareness. We're aware, Cirie thought. We're aware.

"I went down to check on General Petrov," she told Dr. Legare after the supervisor left. "But he was asleep."

"Why not try later?" You never had to explain anything to Dr. Legare.

It was dark when Cirie hurried back to General Petrov's room. "I thought you said he didn't wake up this morning," Risa greeted her. "He's been asking for the angel with the blue eyes, blonde and smiling."

"Oh, Risa, I'm sorry," Cirie said. "He opened his eyes for a second. He didn't really wake up."

Risa shrugged. "What's the difference?"

"So here you are," General Petrov greeted her. "You were here before."

"I'm the surgery nurse. I came to check your incision."

The lines creased around his eyes. "Check anything you like."

Cirie laughed and lifted a corner of the dressing. "That looks fine."

The lines around the eyes deepened. "Are you going to sit and talk with me a few minutes?" he said. "Or possibly longer?"

"Of course." Cirie drew up a chair. "Why not?"

*   *   *

"Let's go down Gleb Street and catch a look at Darius Kyrigen," Olga said.

"I can't," Lily said. They were walking in the road on Elizabeth Street because the snow was still piled high on the pavements. "There's a cigarette line today. Last time it was a block long."

She would love to go but she really needed the cigarettes. With your ration card the most you ever got was a little flour and some grain that Mamma ground in the coffee mill, and sometimes a little kerosene and a scrap of soap—never any meat of groceries. But if you could get cigarettes, you could barter for something.

"Here's Gleb Street. If I see him, you'll be sorry you didn't come," Olga said.

"I know it," Lily said. "But the concerts will start in the spring. I'll see him then."

She hurried on alone, her feet wrapped in strips of curtains. She had outgrown her boots—she was outgrowing everything. Life would be simpler if she would just stop growing. For a few minutes Lily amused herself by studying the tangle of iron pipes poking out of windows, each emitting a different colored smoke, depending on what was being burned—logs, old furniture, paper, wooden fences.

Then suddenly a man just ahead of her turned his head and Lily recognized him. It was Petya! She hurried up to him and touched his sleeve. "Hello."

Petya's face lit up. "Lily! Is it you? You've grown up! You look so much like Cirie. How are you all?"

"We're fine. Well, we're like everyone else." People were walking past and Lily hardly saw them.

"Where are you going?" Petya said. "Walk along with me and tell me all your news. How are things here in Kostyka?"

Lily began to relax. "I suppose the same as everywhere. We don't get enough with our ration cards. They list all those things but you never get them—what are they there for?" Lily was amazed at herself talking like this, but she had always felt at ease with Petya. "The kerosene shortage is worse. Mamma gets very depressed sitting in the dark. I'm glad the shortest days are over. Petya, do you have time to come see her? She always loved you and she doesn't have many visitors since Ulla left."

"Of course I have time," Petya said. "We're old friends. I'll come now."

She would just have to take a chance on the cigarettes.

In the tiny apartment Lily unwrapped her strips and hung them near the stove to dry while she listened to Petya's news. Ulla and Oscar were fine, trying to live inconspicuously. Oscar worked as a doorman and Ulla as a clerk. You would never know they had been well off. "The officials closed down my store," he said. "But those same officials want furs—and so do their wives. I managed to hide some— so I barter."

Gathering her courage, Lily sat beside Petya on the sofa. "We heard there was more food in Poltava."

"Maybe a little. But the Civil War is close to us so we have heavy requisitions. The peasants hide their grain, what little they have, and they trade it only for things they need."

"What do they need? I've been thinking of going there to try to get some butter and a chicken for Mamma."

"You're not going to be a bagger, Lily!"

"Only to Poltava."

"Stay home, Lily. I'll come back and bring you a chicken and some butter."

"Will you, Petya!" Lily cried. "I don't mean will you bring us a chicken. I mean will you come back? It's so good to see you!"

"Of course! If you'll let me, I'll come again tomorrow. I'm thinking of staying another few days."

"How do you manage to get a railway ticket? I've heard they're harder to get than salt."

"It works the same as everything else—a friend at the ticket office wanted a fur hat. I came here to look for some furs I left with friends."

"Good for you!" Lily said. "I can see where you could get all kinds of things with furs."

"Lily is our business woman these days—always trading," Marya said. "Did you find your furs?"

"Some—not all. I'll come back and try again."

"I'm so glad you came here to try!" Lily cried.

"And I'm glad you saw me in the middle of the street," Petya said.

Lily could hardly believe it. Petya was talking to her as though she were an adult, almost as though she were Cirie, and he was going to come back.

*   *   *

Laranov walked along the Nevsky Prospect where once he had strolled and seen a hundred friends. Now the restaurants were closed and the shops abandoned and there was no reason for anyone to go there.

In Petrograd, mansions and palaces had been stripped of their former adornments and had become government offices and wooden houses and wooden sidewalks had been ripped up for fire wood. The streets were peppered with potholes, sometimes two or three feet deep. There was no one to repair them and nothing to repair them with. There was no experienced personnel to supervise the work. The only effort to repair a street hole was started in October, a week before the first snowfall, and abandoned until spring.

The famous Alexandrovna Market was teeming with speculators. All private trade or barter was called speculation and was illegal, but there was no other way for people to survive. Minor government officials supplemented their salaries with bribes and by selling government supplies on the Black Market.

In his unswept hotel room, Laranov described the city in his diary:

16 March, 1920

"Petrograd is a dying city, half-empty, a city of beggars, speculators and bribery. The streets are lined with beggars, many of them old friends—generals, princes, countesses—trying to barter some useless relic or just begging for food.

"My old friends are in rags, starving and begging, my new associates are living off bribes, and beautiful old St. Petersburg—(where, he used to say, the wine was smooth and the vodka was strong and the women in silk and lace created illusions and had the power to excite him if only for a little while)—elegant old St. Petersburg is ragged and falling into its grave of gaping potholes and ripped up pavements and torn down houses and malnutrition and disease."

Two days later he went to Moscow where there was even more poverty than Petrograd.

"A huge bureaucracy," he wrote. "More officials than under the Tsar—and more corruption. More beggars. The destruction of the upper classes has not increased the wealth of the lower classes. It has simply made everyone equal in poverty."

The trams were the only form of transportation left. Even bicycles had been requisitioned. At hours when everyone was riding to and from work, dozens of people hanging onto the outside of cars were pushed off. In two days Laranov had seen a man killed and another lose an arm.

"In Moscow there is a shortage of everything," he wrote. "In the Soukharevska Market, like the Alexandrovna Market in Petrograd, everything is for sale at a price thousands of rubles higher than in the government stores. In a government store the price for a pair of shoes would be ninety rubles—if you had an official order and if they had the shoes. In the Soukharevska Market you would probably find them, but for five-thousand rubles. Even an exemption from military service, properly signed and stamped, can be bought for a price.

"Serious speculators—profiteers—are shot but officials close their eyes to street-corner bartering. Otherwise, the peasants would not bring food into the city. Trotsky has said he is ashamed that the proletariat engages in retail speculation. Others say Trotsky engages only in wholesale speculation.

"At the churches there is still a heavy trade in candles. Across from the Miraculous Shrine of the Iberian Madonna a sign reads: Religion is the Opium of the People."

41

❁

Two weeks after he left the hospital, on a Wednesday evening, General Petrov came to call. "It's a dull business here in Kostyka," he said to Cirie on his last day in the hospital. "We're here to fight the Civil War. Our families are back home. We've been away for six years. Cirie, you're a light in a dark world." He paused. "I wonder—would you permit a few of us to call on you some evening?"

On his first visit General Petrov brought along General Malek, a young general with a hoarse voice, the result of a war injury, and General Bolz, an old-time Bolshevik with hands scarred from burns received at the Moscow barricades in the Revolution of 1905. The following Wednesday evening Petrov brought the two Generals again and the local Commissar. On Wednesday afternoons a box would arrive containing kerosene for light and fish and cheese and black bread for zakuski. Petrov brought the vodka himself. The Wednesday evenings became famous among the officers, eagerly anticipated by anyone who could coax an invitation out of General Petrov. For a few hours war and politics were forgotten and they relaxed and ate attractive zakuski and raised their glasses to the "most enchanting woman in Russia."

On a Wednesday afternoon in March, when Cirie rushed in to prepare for the generals, Theo was there, sitting on the sofa, a gaunt hard-eyed skeleton, almost unrecognizable behind a ragged black beard, with the silent shocked family gathered around him.

When Cirie drew away her hand after rushing to him, she saw the louse on his wrist. "Theo—"

Automatically, Theo popped it between his fingers. "I must have picked it up on the train. I'm always careful about them. I'll go upstairs and check myself out." He began to cough.

"We all go upstairs on Wednesday nights." The usual acid was in Vara's voice. "Madame Vassily Vodovsky entertains the generals."

"Here?" Theo was already picking up his pack and Cirie realized what in fact she had already sensed—that he was living an underground life and could not risk detection.

"Theo, wait. You're safe here tonight."

"I wonder," Vara burst out. "I wonder if any of us is safe here with what you're doing. You and your generals! Shall I tell you the truth—"

"No! I'm not interested!" Cirie snapped. "Theo—" Theo was coughing badly and she wondered whether it was only a cough or the beginning of consumption.

"People are talking about you," Vara plunged on. "Everyone knows where there are soldiers, there's a certain kind of house—and a certain kind of woman."

"Theo, nobody will bother us while the Generals are here. On Wednesday nights this is the safest place in town."

Theo put down his pack. "I only want a place to sleep tonight. Tomorrow I'll be gone."

"Has Agniya seen him?" When Agniya was sober, she was everywhere, spying, eavesdropping, searching their rooms.

"I had to sacrifice half a bottle of vodka but Agniya won't wake up for a while," Stepa said.

"This is something I've wanted to say for a long time," Vara persisted, although no one was listening. "If you don't care about your own reputation, you might consider the rest of us."

Fed up, Cirie turned on her so swiftly that Vara stepped back a pace. "Vara, nobody cares! Nobody is dreaming up scandals except you. And if they were, I wouldn't care about that, either!"

"I don't like that, Cirie," Vassily warned. Then he saw Alexei climbing onto Theo's pack. "Stop that," he shouted. Alexei only looked at him. "Apologize! Bow as I've taught you and apologize." Alexei ran into Cirie's arms. "Do you know how to bow?" Vassily shouted.

"That's the spirit, Vassi," Serge said. "Nothing more important than bowing."

"You stay out of this!"

"What kind of bow did you have in mind, Vassi?" Serge needled him. "Just a nod? Or a deep sweeping bow?"

"My son will be a gentleman!"

"That's quite a trick these days. But you stick with it, Vassi. You've got a fine goal there."

"As for you," Vassily cleared his throat and turned on Cirie. "Our good name is not to be taken lightly."

"Before long they'll say things are going on here on Wednesday nights!" Vara cried.

"Too bad they're not!" Cirie snapped. "I'd get more out of it than I'm getting now! And we need everything I can get—at any price!"

She motioned to Theo to come upstairs. They could move a cot in with Constantine and Georgii. "Theo, where have you been?" she whispered on the stairs. "What are you doing?"

Theo hesitated. Then he whispered, "I'm a smuggler. Don't tell anyone." He cast his eyes toward the family downstairs.

"What do you smuggle?"

"People."

Cirie waited.

"Former officers. Only a few years ago they were willing to give their lives for Russia. Now Russia calls them enemies. They're hunted men. Some are in prison, some are on the run. To get them out we work with professionals."

"Professionals?"

"Smugglers. They'll smuggle anything. It's how they live. They're only interested in money. Not Russian rubles. Good money. Each man pays his own way."

Something clicked in Cirie's brain. This was something she understood. Was it possible it could be that simple? She started to ask more questions but Serge came up the stairs and she broke off. "Right here—" She stopped in front of Constantine's room and Theo went inside.

Serge came up to her. "Cirie, I'm leaving tomorrow."

"I'm sorry, Serge."

"Will you meet me tonight after the generals leave?" Every Wednesday night it was the same. After the generals left, he would be waiting for her at the top of the stairs, believing with a hope born of vodka that this would be their night of love. He took her wrist. "Will you?"

"No, Serge."

At the door to her room he grasped her hand. "Cirie, you can't send me away with nothing."

She didn't have time for this. She still had to fix the zakuski and the generals would be here any minute. She'd have to ask Kyra to help her. The idea was to make it a party for them.

"For six years I've wanted you." His blood-shot eyes were damp. "For six years I've loved you."

"No, Serge, I was just a toy you wanted as a boy and couldn't have."

"Cirie," he mumbled through tears. "I'll never be back."

"Don't even think that way, Serge," she said firmly, as though to a child. "You'll be back."

She changed into her only white blouse and black skirt and brushed her hair and rushed downstairs. While she made the zakuski she thought about Theo's smugglers. If it was only money...

A moment later she opened the door to General Petrov and Malek and Bolz. And an important new guest, a huge mass of a man whom Petrov introduced as General Renkovsky, just arrived from the south. And Renkovsky's young aide, Commander Gorshenko. And with them was Laranov.

With the arrival of General Renkovsky, the mood of the Wednesday night changed. A long-time party member, fresh from the Civil War front against General Denikin, he talked incessantly about necessary atrocities. "Tell me you object to these atrocities and I say you're the enemy," he shouted. "Anyone who asks for justice and leniency today is a Counter-Revolutionary—working for the Whites."

The Whites, under Denikin, had pushed north this year to Orel, only a hundred and forty miles from Moscow, before being driven back, and the Poles and Cossacks, fighting together, had reached Kiev. The Civil War was raging on many fronts and everywhere the atrocities on both sides were sickening, but not to Renkovsky.

"An intellectual! Head in the clouds!" Renkovsky shouted, discussing a former comrade. His fanaticism aside, Renkovsky's most prominent feature was a massive low-slung stomach and he stood, weight on his heels, feet apart, as though steadying all that flesh. His sandy hair was sparse and in the light of the kerosene lamp a swollen scar showed from his throat to his left ear. "Bleating about freedom and justice for everyone! He was found dead in an alley, shot in the head. A fitting end for a traitor!" He flung out his arm in a nervous choppy gesture, ridding himself of the corpse.

Uneasily Cirie thought that Theo and Constantine could hear every new threat that rolled so lovingly off Renkovsky's lips—Constantine with the stolen passport of his dead superintendent, Theo, so far as she knew, with nothing. But even if they were not upstairs, she would be uneasy about Renkovsky. Fanatics were dangerous.

The usual camaraderie was absent tonight. Two separate groups had formed— the sycophants clustered respectfully around Renkovsky and those, including Laranov, who dared to exclude themselves. From across the room his eyes met hers and she felt the same stab of pleasure she had felt earlier, and instantly denied, when she saw him at the door.

"Does a dog chase cats?" Renkovsky shouted. "An aristocrat is automatically a counter-revolutionary." At his side his handsome obsequious young aide, Commander Gorshenko, hovered like a faithful dog.

"Comrade General, for years we've had aristocrats in our ranks," General Malek protested in his hoarse voice.

"For them it was a diversion." Renkovsky's hand worked at his swollen scar. "Destroy them. No sympathy. Wipe them out—wipe them out!"

Renkovsky reminded her of someone, Cirie thought, and groped to place the memory. Laranov was beside her. "When are you coming to see me again?"

"That would be hard to do. But you're always welcome here."

"Here isn't where I want you."

"Ssh-sh!" In spite of her nervousness over Renkovsky, Cirie laughed. "Where have you been? I expected you on Wednesday night before this."

"You don't think I'd stay away from you by choice? I've been away. But you've got everyone else here who can do you any good."

From a few feet away General Bolz spoke to Laranov. "You were gone a long time." He reached for another zakuski. "I love this black bread Petrov gets hold of for these Wednesday nights. Tell me, Laranov, is it true that the moujiks have no grain?"

Renkovsky overheard the question. "They have grain. They have grain!" Abruptly he switched his hatred to this new enemy.

The grain shortage was worse than ever. On city streets and country roads people were expiring from starvation, but to preserve the Revolution, the cities and the army had to be fed. The government demanded ever higher requisitions of grain and the peasants resisted, struggling to hold onto what little they had. Suddenly the clash was on everyone's lips.

"They should know what resistance will cost them—they should see what I have seen." There was no blocking out Renkovsky's voice. "Bodies of hostages lying in the snow—frozen arms sticking out in all directions."

"General, after all—" Bolz objected.

"Bare feet," Renkovsky said in a matter-of-fact tone. "Always the feet are bare. The first thing anyone does is steal the boots. First things first."

"General, these are Russian peasants."

Renkovsky tapped his head. "Here I understand that these scenes are unfortunate. Here—" he tapped his chest where his heart should have been. "It doesn't touch me. These peasants got their land for nothing. We encouraged them to seize it from the corrupt landowners. We've let them keep it—so far. They should work until they drop for the benefit of the Soviet."

"Absolutely," his echo, Gorshenko, said. There was something serpentine about Gorshenko. His voice was hushed and syrupy and even when he stood motionless you felt he was going to sneak up on you.

"Instead, for their government they have no grain! Because they refuse to produce," Renkovsky said.

"Offer them something they want and suddenly they'll have grain," Gorshenko said.

"We'll let the Cheka persuade them—a few lessons they won't forget." Again the nervous choppy gesture, ridding himself this time of the peasants.

Cirie glanced at the clock.

"What are you nervous about?" Laranov said.

She started to deny it and knew that wouldn't work with Laranov. "I don't like fanatics. You never know who's going to be elected their favorite enemy next. Does he remind you of someone?"

"In another age Renkovsky would have belonged to some extreme religious cult," Laranov said. "It's that same passion. The inquisition mentality. When are you coming to see me?"

"Laranov, you know I can't do that."

His voice caressed her. "Shall I tell you how much I want you?"

"Do you think we're the only ones who commit atrocities?" Renkovsky shouted, angrily. "The Whites do it even better. They were trained under the Tsar. In one town they ordered all important citizens to a meeting—lined them up—fired—and left them. They had no more time. Finally someone told the families, go find them. They found them all right—lying in a bloody line—dead." Renkovsky's flat blue eyes glittered as though he wished he had thought of that one himself. "We could take lessons from them."

Laranov took a quick look around and lowered his voice. "Cirie, has Stepa heard from Constantine? I looked for him in Petrograd. Someone said he'd been arrested."

"We had a letter long ago," Cirie said, cautiously. "In 1917."

"Not since then?"

She shook her head. "Why were you looking for him?"

"Why was I looking for him! He was my closest friend."

She would like to reassure him but the decision was not hers to make. Casually, Laranov lit a cigarette and drew on it and said, still in a low voice, "Cirie, how many people live here?"

Did he know something? Was he asking about Constantine to warn her to stop sheltering a fugitive? "Just the family," she said, carefully. "Kyra is with us. Serge goes back to the army tomorrow."

"Does that bother you?"

Bother her! She was relieved. She had become uneasy about the way he sneaked up on her all over the house. She could hardly remember the man she had once thought was her whole life—the tall, charming, still undestroyed Serge.

Laranov misunderstood her silence. "Not still!"

"No—no! I'm sorry for anyone who has to go back to the army."

"Anyone besides the family?" Laranov said.

"Agniya takes transients—you know that."

He touched her elbow and let his hand linger a moment. "I'm leaving. I don't like Renkovsky and he doesn't like me. Walk me to the door. I want to talk to you."

"Why doesn't he like you?"

"He doesn't trust me." In the hall where there was no lamp, the light was dim. "Cirie, fill up the empty rooms with friends or some of those transients will be spies."

"We already have our spy—Agniya."

"She's surely working with the police. And the transients will, too." While he spoke, Laranov's eyes kept track of the movements in the room.

One more step toward exterminating us, Cirie thought. "We don't have any friends left."

"Here is General Petrov, your devoted admirer. Cirie, I can't call on you here. We have to meet in my quarters."

Cirie laughed. "Why do we have to?"

"Because we're fated to belong to each other."

"Fate—that sounds very Russian."

"I am very Russian. And you're the fate I believe in for me. I'll wait for you, darling."

"Why is he leaving?" Renkovsky said as Laranov closed the door. "I'm suspicious of him. He's had too many allegiances."

"I believe his allegiance is to Russia," Petrov said.

"Whose Russia? Only a very small part of Laranov is a Bolshevik—the expedient part." Renkovsky shot a cruel look at the door and turned back to Cirie. "And you, Madame, are an aristocrat?"

"On the contrary, Comrade General. My mother was a moujik and my father was a poor country doctor. I worked as a nurse and I married my employer."

Renkovsky's pale eyes glittered as he studied her, appraising, speculating. "If I stay here, I'll take time to instruct you. When I finish, you'll be a dedicated Communist."

"Thank you, Comrade General." I doubt that, Comrade General. And I will not stay here.

"All our troubles are the work of the Tsar's corrupt bureaucrats. They lined their pockets while they sent millions to their slaughter without guns or ammunition."

"Nobody learned that more painfully that I, Comrade General. I nursed the wounded."

"So did the Tsarina. It doesn't necessarily clear you of suspicion. Every aristo-crat is an enemy. If his class is the enemy he must be destroyed." He was losing control again. "I say attack them again—and again. Hit them until there's no place for them to hide. Again—again—

The memory she had been groping for surfaced. Again! Again! A mammoth she-devil on a horse, a whip cutting the air. Again! Again! Hit him again! Shove him! Roll him! Hit him again!

"Do you hear me, Madame? *Madame*—do you hear me?"

"Yes, I hear you, Comrade General."

Renkovsky studied her with pale greedy eyes. "Yes, Madame. I will definitely make time to instruct you."

As soon as the generals left, Stepa and Constantine and Theo came down to the kitchen, joking now that the crisis was over.

"I checked the exits," Theo said. "From Stepa's room you can drop down to the woodpile and you're off to the alley seen by no one but the cow."

"Even I could do it," Constantine said. "Still, I should try it once to be sure."

"The first time I've heard from an official mouth that this wonderful system isn't working perfectly," Cirie said.

"I feel better now that it's official." Stepa opened the door to check on the resident spy, Agniya.

Cirie put the leftover zakuski on the table in front of Theo. Ordinarily she saved them for the family but Theo looked starved. His tunic hung on his bones like a sack.

"Theo," Stepa said. "Your escape route for the soldiers. How does it work?"

"We're the underground." Theo devoured a piece of bread and offered some to Stepa and Constantine. They were hungry, too, but not literally starving as Theo was, and they would not take it without sharing equally with the family they shared everything with—good or bad.

"We try to outfox the Cheka—and outrun them." Theo's eyes brightened. "With my friends it's a cause. The others are professionals. They'll smuggle any-thing in or out—guns, cocaine, convicts, heroes—whatever pays."

Stepa picked up on that. "They have no cause?"

"No cause, no allegiance. They care only for money. They're good, they're effi-cient, they get through. For money."

He's different from the old Theo, Cirie thought—and different from the rest of us. He's a skeleton but he's tough and hard. And he has a fire in him.

"My friends and I shelter them overnight and send them on the underground route to the professionals. Sooner or later we'll be caught. We can't last forever."

He doesn't expect to survive but the rest of us don't have much more hope. Last week Constantine had said, "We've shrunk to the simplest form of life—a group of cells with one function—survival." Cirie touched Theo's hand. "Theo, you've been knocked down like the rest of us and you came up with a diamond in your hand. With every life you save you taste glory.

Her mind went back to the more urgent matter of the escape route. Stepa asked the question first. "Theo, would your smugglers take Tanya and me?"

Theo hesitated.

"For myself I would stay here and try to help the family," Stepa said, "although I feel our days are numbered. But I want a future for Tanya. I want to take her to Elissa in Paris."

Theo was silent and Cirie froze, waiting for his answer. Why the hesitation if it was only a business to the smugglers?

"It's a hard trip," Theo said at last. "They move only in the worst weather—a blizzard usually—so no one can see them. They fly over the snow and it's understood they stop for nothing. They've never taken a woman."

Cirie's heart fell. If they won't take a woman, they won't even talk to a woman with a baby, an elderly mother and a sister.

"Tanya is young and strong and I'll be with her."

"I'll ask them. I'll vouch for you although they've never taken anyone over forty. Don't tell anyone," he warned. "Not even the family."

The kerosene in the bottle had burned low and they stood up to go to bed. Cirie drew Constantine aside. "Laranov was here tonight. He looked for you in Petrograd. Do you want him to know you're here?"

Constantine shook his head firmly. "I'd love to see him and talk all night again—just one more time. I ache to know what's happening in Russia and the world. But he's a Soviet officer now. And I'm a fugitive. I trust Ilya, but the information could become a burden to him. And it's a risk for you, too. You've sheltered me. I wish I could send him word that I'm alive but it will be better if he doesn't know."

After Stepa and Constantine went upstairs, Theo lingered another minute. "Theo?" Cirie said, "could I deceive the smugglers?"

"With a baby!"

"I'll strap him to my back. They won't have to stop." For the moment she didn't mention her mother.

Theo looked troubled. "It's supposed to be just officers—"

"Tell them I'm a man—a large man. I'll cover Alexei with my cape. It doesn't have to be the next trip. We can take time to plan our deception." She would need time to send Marya ahead. Maybe Lily could go on the sled, unless she was afraid.

"Cirie, I can't. They'll look you over."

"Where?"

"At the meeting point—where we turn people over to them."

"Is it inside or outside?"

"Outside. It's an isolated open shed on a deserted road."

"At night?"

Theo nodded.

"Well, then—! Theo, I promise you they'll never suspect."

"Cirie—" He looked miserable. "I can't."

"Will you think about it?"

A long silence. "Yes. I'll think about it."

Theo started toward the stairs and came back. "Cirie, I'll be gone before daybreak. I want to say goodbye." He bent over to kiss her. "This may be the last time I'll see you. When my luck runs out, there won't be anyone to smuggle me along an escape route."

"Don't say that." Theo was one of the best people she had ever known. He was like Strengov. And like Strengov, he was caught in a hemorrhage that was not of his making and he was doomed.

After he went upstairs, Cirie sat alone in the dark. The knot was pulling tighter and everyone knew it—Renkovsky threatening everyone who still prayed for moderation, Laranov whispering that there would be spies in the house and leaving early to avoid Renkovsky, Theo talking calmly about his own death. But knowing it doesn't help because I can't find a hole we can slip through. Maybe I could bribe the smugglers to take Alexei and me—and maybe even Lily—but Mamma, never. Now that her mind was working, she sat there another few minutes, thinking. There were other smugglers. She would ask Taras, a speculator who turned up in the alley of the black market when he had salt or sugar. He might do his own smuggling. Or know someone. She would find her own smuggler.

At the top of the stairs Serge appeared out of the dark and reached for her. "Serge, don't do that."

"I told you—I'm going to have you before I die."

"Serge, let me go!" She wondered how drunk he was. If she pushed him away would he fall down the stairs or go into a rage? She had seen him like this once before—the day of the gnats. "Serge, speak to Theo—maybe he can help you escape."

But Serge had only one thing in mind. "You were mine and I was denied what was mine."

"Serge, stop it. Don't force me to cry for help."

He clapped his hand across her mouth and twisted her arm behind her and forced a knotted handkerchief through her teeth. He dragged her to the back room Professor Erlat had vacated only this morning and threw her down on the bare mattress. "I've waited a long time for this."

Tonight there were no gnats to intrude while he stripped off her clothing. She struggled against him and he struck her three sharp blows to the face. His hands and mouth devoured her breasts. She wrenched away and kicked him and he slapped her viciously, while he murmured drunkenly, "You're going to love it, you're going to love it. You know you want me—" Desperately, sloppily, he tried to kiss the length of her naked twisting body and suddenly stopped and threw himself on top of her. For years she had dreamed of this moment. Now she felt consumed with disgust.

He fell away from her and she ripped the gag from her mouth and sat up on the edge of the bed Her stomach cramped and she threw up into her rag of a handkerchief. That's what I wanted for so long! she thought. That! That's what I craved and burned for—that's what I gave up so much for and married for revenge and even then burned for! For years! That! *That!* She felt degraded and used. Her nipples stung from his abuse. She stared dully at the dark window and felt that she was going to throw up again. Have I become so hard, so cold, she thought, that I don't even feel shock? Only revulsion and disgust.

She groped for her clothing that was strewn about the floor and put it on and left Serge, naked and limp on the bare mattress, hair matted, bleary-eyed, drunk and spent. Had there ever been a golden-haired, clear-eyed young man in a white suit who stepped off a boat from Paris and lay beside her over the lake?

In her room, still numb, she bent over Alexis and touched a lock of his soft blond hair. In his sleep he grasped the finger she held out to him. There had to be an answer. There had to be a way to get out. She asked herself whether she could really strap him to her back and go and leave her mother and Lily behind. In a sled, with a prearranged route and schedule, you could make it. On foot, in a famine, you would die.

42

❀

In the pale light, furtive figures ducked into the alley of the black market, a narrow opening on River Street, hemmed by sagging houses, where hungry debilitated people came to trade something they would need tomorrow for something they needed more today. Taras was here this morning, leaning against a building, smoking a cigarette. Cirie moved a step into the alley. "Taras—"

Without removing his cigarette, Taras signaled with his eyes into the alley and Cirie saw a dark form in a doorway, a hand extended in the familiar gesture of taking something slipped to him by a ragged victim. "You have to pay bribes now?"

Taras nodded and smoked.

"Who is it?"

Taras shrugged. "An officer. Come tonight."

On the street, safely away from the officer's eyes, Cirie slowed down and a wave of disgust swept over her. The people in the alley were almost corpses, with the hollow eyes and shrunken faces of the starving. And here was this officer, bleeding them. How does a man get this way? she thought. What disease infects this man who is so greedy, whose humanity is so dead, that he demands his pound of flesh from those who have no flesh left to give? Everyone is hard. There is no humanity left anywhere in Russia—not even in the alleys that are the last step before the grave.

Around noon a late winter rain began and after work, during an unpromising let-up, Cirie hurried to Marya's apartment where she found her rearranging the furniture again, a sign of deep distress. "Mamma, what's the matter? What happened?"

Marya sank onto the sofa. "Cirie, Lily wants to get married!"

"Married! She's a baby! My God, she's not pregnant?"

"No—I don't think so," Marya said, as though this possibility had not occurred to her. "She'll be fifteen next month."

"Who is he? Not the boy who gives her extra bread?"

Marya's face brightened a little. "It's Petya."

"Petya!"

"They told me today when Lily came home from school."

"Petya is thirty! Oh, this is ridiculous. One minute she's at school learning her numbers and the next minute she wants to get married."

Marya hesitated. "Lily doesn't want you to know. Petya was so much in love with you."

"That was years ago!"

"Try to understand, Cirie. Lily feels she can never be as beautiful or as clever as you. Next to you she feels plain. And she's mad about Petya."

"It's an adolescent crush! She was always in love with Petya. Talk to her. Persuade her to wait a little."

"It won't do any good. You should see how he fusses over her, Cirie. She's walking on air. In normal times I'd plead with her to finish school first, but these aren't normal times. Although Petya feels things will be better soon, when all the wars are over."

Let her believe it if she can. The rain had eased off again. "Mamma, I have to go. I'll come back tomorrow to talk to her."

"Taras, do the smugglers who bring in sugar and salt ever take anything out?"

"What is there in Russia to send out?"

"People."

Taras' eyes narrowed.

"Would they? If it pays?"

His eyes said he doubted it. "I'll ask. But they move fast."

Something was wrong. As soon as Cirie closed the door Agniya stepped out of the parlor and threw her an accusing look and from the first floor bedroom she heard muffled weeping. Stepa came to meet her, an eye on Agniya, and whispered. "Theo's been arrested."

Fear clutched at Cirie's stomach. "Where? When?"

"Late this afternoon. Constantine saw it. When Theo left us, he stayed in Kostyka."

In the bedroom Kyra was weeping convulsively. "Where have you been?" she cried as Cirie hurried in. "They've taken Theo."

"Ssh—" Madame said and Kyra lowered her voice. "Cirie, save him! You saved Vassi and Serge."

Cirie cracked open the door and saw Agniya eavesdropping from halfway down the hall. Constantine came past her and crowded into the little room. "It was on Gleb Street," he whispered. "He just barely nodded to another man and a second later the soldiers seized him. It happened almost in front of me."

"Oh, God help him!" Kyra cried.

"I followed as close as I dared. I think he's in the military prison. They headed that way. And he's a former officer—" Constantine lowered his voice. "Helping other officers."

"Is that what he's doing?" Vara said, sharply, and Constantine started, regretting his words.

"I'll go in the morning and ask if he's there," Cirie said.

"Go tonight," Kyra begged. "You saved Vassi and Serge at night."

"Oh, I can't!" Cirie gasped. She knew what that would mean. Vara's lip curled into a knowing smile.

"The officer who helped you might still be there," Kyra implored. "Theo can't have done anything serious. Cirie—go now."

"Let me think!" Warring arguments raged in Cirie's mind. Asking Laranov was the only way. But would he do it again? And does Renkovsky make a difference? Should I even go there with Renkovsky in town? She was not ready to acknowledge the other reason—the temptation she knew she would face and the choice she knew she would make. On the other side, there was only one argument. If she didn't go, Theo was lost.

Painfully aware of his weak position, Constantine followed Cirie into the hall. Once he had had so much power. Now he was useless. But he could not watch this brave and beautiful girl, who still looked so deceptively fragile, shoulder the burden one more time for this helpless family. They whispered in a corner of the hall. "Cirie, if you feel you can't go, we'll try some other way."

"How can I not go?"

"You'll go to Laranov?"

She nodded. Her hesitation might simply be born of fear. Just going through the streets at night was reason to fear. Just going to the prison was reason for fear. Especially as they probably had an actual charge against Theo. "Was it Laranov who gave you Vassily and Serge?"

"And told me about our eviction. And about this house."

Constantine realized that he might be intruding into a private matter. Then he told himself that those nice sensibilities were born of different conditions. "Cirie, if you feel you can't go to him again—"

"There's no one else! General Petrov would do me a small favor, but this is serious." Her voice was troubled. "Do you remember how Serge talked about this prison? The filth, the disease, the lice. But you know about that, too."

"Any prison is hell."

The crone of a landlady emerged from the parlor.

"And with Theo that won't be the worst of it. They'll want information. The night Theo was here he said that when he was picked up there would be no one to help him along an escape route. He expected that when he was caught, he would die. If he can give so much, how can I not at least try?"

They moved into the empty parlor. Constantine looked a moment at the rain lashing the window. "Cirie, you're not afraid of Ilya?"

"No."

"I know him. If you go to him for a life, if he wants to give it—if he can—" He stopped. She was too quick not to understand what he was saying—that Laranov would not exact a price.

"I know that," she said.

He turned around, surprised. "Then what?"

"Nothing—it's nothing."

"Cirie, he's cared for you for years! I saw his face when we spoke of you." In all the world she has nothing, he thought. Not even love to support her in this hell. Vassily is no man for her! Once I said that with those eyes and that smile that makes every man feel it's his reward for being so remarkable, she could conquer the world. And now she has no one. "Cirie—" he said, still facing the dark window. "It's different when life offers you a feast, as once it did—" He turned to face her. "God, Cirie, we live in an endless night. If you love him, love him now!"

She touched his arm as though she were helping him in a struggle rather than the other way around. "In this darkness, he's been our only light. Your last light should not be burned too often or too long." She picked up her thin wet cloak. "But this crisis is here and maybe the next one won't come. I'll go around nine o"clock. Things are quiet by then."

"It's raining hard again."

"I've walked in the rain before. Tomorrow might be too late."

"Stepa and I will walk you to the prison."

"No, you'll only get picked up, two men on the street." She gave him his reward—the marvelous smile. "I'll be all right. I know these back alleys like a cat."

*   *   *

At nine o'clock that evening Laranov was at his desk talking to General Petrov who had been here an hour.

"Renkovsky insists that the peasants are refusing to produce while Russia is starving," Petrov said. "Is that true, Laranov?"

The wind threw a sheet of rain against the window and Laranov looked up at it. Every night he had waited, hoping she would come. With this rain he could forget it tonight. Petrov was waiting. "General, you're a good party member. Do you want me to reassure you that all is well or do you want the truth?"

"I want the facts. That's why I ask."

"And will you shoot the messenger?"

Petrov looked puzzled and then understood. "You have my word."

Laranov tilted back his chair. "They're plowing about a third of their land. They have a hundred excuses."

"What excuse could there be when Russia is starving?"

"That the government has taken their horses, that their plows are broken and they can't repair them and can't get new ones." In his mind, Laranov could see a dozen angry resentful moujiks gathered in a muddy field, giving vent to their hatred of the requisitions. "The government tells them that they must meet the requisitions whether they have anything left for themselves or not. And they have not. They don't have enough left to exist. They can't feed their children. They complain that the government doesn't pay anything—fifty rubles a pood when they could sell it themselves for thousands."

Laranov froze a second as he heard a light step outside his door. Then there was only the sound of the hard rain against the window. He turned back to Petrov. "They say the government wants them to break their backs to feed the cities but they get no city products in return. They need everything—machinery, tools, kerosene, matches, soap, petrel, medicines. So they feed their families and hide the rest and barter to keep going."

"Food for the starving cities is life or death for the Revolution!"

"They say that this year the government will take it all, anyway, so they're planting less."

For a minute Petrov was silent. "Renkovsky says the peasants are fighting us and they intend to use food as a weapon."

"The peasants are certainly fighting us. They hate us as much as they hated the landlords. And for the same reason. The same as a decade ago and a century ago. The land. Now that they got rid of the landowners, they believe that the land is theirs. And what they produce on it is theirs."

"No one owns the land! The land belongs to the people!"

That was the battle line. "Their own few acres of land was what the moujiks fought a revolution for."

"Bolshevik plans call for state control," Petrov said.

"You think food is scarce now, General? You haven't seen the worst of it."

Soberly, Petrov leaned forward. "Laranov, they trust you. Talk to them. Renkovsky is convinced they're hiding large stores of grain. His solution is to set higher quotas and let the Cheka show them he means business."

"You want me to tell them to give him their grain and let their children starve?"

"He's a hard vindictive man—Renkovsky." Petrov stood up to leave.

At the door Laranov said, "It might be easier with a carrot than a gun, General. Unchain them. Let them benefit from working their own land."

"Laranov—" Petrov lowered his voice. "Renkovsky will talk to you. He's heard the peasants trust you. Don't tell him this." His eyes narrowed. "Today, Laranov, the important thing is not necessarily to be right. And certainly not to be an independent thinker. A free thinker today is like the fox who's let out in front of a pack of dogs. He can't run fast enough to keep from being torn apart. Here and in Moscow, Renkovsky has real power."

Laranov closed the door behind Petrov. On his travels he had heard it said, privately, that the Soviet had wiped out the aristocracy and the bourgeoisie and that it would, itself, be destroyed by the peasants. He wasn't surprised that Petrov thought trouble was coming.

When he heard the quick tap on his door, Laranov thought that Petrov had returned and then realized it wasn't Petrov's heavy knock. He threw open the door to Cirie, her hair matted into dark strands, her face streaked with rain. He gathered her into his arms and felt her wet cloak against his uniform. "How long have you been out there?"

"I was afraid someone would see me in the corridor." She pushed her hair out of her face. "I waited outside."

He brought a towel and blotted her face. Her blouse was wet against the quick rise and fall of her breasts and her limp skirt sagged against her legs. She was shivering with cold. "Get out of those wet things. I'll give you a robe."

"No, I'm all right." She stood at the stove drying her hair and Laranov's throat tightened at this ordinary act that seemed, in the low light of the lamp, intimate and private. She sipped the brandy he brought her, her eyes unnaturally large in her pale face framed with her wild hair. Rivers of rain poured down the window and beyond it the world was black.

Laranov waited. She had not stood so long in the rain unless she was desperate. It was probably that pathetic doomed family again. Why did she kill herself for them? Why did she even stay with them? Probably for the most insidious of reasons—they needed her.

With an air of defeat she looked down at her wet clothing. "I'm a mess."

Laranov thought that he had never seen her like this—bedraggled and disheveled, her clothes clinging to her thin lithe body that could have been that of a young boy except for the firm breasts, rising and falling in a slower rhythm now. And then he thought that yes, he had seen her like this once before, her face wet then with perspiration, in the lantern light of the Vodovsky stables when she was trying to save the mare and its foal, and he remembered that then, as now, the crystal beauty of the clear wet face and the slender young body as she tugged on the foal, had aroused in him the same desire.

She put down the towel and found a comb in the pocket of her cloak.

"Cirie, why haven't you left that family? Why haven't you left Russia?"

"I will." She gave a little shrug. "Like everyone else, I live from day to day."

"You know the danger. To the Soviets you're a Vodovsky."

In the lamplight, her eyes were almost black. "My sister wants to get married—can you imagine? She's fifteen."

When she left for America, as someday she would if she could hold on long enough, he would be empty without her. He put the thought out of his mind. She was right—everyone lived from day to day and he did, too, and this day—this night—was here. She was warmer now and he led her over to the sofa.

"What about you, Laranov?" she said. "Are you free of danger?"

"Nobody is free of danger today."

"Why don't you get out? You have no strings."

Why, indeed? For him leaving Russia was unthinkable. "When I see that I'm marked for trouble, it will be time enough to get out. Meanwhile I can't abandon Russia." On his travels he had made friends. For a little while, he could find a refuge anywhere. "It's not hard for me to disappear. I've done it before. If I can move, I can save myself."

He drew her into his arms. "Cirie, in all these years, we've never been alone like this—with no one watching, no one listening or waiting, no crisis—"

She moved back to the stove and continued her effort to dry her skirt. Laranov added another log and the fire flared and in its light he studied her profile—the delicate features, the dark blue eyes, the special glow that was part of her. She could be perfectly still, as she was now, and for him the room would light up. "I love to look at you. You have such wonderful fires." He reached for her again.

"Laranov—I've something to ask—" The mood was broken. "You have someone in there." She nodded toward the prison. He waited. "Theo—our cousin—"

Laranov withdrew his arms. "What did he do?"

"People don't have to do anything! And whatever they think he did, it can't be very serious. Renkovsky said the serious offenders go to the political prison.

Maybe somebody recognized him as a former officer. Or maybe it's another case of mistaken identity."

Laranov doubted it was that simple. If Theo was legally out of the army, he'd be living in that house, unless his presence would spell danger for them. He remembered Theo—serious, idealistic. God only knew what he was doing.

"Laranov, while I waited in the rain, I was tempted to go home and try again tomorrow. Then I thought of the prisons I saw when we were looking for Vassi and Serge—all those pathetic faces at the barred windows, like disembodied heads piled on top of each other, just staring out—resigned. Resigned!" Her voice dropped almost to a whisper. "They were utterly without hope."

The rain was beginning again, beating a slow tattoo on the pane. Far down in a wing of the old mansion, a lamp came on and Laranov left the window.

"Laranov, Theo isn't a Czarist. He never was. Don't condemn him to that inhuman misery."

She was pleading so passionately that Laranov wondered what the man meant to her. "Was he your lover, too?"

"Why do you think everyone was my lover?"

Outside, the square of light was gone again and the wet block of the prison loomed. "Perhaps," he said, quietly, "because I have wanted to be, myself, for so long."

He moved close again. The warmth of her, the elegance, the indescribable sweetness of touching her drove everything before it. He bent over her and felt the warmth of her breath on his face and his lips touched her hair and moved to her lips. Stopping—knowing that soon he would not be able to stop, he stopped—and moved away. When he looked at her again she was standing quietly, waiting, her hands at her sides, the serene, inscrutable mask gone from her face.

For a moment Laranov stood perfectly still. Then, tentatively and tenderly, he drew her close again and ran his hands over her face and her throat and his blood raced because her fast hard pulse told him that her concern for Theo was not the only passion driving her tonight and he picked her up and carried her into the bedroom.

Unguarded, Laranov lay quiet beside her, still holding her as though they were one. She had never imagined that a man could show so much passion and so much tenderness. Laranov had taken her to a world she had not known could exist and she had forgotten the other world of fear and prison. We are so many selves, she thought, and a self denied too long can rise up and rule completely. She stirred and Laranov drew her fingers to his lips and then his hands moved over her body on a trip, leisurely at first and then with renewed hunger, as if exploring what he had missed the first time....

Quiet again, she wanted to just lie here, the length of her body, every inch of her body, touching him, until he released her or wanted her again. "Laranov—" Reluctantly she broke the spell. "Before it's too late, give me Theo."

He let her hand slide out of his and lay back, apart now, no longer one, looking at her. After a minute he got up and moved about the room, and her eyes followed the powerful body that had taken her where she had never been.

Dressed, he came back to her. "Stay here. I'll walk you home."

"Theo?"

"Yes." He seemed to be talking partly to himself. "He doesn't have a prayer when they get around to him."

He gathered her close again. "Wait here, darling." At the door he stopped. "And, Cirie, tell your cousin to get out of town. If he's doing what I think he's doing, he could be a victim of mistaken identity again very soon."

43

❀

The news about the trouble on the former Vodovsky estate reached the city after the first murder. A government official had visited the area and demanded fifty poods of grain from each village. The moujiks in the villages were hungry, their children were thin and hollow-eyed. In the third village he entered, the official was shot.

Retribution was swift. Another official went to the village with six soldiers to enforce the requisition. The moujiks were already stretching their meager stores of grain to feed their families until the next harvest. The second official and his six soldiers were shot. Renkovsky labelled the resistance an insurrection and sent Gorshenko to handle it.

Installing himself in the mansion at Rivercliff, now a training center for officers, Gorshenko ordered ten hostages taken. The men were closed up in a small shed at the edge of the village where the trouble had started. Gorshenko waited. The moujiks would not give up their grain.

At the Wednesday night, Laranov was not surprised that the Generals talked of nothing else.

"Taking hostages will cause trouble," Petrov said.

"Locking them up in a shed so crowded they can't even lie down won't get the grain," Malek said. "Let them out. Take what they can scrounge up and say, Not enough—do better next time."

"Let them out!" Renkovsky shouted. "They have grain!"

"How much grain?" Petrov demanded. "Do you know how much?"

Laranov watched Cirie make her way over to him. "I long for you," he whispered. "I waited all week."

"Laranov, have those hostages even had water?" she whispered. "It's two days now."

"No one's allowed near them. Cirie, don't try to do something. This is very serious."

She looked at him, puzzled. What could anyone do? Once you might have reasoned with someone, but now—"Most of them are poor farmers who never had any extra grain."

"The army has to eat," Renkovsky shouted. "These moujiks are the enemy. If a few die, it's no loss."

"No one tried to find out which ones are the enemy," Petrov protested.

"There are enemies among them. Trust no one. That solves the problem."

Laranov leaned closer to Cirie. "Let me meet you somewhere. I ache for you."

"Let them fill the requisition or be hanged." Renkovsky looked around to be sure everyone was listening. "Lenin says, 'Take hostages to insure the collection of grain. Ten hostages, not one.' Lenin says, 'Reward the informers who help locate it. If a village resists, reward the informers for every man who is hanged.' These are not my words—these are Lenin's words!"

"Does Lenin say that?" Cirie said.

Laranov nodded. "Lenin is in love with punishments," he said in a low voice. "They give him a thrill. He sits in a little office in the Kremlin, surrounded by telephones and telegraph machines, and sends hysterical orders far and wide for punishments. 'Immediate, swift, massive,' he says. Death for one offense, prison or ten years hard labor for another—especially for not carrying out his instructions instantly and completely."

"Everyone? Not just aristocrats and bourgeoisie?"

"Anyone who opposes him. Moujiks who won't fill the requisitions are the enemy, whether they have grain or not. They must be wiped out. 'Instantly, finally, totally and without remorse.' To Lenin terror is the most effective weapon. 'Take hostages,' he orders. 'Arrest and shoot whole communities for not obeying orders immediately, to the letter.' It's never shoot one hostage as a warning. Shoot them all. Always hysteria. Always overkill. Destroy everything. Towns, peasants, kulaks, priests, bourgeoisie. 'Everyone—everywhere. The whole world—all—all—all.'"

"But can't he see?"

"He believes that he alone can plan the new order for the whole world and that he has the right to make the whole world obey him."

"Laranov," Renkovsky called. "You're their friend, even though you're a former aristocrat. Tell them men are hanging!"

"They know, General. And they know that drunkards and idiots are rewarded for helping the government take their grain."

"Why not?" Renkovsky came across the room. "These drunkards and idiots are ours. They're landless peasants—exploited—they hate the bastards who have taken the land for themselves. This hate we encourage."

A man uses the weapons he knows, Laranov thought. The Bolsheviks rode to power on class hatred. "Tell a man informers are making vodka from the grain taken from the mouths of his children," Laranov said, "and then hang a few men and you've got a revolt on your hands." He remembered Petrov's warning about the fox chased by the pack of dogs. It was time to leave. Still he said, "From the Ukraine to Siberia, they're calling it the Peasant War."

"They can avoid trouble! They can give up their grain. Tell them about Lenin's orders, Laranov, which we follow to the letter. Tomorrow Gorshenko will announce they have until Friday at noon to deliver. At one minute past noon, the first hostage will hang. When he is twisting on the rope, we'll get the grain. This is Lenin's prescription for the cure and we intend to cure them."

Renkovsky turned suddenly to Cirie. "I see from your face, my dear, that I really must make the time—" his eyes flicked over to Laranov, "— to instruct you. Lenin orders that examples be made so there'll be no more trouble. This is what we're interested in, my dear. Examples! And grain!" Renkovsky rocked his massive weight and looked smug. "You see, my dear, we can't worry about individuals. We're saving the Revolution. As soon as this is settled, you'll be my guest for dinner and I'll explain this to you."

"Don't go near him!" Laranov whispered to Cirie when Renkovsky turned away. "I'm leaving."

At home, sober and discouraged, Laranov reread the notes about Lenin that he had entered in his diary in February after a trip to Moscow:

"He is obsessed with controlling everything," he had written. "Planning everything down to the smallest detail—a perfect machine run by government bureaus. And yet he knows that this dream machine exists only in his head. And that the government bureaus are inefficient and corrupt."

In his mind's eye Laranov could see the ash-gray people with the swollen limbs and feet of the starving, collapsing in the streets. He could see the soup kitchens where a third of a million people ate their only meal of the day. There was a standard portion and workers received four times the standard portion—still too little for good health. Others, the former upper classes and intellectuals, received only a single standard portion and were so listless they were incapable of anything but an effort to survive. Only the workers received an evening meal. He could see the streets of Moscow, empty of dogs and cats—they had all starved to death or been eaten. He could hear the whispered rumors of cannibalism in Russia again.

"Lenin's answer to the devastation is not to reexamine his plan," he wrote, "but to order Russia to tighten her belt and remember that the only salvation lies in the machinery that is not working—the international Socialist Revolution."

Beyond the Urals there was grain. But there were no railways to transport it. With no spare parts and no mechanics the system was almost paralyzed. Train robbery was epidemic. "People are worn out from destitution, sickness and terror," he had written. "Electricity is failing. There is no medicine for typhus. At cemeteries frozen bodies are stacked like logs because the ground is too hard to dig. All this right under his eyes—and yet he is waiting for the world Proletarian Revolution and is puzzled that it does not come."

Laranov closed his diary. He had stopped carrying it with him on his trips and it was dangerous to leave it behind. Where would it be safe from a search conducted in his absence? Or even in his presence? The earlier volumes, dating back to 1914, were safe in a bank box in London where he had left them a year ago while on a covert economic mission. But the current volume, beginning with Lenin's coup, was here. Before long he would have to destroy it.

For now, he locked it away under a false bottom he had constructed in the Vodovsky Oriental chest and his thoughts went back to Renkovsky, disciple of Lenin, who also believed he had the right to make everyone obey him—Renkovsky, who had focused his interest and his insatiably greedy appetites on Cirie.

The next morning, the alley of the black market was empty. With the hostages on everyone's mind, no one would appear with so much as a thimble of grain. As she walked to work Cirie thought about Lily who was going to marry Petya on Saturday. She would feel better about the marriage if she thought Lily really loved him and wasn't merely grateful to him for loving her. Lily had always been so eager for approval, so sensitive to the smallest rebuff.

Near the hospital, a beggar with a toothache lurched up to her, a dirty rag around his swollen jaw, drunk, holding out a hand in the familiar gesture of begging a crust of bread. "Cirie, it's me."

"Theo!"

"Good. You didn't recognize me. Keep walking." Coughing, he staggered along beside her. "Cirie, who do I owe my life to—Petrov?"

"No. Theo, it's dangerous for us to be talking like this on the street. Act sick—as though I'm taking you to the hospital."

"Cirie, will you help me again?"

"Again!"

"My partner was picked up. Our work is becoming so hard. We move only the most desperate cases, who will surely die. It's so hard to get anyone out of the prison."

"It's hard for me, too."

"Every time we fail, a life is lost!" Through his ragged beard Theo's eyes burned.

"Have you heard about the hostages?" Cirie cried. "Some of them fought for Russia, too. Ipat lost an eye. At least one of them lost an arm. Don't you think someone should save them, too?"

"Half the army is guarding those hostages!"

"We're being watched." Roughly, she turned him around. "I don't think you're sick at all! You're only dying for a drink. Come back to the street. Theo," she whispered, "how long have you been back in Kostyka?"

"I never left. It's not safe for me to come to that house." He was seized with another fit of coughing. "How is my mother?"

"Worried about you. Theo, you need care for that cough."

He looked as though he didn't comprehend the suggestion. "Will you help me with my partner?"

"I don't know. I don't know if I still can—"

"Cirie, every man we get out is a life saved."

How was she going to refuse? She nodded to the alley off St. Stephens, where she cut through to Marya's, and told him to meet her there after work and she would give him an answer.

"Cirie—there are so many men in prison who will be killed or sent to Siberia to die."

She realized he was asking for more than his partner. "Theo, I can't!"

"We can get them to the underground, but we can't get them out of the prison."

He looked at her with those burning eyes of a martyr. Or was it the fever of consumption? That Theo had come to this filled her with a feeling of utter hopelessness—Theo, who had lounged on rose-bordered terraces and ridden fine horses and studied and played in Paris, and now was a sick and hounded man in the country he had loved and served. "Theo, you can't survive here. Why do you stay?"

"Survive?" His smile was the smile of a saint in an ikon. "Our whole class is marked for death. It will be sooner or it will be later."

She watched him stagger down the street. He didn't expect to survive. Whether or not to die was not his choice—only the way it would happen. And he had chosen.

At nine o'clock that morning Gorshenko issued the ultimatum: Fifty poods of grain from each village by tomorrow at noon or exactly at twelve o'clock the first hostage would hang. And every hour another hostage would hang until the requisition was filled.

In the midst of the pall cast over Kostyka by the hostage crisis, Ulla arrived after a railway trip worse than anything she could have imagined. "People sitting in the aisles, on the stairs, on the roof. But I couldn't let my little Lily get married without being here. When I heard the news I was so happy I cried. Cirie, don't you think Petya looks marvelous?"

"I haven't seen him but Mamma and Lily say he does." Cirie pulled out Strengov's watch. She wouldn't see Petya tonight, either, because she had just promised to try to help Theo's friend, and she would have to leave soon.

In the alley Theo had said, "His card says his name is Alexander Ivanov—that's all you have to know."

"I'll try to go in about nine o'clock," Cirie had told him. "I don't know how long it will take."

As she left him Theo said, "Cirie, will you help again with some of the others?"

She had hurried on without answering but now, sitting here, only half-listening to Ulla, she hoped he wouldn't ask again because if he did, how would she find a way to refuse?

"Petya fusses over her so," Marya said. "Dresses, furs—"

"Furs!" Ulla cried. "And yesterday she was just a baby!"

She's still just a baby—a baby in a heaven she never dreamed could exist, Cirie thought. Petya had showered gifts on her—a fur hat, a fur muff, beautiful fabrics for Marya to sew dresses—two of them, a wool and a silk, in a shade of blue that had always been Cirie's favorite. Petya seemed able to put his hands on luxuries long vanished from the Russian landscape.

"Petya told his family Lily is his dream girl," Ulla said.

Lily looked up and blushed but she was preoccupied tonight, running her finger over a bit of embroidery on her dress, and Cirie wondered if she was having second thoughts.

"He wouldn't let his family come for the wedding," Ulla said. "His father could never have survived the trip. I thought I wouldn't survive it myself. Cirie, you look more beautiful than ever. How do you manage it?"

Lily threw Ulla a quick look and returned to tracing the embroidery on her dress. What's wrong with her? Cirie wondered. She looks ready to cry. "We didn't realize how shabby we'd all become until we saw Lily's new clothes," she said.

"You shabby, Cirie! In anything you still look like a countess." She lit a cigarette. "On the train the soldiers threw everyone off at a station and told them to go inside and wait for another train. Well, you couldn't go into the station. There was no place to put your foot! Every inch of the floor was covered with people, unwashed, the color of ashes—skeletons."

Cirie glanced at her watch. She had to leave.

"Women were dying on the station floor." Ulla smoked her cigarette as though it were her last remaining pleasure. "When they fell ill they were put off the trains. Some were already dead. People had already stolen their shoes. The government will throw them into mass graves."

Dying in stations, dying for not giving up their grain, dying in prisons, Cirie thought. When Theo asks again, how will I say, No, leave them there—leave them there to die. If I'm not careful I'm going to end up like Theo, always a step away from prison and finally in it.

"Children just staring at their dead parents. The government has a home for orphans who survive," Ulla said. "A soldier told everyone to get on the next train wherever it was going. I thought I was going to end up in Siberia. I hid for a whole day until a train came that was headed this way. Thank God I carried food for three days." Ulla's cigarette was down to a half-inch stub. "Petya isn't here yet, Lily? Lily—?"

Lily looked up. "I told him we'd be busy so not to hurry."

"If not for Petya I never would have gotten here," Ulla said. "I stood in line a whole day and then they said only government officials and Red Army men and baggers could get tickets."

Cirie's thoughts moved to Laranov. You're too hungry to go to him, she told herself. Even before you saw Theo this morning you wanted him. You want to be in his arms—you want to be in his bed. She stirred uneasily. And you're putting your head in a noose. It can only lead to trouble.

Then she thought, No. It's us against them! And Theo's partner will make up a little for the hostages. Go and keep your feelings for Laranov out of it...And how will you do that?...You can still change your mind, she told herself...And will you sleep tonight if you don't try?...You can't save everyone, she told herself.

Footsteps sounded on the stairs and Lily jumped up and flung open the door and Petya came in, all smiles, and swung her up off the floor. "Here's my kitten!" he cried. The cloud lifted from Lily's face. Petya put her down and turned to greet Ulla. Then, for the first time in three years, he saw Cirie. He stood absolutely still and before he thought, before he could stop himself, without taking his eyes from Cirie's face, he whispered, "Why, you don't look at all like her!"

Lily let out a wounded cry and flew into the bedroom and Marya rushed in after her. Lily was weeping as though her world had come to an end.

"Lily, what is it?" Marya said.

"He loves her!" Lily cried. "He really wants her!"

Petya hurried into the bedroom. "Lily, how can you say that?"

"Lily, he adores you," Ulla said.

"You're still in love with her!" Lily wept into the pillow. "You only wanted me because you thought I looked like her. You thought you were getting her all over again."

Cirie sat beside her on the bed. "Lily, you're just having a case of nerves."

"You did it on purpose!" Lily screamed. "You didn't want me to marry him."

"Stop crying and talk to Petya," Cirie said. "You'll see you're imagining all this."

"Go away!" Lily looked at her with hatred. "Go away and shut the door!"

In the small living room there was an awkward silence. A minute later Lily rushed out of the bedroom, carrying all the dresses and furs that Petya had given her and flung them into his lap.

"Lily, no!" Marya cried.

Bewildered, Petya put the clothing aside and stood up. "Lily, it was just the surprise. Please—we're going to be married in two days."

"Oh, you're still ready to go through with it?"

"I want to—"

"No, Petya, I saw your face! You'd go through with it but it wouldn't be the same. You're in love with Cirie. Like all the rest of them, you're mad about Cirie."

After Petya left, Cirie looked helplessly at Lily, still weeping on the bed. She had said all the obvious things—that Petya really loved her, that she was too young, it had been an adolescent crush, there would be others. Lily refused to be consoled. Drained, Cirie thought of the poor man in prison, whose life was closer to an end than Lily's. Suddenly it seemed very important to save him to make up for the doomed hostages and if she was going to help him, she had to leave. More sharply than she had intended, she said, "If he didn't love you more than that, what good was it?"

"He loved me until he saw you! Why did you come here?"

Cirie wished she had not. "Lily, these are terrible times. The man you marry should be ready to die for you—not teetering on the fence between loving you and living in an old dream about your sister." What kind of nonsense am I talking? Who loves anyone like that outside of books?

"I suppose Vassily loves you like that!"

"Of course not. I don't want you to make the same mistake. I want to help you—"

"Don't help me! Leave me alone."

"Lily, listen to me! You're young, you're beautiful—"

"But not as beautiful as you! Well, I'm glad I'm not as beautiful as you! Your beauty is a curse. Look at all the unhappiness you've caused—with your special beauty! Serge and Vassily and Petya and before that, Boris. And probably that general—Laranov! You're a curse to everyone. I never want to see you again."

"Laranov!" Ulla said. "Is he here?"

"I don't want to be beautiful like you!" Lily raved on. "Or clever like you! I don't want to be like you at all. Because I hope in my whole life I won't hurt as many people as you've hurt."

Cirie had an awful headache. In all these years she had never realized how much Lily resented her, although Marya had tried to warn her. She felt too tired to move, and it was almost nine o'clock. She had to go to Laranov who didn't love her either, she thought realistically, in the way Lily wanted to be loved. "Lily, you're becoming more beautiful every day—" Lily shook her off but Cirie went on. "And in any society, in any civilization, there are men with power—" Like Renkovsky? she thought. "Men who can offer comforts," she plunged on. "And everywhere, whatever language they speak, those men love beautiful women. That is stronger than any language or any politics. And one day a man like that will love you," she went on, "because you have a delicate beauty that men adore. Don't ever forget that. Petya was the first, but there will be others—so many that someday you won't even remember him."

Lily only glared at her with so much hatred that Cirie gave up and left the room. Walking with her to the door, Marya said, sadly, "Petya would have taken care of her. She was too young, I know—but you were born an adult and Lily will always be a kitten—"

As she closed the door behind her, Cirie felt her need for Laranov.

"What's the matter, darling?" As Laranov took her threadbare black cloak, her shroud of the back alleys, he sensed that she was upset.

"It's nothing. Laranov, do you have anything to eat? I haven't had anything but tea all day."

He brought her brandy and a box of Polish cakes someone had brought him and while she drank the brandy, she told him about the little girl's fiance. "I told her that if he didn't love her more than that, what good was it—the man you marry should be ready to die for you."

Laranov smiled. "A bit of wisdom out of your own experience?"

"I married Vassi for revenge."

"And all this time I thought it was money."

"That and revenge, too." She put her head back on the sofa. "Revenge! That's certainly the greatest waste in the world. I told Lily that someday somebody would love her like that—totally. One more lie in a crisis."

She drank the brandy and Laranov sensed that she was close to tears. "You don't think someone will love poor little Lily like that?" he said.

"Laranov, you may know there's no such love and I may know it—"

"I don't know it." He gathered her into his arms. "And neither do you."

"But Lily could only love someone she believed loved her and approved of her totally. She needs that."

She had gotten herself under control and her face was a serene mask again, the pale hair a little windblown, the dark blue eyes shining. More than once he had wondered how she did it—insulated herself against the daily barrage of assaults so that she appeared untouched—when inside, he knew, it was another matter.

"Well, the lie was necessary," she said. "But then today we lie about everything—to survive, to get food, to keep from being kicked out of our rooms."

He refilled her glass. "Darling, I can't believe it bothers you to lie when you have to."

"Of course not! You should outwit the bandits every chance you get. The more the better!" He brought her another glass of brandy and she sipped it and rested her head back again. After a minute she said, "What's happening with the hostages, Laranov?"

"Only the ultimatum this morning."

"They're going to die, aren't they?"

"Probably."

For a minute she was silent. The branch of the tree rustled against the window. "I think," she said, "that deep inside, you have to have a little shred of faith that all these horrors will pass—or you wouldn't go on living this way."

Laranov wasn't so sure anymore that the horrors would pass—for anyone, and especially for the upper classes. In Moscow a hardness was setting in—an unfeeling manipulation of huge masses of people by leaders cut off in the Kremlin, trying to solve the Hydra of problems of a country sliding into total chaos.

"If you couldn't believe that someday you won't be hungry—someday you'll be left alone again—someday the senseless killing will stop—if you couldn't hold onto that, you'd follow the others who lost hope and you'd end your life." Presently she went to the open window. "The moonlight is so bright tonight," she said. "And over there the prison, with all those poor lost souls—"

"Come away from there. You're depressed enough tonight." He drew her close, wishing he could promise her that he would take care of her always, that no one would harm her because he was here. But he wasn't sure he would be able to help anyone much longer. Or Russia, either.

"Meanwhile—" she said, "you cling to that little ember of hope and say, Nitchevo—what does it matter? Nitchevo—it will pass. Only it doesn't always work. Do you ever think, Laranov, that it doesn't always work?"

"Cirie, I don't think for a second that you go around saying to everything that it doesn't matter. When you talk about getting the best of the bandits, that's my girl."

She moved back to the sofa and emptied the glass of brandy. "Once I ran into a woman revolutionary named Marushka and it didn't work."

"Marushka! How did you run into Marushka?"

"She came through here with her gang. Her men were tormenting an old man and I cried out for her to stop."

"You ordered Marushka with her whip and her thugs to stop!"

"I told myself to look the other way because I was pregnant but it didn't work. She cracked her whip at me. Stepa pulled me back but it got me across the ankle."

"Marushka wasn't a Revolutionary—she was a bandit, pure and simple. We've had a lot of bandits—some of them are in the government today. Koba, for instance, robbed banks for the party while Lenin was in exile, with Lenin's approval. He was the best of the bank robbers, totally without scruples. Today Koba is Stalin. Marushka's gang stole and destroyed and tormented people for kicks."

"She had the most evil face I've ever seen. She haunts me."

The brandy was beginning to have an effect and in his arms he felt her relax.

"I can't forget her. Whenever I see cruelty running wild, especially in a woman, a voice inside me cries out. 'Marushka.' Agniya turns viciously on her young nephew who comes to help her and a voice inside me says, 'Marushka!' Even Renkovsky, when he talks about killing everyone, reminds me of Marushka."

Laranov kissed her and moved his hand down her throat. "Darling, am I going to love you tonight?"

Suddenly she was herself again, turning to him with soft shining eyes and that wonderful smile—as though she had remembered where she was and why. She touched his lips. "Laranov, will you give me something?"

"Of course, darling—if I can."

"You have a prisoner—"

He stood up. "My God, more family?"

"No—not family."

"Not another lover!"

"You know better than that."

"What then?"

"A nurse in surgery—he's her lover—and she's desolate. What do you need him for? Some poor fellow who stumbled into trouble—"

It was Laranov's turn to stare out the open window at the mass of stone that seemed fated to come between them. "Tell me what he is to you."

"Just a life." She came to him. "Darling, I've never even seen him. He's just a life."

Nothing is honest anymore—she's right about that. The moon was low, hanging just over the tree that was still only a bare silhouette until you looked and saw the tight red buds, full of life, full of promise—

She stood quietly beside him, the tension gone, radiant—waiting. He held out a hand to her and she came into his arms and he thought, Whatever the man was to her, we have tonight and does anything out of the past matter now? She was right about that, too. Nitchevo.

For twenty-seven hours after the ultimatum, while soldiers erected scaffolding, Gorshenko waited for grain. The peasants refused to budge.

At noon, Ipat, father of four sons, was dragged out of the shed because he was a leader and hanged. His body was left swinging on the rope. At one o'clock a second body hung beside it. The peasants stared at the bodies and burned with hatred. As darkness fell, six bodies swung on ropes, guarded by soldiers lest they be cut down. The last man hanged was Popov, who always had been one of them. Not a cup of grain had been delivered to Rivercliff.

When it was dark Gorshenko ordered the hostage shed, where four men were still confined, burned to the ground. He was not finished. He promised he would go through every hut and barn and shed and outhouse until he found the grain. At midnight the moujiks from every village on the estate gathered in the forest and moved in a silent wave to the house and put torches to it and watched it burn.

With thirty soldiers, Gorshenko beat through the villages. They uncovered a total of twenty-eight poods of grain. The moujiks who had hidden these small quantities were shot before the eyes of their families. Half of the seized grain was given to informers. The remaining fourteen poods were added to the government supply at a cost of thirty lives—twenty-two moujiks, two officials and six soldiers.

On the following Wednesday night Renkovsky cornered Cirie. "I'm ready to begin your instruction, Madame. I would suggest this Saturday night for our first lesson."

Cirie shuddered. "Comrade General, I work on Saturday evenings. We're so short of nurses."

"Then we will dine at nine o'clock."

"Comrade General, I appreciate your interest and if only my situation were different, I know I could learn so much from you." She was reciting all the excuses she had rehearsed since he began to bother her. "But, alas, my husband would never permit it."

"Are you telling me, Madame, that you are happily married?"

"I am very happily married, Comrade General."

"And that your husband is still ruler of your household?"

"Of course," Cirie said, demurely.

Renkovsky laughed out loud. "Madame, I don't believe you." Then the hard glitter came into his flat, almost colorless, eyes. "It's my intention to instruct you, Madame," he warned. "I will not be rebuffed."

On Sunday night, under a full moon, Stepa and Cirie and Georgii set out on foot for a last look at Rivercliff. Around midnight they walked up the winding drive, where carriages and troikas never passed anymore, past orchards where unpruned apple and peach trees still smelled of spring, past the grove of tall pines that had not yet been hacked down. As they rounded the last turn in the drive, the great empty space where the mansion had been loomed ahead of them. Only a Vee-shaped corner of a single wall remained. And in the pale light, the marble steps and iron stair-rail, where lions and tigers and monkeys and panthers raced up one side and down on the other, rose like a ghost over the ashes, jutting against the moon.

44

On a July morning, Lily saw a man collapse on the street. For weeks following her shattered romance, she had nursed a broken heart, refusing to go to the concerts, imagining that Petya would return to swear that he loved her. But he did not return. She was certain her life was over.

Then the man collapsed at her feet. Gray-faced people shuffled past, as though nothing unusual had occurred. A healthy soldier with a rifle stood nearby without moving. This was not his responsibility. Other soldiers with a wagon would pick up the dead and throw them into a mass grave. There were no coffins, anymore. If you died in the arms of your loved ones, they could borrow a coffin to walk behind to the cemetery but they had to return it. To Lily this seemed especially horrible—as though the state decreed that an hour after you were dead it didn't matter that you had lived. You were worth nothing.

That day she stood paralyzed on the pavement. Then she pinched off a corner of the few ounces of bread she carried and, clutching her bag lest someone realize it contained bread and snatch it, she put the small crust into the man's hand. But his eyes were glazed and his skin hung loose and she knew he was dead. When she looked back she saw a woman taking the bread from his hand.

Walking on blindly, she nearly knocked over Olga and Tina who hurried up to her. "We've been looking for you. You have to come to the concert," Olga said. "You haven't been all summer."

"I just don't feel like going," Lily said. How could you go to a concert when people were collapsing on the street? She felt guilty, suddenly, that in the face of such pitiful suffering, she had been feeling sorry for herself.

"You have to—there's a reason," Olga said.

"What reason?"

"You have to be there to find out."

At the concert, Olga said, "There he is—over next to the bandstand." Nothing had changed. They still came here to look at Darius Kyrigen. "All the girls still throw themselves at him, but he has no favorites," Olga said. "They call him Dari."

"With those dark mysterious eyes, he knows he just has to look at them and they fall in love with him," Tina said.

"Why did I have to come to see that?" Lily said. "It's the same as last year."

"This year he spoke to us!" Olga said. "He *came over here* and guess what he said!"

"He asked to see you! Which one?"

"He said, 'Where is your pretty little friend with the long flaxen hair?'"

Lily blushed scarlet. She couldn't look up at the bandstand or at Darius Kyrigen or even at Olga and Tina. She stared at the grass and when the piece was over she said, "I have to go now."

"So soon?" Someone said beside her and Lily looked up into the dark eyes of tall handsome Darius Kyrigen. "You haven't been here all summer. Not once."

"No," Lily said. "But I have to go now."

"Then perhaps you'll allow me to walk with you a little way."

Oh, this couldn't be happening! Darius Kyrigen with the beautiful dark eyes, the classic profile, the sensuous mouth! What could you say to someone like that? What would Cirie say to him? Probably nothing! Cirie would just give him a slow smile and let him worry about what should be said. Well, that couldn't be so hard. Trembling, Lily started a smile and Darius Kyrigen took her elbow and walked with her out to Elizabeth Street.

When they came up to the fatal spot, the body was gone. "A man collapsed here from hunger a little while ago," Lily said. "Right in front of me. It was awful. Have you ever seen that happen?"

"Yes, I've seen it a few times." Darius Kyrigen spoke quietly but he had a bright, almost electric quality about him—part of that special charm everyone was so crazy about.

"I saw it once before and it haunted me," Lily said. "I even dreamed about it. In my dream I saw all the gray starving victims lined up against a wall and the healthy-looking soldiers in a row pointing their rifles—and no one moved, no one fired a shot, but all the people fell down."

Darius Kyrigen took her arm again to guide her around a deep hole in the pavement. "I hesitated to speak to you—you seemed so young," he said. "But you're so pretty I had to take a chance." He smiled down at her, that wonderful smile she had seen so often bestowed on other girls. "But you really aren't just a child, are you?"

"No," Lily said. "I'm not just a child at all."

*   *   *

On the empty dock at daybreak a faint breeze mixed the smell of the river with the ever-present haze and the smell of smoke from the forest fires. All over Russia the forests were burning. There were no longer any foresters and the peasants going into the forests to cut wood were careless with cigarettes. Out on the river a fishing boat creased the water—government boat, government worker and, once caught, government fish—while on the street early risers were coming in from picking berries, probably their only food for the day. Presently Constantine came across the street. "Who can sleep in this heat?"

He looked at the empty river where the sun was just showing the top of its head. "At Whitewater you and I used to have some fine conversations at this hour. Now when I watch you, you're a million miles away and I wonder what you're thinking."

"I'm thinking about how I can really be a million miles away!" Cirie said. "And you?"

"I indulge in old habits. I search for answers to questions. Why did it happen this way? Were we fools not to see we were doomed?" The glassy surface of the water warned that the awful heat would go into another day. "And I think about good and evil. The Tsar and the Bolsheviks both paid lip service to 'good.' But that was as far as it went. The Tsar's greatest evil was his weakness."

"Well, they're not weak today."

"They are—in a way. They're a hated minority holding onto their power the only way they can—with force and the illusion of force."

"The Cheka and the prisons and hangings aren't illusions."

"They use terror so the people won't think about resisting."

Over the water, gulls dove for the nationalized fish. On the street the speculators were beginning to show up. It was time to go to work.

"Cirie, you know Stepa has been in touch with Theo?"

Cirie nodded. "What about you, Constantine? Why don't you go?"

"I will—in time."

"Where will you go?" That was always the question when they dreamed of getting out.

"To Paris first, like everyone else. After that, England, maybe. Or America. I'll teach them about the Revolution—how a minority of men pulled it off and how it descended into darkness. They'll think they already know but they won't know anything."

The sun was up now, sitting hot and red on the water, ready to scorch the world. "Cirie, what about Laranov?"

"He's all right, although the other generals are nervous about him. And suspicious." Partly because of his frequent trips to Moscow and partly, she knew, because some of them, especially Renkovsky, suspected their love.

"Ilya is clever," Constantine said. "No matter how much they shake things up, he comes out on top. Like Talleyrand in the French Revolution. He served the king and then the Revolution and then Napoleon and then the king again. I suspect the generals know Ilya is smarter than they are."

Smarter than Renkovsky, whose devious mind was always working? The sun was higher now, shimmering on the river, creating for a moment the illusion that the world was whole again. But only for a minute.

"I meant what about Laranov and you," Constantine said.

Cirie knew the question was not idle curiosity. "I don't want to be in love, Constantine." As though she had a choice. "I want to get out. My mother refuses to go, but if she'd hear from America, she might agree to make a run for it. If not, if I find a way, I'll go alone with just Alexei. If I have a chance to leave, I don't want to stop and think about being in love and tearing myself away. I want to go."

At the street, Constantine paused. "Cirie, I don't think a letter from America will reach her here. Ask Laranov if there are any western embassies yet in Moscow. American, French or British. Or some service organization—Red Cross, anything. Give Stepa a letter to carry out, telling your family to try to reach you through some embassy or organization in Moscow. Later, when the famine is over, you can go to Moscow and make the rounds to ask for a letter."

Cirie stared at Constantine as a new flicker of hope was born. Then her joy was interrupted by a disturbance up the street. At the black market alley a crowd had gathered and a ragged emaciated boy, no more than fourteen, was struggling in the grip of a soldier while a second soldier shouted accusations at him.

"What is it?" someone said as Cirie and Constantine reached the alley. "What did he steal?"

"A chicken," someone else said. "One of two being delivered to a Commissar."

"…Guilty!" the soldier shouted. The boy jerked and shook his head. "Move him over there to the wall."

The terrified boy lunged away and the accusing soldier calmly fired his rifle and the boy fell to the ground.

Stunned, the crowd stared at the dead boy. Then the silent men and women ducked their heads and drifted away. Cirie felt that she was going to be sick. In the alley, she had seen an officer who could have stopped the shooting—probably the one who collected bribes—but he wasn't interested in a petty thief. Taking her arm, Constantine urged her back to the house. "This is what I mean by a show of force," he said. "Now none of these people will ever steal from an official—and who else has anything? Thirty people could have disarmed two soldiers. But no one did anything."

No, no one did anything. No one knows what to do. And neither do I.

When she came up to the alley again on her way to work, she didn't notice Gorshenko until he greeted her. She had an odd feeling that he'd been waiting for her. Then she saw the flicker of a warning in Taras' eyes.

"I understand there was an incident here a little while ago," Gorshenko said in his serpentine voice, walking along with her. "Did you see it?"

"Only for a second." What was he doing here? Was he spying on her as part of some sinister scheme hatched in Renkovsky's seething mind or did he have some other devious purpose? Since the hostages she had avoided him on Wednesday nights, although she knew the orders were Renkovsky's and he had only been the enforcer.

"Tell me the truth, Cirie. Do you barter in the alley?"

Suddenly she understood Taras' warning. Gorshenko was the bribe collector and he was afraid that she had seen him in the alley. "I was out on the dock—it's too hot to sleep," she said. "I saw the disturbance."

"I thought some of the moujiks were about to greet you."

"Oh, I probably once gave them medicine. I can't remember them all." He has to know if I saw him because he's afraid I'll tell someone and he'll have to pay a bribe, himself. "How pleasant to have your company on my morning walk, Commander Gorshenko. Are you driven out, too, by the heat?"

"Please, Cirie, he said, in that soft voice that made her skin crawl. "Please call me Grigor."

He murders for Renkovsky, she thought, but he's lining his pockets for himself.

                    *   *   *

In response to an order delivered by messenger, Laranov headed for the Headquarters Building that scorching afternoon, wondering what Renkovsky wanted now. Some luxury, probably, that he would commission Laranov to find on his next trip. Or a personal report on the political infighting in Moscow, where there was ill feeling between Stalin and Trotsky and only Lenin kept the peace. Privately Laranov had heard that Stalin was planning at the right time to seize all the power for himself. Regardless of who was in power, that Byzantine mentality never changed.

Moving along the hot street, Laranov thought that he had become two separate people these days. Part of him traveled to Moscow and to the provinces where deals were sometimes possible with old friends. The other part lived in his moments with Cirie.

He hated the bargain they had drifted into—a tacit bargain that had developed out of his growing passion for her and out of her strange new passion for saving lives. Each time she would say, as though she had never said it before, "Laranov, I have something to ask—" At first one—Theo. Then, again one. Then two. Three!

He had stopped asking what the men meant to her. The answer was always the same. "Lives. Just lives." Why did she do it? Was it only dedication? Or in these hopeless times, did it give her a reason to live?

And what about him? Was he taking advantage of her dedication to a heroic cause? For so many years he had desired her. Now he ached for her and worried about her and he was haunted by the question: Did she love him as she seemed to when she was with him, or was she only using him while he had not really touched her? As he turned into Elizabeth Street he thought that before long he would know because the bargain was going to have to end. At the prison security was tighter every day and slipping men out was no longer so easy. When the day came that he had to refuse her, what then? Would he lose her? Would she give up her crusade or would she look for another way? He reached the Headquarters Building and went upstairs into the crowded noisy unswept hall. And if she continued, he thought uneasily, who would she go to then?

Renkovsky's office was as much a testament to his greed as his massive stomach. Whereas most government offices were bare and stark in the spirit of the Revolution, here the room was cluttered with fine furniture and little treasures—porcelain boxes, silver trays, figurines. Renkovsky waved him into a chair. "They tell me, Laranov, that your value is that you can lay your hands on anything in Russia. Where would bad chloroform come from?"

"I have no idea, Comrade General."

Renkovsky's flesh butted against his desk. "At the hospital this morning, they were forced to perform an operation with useless chloroform. This was one of my men." When Laranov did not reply, he challenged him. "Who should be made to pay? The doctor? His name is Legare."

"Absolutely not. Doctors are scarce."

"The nurse?" Renkovsky was watching him with sharp hooded eyes. "Who was, I believe, Comrade Vodovsky."

What devious plot was Renkovsky hatching? Was this bastard leading up to something else entirely? Or was he planning some phony accusation against Cirie because she refused his dinner invitations? But it wasn't like him to destroy what he wanted and Renkovsky wanted Cirie. "What are you getting at, Comrade General?"

"This upsets me." Renkovsky clutched his massive belly. "I have an old problem that will require surgery one of these days. I wouldn't like to be the one on the table—"

How would they cut through all that flesh? "I'll look into it, Comrade General."

Renkovsky fastened flat hard eyes on him. "You're spending a lot of time in Moscow. They like you there, eh, Laranov?"

"Moscow has no time for affection, Comrade General."

Renkovsky lowered his voice. "They say Lenin is tired—he never really recovered from that assassination attempt."

"He works long hours, Comrade General."

"Tell me, Laranov, who do you see there? Trotsky? He likes you—Trotsky?"

Laranov knew what was on Renkovsky's mind. Early in the Civil War, while Trotsky was everywhere, reorganizing the defeated army, Stalin was busy in the Kremlin consolidating his own power, and after Lenin, Renkovsky was a Stalin man.

"When I get to Moscow, am I going to find you at Trotsky's right hand, Laranov? In an office next to Trotsky's? Leaning over Trotsky's shoulder, perhaps, and whispering in Trotsky's ear?"

"I doubt that, General."

"You're not in a hurry to leave here, eh, Laranov?"

Laranov stood up. As long as Renkovsky was concerned with his own ambition Laranov was willing to humor him but if he was trying to bring Cirie into it again, Laranov was finished. "With your permission, Comrade General, I'll start the inquiry into the chloroform to be sure it won't happen again, especially when you are on the table."

*   *   *

Nauseated and shaking, Cirie sat and smoked a cigarette in Dr. Legare's office. All day the heat had been building and the air was heavy with the smell of the forest fires. In the foul-smelling corridor, rags of curtains hung limp over the open windows.

Dr. Legare's hand trembled. "This wasn't the worse we've been through in that operating room," he said. "But the other horrors were delivered to us from the war. Not inflicted by our own supply room."

All day Cirie had been upset by the memory of the murdered boy, and now the experience during the fourth operation had left her sick and shaken. The last available bottle of chloroform had proved to be worthless and they had been forced to work on a screaming struggling patient whose surgery could not be delayed. After sewing up the victim, Dr. Legare, beads of perspiration standing on his face, had stormed out of the room and canceled all surgery until further notice. Looking at him now, chain-smoking, struggling to get hold of himself, Cirie thought that he looked the way Strengov had looked before he collapsed.

"They're trying to send me to Moscow," he said. "If things get any worse here, I may stop resisting."

How could things get any worse? A third of the beds empty, patients turned away because of a lack of supplies, now all surgery canceled. In the corridor, the evening meal was being distributed, a watery soup with a few herring heads floating in it. Only high-ranking officers received an adequate meal. At a window, an orderly was swatting sluggish flies.

"This is what happens." Dr. Legare said, "when everybody who knows anything is pushed out and only the most ignorant are put in charge—selected for no reason except that, formerly, they were the lowest and the most unwashed and unquestionably the most ignorant. This supervisor won't even understand our complaint." Always thin, now frail and emaciated-looking, Dr. Legare leaned back in his chair and closed his eyes. "Can they really believe that nothing requires special skills or training? That a former laundress can run a large hospital with political questions? No—they don't believe it. They just don't care. I'm going to Moscow. I can't stay here."

"It'll be just as bad."

"It can't be worse."

Just outside the city was a spot where a little stream left the river and flowed over rocks to a pool below and then fell in a small waterfall to a still lower pool where the sun never reached.

"It's a very small insignificant waterfall," Laranov said when he met her as she came out of the hospital, pale and still nauseated. "But at the bottom the water is always dark and cold and we're going swimming in that icy pool because it's filthy hot and you've had a bad day."

Cirie was so glad to see him and she so longed for the cool water that it didn't occur to her to protest.

"Meet me four blocks from here, at the edge of town. I'll be waiting in an elegant carriage with three prancing horses and we'll fly through the countryside."

"Wonderful," she said. "What are you talking about?"

"I've gotten hold of an old nag and a cart and I have bread and wine in my briefcase and we're going swimming."

Dust rose around the horse's legs and the smell of the forest fires was strong through the trees. "All that wood going up in smoke," Cirie said, as the cart bumped along the river road. "And next winter people will burn their furniture and then freeze to death."

When they came out of the forest the sun was still hot and a layer of smoke hung over the river. "The government says there's no one to put out the fires but the truth is they don't care if a few million people freeze to death next winter. They've killed more than that. I don't know why they bother to kill them? Everyone will die soon enough, anyway. We'll all die before long."

Laranov drew her hand to his lips. "That water will make you feel much better, darling."

"All those spies, all those men running around smashing into houses and arresting people on the streets, they could stop all that and put out the fires!"

"Darling, put your head back and relax. You'll know when we get to the water-fall because I'll carry you down and throw you in."

"You know it's true! Only the State is important. The people are only equal enough to give equal obedience to the leaders."

"On the whole, darling, the Russian people are comfortable with this," Laranov said. "Remember all those people who followed Rasputin?"

Cirie didn't even open her eyes. "God, I've almost forgotten about him."

"Remember how they obeyed his most asinine orders? They loved having someone tell them what to do. It's all they've ever known. Lenin understands this."

"Lenin isn't interested in the people."

"Lenin is interested in his own power," Laranov said, quietly. "Raw power. Lenin is the new Tsar. And more of an absolute dictator than the Tsar ever was."

"And there's more cruelty now than there ever was." Suddenly the whole day seemed to close in on her. "My God, Laranov, I saw a boy shot dead on the street this morning for stealing a chicken!" She clamped her hand over her mouth. She had been about to repeat Constantine's comments!

Laranov reached over to her. "Darling, these are bad times. You have to wait them out. Hold on and wait for a change."

"Nitchevo!"

"Yes, nitchevo."

"Well, it does matter! Laranov, don't you see all the cruelty?"

"Darling, the history of the world is the history of cruelty. In the name of God. In the name of a leader, who is mortal even though they call him the Tsar or Lenin. In the name of property or class or marriage. Give a man an idea and he'll find a way to debase it and then he'll champion it with unimaginable cruelty."

As Laranov's words washed over her, her despair increased. Cruelty in the name of anything. They always convinced themselves it was necessary—for the sake of the cause, for the sake of the future, for the sake of the people who would be better off, if they didn't kill them all first. "Laranov, you're always surprising me. You've never even suggested that you care about all the cruelty. And you do!"

He reached for her hand. "Yes, up to a point, I care. But I'm practical, too. I stop when I have to."

They turned off the road and stopped and Laranov led her down a small ravine where you could hear the falling water. And in the shadow of the tall trees, you saw it—just a tiny waterfall, not very wide, not very high—and in the lowest pool it was dark and wonderfully cool.

She knew—she knew clearly—that she should not feel this way. She knew clearly that she should not be here, lying in his arms like this—on a blanket on the flat ground that smelled of pine needles and damp earth, looking up through the tall trees to night coming into the sky—she should not, while he made love to her, let him drive every thought out of her head so that nothing else mattered and for that brief moment the world seemed whole again. Once she had told herself that she would not make that mistake again. Once she had said, love is a convenience—not forever. Only this morning she had explained it all to Constantine.

Beside her, Laranov stirred and reached for her and she closed her hand over his. She told herself it was only because she had never really known love that she felt this way. That was all it was. Or was she calling it love to justify this affair, entered into for a different purpose? She laughed at the idea. I've sloughed off just about every belief I ever had, so why would I suddenly try to justify anything?

"Darling—"

She turned to him.

"We have to leave now. It's almost dark."

She reached up to his face as he bent over her. She knew—she knew clearly— that she should not be wildly—dangerously—in love.

For a minute the dark river appeared to be empty. Then Laranov nodded and said, "The smuggling has started," and she saw two small boats gliding with silent oars toward a large hulk of a boat in the middle of the river.

"What do you think they have tonight?"

"Probably salt. Salt will bring almost any price today."

By the time they reached the curve in the road the contraband had been unloaded and the small boats had vanished. "I look at those stars," Cirie said, "and I think that they shine on other places that are happier than Russia. And the river runs on to places that are free. And I tell myself that the world will be here after Lenin and the Bolsheviks are gone. But sometimes it's hard."

Laranov dropped the reins to reach for her. "Darling, do you every think about us? About where we're going? You and I?"

"No."

"Never!"

"Where can we go? For us there's no tomorrow—" Her voice trailed off. "But, oh, Laranov—" Suddenly she put her head on his shoulder and thought that in the whole world he was her only rock. "Now—for now—I'm happy to have you."

In the city the smoke from the fires hung low over the rooftops and crept between the houses and sifted in through open windows. Insidious, relentless, it wrapped itself around everything. Nothing could escape it. There was no escape.

When she opened the door, Constantine hurried up to meet her. "Are you all right?"

"We had a bad time at the hospital with some chloroform," she said. "For a while it made me sick."

"Sick?" Vara's smirking face appeared over Constantine's shoulder. "You're not pregnant? How would you ever know who the father is?" Constantine whipped around in disgust and Vara defended herself. "You don't really think she's at the hospital these nights she doesn't come home?"

Realizing there was bad news, Cirie looked at Constantine.

"There's a letter from Serge," he told her. "He's been transferred to a labor regiment." Madame was in the living room with Irene and Stepa, a stricken look on her face, a letter in her hand.

"The Labor Armies are regiments converted from fighting to labor," Serge wrote. "Working on roads and railway tracks, doing field labor, cleaning streets. Your labor book must be in perfect order or you receive no rations. For perfect conduct—extra rations. For punishments—starvation, prison camps and the most degrading jobs. For desertion—death. To many it's the only choice left. Either they will succeed or death will provide, mercifully, another escape."

"My beautiful boy," Madame whispered. "They've made him a slave."

Back in his quarters Laranov thought that he should have told Cirie tonight about the tightened security that would make it impossible to give her any more lives—and he would have told her if he understood what her crusade was all about. What made her take such chances? This afternoon he had asked himself whether it gave her a reason to live. Now, recalling her despair on the way to the waterfall, he asked himself if the reason was something more alarming. Was it a reason to live? Or was it a bizarre form of the suicide she had once talked about? "Deep down inside, there must be an ember of hope," she had said, "or you would follow the others who have given up and you would end your life."

Was it a reason to live—or a way to die?

45

Autumn arrived all at once. The wind changed and blew the smoke of the forest fires in another direction and the first warning chill came into the air. Awaking in the dark, feeling the sudden cold, Cirie's first thought was that the approach of winter meant that Stepa and Tanya and Georgii would leave soon. They would make their way to Petrograd, sheltered in safe-houses, and from there, during the first heavy snowstorm, the smugglers would race across the ice to Finland.

"You have to get to Petrograd on time, but not too early or you'll starve," Theo had said. "And carry bread for the trip. You won't find any food along the way."

Lying in bed, Cirie asked herself whether her mother could survive such a trip. For herself, she was ready to insist that the underground take them—all four of them—on the next trip. They owed it to her. She would strap Alexis to her back and get them out and figure out later how they would get to America.

She got up and put her cape over Alexei and stroked his warm face. "What do you think," she whispered. "Are you tough enough to cross the ice into Finland in a blizzard?"

In the kitchen Stepa was waiting for her.

"Soon it will be time," he whispered. "Before I leave I want to build up the woodpile. Gerzy and I have logs under his haystack. But first, while the wood is low, we should move out part of the vodka and wine. The Civil War will be over soon. If your devoted Petrov is transferred, you'll be favored again with 'visits.' Gerzy says they don't believe we have no wine. Why let them find it all?"

Cirie put two cups of rye coffee on the table. "In a search, no place is safe."

"I thought maybe your mother's place. The tenants have vegetable gardens. Is her garden under her window?"

"There are a few cabbages and late flowers."

"That's the one. We could bury it there. The flowers are gone by, so no one will notice if we disturb them. We'll do it at night when everyone is asleep."

Cirie could already hear Marya's objections—it was flirting with disaster—she had enough to worry about already with food scarce and winter coming and Lily out every night and she didn't know where she went. "The generals come tonight. I'll ask her tomorrow."

"After the generals leave tonight, Constantine and I will begin digging up the bottles. This isn't a one-night job. We've got the whole operation planned. We're nothing if not careful planners." They would dig up twenty bottles a night and store them in the house and over the next two days Constantine would move them to Marya's apartment, ten bottles at a time in the baby pram. After midnight, they would bury them in the garden. Then they would repeat the whole procedure.

"We'll have to rebuild the woodpile every time you touch it or Agniya will be a problem," Cirie said.

"And replant the dead flowers in the garden," Stepa said. "But it's worth it, considering what wine and vodka bring on the black market."

"Have you spoken to Theo again?" Cirie said.

"Every day after work Theo and I walk past each other at a certain dock. When it's time he'll say, 'Good evening,' and we'll leave the next morning. We'll follow Theo to a safehouse to wait until night and then we'll be gone. We can't even say goodbye." Stepa's face showed that he was troubled at going and leaving her behind.

She touched his hand. "You're doing the right thing. Can't you persuade Constantine to go, too?"

"He says not."

"Why does he stay? He has nothing here."

"You'll have to ask him. Although the truth is, Theo won't take him—he says he's too old. Cirie, one other thing—I promised Gerzy the dresser in my room. He didn't ask but he needs it. Will you see that he gets it?"

"Of course."

"Vara will object. But Gerzy has worked hard for our family and has taken great chances. I don't want to leave with a debt unpaid."

*   *   *

Laranov had returned from Moscow this morning and he was writing in the diary that he no longer carried with him. There was a new tear in the Soviet fabric. The Government was suddenly fighting its most loyal supporters—the proletariat. In 1917, when the workers flocked to Lenin's banner and fought and died in the streets for him, they saw him as their leader. His victory was their victory, his government was to be the dictatorship of the proletariat.

"The love affair is over," he wrote. "The government is restricting the freedom of the working classes—freedom of speech and even freedom of action—and is destroying the unions and cooperatives they've always depended on. Now it announces a more drastic step—*Labor Duty*. All able-bodied persons, both male and female, will be forced to work at any kind of labor, in any place, at any time and for any length of time that the Soviet deems necessary. This policy is needed, Lenin says, to save the economy.

"The unions have denounced it as slavery. Union leaders have fled to Latvia or Finland and protest from exile that 'The Soviet Government has double-crossed Labor!' and 'Bolshevism is the worst enemy of the working classes!' and 'Labor must now work for the defeat of Bolshevism!'

"Trotsky anticipates objections from world Labor and has announced that the idea of free Labor is a capitalist concept. The Leaders have the right, he says, to force Labor Duty on the undeveloped masses."

Cirie knew Laranov was back from the way the generals were watching her—expectantly, the way people used to watch at gatherings on her first visit to Petrograd when a woman was about to run into a former lover who was now devoting himself to a younger woman, or when a husband was expected and his wife's lover was also present. It was 7:30 and Laranov had not yet arrived but Petrov was watching and Renkovsky was watching, so closely that she wondered if he knew something that she did not. A moment later Petrov came up to her. "Cirie, I want to talk to you. Don't talk too much to Laranov. You were seen out riding with him."

"When?" she said, puzzled. "Oh, that—he came to the hospital to look into some bad chloroform for General Renkovsky."

"Let me explain something to you," Petrov persisted. "Laranov has jumped the fence too many times. He worked for the Tsar's government, where he pretty much had his own way. Then he jumped into the arms of the Kerensky government. Now he's with us, but he's an aristocrat and you're an aristocrat. With Renkovsky around, if you're seen with your heads together, you could be accused of counter-revolutionary plotting."

Renkovsky, his tongue fueled by vodka, was talking non-stop. "Our Revolutionary courts are not for justice," he shouted. "They make it possible to line up the aristocrats and the bourgeois bastards against the wall with a certificate of approval on the guns."

"You hear?" Petrov said.

"General, you know I'm not an aristocrat. My father was a country doctor. My grandmother traded on the waterfront."

"Cirie, you don't look like a poor girl. You don't talk like a poor girl. You look like an aristocrat. The Vodovskys were among the richest families in Russia. Only my friendship for you has left them unharmed. I've even heard that your husband meets with Tsarists."

"General, you know how much I appreciate all your kindness," Cirie murmured.

"Laranov appears to be wooing you, but even if you were to divorce this dull Vodovsky, he couldn't marry you. He knows this. He knows what would happen to both of you. I don't like this careless toying with your affections."

Once she had loved a man who couldn't marry her because she was considered a peasant. Now she loved a man who, even if she were not determined to leave Russia, would not be able to marry her because she was considered an aristocrat! "General Petrov," she said, softly. "I'm grateful for your warning and I take it very seriously. But no one is trifling with my affections. I have no time for that. After work I only have time for my little boy."

"Why shouldn't the workers work where they're needed?" Renkovsky shouted. "These Labor leaders are bastards. They've left the country. Good. We're rid of them. Political considerations come first. We're building for a thousand years, eh, Laranov?"

Cirie waited a minute before glancing around. With a blurred image of all faces turned to her—Petrov, Renkovsky, Golz, Malek—she picked up the zakuski tray and moved about the room.

"When did you get back, Laranov?" Renkovsky demanded.

"Today." Laranov poured himself some vodka.

"Tell me—" Renkovsky called over to him. "It's an exaggeration, is it not, that Moscow is starving?"

Laranov looked around. "Moscow is starving."

"I suppose you think we're responsible? You never heard of a famine under the Tsar?"

"I believe, General, there were many." After a moment Laranov drifted over to Cirie. "Tomorrow?"

"General Petrov just warned me against you."

"I don't want to wait."

"We have to wait."

"You have good friends in Moscow, Laranov?" Renkovsky was starting again. "I'm surprised they let you come back to us. Come over tomorrow and tell me who you met with and what they told you."

Laranov finished his drink. "If you'll excuse me, Comrade General, I have reports to write." He nodded to Cirie and the generals and left.

Petrov moved back to Cirie. "He's careful. I'll say that for him."

Before he could continue, Renkovsky came up to them. "I understand Laranov is leaving again very soon." He looked sharply at Cirie.

"To Moscow again?" Petrov said.

"To the Crimea. The only active front left in the Civil War." The Crimea! A chill skipped through Cirie.

"I hadn't heard that," Petrov said.

"Oh, he's going all right." Renkovsky smiled that malevolent smile. "I have an old Comrade down there, fighting Wrangle. I'm certain our friend Laranov will be reporting to him. As a friendly gesture I think I'll write a note. I'll give it to Laranov to deliver. That way I'll be sure it gets there."

Cirie saw Renkovsky's frozen scheming smile and Petrov's wary eyes and she knew that someone would be watching Laranov's quarters to see if she tried to warn him.

At midnight Stepa and Georgii began to move the logs. Carefully, they took out the vodka and the wine, a bottle at a time, and passed it through a window to Constantine inside the house, where two transients tonight might or might not be spies. Shivering in front of the house while she watched for passing patrols, Cirie asked herself how she could warn Laranov about Renkovsky's note to the General in the Crimea. For the first time she was afraid to go to his quarters, as much for him as for herself. Maybe she could ask Lily to tell him—but Lily was never home, anymore. Or Marya? Only as a last resort. Tanya? How can I send Tanya? There's no one. I'll let a few days go by and then, if I pull the hood of my cloak down over my face, how will anyone recognize me? More than one woman these days is visiting an officer in there in exchange for food for her children.

She had given Marya strict orders not to come outside, not to even look out the window, while they were burying the wine. "Go to bed," she had instructed her. "When we're ready for the bottles I'll come in and get them—you won't even know I'm there. Don't burn a light and don't come outside."

And yet here she was! Wandering around, waiting for her! *What for?* Restraining her anger, Cirie drew her aside. "Mamma, I told you—"

"Cirie," Marya whispered. "Lily is married!"

"What!" Cirie drew her away, from the house. "Petya came back?"

"Not Petya." A sob burst from Marya's throat. "Someone I don't even know."

"Who is he? When did it happen?"

"This afternoon," Marya said. "I don't even remember his name. 'Dari.' She called him 'Dari.'"

They were finished. The woodpile had been rebuilt and the last bottle was buried in Marya's garden and now, by the flickering light of a wick, Stepa put a bottle of wine on the table. "Theo gave the signal tonight. We go tomorrow. So—one last bottle together before we part." He looked up from working the cork. "Who knows when we'll meet again? But I have faith that we will."

He poured the wine and looked at Cirie. "We've traveled a rocky road since that first day I saw you, standing in Eugenie's study at Whitewater."

He had seemed so large that day, Cirie remembered, and so full of authority with his booming voice.

"You were in front of the Oriental chest," Stepa said. "Later they moved it. Where did they put it?"

"Out in the long hall. I used to touch it for luck when I ran by."

Stepa nodded. "Did you know Irene is trying to go to relatives in the South? I don't know how she'll get there but she hopes they'll find a way to take her to Paris. She's given up hope that Serge will return. I don't blame her. At least she was loyal to him while there was hope."

Poor Serge. And poor Theo. They were both so handsome and carefree that summer. Now Serge is lost and Theo is sick and half mad. She turned back to Stepa. "Do you need anything? Do you have something for bribes?"

"I have British pounds and some gold and I think Elissa will be in Paris." While he refilled the glasses he said, sadly, "To me Paris is like a second home but it can never be like Russia. What can one more cultivated unskilled Russian do in Paris? We'll be like poor relations, although I left a little money there."

"If we make it," Tanya reminded him, "in Paris we'll work to help those left behind."

"It's an obligation," Stepa agreed. "I've heard there are organizations doing this in Paris."

Cirie touched Constantine's arm. "Why don't you go, too? You have no reason to stay."

"I'll go some other time. Maybe next year."

"Go now. A lot can happen by next year."

"I'll go later. They don't want me on this mad dash. They say I'm too old."

"Nonsense," Stepa said. "You're a year older than I am."

"I'll find another way," Constantine said.

Cirie met his eyes. "I'd miss you, but I'd like you to go." She handed Stepa the letters they had discussed. "Write three," he had told her. "We'll each carry one in case I don't get through. These smugglers don't stop for anything."

Stepa took the letters and handed slips of paper to Cirie and Constantine. "Elissa's address, so when you get to Paris, you can find us."

He refilled the glasses and the bottle was empty. "I've left Russia so many times but this time is different." He raised his glass. "We'll meet again on the outside."

The next morning, hours after he was supposed to be in the safehouse, Cirie saw Stepa striding, agitated, back and forth on the hospital walk. Something had gone wrong!

"They've taken Constantine," he said as she rushed up to him.

"When?" she gasped.

"A few hours ago. He was going to his janitor job. A line of prisoners was being marched from one prison to another and right in front of him a prisoner broke out of line and escaped. Constantine was questioned and apparently said he saw nothing—"

"He was arrested because he saw nothing?"

"He wouldn't have said anything. That was the way he escaped in Petrograd. They're holding him as a possible witness or accomplice."

Frightened, Cirie leaned against a tree. "A stranger escapes and Constantine is in prison." No matter how careful you are trouble will find you, she thought. Life is nothing more than an accident—the throw of fate's dice. "How did you find out? Didn't you meet Theo?"

"We were following one at a time several yards behind Theo. Tanya saw it. I sent her on with Theo and I went to Gart for information. Over Theo's objections. Theo is in terrible condition, physically and mentally."

New questions poured into Cirie's mind as she realized how serious this could be. "Do they know who he is?"

"I inquired about Feodor Pavlovitch—the name on his card."

"I can't go in until after dark to ask for him." She shouldn't go even then. It was still too soon. If she saw that she was being watched, she would have to go to the prison instead of to Laranov and try to plead for Constantine on her own—say that he was an old man, simple-minded, fumbling along the street—if he had seen anything he wouldn't have understood it—who would select such an accomplice? "He can't stay here now," she said. "If I get him out, you'll have to take him along."

"Theo says they won't take another old man."

"He has to take him."

"He says the smugglers give the orders and can't be controlled."

"There's nothing a bribe can't control."

"I told Theo to take him in my place. Tanya and Georgii can go with him. I'll go next trip. No one is looking for me."

"No!" Cirie said. "Go home and pack a sack for him. Take his gold or pounds or whatever he has. And tell Theo to meet me after work in the usual place."

Stepa started to hurry away and came back. "Cirie, you should know—Constantine didn't want to leave because of you."

For the first time in months tears stung Cirie's eyes.

"Vassi is no help to you—we all know that," Stepa went on. "Without Constantine, after I've gone you'll have no one. He was hoping Laranov would take his place. Now Laranov is leaving, too."

"He'll be back." She still had to warn him about Renkovsky's letter. At least now it had been decided. She would try to go in there tonight.

She lingered in the hospital until the light began to fade. In the alley between St. Stephen's and Muscovy, Theo emerged from the darkness. "Cirie, he's too old!" Theo's voice was hoarse. "We can't take him."

"You have to," she whispered.

"My partners won't do it. Much less the smugglers."

"Theo—" she said, firmly. "Tell your partners that if they don't take Constantine. I will never again lift a finger to help them."

"But Cirie—" Theo smothered a cough. "We leave in a few hours. We can't travel in daylight."

"Then wait another night."

"The safe-houses won't keep them another night."

"How many men in those safe-houses have I saved?"

"Most—at one time or another."

"If they don't do this for me, they're as good as dead the next time they set foot on the street."

"Cirie, he's only one old man."

"Not to me!"

"We're working to save hundreds. We can't jeopardize everything for one man."

"That's what the Bolsheviks say, Theo. 'The Revolution comes first. We can't worry about one man!'"

"They race a sled across the ice in a blizzard. He won't be able to hold on."

"Tie him on."

"Cirie, I know you." Theo gestured nervously. "You wouldn't leave men to die when you're the only one who can save them."

"Take him."

"Cirie, you've developed the mentality of a killer!"

"That's right."

Theo saw that she meant it. "What time should I meet you to pick him up?"

"I try to go in around nine. I don't know how long it will take. Be there and wait."

Theo struggled again to choke back his cough. "Cirie, Stepa says to give Constantine a letter, too."

Cirie smiled. Stepa had more confidence in her success than she did.

While Laranov worked at his desk, a part of him listened for quiet footsteps and a tap on the door. He knew Cirie was afraid to come here—and she was right—but in two days he was leaving for the Crimea—and he couldn't go away for what might be a long time without seeing her.

He used to be a happy nomad, he thought, and there had never been a place that it had bothered him to leave. Now, wherever he went, a part of him stayed here, and he was asking himself if he could take her to Moscow where nobody would know her and live with her there. Not right away—only an idiot would move to Moscow now—but when the famine was over. Maybe next year. He would get her a card under the name of Strengov—safer than Vodovsky—and she would be anonymous. He wondered if he could work it out. He wondered if she would go. He marveled at the mysteries of a man's heart that he was even thinking this way. If she didn't come tonight, he would go to her.

Laranov looked at his diary, a chronicle of the descent into hell, and thought that every time he went away, the problem was the same. He couldn't take it along and it wasn't safe to leave it behind.

He knew what he had to do. He picked it up and moved to the fire and opened the door. Do it now, he told himself. Why wait? Then he closed the door and locked the volume away again in the Vodovsky chest. He had another day. But he knew he had written his last entry.

For twenty minutes Cirie waited in the shadows, watching the guard walk back and forth until, satisfied that he was alone tonight, she slipped into the building and tapped on Laranov's door.

Moments later she listened with disbelief as Laranov tried to explain why he had to refuse her. "Darling, it's become too dangerous," he said. "They're watching the prison and they're watching us. You know that."

"Laranov, I have to have this one!"

"I can't do it. Cirie, the place is crawling with guards."

"And the people who are in there now?"

"They'll be long gone before things ease up—shipped out somewhere. It's not possible anymore to just slip someone out. Security is too tight. They're passing around daily lists—"

"Then it's a tomb! If no one can get out, it's a tomb!"

Laranov drew her over to the sofa. "Darling, you've developed a bad habit, thinking you have to save all these lives. Most people go a lifetime and never save a life."

He looked startled and wounded when she backed out of his arms. "Laranov, how can you not even try? It's so cruel."

"Because I lay my head on the line every time!" He stood up and walked away. "Because it's impossible! Cirie, you have an Achilles heel—a terrible weakness. You have no stomach for cruelty."

"And you have no weaknesses. That frightens me."

He smiled. "I have a weakness."

"Then give me this one—tonight! I won't ask again."

"I can't." He came back to her. "Darling, I want to talk to you about something—"

"It's because you feel sure of me!" she cried.

He didn't try to touch her again. "Sure of you? No—"

Cirie moved to the window. Should she tell him it was Constantine? That would make a difference. But if getting him out was impossible, then she would have revealed information that could mean death for Constantine. Across the yard, the prison was a dark block. "It even looks like a tomb."

"All right, it's a tomb! For now I can't change that."

Why are you hesitating? she argued with herself. This is Laranov. Tell him. But Constantine is only being held as a witness. They might release him. But what if they've already discovered his real identity? Then there's no hope, she thought with a clutch of despair. And if they still believe he's Feodor Pavlovitch, he's safer if no one knows otherwise. But Laranov won't betray him. Constantine was his closest friend. He might say he's too hot to touch, but he won't betray him.

"Come away from the window, Cirie," Laranov said. "That isn't doing you any good."

She was sick at the sudden gulf between them. For another minute she wrestled with the decision. Then, "Laranov, there's someone in there you know."

He scanned the list on his desk. "We get these damn things every night now." He turned to the second page.

"My God, two pages of new prisoners in one day?"

He glanced up, his mouth set in a hard line. "There's no one here I know."

"Feodor Pavlovitch."

Suspecting an alias, he waited.

"It's Constantine."

"Constantine! Here!" He drew her back from the window. "Come away from there. It's too dangerous. How long has he been here?"

"Always. Laranov, you couldn't have met with him. He wanted to see you but he was afraid for us."

"You've had him all this time? God, Cirie, the chances you take!"

She knew he would take care of it. A fleeting desperate look chased across his face. He didn't know how, but he would do it. "Do you need something for bribes?"

"I have bribes." He took out two bottles of vodka and started to go. "I could hang for this."

"Laranov!" She had almost forgotten! He stopped at the door. "Are you going to the Crimea?"

"I leave day after tomorrow."

"So soon!"

"If you hadn't come tonight I'd have gone to the hospital tomorrow to tell you." He took a step back into the room. "How did you know?"

"Renkovsky told us after you left the other night. I was coming to warn you. He's going to give you a letter to a friend."

"Renkovsky is going to give me a letter?"

"To an old Comrade. He had that evil scheming look and he watched to see how I would react. I'm sure Petrov told him he saw us together."

"It was Gorshenko."

"Darling, the letter—don't deliver it."

Laranov smiled. "It's all right if Renkovsky wants to give me a letter to a friend. I'll know who to watch out for."

"Be careful! Don't trust him!"

"Trust Renkovsky? Nobody would think of trusting Renkovsky! Don't worry. I don't intend to be shot in the back on Renkovsky's orders."

Laranov put down the vodka and took her in his arms. "Cirie, I love you so. I love your beauty—and your agonizing heart—and your cagey mind and your insane courage. I used to think about how magnificent you could have become if not for this upheaval that has destroyed everything. Now I love what you've become because of it."

He knows this is our last meeting for a long time, she thought. How would she get along without him? In his arms she had known her only moments of happiness. "Oh, Ilya—I'll miss you so!"

His eyes searched her face. "That's the first time you called me that."

"What?"

"By my given name—Ilya." Defenseless, he whispered, "You do love me!"

She touched his face and answered with her eyes.

"Darling, listen to me. I'll be away a month. Maybe longer. When I come back I'll find a way for us to go away together."

She nodded.

"You'll go?"

Go? Then when will I get out of Russia? But how can I give up Laranov? "If I can take Alexei."

"Leave Vassily now. While I'm away. Get a divorce. Use the name Strengov again. Will you do it? Will you leave him?"

"Yes, I'll do it."

"When?"

"I'll find the right time."

"For now this is goodbye." He held her as though he would have to remember this moment for a hundred years. "I'll come back for you."

She remembered Constantine's instructions. "Ilya—is there anything yet in Moscow from the West? An embassy—a trade organization? American or English? Or a Red Cross?"

"Why?"

"My family could send a letter there."

His face said he wondered if it was only that. Then he said, "There's a Friends group. American Quaker Relief." He held her again, reluctant to let the moment end. "Darling, isn't it incredible," he whispered, "that in the middle of hell—in this tomb—we've found love?"

Then he picked up the bottles to go and free Constantine.

In Laranov's quarters, the two old friends gave themselves the luxury of a few minutes to talk. Then it was time to go and Laranov gave Constantine a diary and a key for a bank box in London, and Cirie and Constantine left to meet Theo. Just before she kissed Constantine goodbye, Cirie gave him a letter to Anna. "In Moscow there's an American Quaker Relief."

"I'll write your family from Paris."

Then Theo stepped out of the shadows and Constantine embraced her quickly and was gone.

With a heavy heart Cirie climbed the stairs and entered the house. Everyone was gone—Stepa—Constantine—Tanya—Georgii. Laranov. They were all gone and she was alone. In the house she locked the door and headed for the parlor. She just wanted to be alone for a little while with her feeling of loss. Then in the dark room she saw that they were all there—Vassi, Madame, Kyra and Vara. My God, this is all that's left of us! she thought. She sank into a chair without speaking. She was so tired she felt she couldn't move even to go upstairs. Then she became aware that Vara, who was standing, had come in just ahead of her. She was still wearing her coat.

"I told you!" Vara said, triumphantly. "I told you she wasn't spending all those nights at the hospital."

"Where were you?" Vassily demanded.

Exhausted, eyes closed, Cirie didn't bother to answer.

"Cirie, I'm questioning you!"

"Vassi, what are you talking about?"

"Were you at the hospital tonight?"

"No, I wasn't at the hospital. Constantine was arrested and I was out trying to save him. They've gone." She opened her eyes. "All of them."

"We know," Madame said. "Stepa rushed home in the middle of the day and went to Constantine's room."

"I'm so curious to know how you do it," Vara said. "Tell us—which of your men is helping you? Your generals? Your doctor, who adores you so?" With a taunting smile she turned to Vassily. "Have you any idea how many men she has?"

"Stop this, Vara," Madame said. "Our loved ones are facing great danger tonight. We should be thinking of them."

The words brushed past Vara. "Haven't you ever wondered how she saved you and Serge? And then Theo? And why Stepa went right to her when he heard that Constantine was arrested? What an unusual gift. I've thought so for a long time. And tonight, to satisfy my curiosity I followed her from the hospital. Would you like to know where she went? To the officers quarters. And she was in no hurry to leave." Vara's face was distorted with the passion of her accusations. "I told you all along. She's the army whore—the sweetheart of the barracks."

"Vara!" Madame half-rose out of her chair. "Vassi, you know Vara always imagines the worst!"

Vassily only shook his head. This time he believed her.

"Vassi—in the past she's even accused me!" Madame said.

"It was true!" Vara cried. "You and Sacha Borassin."

Cirie looked up. "You can say that, Vara?" she said and Madame looked puzzled at the exchange.

But Vara was beyond hearing the warning. She looked like a mad witch. "I saw her! I saw the whole thing! I saw her watch until it was safe. And then she went in like all the other whores who go there. I waited a long time for her to come out— I got quite tired of waiting—and *she did not come out*." Eyes bulging, she turned on Cirie. "I finally decided you were spending the night. I'm surprised to see you here."

Suddenly Vassily was back in that other world where his word had been law and any infringement on his domain had rocketed him out of control. In a rage he turned on Cirie. "Get out of my house!"

Vara's wide mouth went into a triumphant smile.

"Certainly, Vassi, if that's what you want," Cirie said. The right time was here—sooner than she had expected. She started toward the stairs. "I'll be gone in the morning."

"Where are you going?"

"I'm going to bed, Vassi. I've had a hard day. There are extra beds tonight. Find another one for yourself."

"Don't set foot in that bedroom! I don't want you near my son!"

Cirie came back. "You didn't think I'd leave without Alexei?"

"Alexei is my son." He placed himself in the doorway of the parlor. "Get out—get out now. Go to one of your lovers—any one. Go. But don't go near my son."

"I'll leave now, Vassi," Cirie said, coolly. "And Alexei will come with me. Don't try to stop us."

"I'll stop you! Who are you to give me orders?"

"Vassi," Cirie warned. "You're playing with fire!"

"Nonsense!" Unable to stand still, Vassily began circling the room. "I raised you up from nothing. A servant! And this is my thanks!"

"You took the name Vodovsky and dragged it through filth!" Vara cried.

"It's not nonsense, Vassi," Cirie said, softly. "They know about you. They watch you. They know you meet with Tsarists—they know you're fooling around with counter-revolutionary movements."

Madame gasped. "Oh, Vassi, you shouldn't!"

"I've protected you for months. So don't threaten me, Vassi, because when I stop protecting you, they'll be here."

"Nonsense! Rubbish! *You* protect *me!*"

"And now I'm going to pack. Alexei and I will be gone in half an hour."

"Stop! Don't touch him! I don't want your hands on him!"

"Vassi, don't ask for trouble."

"He's my son. You'll never see him again."

Cirie came back to face him and felt a tug of sympathy as he seemed to shrink before her hard stare. "Vassi," she said, coldly. "You couldn't keep him a day. *I keep you alive!*"

Upstairs she cut open the mattress and took out her jewels and the pouch of gold coins. Half an hour later, with her sleeping son in her arms, she handed a tearful Madame a cloth containing several gold coins. "Guard it carefully,

Maman," she said. "Sew it into your mattress. If trouble comes, it's all you have left." She remembered her promise to Stepa. "Maman, Gerzy is going to build up the woodpile. Stepa promised him his dresser."

Madame nodded.

Cirie closed the door behind her and walked through the alleys to her mother's apartment.

46

❀

In the frozen wasteland no sign of life intruded upon the desolation. Constantine pushed on beside Stepa. The snow made a sheet as thick as frozen milk and blinded him as it sliced his forehead and the skin under his eyes and piled thick on the scarf over his nose and chin.

A few paces ahead Tanya and Georgii trudged through mounting drifts behind the underground guide who seemed to be untouched by the weather and stepped firmly toward the destination he alone knew. Since leaving Petrograd, he had spoken no one. White from head to foot he blended into the falling snow around him. Constantine could barely make him out only a short distance ahead of Tanya and Georgii. He pushed on.

Then the guide turned a little to the left and the lines of a makeshift shelter emerged from the fast-falling snow. The shelter was an insecure roof clinging to three rickety walls. They stepped under the roof and stood there, backs to the wind, moving their arms and legs in the biting cold.

"Theo said the first serious blizzard," Stepa said, beating his hands together, trying to knock off the layer of snow that covered him. "This is a serious blizzard."

"You can see it's safer," Constantine said. "A border patrol can't see any more than we can."

In the cutting cold and wind, talk was difficult and he fell silent. He wondered when the smugglers would show up. In the safehouse in Petrograd—a cellar in a deserted house that any day would be torn down for firewood—men who were more loquacious than this guide had talked about them. "A rough crew," one had said, "but good smugglers. Finnish."

"A bad lot," another had said. "We hear stories about them murdering their passengers, especially if they have anything worth stealing."

Everybody had something. This was not charity. Every man paid for his own trip, through the underground, and every man would carry something to sustain himself awhile on the outside. How do they know if a man has something worth stealing? he wondered. Should we expect to be searched? Where could a search take place in this forsaken end of the earth? Snow froze on his eyelashes and he ran his snowy mitt over them and ducked his head. Constantine was carrying a pistol and a knife. Whenever he and Stepa had discussed a possible escape they had decided that, if possible, they should bring along a gun and a knife and Stepa had brought Constantine's. Constantine could remember a time when he was opposed to violence. But now he did not intend to be searched or to allow his friends to be searched. There would be no compromise. It would only lead to murder. The Revolution had taught him lessons.

Then out of the thick veil of snow the smugglers emerged with two heavy Finnish sleds and four powerful horses. Without a word the underground guide paid them in British pounds and with not so much as a nod, headed back into the blizzard, leaving the four escapees at the mercy of the Finnish outlaws. The valuable cargo tonight was already loaded and tied down—precious furs. The passengers were only baggage. The smugglers grabbed them and pushed them onto the heavy sleds, Stepa and Tanya in the first sled, Constantine and Georgii in the second, where they sat on top of the furs and held onto a bar as best they could. In less than a minute they were on their way.

The magnificent horses, that seemed to have been fed and trained for great speed and endurance, shot like bullets across the deserted countryside. Challenged once by a patrol, the smugglers asked for more speed and left the patrol far behind.

Minutes later they came upon a lone house with a light in the window and turned and came soon to a small town where another light burned in a window. They turned and raced down a dark street. A lone man and his dog stood on a corner. They turned and flew across bumpy fields. Constantine understood that these innocent appearing contacts were organized to signal the drivers about which routes were safe tonight.

They slammed into a frozen snowdrift and he clutched the bar to stay with the sled. It will be easier, he thought, when we reach the Gulf of Finland. Frozen water will not be as bumpy as frozen fields. He was wrong.

Gale force winds swept across the open Gulf. The frozen surface was covered with blocks of ice concealed by high snow drifts. The sleds would crash into them and overturn and the smugglers would hasten to right them and check the furs. The passengers barely had time to struggle back on before the horses flew off. The searchlights began. Long blades of light followed each other across the expanse of the Gulf. The smugglers zigzagged to stay out of them.

Constantine could remember when Russians boasted that Kronstadt with its cannon and searchlights made St. Petersburg the most impregnable harbor in Europe. Kronstadt with its cannon and searchlights are still there, he thought, still guarding it, but we are going the other way. We are the enemy and the searchlights are our enemy.

The blades of light were closing in, searching, moving on, returning. The guns began. The snowfall was suddenly lighter. Vision improved. The smugglers zigzagged and called for more speed from the horses.

Suddenly the first sled hit a huge frozen mass. Tanya flew up in the air and in one motion Stepa leaped up and caught her and in the same instant Constantine, in the second sled, instinctively leaped up because Tanya might fly toward him and the smugglers would not stop.

In that second, in a lull in the storm, the path of a searchlight crossed the sleds and guns fired. Constantine groped for the bar and felt the searing pain in his right arm and saw Stepa fall forward. He saw a smuggler grab Stepa and hold him on the sled. More gunfire from Kronstadt. Then the lull in the storm was over and snow closed in again. The guns stopped.

The smugglers stopped.

"We're out of Russia," one of them said in broken Russian. "The contract was we take you out of Russia. You're out. We're through."

He pointed to the distant searchlights. "Russia." He pointed in the opposite direction. "Finland."

"You can't leave us in the middle of the gulf!" Constantine protested. Pain pierced his arm. He saw that Stepa was in great pain and losing too much blood. "We have a wounded man. He can't walk to Finland!"

"The contract is done. We're through with you."

"No!" Tanya screamed. "My father was shot. He's bleeding badly."

"A woman!" The smugglers stared at her. "No women!"

They threw off the four small bags, almost burying them in two feet of snow, and pushed their passengers off the sleds. They pointed to Finland. "You can walk."

"No!" Tanya tugged at the driver, who shook her off. "Take us. Please take us. My father will die."

"We're through."

"My mother in Paris will pay you a great deal of money!"

They were gone, leaving the four refugees standing in a wake of snow, alone in the middle of the frozen lake.

Georgii picked up Stepa's bag along with his own and they struggled to push on but two feet of soft snow was too much for Stepa. He made an effort to walk, leaning on Georgii and Tanya for support. After a few steps he stopped.

"Leave me," he said. "I'll rest here. In the morning someone will pass and see me. Go on without me. Take care of yourselves."

"Never!" Tanya said.

Constantine shook his head at the unthinkable suggestion, although he knew that with the bullet in his arm he would not be much help.

Georgii put down his bag and Stepa's bag and said, "We'll carry you." He looked a moment at the bags as though considering whether he could carry just one.

"Leave them all!" Tanya cried.

"The gold is in them," Georgii said. "If we make it to Finland, we'll need it—for bribes—or just to pay our way."

"And if the Russians pick us up, they'll steal it all!" Tanya cried.

"We each have a little in our belts," Constantine said. "We'll manage. Stepa comes first."

"I'll try the smallest one," Georgii said as they picked up Stepa.

But the bag threw him off balance and he kept slipping in the deep snow. After a few minutes, without a word, he put it down. They had already agreed this was what he would do.

All night they pushed on in snow up to their knees, carrying and dragging Stepa across the frozen lake, checking the searchlights they knew had to be kept behind them. Then the lights stopped and they trudged on, praying that with their slipping and staggering they had kept the direction. In the morning, as dawn was breaking, they reached a shore and struggled onto land, uncertain whether they were in Finland or had circled back to Russia.

Frozen and exhausted they summoned up their last bit of strength and trudged along the shore. Stepa was barely conscious. Constantine steeled himself against the pain in his arm. He told himself this was not worse than he had known before. He had been weak like this before, he had been frozen like this before. He had never known pain like the pain in his arm.

The sun was above the horizon when they came to a small cottage. Constantine held out his good arm to stop them.

"If we're in Russia there'll be soldiers inside," he said. "We have to take a chance. Stepa needs care."

"I'll go ahead and try to find out," Georgii said.

"No. Stay here to carry Stepa," Constantine said. If one of us has to die, he thought, it's more important that the two young people survive. Their whole lives are ahead of them. "I'll go alone. If they're Russians they'll look for my friends. Try to stay out of sight."

He knocked on the door. There was no sound from within. At least there were no orders from Russian soldiers on guard. His teeth were beginning to chatter. He knocked again. There was a glimmer of a light and the sound of someone coming to the door. He knocked again, hoping to persuade the occupant to shout at him so he could signal Tanya and Georgii to come to the door or to hide. Another hard knock and a man's voice called out—in Finnish.

The man opened the door, took one look at them and asked no questions before carrying Stepa into the house. His wife put on coffee and took their wet clothing to the fire. It was clear that other fugitives had stumbled off the frozen lake before tonight to knock on their door. The husband, Taddeus, sterilized a knife in the fire and removed the bullets from Stepa's back which had entered near the shoulder and had gone very deep. Then he sterilized the knife again and turned to Constantine's arm where the bullet had slanted close to the surface.

For three days Stepa, who had always been a rock, was too weak to speak. He developed a burning fever and became delirious. On the third day he died.

The three grieving beggars had to move on. Taddeus borrowed a horse to drive them to the place where the underground had told them to pick up their documents. Leaving just as the sun came up, Constantine took one last look across the gulf at beautiful old St. Petersburg, gleaming in the early light. Lost forever, he thought, to us and to the world.

Their money was almost gone. Some had been in the bags they left behind on the ice and the rest they had spent to get to Helsinki.

Poor Tanya mourned her father in a daze, almost paralyzed with guilt because Stepa had died saving her, but at the French Embassy in Helsinki, she had enough presence of mind to get word to Elissa in Paris. Elissa spoke to the French Ambassador who was eager to be of service to the wealthy and fascinating countess.

Elissa had money and passage delivered to the Embassy and met them at Le Havre with her chauffeur and rushed them through customs and hurried them home to Paris.

It was night when they arrived in Paris and lights were on. The city was aglow with light, flooded with light. After so many years of darkness, with only the flicker of a wick in a bottle, Paris, where cars raced about and people walked freely without fear in their faces—Paris seemed to be awash in light, bathed in light, swimming in light.

47

The wick flickered and went out and Cirie sat with her mother in the dark. A letter **had** arrived today from Dr. Legare urging her to come to Moscow but warning her to wait until spring. In Moscow this winter it was still the same—no food and no fuel. The letter was dated January 5th. And today? She thought a minute. February 4th. No, February 6th. 1922.

Many times since the Revolution, people had said they had lost track of time, they lived from day to day and could no longer say for sure what happened when. Now she had become one of them.

At first she had refused to believe that Laranov was not coming back. Long after the Civil War was over, she refused to admit that if he had not returned or even sent a message, he would not come back. Even when Theo told her that Laranov's entire company had been destroyed by the Whites she did not accept it. "The Whites never took prisoners," Theo said. "He couldn't talk his way out of this one. He's dead." She could not believe that all that dynamic energy, all that passion and laughter, were still—those arms that had held her, that body that had given her the only pleasure she had ever known. Somewhere, she felt, Laranov was still alive. When she accepted at last that he was not coming back, she lost track of time.

When did Kyra come with the letter about Serge? The usual careful unsigned letter. "Dear Friends. I write from an army work brigade where a fellow soldier turned out to be the husband of your old acquaintance, Irene. Unfortunately he met with misfortune some distance from camp and has perished…"

As she read the letter Cirie thought that Serge had died long ago. That other death he had resisted briefly. This death he had welcomed.

Two days later Kyra came again to tell her that Madame had suffered another heart attack. "She wants to see you and Alexei before she dies." When Cirie attempted to commiserate with her over Serge, Madame said, "I thank God he has been released at last. His suffering is over." This was the prevailing reaction to death, the survivors grateful that for the loved one the suffering was over. And when Madame died, Cirie thought it, too. Her suffering is over—she has been released. In Agniya's house that day Cirie thought, we were thirteen when we moved here. Now only Vassi and Vara and Kyra are left.

She had no trouble believing that Serge was dead. Or Madame. But she could not accept it of Laranov.

When did she sell the cow for them? Sometime after Madame died. Vassi and Vara were going back to Whitewater. In the end, these two, who had always hated each other, were together.

"Whitewater was more than a house," Vassi said. "The forests, the cottages—they'll let us live somewhere. They won't kill us."

"They will kill you," Cirie said.

"Then if I'm to die, that's where it will be." Vassily shook hands with his son and, for the first time, impulsively bent down and kissed him. And kissed Cirie, too. "We had a few good years," he mumbled, sadly.

Years! Four months—from our wedding to the revolution! She nodded. Let him think they had had years. "Vassi, people are still getting out. Why don't you try? Go to Paris."

"I will not be driven out like a convict. Russia is mine—more than theirs. I will not let them take it from me."

Only Kyra would be left, determined to stay at Agniya's where Theo could find her, as though she could will him back to health and sanity.

Just before Vassi left, Cirie sold the cow for them even though technically they didn't own it. Less than two years ago she had bargained for it for a half-million rubles and she had been shocked at the figure. Now she sold it for four million.

Then, in February, 1922, the letter came from Dr. Legare. Cirie asked Kyra to let her know when Professor Erlat turned up at Agniya's and the professor assured her that if they moved to Moscow, they could have cots in the parlor of the house he once owned and now managed until she found a room.

"It's the only way," she said when she told Marya they were moving. "We'll never get to America if we stay here. We won't even get a letter."

For several minutes Marya didn't answer.

"Mamma, I can't leave you behind."

"All right, I'll go! "She said it as though she were consenting to her own death." I don't know what for. We don't know if they're alive—or worse off than we are. America is Bolshevik, too."

"America is not Bolshevik."

Marya shrugged. "Bolshevik or not, you and I will never see it."

"We'll see it."

A date she knew was the date she divorced Vassily. She couldn't believe it was so simple. She went to the courthouse alone and asked to use the name Strengov for herself and Alexei. February 14, 1922.

*   *   *

On an early spring evening, Lily hurried back to the little flat above the pharmacy, walking quickly because she was upset at some of the things Mamma had said. As always Mamma had asked all kinds of questions: "What do you do all day? Are you happy with him?"

"Of course I'm happy!" Lily had cried. "How can you doubt it?"

Mamma hesitated. "He seems a little—I don't know—soft."

Lily was stung. These had been the happiest months she had ever known. For the first time she felt desirable. All the girls still flirted with Dari but he wanted only Lily—not as a substitute for Cirie, but for herself.

Mamma searched for words. "A soft core. But if you're happy—"

"Well, he's not like some of these toughs you see strutting around but he's not soft!" Lily flared. "He's very sensitive."

Going home, she told herself she should have told Mamma Dari was a rock. Mamma hadn't spent every minute of the cold winter with him in the pharmacy and the tiny rooms over it where he always managed to have a few sticks to burn. Mamma didn't sit with him evenings or lie beside him at night while he stroked her shoulder and whispered that she was his beautiful kitten.

Walking down Elizabeth Street, Lily caught the smells of spring coming into the air. Soon the park would be filled with flowers again and she and Dari would go to the concerts together. She loved the smell of spring evenings. And she loved Russia, even though it was hungry and ill right now, and she loved the flowers and she loved Dari and she was sorry she had gotten angry at Mamma. Even though she was hungry, she was in love with the world.

At home Arthur, Dari's closest friend, was visiting. Stocky, with a bouncy manner and a limp from the war, Arthur ran a pharmacy on River Street. Lily rushed up to Dari. "I'm sorry I'm late. Mamma was talking and it was hard to break away."

"As long as it's only Mamma," Dari said. "Arthur has been entertaining me with a story about how he got into trouble playing cards."

"These righteous Soviets arrest ordinary people for gambling but officers and commissars have themselves a fine time. Although when I was arrested, I was playing with some officers."

"Then why did they arrest you?" Lily said.

"I was winning." Arthur grinned. "I saved myself by telling them I had some fine medicine in my pharmacy, meaning vodka. They came back with me. It cost me three bottles."

Dari put an arm around Lily. "Good news, little one. I made a trade today for some horse meat."

"Dari, how marvelous! How long since we've had meat? I'll ask Mamma to help me cook it and perhaps she could stay and have some."

"Of course. And your sister and Alexei, too."

"You have a sister!" Arthur said. "Is she as pretty as you?"

"No!" Dari said.

Lily blushed. "Prettier. She's the famous Cirie Vodovsky."

"Lily doesn't like to have her here," Dari teased. "But she must be hungry. Since she left her husband she looks unhappy."

"You think Cirie looks unhappy!" With a rush of guilt Lily wondered what was wrong. Everything had changed for Cirie. She had stopped entertaining the generals and everyone she cared about was gone. Dr. Legare and all those people from Agniya's house. And Laranov who went to the Crimea and never came back. There had been fierce fighting in the Crimea last autumn. "They tell us we completely crushed General Wrangle and the Whites," Dari told Lily. "But many Soviet units were captured and shot. The Whites never took prisoners and this battle was a last stand before they escaped onto ships. There were heavy Soviet casualties."

Later that night Lily lay in bed, the silence broken only by the faint sound of Dari fussing with something in the kitchen. She wondered what he did in there nights before he came to bed. The occasional clink sounded as though he were mixing a prescription but it couldn't be that. Then her thoughts drifted off to Cirie. All her life everything had gone Cirie's way—and now, suddenly, everything was going against her. People had always buzzed around her like flies and now, except for Mamma and Alexei, she was alone. A few minutes later Dari came to bed.

"What do you do, darling, fussing around in there at night?" Lily said.

"Nothing very important." Dari made light of it. "Just getting a few things organized."

He seemed happy tonight, almost exhilarated, as he slid into bed and circled his arm around her. She turned to him and, as always when he held her close in bed, Dari became very excited. For a few seconds every part of his body was taut and hard. Then the excitement was over. With a groan he flung himself over to the edge of the bed and lay tense, his breathing hard and choked.

Presently, when he was quiet again, he turned back and stroked her shoulder and called her his beautiful white kitten and Lily felt safe and wanted in his arms.

Later—she must have dozed off—she heard him in the living room again and she sat up, shocked. She could have sworn Dari was crying. She wanted to run to him to ask what was wrong but she was too embarrassed and confused. A man crying! A man twice her age! It was at moments like this that Lily felt she was too young to be married—that she simply did not understand men. If she were a few years older, she would know more and understand more. She tried to remember if Papa had every cried. Only that week when Anna left for America. And then it was only quiet tears sitting in his eyes—not these deep guttural sounds. Lily did not understand what upset Dari or what she could do to help him.

48

❀

Moscow. Wake up hungry. Walk through the pot-holed streets. Work hungry, without medicines or pain killers or soap. Walk home hungry at night, sweltering in summer, freezing in winter. Trade in the alleys for food—barely enough for three people. Marya stood in lines with ration cards but rations were little help. Go to bed hungry.

Moscow. Where the opera and the ballet and the theater were still alive. The front entrances of private houses were the public toilets. Terror was commonplace. Arrests before your eyes. For what crimes? You never heard. And over it all, the domes and golden crosses of the Kremlin and the bells playing "the Internationale."

Fall into bed at night and open the door to memories and there was Laranov, waiting to come in. Push him away. Think about getting to America. He returned. At first she would walk in Red Square every day. If he was alive, sooner or later he would come here. It was almost two years since he went away. Think about America.

In Kostyka, armed with a letter from Dr. Legare, she had persuaded the local commission that she was officially summoned to Moscow and she had stood in line for permission to stand in the ticket line and had bribed the ticket seller and sold the wine and vodka for gold and food.

Carrying bread and cereal and potatoes and their few meager possessions in back-packs to leave their hands free, they had pushed into a packed, lice-infested, foul-smelling car with broken windows boarded up, pitch-black at night and almost as dark in the daytime, and on a cold night they arrived at last in Moscow. With no transportation available, they found a spot among the sleeping men and women on the crowded station floor. In the morning the room was damp and steamy from the heat of bodies.

On the street they were turned away from an empty tram. "Do you have workers' passes?" the conductor challenged them.

"We've only arrived on the train," Cirie said.

"Get a pass. They'll mark the distance from your room to your work. You can ride that far and no more."

"But you have only two passengers!" Cirie said. Why am I arguing? Because we're tired and stiff and our packs are heavy and Professor Erlat's house is a long walk. "You have plenty of room!"

The conductor closed the door in her face.

Professor Erlat opened the door cautiously, blinking nervously behind his glasses. When he saw her, his face flooded with relief. A former tenant had been arrested during the night, he whispered, by the GPR. The new name for the Cheka. Whatever you called it, it was always the same. You did not like to think the room was available because of someone else's misfortune, but you were grateful to have it—one room and the right to share a community bath and kitchen and parlor. Moscow, with a mushrooming bureaucracy and crowded with peasants who had fled from the famine to the city, had little available shelter.

Finding the Relief offices—the Quakers or the new official American Relief Administration, the A.R.A.—was not easy. Telephone books had long since disappeared and there were no neighborhood stores where one could inquire whether a certain office was in the area. "I've seen cars with American flags and the A.R.A. letters," Professor Erlat told her, "but I've no idea where their offices are located."

"And the Quakers?" Cirie asked.

"I've heard they've been here for some time, longer than the A.R.A., but I don't know where they're located, either."

Afraid to go to the police, especially to inquire about American agencies, Cirie began to use her few daylight hours away from the hospital to walk through the city, a small section at a time, searching for them.

Walking on the drab broken streets, Cirie remembered the Moscow she had visited in 1917—throngs of people in Western dress or in old Russian caftans or native Asiatic dress, coachmen racing horses through the streets. Now the only transportation was the restricted trams. Even bicycles had been requisitioned for official use. She remembered the busy markets selling vegetables, poultry, flowers, fruits, horses, fish, and the street vendors selling pickles and black bread, and the peasants selling bowls of sour cream and baskets of strawberries. She remembered the shops in the Arcade off Red Square, selling silks and furs and gold jewelry. And the elegant stores selling precious stones and the tea houses and restaurants and the gypsy entertainers. She remembered Moscow as it was—gaudy, robust, commercial, bursting with life. Now all that had vanished and sick, shabby destitute people with grim faces and wary eyes shuffled silently through the gray city. And she was one of them.

"Perhaps the foreign office," Professor Erlat suggested. "The Americans are foreigners, after all."

Not yet, Cirie thought. But as the weeks passed and the fruitless search for the Relief Agencies continued, she realized how alone they were in Moscow. In Kostyka, one way or another, she had always been able to get information from someone—Laranov, Gart, General Petrov—or Stepa or Constantine would hear things. Now, with no friends and far removed from power, she had nowhere to turn.

Whenever she passed the Kremlin she imagined Lenin, as Laranov had described him, somewhere inside, shouting commands into his telephone or issuing orders to committees to punish, destroy, kill—kill—kill.

In fact, Lenin was not in the Kremlin or even in Moscow. By the end of 1921 his problems had exhausted him. While he waited for the world revolution, he was forced to accept food from the hated Western capitalists. His government had grown into a huge stagnant bureaucracy, more corrupt and inefficient than anything under the Tsar. He suffered from insomnia and severe headaches and attacks of nausea. He was only fifty-three and he had burned himself out. In December, 1921, his doctor had ordered a rest and he left Moscow for Gorki.

In March, still ill, he returned to Moscow to attend the Party Congress, less restrained than ever. His program was the only correct program…The stagnation and red tape must be punished…For criticism and opposition, his enemies should be shot. And he appointed Stalin to the office of General Secretary.

Back in Gorki, on May 26, 1922, he suffered a stroke.

In the fall of 1922, Cirie went reluctantly to the foreign office. A homely woman with short straight black hair turned to an official in a shabby brown uniform. "Comrade Melnikov, this woman asks the location of a group she calls the American Relief Administration."

Comrade Melnikov threw Cirie a sharp suspicious look. "Your name?" The woman wrote down her name. Cirie was sorry she had come. "Why are you looking for such an organization?" Comrade Melnikov said. He pretended to read a document while she explained that she was hoping for news of her sister in America. Presently he looked up. "You're still here? What do you want now?"

"The address of the American Relief Administration, Comrade."

Comrade Melnikov gave a nasty laugh. "That's a joke. People actually believe they're here. They're not here."

Of course they were here! Everyone knew they had saved millions of lives. "Or the address of the Quakers?" Cirie said. "The Friends?"

"You're hoping to join your sister in America?"

"We're only hoping for a letter, Comrade."

Comrade Melnikov's voice rose above hers. "The Quakers?" he said, disagreeably. "They were here for a short time but they were a nuisance. They didn't do any good. We threw them out."

What was the purpose of this deception when the American flags on their cars and trucks were seen regularly on the streets? With a stab of fear, Cirie hurried away, realizing again how alone they were—no friends in power, no protection against threats or harassment. Discouraged, she walked blindly through Red Square, narrowly missing other pedestrians who were trudging home at this hour. Someone bumped her roughly and she looked up and was about to continue when she saw a familiar face. Twenty feet away, carrying a leather briefcase, moving with a confident step, his handsome face a picture of composure, was Gorshenko. She froze. Here at last was someone she knew. She took a step toward him and stopped. The memory arose of his hushed oily voice and the outstretched hand in the alley and the horror of the hostages. She turned and walked quickly in the other direction.

Walk through another section of broken streets. Moscow is twenty-seven miles wide. "Somewhere in this city there's a letter," she told Marya.

"There's no letter."

"Sooner or later I'll find the America Relief Agency and there'll be a letter." In her heart, she was sure of it.

"There won't be a letter—now or ever." A sob burst from Marya's lips. "We're lost."

Cirie thought of Gorshenko. In all Moscow he was the only person she knew who could help her if he wanted to—if he could be persuaded to want to. If she didn't find an American agency soon, she would have to go back to Red Square and wait for Gorshenko.

On December 16, 1922, in Gorki, Lenin suffered another stroke.

Late one afternoon, with daylight almost gone and hope gone even more, Cirie stumbled onto the A.R.A. office. She was walking, head down, into the bitter wind that blew down the empty streets when, out of the corner of her eye, she saw an American flag go past. She broke into a run, chasing the car as it pulled away and out of sight. At last, gasping for breath, she slowed down. Then she saw the flag again, far ahead. The car was turning a corner. She raced around the corner. The car was parked at the pavement in front of a pair of ornate twin houses with American flags and the legend:

American Relief Administration

In the reception room of what had once been an elaborately decorated house, Cirie stood a minute, catching her breath, her heart racing. Inside, young men were writing at desks, hurrying in and out, all looking so healthy, so untroubled, so unfearful. She approached a serious-looking young man identified by a sign on his desk as Charles Wellman. "Strengov," she said, handing him a scrap of paper on which she had written the name. Nearby a stocky Russian woman typist with wild black hair glanced up at her. Using the little English Constantine had taught her, Cirie said, "A letter?"

The young man went to a stand where he searched through a stack of mail. All those letters! It seemed incredible that all those letters had reached Russia from the outside. Where are the people they're intended for? Do they even know the letters are here? Are they even still alive? What was taking him so long? The letter must be at the bottom of the pile—it must have been waiting here a long time.

Charles Wellman spoke a little Russian. "Nothing for Strengov."

"There must be!"

"I'm sorry."

"Look again. Please!"

"I checked twice. Nothing for Strengov."

No letter! Cirie gripped the edge of the desk. She had been so sure it would be here—a letter that would solve her problems, tell her arrangements had been made, give her instructions about how Marya could join her family in America. And now there was nothing!

Dumbfounded, she stared at Mr. Wellman. Constantine and Stepa should have reached Paris long ago and mailed her letters. And Georgii and Tanya. They must not have gotten through! What happened to them? Were they dead somewhere in the Gulf of Finland? Or rotting in a Soviet prison? It couldn't be—not all of them. Irrationally she turned her anger on Anna and Anton. It's for Mamma, she thought. She's their mother! Then she collected herself. The Quakers! Constantine was going to write Anna about the Quakers. It was the Quakers that Laranov had spoken about that night more than two long years ago.

"Maybe next time," Mr. Wellman said, less impersonal now.

The Russian woman was watching her and Cirie instinctively turned her back and lowered her voice. "Do you know the address of the American Quakers?"

He wrote it on a slip of paper. Cirie managed a better smile and he came around the desk. "I'll see you out." When they were out of earshot of the other workers, he said, "Are you hungry?"

"Everyone is hungry."

"We're only supposed to feed children," he whispered. "It's our agreement. The Soviets feel we can't corrupt young children."

"I have a child."

"Wait here." A minute later he was back with three cans of chicken and some chocolate. Cirie stared in disbelief. No lavish gift of priceless gems had ever looked more beautiful.

At the Quaker Relief there was no letter, either. Nothing for Strengov.

Go back to your first plan—escape. Get a passport for Mamma, and send her to Finland. Bribe for the passport—bribe for the ticket. Then buy yourself an escape. If you can't get to America, you can get to Paris. Start with the passport.

At the foreign office Comrade Melnikov remembered her and was no more inclined to give her mother a passport than he had been to give her the address of the A.R.A. "So now you're planning a visit?" he said. "It's no longer just a letter."

"Only my mother, Comrade," Cirie said. "To see her children. It's not unnatural."

"Bourgeoisie have no rights, natural or not."

"My mother was born a moujik, Comrade."

With a malicious smile he spoke to a clerk who directed them to a room down the hall to get the necessary forms. After three hours in line they reached the window where, it turned out, Marya was only to add her name to a long list. For the actual application, she was sent to another line. As she reached the second window, after standing another three hours in line, it was closed in her face. "No more today," the clerk said.

"My mother has waited all day!" Cirie protested. "The forms are right there. Can't you hand her one before you close the window?"

"No more today."

The next day when Marya returned, she was told that no forms would be given out that day. On her next visit she was asked for proof that this was her name. At last, when she was ready to give up, unexpectedly she received a blank form. A week later, the application carefully filled out, Cirie went with her to the passport office only to be told to return in a month—the application had to be verified. At the end of a month she was told to get signatures from two relatives who would assume responsibility if Marya spoke or acted against the Soviet government when she was in America. For any traitorous words or deeds the relatives who remained behind would be punished.

"It's all right, Mamma," Cirie said at supper that evening. "I'll sign it and Alexei will sign it."

"Alexei!"

"What do they know? I've signed papers for Dr. Legare a hundred times. I'll sign for Alexei. Nobody ever looks at papers. They're choking on papers."

"But if you're still here and they have your name, even if I say nothing they'll come for you!"

"If they want me, they'll come anyway. I don't intend to be here." She looked down at the thin cabbage soup and changed the subject. "Mamma, when you're out of Russia, what's the first thing you're going to order for dinner?"

"Cirie, you're talking dreams. It's not going to happen."

"It will happen."

*   *   *

Yesterday Lily had stopped in to see Olga, who had married a Red Guard man and now was pregnant, and all morning the visit had been on her mind.

"How is it you're not pregnant yet?" Olga had said, looking at Lily's slim figure.

"I don't know," Lily said, evasively. "I suppose it will happen someday, but not too soon, I hope."

"You've been married two years now. Can't you have a baby? What's wrong?"

"Nothing's wrong!" Lily cried and left.

But she wasn't so sure that nothing was wrong, and she wished there were someone she could talk to. Olga would supply answers galore but Olga was so blunt Lily would be embarrassed to talk to her. She had thought of asking Dari, and ruled that out, although she could not have said why. She wished Cirie were here.

As soon as Dari came in, Lily saw that he was having one of his attacks. He always said the attacks were just nerves and at first she had accepted that. Dari was sensitive and life was hard. But lately the headaches and the almost frantic nervousness had occurred more frequently and Lily suspected there was more to the problem. On this cold, cheerless day he asked her for tea and Lily saw that he was shivering. "Is it that cold, darling?"

"Yes, it's very cold." His hands were shaking.

"Dari, what's the matter?" She led him to a chair.

"It's nothing. Just nerves." Shivering, he sank into the chair. "I've a terrible headache—it's made me weak."

Hastily Lily pulled a blanket off the bed and put it over him and Dari fussed futilely at getting it around him and gave up and left it lying crumpled on his lap. He lifted troubled eyes to her. "Darling, I'm quite ill," he said. "This is a severe attack and I'm out of medicine for headaches. I don't like to ask when it's so cold, but could you go to Arthur—here I'll write a note—and get me the medicine?"

"I'll leave this minute." She pulled on her coat and reached for her babushka. "But will you be all right alone?"

"I don't need company. I need medicine!" Dari's voice rose through chattering teeth. Lily flew to the door. "Darling, take my scarf, too," he said in a low voice. "It's terribly cold."

Outside on the street Lily looked at the note but it was scribbled in Latin and she couldn't read it. In Arthur's pharmacy she warmed herself at the stove while Arthur read the note, quickly controlling a flash of surprise. "Dari's awfully sick, Arthur," she blurted out.

Arthur limped to a chest behind the counter.

"He has an awful headache. He was shivering."

Arthur's usual buoyancy was missing. "This will help him."

Arthur's reticence surprised her—he always had so much to say. A seed of suspicion planted itself in Lily's mind. She remained silent. The idea refused to go away. "Did you know my father was a doctor, Arthur?"

"Yes, you told me."

"I saw a lot of sick people. I never saw a sickness like this."

"There are strange illnesses. People react differently."

Lily's suspicions took a firm hold. "Arthur, what is that medicine?"

Arthur hesitated. Then he said, evasively, "You know pharmacy, Lily. Everything has a long Latin name that you wouldn't understand."

"What does it cure?"

"You said Dari has a headache."

"Is it a common headache drug, Arthur?"

"In a way."

"Why do you suppose Dari was out of it?"

"Drugs are hard to get. Ask Dari. He's your husband."

"I don't think he'll tell me. He thinks of me as a baby."

Arthur looked miserable. "Lily, you're happy with him. Why not leave it alone?" His eyes met hers. "Dari's my closest friend."

His discomfort only nurtured her suspicions. "It has another name that I would understand, doesn't it? Arthur—you have to tell me the truth."

"I think you already know, Lily."

"I have to be sure. Arthur—"

Tears filled the beautiful blue eyes and Arthur succumbed. "Yes, Lily. It's cocaine."

"Dari is an addict?"

Arthur nodded.

For a moment Lily couldn't speak. Then she said, weakly, "Why? Why does he do it?"

"He needs it now."

"But what does it do for him?"

"Lily—" Arthur stopped. Lily waited. "Lily, you know Dari had some problems—and the cocaine—they said the cocaine would help." He avoided looking at her. "I guess maybe it did."

"What kind of problems?"

Arthur turned away. "I guess—maybe he doesn't have them, anymore. At least not so much."

"But what were they?"

"That's something only Dari can discuss with you." He brought her the small package and limped back around the counter. "I can only tell you, Lily, that when Dari and I were very young, they used to say that cocaine made a man feel like—" He hesitated. "A great lover."

Outside heavy clouds had mounted in the sky and a wind had come up. Lily shivered as she walked slowly home. Then she remembered that, whatever the cause, Dari desperately needed the "medicine" and she quickened her pace. "My husband is an addict," she said to herself, helplessly. She had to talk to someone. But who? There was only Olga. An addict! Dari—so sensitive and beautiful and loving—Dari was an addict. "My husband is an addict. I'm lost. My life is over." She was too sore for tears.

*   *   *

At the Foreign Office Cirie was still trying to get a passport for Marya. They asked for more signatures, they accused Marya and Cirie of refusing to supply information they had not previously asked for, they warned them to stop playing games. They threatened to tear up the application that Cirie had worked on for months. If she had asked for three passports, Cirie was sure the Foreign Office would have refused long ago. As it was, they hadn't issued papers for Marya but neither had they turned her down.

With a new letter in her pocket Cirie entered the office of the A.R.A.

"I wondered what had happened to you," Charles Wellman said. "You haven't been to see us in a long time." The Russian typist who Cirie was sure was a GPU spy was watching.

"Is there a letter?" she said.

"I haven't see one but I'll check again."

The typist stood up and left the room. Cirie leaned over Wellman's desk and whispered, "Can I mail a letter to America through you?"

"Do you have it with you?"

She nodded.

"Put it on the desk." He glanced around and slipped the letter into his pocket. Cirie nodded her thanks and started to leave. At the door she stopped. The typist was still out of the room. She hurried back. "Is there anything for Vodovsky?" she whispered.

"What name?"

"Vodovsky."

"Write it out." He handed her a pencil and a slip of paper. The Russian typist returned to her desk. Wellman came back from the mail. "I'm sorry," he said. "Nothing for Vodovsky." The typist's head snapped up as she recognized the name and she left the room again. Fear shot through Cirie. She had made a serious mistake. She whispered her thanks to Wellman and hurried out.

Rushing away from the office, she took a circuitous route home, glancing around every few minutes to see if she was being followed, expecting every minute to have someone jump out of a car and seize her. By the time she reached home she was shaking and struggling for control.

How could I have let us become so powerless—so completely at their mercy?

All night she lay awake, listening for the sound of a car going slowly past the house and stopping a little beyond, breathing with relief each time a passing car moved on. Go to bed hungry. Wake up hungry. Lie awake all night, shaking with fright. Long ago she had learned that the first rule of staying alive with the Soviets was to never let yourself be caught without access to power. Now, because she was in Moscow to escape and wanted to remain unknown and unnoticed, she had let herself violate her own rule. In Moscow, of all places, there is power, she told herself. You have to find someone you know, even if it's only Gorshenko.

The next day after work, she walked past the Kremlin and moved on some distance and walked back again. So many officers had been transferred here after the Civil War surely she would find someone who had come to the Wednesday nights in Kostyka. She recognized no one. For eleven days she came back, searching for a familiar face. On the twelfth day she saw Gorshenko in the distance. She hurried toward him and then she saw a second familiar face and stopped short. Renkovsky! That was too much. She turned away. Then she thought she recognized an older man in uniform just ahead of her—a heavy set man with the familiar limp of the war-wounded. Who was he? Perhaps he only reminded her of someone. Following a little behind, she tried to place him. Then she knew!

"Comrade General?" she called softly. "General Borassin?"

49

In spite of his limp, Sacha Borassin insisted on walking home with her. "I want to hear everything—" He glanced over his shoulder. "Without the presence of my driver's big ears." Borassin had changed since that summer of 1914 when he had been so exuberant and outspoken, spilling over with so much energy that Cirie had likened him to Laranov. Now he was lame and careful and circumspect. But he couldn't get enough of the memories she evoked. "It was always my family. Eugenie. Kyra—I had no other."

When she told him of Madame's death, he gave a sad little moan. "How could it be otherwise? How could Eugenie have survived such conditions? She was so gentle. And in her later years so frail." In those few minutes Cirie sensed that Vara's suspicions about Sacha Borassin and Madame had probably been correct. But in the midst of all the hatred today, it seemed incredible that anyone had ever objected to love.

"Serge gone, too?" he said. "Poor Serge. And Vassi, too?"

"I feel he couldn't survive alone."

"Poor fellow, he couldn't bend—he couldn't accept anyone else's weaknesses. What good did it do him? And poor Kyra—the gypsy—all alone now in Kostyka. Not even packing to go somewhere." He continued to reminisce. "Do you remember that last beautiful summer at Whitewater? Prince Tchernefsky was there, talking nonsense as always. And Ilya Laranov was there. He went on to great service during the war. Ah, he was clever. And you could depend on him. A tragedy that he was lost in the Crimea—in the final battle, at that."

"It's true then?" Cirie didn't know why she needed another confirmation.

"He hasn't been heard of since. And killed by a friend."

Her stomach tightened. "What friend?"

But it wasn't what she had suspected. "Undoubtedly he knew Wrangle. Laranov knew everyone." Borassin's thoughts went back to his own love. "Poor Eugenie. All her life she was cared for like a China doll—so lovingly—she was so beautiful— and to have come on such hard times at the end. And I couldn't go to her. First I was at the front and then in the hospital." He wiped his eyes and Cirie thought that in his early life he had been a member of the nobility—a Count—and very rich and in his later days he had been a national hero but with all that, what had he lived for? Only the Army and the memory of a young love.

*   *   *

Borassin quickly became a regular caller, always bringing food and the latest news and a few necessities—soap, thread or a piece of fabric, mittens or a scarf for Alexei.

In March he reported that Lenin, still in Gorki, had suffered a third stroke that had deprived him of the power of speech, paralyzed his right side and partially affected his left side.

"He's been writing endless letters from Gorki," Borassin said. "He looks at his government and he sees a monster—a huge, stagnant, corrupt bureaucracy. But he knows its enormous power—after all, he created it—and now he's afraid it will fall into the wrong hands. He regrets appointing Stalin General Secretary—he'd like to throw him out. But it won't happen. Stalin has been building a power base for years and the line between Stalin and Trotsky is already drawn. There's little to choose between them. Stalin is totally without principles and Trotsky is arrogant and thinks that he and only he is always right."

"Then there's nothing to hope for—either way?"

Sacha shook his head soberly. "Lenin, believe it or not, had a human side to him. Stalin—" He opened and closed his fist. "Stalin will be worse than Lenin."

Then one day Sacha brought a different kind of news. "I've been approached by two old friends of yours," he said, obviously unhappy with the message he was delivering. "General Renkovsky and Commissar Gorshenko. They saw us walking together one day. Now they ask if they may call on you."

"Gorshenko is a Commissar? In Kostyka he was a Commander—Renkovsky's aide."

"Gorshenko is a nice ambitious young man."

"Don't be fooled by that soft voice and that baby face, darling," Cirie said. "Gorshenko is not nice. He's cold and very greedy. What's his job in Moscow?"

"He's involved in trade with the West and I suppose he's found a way to line his own pockets on the side."

Trade with the West? Cirie's interest picked up. "How much power does he have?"

"Not like Renkovsky. Renkovsky is close to Stalin. But Gorshenko has power."

Renkovsky! Renkovsky could probably do anything! Get a passport for Marya and for herself and Alexei, too, if he felt like it. But at what price?

How could you make a deal with Renkovsky when you were helpless to enforce it? How could she entertain Renkovsky again when she knew he had sent Laranov to his death? And because of her? How could she smile and say, "Of course, Comrade General. Thank you, Comrade General?" She didn't want to look at Renkovsky again. She didn't want to have to rebuff his advances that left her paralyzed with fright at the threat of being forced to become his mistress. "Sacha, do you have any power at the Foreign Office?"

"My influence is only with the military," he said. "With my background, at the foreign office I'm suspect."

Then it would have to be Gorshenko or Renkovsky. Cirie slammed a lid on her feelings. There was room in her life for only one goal these days—getting out. There was no room for sentiment. And she had better move fast. If Lenin was not going to recover and there was going to be a power struggle, the losers would be like all the other losers—dead or in prison. She turned back to Borassin. "Please tell them I'll be delighted."

She could see he was not pleased. "I'll be there, too," he said firmly. "To keep an eye on them."

Inwardly, with little humor, Cirie laughed. What could Sacha, so honorable and upright, do against a pair of venomous snakes like Renkovsky and Gorshenko?

"Cirie, I worry about you being alone like this. I don't like men like Renkovsky or Gorshenko trying to take advantage of you."

"Maybe they just want a place to relax."

"All the same—" Sacha insisted. "I have a friend coming to Moscow soon—a former officer. He's been working beyond the Urals in Tashkent—near the Turkish border—trying to revive the textile industry. A bright young fellow—very promising. Peter Nemerov. You'll like him."

She didn't want to like him. She only wanted to know if he had any power at the Foreign Office. Enough to get her an exit permit—or two or three? And if he was working in Asia, that seemed unlikely.

*   *   *

In Kostyka Lily stood on the street in front of the Army Headquarters, trying to work up courage to go in and ask for General Petrov. If she were not so desperate, she would not think of approaching a general to ask for help.

In the little flat above the pharmacy everything had changed. The easy expressions of love had died and she and Dari were strangers in the little apartment that had once seemed cozy and now seemed too small. Feeling trapped and oppressed, Lily found it impossible to stay home. She walked for miles, thinking about her problem. She should return to school and learn a trade—office work, maybe— but if she left Dari she would have to go to work. And where would she live? She had to get to Moscow to Mamma and Cirie.

Lily told herself to take things one step at a time. Yesterday she went to the City Hall to ask how to get a divorce and came away considerably heartened. You just had to go in and ask for it. This morning she went to the railway station to inquire about getting a ticket to Moscow, which turned out to be a more serious problem. The ticket seller looked her over and concluded, correctly, that she had nothing for bribes. "First you have to get permission," he said. "But we're sold out for three months."

Close to panic, Lily was on her way to see Olga when she thought of General Petrov. A word from him would get her a ticket. Outside the gate she stopped. He didn't even know her! They probably would not let her see him—might even think she intended to harm him and search her to see if she had a gun. She started to walk away. But if she did not force herself to go in there, she was lost.

At the entrance, a soldier said, "Your name?"

"Tell him," Lily said bravely, "it's Cirie's sister."

"Just Cirie's sister? No other name?"

"That's all."

To her astonishment the soldier was back instantly to admit her and when General Petrov stood up to greet her, both hands extended, smiling broadly, Lily knew everything was going to be all right.

She arrived in Moscow on a cold Wednesday evening and found Cirie expecting the generals, exactly as she had in Kostyka.

Lily had not intended to go downstairs while the generals were there but Mamma insisted. "If you had mixed more you wouldn't have hurried into such an early marriage," Marya said. Lily stopped arguing. She wrapped her braids over her ears to look a little older and crept down the stairs.

From where she sat, alone in a corner, she recognized a few of the men. She had seen Gorshenko in Kostyka and the lame old man was General Borassin and she knew from Cirie's descriptions that the fat non-stop talker was General Renkovsky. Lily was fascinated by these powerful worldly men. She watched the way they smoked their cigarettes and raised their glasses and moved confidently about the room and the way Cirie moved so easily among them. She would never be able to do that and she hoped no one would notice her. Then she realized that one of them was speaking to her. "Why are you sitting over here alone in a corner?" he said.

She looked up at a wiry young man with a lean face and gray eyes. "I just came in for a minute," she stammered.

"I know when you came in because I noticed you at once," he said. "Will you permit me to sit with you? My name is Peter Nemerov. And you're Cirie's sister. Why aren't you talking to all these generals?"

Lily blushed. "I wouldn't know what to say."

"You don't have to say anything. As soon as they notice you they'll be here and you won't have to say a word. Just smile and they'll all fall in love with you."

Renkovsky's voice rose above the others. "The peasants have waged a war against us. A war of starvation. We won't forget."

"Stalin's words in Renkovsky's mouth," Peter Nemerov said.

"Were you in the wars?" Lily said.

"Not the one he's talking about. In the other one I was a pilot."

"An airplane pilot!"

"I flew a little open wooden airplane."

Lily stared, wide-eyed. In her life she had never expected to be talking to an airplane pilot! Renkovsky was still shouting. "Is he always so noisy?" she said.

"I'm not one of the regulars. I'm only in Moscow until Friday. I work in Tashkent." With his boyish smile Peter Nemerov did not seem so formidable as the others. "But I understand he can be depended on to make himself heard. There, you see, they're looking at you."

Lily saw that a few of the generals were actually glancing her way.

"So what if their farms are ruined?" Renkovsky shouted. "We'll take their farms. In the end they'll be better off."

Lily frowned. "He's hateful, isn't he?"

Peter Nemerov laughed. "At least he won't stay late. He'll leave for the casinos soon. He's a big gambler."

"Casinos! I thought gambling was illegal."

"That was at the beginning of the Revolution. Now there are casinos all over Moscow. The government doesn't object—it makes the regulations and shares in the profits. Why do you look surprised? If you make a study of revolutions, as I have, you'll find some things are always the same. At the beginning there's fanaticism and high morality, but then the fervor burns itself out and the revolution deteriorates into corruption and scandal, as we have now. There are still some fanatics but they don't come here."

"Why have you studied revolutions?"

"Why?" He smiled his boyish smile. "Because I believed in it. Because I'm part of it. Every man here is part of the Revolution, even if they've forgotten its original purpose. I have not."

His intensity thrilled Lily and her blood raced. "Do you know Cirie?" she said, suddenly.

"Of course I know Cirie. I met her here last Wednesday night."

Renkovsky glanced at his watch and began to edge toward the door. As though released from duty, a few of the officers moved toward Lily.

"You're about to be surrounded," Peter Nemerov said. "Tell me, what time tomorrow shall I come to call on you?"

"Why—" Lily stammered. "Any time."

"We'll go to the ballet," he said. "And the next night we'll go to the opera. And on the weekend we'll walk in the park."

"But you're in Moscow only until Friday."

"I've decided to extend my visit. And the next time I come to Moscow, I'll take you for a ride in a plane!"

They went to the ballet and to the opera and to the theater where the building was very cold and the actors were very intense. Peter left the following week and came back two weeks later—flew back in a little open wooden plane. And flew back a month later and a month after that and by the end of the year Lily married him and went to live in Tashkent.

*   *   *

January 24, 1924. Red flags with black bands lining the streets, whipping in the arctic wind. Heavy snow falling, blocking the streets. Soldiers standing at attention in lines that stretched for miles. The red coffin borne slowly along the snowbound streets of Moscow to Red Square to the Hall of Columns. Lenin was dead.

For four days they kept his body on view and people came to Moscow from all over Russia and stood in the snow, day and night, just to march past his open coffin and look at his waxen face. For four days the snow continued. The temperature was twenty degrees below zero. On street corners bonfires burned for the mourners to warm themselves. People fainted in the cold. Doctors and ambulances stood by. People sang revolutionary songs. Did he really make a better life for all those people? Cirie wondered. Or was their grief only a demonstration of Russian emotion?

Lenin's political heirs made a god of him and fought for his throne. As the winter passed, people who knew predicted that things would be worse. "Stalin is wily and totally without scruples," Borassin told her. "He respects no one and betrays everyone, but not before he has new support to replace them. Against his enemies he trumps up charges and has them arrested—or murdered, if necessary. He stops at nothing. Trotsky has only contempt for his ignorance and crudeness, but contempt doesn't produce political victories. In the end Stalin will come out on top and the ruthlessness he has shown his whole life will have no restraints. With Stalin in Lenin's shoes, all enemies will finally be liquidated."

"Mamma, if we tied you on, do you think you could make the trip across the ice?"

"To Finland!" Horror edged into Marya's voice.

"It will have to be soon. In a few weeks the ice will melt and we'll have to wait another year." From the way Borassin talked, she was not sure they would have another year.

"And Alexei? You'll tie him down, too? He's too big now to carry on your back." Marya's voice rose. "To be shot in the back by guns firing on him while you force him to flee!"

How does she conjure up these horrible bloody images? For them to take Alexei Cirie expected to pay a larger bribe. "Mamma, the smugglers are very good. They're very experienced."

"How do you know? Are they going to tell you how many get shot? Or fall off and freeze to death in the snow?"

Cirie was sorry she had asked.

"You never cared about him," Marya raved on. "You never saw him. An hour a day, maybe."

Cirie had heard Marya's hysterical accusations before. It was true she had never had much time with her son. The enemy—the Revolution—and all those people who became totally dependent on her—had taken him away from her. He had become Madame's and Kyra's darling and now Marya's and she had become the wage-earner and the slave.

She looked at Alexei asleep on his cot, his fair tousled hair across his face, vulnerable and trusting in sleep. She had to make the decision soon—between the smugglers and Renkovsky or Gorshenko. She brushed the fair hair off his warm face. She had to choose between his future and her mother—and she had chosen. She couldn't risk his life in Russia any longer.

Standing at the window, Cirie looked out at the dark night. Today in the yard she had seen the first little blue snowflowers pushing up through the snow. Once she used to say that the first snowflowers were a sign that things would be better. If you will just survive the snow and the wind and the cold, presently the sun will shine on your face and the world will be warm again. Now she thought, That's a lot of nonsense.

She turned from the window and took out her list of English words and phrases that Constantine had given her. "Please—thank you—where is the train?—trolley—telephone—1—2—3—4." Suddenly she could not go on. What's the point? she thought. When am I going to need them? She thrust the word list into the back of the drawer and slammed the drawer shut. She was very low tonight. If she didn't do something soon she would give up. Maybe she could send Mamma to Lily in Tashkent.

"Cirie, I'm too old to flee over the ice," Marya said, calmer now. "Go if you want to. Don't worry about me."

It seemed to Cirie that she had lived with this problem forever. "We'll still try to go together," she said. "But I can't wait any longer."

She would approach Renkovsky or Gorshenko—one or the other. But how would she go about it? She was an old hand at bribes but there had always been a tacit understanding that a bribe was expected. Now she thought, How do you go about bribing a high official?

Then Sacha Borassin offered her a little time. "Cirie, at the moment everyone is busy with political infighting," he said as they walked in the park on a summer afternoon. Roses bloomed among the weeds and uncut grass. Ragged children played in the dirt. The eyes in a faded picture of Lenin stared out at them from a tree trunk. "But when it's over, there will be purges again to get rid of enemies and discourage dissent and to show that the winners are in firm control. The upper classes, the few who are left, will be the first to go. They'll be killed or sent to Siberia." He looked at her, soberly. "Even though you call yourself Strengov, it's known that you're a Vodovsky. Who are you going to trust to keep it a secret? Renkovsky? Gorshenko?"

Renkovsky and Gorshenko? She didn't even trust them enough to risk offering them a piece of valuable jewelry. She was afraid they would decide there was a whole cache of jewelry somewhere and the GPU would be upon her the same night.

"I would like to try to protect you," Borassin said.

"If they decide to come for me, Sacha, no one can protect me."

"I would like to marry you. Then you'll have my name and I don't think they'll bother me. Why attack a war hero who is not interfering with them? We would be married quietly. You'll live in my house and drop out of sight. No entertaining, no public appearances until things are quieter, but you'll be cared for, you and your family, and you'll be protected until you can find a way to leave."

Cirie felt as though a mountain had been lifted from her shoulders. She could hardly comprehend that someone would actually take care of her.

"Once, as your husband, I could have pleased you and made you happy. Now I'm old and wounded and I could not." He looked to see if she understood and she nodded and touched his hand. "I'll try to help you find a way to leave. I won't hold you back." All at once his face lit up the way she remembered it from years ago. "Meanwhile—" he raised her hand to his lips. "In my house, you will be a precious jewel."

She felt that the sun was shining on her face again.

After the brief ceremony at a municipal building, they rode in Sacha's car directly to his house and his driver pulled away. As they walked slowly up the steps, Sacha smiled with pride. "Now you are Countess Borassin and in our home you will be treated that way." He kissed her hand and turned as someone called his name.

"Comrade General!" Two young soldiers of the Red Guard came up the steps.

"What is the problem, Comrade?"

"You are ordered to come with me."

For a second Borassin looked stunned and then recovered. "For what purpose?"

"I am not given reasons," the soldier said, arrogantly. From his tone one could guess the rest. "I believe there are charges to be heard."

Borassin turned away. "You do not arrest me!"

"Comrade General!"

Borassin opened the door. "Step inside, my dear."

"Comrade General!" The younger of the two soldiers seized his arm and raised his gun. "Do you resist arrest?"

"Comrade, you are a Red Guard and I am a General." Borassin drew his own gun. "Don't presume to touch me."

His last words. A second later he was lying on the step, shot through the head.

50

❊

On a tree outside the window, two dry leaves clung to a branch, refusing to fall off and blow away. Cirie had first noticed the left-over leaves—eight, then—as she began to recover from the shock of witnessing Sacha's murder.

For several days, suffering from melancholy and indescribable fatigue, she had sat in the window, staring out at the naked branches while the murder kept replaying itself in her mind. She had knelt beside Sacha and searched for a pulse, knowing there was none. The soldiers who had come to arrest him had fled. Everyone on the street had fled. No one wanted to be accused, no one wanted to be a witness. She rushed to the corner and found a pair of soldiers who followed her back.

"Who are you?" one of them said.

"I—I knew him," she stammered. "It's General Borassin, the War hero. I was passing nearby and—" she managed a mechanical smile. "There was no one else. I couldn't leave him."

"Who shot him?"

"I have no idea. Everyone ran away."

She fled in terror. By the time she reached home her teeth were chattering. Between Sacha's house and this small room, all hope had died.

Then one day as she sat in the window, staring out at the spindly tree, she counted the leaves that had not fallen off—eight leaves that dipped and twisted in the wind and held on. Why these? The same tree, same wind and cold—but these few hold on. Well, don't blow it up into a miracle, she told herself. Probably the next wind will take them, too. When she began to go to work she fell into the habit of counting them every morning before she left the house—eight leaves holding on. And then one day there were only six. She searched the tree twice, thinking she had overlooked two, and a little shock skipped through her—as though it were an omen. Then there were five. She stopped counting. Then one morning only these two. The idea shot across her mind that when the last leaf fell, she would be finished. You're losing your mind, she told herself. They're only dry leaves. You're becoming obsessed with them. You're tired and you're losing your reason.

She left the window. You're talking in the present tense again. What was it Aunt Vayana used to say? "I'm an old woman and I know it doesn't matter." And that was how she felt—she was bone-tired and it didn't matter anymore.

In the end it was Gorshenko who responded to the veiled suggestion of a bribe. "Comrade Gorshenko," she said one Wednesday night. "Have you ever been to Riga?"

"Many times." Gorshenko's green eyes came to attention. "Why do you ask?"

"My mother is having trouble with her eyes and Dr. Legare has referred her to a specialist in Riga." She had decided to stop asking for the moon—the right for Marya to go to America. She would keep it simple. She would try to get her to Riga. Latvia had been recognized as an independent republic but it had been part of Russia for so long that going to Riga did not seem unusual. Once there, she would worry about the rest of the trip. "Involved in foreign trade as you are, I was sure you'd been there recently," she said. "Is it a difficult trip?"

"The trains are slow so it takes a few days."

Gorshenko waited.

"In that case I suppose I'll have to go with her. She's elderly and doesn't see well. She couldn't make the trip alone."

Gorshenko's eyes narrowed. "Do you have a passport, Cirie?"

"Surely one doesn't need a passport just to go to Riga?"

"Oh, yes." Watching her, Gorshenko sipped his vodka.

"How does one get this permission to go to Riga?"

"You go to the Foreign Office."

He knew the Foreign Office would not give her a passport. "Is there no other way?"

Gorshenko smiled his cold little half-smile. "Let me look into it."

The next week Gorshenko watched until Cirie was alone and then, glass in hand, came up to her. He complemented her on how well she looked, he sampled a few zakuski, and casually brought up the subject of jewels.

"I've always meant to ask you, Cirie," he said. "In Kostyka we heard that the Vodovsky jewels were fabulous." He took another zakuski. "Someday you must tell me about them."

"They were not so extraordinary, really."

"They said that Vassily showered his young bride with gifts."

"Oh, that's an exaggeration! You know what gossip is. A pebble becomes a mountain."

Gorshenko sipped his vodka. "What ever happened to all those jewels?"

"I have no idea!"

He watched her carefully. "There's no official record of them anywhere."

"In the early days of the Revolution," she said, "when the moujiks could do as they pleased, they stole a great deal."

"Every last jewel?" His scheming eyes said that the game was progressing.

"Later Commissars were furious. They said the moujiks should have been allowed to take farm tools but jewels should have gone to the State."

Gorshenko smiled his cold smile. "Those things happened."

Then Renkovsky joined them and when Cirie turned to speak to Gorshenko again, he had moved away.

The next day, Professor Erlat met Cirie at the door when she came home from the hospital. "There's a gentleman upstairs with your mother," he whispered. "I sensed something official in his manner."

"And you took him to her! Why didn't you say she wasn't home?"

"I didn't take him upstairs. She did. I told him I'd see if she was in. She came downstairs and spoke to him for one second and then asked him upstairs. He's not Russian. He speaks Russian but he's not—"

"He's not Russian!"

"He speaks fluent Russian but with a foreign accent. And he's too well dressed to be Russian."

Cirie rushed upstairs and found Marya in the company of a well-dressed blond young man. With a look of disbelief on her face, Marya was fingering a letter. "We have a letter!" she murmured. "They wrote to us! We have a letter!"

The blond young man introduced himself as the Finnish consul. He had been asked by a Finnish businessman to find them and had only now received their address.

Mr. Wellman at the A.R.A. had kept his word and mailed the letter.

"Your family has been looking for you a long time," the Finnish consul said.

Cirie's throat tightened. They had been trying! They had not forsaken them, after all.

They had just received the Moscow address, Anna wrote. "Uncle Lawrence's brother-in-law will arrange for this letter to be delivered by hand. A political associate knows someone who does business in Finland and can ask the Foreign Office there to get in touch with you. There are new laws in America—immigration quotas. Mamma can come into the country permanently. A mother is considered a close enough relative. A sister is not. For now, Cirie must enter the country as a visitor and Uncle Lawrence will arrange for her to stay one way or another. As soon as we receive an answer to this letter, we'll send passage and dollars."

"They're not Bolshevik, after all," Marya murmured. "Imagine, Cirie—they have extra. Enough to live and extra to send to us. If they were Bolshevik, they wouldn't be able to help us."

"No, Mamma, they're not Bolshevik." They had waited so long for this letter and now that it was here, she felt so little. Only confusion. She could not comprehend that the door had cracked open, that they might yet be free from fear—free of listening for cars to stop next door in the night, free from hunger and destitution and living only to get through the day with the future a blank wall. They would have civilized lives again, enough to eat, a family—hope. "We have to be careful," she said to the Finnish consul.

"Yes."

"I've been trying to find a way for us to get to Riga. It seemed simpler."

He gave her the address of the Finnish Consulate. "Let me know when you're ready," he said. "I'll have you met in Riga and taken care of. Your tickets and American dollars can be delivered there."

Was it possible that there were still such people in the world, who would go out of their way for strangers—meet them, help them, get them their passage? She remembered that she should answer the letter. "I should write them," she said. "Can I bring it to your office?"

He nodded and rose to leave. "I'll let you know when your tickets are in Riga. You won't want to go there too soon—unless, of course, it becomes necessary."

"Comrade Gorshenko." Now that the door had cracked open she had to take the chance. She waited until he was alone. "I enjoyed our conversation last month. I didn't realize you had an interest in jewels."

"Only as art," he explained. "Without political connotations."

Cirie smiled. "Jewelry can be as much a work of art as a painting."

"Oh, yes."

"My husband loved rare precious gems in unusual settings. He usually selected the stones and approved the designs himself."

"I've heard he was famous for his taste in jewelry." He was making his move again. "And for his generosity to his bride."

"That seems a very long time ago." Then, impulsively, she said, "Let me tell you about his most unusual gift—" She stopped. "But I don't want to bore you."

Bore him! His greed was practically spilling over while he tried to appear calm. "Not at all."

"It was a pair of earrings. He thought it was unusual, since I'm so fair, that my eyelashes are black. As a tribute to them, he searched Petrograd for black pearls. These were very rare black pearls. And he had them made into magnificent drop earrings, three large pearls in each, set with diamonds."

"They sound—" Gorshenko's glass shook. "Very beautiful."

"Very."

"It's too bad you lost them."

"Yes."

"If you were able to locate them, there are people who would go a long way to have them."

"I suppose they would."

He smiled that nervous little half-smile. "Perhaps, even, to Riga."

"Yes." She met his eyes and the bargain was made. "I agree."

51

Before dawn, by a low light in the community kitchen, Cirie was cooking a pot of oatmeal while Marya showed Alexei what to pack. Today was the day. This morning they would board the train and leave Russia forever.

Whispering to Marya at night, Cirie had planned their departure, trying to anticipate everything that could go wrong. The biggest threat was Gorshenko. He had the black pearl earrings and she had three passports and exit permits and tickets to Riga, but she doubted that was the end of it. Gorshenko was shrewd. He would reason that, if she still had the earrings after so many searches, she had more jewels in a good hiding place which she would not disturb until the last minute. "He doesn't believe the earrings are the last of the jewels," she said to Marya. "And he doesn't believe we're only going to Riga. If there's a visit, don't forget about your eyes."

Another risk was that, if they packed in advance, some tenant hoping for a reward might hurry to the GPU to "give information" that they were escaping. "Take only enough for a two-day stay in Riga," Cirie told Marya. "Set it aside. We won't pack until the last second. The next second we'll be out the door."

She had written a note for Professor Erlat, telling him of an opportunity to go to Riga for a consultation on Marya's eyes (lest he be accused of helping them escape) and would return next Wednesday if all went well. She had written Lily the usual ambiguous unsigned letter: "Anna has seen our old friend, Lavrentii. We will see her soon and will write you." She had bartered for bread to carry on the train.

Ordinarily, if the GPU didn't show up by midnight, you were safe for the night, but Cirie delayed cutting the fine stitches in the mattress until almost daybreak. Working by the light of a candle, she retrieved the jewels and Marya carefully resewed the mattress. Now the first light was showing and her gold and jewels were in two pouches in her pocket.

She had just put a bowl of oatmeal in front of Alexei when a car went past the house. Too slowly. Automatically, even though the GPU never came in the morning, she listened. Even before the car came to a stop, she knew. Gorshenko had delayed the search until the last possible minute, knowing that by now the jewels would be out of hiding.

Frantically Cirie looked around the kitchen for a place to conceal them. If the GPU men were looking for jewels, they would certainly search her. Her eyes traveled over cupboards and shelves and boxes as she rejected each one in turn. They would surely search the kitchen. Just as the familiar hard knock sounded on the door she rushed to the stove and dropped the two pouches into the pot of oatmeal.

Five GPU men entered the house. The leader had been here before and directed his men to begin immediately—one in the kitchen, another in the parlor, two upstairs to search their bedroom and their belongings. "We have a report that you're planning to escape."

"Oh, no, Comrade," Cirie said. "One day soon I must take my mother to Riga to an eye doctor. I have permission. But today is not the day."

"Then why are you up so early?"

Cirie smiled at him. He was a young man, not much more than a boy—a peasant who had come to the city and become a policeman. "I'm always up at this hour. I'm a nurse. I have to feed my little boy and get to work."

"We have a report that you have jewels."

"Comrade, you've searched our room at least a dozen times. Do you really think you would have failed to uncover valuable jewels if they were there?"

"No," he said firmly. "But I'm ordered to search again."

"Ah—I think I understand," Cirie said. In a tight spot you had to try something. "Who sent you, Comrade?"

"That's nothing you have to know."

She smiled again. "You don't have to tell me, Comrade. I know." She turned to Marya. "I'm afraid it was Grigor, Mamma." She wasn't even sure Marya knew Gorshenko's name. "Taking revenge."

To her amazement Marya caught on at once. "I told you—" she snapped.

Cirie looked helplessly at the leader. "We were seeing each other," she murmured with a show of embarrassment. "We had a quarrel."

"I told you he was no good," Marya put in. "You should never have taken up with him." She enlisted the sympathy of the GPU man. "He was pursuing her like you never saw. She was—" Marya shrugged as though she could not call it what it was. "Nice to him. Good to him. *Sweet* to him." She turned on Cirie and hissed, "Next time you'll be more careful." Back to the GPU leader, growing more venomous with every breath. Cirie could hardly believe this performance. "A hot young man—jealous—a fight because someone else pays her a little attention—and this is the result." She appealed to the GPU leader and to the heavens, too, for sympathy. "Our house invaded—our breakfast interrupted—our little boy scared half to death—all kinds of accusations—" She began to wander about the kitchen, away from the stove, cursing all hot-blooded young men.

"We heard you had jewels," the leader repeated stubbornly.

"Well, isn't that what they always say when they want to get you in trouble?" Cirie said, lowering and raising her eyes. "All of Russia is walking around laden with jewels."

The leader glanced at the pot of oatmeal. Cirie had a terrible thought. What if they were hungry and wanted to eat? There wasn't enough in the pot to feed five men without uncovering the pouches.

"When they're jealous!" Marya shouted—gentle Marya who never raised her voice, shouting like a crazy old woman! "I'll tell you something—a beautiful daughter is a curse. I don't know what's happening today. Girls used to be quiet, modest. If you keep a man in his place you don't get into trouble. You don't have jealous lovers—" Her voice grew shrill as she launched into a barrage of insults against Gorshenko. "That kind of pig! They take what they want of a girl and then—!"

"Mamma, please." Cirie looked mortified.

"Hot—mean—a sneak—shifty. Well, look what he did to her!" she challenged the leader. "Well? Well?"

"He's a friend?" the leader said to Cirie, trying to make himself heard over Marya's screaming. His man finished searching the kitchen and he sent him to help in the parlor.

"Oh, yes. He was a good friend," Cirie said in a voice that assured him they had been more than friends.

The leader looked uncomfortable. He was a policeman, and he was not interested in a lovers' quarrel. The other men returned. "Did you find anything?" he said.

"Nothing."

"Not even a packed suitcase."

The leader ordered his men to the door. "Sorry we bothered you," he said. "I guess this is a personal complaint."

"Oh, it is, Comrade," Cirie assured him.

"Not a state complaint."

"Our relationship is hardly a matter of state, Comrade," Cirie said.

As he closed the door behind him, Cirie, nerves stretched, smothered her laughter and threw her arms around her mother. "Oh, Mamma, you should go on the stage!" she cried. "What an actress!"

At the station, pleading that she had to guide a blind aged mother and a young child, Cirie bribed the gatekeeper with a gold coin to let them through the gate even though the train would be late, and moved out of sight. Her last bribe in Russia. As the gate closed behind her, she caught sight of Gorshenko entering the station with the GPU men he had sent around this morning.

At ten o'clock the train creaked and groaned and let out a blast of smoke and rolled down the track. At every station she watched for police or the GPU coming aboard to search the train. Two days later, they crossed at last into Latvia and left Russia behind them.

BOOK THREE

THE WORLD THAT WAS FOUND

1934

"*I go into the grounds, the extended mansions of remembrance…On visits there I make request for what I would withdraw, and some are issued instantly, while others must be sought for at some length in deeper vaults. Still others, clamorous, pour out unbidden and…dance before me, saying, 'Wasn't it us you were wanting?'*"
—Confessions St. Augustine

52

❊

Lily stood near the dock at the tip of the city at the tip of Africa and took in the clear blue water of the busy harbor. On this mild sunny day with only a faint breeze off the water she held tightly to her son's hand.

Ordinarily in Capetown, she did not keep such a tight hold on Ivan. In Moscow, even in their apartment which they had shared with another couple and a single woman whom they had suspected were spies, Lily and Peter had been afraid to talk to each other except in whispers in bed. In Capetown she had begun to feel safe again and she would let Ivan run and play in the park or walk freely beside her on the street.

Now a telegram had arrived instructing Peter that he was being transferred to Argentina—the Soviet extending its awful power over them again. The old fear settled in and Lily held Ivan's hand in a tight grip, as though that would protect him.

Lily loved Capetown. She loved the British formality and the Dutch tidiness, the Parliament building with its white columned front and neat windows and low fence, and the small neat white houses built by the Boers with steep roofs and picket fences. And all the automobiles and the palm trees. And the mixture of so many peoples. The British and the Boers, who called themselves Afrikaners, the Hindus and Moslems from India, the Coloureds of mixed European and African blood, and the Natives—pure-blooded Negroes. She loved having tea with other diplomatic wives at the hotel where elaborate formal service was the rule, and the ladies wore hats and gloves. She would miss Capetown, but Argentina would be all right, too. As long as she had Peter and Ivan she would be happy anywhere.

"Another ship," Ivan said. He pointed to a freighter slowly making its way into the harbor. "Do you think a ship ever just goes past us and doesn't stop?"

"I don't think so," Lily said. "Papa's friend, Mr. Foster, told us that almost five hundred years ago a captain from Portugal found this harbor." Richard Foster, Peter's closest friend in Capetown, was the American consul. "Since then all the ships have stopped here for fresh water. Five-hundred years is a long time."

Ivan nodded soberly. He was only six and had no idea what Portugal was or how long five-hundred years was, but Lily liked to talk to him this way. In Moscow she would be afraid to speak so freely.

"And today many of them stop to deliver or pick up a great deal more than fresh water."

"Do any of them go to Russia?"

"You know Papa buys things that people need in Russia, especially wool. And sometimes sugar. And some ships will deliver them to Russia."

"Are we going to Russia?"

"No, Ivan. I told you that only Papa will go home to Russia to talk about his work in Argentina." The government, because money was very tight, would bring the diplomat home alone for instructions. He was to send his family directly to the new post. "You and I will go to Argentina and Papa will come there after Moscow."

The thought of the separation, of Peter going back to Moscow, worried her. It worried Peter, too, she knew, although he had not mentioned it. In the embassy all servants were spies and Lily and Peter had lapsed into the old habit. They discussed it only in bed—in whispers. In Moscow several heads of departments were in trouble—several of their friends had been liquidated and the reports from home indicated that Stalin had begun a systematic purge.

Peter would be home soon. Lily took Ivan's hand and they started back to their house.

When Peter came in Lily could see that something was wrong. Whenever he was upset his gray eyes were almost black and his lean face was taut. He signaled to her not to ask any questions.

Later in bed, in a whisper he told her. "I answered their telegram." Peter held her hand tightly, a warning not to cry out. "I wired that I would come home and I would send my family directly to Argentina."

"What happened?" Lily whispered.

"They wired back that I should bring my family home with me."

Lily gasped and clutched her hand over her mouth.

"Do you know what that means?"

Lily nodded in the dark. "Yes," she whispered.

"It means I am to be liquidated. They want my wife where they can watch her. I probably won't even have a trial. What could they accuse me of? If there is a trial it will be a mass trial with dozens of other people they want to purge. A mock trial, a quick verdict and a quick imprisonment in Siberia."

"Darling, we can't go home," Lily whispered.

"We will not go home. We have to defect."

Peter laid out the steps of their defection as meticulously as he had ever planned anything in his life.

For the four years he was in Capetown, while purges in Moscow grew worse, he had planned it in case it became necessary. He bought gold. Even in Tashkent he had bought gold. He sent Lily to put it in a box in a bank.

He took Richard Foster into his confidence. The American consul was the only man Peter trusted enough to enlist as a co-conspirator. He asked Richard to buy a small suitcase for him and take it to his own home. Peter and Lily could not walk out of their own house carrying a suitcase without arousing suspicion. He was sure the servants, Flora and Lavri, who were spies, had been alerted.

Every few days Peter and Lily would call on Richard and his wife, Louise, gradually packing their suitcase. Each time they went they added something—only articles they could wear or carry in their pockets or in a purse.

They wore extra underclothing and hosiery and removed them in what had become their room in Richard's house and packed them.

He bought more gold. He was worried about Lily. She was becoming nervous and tense. Just her manner would arouse the suspicions of Flora and Lavri.

"Darling, you're getting too nervous," he said at dinner one night in front of Flora. "You're letting this packing to go home upset you."

Lily looked shocked and wounded and then recovered. "It's just that it's such a huge job," she said. "You know how I am when there's so much to do and there seems to be no end to it and it's all so hard. I've never been very good at moving. But I'm excited at the thought of going home." She had understood his warning.

They wore extra sweaters to Richard's house and packed them. They carried toilet articles and packed them.

When the suitcase was filled they had packed a single change of clothing for each of them, sweaters, and a minimum of necessary toilet articles.

An American freighter docked in the harbor. It was perfectly natural for Richard to call on the captain. While there he arranged passage to the United States for an anonymous couple with a child. On the day the freighter was scheduled to sail Richard carried a suitcase aboard. He remained less than five minutes and shook hands with the captain and left.

At lunch Peter said, "Darling, it's such a beautiful day. All morning I've had a headache." He pressed two fingers over his eyes. "I think it's my eyes. A lot of paperwork. Would you like to come for a short walk with me before I go back to the office? Or are you busy? I don't want to upset your plans."

"Of course I'll go for a walk with you. I have no important plans. No tea with the ladies." She laughed. "I've been in all morning, checking the packing. I'm afraid I'm not doing too well. Darling, won't it be exciting to see Moscow again?"

"They say no matter how far you travel, you dream of home. Yes, it will be very exciting."

Lily stood up. Flora, cleared the table and eyed her suspiciously.

"Darling," Lily said impulsively. "Let's take Ivan on our walk."

"I don't know—I don't have a lot of time."

"He'll trot right along with us. He's been indoors all morning." She had kept him in deliberately to have a natural-appearing excuse. "Let's go for a walk, Ivan. Just a short one."

"Why short?" Ivan said.

"Because Papa has to get back to work. Maybe later I'll take you to the park."

Flora finished dawdling and left the room.

Peter stood up and Ivan slipped out of his chair and Lily got her purse. They walked out the door, carrying nothing with them, leaving behind their half-packed suitcases open in the bedroom, and walked to the dock and onto the freighter and the freighter sailed.

53

❀

Time—the wonder machine, Cirie thought. It dulls the bright colors of memory and buries what was never to be forgotten. It cuts down your irresistible dream and quiets your passions and wrings the juices out of your hopes. Or so they say.

On these spring mornings in New York, there was a fresh smell in the air, with the streets newly washed and a breeze from the river and the pale green of small city trees, that could stir in you an irrational optimism you had no reason to feel. On mornings like this Cirie would get off the subway a stop early and walk west to the park and then down Fifth Avenue to the store where, in a city where people were selling pencils and apples on the street, she was supposed to sell perfume. Today in the park the dogwood and tulips were in bloom, bold red against a shower of white, with pigeons and sparrows pecking among them, and Cirie felt a little tug of nostalgia as the canvas, painted in shades of green and white and red and yellow, reminded her of parks she had left behind. She hurried away. It was eight years now. She had put all that behind her. It was past, both the good and the bad, and most of the time she did not think about it, anymore.

Eight years. She had arrived in America with a trusting Alexei and a tearful Marya and a hundred English words. She had a memory of the immigration building with American flags and steel posts and uniformed officers and doctors and a long line of frightened people speaking every language, women with shawls and babushkas, men with derby hats and ill-fitting suits, crying babies, pale children, and an official who left off the last syllable of their name and wrote down Strong. A new name—an American name. And a memory of Anna and Anton meeting them, embracing them, taking them home. They were in America—they were free—they were in heaven. Marya cried at seeing the son and daughter and brothers she had never expected to see again and cried some more at the news that over the past two years Grandma and Grandpa had died.

Their American family came to visit them—Uncle Lawrence, treated with special deference because he was the richest, and Charles and Oscar, and their wives and sons—aunts and cousins who had been just names in letters received long ago—and attractive young women married to her cousins, smart, slim, fashionable young women who drove cars and played golf and considered themselves part of society in this little Connecticut town. The relatives came to Anna's to visit them and drove them around in automobiles to see the local landmarks and invited them to dinner, each in turn, once. It was paradise. The meaning of family shone like the sun.

It took a little while to realize that the attention showered on them when they arrived, poor and dowdy and undernourished, had been motivated by a sense of duty and that, in fact, these attractive Americans were not eager to present these poor immigrants to their friends, several of whom employed similar immigrants as maids. When they realized it at last, Marya was deeply wounded. "If they came to Russia, we'd have welcomed them with open arms."

"Russians are different, Mamma," Cirie said. "Anyone who came to us was welcome. Madame always had relatives living with them. They thought Aunt Vayana was dotty but their home was her home."

"Look at how Ulla took us in," Marya said. "Papa's second cousin. And Papa always took in everyone."

"They didn't come to Russia. We came here." Memories of the early snubs at Whitewater and of sitting on Pegasus, looking at the river, and saying to herself: Inside there is a place where I am the ruler, I am the Tsar...And as long as that is mine, I can survive. No one can humiliate you if you refuse to be humiliated. No one can touch you if you won't let them. "Your brothers helped us come here, they're helping us get on our feet. That's all we can expect. If these aunts and cousins think we're not good enough for them, we can live with that."

"Cirie, you're so thick-skinned. Doesn't anything touch you, anymore?"

Cirie shrugged. "We survived a revolution, Mamma. We'll survive a few snubs. Things will change."

"If Grandma were alive she wouldn't permit it," Marya said.

Cirie doubted that Grandma had carried much weight with these smart, brittle young women. "Mamma, Anna is overjoyed that you're here. You can learn English and help her in the store."

Suspicious, Marya looked at her quickly. "And you?"

Me? Cirie thought. I'm going to learn English and I'm going to get rid of these dowdy clothes and get out of this little town. I'm going to New York.

Realizing instantly what she had in mind, Marya was distraught. "Cirie, you're always looking for something better somewhere else. You won't find it anymore. You're not seventeen—you're in a foreign country—you don't know the language—"

"I'm learning it."

"You don't know their ways."

"I'm learning them, too."

"Cirie, settle down where you have family. Stop running." Marya's voice rose. "You always intended to see everything. You always meant to have everything. It brought nothing but trouble."

Eight years. Three times when her visa expired she went to Canada and Uncle Lawrence succumbed to his sister's tears and paid someone through his brother-in-law, Harry, the politician, for a new visitor's visa. Then Harry and his political cronies became involved in a corruption scandal and went to prison and Cirie, to become a citizen, married a strangely foolish American and thanked God when he gave her a reason at once to throw him out. "It's strictly a business deal," Uncle Lawrence had told her when he outlined the necessary moves. "He's Harry's cousin—Alfred, Alfie." A totally foolish man who smiled and smiled. An hour after the ridiculous ceremony in City Hall, he stole Strengov's gold watch from her. She could still remember the scene:

"Alfie, where is my watch?"

Alfie smiled. "What watch is that?"

"Give it to me, Alfie."

"Cirie, I'm your husband." He smiled. "If you loved me you'd want me to have it." A wider smile, pleased at his clever response.

"You are not my husband, Alfie. This is a business deal. You were well paid."

"That was before. Now that I've seen you, I've decided to be your husband."

"That was not the arrangement. Give me my watch."

"I can't. I pawned it." He took a few bills from his pocket. "We'll celebrate, Cirie, and then have a wonderful wedding night." He moved to take her in his arms.

"Give me the pawn ticket," she ordered, so sharply that he stopped smiling and took the ticket from his wallet.

"Goodbye, Alfie."

"Lady, I mean to be your husband," he said, pointedly. "If you refuse to honor this marriage I can get you deported."

"And I can get you in jail."

"*Put* me in jail," he corrected her. "Not *get* me in jail."

"Put or get, Alfie, you'll still be there."

"For borrowing my wife's watch?"

Cirie looked at him narrowly. If he had stolen her watch in less than an hour, he had stolen before. He had itchy fingers. He was in practice. He had known where to find the pawnbroker. "Alfie, I know all about you," she said, "and all those other things you stole. Your cousin Harry is in jail, he can't save you, anymore, and if you give me any trouble, now or ever, until I have citizen papers, I will go to the police. With the whole list."

End of Alfie. She never saw him again and Uncle Lawrence arranged a divorce. The whole episode didn't touch her very much. Right after that, Roosevelt became president and closed the banks and she was far more upset at that because she remembered that when the Bolsheviks came to power, they closed the banks, too. Eight years. They were easy to forget.

She left the dogwood and tulips behind and walked down Fifth Avenue, look-ing in windows at things she couldn't afford. Coming up to a magazine store, she glanced at the newspaper headlines. Well, here was something. A Soviet trade mis-sion had arrived in the United States. They were going to do business with the bandits! Lately, there had been a rash of news about the Soviets. More reaching out to the West—more ambassadors, ministers, trade delegations—and more people imprisoned or killed at home—with or without kangaroo trials. Stalin had consolidated his power and was getting rid of his enemies. Kamenev was out—Kamenev who had once edited Pravda with him. And Trotsky, his arch-enemy, had fled Russia.

On the front page of the Tribune was a picture of four men being greeted at the boat, their faces partly hidden by the hats of the welcoming American officials. Cirie looked at the indistinct, partly concealed faces. She didn't know anyone in Russia anymore, she thought, and she didn't know anyone here, either. In New York she was just one more person on the subway, one more person walking along the street to work, lucky to have a job in the middle of a depression, and going home at night to an empty apartment. Alexei and Mamma were with Anna, where they were better off, and she knew only Dixie, the girl at the scarf counter next to the perfume counter, and Jed, the college boy who worked evenings in the grocery store near her apartment. And Norman. Did Norman remind her of Petya because he was quiet and sober and not very interesting? Or because he wanted to marry her at a time when life held little promise? Why is everything coming back to me today? Tulips bloom in the park, a Soviet Delegation arrives—the window of an antique shop last month—suddenly everything brings back memories I'm not looking for and don't want. Or is it that when there's nothing in your life, you remember a time when there was? You're in fine condition, she told herself. This will do you a lot of good. It's spring fever, she told herself. The world is waking up and you have no one to wake up to. Or with.

The difference between Petya and Norman was that back then she had still believed, in spite of their poverty, that somehow she could still seize hold of life and live it, that she could conquer the world. Now when she thought like that, it was just an old habit and mostly, now, she just thought about holding on and about being alone. She would probably marry Norman out of loneliness. As Mamma kept telling her, she was no longer eighteen.

In front of the Cannon Building a limousine stopped and the passenger, without waiting for the chauffeur, threw open the door and strode toward the building. This man arrived at his office every morning at this hour, usually hatless, today coatless, about fifty—maybe a little younger. She had noticed him because he moved with so much energy and because he seemed to be the only man who could still afford a chauffeur who came to work so early. Imagine anyone still being able to afford a chauffeur and a limousine.

She passed another magazine store and again sought out the pictures of the Russian delegation. Probably Lily knew them. Now it was Lily who knew everyone. It was more than a month since Cirie had heard from Lily. She wondered if they had gone home and hoped that nothing was wrong. You could be in favor one day and in the Black Maria the next, on your way to Lubyanka. Another fine memory.

At the store Dixie leaned over from her counter on the center aisle. "That aisle is nothing but a street," she complained. "Everyone just walking and looking. Go up to them and they run." A willowy auburn-haired girl, Dixie steadied herself on the counter and flexed her foot. "I went dancing last night and my feet are talking back. Boy, I never thought I'd be working like this again—on my feet all day."

"What did you do before?" Cirie asked.

"Nothing. I had a friend who took care of me. You got your courage letting them stick you in perfume. Almost anything would be better than perfume. Still, you manage."

Even in hard times there are people who have bread, Cirie thought. In prohibition there are people who have liquor. While some people are freezing, there are people who have wood. And while people are begging on the street, there are people who can buy perfume. The personnel woman had told her that her accent belonged in perfume or fashion. "But for fashion you'd need more experience." In America you needed experience to sell fashions but for nursing, experience made no difference. ("You don't speak the language well enough," they had told her at the hospitals. "You won't understand the patients or the doctors or the instructions. We like to train our nurses our way." Their voices suggested she had probably never heard of such high standards. "We have nothing for you here.") What good did it do to argue?

"What happened to your friend?" she said to Dixie.

"The crash is what happened. My friend before this one was even better to me. But he died." She gave a wistful little smile. "I'm snake-bit."

"Snake-bit?"

"That's a gambler's word. My friend that died was a gambler. It means unlucky—nothing goes right for you. Snake-bit." Dixie flexed the other foot. "Boy, that crash—that was one of those days you always remember where you were. What were you doing that day?"

"I was getting rid of a husband—"

"Oh, God. You must have been really down."

"I was delighted."

"At least now you have someone else. Did you decide yet? Are you going to marry him?"

"I don't know." Why did she hesitate? She was fond of Norman. He was responsible and nice-looking with brown hair and worried brown eyes, but then everyone was worried these days. She understood Norman. He took everything a little too seriously but he was honest and dependable and not unkind. "I suppose I will."

"Listen, don't be so negative about it. Can he support you?"

"Yes, he's a lawyer. His wife died. He has two children."

"Don't let that stop you," Dixie advised. "Marry him."

"You sound like my mother," Cirie said. "But I probably will." When it came to wiping out memories, time didn't always do its job, but when it came to cutting your dreams down to size, oh, there—there!—time was a wonder.

At lunchtime Norman was waiting for her on a bench near the park entrance.

"Hello, darling." She sat on the bench. "Did you have a good morning?"

"I was with a very difficult client," he said.

"I'm sorry—" Cirie murmured. He wanted to complain a little and that was all the encouragement he would need.

"Claude is a strange personality. The smallest slight and he's furious. And he holds a grudge."

The dogwood nodded in the breeze. On the bench across the way a worn-looking young man sat staring at his worn shoes.

"Now he wants to divorce his wife," Norman sighed. "It'll be a miserable case. But he pays his bills—one of the few who do these days."

Under a tree a young man and woman had spread a blanket and were opening a lunch basket. "Norman, we should do that sometime, on one of these beautiful days. Bring a lunch and eat in the park. We wouldn't have to sit on the grass. We could sit on a bench—"

Norman examined the picnic for a minute and said, "Eating outdoors can be a very buggy affair." He unfolded his New York Times in order to fold it more compactly and Cirie saw the picture of the Soviet Trade Delegation. Beside the dogwood tree, tall red tulips stood like Red Army sentinels. "Old Vodianoy is really waking up," she said.

"Who is that?"

"That's an old Russian saying for the coming of spring. To the peasants the Vodianoy is the spirit of water. He lives in the river and he can help you with fishing or give you trouble, like churning up rough waters. In the fall he goes to sleep and then when winter is over, the river melts—with a boom like gunfire—and the peasants say, 'Old Vodianoy is waking up,' and they get into their sledges and come into town. It's a saying of spring."

"It's interesting the superstitions the uneducated mind clings to," Norman said. "It's a result of ignorance."

"Norman," she said, impulsively, "it's such a beautiful day. Let's walk over to 57th street before we go to lunch. I want to show you something."

"What is it?"

"An Oriental chest."

"Why would I want to see an Oriental chest?"

"It's only two blocks and it's a nice day." And because I asked you to. "Sometimes I get off the subway and walk over here to the park and then down Fifth Avenue, just window shopping—"

"Yes, you told me that. The walk is probably healthy but you shouldn't be mooning over a lot of things you'll never be able to afford."

"Norman, if the people who could afford those things were the only ones who could look, you might as well cover the windows. Window-shopping is fantasy land."

"I suppose so."

"Then one day last month I took a different route just for a change of scenery, different shops—" She checked herself. If I marry him will I always have to be so careful? Worse, maybe. A depressing thought. "I walked across on 57th street and I passed an antique shop—"

She had only glanced at the window of the shop—the Persian rug and the delicate tables and chairs were too painful a reminder—and she was well past it when she realized what she had seen. She came to a dead stop and hurried back and stared at an Oriental chest. The Vodovsky Oriental chest. It's as though it were following me, she thought—as though it had a life of its own. First it went from Whitewater to Kostyka and then, in 1917, it was one of the first things the moujiks stole. One of them was going to use it as a log-box. Then it turned up in Laranov's room. And when he didn't come back, where did it go? And how did it get here, moved away from trouble again, to 57th Street? She had read that the impoverished Soviet State had sold many treasures for British pounds and American dollars. The teak finish, unmarred by all the moving, was the same—and the pattern of the jade and mother-of-pearl. In the shop window it rested on a Persian rug, between two French chairs as though it were a coffee table. This antique dealer did not realize that all its life it had been displayed on a table.

"When I first went to Vodovsky," she told Norman, "there was an Oriental chest in the study and I fell in love with it. It was the most beautiful thing I'd ever seen. And, Norman, I could swear that chest is in the window of an antique shop on 57th Street."

In the past month she had returned twice to look at it. She told herself it might not be the same chest—there could be others like it—if she looked carefully she might see that it was different from the Vodovsky chest. "Later, of course, I realized that many things in the house were far more valuable."

She had stared at the window of the antique shop, overwhelmed by memories—Stepa in the study that first day, shouting to Georgii and Tanya, Constantine talking to her about the origin of the chest and about so many other things, educating her without letting her know she was lacking. Where were they all now? The letters they carried to mail to Anna had never arrived. She had written twice to the Paris address Stepa had given her but there had been no reply. "Now everyone I knew that summer is dead," she said. "Norman, let's walk over to see it."

"Cirie, I don't think you should keep going back to look at it. I think you should stay away from it."

"Norman, someday if that chest is still there, I'm going to buy it!" she announced, to her own surprise.

Norman's eyes shot over to her. "Where would you get enough money for that?"

Cirie regained her composure. She wasn't ever going to buy that chest. Until this moment the thought had never occurred to her. But still she said, "One thing I've learned, Norman. If something seems impossible, wait a little. The odds will change."

"I don't know why you would want it," he said, dismissing the notion. "What use is it?"

Stubbornly she didn't answer.

"Cirie, forget about it. Why do you cling to memories of those days? They weren't good days."

"Some of them were very good days."

"You shouldn't dwell on memories. You'll only become depressed. I worry about you." Sometimes he showed a flash of warmth and she would think, maybe he's more than I give him credit for being. "Forget them," he advised crisply. He refolded his newspaper and stood up to go to lunch. "You shouldn't think about the past so much. It's not healthy."

At lunch Norman placed his newspaper on an empty chair and it unfolded a little to reveal another picture of the American officials greeting the four men in the Trade Delegation—three stiff-looking Russians wearing ill-fitting suits and one of them taller, broad-shouldered with a mustache, wearing a better fitting suit. Three sober unsmiling Russians, certain of the justice of their mission, uncertain of themselves, and a fourth one in a well-tailored suit, his face partly cut off by an American official's hat, who seemed to be taking it all in, confident that he would get what he came for. Cirie stared at the fourth man.

"What are you looking at?"

Three strangers and one with his face half-blocked by an American hat, who looked like someone who was not a stranger at all.

"Cirie, what are you looking at? You're pale."

Slowly her eyes came away from the picture. "The Soviet Trade Delegation. One of them looks like someone I know—knew."

"I'm sure it can't be. It must be a resemblance."

"Yes," she said. "He died in the Civil War. In the last battle. The likeness startled me." She dropped her purse.

"Why does it upset you?" he said, rather sharply.

Without answering, she bent over to pick up the purse. The waiter brought their lunch.

"What was he to you?" Norman said, after the waiter left.

"Nothing special. Some of the generals and commissars used to call on me." She smiled to quiet his suspicions. "So many people we knew are dead. When something reminds us, we feel our loss."

"Generals and Commissars! Cirie, you weren't a Communist?"

"Norman, do I look like a Communist?"

"Well, they're devious. If we're going to be married, I have to ask. After all, I have young children. Eat your lunch. I have to get back to Claude and his nasty divorce. Why would any man want to inflict the disgrace of a divorce on his family?"

"I suppose sometimes there are reasons," Cirie said. Her eyes went back to the newspaper.

"I don't approve of divorce," Norman said.

She forced herself to give him her attention. "What did you say?"

"Divorce. I don't trust people who've been divorced."

Cirie told herself not to say a word—at least not when she was upset and feeling suddenly perverse. "Norman—" She stopped and then said it. "I've been divorced."

"You said you were a widow."

"I was. My husband was murdered—shot on the steps of his house."

He looked at her horrified, as though she were a jinx.

"And I was divorced, too. Actually I was widowed twice." Perversely, she included Laranov. Why not? He was more a husband to her than any of the others, certainly more than Alfie. He had loved her, he had taken care of her. He had given her all those lives. "And I divorced two husbands."

Norman was shocked. "How many times have you been married?"

"I don't count any more."

"Why?"

"Why have I been married so much, or why don't I count?"

"Why have you been married so much? How can you not count!"

Cirie gave a little shrug. "They were desperate times and you did what you had to do—what you could do. My father always said a woman should be able to do something well so that if fate were unkind to her, she could take care of herself. Getting married was something I did well."

He stared at her and looked at his watch. "I have to get back. Cirie, I have a meeting tonight. I'll call you as soon as it's over and we can talk about this if you want."

If I want? I don't know what I want. This morning I had made up my mind to marry him. Why did I tell him all this?

She stood up and her eyes went involuntarily to the paper again. He handed it to her. "Keep it. I'm through with it."

Outside the subway station near her apartment, men leaned against the wall, cigarettes hanging out of their mouths, shabby caps like the Bolsheviks used to wear, and always that look of defeat and despair that Cirie had come to know so well in Russia—men without work and without hope.

Walking to her apartment, she thought about Norman. Why did I inflict all that on him at lunch? Who would think anything so dull as a Trade Delegation could cause so much trouble? And the chest! He thought you wanted him to buy it for you! Well, she would explain the marriages and never mention the Oriental chest again and everything would be all right. The past is dead, she told herself, and it won't come back. And life is hard—and Norman is here. You could have a home instead of living alone in this dreary flat in a big anonymous apartment house. You could have Alexei with you. Now a few bottles of perfume—the most superfluous commodity in the world—are all that stand between you and walking around with that awful look of despair. She came up to a soup kitchen, filled with people waiting for their evening meal, and hurried past. More than anything the soup kitchens evoked a fear she was unable to set aside. Soup kitchens were part of the Revolution.

In the grocery store she bought soap (in her mind still a luxury) and bread and six eggs and a half-pound of hamburg for a meat loaf that would last two nights. While she was carefully checking the prices, she heard the music from the record store across the street where the two clerks, Freddy and Rosa, played a Victrola all day and into the evening.

Freddy, nineteen, played lively optimistic songs and Rosa, thirty, played romantic songs about lost loves.

In her apartment, Cirie looked again at Norman's newspaper—three strangers and one who looked like someone who was not a stranger at all—and her eyes filled with tears. In the music shop Rosa was at the Victrola now, playing a song about somebody needing someone. Cirie closed the window. For a long time she stared at the paper. After a while she ran her wrist across her eyes and without much interest, read about the Trade Delegation. They would be in America for two weeks, first in Washington and then in New York. The apartment was getting stuffy. The heat came in from the hallways. She opened the window again and heard that Rosa still needed someone and slammed it shut again. The telephone rang. Ten o'clock. Certain that it was Norman, she remained at the window. Answer it—what's the matter with you? She let it ring.

Now, suddenly, it was hopeless. Memories were rushing back of Laranov—the dark tomb beside the prison, the passion that turned to surprising tenderness and rose again to wild passion—the tenderness of his kiss, the tenderness of his hands. "He's dead—he's dead!" she cried out while she wept uncontrollably.

At five past eleven Marya phoned—a follow-up to a long letter that had said, in effect, one thing: Marry him. Marya telephoned only in a crisis and then she waited for the low rates and came to the telephone with a three-minute egg timer. When the last grain of sand reached the bottom, the call was over. "Cirie, he's a lawyer—he'll support you," Marya said. "Alexei is growing up, he'll send him to college."

"He has children of his own, Mamma."

"What will become of Alexei with no education? Do you want him to work in the grocery store like poor John?"

"Don't worry about John, Mamma." Anna's son had a business head like Grandma. Before he was through he would have a bigger store or several bigger stores. Maria, Anna's daughter, was like Vogel. She was lazy and beautiful and wanted only to get married.

"Cirie, you're not eighteen anymore, when you could break any heart you decided in your shrewd mind to sink your teeth into." From this unrestrained language, Cirie knew Marya was extremely worried lest this excellent catch slip away into the hands of a more sensible woman. "Time passes."

Time! It doesn't give you peace. Only age.

"Cirie, you haven't heard from Lily?"

"Not lately."

"I'm worried. There hasn't been a letter for a long time. The sand is down—I have to hang up. Cirie, soon you won't be able to get anyone. Think of Alexei. Marry him."

Oh, wonderful! She doubted that Norman wanted to educate Alexei. Sometimes she thought that all he wanted was someone to take care of his motherless children.

Presently she picked up the newspaper again. When the Russians returned to New York the officials were going to show them the city—stores, factories, monuments, museums, concert halls. Maybe things are better over there, she thought. if they're letting them stay to see all that. The article was continued on page twelve. In the lower corner, before she turned the page, she saw a small item to the effect that a Soviet diplomat had defected. Someone else on the run, so maybe things weren't better. Probably things were just the same. You had to be in the ruling circle and you had to know how to get along. Clearly this Trade Delegation was considered an important event. On page twelve was a box three columns wide, reporting some opinions on what could be expected to develop out of this Russian-American conference.

And at the top of the second column was the opinion of a professor at Columbia University—Constantine Paklov!

54

✿

Cirie approached the door of a lecture hall at Columbia University. Constantine's name was not in the telephone book and when she tried to telephone him at the university she was told that his lectures were over for the year. Through Jed at the grocery store, a student at Columbia, she learned about this public lecture tonight, the last of a series Professor Paklov was giving on the Russian Revolution.

As she opened the door, a student usher turned to her. "The lecture's almost over."

"That's all right," she said.

"You won't learn much."

I know all I want to know, she thought. "How much is it?"

"Two dollars."

She hesitated. "I'm an old friend. Can I see him later on the way out?"

"You can't see him at all. No one can approach him."

She held out the two dollars. No groceries tomorrow.

"It's almost over so I won't charge you," the usher said. "Sit in the back row so you won't have to climb past people. He's just summing up."

"From the start the Bolsheviks were a secret organization," Constantine was saying as she sat down. "Small, tightly controlled, admitting only fanatics ready to follow the orders of their absolute dictator, Lenin…"

Constantine looked older and his voice was less firm. Could it really be so many years?

"…They had the mentality of conspirators. They trusted no one. They saw enemies everywhere and they were old hands at terrorism."

A group of people in front of Cirie exchanged oddly triumphant glances, as though taking pride in this. An aggressive-looking woman wearing large diamond rings, whispered to a small nervous man beside her.

"…Even extreme violence did not repel them," Constantine continued to summarize. "It was the psychology of the Inquisition—the religious fanatic who believes his faith is the only true faith—and in the name of this one true faith murder, torture, and the most inhumane imprisonment became virtues."

Constantine adjusted the light on the lectern. There was something unfamiliar in his motion.

430

"…They were a very small hated minority. How could a few men force all men to become slaves to their theories, except by terrorism?"

"I don't believe it!" the woman in the next row muttered.

Constantine turned a page of his notes and Cirie realized suddenly what was bothering her. He had not been left-handed—and now he was using only his left hand. He did not appear to have suffered a stroke but he was unable to use his right hand. Her thoughts flew to the trip that she had thought for years must have sent all four of them to their death or to a Siberian prison.

"…Under the autocratic Romanov dynasty, the people never developed a political sense of give and take, of compromise and accommodation—"

What of the other three—Stepa and Tanya and Georgii? Cirie thought. What happened to them?

"…The first revolution, in March, overthrew the repressive Romanov rule and produced the democratic Provisional Government. That was the real revolution."

"Not true!" the woman said in a hoarse whisper. "He's a fascist!"

"…But the Provisional Government had little political experience and foundered. That made room for the moderate but weak Socialist, Kerensky…And it was Kerensky's weakness that made the great coup possible—Lenin's coup…It was not a people's Revolution—it was a coup.

"Without Lenin's thirst for absolute power, without the machinery of terrorism that Lenin established to preserve his power, today we would not have Stalin. Stalin inherited Lenin's government. He inherited his machinery of government—terrorism—and used it for his own ends. He purged Lenin's colleagues. Today he is purging his own followers. He has murdered millions. In the Ukraine he deliberately starved a whole people, robbed them of every scrap of the abundant grain they produced, shot them for attempting to gather the remains left in the fields, reduced them to *cannibalism*, drove them to suicide. Stalin today is more ruthless than Lenin ever was…"

Constantine leaned forward over the lectern. "It shouldn't have happened. The vast majority didn't want it. But here was a people who were hungry and wounded, weary of war, without hope—and a charismatic leader enticed them with promises. The result was the Revolution that nobody wanted. That shouldn't have happened. And did."

"Not true—not true!" cried the woman in front of her.

"It is true—every word of it!" Cirie told the astonished woman who was on her feet trying to argue with Constantine. A gentleman on the platform reminded the audience that there would not be a discussion period.

Cirie started up the aisle and felt the hand of the young usher on her shoulder. "Sorry, ma'am. No questions."

"I'm an old friend. He'll want to see me."

"You'll have to see him some other time."

"No!" Her chin tilted in a perfect imitation of Irene. "Please take your hand from my arm!" To her amazement he obeyed. "Thank you." She darted into the crowd that was moving against her toward the exit. By the time she reached the platform, Constantine was leaving through a side door and the usher was grasping her arm again. "You'll have to leave, ma'am," he said. "Now."

"Constantine! Darling!" she called out in Russian.

For a minute Constantine stood perfectly still. Then, slowly, incredulously, he turned and peered into the hall.

"Darling," she called again. "It's Cirie!"

He came across the platform, looking for her, and hurried down the stairs. "Is it you? Is it really you?" he said. He gathered her into his arms and his eyes filled with tears. "You're alive!" he murmured again and again in Russian. "Thank God, you're alive!"

In Constantine's living room Cirie felt she was back in one of the Russian drawing rooms they had left behind.

"The smugglers were as rough a crew as I've ever seen," Constantine said. He was describing their escape. "They're a bad lot but their organization and efficiency were fascinating. Their horses are fed and trained for great speed and endurance and they go like the wind. If they're challenged to stop, they go faster." Constantine paused, reliving the trip. He told her about the wild ride on the Gulf of Finland with the searchlights and cannons of Kronstadt pursuing them, and about the sled slamming into a huge frozen mass, throwing Tanya into the air just as a blade of light found them and the sailors on Kronstadt fired. "They caught Stepa in the back and me in the arm."

He described Stepa's condition while they struggled to reach land and the good Finnish fisherman who took them in and Stepa's death three days later.

"In Helsinki it was my turn to become a problem. I developed an infection. Our money was almost gone. Some had been in the bags we left behind on the ice and the rest we had spent to get ourselves to Helsinki—three exhausted grieving beggars. That's what happened to your letters, Cirie. The others had carried theirs in their bags that were left in the snow. We prayed someone would find them and mail them. Did any of them arrive?"

Cirie shook her head.

"I suppose it was too much to hope for," Constantine said. "Mine was in my pocket and was so soaked with snow and blood the address was illegible. When I reached Paris I tried to remember it and wrote several letters to different addresses I thought might be correct. None of them arrived, either?"

Cirie shook her head. Poor Stepa. He wanted a future for Tanya. At least he knew he had done that. She told Constantine that Madame and Serge had died soon after he left.

"Poor Tanya was almost paralyzed with guilt because Stepa had died saving her, but she had enough presence of mind to find the French Embassy in Helsinki and get word to Elissa. In Paris for the first time in years, we lived normal civilized lives again. Food, comfort, old friends. Kurasin is there. He gives concerts and is busy being unfaithful to Lydia. Irene made it to Paris with her sister and Christina. They're living with Prince Tchernefsky, who is past ninety."

"What has happened to Georgii and Tanya?"

"Georgii went to work in a vineyard. He always preferred farming to city life. He married the daughter of an influential wine family and he has become very good at what he does. Even Vassily would approve. Tanya had a hard time of it for many years because of the way Stepa died. She lived with a starving artist for a while and left him and moved in with an equally impoverished poet—again a very brief romance. Then Elissa said that was enough guilt and enough of a fling and took her back home—and she began to heal. In Elissa's clever hands she became very striking and she married a wealthy silk manufacturer from Lyons, where she seems to be happy. She has two sons, an estate, an apartment in Paris—she's all right now. And I am here. Now—about you? You came to your family at last?"

"For a little while," she said. She told him about poor Sacha Borassin and they laughed together over Gorshenko's treachery. "From Riga we came directly here and I learned that family can be wonderful—for a little while. I had a grandmother, an efficient little machine of a woman who used to say, 'Families must stick together. If you're up today, help the others—tomorrow you may be down and they'll help you.' That's a Russian idea, you know. But here it has its limits. Our family arranged our passage and they helped us until our wounds healed a little but then—"

Constantine nodded and she thought how good it was to be talking to him again, and how much she had missed him. "The uncles had their own families— wives who resented the charity their husbands were giving us. We weren't very acceptable socially—"

"You not acceptable socially! A Russian countess—twice!"

"We were poor and dowdy and we didn't speak the language. I had only your hundred words that you began to teach me. So we weren't the kind of people they wanted to present as their relatives—"

"I remember the night you danced with a Grand Duke and he was enchanted!"

"Ah, Constantine, you were always good for me," she said. "It bothered my mother. I had a bigger problem. I had to become a citizen. My uncle used a political connection—a brother-in-law—to get my visitor's visa renewed a few times. Then the political connection and all his cronies were involved in a corruption scandal and went to prison. It upset the family. I told them prison was nothing— most of my friends had been in prison. They didn't think that was funny. Here they haven't learned about real political corruption yet." She laughed. "But my visa expired so I did the only thing I could. I married an American—and got rid of him so fast I hardly had time to find out his name—which was Alfred. Alfie—"

"What was wrong with him?"

"He was a very silly man. And he was a thief." Laughing, she told Constantine about Alfie. "The pawn broker was very nice about it. He was upset at first because he thought I was accusing him of buying stolen goods. How could he have known? Then he said he'd try to hold onto it until I could get the money to redeem it— and I finally did." She pulled out the watch.

"It's an amusing story now." Constantine's bright eyes were as young-looking as on the day she first saw him at Whitewater. "But I'm sure when it happened it wasn't funny."

"It didn't touch me very much. The past was still fresh in my mind and this was still paradise." How long had it been since she had had someone she could talk to like this? Someone who knew her so well, there was no confusion or misunderstanding. "You can never leave it all behind, can you?"

"No, some things you don't leave behind," Constantine agreed.

"When Roosevelt closed the banks, all I could think was that in 1917 they closed the banks and then took them over and after that I paid a half-million rubles for the people's cow. Later I sold it for four million. In a newsreel at the movies, a politician shouted, 'Seventy-five percent of the American people are farmers and they're in terrible trouble,' and I thought, Oh, God, it's just the same! I was actually shaking."

Constantine recognized the reaction. "The scars last a long time. And they come back when you least expect them—sometimes the ones you had most completely forgotten. What about you, Cirie? Are you all right?"

"Yes. I smuggled out some gold but it's almost gone. And some jewels, but you don't get a good price these days. I had to sell most of them just to keep going these past years. That's been our life for so long, hasn't it? Just to keep going. I can hardly remember anything else."

"It's not such a bad talent. We're what the dark years made us—and it's not all bad. You have a job?

He was shocked to hear she was selling perfume.

"At the hospitals they said I didn't understand the language well enough and they like to train their own nurses. They suggested my standards probably were not their standards."

"Didn't you explain that you worked through a war and revolution? You worked even when there was nothing to work with!"

"They weren't interested. Why argue? You can't win."

Constantine smiled. "You won quite often, Cirie."

"But how many things did we fight for all those years? Only to keep from starving and have a roof over our heads. Only to go on another day."

"You fought for more than that. And at the time even that was quite a lot. Since you had a whole family on your hands."

"Mostly we said, 'It doesn't matter.' We learned that we could do without almost everything. It's how we survived."

"All the same," Constantine said. "I'm not sure it should be a guiding philosophy for life. Cirie, I thought you would divorce Vassi and marry Laranov."

"He was already lost."

"Lost? Lost how?"

"He died in the Crimea in the last battle."

"Died in the Crimea!"

"I forgot you couldn't know."

Constantine stared at her. "Cirie, Laranov isn't dead!"

She sat up. "What are you talking about? He went to the Crimea and we never heard of him again. Everyone said he was dead."

Constantine held out the evening newspaper with a picture of the Russian delegation in Washington. In this picture the face was not blurred or half-concealed. The face was clear. Laranov was alive!

"What made you think he was dead?"

"He never came back!" He's alive! Laranov is alive! "Everyone said he was dead! Renkovsky was jealous of him because of his influence in Moscow and because of me. He had him sent to the Crimea. He even sent a letter to an old comrade. He said it was to introduce him but he probably suggested that he wanted Laranov killed. When he didn't come back I thought the plot had worked." She still couldn't grasp that he was alive. Her eyes lingered over the picture. "I don't understand it," she said, softly, "I never heard from him again."

"He probably went into hiding until Renkovsky was liquidated."

"Renkovsky liquidated? Renkovsky is dead?"

"Stalin has purged more than one of his old comrades. After Renkovsky went, Laranov probably reappeared."

"How can we reach him?" She searched through the article. "Where is he staying?"

"Cirie, I don't think you can try to reach him!"

"But he won't find me! He doesn't know I'm here! He doesn't know my American name."

"Cirie, have you forgotten how suspicious they are? They watch each other."

Cirie stared at Constantine. "Don't you want to see him, too?"

"Of course I want to see him. I wanted to see him in Kostyka. But I would only spell trouble for him. I write articles against Stalin's regime. I make unfriendly speeches. If he met with me, he'd be purged the minute he returned to Russia. For you, I admit it might be different. A meeting with a beautiful woman can look like what it is—a meeting with a beautiful woman."

She read quickly through the article. "They want to see subways and factories and stores. They'll take them to Macy's because it's the biggest—a store for the people—and they'll bring them to us. We're the newest. They always bring visitors there."

"Cirie, if he comes to your store, be careful. If he doesn't speak, don't speak to him. Don't get him in trouble."

"How can I not speak to him!" But she knew he was right. You think you remember it all, but how quickly you forget. "They'll take them down the main aisle in the center. He won't pass me. He won't see me. They won't let me approach him. I can't let him walk past twenty feet away and not call to him. That's impossible!"

"Laranov will go back, Cirie," Constantine said. "He went back after he was in hiding and he'll go back now. If he had friends to hide him, he had friends to smuggle him out of Russia. He didn't leave. Or if he did, he went back. You know how he feels about Russia."

"But he's here! I can't let him go back without seeing him." She read the article again. "They're still in Washington. I have a little time to think of something."

55

A mild stir rippled through the store as the Trade Delegation came up the center aisle. Dixie, on cue, called loud and clear to Cirie, "Cirie—Cirie—here are your countrymen. Cirie!" Cirie saw Laranov's face when he saw her.

He recovered and turned to his colleagues. "Just a minute," she heard him say in Russian, "I think I see someone from my home town." He looked the same, lean and fit, he walked the same. He came up to her and smiled the same irreverent smile. "Are you from Russia?"

"Yes." She steadied her hand on the counter.

"From Kostyka?"

"For many years." She remembered Constantine's warning and waited for him to go on.

"You didn't wait," he said, softly.

"I waited. You didn't come back."

"I couldn't come back."

"Where were you?"

"In hiding. I told you I had friends who would hide me if it became necessary."

"Everyone said you died in the Crimea."

"I was taken prisoner. Wrangle was an old friend. He let me talk my way out of it." He bent closer. "Darling, I wrote to you. Didn't you get my letters?"

If she had, she would still be in Kostyka. "What did you say?"

"I said, 'I love you. Wait for me.' As soon as I could, I went back to Kostyka. You were gone—all of you."

"Comrade Laranov," one of his comrades called.

"In a minute," he answered. "Darling, meet me tonight? Two blocks from here—the hotel Waldorf Astoria. Sit in the lobby at nine o'clock. I'll find you." His voice became impersonal again. "It's good to see you after all these years." He bowed and whispered, "Tonight at nine, darling."

"He's here!" Riding home on the subway, Cirie was oblivious to the noise, the faces, the crowd. "He's alive! He's here! I'll be with him tonight."

An impossible question pushed into her thoughts. Was there a chance—in spite of Constantine's warning—was there the smallest chance that Laranov would stay? Had he ever considered it? Could she persuade him? He would not be the first Soviet official on a government mission to fail to return. Or am I meeting him only to lose him again? I can't think about that now. That's tomorrow. All I know is today—this moment—tonight. Life that had been barren and hard was bright again. She would have tonight with Laranov.

She passed the music store where Freddy was playing Happy Days Are Here Again. She laughed out loud. For once, no argument. The years melted away. The pain melted away. She was alive again.

As she turned the key in her door a man and woman and a little boy, hats pulled down over their eyes, came around the corner of the corridor.

"Cirie—" the woman whispered.

Cirie stared. "Lily!"

Lily and Peter and a little boy who looked like Alexei hurried up to her.

"Quick—open the door," Lily whispered as Cirie embraced her. "Let us get inside."

"Lily, why didn't you let us know you were coming?"

"We couldn't. Open the door. Open the door."

Cirie opened the door and the three of them darted inside. "Is anyone here? Do other people live here?"

"No! I live alone."

"Who comes here?"

"No one, really. Lily, what is it? What's wrong?"

They sat together on the sofa. The little boy, Ivan, buried his face against his mother's arm.

"We've left," Peter explained, nervously. "We're in hiding."

"You're the diplomat who defected!"

"They've questioned you!" Lily gasped.

"No! There was a piece in the paper." At their look of alarm he added, "A very small piece. How long were you waiting for me?"

"We docked early this morning," Peter said. "We came on a freighter from South Africa—it was the only way we could remain undetected. Then the captain told someone he had a Russian who was escaping and we had to avoid the reporters. We ran several blocks and got a taxicab and came here."

"You waited in the hall all day?"

"When someone came to this floor we went to the elevator and went down to another floor and later came back."

"You must be exhausted. And starved. But you're safe now. I'll go out and get some groceries. I have to go out tonight but I'll fix you some dinner first." For a few minutes Lily's arrival in this terrified condition had driven Laranov from her thoughts. "Of all people, Ilya Laranov came into the store today. I'm going to meet him later."

Lily paled. "You can't!"

"Lily, I know I haven't seen you for years but we'll have time together now. And Laranov is here for only a few days."

"Cirie, you can't meet Laranov! They'll be watching!"

"Laranov will slip away from them." Remembering, she smiled. "We're both good at that."

"Not Laranov! They'll be watching you!" Peter said. "They're trying to find us through you. That's why he's meeting you."

"Peter, Laranov wouldn't do that to me. He loves me."

Lily looked away. "I always thought you were having an affair with him," she said, disapprovingly. "While you were married to Vassily."

Can she possibly think that's an accusation that would bother me?

Peter leaned forward and fixed tired, piercing eyes on her. "Why do you think he came to your store?"

"There's a Trade Delegation here. They're showing them the city. Subways, museums, factories, stores—"

"But why that particular store—where you work?" Nervously, he tapped his knee with his middle finger, to drive home his point. "Why today?"

"Because today they were showing them stores."

"No! Because today we landed here. They came to you to lead them to us!"

"Peter, Laranov didn't know I was in that store. He was astonished to see me. He was dumbfounded."

Peter laughed. "Everyone in Russia is a consummate actor today. How else would you live—except by always affecting innocence?"

"Cirie," Lily whispered. "They know where you are every minute. They're everywhere. They're watching you. You can't go to Laranov."

What has happened to them to produce this irrational terror? They were never so frightened, either of them. But whatever the reason it has nothing to do with Laranov and me. That wasn't a trap today. He was astonished to see me—and overjoyed. "Lily, you're safe now. You can hide out here as long as you want. But long ago Laranov and I were in love. I thought he was dead. After all these years I've just found him again and I'm going to see him tonight."

"For what!" Lily burst out, frightened and angry. "Are you going back with him?"

Would she go back? Could she? For Laranov? "I only know that I'm going to have this night."

"No!" Peter moved to the door.

"Cirie, one night!" Lily cried. "Laranov isn't going to stay here with you! Not Laranov! He has power now. Are you going to sacrifice us for one night?"

"I am not sacrificing you. I'm going because we're in love."

Peter stood firmly against the door. "I can't let you go."

Cirie stopped arguing. She went into her bedroom and, without speaking to them, into the bathroom and showered and returned to her bedroom. She could hear Peter and Lily speaking urgently in low voices—Peter who was always so confident and amusing and Lily who was always so quiet and meek. When she returned to the living room to leave, Peter moved back against the door.

"Step away from the door, Peter."

Peter shook his head. "Cirie, you and I were once good friends."

"Peter, step aside!"

"I can't let you jeopardize my wife and son."

"You've lived in fear so long it's made you a little crazy, both of you!" Cirie cried. "Nobody is going to follow me. Nobody cares."

"They care," Peter said, firmly. "You're naive if you think it was coincidence that Laranov came into that store. Or that, after all these years he would risk meeting you tonight because he's still in love with you."

"Cirie," Lily said, pathetically, "it's so much worse over there now—under Stalin. You can't imagine. Even before we went to South Africa we lived in fear. We shared an apartment with another couple and a single woman—are you sure no one lives here with you?"

"No one lives here."

"In Moscow, in our own apartment, Peter and I were afraid to talk except about very ordinary things. We never knew who was eavesdropping—who was a spy. Anything important we whispered to each other in bed. Nights we would lie there and listen for the Black Maria. When we heard it we would think who are they taking away tonight? You never knew who would be next. Cirie, it's so awful to be afraid."

"I know about that, too," Cirie said.

"But you weren't scheduled to be liquidated! Peter was on their list. They ordered him to come home and bring his family. That could only mean he was to be liquidated."

"We left with next to nothing," Peter said. "A change of clothing and a few necessities for each of us. And a little gold. We don't ask for charity. Would we do that without good reason to be afraid? I am not easily frightened, Cirie. I flew a little open plane all through the war. When I speak of fear there's a reason."

"Peter, nobody is trying to reach you through me. If they'd wanted to do that, they didn't need an elaborate scheme. They could have just followed me home from work."

"Are you sure they didn't?" Lily paled.

"Of course they didn't. Do you see anybody bothering us?" She understood their fear but she would not give up Laranov. "Peter, please move away from the door."

"I can't let you go out, Cirie."

"You have no right to come here and interfere with my life!"

"On the edge of a precipice, one doesn't discuss rights."

"Let me out!"

"No! I can't take that chance."

"Let me out!" she screamed as she realized that they would actually keep her here by force if they had to.

"No, Cirie." Peter met her anger with cold grey eyes. "I regret it but I will not."

56

❁

The woman behind the desk at the Employment Agency snapped up Cirie's job application with long red fingernails. "You're a nurse?"

There was no question of going back to the perfume counter. When she had tried to go to work the morning after the entire Russian Delegation had seen her in the store, Lily had wept and begged and collapsed in hysterics. "They'll follow you home! You won't even know it until they step up beside you at your door. They'll force you to tell them where we are. They know how to do it." Lily's voice rose. "If you go back to that store, we can't stay here. We'll have to move and they may be on the street watching for us. And where will we go? Where will we go?" Weeping hysterically, Lily rushed into the kitchen and for some reason turned on the water and sobbed convulsively at the sink. Peter, ashamed of his own terror and of moving into Cirie's home and disrupting her life, wrestled with his conscience but nevertheless asked her not to go out until the Soviet Delegation had left New York.

After being held prisoner and kept from Laranov, and exhausted after crying all night, Cirie had little desire to comfort them. But how could she send them out to wander the streets?

The interviewer's red mouth was wide and busy. "Russia!" she said. "You were trained in Russia?"

"I worked in surgery for twelve years before I came here."

"Do you have papers to prove it?"

"No," Cirie said. "We had a Revolution."

"What I have for you," the woman said, with the arrogance of one who knows her power, "is a nice job selling washroom supplies. You might wear your uniform—you'd make a nice impression in it."

"What!"

"Do you think you're too good to sell washroom supplies? You girls think just because you have a pretty face, everything should be easy for you. I have no way of knowing whether you were a nurse in Russia, do I? And neither will any hospital. But I do know you'll sell washroom supplies—especially to men purchasing agents. Just don't let them get too intimate because you're selling intimate articles." The woman smiled a wide, toothy smile. "Soap, toilet paper, towels, Kotex. Take it or leave it. If you don't want it, someone else will."

"How much does it pay?"

"You work on commission. Here's where you go." She thrust a referral slip into her hand and called, "Next—"

"Cirie, you've always known how to wait out the bad times—wait for the odds to change," Constantine said. "You taught the rest of us."

"I don't feel that way, anymore," Cirie said. After being hired and told to report for work the next morning, she had taken the subway up to see Constantine rather than go home to Lily and Peter. "When they kept me from Laranov, something went out of me. But I held on. As long as he was still here I thought he would find me—he would telephone and say, 'Where were you? Where are you?' And I could have explained. And then yesterday they sailed and I just went flat."

"He didn't know where you were."

"Have you forgotten? Laranov was the one who could track down anything. Maybe Peter and Lily were right. Maybe it was a trap. I'm beginning to feel it will always be this way for me. Nothing works out. I'm snake-bit."

"Snake-bit?"

"A gambler's expression I learned at the store. It means unlucky—things never go right for you."

"Cirie, this is nonsense—you're just depressed."

"I'm resigned. No, you're right. I'm depressed, too."

"Stay here and have dinner with me. We'll eat by candlelight and talk about life and luck, which can change, as you used to say, as fast as a magician's hand—"

"I was young then—I didn't know any better. No candlelight. I had enough of rooms as dark as my life in Russia."

"Then we'll have bright lights."

"I'll have to phone Lily. They'll think I've been picked up by the secret police." A moment later she hung up the telephone. "I should have known—they're afraid to answer. Constantine, I'm beginning to think I should marry Norman and be done with it."

"Don't tell him yet."

"There's nothing wrong with Norman. He's bright and attractive and he works hard." She said it as though she were convincing herself.

"Cirie, right now you're very low. You feel luck has run out."

"Luck ran out a long time ago."

"A wonderful time to make a decision."

She laughed in spite of herself.

"Would you like to stay with me for a while? It must be very crowded there and obviously they depress you."

"Thank you, darling. But how can I leave them? They're afraid to go out even to buy food."

"That will pass. We were all a little wary when we first came out. We don't leave our fears behind so easily. Cirie, I hope you won't work at this selling job too long."

She shrugged. "Perfume or washroom supplies, what's the difference?"

"I can't agree with that. Cirie, it's not like you to give up this way."

"Constantine," she said, struggling not to break down. "This isn't the worst I've known but it seems like rock bottom."

*   *   *

At her apartment as she jammed the key into the lock, Lily, distraught, flung open the door. "Where have you been?"

"I tried to phone you," she said coldly. "You didn't answer."

"How can we answer!"

"We'll have to work out a signal." Cirie's eyes fell on a large flower box and her heart leaped. "What's that!"

"It arrived for you late this afternoon. We called for the delivery man to leave it. We were afraid it was a bomb. After an hour, we took it in."

Cirie tore open the box to uncover a mass of long-stemmed roses. Almost spilling them as she picked them up, she hurried into her room, away from Lily and Peter—she could not share this moment with them and their fear—and broke into tears. He found me, she whispered. He cared. He found me!

She reached for the card, written in Laranov's familiar handwriting:

"...I loved thee once—long, long ago—
Long long ago—the memory still is clear
Stand face to face...and unveil thy eyes
Look deep in mine and keep the dead past clear of all regret. *

               I love you.

 *Sappho of Lesbos "

He knew, she thought. And he knew why I couldn't come. And he knows the world we are caught in. She remembered the night he showed her something he had written in his journal—the night he asked Constantine to take it out of Russia. "First and in the end I am for Russia," he had written. "A creature of beauty, vitality and infinite variety. I am caught by her challenge—I am tantalized by her possibilities—I love the promise of how magnificent she could become."

Now he was a lover watching his beloved sink into misery, insanity and death, but he would not leave her. His love for Russia was his religion. It was his passion that fired his thoughts, his deeds, his courage. If he left Russia, the passion would die and what would replace it? She thought of Peter in the next room, gray and fearful, Peter who had been so brave, so full of life and laughter, Peter who had believed passionately in the Revolution which Laranov had not. And Peter was a frightened and beaten man.

If Laranov left Russia he would only exist, as she was existing now, turning her back to affronts and rebuffs and saying it did not matter. Laranov could not do that. If he did, his very being would die. He would be just another man—no longer Laranov. He had given his life to a hopeless dream, she thought, and he would stay with it to the end.

And if he had asked her to come back with him—to him and his dream—so they could be together, could she have gone? Back to what she had fought and schemed all these years to leave? She turned the card in her fingers. "I love you."

Here I have nothing, she thought. No love, no money, not even Alexei is with me. But no one comes in the night. There are no visits—no hands violate me—no fear. No Black Maria in the night. If she were to go back to be with Laranov, someone would find her out—that she had been a Vodovsky—and she would finish her life in Siberia. "I would go back with you and suffer with you," she said aloud, eyes on the card. "But if I go back I will suffer and it will be without you."

Later, when she was at peace again, she went out to the kitchen to make a cup of coffee.

"You see," Lily said. "He knew where you were. They always know."

"Yes, he knew. But he didn't do anything about it, did he?"

She carried her coffee back into the bedroom. She could not bear to look at them tonight. He knew, she thought, and he knows the world we're caught in. And he's saying goodbye.

"Keep the dead past clear of all regret."

For the first time she accepted it, too.

57

❀

On a hot midsummer day Cirie stood in the lobby, looking at the directory of the Cannon Building. In some companies, the washroom supplies were ordered by a purchasing agent, more often they were ordered by a housekeeper who was in charge of washrooms. The listing for Cannon Realty began with J.K. Cannon, President, who owned the building—and many other buildings, according to Lily who still had not stepped out of the apartment. Lily had learned English in Capetown and she spent her days reading magazines and newspapers. On the twenty-second floor, the receptionist directed her down a long corridor to the washroom supervisor's office—a small cubby-hole, hot and close on this hot day, with an unpleasant odor which Cirie suspected emanated from the woman herself who was obese, with a fleshy red face and enormous breasts spilling over the belt of her trousers.

Mary Raijerhorn was sitting at a disorderly desk on which were strewn the remains of a mid-morning snack. As soon as Cirie started to speak, Raijerhorn cut her off. "What are ya, anyway, with that accent?" Resisting the urge to hold her handkerchief to her nose, Cirie opened her case. "Yer wastin' your time, sweetheart," Raijerhorn said. "I don't buy from no accents." She looked up as a very old woman, with wispy yellow-white hair and a vein-marked face entered. "Now what?"

"I'm finished." The old woman stood tentatively near the desk. "I'm going."

"You're finished when I say you're finished," Raijerhorn shouted. The old woman blinked as though half-blind. "You think I can letcha go without checkin' on ya?"

The old woman stared into space.

"Well? Well?" Raijerhorn half-rose out of her chair and leaned menacingly over the desk. "Can I get an answer here? Or you deaf, too? Blind ain't enough?"

The old woman steadied herself on Cirie's chair and Cirie stood up to let her sit down.

"Hold it!" The supervisor reached across the desk and whacked the old woman's shoulder. "*Hold* it! *Hold* it! *Hold* it! I ain't told ya to sit."

The old woman blinked and said nothing. One of them is simple-minded, Cirie thought, and the other is insane. "Well, I finished," the old woman said, again.

"*Hold* it! *Hold* it!" Raijerhorn punched the old woman's shoulder again. "Do I get an answer here? Whadayasay? Whadayasay?"

The old woman thought a minute. "I'm comin' back," she offered.

Raijerhorn laughed wildly. "If you wasn't so funny you'd make me mad," she yelled.

Horrified, Cirie stared at the huge woman—the mammoth breasts, man's trousers, yelling, laughing wildly—and suddenly an image of another huge-breasted, red-faced, insane shouting woman surfaced out of buried memories. Marushka!

Raijerhorn punched the old woman's shoulder again and Cirie exploded. "Stop that! Don't hit her again! What gives you the right to punch her?"

"I'll punch you, too!" Raijerhorn-Marushka lunged across the desk toward Cirie as though to strike her and instead snatched off her hat and threw it on the floor. In her mind Cirie could see the whip and feel the welt on her leg.

"Dincha hear me? Dincha hear me? I don't buy from no accents. I don' trust none of 'em. And God knows I don' trust sluts. Get out! Foreigner! With your accent!"

"Have you listened to your own?" Cirie said, coolly.

"You're as deaf as the dummy! Get out."

At the door Cirie stopped. "Marushka," she said. "I intend to have you fired!"

I am sick of this. She stormed up the corridor. I am sick of cruelty. I am sick of seeing people cringe. The bullies are everywhere, abusing people and getting away with it because no one fights back. They know who to pick on—all the people who are too weak, too uncertain, too simple-minded to fight them. I'm sick of it! And that's what you looked like, too, she told herself—so courteous, so full of deference, so worried that you might not sell a few boxes of toilet paper or Kotex, trying to be American, accepting insults about being a foreigner, turning your back on the bullies and always saying, Don't answer back, it doesn't matter. Don't argue, it doesn't matter. Don't get upset, it doesn't matter. *It matters!*

"Mr. Cannon—" Furious, she moved past the secretary's desk outside the gold-lettered oak doors. With all the iciness learned from Irene, she raised her chin as though to challenge her would be unthinkable. One of the gold-lettered doors was ajar. She could go right in.

"Do you have an appointment?"

Chin high, Cirie kept walking.

"Just a minute! Your name?"

"I am Countess Borassin." Without breaking stride, she sailed through the open door.

Cannon was talking on the telephone when she burst into his office, no doubt being warned by the secretary that she had crossed the barricades. So that's who he was—the dynamic man with the limousine who came to work early. He swung away from the telephone. "You have an appointment with me?"

Cirie revised her strategy and offered him a slow-starting smile. "You know I don't."

"All right." He smiled a quick smile charged with energy. "Sit down and tell me what you want. What's in the case? You don't mind a few minutes, Charlie?"

For the first time Cirie noticed a younger man standing at the window.

"Charlie—" Cannon started to introduce her. "Is your name really Countess Borassin?"

"It is." Up went the chin. I never gave Irene enough credit, she thought. Sometimes this is a very good idea.

"You can bring back your chin. I believe you."

"I am here because I am furious—"

"O.K."

The man at the window moved closer.

"This is my lawyer, Mr. Korloff—"

Cirie gave him her best slow-starting smile. A man's lawyer might as well be on your side.

"Are you Russian?" Korloff said with an interested smile.

"I am," Cirie said, coolly, daring him to make a disparaging remark.

"I was born in Russia," Korloff said. "Where are you from? What part of Russia?"

"A small town in the northwest called Novotnii. A little town. Then I married Count Vodovsky."

"Vodovsky!" he said. "I remember the name."

"I was Countess Vodovsky."

"I thought it was Borassin," Cannon said.

"Count Vodovsky first. Then Count Borassin."

Cannon stood up. "Come to lunch with us, Countess. You two can catch up on Russia." He smiled the infectious smile. "And you can air your complaints."

"I remember those muddy little district towns so well," Korloff said as the waiter brought their drinks. "Ten stores, a roof over the fire wagon, the police station next to the store where they bought that rot-gut vodka."

"My father was the local doctor," Cirie said to Cannon, who had listened patiently through ten minutes of reminiscences which she had a feeling was all that could be expected. She had stuffed her severe hat into her case and brushed her hair to fall loose to her shoulders and fixed her face and she was satisfied that she looked very well, indeed. "Isn't it amazing," she said, "that memories find their way back across half a world and half a lifetime?"

"What's amazing to me is that you grew up in a muddy little town with ten stores," Cannon said. "When do I get to hear your grievances that brought you crashing into my office?"

Sipping her vodka, Cirie smiled at Cannon. "I'm afraid that's part of a memory, too—a different kind—a different time."

"O.K."

"To explain it I'll have to tell you a long story."

"Were you going to tell me a long story in my office?"

"No." In a way she used to know so well and had forgotten, Cirie let her eyes rest on Cannon. "I was just going to protest."

"Just a minute before you begin." Cannon handed Korloff an envelope and they talked a minute in low voices. No smile now, Cirie saw. Now he was firm and serious and the dark eyes were sharp. He looks like the last person you'd want to tangle with, she thought and tried to remember what Lily had read about him. In her newspapers and magazines Lily read the news about Russia first and then the gossip columns and society pages of New York. What was it Lily had said? Something about American girls making themselves too available. "Here is this man, Jake Cannon, who is apparently one of the wealthiest men in the city," she had said. "This isn't the first time I've read about him. He didn't suffer in the stock crash. And he has a different girl every night. They leap to go with him." Lily had turned the pages of a newspaper to find the gossip column about Cannon. "Here it is. 'The most beautiful girls in town…But marriage is not in his plans. Some of his friends say charming, tempestuous Jake is fearless in business and gun-shy about marriage. He tried it once. Others say this dynamo wants the impossible— a woman who will keep him eternally fascinated.'"

While Cannon was speaking to his lawyer, a fashionable older man and two women detoured across the room to his table to tell him they had missed him at an event the night before.

"I tried," he assured them, rising. "Something I just couldn't get out of."

The trio moved on. "What couldn't you get out of, Jake?" Korloff said with a laugh.

"Hell, I like to stay home." He turned back to Cirie. "All right, tell us your story."

"Well, at the start of the Revolution," Cirie said in her low exciting voice, "there were half a dozen different factions in Russia—Tsarists, Socialists, Communists, Anarchists—it was a many-sided Civil War. And besides that there were gangs with no politics, thugs who just rode into town and robbed everyone and abused people—it gave them a perverted kind of pleasure—and rode out again. One of these gangs was led by a woman, a huge bawdy woman who wore men's clothes and carried a gun and a whip—Marushka. Marushka looked like a man, she yelled like a man and she drank like a man. She was a famous outlaw."

Holding Cannon with her eyes, Cirie paused to give him a chance to cut her off, but he was listening totally, the dark eyes searching her face, and she thought that whoever said the eyes are a window to the soul was thinking of a simpler man.

"One day," she went on, "Marushka and her gang rode into town and after they'd finished robbing and thieving, they started to enjoy themselves. They cornered a gray-bearded old man and they were butting him with their guns and reeling him back and forth, and Marushka, drunk and insane, was prancing on her horse, cheering them on, shouting, 'Hit him again—hit him again—*again— again.*' When the old man fell down, she yelled, 'Pick him up, hit him again, roll him again, hit him again.' And I cried out, 'Stop, you're killing him!' And Marushka turned her horse on me and lashed me with her whip. My husband's uncle pulled me back and the whip only caught my ankle and raised a welt." Cirie let her eyes rest again on Cannon who was listening, spellbound. "And you have Marushka supervising your washrooms—and she shouldn't be there."

"Not the same woman!"

"No, that Marushka is probably dead. This woman's name is Raijerhorn—but she could be Marushka's twin. While I was trying to sell her some supplies—she wouldn't even talk to me because she doesn't like foreigners—a simple-minded old cleaning woman came in to report that she had finished her work. And Raijerhorn-Marushka plagued her and punched the bewildered old thing and kept shouting, '*Again—again—again.*' And every time she punched her, I saw Marushka's whip and I felt the sting on my leg and—" Cirie paused and sipped her vodka and let her eyes do some of the persuading. "I told her I intended to have her fired."

"I'll be damned!" Cannon said. The quick smile crossed his face. "Let me get this straight. You don't like the woman in the washrooms and you crashed into my office to get her fired."

"What right does she have to abuse people? These poor people can't fight back or quit because they need the job, even a job cleaning a washroom. She shouldn't have the power to abuse people."

Fascinated, Cannon stared at her. "First I want to know—what in hell are you doing selling stuff for washrooms?"

She polished up the slow-starting smile that Constantine had once said made a man feel he had somehow earned it and it was his reward. "This is marvelous vodka."

"You want some caviar with it?" Cannon said. "Don't Russians eat caviar with vodka?"

"I would love some caviar."

He signaled the waiter who was never far away. "A bowl of caviar."

"A bowl, sir?"

At Cannon's look, the waiter hurried off.

Cannon turned back to Cirie. "How the hell would I know what's going on in the washrooms?"

This is ridiculous, Cirie thought. We're sitting in Reynaud's, the most elegant restaurant in town, with a captain and waiters hanging around, leaping at every flick of his finger—and we're talking about washrooms. "The people at the top never know what's happening at the bottom," she said. "That's where Revolutions come from."

"I'll be damned!"

The waiter was back and for a moment Cirie gave herself up to the pleasure of savoring marvelous caviar again.

"God, is it that good?" Cannon said, watching her.

"During the revolution I learned to enjoy totally even the smallest delight that came my way. Not that a bowl of caviar is so small. Won't you have some?"

Cannon sipped his Martini. "You're eating memories."

"I suppose so. Memories of crisp cold air and snow higher than the windows—" Suddenly it seemed important to talk about the past that had not been an American past and to respect it. "And forests and rose gardens and crystal chandeliers and gleaming silver and waiters in white gloves. And people who didn't know they were living on the edge of a volcano." She smiled. "It was a long time ago."

Cannon was looking at her with a look she recognized and had not seen for a long time. "There's nothing on earth that would make me give you that order for washroom supplies. You don't belong in washrooms."

She raised her thick black lashes. "I didn't go to your office for an order. I went to get Marushka fired."

"That you've got."

At two o'clock Charlie left for an appointment and Cannon turned back to Cirie. "Have some more caviar."

"No!" She laughed.

"I like to watch your eyes light up when you look at it—"

"Well, it's marvelous caviar."

"You have incredible eyes."

The restaurant crowd was thinning out.

"You can have some more for lunch tomorrow," he said. "So I can watch your eyes again."

She gave him his reward for being so clever, so thoroughly excellent.

"Tell me something," Cannon said. "If it was so bad over there, why don't you let it go?"

"I suppose finding Marushka today brought everything back."

"Will there be anything else, Mr. Cannon?" the waiter said.

Cannon waved him away. "Just today? No other time?"

"Of course other times, too." The restaurant was almost empty. She had not noticed people leaving. For the first time in a long time she felt alive and exciting. Things she used to know long ago, when all she had to worry about was being exciting, came flooding back out of brutally buried memories.

"Some things you don't forget," she said. Rows of wounded men when you had no medicine and nothing for pain. Starving dogs looking at you for food—and starving children with old faces and bloated stomachs—when you had no food to give. Cars stopping beyond the house and the hard knock on the door. Love in a tomb. "Don't you have memories?"

"For me the past goes when it's over." He laughed. "No, that's not true. I remember. But you're holding onto memories of bad times."

"There were happy times, too. Things seemed worse at the end of a hard winter, especially when food and fuel were scarce. When I was a little girl, I used to look out at the blue snowflowers lifting up through the snow and I'd think that they teach you if you will just draw yourself in when the snow comes, if you will just hold on, presently the world will be warm again. After the winter you'll look up and feel the sun shining on your face again." The smile that had been rusty was working fine now. "The problem is that life isn't as regular as the seasons. Sometimes you have to wait a little longer for spring."

Cannon was turned toward her with his arm over the back of the corner banc. The restaurant was empty now. Cirie ran her hand under her hair.

"You have marvelous hair," Cannon said.

She smiled.

He raised her hand to his lips. "Cirie, you're driving me crazy, you know that, don't you?"

She let her eyes with their black fringes talk for her.

"Are you going to have dinner with me tonight?"

Not too fast, she cautioned herself as older memories danced up out of their burial ground and she saw the long table at Whitewater and Serge's eyes talking to her over his wine and she was sixteen again and saying to herself, The scales are out of balance—this is a game in which he holds all the cards.

She could hear Stepa saying, "A Russian is guided by emotion, not by reason. He'll pray all day for God's personal intervention, but he won't figure out what he can do himself about his own fate."

And Serge saying, "Cirie, meet me later. At the river." And she had refused and said to herself, The scales are too uneven—you can't win. And had realized that she didn't believe it. "In an hour," Serge had said. "I'll wait for you." And still she had refused, telling herself that she didn't believe she could not have him. But rushing to him tonight was not the way.

All life is a dress rehearsal.

"Cirie—" Cannon said. "Are you going to have dinner with me tonight?"

Be careful, she told herself. He's half again too clever and charming. "Thursday nights I visit an old friend. I can't disappoint him. He looks forward to it."

"He?"

"My closest friend. I met him when I was sixteen and he was fifty and very famous in Russia. And he was wonderful to me. Now he's alone. But I don't visit him out of charity. I love him. He's very wise."

"What does he do?"

"He's a professor at Columbia."

Cannon laughed. "Your closest friend a seventy-year-old professor at Columbia? I'd have guessed anything but that. Are you going to have dinner with me tomorrow night?"

"Of course," she said. "Why not?"

58

❀

On a brilliant September day Lily sat at the table in her housecoat. "At home they're getting ready for winter. Getting out the double windows. Tying birch twigs along the roads."

Lily's skin was pale, her eyes dull. She really looks awful, Cirie thought. They all do—even little Ivan—and why wouldn't they? They walked through that door in May and they haven't been out since, not even on the hottest summer days. And now it's September.

Lily lit a cigarette and stared over her cup. "Remember the beautiful moss we used to collect to put between the double windows—silver, russet, so many shades of green—" With no present, and stubbornly resisting a future, Lily lived more each day in the past.

"What would you like from the grocery store?" Cirie said. "I won't be home after work."

Resentment played around the edges of Lily's sigh. "I suppose you'll be with your playboy again."

She knows his name, Cirie thought—she devours the papers for news of him. Why does she insist on calling him my playboy? A playboy, which he isn't, and mine which he probably won't be, either. J.K. Cannon figured often in the news. With construction at rock bottom, he was starting a large midtown complex of buildings and the papers were full of it. Rowing against the tide, they said. "It's Thursday," Cirie said. "I go to Constantine tonight."

Lily dragged on her cigarette the way Ulla used to, as though it were her only remaining pleasure. "Cannon, Constantine, Norman. Do you always run around like this?"

Cirie knew that Lily felt she was avoiding them, and it was partly true. Their self-imposed confinement was giving them claustrophobia. They had too little to do, they analyzed everything, and they were hard to get along with. "Lily, it's a beautiful time of year. Why don't you take Ivan to the park today?"

Lily only tapped her cigarette nervously. "Why do you say that when you know we can't?"

"Lily, no one is watching this apartment. Nobody ever says a word about strangers in the neighborhood—not in the grocery store—not in the music shop—"

Lily's eyes flicked toward the window. "After four months they wouldn't be strangers."

"I'm in and out all the time. I don't see anyone."

"Mostly out. Cirie, don't you think you're seeing too much of this man?"

Too much! How long since she had known a summer like this one—weekends at Jake's waterfront estate, trips on his boat, the races, dinner, champagne? How long since she had known a man with so much energy, a man who was a force, who made decisions and made things happen? She was young again and tan and blonde and she wore smart clothes. She was alive again. Too much? Not enough!

"I read about him in the papers and magazines. Peter says he sounds very tough."

"I know he's tough."

"Then you should give him up."

"Lily, you and Peter kept me from Laranov. You're not going to keep me from Jake."

"You're asking for trouble."

Cirie shrugged. "He likes to get his way. Why not, if he can? And he has no patience with fools. And you don't repeat yourself because he gets it the first time." And then, she thought, there's the way his whole face lights up when he smiles and when he holds you and says, Damn you, Cirie, you're still driving me crazy! The way another man might say, I love you. And he can be as passionate and as tender as any man I've known. And if I say that to Lily, she'll fire back, And how many men have you known?

"Peter says that kind of man usually gets anything he wants."

"I suppose he does."

"He won't marry you, you know."

Cirie took her cup into the kitchen. Lily was touching a nerve and she didn't need the gossip columns to tell her about Jake. He didn't conceal his infatuation and he didn't conceal that another marriage was not in his plans.

The kitchen window looked out onto a little backyard garden with fat round cabbages and big red tomatoes propped against sticks and, tucked in a corner of the yard, a flaming sumac—a red flag warning that summer was over. September—more a new beginning than January. A time for settling down to winter schedules, winter plans. Changes.

When she came back to the table Lily was searching with nervous unspent energy through a magazine. "At least this one says a different girl every season, not every night." Cirie wondered where these people got their information. Jake wasn't even interested in being with a girl every night. He was too busy. "Listen to this," Lily said. "'This summer a new blonde with an accent and heavenly eyes. Heavenly eyes but no wedding bells.' That's you. You're only this season."

"He showed me that one, himself."

"He was telling you!"

"Mmm-hm."

"What a bastard he must be!"

"I suppose he is, sometimes."

"Cirie, he's only playing."

"Maybe I'm only playing, too." Cirie picked up her coffee to go to her room to dress.

"Why? What's the matter with him?"

"Nothing's the matter with him. He's wonderful and brilliant. And stormy and difficult." And when he talks the room lights up and sparks fly and other conversations stop. And the eyes—the sharp black eyes that sparkle like diamonds—and tell you that, however well you know him, you'll never know it all.

"Cirie, don't you care that he's only playing with you like all the others? Any day now he'll end the whole affair."

Well, not really like all the others. Deep in her sixth sense that she had always trusted, she knew that. And she knew, too, that Jake was not ready to end it. He was going to try to change it. A new season, new plans. New arrangements.

When she came out of the bedroom, Lily looked at her high-necked black silk sweater and smart beige gabardine suit, both gifts from Cannon. "You are seeing him today!"

"Lunch."

"Cirie, this man is using you. A little fun and you'll never see him again."

Cirie took some money from her purse. "I'll bring you something for dinner."

"You should grab Norman. If you lose him you could end up with someone much worse. Mamma is right. You always intended to have everything and you never think ahead."

"Too many people live for endings. I live for today. I don't ask anymore how things will come out."

Lily looked at her narrowly. "Cirie, I know you. You think you can do anything. You think Cannon is going to ask you to marry him. He won't."

"No," Cirie said. "He's going to ask me to move in with him."

*   *   *

At his regular corner table at Reynaud's, Cannon broke off talking to Charlie to look at his watch. "She's late."

Charlie looked up from his notes. "What about Cirie, Jake?"

"What about her?"

Charlie did not answer. He would not say more unless Cannon wanted to talk about it, and Cannon did not. He was already spending too much time wondering where she was and what she was doing and whether she was with someone else—that lawyer who was after her and wanted to marry her, damn him. Or just thinking about her. Like now. She was a few minutes late and already he was wondering where she was and feeling the exhilaration that came when he knew he was going to see her. "Why do I have to do anything about her?"

"Only if you want to," Charlie said.

"The world is full of beautiful women, Charlie." Cannon sipped his martini. "She's different—I'll admit that. When I get used to her she won't be so different, anymore."

"Don't bet on it."

"It's just taking a little longer than usual." Cannon was silent a minute. "Well, I have time to find out. She's not going to walk away from me."

Charlie looked as though he were not sure of that, either.

"Come on, Charlie. What else does she have? A job calling on the washrooms of Manhattan. Maybe she even goes to Brooklyn, too—I don't know. And a lot of scared relatives. I'm good to her. Why shouldn't she stick with me?" He looked at his watch again. "She's always right on time."

"What is it now—four months?" Charlie said.

Cannon looked at him sharply. "Am I getting serious? The answer is no. You know how I feel about that. Hell, you know better than anyone. Marriage gets in your way." He nodded at Charlie's briefcase that held the plans and contracts they'd been talking about. "This project is going to take a lot of my time. I don't want to have to call home to say I'll be late. I don't want trouble when I work half the night. I don't want arguments at breakfast. I don't need it."

"I've heard you call women a hundred times to say you're tied up—you'll be late."

"That's different. Your dates tell you not to worry about it. You send flowers. And if they're sore, what have you lost? There are plenty more. But a wife thinks she owns you. If you say you're tied up, she says, 'What about my plans?' You say, 'Go alone.' She says, 'You promised me. You'd better be here or else.' You hang up. When you get home you get a lot of complaints and accusations. And more at breakfast. Like a damned radio serial. And the `Or else' is usually that she's going to deny you her wonderful body for a few weeks—as if there weren't another woman in the whole goddam world."

Cannon laughed at his own outburst and relaxed a little. "Now it's quiet at breakfast. I read the paper, map out my day and I'm out. Why should I get married? I'm not eighteen, anymore. I don't owe it to anyone to get married. I'm not in the morals business. I've been straight with Cirie. She knows how I feel. If you're worried about her, you can tell her I mean it."

"Here she is," Charlie said.

"There was an accident on 57th Street and I got out and walked," Cirie said, by way of apology. "And I stopped a minute to look in a window."

"What kind of window?" Cannon said.

"An antique shop," she said. "There's a chest in the window that I think used to be ours." She told them about coming on the Oriental chest only a block away from here. "My first hour at Whitewater I fell in love with it. At first when I saw it in the window, I kept going back to see if it was really the same chest. Then I decided that wasn't such a good idea and I stopped going down 57th Street. Today I was sure it would be gone."

"And was it?" Cannon said.

"I came up to the window and there it was!"

After Charlie left, Cannon said, "Your sister and her husband go out of the house yet?"

"They have claustrophobia but they won't get out of the closet."

"You find it hard to live with that?"

Cirie sensed that he had something on his mind today. "You can't judge them by American standards, Jake. You don't see the terror here that they have seen—you don't understand the fear."

In the restaurant the ladies were in black city dresses or smart fall suits and fall mums filled the vases. "There's a different look here today," she said. "A look of fall—everyone settling down to the business of the new season, even if the business is only pleasure. When we first came here, people were bright and relaxed, enjoying spring." She smiled at Cannon and found him studying her. "That day I burst into your office to have Marushka fired."

"And you said you were Countess somebody or other."

"Borassin."

"I've never asked you about that. What made you pick that name?"

He hadn't asked her because he didn't like her to talk too much about the past. "I was Countess Vodovsky first and then I was Countess Borassin for about an hour. Sacha Borassin was a famous general."

"That Borassin? We heard about him in France."

"Sacha thought as a Vodovsky I was in great danger, which I suppose I was. He was an old friend and he married me to try to protect me."

Cannon laughed. "That's one reason I haven't heard before. How would that save you?"

"He thought they'd respect his home because he was a war hero. I was supposed to move in and stay out of sight until things quieted down."

"He didn't have to marry you for that," Cannon said, a little too quickly.

"No, he didn't." She looked at him steadily. "He was shot on the steps of his house a half-hour after we left the city hall."

"Jesus!"

"Yes."

"What happened?"

"Stalin and Trotsky were in a power struggle and I suppose one of them—probably Stalin—thought Sacha might use his influence against him. After that, when I would look out at the snowflowers, I didn't believe anymore that if you would just hold on, things would be all right again." And what about now? she thought. Do you believe it now?

"I knew then more than ever that I had to get out. I used to entertain some Generals and Commissars on Wednesday nights and I found one who was corrupt enough to be bought. I think a lot of them were corrupt but I settled on this Commissar because I was sure he was corrupt and I bribed him for passports and some railway tickets to Riga."

"What'd you bribe him with?"

"A pair of black pearl and diamond earrings."

He was wondering whether to believe her.

"The jewels that Count Vodovsky gave me were famous and the Commissar was very greedy." The image arose of Gorshenko's sly crafty face frozen in time—greedy green eyes, glass in hand, at the Wednesday night.

"You're leaving me again, darling," Cannon said. "I never saw anyone slip off the way you do. You hypnotize yourself."

"I'm sorry, darling." She touched his arm. "It's strange that when I see images of those people, they're almost never in motion. They're frozen in one position, with one expression, as though everything about them—everything good and everything bad—had crystallized in that one moment. Do you ever think of people that way?"

"Only you," Cannon said, with a grin.

"I see Gorshenko, with his greedy eyes and his sly face and his oily smile as clearly as I did then."

"Gorshenko?"

"The man I bribed. And then I see him again in the doorway of the railway station, this time with a predatory look because he was chasing me. He'd come in with four of his men and he must have moved a second later because he was trying to catch me—but for me, he's frozen in that moment—all the greed and treachery frozen in his face, turned toward the tracks, all keyed up, ready to move."

"Why was he chasing you?"

"He thought I must have more jewels. He'd sent some men to search our rooms and they didn't find them. But I had them and he knew it."

"Where'd you hide them?"

"In the oatmeal."

Cannon burst out laughing. "A box of oatmeal?"

"A pot of oatmeal cooking on the stove. They'd always been hidden in the mattress. I waited until the last minute to cut them out and they were in my pocket when the GPU men came to the door. I knew they would search me. I was cooking breakfast for Alexei and I dropped them into the pot of oatmeal."

When he finished laughing, Cannon said, "Am I frozen in some unguarded moment, too?"

"It's only the past that's frozen. Sometimes I think we always knew our beautiful world would be wiped out and that we would have it only in memory, so we remembered. After that we remembered the horror, too."

Cannon raised her hand to his lips. "Cirie, come have dinner tonight at my place. I want to talk to you. Tell Constantine you can't make it tonight."

"Darling, I would but he's been sick. What do you want to talk to me about?"

"For one thing, I want you to quit peddling that washroom stuff. Let me take care of you."

"How do you mean that, darling?"

"Exactly the way it sounds. Let me support you. Let me pamper you."

"You mean you'll keep me?"

"In wonderful luxury."

"No, thanks, Jake."

"You turned me down awfully fast. Don't you want to think about it?"

"No."

"Come on," he said, impatiently. "Let's get out of here."

As they stepped out into the clear warm September air, he said, suddenly, "Let's go look at your Oriental chest."

59

"When I saw it here, I suddenly felt that it had a life of its own and it was following me," Cirie said as they walked to the antique shop. "I saw it first at Whitewater and then Kostyka. During the first Revolution the peasants stole it and then it turned up in the quarters of a General I knew. And then there it was on 57th Street." They came up to the window. "Here it is," she said. "It's supposed to be on a table, not on the floor. We never put it to any use. It was enough that it was beautiful."

"Let's go in and take a look at it."

Close up, there was no question but that it was the same chest. Cirie ran a finger over it. "I used to touch it for luck when I ran past it."

Cannon stood with an arm lightly around her waist and Cirie wondered whether the gesture was affectionate or possessive. "What kind of luck were you looking for?"

"I was sixteen! Almost any kind of luck would do!" In memory she could see herself running her hand over it as she returned mornings from meeting Serge.

"And now?"

"Now?"

"What do you want now?"

"Now I don't think about it." She gave him a slow smile. "At sixteen I wanted to see the whole world."

"That shouldn't be so hard." Cannon looked at her, thoughtfully, and then at the chest. "You want it?"

"No! Oh, no, darling. But thank you."

She wouldn't accept it but if she could, would she still want it? "At first I couldn't tear myself away from it. Now—"

This quiet shop, crowded with the polished survivors, as she was, of other days, was permeated with a sense of lives that had been lived, of time that had passed, of relinquishings and partings. Jake was right. You could hypnotize yourself with memories. She touched the chest one last time and turned away and Cannon reached past her to open the door.

"Darling," he said when they were out on the sidewalk. "Come home with me now and let's talk."

Her instinct told her to beg off, delay awhile, but she knew that once Cannon had brought it up, it was not his way to leave the matter unsettled.

It was almost five o'clock by the time he had stopped at his office and returned to the car and the elevator shot up to the penthouse of one of his apartment buildings. He led her through his quiet, elegant sparsely-furnished living room and out to a terrace with a lush garden of potted trees and ivied trellises and boxes of fall mums. Cirie stood at the railing, looking down at toy-like cars and the park that was a green carpet with dark green patches of trees.

"Do you like that room?" Cannon said, after a minute, nodding toward his living room, where soft grays and blues and touches of pale yellow were catching the late-day sun.

"You know I do." The first time she saw it she had thought it was probably the most beautiful home in New York. And then that she was sorry he had brought her here. This quiet room with its old Italian and English paintings that reminded her of Rivercliff and its French Impressionist paintings—a Monet, with a woman like Madame in a garden like the one at Whitewater, a Cezanne with a window revealing private desires, and a Renoir—that brought back the mansions of the Moscow millionaires, this serene room revealed a more sensitive man than she had, until then, come to know and she had begun to fall in love in a different way.

"You can see the scaffolding of my new building from here." Cannon's eyes lingered a minute on the skyline and came back to Cirie. "The last girl who was here hated that room. She said it gave her the creeps—it needed more furniture."

Seated on the wicker sofa, Cannon fell silent again. Cirie had seen him like this before, when he broke long silences with random thoughts that had nothing to do with whatever was on his mind.

"Out on the job," he said, toying with her hand. "I ride the lifts to the top of the scaffolding to be sure things are right. Foremen and inspectors, like your Russian Commissar, aren't always above a quiet little bribe." Easing deeper into the wicker sofa, he put his feet up on the coffee table. "I'm comfortable up there, as comfortable as behind a desk. I can ignore the dirt and the noise and the clatter. But here—here I like it quiet. This is my refuge. I like to come home and change into old clothes and just sit here and watch the sun drop below the buildings—some of them mine." He studied her again. "I don't mind being alone. I like it."

The sun was already sinking below the tops of the highest buildings. He kissed her lightly and leaned back again. "I think I'll try to find your black pearl and diamond earrings. And if I can't, I'll have another pair made. After all, they brought you to me."

Cirie only smiled and met his eyes.

"I'd like to see them with a black velvet gown," he said softly. "An elegant black velvet gown. And sables—"

These are no longer idle random thoughts, Cirie told herself. This is bait.

Cannon reached up to kiss her again. "Cirie, move in with me. Live with me."

It was the September song that she had expected.

"You'll have everything—jewels, clothes from Paris. Furs. A limousine and chauffeur." When she didn't answer he went on. "You'll have to put up with my moods and not get in my way. You'll have to amuse yourself nights when I'm busy—"

Did he mean there would be places he couldn't take her? Of course there would be places he couldn't take her.

"I don't always end my work at five o'clock," he said, reading her mind. "When there's a problem, if I can do anything about it that night, I do it. I work until midnight. Or all night if I have to."

That was nothing new. He had done that a few times since she'd known him.

"And even when I'm free, I won't go out every night. I like to stay home. I may just want to sit here like this and talk. Or I may go into my office and shut you out. I can't give you all of me. You'll have to put up with that. You can't own me."

Cirie looked through the open door to the beautiful serene room and thought of the rooms that lay beyond—the library, the smaller drawing room, the dining room almost as large as the one at Rivercliff, the master bedroom where doors opened out to another terrace and, at night, to a sky showered with a million stars—everything soft and beautiful—everything quiet. She thought of the crowded apartment uptown with the small rooms and the ordinary furniture and the hot hall and the noise from the street—the Victrola playing in the music shop and mothers screaming and brakes screeching. She thought of the clothes she had scrimped to buy or that, more often, Marya had made. She thought of the washrooms. Why not? she thought. Oh, my God, why not?

"Or I may just want to sit here with you and say nothing. Like you're doing now."

The sky began to take on the color of the end of the day and a cool breeze drifted across the terrace. Hot halls and hot rooms and the men sitting without hope on boxes outside the subway station just before you came up to the steamy smells of the soup kitchen. And those washrooms. Once, lying beside Serge at daybreak on the little hill, she had said, Why not? We're in love. It's only natural for people in love. Why not? But now when she spoke, it was not to say yes or why not, my God, why not? When she spoke at last, she said, "And will we be married, Jake?"

"You know me better than that. Darling, I'm crazy about you. Since the day I found you, every other woman has bored me. Every other woman has seemed over-eager, over-nervous, over-painted. Next to you, there's no one. I want you." His voice changed. "I don't want to spoil it. I want it just the way it is."

Nothing stays the way it is. Still she said nothing. What could she say? Not, Why does it have to spoil it? How many times had he heard that? Is that even his reason? Or does he only say that, and maybe tell himself that, maybe even believe it, because he knows his own power? He doesn't have to marry anyone. Long ago, with Serge she had thought, What a one-sided affair—such vast power on one side and no power on the other. Where is my weapon?

The black eyes were fixed on her, waiting. Why not? she thought. Who would it hurt? And who could hurt us? Why not? I've never lived by the rules any more than he has. I loved Laranov in a tomb and never thought about marriage. But then there was no hope! She spoke at last. "No, Jake, I don't think so."

Still he waited.

"It just wouldn't do," she said. Beyond the September chrysanthemums the sun was flaming the sky. Don't waver. The scales are so uneven, you can't give an inch. "It wouldn't work. I couldn't live here like that—a visitor—until you grew bored. Like a hotel guest, expected to leave after an appropriate time."

"I'll give you the moon. You wanted to see the world. I'll show you the world."

Why not? Why not? The shabbiness will be over, the noise, the dirt, the pennypinching. Life will be a garden again. For a little while you can have the life that once you had, long ago, for a brief time that ended too soon. And who knows whether any of us will be here tomorrow—next week—next year? We could all be dead! She caught herself. This is how we used to think in Kostyka. And only a few hours ago I said the past was over.

"Darling, why don't you think about it?" The eyes that missed nothing were searching her face for a different answer. "You're not going to be happy just selling that junk."

A sour note vibrated. That's the whole point, she thought. If he were in love with one of his society friends, he would marry her or he would break it off. But does it really matter what he would or would not do with someone else? Yes, it matters! Careful, she told herself. Don't say what you're thinking.

"You've gotten used to the good life, Cirie."

"I've had the good life before."

"You won't go back to that God-awful job—and that crowded depressing apartment."

"No," she said, softly. "Not for long." She turned the black-fringed, deep blue lights on him that Constantine used to say could conquer the world. "Not for long."

Surprise flickered across his face as though it had not occurred to him that he could lose her. "Darling, I'm crazy about you," he said, softly. "But you can't change me."

"You'll be what you want to be, Jake. You don't need my help."

"Cirie—" he murmured and bent toward her. "Darling, you're too beautiful to be knocked around. What will you do?"

"Something will come along."

"Is that something else you learned in the Revolution?"

"That's how I survived the Revolution." Tell yourself that now, she told herself. Just get through these few minutes and get out. Don't waver. Don't show a flicker of doubt. Don't listen to him too long. "To survive you had to give up wanting everything. You had to be able to get along without everything. And know you could do it."

"What the hell good is that?" Cannon exploded. "Knowing you can do without everything? You don't have to do without everything! You could be here."

She didn't answer.

"Goddammit, Cirie, these are hard times. There's nothing out there. How long have you been peddling that junk? At least four months now. Are you going to do it forever? Spend your life in the city's washrooms when you could be here?"

Restraining her anger, Cirie lifted her chin. "Jake," she said, her voice soft, her eyes blazing. "I have starved. I have fought a world gone mad. I have sneaked through back alleys in the night, listening for gunfire on the streets. I have patched together a hundred men in a single night—men who had lost arms or legs or eyes or stomachs, men with a tube where their nose should be or a tube where their organs should be—without ether or morphine."

She paused as the terrible pictures unrolled like a high-speed movie before her eyes. And done things that as a girl I would have found unthinkable. Well, don't tell him that. And married men I didn't love—to survive, to stay alive, to stay here. And survived loving one man who was afraid to marry me. And traded love for lives—and then fell in love. Don't tell him that, either.

"I have seen homes burned and hostages hanged. I have seen whole villages dying of typhus when I had only raspberry tea to treat them with. Hell can hold no surprises for me! I've been there. So a few months more or less in this marvelous job that makes you so uncomfortable don't matter very much. I'll survive."

"You'll give up all this?" Cannon shouted. "For a piece of paper and a few words mumbled by some seedy justice of the peace?"

This is not going right, Cirie told herself. Don't drag it out. She started toward the door. "Good-bye, Jake."

"Cirie, what will you do?"

"It won't be the first time I've closed a door without knowing where the next door would open." She paused in the doorway and looked at the lovely serene room and then back at Jake who was standing now, silhouetted against the flaming sunset.

"Cirie, I can give you so much. What do you have now?"

Don't turn around, she told herself. If you turn you're lost. She took her jacket from the closet and he came up behind her and helped her into it. His hands stayed on her shoulders and in that electric moment she knew he wanted to hold her and she wanted to be in his arms again. She started toward the door, slowly, waiting for him to say, Don't go. But he was angry and silent. Keep walking. Don't look back. At the door she said, "I'm worth more than the crumbs, Jake."

"Crumbs!"

"I'm worth the whole loaf."

He remained at the other end of the hall. "Where are you going?"

"It's Constantine's night. And he's sick." Constantine, who had always been there.

"I'll send you in the car."

"No."

"Damn it, Cirie. I could make you happy."

"Mostly, Jake, happiness is something just a little better than before."

"Cirie—" he called. She stopped. "When you change your mind, the door is open."

He was so confident, so sure she'd be back. "And you, Jake—if you change your mind, come to me."

60

When Constantine did not respond to his buzzer, Cirie tried the door and found it unlocked. She hurried through the apartment and found him in bed, lying so still that at first she thought he was dead. At her cry, he forced open his eyes and coughed a weak croupy cough, struggling to breath.

Cirie hurried down to the first floor where she had noticed a doctor's office and returned with Dr. Schurz who diagnosed the illness as a severe case of flu. "It's a mean bug," the young doctor said. "He needs care and absolute rest. Does he live alone? I should put him in the hospital."

Cirie read the protest in Constantine's eyes. "I'm a nurse. I'll stay with him."

The doctor wrote a prescription and motioned Cirie into the living room. "These older people are in real danger with this. He's very frail. He could get very sick."

He may be old, Cirie thought, but ordinarily he's not frail. And he's very sick already.

A few hours later, she lay on the sofa in Constantine's study, surrounded by his books, and thought that of all the people she had known, Constantine had been her rock. He had always understood her, even understood what she was thinking. If she were to lose him—she closed off the thought. She refused to admit the possibility.

Her mind moved to Cannon and the rift she had known was coming. In the end it comes down to one question. Do you want him and the good life for as long as it lasts? If you want it, grab it. Only this morning you decided to take it. Why did you change?

Unable to sleep, she got up and stood at the window. At the corner a boy and girl stood under a street lamp kissing a lingering kiss—probably saying good night, going home to hot little apartments crowded with family. Why else would they be saying goodnight at the lamppost?

She knew that she had not really changed her mind. Not irrevocably. She had succumbed to that old instinct for taking the calculated risk—that take-a-chance-shoot-for-the-moon-at-least-give-it-a-try instinct. You're an incurable gambler, she told herself, always thinking maybe you can win. And if you lose? If he doesn't come after you then what? Then do it his way.

She went back to bed. On the street a siren wailed and she thought of the lovely silence in Jake's quiet serene apartment that could be hers. Why wouldn't it work, she thought—if he really cares and all those other women seem dull and over-nervous and over-painted? And if it doesn't last? Then you can enjoy the here and now. And when it's over you can still find that door that always opens somewhere. As you have done so many times before. After Serge. And after Papa died, and after Laranov rushed you away from home in the middle of the night. And after the Revolution and after we were thrown out of Rivercliff and after you lost Laranov. Your whole life is playing before you, she told herself. They say that happens when people are about to die, although she had never believed it. But what if you were to die tomorrow or next week? Why not live while you can?

Horns blasted on the street—someone was tying up traffic. Maybe if she lived with him, she could become important to him. In a hundred subtle ways she could fill a need and he wouldn't want to lose her.

Long ago she used to say to herself, If you lose will it hurt any less if you don't try? Take a chance. But which way? Live with him and take a chance that you'll change his mind? Or stay away and take a chance that he'll miss you enough to change his mind?

Lily stepped furtively out into the hall, looked both ways, and rang for the elevator. She waited, trembling. If there was someone in it, she decided, she would turn away as though she had forgotten something and go back to the apartment. The hall was silent and empty. Staring at her feet, she forced herself to stand there. Cirie had not been home for almost a week. Last Thursday night she had found Constantine seriously ill and she had been with him ever since. Lily did not blame her—the poor old man had no one else in the whole world. On the telephone, Cirie had been close to tears. "He was always there when I needed him—he was so wise and so kind," she had wept. Lily noticed that she spoke of him in the past tense, the way you used to speak about people who had been picked up overnight in the Black Maria and you knew you would never see them again.

As the days passed and Constantine grew worse, Lily became alarmed, both for him and for her own family. In the little apartment they were running out of food and one of them would have to go out. Lily pointed out that if the Soviets were still watching the building, it was Peter they were looking for. And besides, they might mistake her for Cirie who was in and out every day. Especially if she wore Cirie's clothes.

In the hall, the elevator clicked to a stop at the floor above and Lily controlled an impulse to run. She had to go out, whether it was now or an hour from now. There was no food for her son or her husband. The elevator came. Lily stepped into the car and nodded to a very fat old woman with a fat old cocker spaniel. The door closed and she looked at the old woman, terrified, to see if the age and the obesity could be a disguise. On the first floor the old lady muttered to the dog in a language Lily did not understand and left the elevator and Lily stepped out and into the sunlight.

When she came back with her bundles she let herself into the apartment with a sense of exhilaration she had not felt since Capetown. "Darling, there was no one!" she cried. "I watched very carefully. No one looked at me—no one was leaning against a building or hiding in a doorway or walking back and forth. Nothing!"

The telephone rang and Lily waited to see if it was Cirie ringing the prearranged signal—one ring and hang up, three rings and hang up, then answer the next call on the fourth ring. The ringing continued, uninterrupted. She looked at Peter. "Shall we answer it? I feel it's all right."

"No, I think not. They might have grown tired of sending a man day after day to watch this apartment. But it's easy to phone a few times a day. If we answer, they'll send someone around again."

"You're right, of course, darling," Lily agreed. "Help me carry the bundles into the kitchen. I'll cook you a wonderful dinner tonight."

"Cirie phoned," Peter said. "She sounded very tired and I sensed she had been crying. When I told her you went to the store she asked that you pack a suitcase with some of her clothes and ask the young man, Jed, who works there nights to bring it to her. Do you think, darling, you are up to going to the store again tonight?"

"Oh, I think so," Lily said. "Peter, you must go out soon. it was so wonderful. And darling," she picked up her little Ivan. "Tomorrow we're going to the park."

"Are we going back to Capetown?" he said.

He doesn't even know there is a park in New York, Lily thought, sadly. He thinks New York is only this apartment and the street.

The phone rang again—a steady ring—ten—eleven—twelve times—she counted them. She let it ring.

"I don't know why I reacted to Jake the way I did," Cirie said. For the first time in a week Constantine was well enough to be propped up in bed. "Maybe it goes all the way back to being told I wasn't good enough for Serge. You heard about that?"

"Only second hand—from Stepa."

"I threw a spectacular scene." Remembering, she laughed. It was so long ago that in her own mind she, herself, was frozen in time, weeping on the floor next to

Serge's chair. "I screamed and cried and insulted everyone—Vara, Vassily. Well, they insulted me, too. In the end, after crying all night, I told myself nobody was ever going to be able to say that to me again. And I vowed revenge. Those particular lessons were not exactly the best equipment for the Revolution, were they? Or for America, either?"

"Oh, I don't know." Constantine's voice was weak but his eyes were bright. "They're not so bad. And now?"

"Now—am I playing the same scene with Jake? Then I was young. I still thought I could grasp the world and hold it in my hand. Now—with Jake, what can I prove?"

"Maybe more than you realize."

"Do you know what went through my mind last week when he asked me?" Cirie settled back in the chair, making conversation because she felt he wanted it. "That I would be a stranger in the house I lived in. It would be his home, not mine. And I thought suddenly of Agniya's and that even in the worst of times, we could close the door and feel we had a home. Even with the transients, even with Agniya's snooping and spying—"

Constantine laughed at the memory.

"We belonged to each other. In a crisis, you and Stepa and I had each other. And Tanya and Georgii. And bad as it was, those shabby rooms were ours."

By Saturday Constantine was well enough to sit up in the living room and was growing concerned about her. "If you were to ask my opinion," he said, "I'd say he was behaving like a man in love—a certain kind of American-type dynamo, which is a little foreign to us, but nevertheless, a man in love."

"He cares enough to give me everything, but for him that isn't hard. He enjoys dressing me in the most elegant gowns he can find—like his private doll. But otherwise he doesn't care enough—not enough to marry me."

"And if you were to marry him do you think that would be a happy ending?"

Cirie was silent for a long time. Then she said, "I'm not sure there's any such thing as a happy ending. But I think after Jake I probably would not be able to marry anyone else."

"Darling, I don't think he knows himself yet that he cares enough. He wasn't forced to think about it until now."

"Laranov loved me enough to risk his life when I asked it, to give me lives." She was silent a moment. "Remember?"

"How can I forget? One of them was mine."

"It isn't that it's breaking some kind of rules," Cirie said suddenly. "That's the least of it. I've climbed too many mountains and chased too many El Dorados to follow the rules and I guess I've broken them all. Whitewater. Then Serge. Then Kostyka—God, how I wanted to go to Kostyka—and Vassi—and Moscow and Petersburg—and then America. El Dorado keeps changing—and slipping away. At least for me it does."

Reflectively, Constantine smoothed the quilt. "Cirie, you've had a glorious life." She looked at him, astonished.

"You told Theo that he had been knocked to the ground like the rest of us and he came up with a diamond in his hand because he was saving lives. How many lives did you save?"

"In the hospitals? How can I count?"

"And in the prison?"

She shook her head. "A hundred, I suppose. Maybe more."

"You used to say you wanted to see the world—everything. Did you mean just the good part or did you mean everything?"

She thought a minute. "I honestly don't know. It wasn't to <u>have</u> a lot of things—it was to see it all. It was to live."

"And haven't you seen it all? The most elegant society in Europe. The greatest upheaval the world has ever seen. You've seen the best and the worst. You gave their lives back to more than a hundred lost men. You knew the old leaders and the new leaders. You were adored. You had a great love."

For a long moment Cirie was silent. "If that's true," she said, "maybe it's time to let go. Forget the big gamble. Enjoy what I have while it lasts."

"Cirie," Constantine said, after a minute. "What if there were a Revolution here? And everything were taken away and you were tied to him, as you were to Vassily who wasn't enough?"

"Cannon is like Laranov. He'd figure a way out."

"We say it couldn't happen here, but why not? Is it so different? Too many people without jobs and not enough to eat and no hope. Beggars, soup kitchens. Hungry people with that gray look. Discouraged people with empty eyes."

"It's not the same! It's not as bad."

"All it takes is an ambitious charismatic leader with promises. Promises that things will be different, that things will be better, that with him they'll have what they don't have now. He whips up their emotions. He thrills them. The good life he promises seems very real—revenge against those who have the good life now will be sweet. Have you forgotten?"

She could see the empty faces outside the subway as you reached the steamy smell of the soup kitchen. She thought of the faces of bloated children and starving dogs and of Mita, the horse, accepting the lashes, past struggling, past caring, and the awful agonizing pain rose up in her as she felt again, after all these years, that she was kin to them.

"If there is to be nothing," she said softly. "If here, too, there is to be nothing—then one should enjoy the here and now. I was here almost eight years before I met Jake. I lived on dreams of Laranov that couldn't come true. I don't want to wait another eight years."

She stood up and went to the window. "Jake said if I changed my mind the door was open. After you're well again, I'll go back and live with him."

Constantine made a motion to object. "If you're not important now—" he cried.

"Once you sent me to Laranov and you said, 'God, Cirie, if you love him, love him now.'"

"There was no future then for any of us. We were threatened. We lived day to day. Cirie, this man is not an automaton. He's not an adding machine counting up his millions. He's a man. A very busy man. In America these men never have enough time. And he has been with you almost every day for four months. That's a man in love, whether he realizes it yet or not—"

"That was play—not a life contract. I told him if he came to me, it should be to marry me. He's not going to come."

"Are you sure?"

"After you're well, I'll go to him."

"You've decided?"

"I'll enjoy it while it lasts. After all, we don't know how long anything will last, do we?"

"You and I may think that way when we're tired or discouraged—it's what the bad years made us, we are what we are—" He broke off and for a minute sat perfectly still, holding the chair unsteadily, as though he might faint.

"And now, darling," he whispered. "I'm sorry. I must go back to bed."

*   *   *

For another five days Constantine lay in bed, coughing, his eyes dull, his voice a whisper, seeming almost too weak to move. Cirie was alarmed and puzzled at the relapse. His temperature was normal, his heartbeat was regular. The doctor assured her that his lungs were clear. "He probably got up too soon," the doctor said. "He's an old man—frail. He needs bed rest and care."

After five days during which Constantine's condition did not improve but did not grow worse, Cirie decided he ought to sit up a little while in the living room and see that there was still a beautiful world out there. And indeed, for all his frailty, once established in his chair near the window, he did seem a little brighter. But Cirie was alarmed when, a few minutes later, he asked whether she'd spoken to Cannon because he had asked the same question every day, never seeming to remember the answer.

"Have you given him up then?" he said.

"No," she said. "I'm going back."

"Don't hurry to do that. Take your time."

"Darling, where would I find anyone else like him? I couldn't marry someone like Norman now. It would be impossible. And very unfair to Norman."

"Before you found Cannon it would have been unfair to yourself."

Cirie smiled, a little sadly. "All life is a dress rehearsal," she said. "I went through the same thing with Serge."

"But if the actors change, the scene doesn't play the same."

"As I look back," Cirie said, pensively, "if I had to go through the Revolution, I'm glad I had that little while of seeing the old Russia in all its elegance. I'll enjoy living with Cannon as long as it lasts and when it's over—" The ringing telephone interrupted her thoughts. "Maybe someday I'll look back and be glad I had it, if only for a little while." She went to answer the phone.

"Cirie!" Lily cried. "The most amazing thing! There's a chest here."

"A chest! What kind of a chest?"

"Why are you alarmed? A black Oriental-type chest—very ornate—jade, mother-of-pearl. It must be a mistake—what should I do? Cirie, my God, what a morning! I took Ivan to the park and when I came home there was the chest in the hall and a man waiting for me to sign for it. I made him open it before I'd let him bring it in. I was afraid there might be a bomb. He said he had to open it, anyway, because there was a package inside and I had to sign for that, too. I had to open it. I was terrified but it was only a small box from Cartier."

"What was in it?"

"Earrings. Black pearl and diamond earrings. Like you used to have. They could even be the same ones. But wait. That's not all."

"What else?"

"*He* came here."

"Who came?"

"*He* came. I saw him from the window, getting out of his limousine. He raced up the stairs and pounded on the door. I opened it because I knew who he was. All he said was, 'Where is she, damn it?' I didn't know what to say. I didn't know whether to tell him. He said, 'Doesn't anyone live here? Don't you people ever answer your telephone?' The phone has been ringing constantly for days but we were afraid to answer. Why didn't you let him know where you were? What's going on?"

"Lily, what happened?"

"Finally I said, 'She's with Constantine—an old friend who's very ill.'"

"'Damn it,' he said. 'Where does he live? What's his address? This is taking all my time.' I didn't know whether to tell him. But he's not the kind of man you can say no to."

"It's not easy," Cirie agreed.

"At first I said I didn't know. Then I gave him the address. I hope it was all right. It was about fifteen minutes ago."

"He called?" Constantine was waiting with a smile of satisfaction.

"For days. He finally went up there." She sank into the chair beside him. "Don't ever tell a Russian there's no such thing as fate," she said, laughing while tears sat in her eyes. "If you hadn't had a relapse, I wouldn't have held out. I'd have gone back."

She hurried into the study to change her clothes and brush her hair. When she returned she realized that a suddenly spry healthy Constantine was walking across the room. "Constantine!"

"I'll get out of your way."

"Constantine, you tricked me!"

Constantine stopped.

"It wasn't fate! It was you!"

Constantine came back across the room. "How else could I be sure?" He took her hands in his and kissed them. "To me, where you are concerned, he has no right to be bargain hunting."

Constantine started out of the room. "He'll be here."

"He's here." Outside she could see Jake getting out of his car and striding toward the building.

An urgent ring of the bell and a sharp knock and Cirie opened the door, the slow smile starting on her lips that had carried her through hell and through glory.

"Damn it, Cirie, you knew I couldn't just forget you," Jake murmured. He laughed at his own folly as he took her in his arms. "God help you, darling, if you get in my way. I haven't got time—"

Time. The new world. The American world. Not her past but her future. Some spring, she knew—some spring day in a sweet smelling grassy park, she would still meet Serge in the early wet morning. Some cold day she would wrap a coat around herself and still see, frozen in time, hungry suffering men in a cold hospital, she would still see the cold tomb of a prison in the eerie moonlight, she would still see a dog's eyes begging for food and the dull eyes in the old faces of children and Sacha's still eyes as he lay on the steps. Some night she would still feel the power in Laranov's arms and hear, "Damn you, Cirie, and your hold on me." In her mind's eye she could see the handwriting, "Keep the dead past free of all regret."

0-595-21894-6

Printed in the United States
1428300002B/95